# GILGAMESH

# GILGAMESH

STEPHAN GRUNDY

William Morrow
*An Imprint of* HarperCollins*Publishers*

HarperCollins books may be purchased for educational, business, or sales promotional use. For information please write: Special Markets Department, HarperCollins Publishers Inc., 10 East 53rd Street, New York, NY 10022.

FIRST EDITION

*Designed by Joseph Rutt*

Printed on acid-free paper

Library of Congress Cataloging-in-Publication Data has been applied for.

ISBN 0-380-97574-2

00 01 02 03 04 QW 10 9 8 7 6 5 4 3 2 1

This book is dedicated to John F. Prendergast, the eternal seneschal, and his noble and beloved cat, Prince Mordred

The one who goes on ahead saves the comrade,
The one who knows the route protects the friend.
　　　　　　—*The Epic of Gilgamesh*,
　　　　　　　trans. Maureen Gallery Kovacs

A cat—for its thoughts. A mongoose—for its actions.
　　　　　　—Sumerian proverb

# GILGAMESH

I

The shadow of the city walls was beginning to stretch long across the plains around Erech. Although the spring feast of the New Year was nearly upon them, the fields ripening toward green harvest, there was still a touch of chill in the evening breeze. Puabi pulled her woolen cloak more closely about her, gripping her shepherd-crook firmly. The flock of Inanna's sheep that she tended were milling all around; now and again one would raise its head, bleating mournful and low beneath the high echoes of gongs and bells that floated from Erech's temples.

"Hush, silly things," Puabi said. "Enjoy your grazing while you have it, for your shepherds will be busy feasting tomorrow."

As she spoke, she could feel her jaw tightening. It would be a great New Year's celebration indeed: instead of the Sacred Marriage being carried out as it always had in the years of her memory, between the old En who was Inanna's high priest and the Shamhatu who was the voice of the goddess on earth, young Gilgamesh would take the Ensi's crown in place of his long-dead father Lugalbanda. Tonight the Shamhatu, his mother, would step down from her place to become Rimsat-Ninsun, the Old Woman of Erech, and a maiden would be chosen from among the temple-women to bear the might of the goddess. And at the end of the New Year's Feast, Gilgamesh would become En, as well as Ensi, and he would go in to the new Shamhatu, dedicating his life as an offering to be taken at Inanna's pleasure even as he took the goddess' maidenhead anew, as his father Lugalbanda and his grandfather Dumuzi had done before him.

The pointed tip of Puabi's crook had twisted deep into the earth, digging a dark scar through the short-cropped grass. Gilgamesh, that arrogant little worm . . . As children they had sat beneath the watchful eyes of Inanna's scribes together, for all the temple's children, from the heir of Erech to foundlings such as Puabi herself, learned reading and writing, numbers and wisdom-sayings, in the one school. Though three years younger than she, Gilgamesh had always pushed himself forward, demanding loud-voiced to be recognized as best, strongest, of noblest blood . . . She had hated him then, and, when other temple-duties took her away from the school at the age of fourteen, she kept a close eye on him whenever she could. It did not seem to her that being allowed to train with the warriors, and schooling in the arts of battle and strategy, had made him any better: as his strength and skill grew to quickly make him the equal of most of the men in Erech's warband, Gilgamesh had only grown more arrogant and overbearing.

"Inanna be thanked," Puabi said aloud, "that I am only a shepherdess. Pity the poor woman who is chosen as his Shamhatu!" She dug her crook into the ground again for emphasis, looking about at the sheep as if daring them to argue with her. But they only swung their heavy heads away, their dark eyes lowering meekly as they tugged and mumbled at the grass beneath their hooves. Although the choice of a new Shamhatu would be made that night by reading the liver of a ewe, Puabi knew full well that Urgigir, the sacrifice-priest, was high in the counsel of the great ones of Inanna's temple, and that they would have talked much in secret regarding the Shamhatu's successor: it was the way of all temples, that chance and the will of the gods be tempered by the sense of men.

There were two maidens whom everyone reckoned were the most likely choices: the young trance-priestess Geme-Tirash, through whose mouth the goddess had already spoken more than once; and the willowy and vixen-eyed singer Shubad, whose high soprano voice set cymbals vibrating in answer when her notes rang out above the others in the evening hymns to Inanna—*though she is no maiden*, Puabi thought with a faint trace of unkind satisfaction. Shubad's body and face were as lovely as her voice, and Puabi could not have kept track of the number of times she had heard the other girl rustle out of the pallet beside her own, her slender feet whispering over the mud-brick floor on the way to keep a night-meeting. If she were chosen, it would go hard with her, for the Shamhatu was allowed no beloved of her own, but must take those men who had earned or—at certain times, under certain circumstances— bought the favors of Inanna. But Shubad was beautiful and accomplished, a nobleman's daughter brought to the temple at the age of thirteen when her gifts of song and dance showed too clearly to deny, and there was no doubting that she would fill the office finely. Geme-Tirash, as well: if not as showy, her manner was quiet and deep, her trance-sight beyond questioning. She would grow quickly into a respected woman, the voice of the goddess—perhaps even one to whom Gilgamesh would listen.

"And I shall stay with you, silly sheep," Puabi said, tossing her head. She had made the rounds of the temple-duties: baking, weaving, tending the foundlings, scribe-work, singing, and playing. Only at singing had she been talented. She had begun well in the choir, and might have been given solo parts in time—until Shubad came to the temple, with a voice in the same range as her own but, as it had been set out to Puabi in the music-master Elulu's ruthless manner, much better. Given the choice between staying among the *gala*-priests as Shubad's understudy and going to another task, she had left. Elulu's harshness she had grown used to, but the scorn of a highborn girl two years younger and three times as gifted, who could always find her wanting, she could not bear.

So now she herded, and would do so until one of the priests or priestesses noticed her and called her to learn a craft—sacrifice, perhaps, or kindling holy fires, guiding the prayers of those who came with offerings, reading the sheep's liver . . . there was no shortage of tasks in the service of Inanna. Or else she would leave the temple and make her own way in the world, though unless she caught the eye of some man who offered her a good marriage, there was little chance of that. And, truly, she was freer and better fed as a temple herder than most of the women who toiled at spinning and weaving and cooking within Erech's walls: she had no real wish to leave the life that had been her only home.

Puabi put two fingers in her mouth and whistled, two short blasts. The dog that had been lying still as a big shaggy boulder in the grass bounded to its feet, running in a big circle to round up the few sheep that had straggled away from the flock. Puabi waved her crook to head off another, and together she, the dog, and the sheep, started back toward the sunset-reddened walls of the city.

GILGAMESH PACED IN his room, tossing a small ball of feather-stuffed sheepskin from hand to hand. He had been cooped up within the *gipar*, the great building within the holy precincts of the Eanna, for nearly a week, undergoing the purifications that would make him ready to take up his father's place as Ensi of Erech. *And Lugal as well*, he promised himself for the thousandth time. *Erech needs a war-leader as well as a ruler: our swords have been sheathed for too long. The tributes from Ur have diminished since Lugalbanda's time, for they knew they had nothing to fear from a city ruled by old men, and think that I am yet a child. Though I am but fifteen, they will find out that they are wrong!*

He tossed the ball to the side, drawing the short bronze sword at his side and dropping into a fighting crouch. He had not been allowed to train with the men for the last week, but had been careful not to let his speed or strength slacken. Lunge, retreat, parry, lunge . . . Gilgamesh could see the foeman before him, broad shoulders and shaven skull, black eyes with the dull sheen of fresh-welling bitumen. Stab and back, step sideways out of line while slashing quickly at the other man's outstretched arm; shield up under his wrist to block as he stepped in, his sword hooking up in a ripping rush through the belly. Gilgamesh yanked the blade free of the air, whirling to meet a second foe . . . and the tip of his sword whistled inches before the waistband of the old En's simple linen kilt.

The old man did not jump back, only stood calmly looking up at Gilgamesh, who flushed, sheathing his blade again. Though Gilgamesh's eyes were a full handspan above the top of the En's silver-gray head, he felt himself shrinking before the priest's gaze, as if caught using his writing-reed to play at swords instead of working at the tablet he had been set to copying out.

"Does the waiting chafe on you, Gilgamesh, son of Lugalbanda?" the En asked. His deep voice was dry as years of desert dust, hardly more than a husky whisper.

"There is not much longer to wait," Gilgamesh replied boldly. "I hear the songs of sunset . . ."

"And at sunrise you will be led forth to have the crown of Erech set upon your head. Yes, and you will be given wives, three fair temple-maidens—your own votive-priestesses, overseeing those offerings of butter and oil and honey that the people give to their Ensi. I do not doubt that you are ready for them: as well that you are not expected to go virgin to their bed."

Caught between pride and embarrassment, Gilgamesh found himself reddening again. Would he be expected to service all three of them at once? he wondered. An image came to his mind, warm breasts pressing against him and soft thighs spreading for him, and he shifted his legs uneasily, hoping the En would not glance down to see the proof of his words. But it was true: he was a man, he was ready.

"And you will be ready as well," the En went on, "for she who will be chosen Shamhatu in your mother's place—even as you take my place in the marriage, and let me step down from my work in my old age."

The air went out of Gilgamesh's lungs as if the priest's thin brown fingers had stiffened into a spear-point, jabbing him beneath the breast-bone to paralyze his breath and limbs. He had known that someday he would have to go in to Inanna; but somehow he had thought, told himself, that it would not be this year. Not at once upon his ascension, not before he had a chance to grow older, and stronger, and famous among men . . .

Without knowing it, Gilgamesh had stumbled back a step, then another. He clenched his hands into fists to stop them shaking, but he could do nothing about the blood draining from his face, nor the trembling of his heart.

"So," the En said softly, as if to himself. "So, I see. You do understand. I had thought that I would have to put fear into you, so you would be able to offer yourself to the goddess with a fully opened eye, knowing the price her bridegroom must pay . . ."

"His death!" Gilgamesh broke out, his voice cracking to a high squeak on the last word. "Did you think, because I was a child, that I never listened to the songs of Inanna and Dumuzi, or that I did not hear what folk say of my father's death—that the goddess took him as a sacrifice as soon as my life had quickened in my mother's womb?" He was shivering hard now, the words spewing from him against his will, as if he were vomiting up the curdled clots of tainted milk. He did not know how long it was since he had first seen the dark shape of his doom lying over him like the shadow of Inanna's great statue in her temple; it seemed to him that he had never been without that fear in his path, that bitter tarnish upon the layered horns of Lugalbanda's crown where it shimmered ahead of him, though he had never spoken of it to anyone. That secret had lain cold within him through his childhood, stirring like a serpent unstiffening from the night's chill as he became more and more a man, with the need to sate his body as a man—the knowledge that someday Inanna would use his own desire to snare him like a bird in a net, then strike him down, like all her other lovers.

The En touched the great medallion that lay over his bare and bony little chest—the sign of his office as Inanna's husband, electrum set with polished stones of dark and clear crystal. "Though we mourn Dumuzi each year, I have gone into Inanna's chamber many times since Lugalbanda's death, and yet I live. This is her city, and you were born to be her bridegroom. I have always heard that you are brave: are you not ready?"

He lifted the medallion, as if to take it from his neck, and Gilgamesh recoiled. Desperate with shame and rage, his guts knotting within him as though they tightened about the cold bronze of a blade sliding in, he cried, "Let me prove myself first! By the strength of my arm I will restore Erech to its old greatness—till then, you may be Inanna's bridegroom!"

The En's hand dropped. "We cannot force you as an unwilling sacrifice," he said mildly. "Yet . . . for the sake of your fear of death, will you give up the rule of Erech?"

Gilgamesh looked at the floor, shaking his head mutely.

"You can yet choose. I know of a caravan that will be leaving the city tonight, going to the Black Land. Say the word, and I will see that you have a place on it."

"No. No, I will not leave."

"You speak out of habit, and training. Think again: if you choose wrongly now, you will suffer all the more for it later. Fly, and live free— or stay, and be bound by all the chains of rulership, and give your life to Inanna."

"I will stay," Gilgamesh said, his voice stronger. "And yet I will not go to Inanna this year. Ask me again next year, when my rule is set firmly and I have done more."

Gilgamesh stood braced, waiting for the En's next words. Some subtle and cruel words, so neatly phrased in the old man's dry murmur that Gilgamesh could not reply until their full weight had hit him—some sentence that would twist him inside out again, have him weeping without knowing it . . . But the En only bowed his head.

"As you will it, then. I shall keep the Sacred Marriage this year, and hold Inanna's husbandship in trust for you until you are ready to take it—unless she who becomes the Shamhatu can move your heart, for the goddess will live through her. Wash your face now, for the eunuchs will soon come for you, and you have much yet to purify yourself of."

The painted mat of woven reeds across the doorway swung shut behind the En as silently as it had opened, leaving Gilgamesh staring and astonished at the place where he had been. Seething with anger beneath the reeling shock, he did not know whether to curl up and weep or strike the walls with his sword till the mud-bricks shattered in puffs of dust and the bronze edges grew dull.

"How could he speak so?" Gilgamesh whispered. And then, "How could he do this to me now?" Now, on the eve of his ascension—now, when he was about to take his seat beside the gods—why had the En chosen to come to him so, to make him feel like a wretched and unworthy child? The old fool, the misbegotten son of a goat! And the En had meant to frighten him: he had said so.

"I must not be weak," Gilgamesh said to himself. "I must not show fear, else I will be devoured . . ." It came to Gilgamesh now that it had been no cowardly thing to stand up against the En, to claim his rule in his own right while still refusing to do the one thing he would not do— deliver himself to Inanna like a goat bound for the jaws of a lion. He grasped the hilt of his sword, drawing it white-knuckled from the gilded sheath-leather. "I will be Ensi," he said, careful to keep his voice from cracking, to hold it to a man's depth. "And I will be Lugal, and restore Erech's greatness in the name of my father Lugalbanda."

AFTER PUABI HAD delivered her sheep into their fold, she hastened to the communal baths where the other temple-folk were washing themselves to prepare for the ritual of the night. Gratefully she shucked off the old woolen gown, full of the stink of sheep and sweat, and slid naked into one of the large water-pits. The bathwater was no better than luke-warm, but it was scented with fresh tamarisk branches and sweet oils, smoother against her skin than the finest linen. She scrubbed and scraped, ducking her head beneath the water and flinging the mass of wet dark hair back over her neck in a spray of droplets.

"Watch where you're splashing!" Shubad's silvery voice called out from behind her. "I was nearly dry, and you still reek of the sheep-fields."

Puabi turned to look at the other girl, lounging gracefully on a mat beside the bath as she rubbed a scented linen cloth over her lithe, naked body. A few drops clung to the rounded slope of her left breast; Shubad flicked them off ostentatiously.

"If you don't want to be splashed," Puabi replied, "then find a better place to dry yourself."

The singer smiled—a soft, languorous smile, as though she had just bidden farewell to one of her lovers. "Perhaps I shall." She reached down to towel a last splotch of glistening dampness from the back of one slender thigh, then linked her hands behind her head and arched backward for a moment, touching her shoulders to the mat before rising, in a slow, controlled dance-movement, to her feet. Tossing her waist-length fall of gleaming black hair back behind her, Shubad glided off without looking back.

Puabi gritted her teeth. Prideful as she was, even Shubad would not dare to boast of the favor of Inanna before it was spoken—but tonight she was acting as though sure of it. If she were chosen as Shamhatu, the singer would have her own chambers, with her own bath, and eunuchs of the temple to wait upon her; she would no longer have to put up with the splashing and noise of the others. *She and Gilgamesh would make a fine pair!* Puabi thought. *I hope it is Geme-Tirash who is chosen.*

She looked around for the young trance-priestess, but could not see her plump form anywhere. But Geme-Tirash's duties never took her outside the Eanna: she had undoubtedly been one of the first to bathe, and was likely to either be in her place in the shrine already or have gone elsewhere to meditate. Anyway, the water was cooling swiftly, and the others had already gotten out, drying themselves in haste and reaching for the clean dry robes that had been laid out at the far end of the baths. Puabi made her own way over, ruffling through the robes until she found one that was close enough to her size. It was often said among the temple folk that they always had clothes, but never clothes that quite fit; and for the lesser servants of Inanna, who had to make do with temple issue, that was true enough.

She fell in behind the other young women, listening to their scuffling and soft giggling. "It could be you!" one whispered. "It could be me."

"And wouldn't you like that, if you could take Gilgamesh to bed?"

"Oh no, for that would only happen once a year. Let me be one of his votive-wives, and sleep with him every night."

Another girl laughed. "He is only fifteen—he may be randy, but you'd have a better time with a ram in your bed, bang bang bang. Give me a man who's old enough to know what he's doing, I say. And I wouldn't like to be the Shamhatu: can you imagine that, never being able to choose who you lay with, or fall in love with a man?"

"Oh, but she must fall in love sometimes. Everyone does."

"But the Shamhatu isn't allowed to marry, or sleep with men except when her duty calls her to. Nothing in Erech would be worth that, for me."

"Then surely the goddess won't choose you—she'll find someone prettier!"

"Like Shubad? Well, Erech is called Inanna's Vulva—and they might as well set Shubad's thighs up as the city gates!"

"Jealous cow, jealous cow . . . I know who's a jealous cow!"

Puabi could not help laughing, but now they were beginning to climb the steps of the earthen platform on which the shrine stood. "Hush," she called softly to the other girls. "They may be able to hear us inside."

The others subsided slowly as they climbed. A single bass drum was sounding softly within, the slow thump of a heartbeat almost beneath hearing.

As Puabi stepped into the shrine, she had to blink, the flames of the hundreds of little oil-lamps set within every nook and cranny bursting into a million tiny points of light behind her eyelids. The warm air was sweet with the scents of incense, hanging heavy with anticipation as a dark cloud about to burst into a storm. All the temple-folk were gathered there, each in his or her own place according to duty and rank. But the lights burned brightest at the end of the long hallway: there stood the great statue of Inanna with her two lions, fine-carved stone painted to the warmth of a living face, and beside her, the Shamhatu, her features pale and set as alabaster. The oil-lamps dazzled a golden halo about the two of them, statue and living woman, and the awe of the goddess shone forth from them.

*And yet the Shamhatu is old,* Puabi thought in sudden shock. She had never before been able to see the lines scoring the face beneath the gold-starred diadem with its carven lapis beads, nor marked the strong shoulders of the high priestess slumping with exhaustion. Yet now strands of silver glimmered below the gold tamarisk leaves dangling about the rim of the crown, and even she—even Puabi the shepherdess maiden, who had never been gifted by Inanna with holy sight or wisdom—could see clearly that this woman was no longer the Maiden of Erech as she had been at the last feast of the new moon, but an old woman . . . a woman whose son was grown.

The Shamhatu moved; her mouth opened, a dark cavern in her pale face, and her low voice sounded over the whispering beat of the drum.

"Hear me, my people—children of the Eanna!" she called. "Gil-gamesh, Inanna's son and Lugalbanda's, is a man now: he is ready to take up the regalia of his father, to became Ensi and En of Erech, and hus-band to Inanna. As he has grown, I have grown older, as the gods decreed for mortal folk. Maiden no longer, I am no longer a fit vessel for Inanna: the drinking-skin is too old for the strength of her new beer. Now the goddess must choose whom she will have, to wear the crown of the Queen of Heaven, giving up earthly life and love that Inanna may have her will among men."

Behind her, Puabi heard a faint rustling, then a soft bleat. The En walked at the head in his full regalia—pointed crown made up of layers of overlapping horns, long white robes of linen blended with wool, embroidered about the hems with the symbols of the goddess, and the smooth crystal stones of his electrum medallion flaring bright with lamplight between the black onyxes. He led a glossy-wooled ewe, her white coat shot through with flecks of black that seemed to whirl and dance in Puabi's sight like tufts of night spinning among brilliant-wheeled stars. Behind him came the sacrificial priest, Urgigir—a tall dark shadow against the little flames lighting the shrine, with the bronze knife in his hand glowing cherry-red as though the casting-mold had just broken away from it.

*That is one of my sheep,* Puabi thought suddenly. *That is Queen Sheep*—for the ewe bore a unique mark: a pure white ring around the top of her mottled skull like a crown. Thus Puabi had named her, and thus, she was sure, the ewe had been chosen. *Poor thing: had I known you were to die tonight, I would have stopped in the marketplace to buy you fresh lettuces for supper. But do not fear for your children, for I will make sure to give them milk until they are big enough to live all on grass, and watch them carefully to keep them from wandering into the jaws of a wolf.* Though the temple sheep were, as a rule, doomed to die either as offerings or simply to feed the folk of the Eanna, Queen Sheep had been a good and biddable ewe, and a good mother to her two fat lambs, and Puabi was a little sad to see her walking so calmly to her doom—though it was as noble a death as a sheep could expect.

When the two men and the sheep stood before the statue of Inanna, the Shamhatu stepped forward, her arm upraised, thin outstretched finger wavering like the nose of a hunting dog casting about for a scent. *There*, she pointed, and *there*, and *there;* and as she pointed to each young woman, the chosen ones hurried softly forward like doves flocking home in the evening to stand behind the En and Urgigir, whose dagger was scratching each name lightly on a section of the clay model of a sheep's liver he held. Shubad was one of them, Puabi saw with no surprise, and so was Geme-Tirash, but there would be nineteen others, for it had to look right . . .

She was so busy thinking about the others whom the Shamhatu had chosen, she did not notice for a moment that the priestess' finger was pointing directly at her.

"Go," the Shamhatu whispered—or was it a flicker of the lamplight that had made her lips seem to move, and a rustle of breeze from outside that had made the soft noise Puabi heard. But the maiden gathered her skirts and stepped forward to take her place among the rest. *We are no more than oil-lamps to light the temple's choice*, Puabi thought. *I do hope it is not Shubad . . .*

"Inanna, hear!" the En called out. Though his dusty voice was quiet, deep without resonance, it sounded clearly through the shrine. The *gala*-priests and priestesses, the ritual singers, took his words up, their voices shivering octaves above. "As you set one cup aside, choose another to fill; as your old ewe goes out to pasture, choose you another for your ram. Queen of Heaven, the black-headed maids of Sumer stand before you: let your judgment be known. Give us a new Shamhatu, a bride for your blessed groom; give us a woman whose flesh you may wear, to bear your holy *me*, the gifts of civilization, to Erech again. Who will wear your diadem, Inanna? Inanna, who shall wear the crown of holy heaven's queen?"

The Shamhatu lifted her hand, stilling him. For a moment Puabi could see the brilliance flaring from the old woman's eyes in their twin nests of wrinkles, her bones showing clear through the transparent flame of her flesh; and for that moment she seemed young again. She set her hand on the side of the ewe, just above the liver—and then the brightness faded: the Shamhatu's shoulders slumped once more, and again she was an old woman.

Fascinated by the transformation she thought she had seen, Puabi missed the flash of Urgigir's knife sweeping through Queen Sheep's neck. She only heard the bubbling bleat, then saw the kicking of hooves behind the skirts of the two *ishib*-priests who had come forward to assist Urgigir in the sacrifice. Then the other girls were crowding in front of her, pushing and jostling as much as they dared before the eyes of the temple-folk in the holy shrine, and she was shorter than most. Though she stretched up on her toes, she could see nothing of what was going on, only hear the soft sucking noises as Urgigir reached within the body of the sheep for the liver.

The big sacrificial priest straightened up again; he held the dark, dripping mass carefully in both hands so that no clumsiness of his would blemish it. Laying it on the mud-brick table between the two heads of Inanna's stone lions, Urgigir bent over to wipe the liver clean with a white cloth, then scanned it carefully, his eyes flicking back to the clay liver with its inscribed names. Puabi could hear nothing save the soft rustle of air through her lungs and her own heartbeat pounding in her ears: the drum had stilled, and no one dared to move or speak as they waited for the sign of the goddess' will.

"The goddess has made her choice," Urgigir cried. Though his deep voice was powerful and clear, it sounded muted to Puabi, as though he called out over a great distance to her. "Behold, we are blessed, for the liver shines glossy and clean; surely the favor of the goddess is with us. Trees grow old and wither, and mortal lives fail, as the gods have decreed it, yet for worn lives they give us new again. One Shamhatu passes away, and another is chosen to take her place: come forth, Puabi!"

His words knocked the breath from Puabi's body, like a ram butting her full-strength in the stomach. For a moment she could only gasp and gape, even as the gazes of all the temple-folk turned toward her, the lamp-flames reflected from the rows of shining dark eyes. Shubad's mouth hung wide open, she noticed, the other girl's shock mirroring her own; Geme-Tirash's eyes were closed, as though the young trance-priestess had retreated already into her own meditations at the news that she was not the chosen one. *There must be some mistake*, Puabi thought. *Urgigir has read the liver wrong, or misremembered his instructions: he cannot mean me!*

"Come forth, Puabi," Urgigir repeated. "Come forth—or, if your heart is too weak to bear what the goddess asks of you, leave this place forever. It is not for temple-folk to question the will of Inanna."

Puabi stepped forward on shaking legs to stand before the offering table. Even with only the flickering flames of the oil-lamps, she could see the little streak of bright blood standing out like a glowing carnelian on the smooth dark surface of the liver. No clearer sign could be given, and now she knew what she had doubted: though it was human folk who read Inanna's messages and brought them forth, even the plans of the great could not flout the will of the goddess.

"Will you serve Inanna's desires?" the dry voice of the En husked. "Will you give up your name, your earthly life and loves, the children unborn in your womb? Will you give yourself only as the goddess chooses, and be but her holy vessel in Erech?"

"I will," Puabi answered, her voice strong. It seemed to her now that she stood at the end of a long passageway, the door opening before her to light the hallway behind; and though she had thought she wandered aimlessly, or at her own will, now she could see that she could have taken no step that did not lead her here.

*So the gods guide us, though we know it not, like blind men wandering in the night.* The thought shook Puabi to the bone, rushing over her in a wave of the profoundest humility, such as she had never known before. *This is what it is to know oneself in the power of the gods.*

Yet even as Puabi thought, the old Shamhatu bowed her head before her, and the En knelt to her.

"Take off your robe," the old priest whispered softly, so that only she could hear it. "You are about to receive one more fitting."

Though Puabi was used to being naked in the baths with the other temple-folk, as she bent to grasp the hem of her robe, her hands were shaking so badly that she could barely hold on to the folds of soft white wool.

*It is the will of the goddess,* Puabi repeated to herself. Not allowing herself to think any further, as if she were plunging full-length into icy water, she grabbed the edges of the garment and pulled it up over her head. A soft breeze played over her chilling skin; she could feel her nipples hardening beneath it, as if to a lover's touch, and the muscles of her buttocks tightened as she handed the white robe to the En who knelt before her.

"Take the crown from my head," the old Shamhatu murmured, "for it is Inanna's."

The diadem was heavy in Puabi's hands, the great eight-pointed star of solid gold dazzling her eyes for a moment before she raised it to set upon her own head. The golden tamarisk leaves brushed her cheeks, warm from the other woman's skin.

"Take the pendants from my ears, for they are Inanna's." Slowly, as if dancing in a dream, the two of them went through the ritual: the chains around the old priestess' neck, the ornaments of spiraled gold upon her breasts, the girdle of birthstones about her hips, the bracelets ringing wrists and ankles, the robe of pale blue linen—its fringes sweeping the ground before Puabi's feet when she had put it on—and, lastly, her fine-woven breechclout, until the older woman stood naked before Puabi, drooping breasts and slack belly exposed to the gazes of those within the temple. Though she had not borne Gilgamesh herself—it had been the Shamhatu before her who gave birth to Lugalbanda's heir, dying in the birthing—the long years had pulled her body just as surely, if more slowly, into the sagging shape of an old woman.

"Now you are the Shamhatu, Inanna-on-earth, the Maid of Erech. And I . . ." She reached out for the white robe, held up on the En's outstretched palms, and slipped it over her head. ". . . I am Rimsat-Ninsun, the Old Woman of Erech, mother to the Ensi. May Inanna wear you well, my daughter."

Rimsat-Ninsun reached out to Puabi, holding her tightly in a warm embrace. The younger woman's eyes prickled hot with tears—had a mother never held her so? She felt as if she were a newborn babe, the memories of schooling and sheepherding fading from her mind like a trail of incense smoke tossed on the wind.

"I am the Shamhatu," she said, her voice firm and loud enough for all to hear. Before her, the En touched his forehead to the floor, then rose to take a bowl of scented oil from one of the white-robed assistants who had moved noiselessly to his side. Head and hands, heart and vulva and feet, he anointed her, then turned to give the same honor to the statue of

Inanna that towered above them, the marks dark against her painted face and the light blue linen of her robe.

"So it is done," he said. "Go forth in peace and gladness, all Inanna's folk and the blessing of the goddess upon you."

The voices of the *gala*-singers rose as the temple-folk filed out of the shrine, until at last the singers themselves were gone and only the En and Puabi—she could not yet think of herself as the Shamhatu, for all she knew she must forget her name—stood before the stone eyes of Inanna.

"Why—" Puabi began to ask, but the En silenced her with one finger on the thin line of his lips.

"Come with me," he husked.

She followed the En down the steps of the shrine, into the *gipar* where his chamber was. Somewhere in this building, she knew, Gilgamesh was being readied for his ascension . . . No, she would not think about that yet, lest it spoil the awe and joy that were upon her.

The En's room was warm, a little fire burning in the hearth. Bunches of drying herbs hung from the ceiling; the walls were lined with chests of inlaid cedar. Several cats lay sleeping upon the bed—shorthaired cats, spotted and striped, all descended from the pair he had brought back from the Black Land when he was still a young man and had made the long trek across the desert. One looked up as they came in and yawned hugely, its teeth little slivers of ivory shining bright against the pink insides of its mouth; another meowed and leapt to its feet, twining about the En's ankles and looking up into his face. He bent to pet it, though Puabi could see the faint wince of pain across his eagle-nosed face as a twinge from his back caught him. There was a small golden bell on the table; the En lifted it and rang it thrice, its high voice chiming through the room.

"Sit," he said, pointing to the soft mat of creamy wool before the fire. "Beer will be brought to us soon, for I think you have need of refreshment."

Wondering, Puabi squatted down on her heels, and the old man settled himself cross-legged beside her. It was not long before the soft knock sounded on the door-frame.

The young man who entered, bearing two silver cups, was not one of the usual temple servants, but the scribe Shusuen, the En's great-grandson. He was a handsome youth, lithe-built and fine-featured, with thick brown hair and eyes of an unusual light blue—the legacy of his great-grandmother, whom the En had brought back with his cats. Though two years younger than Puabi, he overtopped her by nearly a head; and his height, together with the studious lines of his face and his calm bearing, made him seem like a man full-grown. He was bare-chested, wearing only a short kilt; the small dark nipples stood out clearly against the pale skin of his slim chest, and Puabi could not help looking at the well-shaped muscles of his calves and thighs flexing as he bent to serve them their drinks . . . *but I can no longer look at men so,* she thought, flushing as she turned her face away. Another shorthaired cat, a half-grown, leggy tom, had followed Shusuen in, yowling plaintively as it looked about the En's room, and Puabi was grateful to the cat for distracting her gaze.

"Thank you, great-grandson," the En said, taking the cup from Shusuen's long fingers. "But have you finished your account of the night so soon?"

"Half finished, Great-grandfather," Shusuen replied politely. "I only hoped to see if there was anything more you wished me to record."

"Nothing that is worthy of the annals of the Eanna," the En told him. "Go back to your work; you will find yourself busy tomorrow, for I wish you to stand by Gilgamesh's side. A young man should write of a young man's triumphs, and I judge your skills great enough for the task. Now hurry on."

Shusuen's face lit with delight, and for a moment Puabi felt a twinge of regret—*I will never bring a man joy, only the goddess through me.*

"Thank you, Great-grandfather!" the scribe said, retreating quickly with his cat trailing behind. The woven tapestry hanging from the door-frame fell back into place. The En waited until its fringe no longer trembled against the floor before he spoke again.

"You wonder why the goddess chose you, no doubt," he said quietly.

"I did not think I was the first choice in anyone's mind."

The En's thin lips curved in a dry smile. "As you may have guessed—and you will know, soon enough—often the gods leave choices to men, but we must be sure not to get in their way when they have made their own decisions. You will not, I think, be too surprised if I tell you that had the liver not shown very clearly otherwise, it would indeed have been Geme-Tirash to wear the starred crown."

"And not Shubad?"

"She is beautiful and talented—and headstrong, and indiscreet. Though the Shamhatu is Inanna on earth, there are many folk who must carry out the administration of the temple and settle its politics, within and without the walls of the Eanna. She would not work well with us, nor easily learn to leave alone those who are doing their duties as they ought."

The En's eyes were dark as the unplumbed depths of an old well, and something in the rustling of the voice set Puabi's nerves on edge. Her head still buzzing from the shocks of the night, she did not stop to cool her throat with a draught of the good beer, or to think what she was saying.

"You mean, Shubad would not be an obedient figurehead?"

The En's lips parted, and Puabi could see the bright shadow-edge of his teeth against the blackness within. She braced herself, trying to keep from recoiling in fear, as though she had set her hand upon a warm stone wall and felt a snake squirm beneath her touch. Then she heard his soft breathy chuckle, and knew that she had not spoken wrong.

"What the Shamhatu is—depends on the woman who fills the office. One may be an empty vessel, content to sit and nod until the goddess is called to speak through her at holy times; she is no less the Shamhatu than the woman who weaves her way with tongue and plot, to give advice to the Ensi and further the desires of the Eanna. What manner of priestess you shall become is for you to decide: now you shall take the first steps on that path. But whether you are figurehead or leader, you must learn to deal with the folk of the temple, else you shall not last long . . . Now, what do you think of Shubad? What will she do this night?"

"She is proud, and felt that she should have been named as Shamhatu," Puabi said slowly, choosing her words as carefully as she would choose steps over a half-broken trail on a moonless night. "If she had more close friends, she would be accepting their sympathy and encouraging them—oh, so gently—to mutter ill things about me. But I think she will go off alone, to brood, and plot what revenge she may take without risking herself too greatly."

"And how could you deal with that? How can you turn her mind away from the wrong she feels you have done her, without confronting her or waiting until she does something that will force us to drive her away? For she would be a great loss to the temple."

Puabi grimaced. *Are you, even at your age, seduced by her beauty and her voice?* Yet, forcing herself to think within the dictates of her new office—responsible for all the temple's doings, from the great ritual performances to the children sweeping the shrine—she could not deny that the En was right; had she not left the singers because she knew her rival was matchless?

"If some great honor were given her . . . something that brought her a chamber and servant of her own, and set her among the high ones of the Eanna; that is what she wants. But she is too young, and there are those who deserve honors far more than she."

The En smiled. "Ride a donkey, but harness an onager to the war-chariot. Tomorrow Shubad will find out that Inanna has chosen her to be the temple's chief soloist by the next feast of the New Year—if she can learn the parts to the satisfaction of Elulu. She has known the feeling of the *gala*-master's rod against her palm since she, as a simple choir-girl, first answered back to him; she fears his sternness, but knows that she must please him. And he knows that the part is within her powers, but only just, and will be the harder on her; and caught by her desire to sing it, she will turn all her thoughts, good and ill, toward Elulu, and have no strength left over to struggle against you. When guiding the deeds of others, give no thought to what of their traits are strong or weak, or good and bad: look only at what they are, and how they may serve."

"What of Geme-Tirash? I do not know how she thinks, except that she, too, is talented, and had good reason to think she would be chosen Shamhatu. The best reasons," Puabi added, looking closely at the En. But his face betrayed no sign of the confession he had made to her earlier: there was not so much as a twitch at the wrinkled corner of one eye, as if his skin were worn too close to the dry skull beneath to shift with any expression.

"What of her? Perhaps you should speak to her yourself."

Puabi lifted her cup, sucking a long draught through the golden straw that clinked against its silver rim. The beer was sweet and cool, its malty flavor rich on her tongue—smooth, well-aged beer, such as she had seldom gotten to taste. *I shall be given beer like this from now on,* she thought; and the thought was more dizzying than the warmth of the drink in her empty stomach.

"I shall do that," she said.

"But now there is a matter you must think on most seriously . . . yes, and ask for Inanna's wisdom."

Though Puabi had not noticed the hint of sly humor in the En's voice as he spoke before, she could hear it dropping away. Now his dusty voice was hard as stone, cold as desert rocks frosted by the glittering ice-stars of a winter's night. "I spoke with Gilgamesh this day. He says that he will not come to Inanna's marriage-bed this year."

Puabi's mouth dropped open. She shut it again, the harsh snap of her teeth jarring through her skull. "He . . . why? How could he?"

"He fears the goddess. He fears death—and he is very young."

"How can he think . . . He cannot rule without Inanna by his side! He must be her bridegroom, else . . ." Puabi did not know what would happen if a year went by without the marriage.

"You must go to him tomorrow night, and speak for Inanna. You are the Shamhatu: this is a task that no other can do for you. Else . . . until he is willing, I may fill the office of En, and Inanna's husband, for a little time longer. But I am growing old, and my body weakens, and it will be sooner rather than later that I can no longer fulfill the bridegroom's duties."

Puabi sat a moment, still with horror. For this to be on her so quickly—if to succeed meant yielding her maidenhead to Gilgamesh's rough fifteen-year-old clutches, when he liked her no more than she liked him, while to fail meant failing the En, and Inanna, and Erech—

*My goddess,* she prayed silently, *why did you choose me, when you knew that this lay before me?*

Mercifully, the En said only, "You must think on it: how to bring Gilgamesh to Inanna's bed, how to ease his fears."

"But he is afraid of nothing," Puabi said bitterly. ". . . Or nothing he will admit to. I know him: he is like a wild bull. There is no challenge, no matter how stupid, that he will not back down from, nor any voice of reason that will turn him aside from proving that he is fearless."

The En shook his head. "You must think on it," he repeated. "Go, now. You have served here in the *gipar;* you know where your new chambers are. By the time you get there, they will have been readied for you."

In her confusion, Puabi could think of no more to do than follow the En's orders. Yet when she reached the woven mat that hung before the Shamhatu's chambers, she found that she was trembling with cold and fear, and could not bring herself to step within. The starred crown weighed hard on her head, heavy and prickly, and the palm of her hand thrummed painfully as she lifted it to move the mat aside. One step forward, two back: this seemed to her the last irrevocable moment.

"I swore before the goddess and the temple-folk, in the holy shrine," she said to herself. "Why am I afraid now, when it is done?"

And yet it seemed to Puabi that she could see the Shamhatu's bed, its ivory frame and clean linens scented with sweet flag; and it seemed that she could also see Gilgamesh reclining upon it, his hateful, self-confident grin stretching to a challenging leer. *This, for the goddess?* she asked bitterly.

*This, and everything,* she replied. At worst, it would be a little time of annoyance while Gilgamesh pawed her body, a few minutes of pain while he entered and satisfied himself. But once it was over, it would be done for another year. And she would be . . .

. . . not free of him, for the Eanna must deal daily with the Ensi: they were the two great powers in Erech. But bedding with Inanna would put Gilgamesh in her power while he ruled, even as the Shamhatu's body was in his power for that one night a year, and that, truly was the goddess' will.

Puabi stepped through the door-frame into the Shamhatu's bedchamber. She was alone there, with the clean scent of the rushes on the floor mingling with the sweet oils of the lamps that burned across the room. Another cup had been set out for her on the table beside the bed, one of silver panels inlaid with lapis, and beside it was a platter of pale melon slices interwoven with thin white strips of cheese. By the bed stood the stone statue of Inanna, naked and pale in the dim light. Slowly, piece by piece, Puabi undressed, setting the crown on Inanna's head, the earrings on her ears . . . everything, down to the breechcloth about her waist and the robe of pale blue linen. The robe's fringes were dusty from trailing on the ground—she would have to have it remade, for the old Shamhatu had been a larger woman than she.

Sitting down on the bed, Puabi felt a strange emptiness. After a moment she knew what it was. She was alone, with no other girls to whisper to until they fell asleep; for the moment, she had no duties. Before, in such rare times—before anyone could set her to one of the myriad small tasks that always needed doing about the Eanna—she would go to the room where the practice instruments were kept, take up a lyre and sing to herself for a while. But now . . . "I will have a lyre made for me," she whispered. A fine new instrument, with no clumsy fingers jangling it constantly out of tune, or careless hands knocking its scarred and scratched frame against things, such as she had once dreamed of before realizing that her talent as a player was middling at best . . .

Yes, that would come in time, and other fine things as well. But now she was hungry and thirsty, and, she realized as a great yawn stole over her, exhausted as well. Now she would eat, and sleep, and leave all her thoughts and worries for the morning . . . for Gilgamesh's ascension.

"AWAKEN, MY MASTER," said the soft high voice in Gilgamesh's ear. His body jerked convulsively, his eyes starting open as the words flung him out of the depths of sleep. His eunuch Enatarzi stood by the bed, plump chest and swelling belly pale above his short gray kilt. In his hand he held a gold cup—all the breakfast Gilgamesh would have, for he must go fasting to his ascension.

Gilgamesh took the cup from the eunuch, ignoring the gold straw to gulp greedily at the clear water. Its cool stream washed the staleness of sleep from his mouth even as he blinked the stickiness from his eyes. He had lain awake long into the night, thrashing under his blankets as if he sought to battle against the En's ill-timed words with body as well as mind; when sleep claimed him at last, it had been drowning-deep.

"Your bath awaits," Enatarzi said. "Make haste: the sky is still dark, but the dawn is not far."

Naked, Gilgamesh followed his servant down the corridor to the bathing chamber. It was all lamplit within, and as he entered, the three *gala*-priests—two eunuchs and one bearded man—began to sing. The eunuchs' voices, alto and soprano, rose chillingly pure over the deep bass of their companion.

"An of the Heavens, father of the gods, hear us!
Enlil, Mighty One, knowing all in wisdom,
Inanna, Queen of Heaven, goddess of Erech, hear us . . ."

Beside them stood the En, a bundle of reeds in his hand—the reeds of holy purification, but also just such a bundle as was used to whip the children of the Eanna when they misbehaved within the precinct of the gods. Looking into the impassive black eyes of the little old man, Gilgamesh felt a slight shrinking within, as if he were still a boy and the En meant to beat him for refusing Inanna.

The youth gritted his teeth. Here he was, on the threshold of being confirmed as the ruler of Erech, and yet he had to obey old men like a child, perform the rituals that had been drummed into him by rote as if he were a slave being trained to address his masters properly and bow before them. For a week he had been the En's prisoner, suffering the endless bathing and chanting, scant food and lengthy lectures meant to bank the fires of his pride and force him to bend his neck to the wills of the temple and the assembly of elders. All his life, since Gilgamesh could remember, it had been the same. *You shall be the Ensi, you must learn . . . you must do . . . you may not do . . . Remember that you shall rule, and therefore . . . What you desire does not matter, for you shall be Ensi and En.*

And yet, for all Gilgamesh had grown to hate the endless rites and the nagging that companioned them like flies about souring milk, he could not protest, or leave out any of the steps he had learned, else . . . he could not simply ascend the steps of the shrine and say to the folk of Erech, *I am your Ensi now*, without blessing and ritual and regalia. *If you would rule*, Gilgamesh remembered the En saying to him over and over again, *you must give your people what they expect of you, lest in their disappointment, they decide it is better not to obey.* And, galling as the source was, Gilgamesh knew that those words were true. Thus, now, he could do nothing except say as he had been taught, "Here am I, a mortal before the gods. Cleanse me and purge me of all evil, I pray, that I may be a fit vessel for their exaltation."

The En lifted his reeds. He struck Gilgamesh lightly, barely tapping him with some blows; yet each touch seemed to sting more than its weight should allow, as though the supple stalks had been dipped in bees' venom. Forehead and mouth and throat; shoulders and palms and heart; belly, groin, thighs, and feet. Lastly, Gilgamesh received three heavier blows of the scourge on his back, and these were hard enough to leave red welts—these, to remind him that for all he might be exalted before men, to the gods he was no better than a slave. Proudly, Gilgamesh bore these as he had the others, without flinching or making any sound; but he was glad when the En laid his bundle aside and smoothed sweet oil over all the places he had struck. His back stung again as he slid into the hot water of the bath, but the pain quickly faded as he took deep breaths of the scented steam. Yet the humiliation of the beating, symbolic though it was, still ached within him.

*Patience*, Gilgamesh counseled himself as Enatarzi knelt beside the bathtub to scrape the wispy beginnings of whiskers from his chin and cheeks. *Soon this will be over. And things will be different once the crown is on my head.*

Stepping out of the water, Gilgamesh stood still as Enatarzi whisked him with softly budding tamarisk branches, then dried him carefully and began to dress him. Today Gilgamesh wore the floor-length kilt of a ruler, rustling with many overlapping layers of linen fronds. A shining bronze breast-plate was set over his chest, and heavy gold bracelets upon his wrists; his long, wavy black hair was combed out carefully and oiled into place with frankincense. Lastly, he was given the great bronze axe that his father Lugalbanda had borne, to be strapped into place at his waist. Although Gilgamesh had never been allowed to do more than look on it before, its weight felt comfortable at his hip, solid and reassuring—proof of his own power, that he would no longer have to come and go at the will of any other.

The first deep notes of the gong shivered through the hard-packed earthen floor, tingling in Gilgamesh's bones.

"The light of dawn has been seen," the En said quietly. "Come, shepherd of Erech: your flock awaits you, and it is time to take up your crook."

Gilgamesh walked proudly out of the bathing room, the morning air cool against his fresh-shaven face. The path from the *gipar* to the shrine was already lined with people, all clad in their festival best—gold and silver for the rich, bronze and copper and clay beads for the poor. The *gala*-priests and musicians were arranged along the sides of the steps leading up to Inanna's shrine, and at the sight of him they struck up a song—a song he knew, the praise of his father Lugalbanda, who had crossed the great mountains in his time, and under whose rule Erech had grown mighty. *And that is well*, Gilgamesh thought, swelling his chest until the breast-plate felt tight upon his growing muscles. *Lugalbanda did great deeds, and his greatness shall live again in his son . . .*

*And he died at Inanna's will.* The thought shuddered cold down Gilgamesh's spine. With a great effort he turned his eyes upward again. The Shamhatu was waiting by the shrine's door—no, not the Shamhatu, though it was the woman who had held that office and been as a mother to him. Her robe was not Inanna's pale blue, but dark, and the crown she wore was not the gold-starred diadem of the Queen of Heaven, but a high cap with the horns of a wild cow wrought small in silver upon it. Behind her were three young women in fine linen dresses, with bridal wreaths of young green palm leaves upon the coiled black braids of their hair. Looking at the heavy curves of their breasts, the nipples dark through the sheer white linen, Gilgamesh felt his manhood swelling: for these, he knew, would be given to him as his votary-priestesses, sisters and wives and worshipers, and after the ceremony . . . Traditions and rites, he reminded himself with a slight smile, were not always unpleasant.

But now, beneath the growing brightness in the sky, he was climbing the steps up to the shrine. And although he had run up and down them since childhood, now Gilgamesh felt as though he were burdened with more than his own weight and half again, his calves aching and breath burning hot and harsh in his lungs. His empty stomach tightened hard, and he was glad that he had been given nothing to eat that morning.

*Am I afraid?* Gilgamesh asked himself. But the eyes of all Erech were upon him; Utu, the mighty sun, was rising before him, and he could not fail or show weakness now. Back straight and proud, he mounted the last step, turning to face his people and lifting his hands in a gesture of blessing upon them. The musicians fell silent; the En began to speak, the *gala-*priests singing out each sentence after him to carry his words far beyond the strength of his thin chest.

"Great gods of heaven, behold! Mighty ones, who made all things, who shaped the race of men, the black-headed people of Sumer . . ."

The words of the invocation washed over Gilgamesh, familiar as the high whine of flies in the summer heat. Though he stood without moving, still as a god carved of stone, his eyes flickered over those on the steps below. The sunrise light gleamed dully from the bald pate of Ur-Lamma, Gilgamesh's chief general and tutor in the arts of war. Gilgamesh could see the slight smile hidden in the older man's grizzled beard—for he agreed that it was time to march on Ur, as soon as the spring harvest had been brought safely in; Ur-Lamma's skills had seldom been called on, in the long years while Lugalbanda's heir grew to manhood. It was a comfort to see him: Gilgamesh had talked with him often of late, and knew that whatever others might disagree with his decision to go to battle, Ur-Lamma was his man, and a mighty voice to argue his case.

Looking farther, to Gilgamesh's surprise, it was the young scribe Shusuen who squatted on the step just below his own, the reed in his hand pecking quickly at a wet clay tablet. He had thought that one of the older temple scribes would have been chosen to record his ascension—*but why not a young one? The time of old men in Erech is past,* Gilgamesh thought. And he had always liked Shusuen when they sat together in the school of the Eanna: the other boy's dry, devastating wit, turned upon their teachers when the old men were out of earshot and on his peers when they tried to tease or bully him for being scrawny and more clever than the rest, had been one of Gilgamesh's few sources of amusement during his schooling. Yes: when the day was over, he would inform Shusuen that he had been chosen as the Ensi's personal scribe, to write down all his deeds and pronouncements. *If only,* Gilgamesh thought, smothering his smile, *he can keep from likewise writing his parodies of every official report on my doings.*

The En's lengthy speech came to an end at last; the gongs shivered a deep note through the air, and Gilgamesh felt a rush of wind as the doors of the shrine swung open behind him.

"Behold the Shamhatu of Erech!" the En called out. "Behold Inanna on earth!"

Though Gilgamesh was quivering with curiosity, he did not turn his head to look; he waited until the Shamhatu, bearing his tall crown and inlaid ceremonial mace, had walked about to stand before him. The gold of all her jewelry flashed and dazzled in the new sunlight, so that at first he could see only the bright light rippling over the pale blue robe. A small woman, whose head came only to his chin, and slightly built . . . Then Gilgamesh's eyes blinked clear of the golden burning and he saw the pale oval face beneath the crown's eight-pointed star and dangling gold leaves.

"Puabi!" he hissed.

Puabi did not blink, nor did her delicate features twitch in response to his breach of ritual and custom. It was as if she had forgotten her name already, to become one with her office—save that Gilgamesh was utterly sure that her nature would not have changed. It was she, the temple foundling, who had always leagued gleefully with their teachers to silence him when he would speak, to reprove him when he would act, as if her three years more of age somehow made her superior to him, despite the fact that he was born to rule and she had been left at the Eanna's gates in a basket. At eleven, he had rejoiced when she was taken away and set to the simple duties of baking and cleaning and herding; but four years of separation had not dimmed his memories, nor, from the gleam in her eyes—black and sharp as a flake of obsidian—had they dulled hers.

The rage began to grow within Gilgamesh's heart, like banked coals slowly fed into flame again. What jest of the temple or Inanna was this, to set Puabi against him again? Had the En planned it, thinking that because she had bullied him as a child, she would be able to bully him now that he was a man? That she would once more act as if she had been personally set by his teachers to keep him dull and obedient?

But Puabi—no, the Shamhatu now: Gilgamesh told himself he must remember that, though he knew that to him the title would always mean the woman who now stood as Rimsat-Ninsun. It was she whose warm arms had enfolded him as a child when he fell and scraped his knees, she who had given him honey-cakes at festivals, and sent him away only when she had to perform the duty of the goddess toward those men who came alone to the shrine with offerings, or else need, great enough to win Inanna's favors. The Shamhatu lifted his crown, a high-tiered structure of layered horns similar to the En's ceremonial cap.

"Gilgamesh, son of Lugalbanda," she called out, her voice carrying through the cool morning air, "ruler of men, servant of the gods, kneel, that you may be exalted."

Reluctantly, Gilgamesh knelt before her. A rich sweetness filled the air as the En poured scented oil upon his head, the rivulets running down through his hair to drip golden and shiny as honey onto his breast-plate.

"Anointed of the great gods of heaven," the Shamhatu said, "Inanna crowns you Ensi of Erech, shepherd of Erech the Sheepfold." She lowered the tall cap slowly onto his head, holding it a moment to be sure it was settled firmly. Even with his neck bowed, Gilgamesh was uncomfortably aware of her closeness: the curve of her hips and slim belly beneath the fine blue linen, the scents of sweet flag and incense and the Shamhatu's own warm flesh—if he raised his head, his face would be nearly in the fork of her thighs. It was well that he was kneeling, for he could feel the swelling in his loins, even as the thought sprang unbidden to his mind: *I could have her tomorrow night!* And if he did, perhaps it would not be Inanna to whom he submitted, but Puabi whom he overcame at last; and thus he could fulfill all that was expected without delivering himself to death . . .

The Shamhatu stepped back; Gilgamesh straightened, careful to keep his heavy crown balanced.

"Ensi of Erech, betrothed of Inanna," she said, "exalted of the gods, receive the mace of judgment. May your rule be filled with wisdom, your mind enlightened by Enlil the mighty, An of the heavens. May the demons of the waste places and the Netherworld have no power against you; may your days in the land be long, and Utu ever shine upon you with favor. Hail to you, Gilgamesh, Ensi of Erech, son of Lugalbanda and Rimsat-Ninsun—two-thirds god and one-third man."

A great cheer went up as Gilgamesh took the mace in his hand, lifting it high. Now Rimsat-Ninsun stepped forward, the three young women behind her.

"Gilgamesh, Ensi of Erech, two-thirds god and one-third man," she repeated, "I bring these women to thee: wives and beloved sisters shall they be to you, votary-priestesses of the Ensi. Enmebaragesi and Peshtur and Kubaba, let them come with you to the wedding chamber, brides of your delight, for now you are a man, and must take up all a man's duties. Come forth with us, Gilgamesh, Ensi of Erech: your brides are ready to receive you."

To the applause of the crowd, Gilgamesh kissed each of the three girls in turn; then Rimsat-Ninsun took him by the hand, leading him down the steps with the women following after. Blossoms showered their path, the pale soft petals fluttering through the air around them like a flock of tiny doves, and behind him the singers raised their voices again. Gilgamesh, though, was aware of little more than an overwhelming sense of relief, mingled with his growing desire. It was over, at last: he was confirmed and crowned. Tomorrow he and Ur-Lamma could confront the elders of Erech with news of the coming war, but today—today he would enjoy his rewards.

The chamber to which Rimsat-Ninsun led him was sweet with flowers, the walls green with fresh palm-leaves and branches of tamarisk. An alabaster pitcher of beer stood on the small table beside four ivory cups; a selection of small pastries and cheese and bread was laid out upon a cedar tray inlaid with mother-of-pearl.

"Congratulations, my son," Rimsat-Ninsun said softly to Gilgamesh. "I have long awaited this day, when you should take your rulership. Be strong, as you are always—but remember in your strength that others are weaker, and be wise and gentle as well." She kissed him softly on the forehead, departing silently as Gilgamesh's three new brides filed in.

Gilgamesh stood by the bed, looking at the three of them. Two were short and plumply curved, their round doe-eyed faces so alike that they might almost have been twins; the third was taller and slimmer, apple-sized breasts high and hard-nippled beneath her linen dress. Enmebaragesi and Peshtur and Kubaba—but when she spoke their names, Rimsat-Ninsun had not shown him which was which. Suddenly he felt tongue-tied as a virgin, unable to meet all three gazes at the same time.

The taller one went down on her knees, prostrating herself gracefully before Gilgamesh. "Mighty Ensi, exalted one, worthy of worship, I am your priestess Kubaba," she said. Her voice was soft and mellow, soothing Gilgamesh's nervousness even as his excitement rose. "Before the goddess your mother chose me for you, I was an *ishib*-priestess in the temple of Inanna; now I shall bear the offering bowls to you alone, with my maidenhead the first gift. The sisters of Enmebaragesi and Peshtur"—she gestured, and the two prostrated themselves in turn—"were *naditum* of the temple; now it is you to whom they will bring the delights that the goddess offers, and while their wombs lay fallow before, we pray that your seed will quicken them."

As she spoke, Gilgamesh could feel his staff rising hard from between his legs, throbbing as it pressed against his fronded kilt. The two *naditum* would have been trained in every skill of pleasure that a woman could practice on a man, and Kubaba's warm tones promised welcome; he thought that his mother had chosen well.

"Rise, and come to me, my brides," he said, sitting down upon the bed. The three women did as he had commanded, Enmebaragesi and Peshtur flanking him with their warm thighs pressing against his own and heavy breasts nestled against his arms while Kubaba filled the ivory cups with beer, holding Gilgamesh's up so that he could sip from the straw of gold. The beer was sweet with honey and date-syrup; the warmth it kindled within Gilgamesh's belly mounted quickly to his head, so that he could feel the hot flush rising in his cheeks. Kubaba lowered the cup, leaning in above it to kiss his mouth even as the light touch of Peshtur's fingers trailing over the linen fronds of his kilt sent a shiver of pleasure through his body.

"Come, my love," Enmebaragesi whispered to him, her lips soft and moist against his left ear. "Let us take off your breast-plate; you need no armor against your wives."

Gilgamesh let them unfasten the heavy bronze and set it aside. Enmebaragesi and Peshtur stroked his chest with delicate fingernails, murmuring softly at its breadth and strength, but it seemed to him that they were holding back, waiting for something. Then he remembered that he was still wearing his high crown, and only he had the right to lift it from his head. He did so, placing it carefully on the table. Then the two sisters were upon him, one straddling each of his thighs with their legs linked inside his own; he turned his face from the kisses of one to the kisses of the other as Kubaba, kneeling behind him, stroked his shoulders and back. Enraptured by the sweet taste of Peshtur's mouth and the liquid glimmer of her dark eyes, Gilgamesh found when he looked back at Enmebaragesi that she had somehow managed to strip her dress away unnoticed, and now sat naked upon his lap, her big plum-dark nipples brushing against his chest; and while his gaze was captured by her sister, Peshtur had cast her garment aside as well.

Gilgamesh drew both of them nearer, holding their yielding bodies close to his own. Enmebaragesi reached down, and Gilgamesh found that Kubaba had unfastened his kilt, so that Enmebaragesi only had to lift aside a fold of linen to expose his full-rearing staff. He groaned as her hand closed lightly on him, stroking the hood back and forth on his swollen head in an unbearable silken caress. Gilgamesh bit his lip hard, forcing back the hot cloudburst gathering in his loins. Dazed, he hardly noticed the look that passed between the two sisters; but Enmebaragesi, still stroking his scepter, shifted the warm weight of her buttocks to the side as Peshtur rose slightly, arching her back so that her breasts pointed to the heavens. Enmebaragesi guided Gilgamesh's thrusting rod, stroking the tip lightly over the dewy petals of her sister's vulva before allowing Peshtur to sink slowly onto him. Gilgamesh gasped as he felt Peshtur's body rippling around him, as she curled upright again, kissing his mouth even as she began to move upon him. He thrust up strongly to meet her, again and again, her eyes half closed in ecstasy, a series of little moans issuing from her mouth. She tightened hard upon him, and again, and Gilgamesh could no longer hold back; his hips drove hard upward, one last time, and he cried out loudly as he spurted into her.

Peshtur held Gilgamesh within her as he slowly softened, while the other two women stroked him.

"Our husband, you fasted this morning," said Kubaba. "And . . ." She smiled slyly at him. ". . . you have already worked hard. You must be hungry."

Even as she spoke, Gilgamesh became aware of the vast emptiness within him. Drained and starved, he reached out for the tray of food on the table, but the gentle hands of his wives pushed him back on the bed.

"Oh, no, we will feed you," Enmebaragesi crooned, giggling a little. "You are married now, you need not worry about anything." The three women took turns putting tidbits into his mouth: savory pastries filled with the rich meat of duck and small birds, cheeses smooth and mellow, or so salty that each bite had to be followed at once with another sip of beer, and bites of flaky honey-cake. As they served Gilgamesh, the two sisters leaned over him, brushing their nipples over his skin and kissing him while they fed him, so that it was not long before he felt his manhood stiffening again under their ministrations. Enmebaragesi reached for him, but Kubaba slapped her hand away lightly, laughing.

"Come, it is my turn now," she said. "You two have known the delight of lovers' bodies in plenty, but I am yet a maiden—would you make me wait longer? Gilgamesh, my husband, have you ever made love to a virgin before?"

Though Gilgamesh had not thought that a woman could make him blush, he knew he was blushing now, and his three wives giggled harder.

"Well, have you?" Kubaba pressed.

"Once . . . yes."

"And did she enjoy it?"

"Now, that is not fair to him," Enmebaragesi broke in. "How would he be sure of that? No, but we will teach you, dear husband, all the skills of loving a maiden." She bent to pull the entangling folds of Gilgamesh's kilt away from his legs, then tugged the pins and ribbons from Kubaba's braids so that her hair tumbled loose in great black waves. "Now, even before you take her dress off, hold her close to you and kiss her—kiss her gently, lest you frighten her away. And you may move your hand upon the curve of her breast and stroke her nipples, but be careful not to pinch or twist too hard, for they are very delicate, and not used to the touch of a man. See, I will show you." Enmebaragesi sat down on Kubaba's other side, pulling the slimmer girl close and kissing her on the mouth, running her tongue softly around Kubaba's lips as her hand gently caressed one of Kubaba's small rounded breasts, and then turning her head toward Gilgamesh. As best he could, the young Ensi imitated Enmebaragesi's movements. He could feel Kubaba's nipple hardening beneath the palm of his hand, and she kissed him back eagerly, her little pointed tongue flickering wetly into his mouth.

Enmebaragesi's hand slipped down the curve of Kubaba's hip and around, stroking her thighs, and Gilgamesh did the same, gently delighting in the warm tautness of her flesh beneath the thin linen even as his fingers brushed again and again over the soft fingers of his other wife.

"Now see," Enmebaragesi said, "how my hand moves in her lap, how I press, ever so lightly, against the gateway of life . . ." Though she only moved her fingers slightly, Kubaba drew a deep breath, leaning her head to look up into Gilgamesh's eyes. Her lips slightly parted, she drew away from the two who stroked her.

"Undress me now, my husband," she said to Gilgamesh.

Slowly, Gilgamesh removed the light dress from Kubaba's body, revealing, bit by bit, all it had half hidden: slim pale thighs and the neat triangle of dark thatch where they met, the gentle rounding of her hips and smooth low curve of her belly, pink-nippled breasts and graceful shoulders . . . He wanted to seize her and toss her down on the bed, to plumb her depths straight away, but he knew that he must hold back for her sake, and that inflamed him further. Her delicacy, her nervousness despite her bold words—he knew it was so, for she trembled even as she reached out for him—spurred him on like the scent of blood inflaming a lion. He embraced her naked for a moment, moving slowly against her body, then carefully eased her down onto the bed. She lifted her knees, waiting for him.

Enmebaragesi and Peshtur moved close on either side, stroking Kubaba where she lay. Peshtur reached out, taking Gilgamesh's hand and setting it on the soft pelt between Kubaba's legs.

"Here, too, you must caress gently," she instructed. "One finger first . . . even that is a great deal, for an untouched maiden." She looked down into Kubaba's eyes—"Be at ease, my sister: the less you fear, the less your pain will be"—and then back up at Gilgamesh. "And just above, carefully . . ." Kubaba suddenly shuddered, her hips arching a little beneath Gilgamesh's touch. "Now you may begin to enter. Press in slowly, but surely, and do not stop: it is best over with in a single thrust."

Gilgamesh lowered himself carefully over Kubaba, easing into her as gently as he could. She tightened as he entered, a single burst of pleasure rushing through him, but he kept pushing. Suddenly he felt something give within her, her body opening to his with a soft cry and the tears welling in her eyes. Fully sheathed in her hot depths, he waited to pull back and thrust slowly again until she began to move against him, rocking back and forth in his close embrace.

When he was done, Gilgamesh held Kubaba to him for a while longer. He did not know whether she had reached her own peak or not, nor could he bring himself to ask; but her eyes were half closed, and it seemed to him that her soft breathing against his neck was a sound of pleasure.

"That was well-done, husband," Kubaba said at last. The other two women murmured agreement.

"You are lovely," Gilgamesh answered sincerely. "I am glad that you were chosen as my wife."

"Well-done, indeed," Enmebaragesi broke in. "But now, husband, what of me? Young and strong as you are, there is much for a man with three wives to learn—for you are expected to do your duty by each of us every night."

Looking at his face, Peshtur burst out laughing. "No, that is not so. But if a little rest does not restore you, you shall learn something new. For everyone knows that a woman can wear out the strongest man, and, potent as you are, there may come a time when your strength fails you. And is this not the most pleasant schooling you have had?"

Though Gilgamesh knew she jested, there was something in her words that galled him. Yet he was too pleasantly tired and sated for the sting to be more than a prickle, and so he only laughed and said, "So it is. Well, teach me more, as you can."

THE RITUAL DONE, Puabi retreated into the cool shade of Inanna's shrine. She did not go straight through to sit by the feet of the goddess; instead, she made her way among the pillars to one of the many little private nooks recessed into the thick mud-brick walls, squatting down before the little table where an empty offering bowl rested and letting her breathing slow to near-stillness.

Gilgamesh had played his part well enough—though in truth, there had been little enough for him to do. But she saw his face when he gasped out her name: he had not forgotten their old rivalry. Yet she knew she must put it from her mind, and pray that he would do likewise, or it would not be long before the desert winds blew dust through the empty shrines of Erech, and the voice of the screech-owl howled where now the *tigi*-hymns were raised. And, one way or another, she must bring him to the goddess' bed.

*Reminding Gilgamesh of his duty will not move him,* Puabi thought. *He will only struggle harder, pressing as strongly as he may to find the limits of his freedom.* And for all he had resented the days of his schooling, he would find, she knew, that the bonds holding the Ensi were drawn far tighter than those binding the heir before his ascension.

No: she would have to come challenging, to set it to Gilgamesh that he must come to Inanna—or admit his fear to her. And there was another weapon she could use: for everyone knew his eagerness for the bodies of women. Puabi wished now that she had asked to be trained in the arts of the love-priestesses of the Eanna, skilled in inflaming men despite their awe or fear, age or infirmity. For her duty's sake, she would have to undertake that training now—it was the Shamhatu's responsibility to be sure that the men who came to her in search of Inanna's blessing were able to receive what the goddess gave—but all she knew of the ways of men at the moment were what she had heard from the other girls of the Eanna, and the clumsy kisses she had exchanged with Utuhegal in the secret crannies of the shrine before his father died unexpectedly and he left the temple to take over his family's firm of builders.

Puabi had almost made up her mind to go to one of the older *naditum* who trained maidens and ask for advice when she heard the soft rustle of sandals on the floor. She bowed her head, pretending to be deep in prayer, but the footsteps stopped just behind her. With a sigh, she looked up.

Behind her stood Geme-Tirash, her dark curly hair hanging disheveled over plump shoulders, her hazel eyes wide. A thrill of nervousness shot through Puabi's body, and her glance went at once to the other maiden's hands, to see whether she held a weapon. But her hands were open, fingers splayed out hard, and the dazed look on her face was not tainted with hate or rage.

"Exalted Lady," Geme-Tirash said softly, "the goddess came to me. She gave me a vision."

"Tell me."

Puabi watched Geme-Tirash carefully as she spoke. It would not be strange if she sought to advance herself so early, with a new and inexperienced Shamhatu; the words of a trusted trance-priestess could quickly become the power guiding the deeds of a temple or Ensi, and whether it was truly a god who spoke or merely—whether good or ill—the heart of the visionary . . . none who trusted too fully could know. And yet the words her low voice spoke filled Puabi with trembling, with a horrible unsureness.

"Gilgamesh stood upon the steps before the goddess' shrine," Geme-Tirash said. "And I did not hear the words you spoke, for a great rushing of wind filled my ears, and my eyes were shadowed as if it were dusk instead of dawn. But there was a strange light above the shrine, a star burning like sunlight and searing a long path across the sky. Then I heard the voice of Urgigir, as though he cried out from a distance . . ."

"What did he say?" Puabi asked, leaning forward breathlessly. Though a little corner of her mind was irritated—it was an old seer's trick, to force the listener to take part in the prophecy so—she could no more have kept herself from asking than she could keep a falling stone from striking the earth.

" 'The omens are not good.' " Now Puabi started back, for the other maiden's voice had dropped nearly to the bass register of the chief sacrificial priest. " 'The gods are displeased; there is wrath in the gazes they turn upon us. Enlil is displeased . . . ' "

"And then," Geme-Tirash went on in her own voice, "I heard another man saying, 'The Ensi of Erech is dead. Go to the city walls and tell it so, scribe.' And the shadow cleared from my eyes, and I could see and hear again."

"This is a vision of great concern," Puabi said carefully. "Tell me— did you see Gilgamesh himself, or did any speak his name?"

Geme-Tirash shook her head, her lapis earrings swaying like date-clusters in a storm.

"It is well that you have told me of this," Puabi went on. "Go and meditate upon it further; if more comes to you, tell me at once."

Geme-Tirash knelt briefly to Puabi, then rose and departed silently.

Puabi bit her lip, staring after the trance-priestess. If this were a true vision . . . She should go at once and seek the counsel of the En, talk to him and to Rimsat-Ninsun, perhaps summon Urgigir and ask him to read the omens on it. And yet, what if she did? If it were accepted as true, and Geme-Tirash then came back to her, speaking this or that demand from the gods in order that the ill fate be averted, and then another and another?

No: she would go first to Gilgamesh. If Geme-Tirash's vision were true, it took little wisdom to see how Gilgamesh might have displeased the gods and brought about his own death. His own life, as well as

Erech's, was in his hands, and it was up to her, more than any other, to see that he did not carelessly cast them away.

GILGAMESH RESTED WITH his three wives, laughing and talking, for a long time. He was surprised by how easy it was to simply speak with them after all of their desires were slaked; it went a long way toward stilling the niggling annoyance that came to him whenever he remembered that he had no part in choosing them. Enmebaragesi and Peshtur were full of stories of their time as temple *naditum:* the training that they had undergone to teach them how to use not only their bodies, but their wits and wills, in order to bring blessing to all of the men who came to them; the men themselves, proud middle-aged merchants whose boasts vastly outstripped their strength, virgin boys too frightened to lift a hand and touch the bodies of the priestesses, old men who desired, just for a little time, that their youth be returned to them . . . Though the sisters were only four years older than Gilgamesh, in that time they had seen, it seemed, half the men of Erech naked and vulnerable before them. Kubaba seemed quieter, more serious and intelligent; and Gilgamesh knew that his lovemaking had moved her, for now and again her hand would move to touch herself where he had been, and then she would look up at him and smile softly.

*Such is the wedding of the Ensi,* Gilgamesh thought when at last the three women had put their dresses on again and gone off together to bathe. In a little time he would call for Enatarzi to bring him a basin of fresh water so that he could wash himself, but now he was content to lie naked on the rumpled bed, every muscle in his body warm and loose, slowly breathing in the mingled sweetness and musk of the long lovemaking.

Gilgamesh was almost asleep when he heard the soft tapping on the door-frame. Likely it was only his eunuch or one of the other servants come to see if he wished for anything; but still, he pulled his kilt up to his waist again and fastened it before calling, "Come in."

The white woolen hanging swung aside, and Gilgamesh jerked upright at once. It was Puabi—the Shamhatu—in her full glittering regalia. Though Gilgamesh's warm well-being was too strong for him to be angry with her, even when he wondered if she had been spying to see his wives leave, he nevertheless hardened his face, asking as coldly as he could, "What do you wish of me?"

"Should I not come to speak to you, when it is we two whom the gods have set as the guides of Erech the Sheepfold?" the Shamhatu replied formally.

Gilgamesh sighed beneath his breath. And yet he knew she was right, for they would have to deal with one another every day. And too, he was not the boy with whom Puabi had ceaselessly struggled and sparred in the schools of the Eanna, and perhaps she was no longer the girl who had divided her time between reporting his misdeeds and shouting at him herself. They were both grown now: perhaps they could treat together.

"That is so," he agreed. There were no thrones in the room, such as there ought to have been for a formal audience, but he rose from the bed and squatted politely upon the rug, and she did likewise.

"You will want to know," Gilgamesh went on, careful to keep his voice low and adult, "what I mean to do as Ensi. And this is a matter that concerns the Eanna, since you have much to do with the clothing and provisioning of the army. After much discussion with our wise general Ur-Lamma, I have set it in my mind that when the harvest is done, I shall take on the title of Lugal again, for a war-leader is needed. I shall call up our forces and march upon Ur, to remind them of the discrepancies between the tribute that our old treaties with them call for and what they have sent in recent years. I trust that I shall have the support of the temple in this, since you benefit as much from the flow of tribute as does anyone in Erech." Gilgamesh smiled at her as charmingly as he could. He knew that his words had sounded well, for he had thought them over often in the night, though he had never expected to be speaking them to her.

But the Shamhatu's thin-arched brows drew together darkly and her mouth tightened. "Lugal of Erech—yes," she murmured. "But Gilgamesh, you know that there is something more you must be."

*The En has spoken with her,* Gilgamesh thought. He could feel his sinews tightening again, and the back of his neck prickled unpleasantly. Still he strove to master himself: if he appeared as a child to her, she would never cease to treat him so. He forced his muscles to relax, smiled at her coolly.

"You speak of the Sacred Marriage," he said. He was about to go on, ready to talk it over calmly with her—to see what truce, what compromise, they could arrange between them. His mouth was opening to speak when the Shamhatu leaned forward, so close that he could see her pupils swelling black to swallow the irises of her eyes, and himself reflected tiny in them.

"You must come to Inanna's bed," she hissed urgently. "There is no other choice: not for the ruler of Erech, not for Lugalbanda's son. The En told me that you were afraid, but I know you, Gilgamesh. You have always said that you fear nothing. Is it true?"

"I am not afraid," Gilgamesh said. But he knew that he lied; he was already trembling within, deep muscle-tremors that took all his strength to still.

"Prove it, then," she challenged. "Swear to me that you will come as the bridegroom in the Sacred Marriage tomorrow, and become the En—Inanna's husband."

Gilgamesh's anger was rising now, its welcome heat overcoming the cold sick terror in his belly. "I will swear nothing to you, Puabi."

"I am no longer Puabi!" she snapped. "I am the Shamhatu of Erech, and I speak for Inanna, to whom you belong by right, and whose laws you must obey. Do you fear her? Will you admit to me that you are afraid to come to her bed?"

The two of them stared at each other. The Shamhatu's eyes were wide, dark pits in the pale clay of her face; it seemed to Gilgamesh as though her words had shocked her as much as they had him.

"I am neither a slave nor a child," Gilgamesh told her harshly. "I am a free man, ruler of Erech."

"You are a spoiled child who thinks he is a ruler!" the Shamhatu shouted at him. "Not an Ensi even a day, nothing worthwhile done in your life—how can you even think of denying the goddess, when both she and your people demand your services?"

Gilgamesh bit back his first reply, answering only, "I am not a stud donkey, either."

The Shamhatu swept her arm out toward the mess of tangled and damp-stained linens atop the bed. "You seem to be trying hard enough to be! Already you are known through the taverns of Erech; you seem willing to bed every woman in this city except Inanna."

"Except you!" Gilgamesh shouted back, the squeak in his voice cracking into a sudden roar. He clenched his fists tightly, forcing down the next words in his mind: he knew better than to curse the goddess of Erech, or her priestess, but he did not know how long he could hold his thoughts back. Instead he breathed deeply, then said, in as calm a voice as he could muster, "Get out. Go away. We will talk of this at another time, but I have spoken with the En and he assures me that I do not need to wed Inanna this year. He will come as the bridegroom in the marriage, as he has for these many years, and the goddess will still be satisfied with her husband."

The Shamhatu stared at Gilgamesh for several moments more, then whirled, grabbing a half-full ivory cup from the table and holding it as if she were about to fling it at him. Gilgamesh lifted a hand as he would raise a shield in readiness to stop an arrow or stone, but she put the cup down very carefully, then turned and walked from the room in silence.

Gilgamesh sagged to the floor, his head in his hands. *I won,* he said to himself. Yet he felt . . . still powerless, the sudden silence in the room swallowing everything he had said. Nothing had changed, after all, between him and Puabi. For all he had tried—tried to apply all the adult self-restraint, all the crafts of rulership he had learned—he might as well have been arguing with the desert wind, or parleying with the storm. And yet she and he were still yoked by their offices, like an onager and an ox set to draw the same chariot, and his only hope of gaining his way was to pull against her more strongly than she could pull against him.

PUABI WALKED TO her chambers, back held straight and face rigid until she had passed into her room, out of the sight of any other. Then she flung herself facedown on the bed, weeping furiously into her pillow; and she did not know whether she was angrier at Gilgamesh or at herself.

"I failed," she cried aloud. "My first true task as Shamhatu—and I failed!" She turned over, staring at the statue of Inanna standing naked by her bed. Her diadem had fallen off; now she picked it up, setting it on the head of the goddess with shaking hands.

"Inanna," Puabi asked bitterly, "why did you choose me? I am stupid, I am useless—I thought I knew Gilgamesh well enough to sway him, and instead I have only ruined my hopes of bringing him to you. Whatever ill may come, I could not avert it." As if to scour her wound with salt, she thought back on how he had looked: clad only in his kilt, hair disheveled and eyes half lidded with voluptuous exhaustion, in a room reeking of the pleasures he had just taken with his three wives. How could he scorn her after that? How could he scorn Inanna?

Angrily, she tore her regalia from her body, piece by piece, setting it back upon the statue, until she was naked and the goddess was clothed. "I am not worthy of what you have given me—O Inanna, take it back: choose another in my place!"

But Inanna's stone face was silent, her stone eyes impassive as she watched Puabi weep and writhe before her. And gradually the storm that shook the priestess abated, tear by tear, until Puabi lay, exhausted and trembling, at the goddess' feet.

"Inanna," she asked, her voice very small, "what must I do? How can I set matters right—with *him* as Ensi?"

Still Inanna did not answer. Finally Puabi got up from the floor, pulling a simple robe on over her body. Her muscles ached painfully, as though she had spent the day carrying and lifting and cleaning, but that was little to her. Worse was the knowledge of what she must do now: she must go to the En and tell him what had happened, and that he would, after all, remain as Inanna's bridegroom for that year—and the years to follow, unless Gilgamesh could somehow be made to change his mind.

But once she had gathered her thoughts a little more, Puabi did not go in search of the En. Instead, swathing herself in a cloak so she could not be easily recognized, she made her way across the city to the temple of Rimsat-Ninsun. She did not have to speak when she reached the door of the shrine; the moment she folded aside the light wool draping her face, the old woman who watched the entrance hobbled off to fetch the new goddess.

"What is it you seek?" Rimsat-Ninsun said when she came out to Puabi. "You seem troubled."

"I would speak to you in private, for matters have gone ill with Gilgamesh."

Rimsat-Ninsun led her back to her own chambers, squatting on the rug beside her. Calmed by the quietness of the older woman, Puabi was able to tell her what had happened—Geme-Tirash's disturbing prophecy, and all that had befallen when she went to Gilgamesh. Rimsat-Ninsun listened, only nodding her head now and again.

"This does not bode well," she said at last. "And yet there is little that can be done. I do not think we can sway Gilgamesh's mind before tomorrow, nor can any shift what the high gods have decreed, only prepare for it. You are wise to be careful of the prophecies of a trance-priestess, though I believe that Geme-Tirash may be trusted. Yet ambition and disappointment may change the natures of many: watch her, as you mean to, and her behavior will show her truth. As for tomorrow . . ." She closed her eyes a moment, as if gazing inward at a memory. "Are you still a virgin?"

Puabi nodded.

"So, you do not know the ways of men, and your first night may come hard to you. The more so, because the En is an old man and, though his rod still stands, even the gentlest of lovemaking is a strain to his body. It will be best for you to lay him upon his back—do not blush! You must learn not to be shamed or abashed by anything that passes between men and women, for you will not only have to do them, but you must do them gracefully, without any thoughts in your mind that will block the presence of Inanna, or let you seem less than the goddess to any man who comes to you. You must lay the En on his back, and lower yourself onto him; you must not rest your weight on his chest if you can help it, for he no longer breathes easily. Then you must move upon him, so that he does not have to thrust up into you, which would strain his ancient back. If he cannot finish thus, take him in your mouth, or your hand. It matters only that he spill for Inanna, not that the seed find your womb. But be gentle, for men's private parts are very sensitive, and if you scratch him with your teeth, or your fingers are rough upon him, he may soften and not be able to stiffen again." She paused. "Let me see . . . In the chest in your chamber, you will find a small bottle: that holds the potion that will keep you from quickening. Drink half of it in the evening before the En comes to you, and half before dawn the next day. Do not forget to ask him to mix you up a new batch afterward, for you must take it every time a man comes to you."

"Is that all?"

Rimsat-Ninsun chewed her lip for a moment. "It has been so long since I was first trained . . . Yes. You may be frightened when he first comes to you, and you must learn how to lie with a man who does not excite your loins. Go to Shibtum, who teaches the *naditum*, and she will give you a share of the oil they use, that he may enter you easily. And . . . if you are still a virgin, your maidenhead will not be easily breached. It may be best for you to break it beforehand."

"How should I do that?" Puabi asked, shocked. "Must I look for a man?"

Rimsat-Ninsun laughed, though kindly. "My dear, how have you lived in the Eanna so long and learned so little of what other women know? Ask Shibtum for a pestle, and she will tell you how to use it— even do the duty for you, if you wish. You must not be ashamed to let her touch you, for she will be teaching you all you must know, and you cannot learn it if you are afraid of her."

Puabi said nothing, but her face must have shown something of her thoughts, because Rimsat-Ninsun leaned forward and patted her shoulder gently. "I know you are wondering if the marriage might have been easier with Gilgamesh. Take heart: though less might have been asked of you, you would surely have suffered more pain. Though the En is old, he is also wise in the ways of women, and was always a joy to me when I lay with him. Come to him with love and gladness in your heart, and Inanna will surely fill you with her blessings. And you could have no better start in learning the office that you must carry out."

"I thank you," Puabi said. "You have calmed my heart; I know now that I can do what I must."

Rimsat-Ninsun kissed her lightly on the forehead. "That is a good beginning. And who should know better than I, who once sat where you do now, to hear the same advice from an old woman?"

## 2

The Shamhatu sat on her inlaid stool at the feet of the goddess Inanna. Though the shrine at the summit of the high terrace was warm with the heat of the day, the shadow of the great stone image and the lion bearing her up cooled Shamhatu like a breeze whispering from the river across the baking plain as the evening's shadows lengthened. She did not have to look up to know Inanna there: she knew the goddess' chiseled face beneath the great eight-pointed star of her gold diadem better than her own, and her fingers had rippled down the lion's stone mane since she had been a small child stealing a few moments of her own from her duty of sweeping the old rushes from the shrine's floor.

The Shamhatu blinked herself awake as she heard the feet rustling through the reeds. Before her stood a maiden of some thirteen or fourteen years, her little breasts pressing softly against the sweat-stained woolen shift she wore and her dark hair tied back in a plain tail—just as Shamhatu's had been at that age, when she tended the temple's sheep. In the maiden's hand was a clay tablet.

The girl sank gracefully to the floor, brushing her forehead against the long leaves that strewed it. "To the Shamhatu, Inanna's voice and body within Erech the Sheepfold, servant of the mighty goddess who brought the *me* to mankind, Divine Lady, Queen of Heaven, terrible as the storm on the plain and beautiful as the palm trees in full fruit, bride to the tender of Erech's sheep, is sent this message from Lugalbanda's son Gilgamesh, Ensi and Lugal of Erech, protector of the flocks, undefeated in war and mighty in peace, two-thirds god and one-third man!" She rose, handing the clay tablet to Shamhatu.

Shamhatu took it carefully, for it was still a little wet: Gilgamesh had not bothered to have it baked or even let it dry. She scanned sharply down the lines of markings in the damp clay. Gilgamesh had scribed it in his own hand—a hand she knew well, his reed digging in so deeply that it was sometimes hard to read what he had written. *Young idiot,* she thought scornfully. For all he was only a few years younger than she, and Lugal of Erech, undefeated in his three short wars, as well as Ensi, ruler and lawgiver of the city, Gilgamesh could not rein himself in even so well as to write clearly, though the old En, the chief priest of Inanna's temple, had worn himself out rapping the youth's knuckles.

*To the Shamhatu and the temple of Inanna . . .* Yes, the usual greetings and titles, for both herself and him: even Gilgamesh was not so rash as to leave those out, but Shamhatu skimmed swiftly over them. *The Lugal, defender of the sheep of Erech, wishes to call upon his shepherds for aid . . .* Dear gods, what now?

*. . . Five thousand soldiers' kilts of sturdy wool will be needed by the end of next month. I therefore bid you to set all your temple workers to spinning, weaving, and sewing, for by that time my new recruits shall be ready to receive their issue; also one clay bowl and cup apiece must be made . . .*

Shamhatu lifted the tablet, then hurled it as hard as she could, face first, at the nearest wall. It stuck for a moment, then dropped to the floor, leaving a dirty smear of fresh clay across the mosaic-plugs of red and black that adorned the mud-brick walls of the shrine in geometric patterns. No one else would read his message now; too angry to remember her dignity, she surged to her feet.

"Call Gilgamesh here!" she shouted at the pale-faced maiden, who cringed away from her voice like a starved jackal-dog on the street cringing from a kick. "And tell him for me—" Shamhatu checked her temper: it was not fit to ask the child to bear such a message to the ruler of the city. *Though Gilgamesh will do her no harm, especially since she is not old enough for him to seek her maidenhead.* "No: simply summon him, for I will have speech with him. And call to me the En as well, and then go through the streets to the temple of Rimsat-Ninsun, for the counsel of that kindly goddess, mother to the Ensi, may also serve us well."

Shamhatu sat back down, folding her hands upon her lap and trying to still her breathing from the harsh, angry bull-snorts that echoed through her ears, as the maiden brushed her forehead to the floor once more, then rose and hurried out.

The priestess waited and waited, long enough for her heart to still to a dull thudding in her breast, then quicken again with rising impatience as the sunlight through the door grew longer and ruddier with no sign of Erech's Ensi before her. When a shadow darkened the lengthening rectangle, it was not the broad-shouldered silhouette of Gilgamesh, but a much smaller one: it was the wizened little body of the old En that half blocked the sun, its light still streaming over his silver-gray head. He was not breathing hard, but Shamhatu knew that he must have come in a hurry: he was not wearing the three-tiered kilt of linen fronds that showed his high rank, but only a simple skirt of wool, and the thin bones of his sunken chest stood out sharp and naked, not hidden by the great disk-pendant of electrum and polished clear and dark crystal cabochons that was his sign of office.

"Where is Gilgamesh?" Shamhatu demanded before she could rein herself in.

The En did not shake his head at the young priestess' failure to control her words, but Shamhatu thought she could see the reproach in his great dark eyes, and was ashamed. *He must have been sleeping through the heat of the day; he is growing old, after all,* she thought.

"Gilgamesh has gone out," he said mildly. "His body-slave Enatarzi tells me that he paused only long enough to scribe a tablet to you: now he is inspecting the building of his walls, for he says there is much work to be done before the armies of Kish march against us, if Erech is to hold."

"Building of his walls!" Shamhatu spat. "As if he had not already taken half the young men from tending barley fields and palm trees, so that oldsters must break their backs and women leave their hearths . . . he cannot feed his workers on grass, and that will be all that is left if this goes on, but do you know what he has done now?"

"Something of note, I gather, to have you spitting like one of my shorthaired cats from the Black Land," the En answered. It seemed to Shamhatu that she could hear a note of amusement in the dry husking of his deep voice, and the sound only made her angrier. "Well, tell me: what fence has the young bull broken down now?"

"He has written to ask for five thousand soldiers' kilts by the end of next month—that would be hard enough to manage, but he says that he needs them for five thousand new recruits! Where does he mean to find them, I ask, when almost every able-bodied man in Erech's fold has already been pressed into his service, for building his accursed wall or for his army or both? It is clear to me that he means to go on with his mad scheme of denying Agga of Kish his yearly tribute—and for what?"

"My bones are old," the En pointed out, rubbing a fist over the brown ridges of his ribs. "Shamhatu, Divine Lady, do you wish me to stand throughout the day while you shout at one who is out of your hearing?"

"Your pardon," Shamhatu said. She raised her voice, calling for a chair. In a few moments two temple servants had dragged a lapis-inlaid stool out of one of the small niche-rooms that furrowed the shrine's inner walls and set it down beside her. "I am only angered at our mighty Lugal's lack of sense. When he sends to the temple for the grain in our storehouses, he seems to know well enough that soldiers must eat; but does he think that the barley springs from the ground of its own will, grows without tending, and falls without reaping? The canals that bring water to the field need repair as badly as Gilgamesh's siege-wall, and though we have seven years' worth of grain laid up in our storehouses, it is daring the gods' wrath to call upon it when they have given us fair weather for growing more. A strong Lugal he may be, who summons up the troops and wins his battles, so that Erech is now chief of the cities here, with only Kish as our lords; but as Ensi, who should guide Erech's sheep to green fields and clear water as well as fight away the wolves and lions, he is no better than that most foolish of our temple servants who can barely be set to sweeping without someone to watch his work."

"How dare you speak so?" The low baritone voice boomed out from the doorway, where a huge shadow now blocked out the sun's light. Gilgamesh, his bare shoulders glistening with sweat, stood at the mouth of the shrine, glaring down its long central passage at the two who sat there. He strode down toward them, the fronds of his long kilt swirling above the thick-corded muscles of his sun-browned legs; the heavy muscles of his arms and shoulders stood out starkly as he clenched and unclenched his gold-ringed fists. "I sent to you for those things which the great flocks and many servants of Inanna's temple are bound to provide for Erech's ruler, not for insults that you would scorn to heap on the meanest dog in the street."

Shamhatu clenched her own fists: if she had the offending tablet back in her own hands, she would have hurled it at his face. But she knew that it was unseemly for Shamhatu and Ensi to shriek at each other like fishwife and date-merchant haggling in the marketplace, and so she straightened her back and said coldly, "If you wish the respect due your offices, you were better to carry them out more fully. Are you aware of the fields of Erech, which must still be worked—whether or not you are stupid enough to thumb your nose at Agga of Kish for your own pride's sake? Your soldiers may cool themselves with cucumbers and melons in the heat of the day, and eat good barley stew with lamb in the evenings, but someone must see that the canals through the fields do not leak their water upon the ground before it can reach the fields, and someone must dip the water out for the lettuces and onions with the *dalu*. Siege-walls will do us no good if those within have already starved because you took all the men from their work when they were needed."

"Not seven days ago," Gilgamesh answered, the noble curves of his face now as frozen as Shamhatu's own, "you swore to me that all the storehouses of Inanna were well-stocked, finer than they had even been since Lugalbanda's death—for all I have not come to Inanna's bed," he added harshly. Shamhatu's jaw tightened, teeth pressing painfully together, but she did not kick against the goad, for she knew that Gilgamesh sought to turn her from the question at hand by bringing up an older argument. The Ensi waited a moment, and Shamhatu saw the faint creasing of his broad brow, like a smooth clay tablet beginning to crack before any words could be pecked into it. Yet she said nothing, and at last Gilgamesh went on. "Well: the war can be looked for just after planting next year, and, if the Queen of Battle fights beside us, shall finish there as well. Then what we make up by not paying tribute to Kish will more than fill the storehouses again."

"Yes . . . if the rains come on time, and if the Buranun does not rise and flood us; and why should the gods grant us such mercy, when Erech's Ensi does not carry out his share of the rites?"

"Rites will be carried out duly in thanksgiving when we have won our battle," Gilgamesh said. "I take my part at the feast of the new moon each month; does not the En do the rest, as the gods have ordained for him?" He tossed back his glistening mane of wavy dark hair, crossing his arms across his chest; the reeds rustled and broke beneath the tapping of his sandaled foot, the scent of sweet flag rising up from the crushed leaves to blend with the lingering smoke of fine gums and oils that pervaded the temple.

Shamhatu opened her mouth to reply and closed it again, for she saw how she had nearly run headlong into his snare. *The great bull, he is not as foolish as he seems,* she told herself severely, looking up at Gilgamesh. *How did the gods shape such a son, to stand head and shoulders above other men, with the strength of the Buranun in floodtide, and yet scant him in the giving of wisdom?* Hardening her heart, Shamhatu said, "This is a matter for another time. We are here to talk of the tablet you sent me—"

"You called me in from Erech's walls," Gilgamesh broke in, "and the day is hot." With an exaggerated gesture, he wiped the beads of sweat from his forehead: even standing still, more little rivulets were trickling between the broad low curves of his pectorals and winding down through his heavy arm-muscles. "Has Inanna's shrine no beer that may be shared with the shepherd of her folk—or, at the least, cool water?"

"Cool water will do us all good," the En whispered, his deep, desert-dry voice rustling like the paws of a wolf treading through dead grass, "for this is a matter for sober thoughts and cold heads, not for the warmth of beer. But let it be fetched, for it will be a little time yet before Rimsat-Ninsun has made her way here . . . ah."

The figure who now stood in the doorway was slight, wrapped so thoroughly in deep blue wool that only her dark almond-shaped eyes could be seen.

"My son," Rimsat-Ninsun said, turning her black gaze upon Gilgamesh, who shifted his feet beneath it. "What have you done, that we must all be called here?"

"I have carried out my plans for the safety of Erech!" Gilgamesh answered hotly, and even beneath his deep-bronzed tan, Shamhatu could see the blood flushing red along his high cheekbones. "Why am I being treated like a boy who has shirked his writing lessons? For Erech to defend itself and win its freedom, we need a strong siege-wall and a soldiery made up of trained men, not youths who are more used to dipping out water with the *dalu* than to holding a sword's handle. Well do I know that our numbers are fewer than those of Kish: therefore, we must use all we have, and see that our warriors are better taught and better disciplined than Agga's, so that leadership may win where force would lose. I ask you to hold it in your minds, that I did not win my first battles by being foolish. Ordained of the gods, I keep my place as Ensi and Lugal; ordained of the gods, I shall hold Erech the Sheepfold safe."

"My son," the older woman went on, softly and remorselessly, "the weeping of women has risen from the shrine of Rimsat-Ninsun until the goddess' wooden shape is like to crack from the flood of salt tears. They come because their husbands have been taken away and their young ones have no bread; they come because their sons have been wrenched from their work, so that the baker no longer tends his oven nor the herdsman his flocks, and the aged mother must stand among the sheep in the early morning with the damp eating at her joints or break her back lifting the shovels of barley into the malting ovens. Young girls weep because the men they love cannot earn their bride-prices, being bound to the meager wages of soldier or brickmaker, and all of them come to my shrine, making those little offerings they can afford in this time when their men have been taken from them."

Rimsat-Ninsun cast back her cloak. Though not ancient, she was no young woman, and the adornments she wore this day made her look older. On most occasions when Shamhatu had seen her before, her silver-threaded black hair had been bound back beneath a circlet of gold, and it had been bangles of gold and electrum that ringed her slim soft arms. Now Rimsat-Ninsun wore necklaces of pottery and agate beads, bracelets and earrings of twisted copper wire—a great mass of the cheap necklaces hung over her sagging breasts, gaudily bright against the simple white wool of her dress, and the copper and bronze bracelets covered her arms so that no pale skin showed beneath them: she looked like an aging vegetable merchant's wife decked out as showily as his meager wealth could manage for the New Year's feast.

"See, I come wearing the gifts that have been given to me—all the women of soldier and brickmaker can afford, when before gold shone at the feet of Rimsat-Ninsun's statue and silver sparkled brightly beneath the smoke of my shrine; it is palm oil that burns there now, not olive oil from the mountains nor any precious gum. The hearts of those who come to me have grown no less generous, but none can give more than she has. Only those whose kin are rich enough to serve your will in other ways can still keep the forges of Erech's goldsmiths burning; only those lesser folk who can buy themselves free keep the hammers of the silversmiths tapping—those artisans who have not themselves been torn away to lift rude stones with their skilled hands or leave their forging of fine gold leaves to shape sword-molds and blow up the fires to melt copper and bronze."

Shamhatu could see the little muscles jumping at the side of Gilgamesh's clean-shaven jaw; she fancied that she could hear the soft grinding of his teeth, like rock rubbing on rock beneath a careless footstep in the distance.

"Better that," he answered, "than that those men lie slain, and that none come to a broken shrine, or that no goddess held her court at the feasts of month and year. The counsels of women are fit for matters of women, and the redes of priests good when we stand before the gods, but in things of war, it behooves all to listen to the voice of a warrior— and that I am, with none to match me within five days' march. It is for Rimsat-Ninsun that I ready Erech to stand and its armies to fight—and for Inanna, that she stand eternally above our city and its lands, Divine Lady of the sheepfold as well as Queen of Heaven."

"If this is what you wish," the En murmured, "then why do you not spend a fraction of what you are wasting on war and walls in sending our year's tribute to Kish, as we have done since before Dumuzi's time, and leave all in peace and health? Then Rimsat-Ninsun's shrine will sound with the joyous voices of mothers and the cries of babies, and there will be neither wailing of widows nor lamentations of the old."

Gilgamesh half turned toward him, his kilt-fronds swinging; Shamhatu saw the young Ensi's dark eyes narrowing, the thick muscles of his shoulders humping up like the shoulders of a taunted bull readying himself to charge.

"Why not, Gilgamesh?" Shamhatu echoed.

He turned on her at once, swift as a snake striking between the mongoose's paws. Gilgamesh's dark brows beetled as he glared down at the seated priestess; but even in his rage, he could not keep his glance from flickering up to the stone figure of the goddess above her.

"How long shall we pay tribute to the northern king?" Gilgamesh demanded fiercely. "This year he asked more than last year, and last year more than the year before. If you are all blind, I can see it; before the first silver touches my hair, we will be able to ransom ourselves only by going into slavery, beaten down as surely as if we had lost the battle. Agga is not blind, either, and he knows how Erech has grown in strength—he seeks to bleed our might away before we can gather it to raise against him, to keep us from raising our heads higher than those of the cities around us. I tell you, Agga already knows me his foe, and the simple tablet bearing his list of what he will have from us is no less than his strangler's noose tightening around Erech's throat!"

Gilgamesh slammed fist into open palm with a resounding *thwack*, glaring from one to the other of his counselors as though daring any of them to speak against him. His upper lip had lifted a little, showing a glimmer of white teeth, his wavy black hair flaring out like a sweat-matted mane about his head and shoulders. Shamhatu felt the cold trickle of sweat dripping down her own back, as though she had just heard a lion's cough coming from the edge of her sheep-flock at night. But even when she had been sweeping the temple and guarding the sheep, she had seen Gilgamesh, bigger and stronger than the other children taught in the House of Knowledge within the Eanna's walls, taking honey-cakes from their rightful owners and dealing out blows to nose and ear when thwarted. He had not frightened her then, for, at five years older, Shamhatu had still been enough larger than the young Ensi to box his own ears and teach him a healthy respect for the sting of her slaps. That had taught Gilgamesh a lesson then, and he had bullied his school-mates no more—and it was in Shamhatu's mind at this moment that he needed a like lesson now. Though, as a grown woman, her head came no higher than the middle of his massive chest, and Gilgamesh could have lifted her one-handed and never noticed the weight, Shamhatu thought that she still might have a few things to teach the boy.

"Agga is, as you say, not blind," Shamhatu answered, "and he knows how Erech's riches have grown since we started calling for tribute in our own right. What he asks is no more than a thirtieth part, as he ever has. It is you who would make a foe of him, and you should know best of all that nothing is more foolish than the weaker setting out to make a foe of the stronger: what do you do when a lesser man will not be held back from wrestling with you?"

"I am no lesser man!" Gilgamesh roared. Then Shamhatu could see that he had heard his own words, and knew their folly. His fists unclenched and, though the blood still darkened his cheekbones, his wide brow slowly unfurrowed. "Aye: the smaller and weaker often wres-tle against the bigger and stronger. And when the two are matched in wit, it is the greater man who wins—but I learned to wrestle as a boy, before I had a man's size, and learned then that skill and cleverness win the day as often as muscle and weight. And *therefore* must I gather and train my troops, though time be lost from tending the fields: this is not folly, but wisdom, and you do nothing for Erech when you try to turn me from this course—as well seek to divert the Buranun from its bed."

"Not to divert," the En husked softly as he looked up at Gilgamesh. The wrinkled skin seemed to have fallen away from the bones of his face: from the frame of long silver hair to the proud curved nose, it might have been a bronze axe-blade lifted toward the Ensi—save for the glittering dark agates of the old priest's eyes. "But when the river flows too strongly for its banks, it bursts them; and then the water is not life to the fields, but death. And you must remember that your strength is matched by none in Erech, neither your stone-layers nor, more to the point, your soldiers. You cannot make them an army of Gilgameshes, no matter how you tear them from tending palm and fig and barley-field and set swords into their hands."

Gilgamesh's eyes rolled in his head. For a moment it seemed to Shamhatu that she stared upon a carven mask of gray stone set over the Ensi's own face; it seemed to her that she could feel the despair in his limbs, a sudden cold weakness like the unexpected blooming of sickness in the bowels.

"My strength is matched by none in Erech . . ." he echoed softly. Then Gilgamesh's dark eyes were alive again, and he said angrily, "Well, I can take what I have here—I have led these men before, and know what they can and cannot do—and, unless it is a plan of the gods that Kish bring us under. I can lead them when the armies of Kish are camped on the river-plains around Erech. It is the might of the many together, not of any one, that will win the battle: but the many must be gathered and trained now, or they will never work as one."

"But why so swift, Gilgamesh?" the En questioned, tilting his head to the side. "If you move more slowly, gathering your might and training your men as Erech can support it, without calling away all the workers from the fields, then surely—in three or four years, perhaps—you will be more certain of a victory, and able to get it at less cost to the city."

Gilgamesh shook his head, his dark ringlets flying. "I have thought on that already. There is some wisdom in it, for it is true that a stronger force could be built thus—but Agga is no more deaf than he is blind. For us to gather ourselves slowly would be to send him the message of what we mean to do, long before we are able to stand against him. He would need no excuse to crush us then, and there is no doubt that that would be the first thing in his mind. I have no doubt of it," he added. "I should do the same myself."

"Then why not give over, Gilgamesh?" Rimsat-Ninsun asked. "Why must you crush your people beneath your sandals as though you were not Erech's shepherd, but her conqueror, only to save them from a threat that is no threat save when you provoke him? The meeting of armies, as you say, is no clashing of the two wild bulls Gilgamesh and Agga, but a war of many against many; and yet it is not the will of those who fight and fall for Erech or Kish that says, 'There shall be battle.' Whether you speak to the elders of the city, or the men who heave up stones for your wall, you shall hear them saying, 'We would have peace: we would have Erech governed well, bright beneath Inanna's star, a mighty fortress in the favor of the gods.' "

"Old men may say so," Gilgamesh answered. "The elders of Erech, though men call them wise, have long since lost the strength of their arms, and the strength of their hearts has withered with it. But when I speak with the young men, the soldiers and the strong ones, then they are ready for war, to throw Kish's yoke from our necks and raise our heads high in the land."

"And if you ruled a city of young men alone, all should be well and good," Shamhatu said tartly, crossing her arms across her breast. "But it is the duty of the king to care for all the black-headed people: to do justice to all, to do evil to none. The king should establish safe travel, build houses and plant gardens beside them; he should reinforce the canal walls, that all, from slave to priest, have fresh water to hand, and he should deal out barley and beer to apprentices and workers, that none go hungry within his city's walls."

Gilgamesh crossed his own arms, glaring down at her. "Now you mouth the words of a clay tablet set to children for copying. I shall give them back to you: Inanna has exalted me above men; An set the holy crown on my head, and made me to take the scepter of lapis. On the shining dais, he raised my fast-set throne to the heavens, and lifted up there the power of my rule. The gods did not give me my place that Erech should have a timid ruler: the line of Lugalbanda and Dumuzi is not one of donkeys beaten and broken to the burdens of the farmer's cart, but of the most noble and purely bred wild asses, fierce as the hailstorm rolling out of the desert." He clapped his hand to the gold-bound hilt of the gold-sheathed sword that swung by his side, half drawing it. The temple servants were starting to kindle the evening oil-lamps, and the little flames glittered red from the polished bronze, shining paler from the thin line of the blade's keen-stroked edge. "Here, before Inanna, Queen of Heaven and Lady of War, I say that we shall have a battle, and that neither the moaning of old men nor the whining of women shall turn me back from it! Shamhatu, finish those kilts, for I must have them for my soldiers—I, Lugal of Erech, have ordered this." Gilgamesh slammed his sword back into its sheath.

Shamhatu rose to her feet, looking straight up into his eyes. "As you are Lugal, leader of the war-host, you may order it—but as Ensi, ruler of the city, then you must do your duty by Erech's goddess Inanna! Inanna's temple will give you nothing, neither kilts to clothe your soldiers with nor grain to feed them, until the goddess has your oath that you will come to her bed as husband at the feast of the New Year."

"If I give that oath," Gilgamesh answered, his voice tight, "will you, in turn, swear to give me the help I need, and freedom to call whatever able-bodied men I need, for the war that must come and the wall that will hold Erech safe?"

Shamhatu stood a moment, poised and trembling, like a falcon about to swoop from her high crag, staring up at Gilgamesh's face. She could see the white rim all around his dark eyes, wild as the eyes of an onager kicking against the taming ropes that had caught and bound it; the tiny beads of sweat sheened his skin like fine oil. Shamhatu nodded sharply once. "I will."

"Then so I swear it," Gilgamesh said.

"And I in turn."

Without more words, Gilgamesh turned on his heel and strode from the shrine. Shamhatu could hear the fading clatter of his sandals down the mud-brick steps of the terrace. Now her legs were shaking so hard that she had to sit, and her own breath rushed loud through her ears.

Rimsat-Ninsun sighed. "As well seek to harness the wild bull to a plough," she murmured, and turned to Shamhatu. The cheap bracelets hanging from the older priestess' arms clattered and jangled as she brushed a few wisps of sweat-damp hair away from her forehead. "That was well-done indeed, to rein him so. It is no fault of yours that you cannot altogether tame him, do not fear that. Gilgamesh is mightier than his father, and came to rule so young . . ."

Shamhatu stared at her, stung to fresh anger. Well she knew, indeed, that one of the duties of the Shamhatu was to temper the Ensi with counsels of wisdom as well as the words of Inanna: that had been told her in soft whispers by the old priestesses who scoured her with tamarisk leaves in the bath of purification before she took on the goddess' robes. And yet . . .

"No wisdom is great enough to prevail against determined folly," Shamhatu said hotly. "If he will not listen to you, or the En, or myself, what is there that we can do?"

The En reached out, touching Shamhatu's arm with a hand like a spray of dry twigs wrapped in linen. "Shamhatu," his deep voice husked, "since Gilgamesh will not be turned aside by words, we must pray that the gods will instruct him in the ways of wisdom and lead him upon safer paths than those upon which he seeks to lead his city. As for the rest: we must not gainsay him before the folk of Erech, for then the sheepfold will truly fall to the wolves. We have enough in our stores, indeed, to hold us for seven years, so that we may grant Gilgamesh his year. As for what shall come after: it may be that Gilgamesh will win his battle, and then we shall rejoice in Inanna, fighting for her city. It may be that he will lose, and then we must seek to sway the heart of Agga, that he not break down the goddess' shrines, nor still the singing of her *gala*-priests with his sword. None can fathom the ways of the gods: their minds are beyond ours, and their knowledge farther yet. Yet you have done well, to win his oath that he will come to Inanna's bed, which will surely be pleasing to her. But as for us, we must wait, and carry out our rites as is fitting, and see what comes of this."

"We shall wait, indeed," Shamhatu said, her throat tight with fury. "But now I must go, and call for a bath to purify me, for I feel in great need of purification—lest I speak words that I should not about he who must be the husband of Inanna at the New Year." She rose, the blood rushing back into her cramped legs in a torrent of little stabbing pains, and stalked out of the temple, narrowing her eyes against the red sunset as she began to make her way down the terraced steps of the shrine's platform.

GILGAMESH STRODE THROUGH the streets of Erech, casting his gaze neither right nor left. The cries of the merchants were growing fewer, like the humming of bees dying down at the settling of evening; the sky was deepening into twilight's blue above the last red light of the sun. The flush of anger still bit through his body, stinging as though he had rolled in a thornbush.

*How dare she speak to me that way?* Gilgamesh thought. Though he had never struck a woman, when Shamhatu had sat with her arms folded across her chest and smugly reminded him of the Ensi's duties—as though he had not had them drummed into his head from his first day as a boy in the House of Knowledge, been forced to copy and recopy them while the En stood ready to crack a stick across his knuckles for each error—then he had ached to slap her mouth silent, to teach her that the gods had not lifted her up only that she might stand upon the prone body of their chosen ruler.

"Women and old men," the Ensi murmured to himself. The words left a bitter aftertaste in his mouth: he spat, the gobbet striking a house's smooth mud-brick wall and dripping slowly down. "What advice can they give me? It is a man's counsel that I need now, and for that I have . . ." Gilgamesh stopped. The light evening breeze blowing from the Buranun's wide banks was cooling the sweat on his shoulders and back now; he stood in an island of silence on the busy street, for the men and women who laughed and jostled each other as they hastened home to their families or out to the taverns trod carefully around him, not daring to brush too close, lest they rouse the Ensi's wrath.

". . . only myself," he finished.

Gilgamesh stood a moment longer, irresolute. His wall-builders would be coming in from their labor now, each ready to receive a rough clay bowl of barley and fish stew and to have his mug filled with fresh beer; his soldiers would be laying down their training weapons and heading, sweaty and tired, for the barracks, where a like meal was waiting for them. He had eaten that meal often enough himself, laboring all day in the sun beside his men or swinging the weighted practice-sword even as he shouted orders to his troops. There were men he could talk to: the grizzled old veteran Ur-Lamma, his bright young second Ninshubur— they could speak about war, about battles they had fought in or heard of, and the thoughts of fighting men.

But that promise did not lure Gilgamesh as it might have: it seemed to him that he was not willing to go so quickly from shrine to barracks, from his harsh words with the great priestesses and priests of Erech to the laughter and easy hailing of his soldiers—most particularly, those who were eager for war. That seemed too simple to him, and even a little cowardly, like fleeing the wounds and heat of battle to sit in a cool inn, drinking beer and flirting with the tavern-maids.

"I am Ensi of Erech, son of Lugalbanda and Rimsat-Ninsun," Gilgamesh said to himself, "two-thirds god and one-third man. And neither Shamhatu nor Rimsat-Ninsun spoke with the voice of a goddess this day: they are, indeed, but women."

He thought on that a moment, and smiled. Women, indeed, had plagued him all through that afternoon—should he not find easing from a woman? He could go to his votive-wives, any or all of them, and they would welcome him gladly, as they always did. And yet . . . they were the women chosen for him, reminders of what his mother and the others expected of him as well as rewards for his duty.

No. Though Gilgamesh had his wives, he knew that any woman in the city would open her thighs for him, there was one best fit to receive the blessings of the Ensi that night. Naram-Sin's daughter Sululi was to be wedded the next morning: what better gift for her than to have him come to her bride's chamber that night? And she was a highborn maiden, fit indeed for that honor.

Naram-Sin's house was one of the largest and newest in Erech, built not of mud-bricks, but of stone. Gilgamesh put his hand out, pushing against the door. It swung back on its peg; the muscular, shave-headed slave who stood beside it stepped forward, as if to forbid him entrance. Gilgamesh only stared down at him a moment, and he gave way, sinking down to his knees and touching the floor with his forehead, recognizing the guest at last, Gilgamesh thought with a grim chuckle. The Ensi pushed his way through, following the corridor's path by the light of the little oil-lamps that stood in niches down its length. Farther along he could hear the sound of laughter and singing, the plinking of the lyre and voices raised in merriment. He followed that sound out to the square garden around which the house was built, stepping into the flickering darkness and light of the wedding-feast.

A large fire burned in the middle of the garden, hissing out an occasional flare of brightness as the sheep's carcass roasting above it dripped fat into the flames. The arching palm trees stood as slender, frond-headed black shadows against the pale limestone of the house's smooth walls; the people moved as kilted and gowned silhouettes, lifting goblets that glittered with silver and gold in the fire's leaping brightness.

Naram-Sin sat on a great carved cedar chair, Sululi beside him, and the bridegroom—Gilgamesh could not remember his name—at his other side. The maiden was decked modestly, but finely wrapped up against the cold in a tufted shawl of the finest white wool and crowned with leaves of beaten gold and silver; the same leaves dangled from her ears. Even in her wedding adornments, Sululi was not beautiful of face or shape: the dark paint about her eyes and the thick dark coil of her braid around her head only played up the sallow paleness of her skin and the low coarse lines of her wide cheekbones. Her shawl could not hide the straight lines of her clumsily long-limbed body, and her face was dotted here and there with the ruddy pustules of youth. Yet she seemed beautiful to Gilgamesh at that moment, for he knew now that it was ordained for him to carry off her maidenhead and for her to have such blessings as his touch could bring to her—no maiden, he knew, was ugly on her wedding night, nor when a man's desires rose as his were rising now.

As Gilgamesh drew nearer, Naram-Sin rose to his feet. The firelight shone from his shaven head as he bowed low before his ruler, the fronds of his kilt and the curly ends of his silver-threaded black beard almost sweeping against the ground. "Greetings to Gilgamesh, Ensi and Lugal of Erech, born of the goddess Rimsat-Ninsun," Naram-Sin's soft voice murmured. "Your coming brings joy; the light of your face is a blessing upon this wedding. Drink of our aged beer and date wine, eat gladly of our food, our lamb and cakes and fruit, for no more welcome guest could have come to our house this night."

The older man straightened easily. Naram-Sin was tall, only a few finger-widths shorter than Gilgamesh, and though the muscles of his shoulders and arms were beginning to go stringy with age, Gilgamesh knew that he could well wield the sword by his side. There was something of challenge in the way Naram-Sin fearlessly met the Ensi's eyes;

Gilgamesh had no doubt that he well knew why his house had been graced with this visit that night.

"Blessings indeed, upon you and yours," Gilgamesh answered. A slim serving-maid, her eyes turned away, placed a cup in his hand. The triangles of gold inlay around the rim of the patterned olive-wood vessel glittered as the Ensi raised it to his mouth; the date-honey wine left a sticky-sweet taste on his tongue, but glowed warmly down into his stomach. Another servant handed him a platter of meat fresh-sliced from the roasting sheep, its fat spreading in little shimmering globules through the sauce. Gilgamesh put a sliver into his mouth and chewed slowly, savoring the tastes of garlic and mint and honey blending into the rich tender lamb, then broke a warm piece off the bread stacked beside it, rolling it up to keep the melted butter that drenched it from dripping all over him.

Over to the side of the courtyard, the musicians were beginning to play, their voices rising above the plinking of the lyre, the keen high jingle of cymbals and thumping of little drums, and the soft plaintive singing of the wooden pipes.

"See, the bride blushes in the warmth of her beloved,
Like a pomegranate ripe for plucking,
His arms arch above her as the branches of the palm,
To shelter her from wind and rain.
Fly, little doves, fly, you two doves,
Cooing to your nest, as evening comes.
As the nanny to the buck, as the ewe to the ram,
As lioness to lion, in the cool of the day.
See, the bridegroom yearns for his beloved,
Her breasts sweet as date-honey, kisses like clear water . . ."

It was a wedding-song that Gilgamesh had heard many times; this was not the first time he had sat like this beside a new bride whose color rose at the words, whose fringed woolen shawl rode down over her one bare shoulder in the warmth of the summer evening to show the upper curve of her breast as she glanced across at her betrothed . . . or, through the corner of long black lashes, at him. It was a song that he would hear again—and here a tiny cold prickle, like the light-footed scamper of a scorpion, ran down his spine—at the New Year, when, between winter and summer, he was brought to Inanna's wedding-house, as Shamhatu had trapped him into swearing he would be.

"Is all not well, all-bountiful lord of Erech?" Naram-Sin asked. "If the food or drink does not please, we can find something else for you."

"All is well," Gilgamesh answered. "When war threatens soon and the city is still in great need of preparation, it is hard to turn the thoughts from battle to rejoicing: that is all."

Gilgamesh did not hear the faint rustle of Naram-Sin's sigh, but he saw the cords of muscle in the older man's shoulders loosen a little as he answered, "All goes well, so far as I know. Certainly I have not shirked my duty, and my son-in-law to be, Ishbi-Erra," he gestured significantly, "has lately taken command of a sixty in the army, and is eager to do more, as it shall be decreed."

Gilgamesh's glance flickered over the young man. He knew that he had seen Ishbi-Erra's narrow, clean-shaven face before: there were two hundred commanders of sixty in his army, but most were new-minted, so he did not yet know them all by name.

"That is well-done," he answered. Yet it was the glimmering crown upon Sululi's dark hair that drew his gaze back, and the glistening brightness of her paint-lined eyes. It seemed to him that the tufted white shawl lying over her little breasts rose and fell more quickly as he looked upon her, and his own breath quickened in answer. Yet there were certain things that even he, Ensi of the city, could not do or say before the eyes of the folk gathered there.

And so Gilgamesh sat, eating and drinking and making polite speech with Naram-Sin as the musicians sang and played, until at last the women, cooing and fluttering their shawls and long skirts like a flock of doves, took Sululi away to the chamber where she would spend the night, waiting for her bridegroom to come to her in the morning. A little while longer, then he rose.

"I must go to bed as well," he said. Ishbi-Erra's face was still; the young man stared into the glow of the low-burning coals, without looking at his ruler. But Naram-Sin nodded, the corner of his mouth flickering.

"Sleep well, Ensi, uplifted one of the gods. May your blessings bring Inanna's favor upon all those gathered here, bridegroom and bride and noble families both."

"May it be so," Gilgamesh replied absently as he strode away, following the path the women had taken.

The way to the bridal chamber was strewn with sweet flag, the long rushes rustling beneath Gilgamesh's sandals as he walked through the cool corridor to the stone archway hung with blossoms and tamarind fronds. The door swung back upon its peg; a single oil-lamp burned within. Sululi had let down her braid, and her long fall of dark hair glistened with sweet-scented oils; but at the sight of him, she shrank away and pulled the sheets up over her small bosom, her eyes shining huge and tear-bright in the gloom.

"Mighty Ensi," she whispered, her voice a soft, breathless squeak. "Tomorrow is my wedding . . ."

Gilgamesh crossed the room in three quick strides, sitting down on the bed beside her. Even as her long limbs tightened beneath the thin woolen coverlet, he could feel the heat of her body. "It is, indeed," he murmured back to her. "And I have come, not to bring you any pain or disgrace, but the blessing of the gods who set me upon the ruler's seat above all men. You need not fear: I shall make you ready for your bridegroom with gentleness." He reached out to caress the bare curve of her shoulder with the tip of one finger. The little goose bumps rose on her skin beneath his touch, but she did not shrink away. Gilgamesh smiled to himself. He had lain with such virgins before; once or twice he had turned away, when the maiden was truly unwilling, but he knew—by something in Sululi's breath, or perhaps the scent of her body beneath the fine oils that anointed her—that she would welcome him, if he warmed her softly enough.

"My mouth is too little," Sululi whispered, "it knows not how to kiss. My womanhood is too little . . ."

"What is fit for the gods," Gilgamesh answered, "is often beyond human grasping; but this they have given us, among the many *me* that Inanna brought to Erech, all those gifts of lore and craft that make us more than beasts. Rulership and godship, the exalted and everlasting crown, the throne and scepter and insignia, the uplifted shrine, shepherdship . . . and the love of man and maid, that humankind not pass from beneath the sight of the gods." The words that he had written over and over, his knuckles aching from the blows brought by each mistake, now dropped from his mouth like ripe sweet dates dropping from the palm tree, and he could feel Sululi's trembling ease into softness beside him, lulled by the familiarity of the list that she, too, had heard from childhood.

Now he bent to kiss her, and she reached up toward him. Sululi's mouth was still and cold beneath his at first, clumsy of nose and tongue: she was truly a virgin and unkissed, for all her words had only echoed those of the maiden goddess Ninlil before the god Enlil fathered the moon upon her. For a fleeting moment, Gilgamesh wondered if Ishbi-Erra truly cared for more than Naram-Sin's wealth and influence, for what lover could have left his beloved so untouched before their wedding?

Thus bidden against Gilgamesh's will, words from the liturgy of Dumuzi and Inanna stole into his mind—the words of the two lovers before their wedding, speaking, as true lovers must before the paying of the bride-price.

> *"Dumuzi, set me free, I must go home, What can I say to deceive my mother?"*
> *"Inanna, most deceitful of women, I will tell you.*
> *Say, 'My girl friend, she took me with her to the public square,*
> *There a player entertained us with dancing,*
> *His chant, the sweet, he sang for us,*
> *In sweet rejoicing he whiled away the time for us'*
> *Thus deceitfully stand up to your mother,"*

"While we," Gilgamesh whispered against Sululi's cheek, "by the moonlight take our fill of love. I will ready for you a bed, pure, sweet, and noble, and the kindly day will see your joy's fulfillment."

He brushed a tendril of hair from Sululi's forehead, stroking down over her shoulder, his fingers tracing the small curve of her breast down to the little hardening nub of her nipple. Sululi drew her breath in with a sharp hiss, still as a half-wild cat beneath Gilgamesh's large gentle hands. Carefully he put the other arm about her, drawing her close enough to feel the beating of his own heart in his chest, the hardness of his thighs beneath the linen fronds of his kilt, then kissed her again until her lips began to move to meet his, until the hot salt of her tears ran down into the sweet warmth of their kisses. Then Gilgamesh's heart swelled, for he knew certainly now that she had never been touched by a man's love before. *I, too, know what it is to be alone*, he wanted to say to her; but he knew that she would never believe it, for was he not Ensi and Lugal, who could bed a different woman every night as he chose?

"My fair one," he murmured to her, one fingertip still tracing the tightening ring of her nipple as his other hand stroked down over the thin sheet of wool covering her taut belly, down to rest upon the low curve of the little mound between her clenched thighs, "my turtledove, my gazelle drinking at the clear waterhole. Your breasts are sweet as clusters of dates, and the honey of wine flows from your lap. You are tall and fair as a palm tree in the midst of thornbushes, welcome to the traveler on dusty ways; clean and fresh as the fronds of tamarind scenting a cool bath in summertime."

Sululi said nothing, but turned her tear-sheened face up so her lips met Gilgamesh's again; then her arms went around him, clasping him tight to her, and he felt her shuddering against him. Slowly he raised his hand from her breast, drawing her light cover down so that her long body shone pale in the low light of the guttering oil-lamp. Lowering his head, Gilgamesh took her other breast-tip in his mouth, sucking softly as he stroked the hard nib with the tip of his tongue. Sululi gasped, and Gilgamesh felt her thighs parting under his hand, so that his single finger could find its way through the soft mat of curls to the damp warm treasure beneath.

"As ram to ewe, as shepherd to shepherdess," he whispered, unloosing his kilt-string with his other hand and letting the linen drop from his body. "Daughter of Erech, you are safe within the fold."

For a time Gilgamesh only lay against Sululi to let her feel his desire against her, suckling at her breast as his hand moved gently between her legs. Then her hand fluttered over his back like the wing of a moth circling tentatively toward the lamp-flame, at last reaching down to clasp his hard scepter in a virgin's rough grip that made him gasp half in joy, half in pain.

"Gently, gently," Gilgamesh whispered to her, reaching down to ease the tightness of her hand against him. "For all his strength, a man can be hurt as easily as you."

Sululi let go at once, staring wide-eyed at him. "Have I . . . hurt you?"

Gilgamesh guided her hand carefully back down. "Feel, you have not. But go easily; I shall show you. Thus, and thus: caress as you would have me caress you . . . so," he breathed, echoing her motions with the fingers that lay between her legs.

"Oh . . . Oh, my Ensi. Will Ishbi-Erra touch me so?"

"If he does not," Gilgamesh answered, his heart clenching within him in a sudden sorrow for her, "you must teach him how." His next words came without his thought, drawing the blood back into the pit of his body: "After all, it is Inanna who brings the *me* to men."

"I have hurt you!" Sululi said, drawing her hand back from his softening rod. "Oh, Gilgamesh, I am sorry, I did not mean—"

"No, it is not your fault," Gilgamesh answered. He lifted his head to still her words with his lips again, fluttering kisses up to her soft eyelashes and down again. *At New Year's I must . . .* The thought sparked in him a sudden violent desire, to take Sululi as he would take Shamhatu, forcing her beneath him. But though he hardened again, he forced himself to keep his touch on her body light: this maiden, lonely on her bridal night, deserved nothing other than the joy he could give her.

"Then let me . . . Gilgamesh," she murmured. "I am ready, please let me . . . You have made me so happy, my Ensi."

Gilgamesh did not yet move onto her, but he touched her more closely, until he felt Sululi blossoming within. Then he lifted himself up on his elbows, slowly pressing himself against her, letting her own movements guide him on like a ram coaxed step by step into the sheepfold. For one moment she paused, and he felt the tight caul of her maidenhood: a single thrust, and he was through. Sululi cried out softly, but did not pull back; and Gilgamesh waited, reaching down between their bodies to caress her until she began to move against him again.

At last Sululi tightened around him, grasping Gilgamesh within her again and again until his tears flowed free with his seed and he let his head droop upon her small soft breasts. Then he wept freely, clasping her to him until her breath came uneasily under his weight. He rolled to the side, but did not let go of her.

"My Ensi . . . my love. Will you come back to me again?"

Gilgamesh caught his breath, the great sobbing gasps slowing until he could speak clearly again. He said, "You are to wed Ishbi-Erra. I may come back again . . . but remember, I am the Ensi of Erech, and her lover . . ."

"The lover of Inanna," Sululi finished.

Gilgamesh's fists clenched and he wanted to cry out. Yet he remembered that he was in bed with a young woman whose maidenhood he had just claimed. And to her he was the Ensi of Erech, the heir of Dumuzi and Lugalbanda, whose life was forfeit within the thighs of the goddess: he was Gilgamesh, two-thirds god and one-third man, and though he might understand her sorrows in his heart, to her he was beyond any such pain.

*And so we come to each other lonely, and leave still alone,* Gilgamesh thought. But he kissed Sululi once again, and said, "So it is. But you, too, are Erech: for without its folk, Erech's towpaths would grow only weeds, and the chariot roads only wailing-plant; where the heart-soothing herbs spring, only tear-reed would sprout, and bitter water flow. Without you, who says 'I would dwell in Erech' would not find a good dwelling place, and who says 'I would lie down in Erech' would not find a good sleeping place. I have come to you, for you are beautiful; if," he added, and he could feel the strain of desperation in his softened voice, "the gods give blessing through men, you have it through me."

"My Ensi," Sululi cried softly, "I know that it is so; I could not have dreamed of better for this night. If there is more I can do for you—"

Gilgamesh laid a finger upon her lips, feeling the tender flesh still beneath his touch. "You have given me great joy, my beautiful one; you are a lover worthy of your Ensi. For even," he added unwillingly, "even the gods are not always joyful. I came heavy-hearted to you, and I go away gladly. Sleep now, and remember this while you live," and now his face pulled into a painful grin, "where the Shamhatu of Inanna failed, you have succeeded, for she could not give me what you have given."

Sululi's lips trembled into a smile; Gilgamesh bent to kiss her one last time, then drew his kilt up and fastened the string again.

The night wind was warm against Gilgamesh's naked chest as he made his way home to his chambers beneath Inanna's raised shrine. An owl's wings brushed softly overhead; without thought, he made a warding gesture against it—against the *lilitu*, the night-demon who stole babes from their mothers and the manhood from men.

THE SHAMHATU HAD adorned herself in the goddess' regalia; she had readied her body, touching herself with oils, and now reclined on the soft sheets of the cedar bed in the chamber where men came to Inanna. The room was dark save for one small lamp. The goddess' suitors looked upon her only in the shadow, lest they be blinded by her might—or, more practically, disappointed by too clear a sight of a body that was less than divine. The man who was coming to her was one of the elders of the city, whom the Shamhatu knew from Erech's councils: Naram-Sin, prudent in his judgments, yet never shy of putting his thoughts forward. He had made a great offering for the blessing of Inanna that morning, and the Shamhatu knew that it would be wise not to refuse him, or pass him off to a lesser priestess, for he was also known to be sparing with his money, and therefore whatever he sought must be of real importance.

Naram-Sin prostrated himself before the goddess as he entered, his silver-black beard spreading out across the floor and the lamp's flame gleaming from his oiled and shaven head. "Holy Inanna, Queen of Heaven," he began. The Shamhatu listened to his litany of invocation, breathing deeply to draw the power of the goddess into her, until at last she felt the tingling through her body, the warmth in her loins that spoke of Inanna's presence.

"Arise," she breathed, her voice humming deep through the room.

She reached down for Naram-Sin's hands, drawing him to his feet. It pleased her to feel the strength in his sinewy arms and shoulders; though he kept his eyes turned down, so as not to look rudely into the face of the goddess, she could feel that he was not abashed before her.

Slowly the Shamhatu unfastened her breechcloth and drew up the hem of her dress, the air warm against her naked legs and belly. "Behold, my vulva is the Boat of Heaven," she said. "Behold the beauty of the Boat of Heaven; I bring it to Erech, laden with blessings and holiness for the children of men."

Naram-Sin knelt before the Shamhatu, kissing her reverently between the legs. Her loins stirring at the warm damp touch of his bearded mouth, she drew her dress up farther. "Behold, my breasts are a fertile plain. They pour out milk; they pour out grain and honey for the children of men."

He rose, cupping her breasts in his hands. Suckling gently at one, then the other, he caressed her nipples with his tongue so that she felt them swelling hard in his mouth, little pangs of pleasure flashing from her breasts through her belly. As Naram-Sin kissed her body, the Shamhatu cast her dress aside, then lay back upon the bed, careful not to dislodge Inanna's crown. Naram-Sin dropped his cloak, unfastening his kilt. The ropy muscles of his shoulders and little ridges of his chest and abdomen stood out starkly beneath the skin, for age had thinned him; but his rod was hard and swollen against his belly like a youth's. The Shamhatu lifted her knees, reaching out to him. "Inanna calls you to her," she said breathlessly. "Come to my garden: the pomegranate is plucked for you, the sweet fig awaits." She embraced Naram-Sin, pulling him toward her and lifting her hips to meet and grasp his first thrust, holding him tight within her.

"Inanna, Inanna!" he cried out as they rocked together. The Shamhatu thrust upward more urgently, gripping him hard: she could feel the goddess' power swelling in her body like a bud warming to flowering.

"Now," she sighed into Naram-Sin's ear. "Now!" He clenched her tightly, hips spasming; it seemed that she could feel his seed spurting within her, releasing her own flooding burst of pleasure. Though he was already beginning to droop inside her, she did not release him.

"Great man of Erech," she said breathlessly—for the question must be asked before the power of Inanna has faded—"what is it you desire of the goddess?"

"Divine Lady, Queen of Heaven, I would speak about the Ensi of Erech." Naram-Sin's breath was already smooth again, and the Shamhatu could tell that she would not be able to keep him within her much longer.

"Speak swiftly."

"Divine Lady, I speak of the duties of the Ensi. Great One, Queen of Heaven, the mighty one of Erech, whom the gods have raised above us, came to my daughter on the night before her wedding, as she lay alone in her bridal chamber . . ."

"As is his right," the Shamhatu forced herself to say. For a moment she thought of Gilgamesh, sating his desires on the body of a virgin as Naram-Sin had just done upon her, and her teeth crushed against each other as though she had bitten on the unexpected pit of a date within its soft sweetness. She pulled away from him, sitting up. Though it was unseemly for the goddess to wipe her body, or do any such human thing, before the men who came to her, Naram-Sin's seed was trickling down her thigh in a slimy trail, and she heartily wished that she could dry herself now.

"He has sent her due gifts, and more than her due, since only three weeks have passed, and it is not yet sure whether she bears a child . . ."

"That, too, is as it should be: the heart of the Ensi is open." *And if I lie*, the Shamhatu whispered to Inanna, *it is only for Erech's sake.*

"But, Divine Lady, though the visit of the Ensi is said to bring blessing to all the family, none of that has come upon us. My son-in-law, Ishbi-Erra, is still but the commander of sixty, although I know how Gilgamesh's army has grown; my fortunes have become no better, though I welcomed the Ensi to the wedding feast, knowing full well what he sought within the walls of my house. On the sheepfold of Erech he raises his gaze himself, like a wild bull rising up over all, his head high."

The Shamhatu nodded slowly; she had heard this complaint before.

"Inanna shall reward you," she said heavily.

"May those rewards come swiftly. O Divine Lady, I take it as no little thing, that my daughter's maidenhead was given to the chosen one of Inanna, the mighty one of Erech. For Gilgamesh is indeed as a wild bull, whom only the gods can rein; yet he is also the Ensi of this city, and without the help of the strong, how can he stand?"

"Inanna shall reward you," the Shamhatu said, more firmly. "Have no doubt of the goddess: does not Erech prosper, and have you not done well here?"

"I have no doubt of the goddess," Naram-Sin answered. "My lady, I trust in your word."

The Shamhatu reached out to lay her hand on the top of his head. The little bristles pricked against her palm, and she could feel the smooth sheen of the oil he had rubbed his shaven scalp with. "That is well. Go now, and trust that all will go well with the kin the Ensi have blessed."

Naram-Sin prostrated himself before he dressed, and prostrated himself again before leaving. It was in the Shamhatu's mind to go straight to her bath, but when she had left the chamber, as if the ringing echo of Inanna's presence in her body were still driving her, her feet turned instead to the shrine atop its high stepped platform, where petitioners from all over the city and its surrounds gathered at this hour to make their prayers and offerings to the goddess. She should, she knew, sit down in her throne to witness the supplications, her presence promising Inanna's, but instead she paused in an empty alcove, her gaze turned upward to the plain mud-brick ceiling of the shrine. She could not keep from seeing Gilgamesh, his broad shoulders brown above his white kilt, his dark glossy ringlets curling down his back as he strode without care into one or another bridal chamber. *And I shall never have my own, save as the goddess desires it through me . . .*

"The raising of his weapon has no match," Shamhatu murmured bitterly, "and with his drum the folk are roused. With the young noblemen of Erech he runs wild through the holy shrines . . ."

Abruptly she walked out into the middle of the temple, clapping her hands to still the soft susurrations of the petitioners gathered in the shrines.

"Be silent," Shamhatu called out, her voice strong and piercing as a note blown on a ram's horn. Then it seemed to her that a great wind lifted her up, as though she were a cloud on the wings of the storm, and the words sang through her throat without her thought. "Nay, speak: speak what is in your heart, the goddess Inanna commands it!"

For a moment there was silence in the shrine indeed, as though the walls had melted to collapse in with a soft rush of clay. Then the voices rose again, one from this place, one from that, the high voices of women's keening underlaid with the deep current of men's calls.

"Gilgamesh does not allow the son to go with the father . . ."

"Day and night he oppresses the weak . . ."

"Gilgamesh, who is shepherd of Erech the Sheepfold!"

"Is this our shepherd, strong, shining, filled with wisdom?"

"Gilgamesh does not let the maiden go to her mother . . ."

"The maid to the soldier, the bride to the young bridegroom . . ."

Shamhatu stood swaying on her feet; it seemed to her that each voice struck her hard across the cheek, so that she could hardly stay standing. Then she cried out, and it seemed she could hear her voice echoing through the sharp tin voice of the sky, and the deeper voices of Rimsat-Ninsun and the En singing with her.

"Gods, did you not make this mighty wild bull?
The raising of his weapon has no match,
And with the drum his folk are roused.
He, Gilgamesh, does not let the son go with his father by day or
    night,
Is this the shepherd of Erech the Sheepfold?
Is this the strong and shining shepherd, filled with the wisdom of
    the gods?
Gilgamesh does not let the maiden go to her mother,
The maid to the soldier, the bride to the young bridegroom."

Then Shamhatu knew that she heard the voice of Rimsat-Ninsun answering her cry, the older woman's alto ringing off the mud-brick of the elder goddess' shrine.

• • •

"Gods, did you not make this mighty wild bull?
Gilgamesh, shepherd of Erech, he has no match.
Two-thirds god and one-third man, Gilgamesh raises himself
    above all the folk.
Ye mighty ones, hear our lamentation.
The widows weep, the maidens cry out,
The young men fall beneath his strength, for he has no match,
Furious as a wild bull roped to a plough, he drives the furrow into
    the river,
Breaks open the canals, stamps the Buranun to flood tide,
Wastes the earth of Erech beneath his feet,
Yet is he not the chosen one of the gods,
Who lifted his crown and rod above the heads of men?"

And, though Shamhatu yearned in her heart to answer, it was the En's
voice, husking deeply, that replied; his long journeys across the desert
had dried the music from his throat, but his words thumped like the
beating of a drum, like the beating of the blood in her ears:

"Gods, did you not make this mighty wild bull?
Gilgamesh, shepherd of Erech . . . Gods, let him find his match!
Two-thirds god and one-third man, ye who have set him above
    the folk,
Ye mighty ones, hear our lamentation!
Inanna, Queen of Heaven, Shepherdess of Erech,
Enlil, who brings life to the earth, water to the crops,
An, lord of the sky, bear our prayers forth!"

Shamhatu raised her voice, and heard the murmuring of the folk behind
her as her cry rose, blending with those of Rimsat-Ninsun and the En,

"Inanna, Queen of Heaven, Shepherdess of Erech,
Enlil, who brings life to the earth, water to the crops,

An, lord of the sky, bear our prayers forth!
Let Gilgamesh find his match . . . two-thirds god and one-third
    man,
Shape a match to Gilgamesh, equal to the time of his heart,
Let them battle one against the other . . .
May Erech have peace!"

# 3

The long morning-shadows of the hills lay over the plain like loose drifts of black fleece, the sun's brightness dazzling between them. Akalla the trapper strode along, letting the waves of sunlit warmth and shadow-coolness wash over him. Above him fluttered a twittering flock of sparrows, black against the pale blues and pinks of the morning sky. The edge of Akalla's spear-point flashed golden in the sunlight, the bronze honed to glittering brightness. He had been sharpening it late last night, for gazelle and ibex were not the only beasts that walked hill and plain. Of the lions, hyenas, and wolves, Akalla had little fear: save when a lion went rogue, these beasts were far more of a threat to sheep than to men.

But something else roamed here: something with hands to fill in the pits Akalla had dug, to wrench open his traps, to set free the game from which Akalla and his family lived. The trapper did not know what this creature might be, whether madman or ghost or one of the *gallas* that guarded the laws of the Netherworld. Because Akalla was no coward, he was set on finding out the answer before he gathered his family and left for less troubled parts—and if the gods had set it upon him as a curse, only sacrifice and entreaties might melt their hearts; and the fat temple oxen and sheep did not come cheaply, especially for one who had been able to sell no game for nearly a score of days now. Because he was no fool, he had carefully sharpened his spear and gone over the fletching of his arrows, making sure that the feathers were unbroken and the shafts

straight and unsplintered: though he had paid in sleep lost, he had
bought a little more peace of mind. Akalla scarcely noticed the straps of
bow and quiver over his bare shoulders; his deep-tanned back was callused from the long rubbing of his hunter's weapons, just as the shoulders of a brick-carrier or the hands of a stone-carver would be callused
from their work.

Turning up into the stony hills, Akalla walked more carefully. The
little scorpions were scurrying about the shadows of the rocks now; the
snakes, still heavy with the torpor of the cooling nights, would just be
stirring. Although the thick soles of his sandals were good protection
against the black-armored insects, it was better to be watchful. As his old
father often said, the gods might curse a wise man, but a fool was already
his own curse. Akalla moved quietly; the fringe of his woolen kilt did
not rustle against his legs, for he had tucked its ends up under his belt—
as he usually did when going to check his traps, because it made walking
easier and protected his privates from dust and bugs and thorns and all
manner of other insults.

He paused a little below the crest of the hill, running a hand through
the short-cropped pelt of black bristles on his head. City folk often
shaved their heads; Akalla, who was abroad for much of the day, knew
better than to let the sun beat down on his bare skull. Now the rising
light showed him something strange. The broad padded tracks of lions,
crisscrossing here and there as they did in a pride, weaving about each
other, sleeping, and mock-fighting, were well known to Akalla. He could
tell that the group that had passed here two nights ago was a roving
pride of young bachelors, with no great king-lion tracks nor the more
delicate paw-marks of queens. That would bring no joy to the shepherds
of his village, when he warned them to set an extra watch on their sheep
for the next few nights, but it was not strange. No: what made Akalla
rub his head in perplexity was the sight of a man's bare footprints going
in and out among the tracks of the lions—nor had he simply passed
later, moving about to examine the spoor as Akalla was doing, for
though his tracks overlaid the lion-prints here and there, in other places
it was the lion-tracks that marred the footprints of the man. Moreover,
if his feet were in proportion to the rest of him—and from the depth of

the tracks, which sank twice as deeply as Akalla's, for all the ground was damp with dew now and must have been dry as a desert-buried bone when the lions and their strange companion passed two nights before—it struck Akalla that he would do better to turn back to his village, to call out some of the other men and see if they would make a search. But he could already hear the mocking words if he did. "Akalla is a bungler and a windbag! A trapper who is too clumsy to trap, he calls the rest of us out to back up his tales so that he will look less of a dolt! The one who cannot read or write letters baked in clay, he thinks he can read the writings of lions baked in dirt!"

Though there was no great ill-will between Akalla and his neighbors, the work of the trapper was not the work of the shepherd; and though Akalla knew his own affairs well enough, he also knew that he was not as quick-tongued as other men, while the scratches birds left in the mud around the watering holes would forever mean more to him than the scratches men made on their clay tablets, for all he had tried to learn to read and write those simple words that even most shepherds could master. So it was that he straightened his back, gripping his spear more tightly, and set himself to following the strange tracks through the hills and down onto the next plain.

As Akalla walked, he wondered further. The footprints of the man—if indeed he was a man—wandered away from the bachelor pride now and again. If the tablet of dust and grass spoke truly, the strange one had come upon a herd of gazelles, and perhaps wandered for a little while and torn up grasses with them; judging by the confused mass of tracks around a nearby watering hole, he had jostled among the animals for his turn to drink, just as if he were one of them in truth. Akalla sat himself down at the same watering hole: the sun was nearly overhead, and it was some time since he had breakfasted on a piece of his wife's good bread and a little dried goat meat. His midday meal was almost as simple: more of the same flat bread rolled around a cylinder of salty sheep cheese, and two precious dates, squashy and sweet beneath their thin dry skins, washed down with cool, slightly muddy water from the drinking hole. By the time Akalla had finished, the food and the sun's warmth on his bare shoulders had lulled him to near drowsiness: though he knew he should rise and seek shelter from the heat of the day, or else go back to his search, he sat and pondered; and his eyelids drooped as he thought.

The rustling of the grasses; the sound of lapping; the rich musky scent of male lion: all struck Akalla at once, snapping his head up from his chest and propelling him to his feet with his spear braced. A mass of tawny fur and lashing tail-tufts across the waterhole—and standing in the middle of it, like a farmer in a field of living grain, was the being Akalla had hunted, now come to hunt him in turn. Akalla's bowels spasmed cold even as his heart clenched, holding every sinew and muscle of his body in a death-grip: he could not move nor speak, staring at the one who stood amid the lions. The stranger stood a head and a half taller than Akalla, who was no small man; the muscled thighs beneath his kilt of half-tanned gazelle hide seemed thick as the trunks of old date palms, and Akalla could not have closed a hand around the heavy bones of his wrist. His great mane of matted hair, golden as ripe barley beneath its streaks of mud and grease, fell past the small of his back; above his tangled golden beard, his cheekbones were wide as a lion's and his eyes the pale green-brown of fields just beginning to sprout. A thick pelt of curly fair hair grew all over his body, so that it was hard to see where his skin garment left off and his own hide began.

And yet, though Akalla's trembling knees could hardly hold him upright and his lungs could draw in no more than scattered gasps of air, he did not fall down in worship. The trapper's spear, more trustworthy than his failing legs, held him upright long enough for him to see the burrs embedded in the wild man's tangled hair, as well as the bruises, deep scratches, and runnels of crusted blood that must have come from the lightest taps of the lions' paws: Akalla was not the cleverest of men, but it flashed through his mind that a god would not suffer such simple harm from his creatures. The wild man, whether he were mad or some last survivor of the long-lived folk who dwelt on earth before the Great Gods sent the Flood to drown humankind, was surely still a man.

Yet, thinking so, Akalla still could not meet the wild man's green-brown gaze—not until the strange eyes widened a little farther and the trapper heard his soft gasp. Then, as though startled by a single tongue of fire leaping out of the dry grasses, the lions and their companion whirled at once, running so swiftly that Akalla still had not drawn breath by the time they were gone from his sight.

The trapper dropped his spear and sat down hard in the mud at the edge of the waterhole, shaking so badly that he could not move. The stink of his fouled garment filled his nose, but that mattered little: he knew that he had not dreamed, for he could still see the footprints of the lions in the mud on the other side, and sharp among them, the huge track of the wild man.

After a time, Akalla dipped his clay cup into the pool and poured some water over his head, then arose and stripped off his kilt, laying it out carefully a little way from the water's edge. Though few folk came out here, the gods hated the fouling of good water, and now would be the worst time of all to seek their wrath. Instead, he carefully scraped the wool as clean as he could with his left hand, then poured cupful after cupful of water over the garment until it no longer smelled as if it had just come from the fuller's vat. It would dry quickly in the heat of the afternoon; indeed, its coolness was welcome on Akalla's waist and thighs, heavy and scratchy as the wet wool was. Lastly, he dipped out one more cupful of water, letting the clear drops drip slowly to the ground.

"Enlil, whose command is far-reaching, whose word is holy," Akalla murmured—one of the few prayers of praise that his father had been able to instill in him,

"The lord whose pronouncement is unchangeable,
who forever decrees destinies,
Whose lifted eye scans the lands,
Whose lifted beam searches the hearts of all the lands . . ."

THERE WAS MORE that he knew, but the words had been frightened from his memory; he hoped that Enlil would understand, and accept the offering.

When the cup was empty, Akalla looked up at the sky. Against its burnished blueness, a black shape soared slowly, tilting its wings to circle up higher: a vulture, waiting patiently for its share of a kill. What the lions left behind, what was left when the wild man had fed, or the jaws of the hyenas and wolves had cracked the bones for their marrow . . . Akalla thought of his own bones breaking beneath the great teeth of the beasts, of his spirit drifting down into the cold of the Netherworld like a dove drifting to its nest in the evening chill, his arms changed to wings as he cooed lamentations to the other dead. He knew that he had escaped death by less than a feather on the vulture's tail: who, he wondered, could fathom the ways of the gods?

Still shivering despite the heat, clenching his hand white-knuckled on his spear, Akalla began to walk home.

"MY SON, WHAT has come upon you?" Akalla's father said as the trapper entered the door of their hut and made to set aside his spear and take off his bow and arrows. "Though the fire has burned down to coals and the evening is near, I can see that your face has lost its color; you look as though you have made a long journey."

Akalla looked down at the old man, who sat cross-legged by the fire plaiting new leather thongs for his battered sandals. His bald spot gleamed through its fringe of black hair like polished cedarwood; the ropy muscles of his shoulders and arms stood out as he pulled the strands of leather more tightly. He was a wise man, who in his youth had herded sheep for the temple of Inanna in Erech; though age had creased his dark face and sharpened the great beak of his nose, his black eyes still glittered like a knife-edge of obsidian from the North. If any would have advice, it would be he; and Akalla's father never scolded his son for his tanglefoot tongue, or doubted his words, which in turn brought the speech more easily from Akalla's mouth.

"My father, a certain man has come out of the mountains. He is the mightiest in the land, his strength is as mighty as the shooting star of An. He goes over the mountains, he jostles at the watering places with the animals, he plants his feet opposite the watering place. I was afraid, so I did not go up to him. He filled in the pits that I had dug, wrenched out the traps that I had spread, loosed from my grasp the wild animals. He does not let me make my rounds in the wilderness; it is because of him that I cannot bring in game. I saw him standing among the pride of young lions at the watering hole, and I have never felt such fear: he seemed as much a lion as a man, with billowing hair as golden as the tresses of the goddess Ashnan, whose hair is the abundant sheaves of barley."

Akalla's father set his sandals aside, twining his bony fingers together for a moment; then he stood, lifting the small wooden shovel beside the hearth and tossing a few shovelfuls of dried sheep dung onto the fire. When the dung was burning well, its thick smoke curling into the air, he sat down again and said, "My son, a certain Gilgamesh lives in Erech. There is no one stronger than he, he is as strong as the shooting star of An. Now I have also heard that he is a rash young man, who continuously seeks toward new wars and new women, and for whom the strange and new is ever more livening than the old and familiar: though he is Ensi and Lugal, I think he will hear your story. Go, set off to Erech, and tell Gilgamesh of this man of might. Gilgamesh will give you a priestess, the Shamhatu of the temple, and you shall take her with you: the woman shall overcome the man as if she were strong. When the animals are drinking at the watering place, have her take off her robe and expose her sex. When he sees her, he will draw near to her, and his animals, who grew up in his wilderness, will seem strange to him."

"How do you know this, my father? Have you heard of such a wild man before?"

"If he lives with the lions, and is like to a lion, I know this: a young lion roams with his fellows, but when he gets the scent of a pride-queen—if he is strong enough—he forgets them and they become his foes; he is part of the pack, with his own cubs to rear and protect. Once this wild man has scented a human queen, it will be the same for him: he will come into the pride, and turn against his own friends who roam without mates, lest they seek to take his place and kill his cubs for the sake of fathering their own."

This was so: Akalla knew all the ways of lions. He had once even heard what few had (from the distance of a safe hilltop): the piteous mewing and cries as a new pack-king slaughtered the young cubs of his dead rival. Though the shepherds laughed at the way he used his fingers for counting, they trusted Akalla to know the lions in the lands he roamed, to warn of intruders and track down habitual sheep-slayers. Of this wild man, this lion, he was sure that his father spoke truth.

"I shall leave for Erech tomorrow at first light," Akalla said. "But who shall I speak to? Does the king walk the streets like any man?"

Akalla's father grinned, showing a gleam of yellow teeth still standing amid the blackened sockets in his mouth. "Something I will give you, that has never left my side since I departed the temple of Inanna and came to tend my own sheep here in peace." He reached into his belt-pouch, dug out a small cylinder of polished brown agate with signs carved around it. "Here is the seal I used as a temple servant. It stood me in good stead then: you are unlikely to be questioned while you bear it."

Akalla took the seal reverently. It was smooth and cold in his palm; as it warmed to his touch, it seemed to tingle slightly. He had never felt anything that was so close to the gods as a seal from one of the great city temples. Though the Great Ones deigned to accept sacrifice and give blessing at their little houses in the village, it was, everyone said, the cities that were their true dwelling places: Inanna in Erech, Enlil in Nippur, Nanna in Ur, Enki in Eridu, and all the rest. "I will care for it well."

"I know you will, my son."

The door swung open again; Akalla's wife Innashagga walked in, a jug beneath one arm and a woolen bag in her other hand. "My husband, you have been out all day; did you find that which you sought? You seem to have made a long journey. Sit down, drink and eat. There is even beer today, and will be for some days yet, for the brewer's wife is losing her milk early, and our nanny goat has milk to spare," she finished breathlessly, blinking quickly several times so that her eyelashes fluttered like the wings of a captive butterfly. Innashagga's words always seemed to outrun her breath; but that was well enough, for Akalla preferred listening to speaking, and Innashagga was pleased to speak for two.

Akalla and his father squatted before the fire, each selecting a clean straw from the heaps on the floor and trimming the ends neatly with their knives so that they could drink the beer without any risk of spilling. Akalla trimmed another straw for Innashagga as she brought out more bread and goat cheese—bothersome as the goats were, he had to admit that they had kept the family from going hungry during these days when the wild man was keeping him from hunting. Taking a long pull from the beer, the aromatic sweetness of malt mingled with dates sliding smoothly down his throat, Akalla began to tell his wife the tale of what he had seen as they ate. For once, Innashagga sat silent, her charcoal-rimmed eyes widening; she gasped as he spoke of the lions milling around the wild man without harming him, but said nothing more until he finished by telling her of his father's advice and what he meant to do.

"It is good advice, surely," Innashagga mused. "But to ask for the temple's Shamhatu, in whose lap men seek the blessings of the goddess—should I let my husband go alone among such priestesses? Will he come back to a simple girl from the country, when he has once tasted the offerings of the temple-women? Or will he, too, forsake the wilderness and his animals, and turn his face toward the town, his back to the smell of sheep and goats?"

Akalla reached over the jug to stroke her soft black hair. "The priestesses of Inanna are not for me: they are women for kings and noblemen."

"Not always so," Akalla's father interrupted. "But Innashagga, you need have no fear. They serve when there is great need, and when the price can be paid for calling the goddess; and that, I remember, comes dearly. In my twenty years in the temple of Inanna, I lay with a priestess only thrice, and that because the temple sheep were sickening and her blessing was needed there. Nor do they ensnare men with their charms: it is the goddess, not the woman, who comes to her lovers, for the priestess' hope of love and wedding of her own is her offering to Inanna. You need have no fear."

"Then go, with my full blessing, my husband," Innashagga said. Even in the dim light, Akalla could see the tears welling in her dark eyes. He did not know what to say, but he took her soft plump hand and held it against his breast so she could feel the beating of his heart.

There was a rustling of straw, then a breath of cool air as the door swung open and closed again: Akalla's father had gone out on some errand of his own. Akalla got to his feet, bending to kiss his wife as she stood to meet him. Her lips were warm, sweet with the beer; the touch of her hand on his belt seemed to ease all the fears that had flashed through him like heat lightning in the summer skies, calling him to cleave to her as to a refuge from the fierce winter storms, a green-fringed well of water in a dry desert land where he could drink and be safe.

GILGAMESH AWOKE SWEATING, his heart pounding as he stared into the darkness. His linen blankets were twisted and wrapped around his limbs like swaddling cloths, his hair plastered damply on his forehead and shoulders. The oil-lamps had gone out, though when he reached for one on the table beside his bed, the bottom was still warm; it was not long past the middle of the night.

He lay there until his breathing stilled, letting the night air cool the sweat on his body as he thought upon his dreams, setting them in his mind so they would not melt away with the morning's warm mist. After a time he reached out to strike the small bronze gong that stood beside his night-lamp.

The slave Enatarzi was beside his master's bed by the time the last ringing echo of the gong had died into the clay walls, his bulk a comforting shadow behind the small yellow flame of his oil-lamp. "The Ensi commands, holy lord of Erech?"

"Bring me water, that I may wash my face and hands; bring a comb, that you may comb my hair," Gilgamesh told him. "And bring my best kilt of white linen, and a necklace of lapis lazuli; and some gift fitting for the goddess Rimsat-Ninsun, my beloved mother, for I go to seek her counsel."

"As the Ensi has said it." Enatarzi prostrated himself briefly, then rose and trotted away, leaving only the red image of the lamp's flame to burn lightless between Gilgamesh and the darkness until he returned.

The cool water soothed Gilgamesh's forehead, chilling the back of his neck like morning dew, so that he felt himself fully awake. Enatarzi's gentle plump hands tugged through his tangles, straightening the matted strands until Gilgamesh's hair once more fell about his shoulders in rippling waves. The Ensi stood up to step into his long kilt, Enatarzi brushing at the three long layers of white linen fronds until they fell straight as the leaves on a carven palm tree; then the slave clasped the heavy dark necklace about Gilgamesh's neck and bent to wrap his sandal-thongs about his legs and tie them carefully above the bulging muscles of his calves. Lastly he set a bag into Gilgamesh's hand: small but heavy, jingling when the Ensi moved—a fit offering for the goddess, to adorn her priestesses or be sold to pay for the care of the foundlings brought to the temple, as Rimsat-Ninsun decreed.

Although the elders of the temple considered it ill-fitting and dangerous for the Ensi to walk alone at night outside the bounds of the little temple-city, Gilgamesh did not bother to wake any of his chosen troops, only nodded and laid a finger on his lips to the warriors who guarded his dwelling. The moon was down, the shadow of the high terrace-shrine behind him blocking the starlight; in darkness, Gilgamesh made his way through the buildings where the folk of the temples of Inanna and An lived and worked and carried out trade for the temple's sake, passing unseen from the Eanna into the Erech of men. His sandals whispered on the hard mud road, scuffing through the old ruts made by the wheels of heavy-laden carts. Now and then a glint of light showed through the open door of a tavern, muffled gusts of laughter bursting out into the darkness only to be cut off as the door closed. Once in a while a drunk would stumble by, muttering or singing or shouting curses at the silent windows above him; but if Gilgamesh's long, triple-layered kilt was not enough to warn fools away from accosting him, his size and the sword at his side surely were.

The temple of Rimsat-Ninsun, the Old Woman of Erech, was across the city from the temple of Inanna—perhaps, Gilgamesh thought irreverently, to keep the older head priestess from meddling in the affairs of the young woman who must always succeed her when her son was grown, or her bearing years over, though the mother who had raised him and the Shamhatu seemed to speak with a single voice too often these days. His sandals rang on the bridge over the canal that ran through the city; a party of drunken revelers stepped aside as he walked past, the rich scent of fermented malt wafting from them like a breath of wind from the temple of the brewer-goddess when the new beer flowed out frothing like the Idiglat and Buranun in flood. On another night, had he not washed himself and dressed in his ruler's finery, he might have joined them, or let his feet lead him into a tavern where he might drink rough fresh beer through a plain piece of straw and still his restlessness for a few minutes in the body of one of the pleasant inn-women. The dreams that had awoken him had left his own body stirred, so that his path almost wavered for a moment as he thought on it; but the strangeness of the signs he had seen in his sleep and his own curiosity drove him on.

Rimsat-Ninsun's temple was smaller by far than the temple of Inanna: even without the great terrace lifting it high above the city, Inanna's house could have swallowed that of the older goddess' twice over. Gilgamesh slowed as he came nearer to the door. The first time he lifted his hand, it fell back: then he caught hold of himself, banging so that the wood shook and groaned beneath his fist.

The Ensi did not have to wait long. There was always a priestess by the door of Rimsat-Ninsun, for—it was a sort of grim jest among the women of the temple—while foundlings of lesser folk might be left there at any hour, those of higher birth were sure to come in the dead of night, when the moon was down and the lamps out. The face he saw shadowed in the lamplight through the door's crack was an old one, nose curving down over a toothless mouth framed by a few strands of silver hair: Bau, who had served the goddess since before Gilgamesh's conception, and been midwife when he was born, cutting the child free from the womb of the dying priestess of Inanna when there was no other way to bring him forth.

"Welcome, boy," her cracked voice murmured. "Why come so late? I see no child in your arms."

"I seek the counsel of Rimsat-Ninsun, my mother," Gilgamesh answered. "I have had strange dreams, and must know what they betide."

The leather hinges of the door creaked as it opened; Gilgamesh stepped in, ducking his head beneath the lintel. He followed the light flickering around the hunchbacked shape of old Bau as she led him through the corridor to the shrine of the goddess. "Sit and be patient," Bau said. "Rimsat-Ninsun will come to you soon."

A half circle of oil-lamps burned low on the mud-brick table before the niche where the statue of the goddess stood, their flames glimmering dark from the polished triangles of lapis lazuli that formed the folds of her dress, and bright from the rings of gold at her fingers and ears. Rimsat-Ninsun's eyes were dark, the painted blackness of her hair sucking in the light so that she seemed to be hooded in black wool; but the pale olive-wood of her face shone with scented oil. On the table in front of her stood a platter of cheese, white as limestone in the lamplight, and a bowl of honey, the firelight gleaming deep gold from its surface. Composing his thoughts, Gilgamesh waited as he had been taught to, still as a relief-carved image of stone on a wall-frieze: the Ensi must often sit so, without twitching or shifting, while the priests and priestesses carried out their rites or the people gathered before him at the holy moon-feasts each month. With the unruly jerking of his young body long stilled by harsh cracks of the rod across his shoulders, forcing himself to sit like this now was a calming exercise to Gilgamesh. He breathed deeply, sucking in the scents of frankincense and myrrh and olive oil, palm wine and the sweet aroma rising from the calamus-rushes that strewed the floor.

Gilgamesh heard the rustle of a long wool dress behind him, but sat still, waiting for his mother to come before him. Like the goddess, the priestess Rimsat-Ninsun wore a robe of deep blue and was adorned at ears and hands with gold rings; but her black hair was streaked with silver now, and the shadows of the goddess' lamps deepened the little wrinkles about her eyes to deep crevasses. Her pupils had swollen so that her eyes seemed as flatly black as the statue's. This was more than the dim light: Gilgamesh knew that the goddess would speak through her priestess' mouth. Rimsat-Ninsun's voice was slow and deep, each word falling still against the mud-brick walls.

"My son, you have come to ask my help. Tell me, what troubles you in the depth of night; what brings you to my dwelling when the moon is down and the lamplight snuffed?"

Gilgamesh opened his mouth, and the words came out in a great rush, spilling from his heart. "Mother, I have dreamed a dream. Stars of the sky appeared, and a great shooting star of An fell next to me. I tried to lift it, but it was too strong for me; I tried to turn it over, but could not move it. The land of Erech was standing around it, the whole land had gathered about it. The populace thronged around it, the men clustered about it, and kissed its feet as though it were a little baby. I loved it and embraced it as a wife; I laid it down at your feet, and you made it compete with me." He was breathless when he stopped, the strange dizziness of the dream spinning in his head again—the longing for the fiery stone hurtling from the heavens, the feeling of his muscles straining against its thrumming might.

Rimsat-Ninsun's mouth curved slowly into a smile, the edges of her teeth gleaming behind her dark lips like shards of white-glazed pottery. "As for the stars of the sky which appeared, and the shooting star of An which fell next to you: you tried to lift it, but it was too strong for you; you tried to turn it over, but could not move it. You laid it down at my feet, and I made it compete with you, and you loved and embraced it as a wife. There will come to you a mighty man, a comrade who saves his friend. He is the mightiest in the land, he is the strongest, his strength is as mighty as the shooting star of An. You loved and embraced him as a wife, and it is he who will save you time and again. Your dream is good: it bodes well."

The wind hissed from Gilgamesh's lungs in a deep sigh; and with it, like blood spurting again from a deep leg-wound when the bandage loosened, came another burst of words. "Mother, I have had another dream. At the gate of my wedding-chamber there lay an axe, and people had gathered about it. The land of Erech was standing around it, the whole land had assembled about it, the populace was thronging around it. I laid it down at your feet, I loved it and embraced it as a wife, and you made it compete with me."

Now Rimsat-Ninsun laughed, a soft sound like the rustling of wind through dry palm leaves. She put out her hand to stroke Gilgamesh's hair back from his forehead; he could smell the sweet oils on her skin, olive and frankincense and myrrh. "The axe that you saw, my son, is a man. You will bring him to me; you will love and embrace him as a wife, but I will also have him compete with you. He will be a mighty man, a comrade who saves his friend, and his strength is as mighty as the shooting star of An."

"Who is this man, and why does he come to me?"

"Because the gods would have it so. Do you wish that he not come?"

"Never should I wish that!" Gilgamesh answered. The longing of his dreams still thrilled through him—the rough warm strength of the stone, the shining bronze weight of the axe—and it seemed to him that he could see the great gates of his duties opening before him, to let him free in the bright desert sunlight for a little space. "By the command of Enlil, the Great Counselor, so may it come to pass! May I have a friend and adviser, a friend and adviser may I have! You have read the dreams about him for me; you deserve the greatest praise, Rimsat-Ninsun, offerings of lapis and carnelian and gold, goats and sheep and the smooth aged beer." Gilgamesh rose and laid the bag Enatarzi had given him on the offering table, between the platter of cheese and the bowl of honey.

"A friend and adviser you shall have, my son, for the gods have decreed it." Rimsat-Ninsun walked around behind Gilgamesh again; her voice grew slower and softer yet, as though she whispered from across the Buranun, her words borne to her son on a whisper of river-mist. "They called out to the goddess Aruru, who created mankind; they called on her to create an equal for you, one matched to your stormy heart and strong limbs. Within herself Aruru created the decree of An: she washed her hands, she pinched off some clay, she cast it into the wilderness. In the wilderness she created him for you, born of Silence, given strength by Ninurta. You shall know him when you see him, for even now he is not far. Wise words and wise counsel shall be given you; when joy is upon you, Inanna shall set you hand in hand, and when peril is upon you, I shall speak the words that give you each to the other . . ."

Gilgamesh waited, but his mother spoke no more; and when at last he turned his head, there was no one beside him in the darkness. Yet he was not satisfied: he rose, pacing about the darkened temple like a nervous lion, as though Rimsat-Ninsun might be standing unseen in one of the black nooks that lined the walls, waiting for him to come to her. But there was no one there, and no more answer than his mother had given him.

At last Gilgamesh saw a light in one of the small archways. He turned to face it, standing still.

"The goddess has gone to bed," croaked old Bau. "And so should her son, though he was born with great omens and great prophecies surround him, for he must rise early tomorrow and sit all day at judgments. Will you have a sleeping draught, Gilgamesh? Your hair and eyes are wild; you do not look as though you will rest easily."

"I will rest easily enough!" Gilgamesh answered, though he knew the words were foolish even as he said them. But he had passed eighteen years; as Erech's Lugal, he had won three great battles, over Ur and Eridu and Lagash, and it was not for Bau to cosset the Ensi of Erech as though he were still a boy with scraped knees.

Bau coughed and muttered, but when Gilgamesh said nothing else, she lifted her lamp again to light his way from the temple. Though he wished to leave in dignity, the Ensi could not keep from casting a last glance over his shoulder to the statue of Rimsat-Ninsun, the black pools of her eyes gazing gravely into the darkness above the guttering oil-lamps. The counsel of the gods is like strong palm wine, Gilgamesh thought as he walked back toward the raised platform-shrine that loomed like a black shadow against the stars. A little may warm the heart; too much dizzies the head, and leaves the drinker knowing less than before. Yet to have a friend who is my equal, one whom I love as I loved the heaven-fallen stone in my dream, the axe I saw in my sleep . . .

The sky was beginning to gray by the time Gilgamesh got back to Inanna's temple-city. He could hear the bleating of goats above the baaing of sheep; for a few minutes he had to stand to the side to let one of the assistant herders drive his small flock by, for the sheep neither knew nor cared that the Ensi of the city was among them, and would not part for Gilgamesh. He knew that he should feel sleepy, but when he got back to his own house, where Enatarzi was waiting for him with a cup of rich milk still warm from the goat's udder and a plate of fresh figs and honey to eat before he washed himself and shaved his face and body for the law-court, Gilgamesh was as wakeful and strong as though he had slept deeply all night and only risen with the dawn.

AKALLA SAW THE walls of Erech standing high above the plain when he was still more than half a day's walk away; above them rose a pointed hill with a building atop it. His father had given him two little pieces of copper, one to pay the ferry over and one to pay his way back: the ferry-man, a short squat fellow whose bald head gleamed like polished bronze, took the first piece without haggling, grunting instead and waving Akalla to sit in the bottom of the skin-covered reed boat as he dug his punting pole in and shoved off from the banks.

By the time he stood on dry land before the arched gateway, Akalla was wordless with awe. The painted bricks of the wall rose high as a cliff above his head, taller than the date palms that stretched away on the field to his left. From within he could hear the sounds of voices blending into a great deep buzz, as though he stood beneath the beehive that gave honey to the gods; people passed back and forth beyond the gate, tight-packed as any herd of gazelles.

A guard stood on either side of Erech's gate, the reddening sunlight blazing from their bronze helms and wristlets. They were tall men, the sweat gleaming on the heavy muscles of their chests and arms above their clean linen kilts; but their dark eyes were slitted like sleepy lizards' against the lowering sun.

"Your business in the city?" the one on the right asked, his voice slow and bored.

Akalla's throat choked on what he had to say: his father had told him to save his tale till he reached the temple. *Enlil, help me!* he cried out in his heart. The guards were both looking at him now, their brows lifting a little.

Desperately scrabbling in his waist-bag, Akalla's fingers brushed the tingling cold smoothness of his father's seal. He brought it out, holding it up to the guards like an amulet to ward off the *gallas* of the under-world.

The guard to the left bent closer, looking at it. Then he straightened up and lifted his spear-point to the sky in a single crisp movement. The guard on the right did likewise, almost mirroring his companion's motion.

"Inanna, mother of Erech, welcomes you back to your home, temple-man," the left-hand guard said. "Is your business in the Eanna alone?"

Akalla nodded, not daring to risk his voice.

"Pass through, and ask blessings on us."

Akalla stepped under the gate. A cold shadow fell across his neck as he passed beneath it; it seemed that he could feel the huge weight of brick on brick straining high above him, crushing him to the size of a beetle as he walked beneath it. So are men before the gods, he thought: truly this is a city of holiness.

On the other side, the road forked into three streets, all full of carts, donkeys, oxen, and people jostling for a place. Akalla turned toward the right, but had not walked three steps before a whistle and call from behind jerked him up shortly.

"Hey! Temple-man!"

It was the right-hand guard, waving him back. Akalla walked to him, dewy sweat chilling on his palms and forehead.

"You've been away too long, or maybe too long in the sun, eh?" the guard said, winking at Akalla. This close, the trapper saw the small pink wen at the corner of his eye, twisting his gaze so that one eye seemed to look over Akalla's shoulder. The guard picked up a thin slab of clay. "Look: here is the gate, where you stand now . . . do you understand me?" he said, slowly and carefully. Akalla had no liking for his tone; it seemed too much like the mocking way the shepherds spoke to him when they made fun of his slow-moving wits. Yet this man's face was kind, and Akalla had none other to show him the way in this strange place. He looked down at the slab, the lines and tiny pocks, then back at the streets—yes, he could see how they were laid now, though the little lines and triangles of writing on the slab often crossed over the longer lines of the roads and made the tangle of alleys almost impossible to pick out. "You go here, along the center road. See the road, there?" He pointed. "You will pass the fishmongers and the brewers and the bakers, then you will come to a big street running across it, just like on the map here . . . see? There will be oxcarts bearing their loads along to the Eanna: there always are. Show your seal to one of the drivers, and he will take you there and save you a little sandal leather. They work for the temple, so if one asks you for money, he is a scoundrel. Can you remember that?"

"I can. Thank you."

Akalla made his way through the streets, careful to avoid jostling other folk or the stalls of fresh melons and cucumbers that lined the roadside. He looked longingly for a moment as the hairy-lipped old crone behind one stall split open a melon for herself, sucking noisily at the sweet wet flesh within—the thirst scratched harsh in his throat, and he could almost feel the cool melon-juice soothing it. But he had nothing to buy with, save the copper bit that he would need for paying the ferryman on the way back over, so he passed on, thinking only what a wonder it was, that a thirst which would seem like the least of accustomed annoyances in the barren desert should loom so greatly in the city with all its riches.

Akalla did not ask any of the oxcart-drivers for a ride: though the lengthening shadow of the terrace-shrine now stretched nearly to the western wall of the city, the walk did not seem far to him, and he did not wish to be taken for a witling a second time. When he reached the sprawl of buildings around the foot of the terrace, however, Akalla stopped in confusion. They were all tall and fine structures, many two-storied, adorned with colored bricks and paint. The herds of sheep passed around him, paying him no mind. He stepped aside as a flock of goats passed, butting and bleating beneath the stick of the young man herding them. A cool evening breeze had sprung up, rustling sharply through the fronds of the palm trees and more softly through the delicate scaly leaves and twigs of the tamarisks that grew around the great well in the middle of the courtyard; though it was not yet cold enough for Akalla to unfold the cloak that also served him as blanket and travel-bag, the soft wind chilled the trickles of sweat on his chest and back, leaving his skin stippled and naked-feeling as the skin of a plucked waterfowl.

Atop the terrace, a door opened. Now Akalla could hear the sound of a ram-horn blowing, followed by the sound of music—many voices singing together as one; though he could not make out the words, their wailing tone sent a chill of beauty down his spine. He walked around until he found a pathway through the temple buildings, a pathway that led all the way up the terrace's stepped side and to the shrine at its height.

Stepping in through the open door, Akalla thought he would swoon. Oil-lamps burned everywhere, so that the shrine seemed warm and bright as noonday; the air was thick with heavy sweet smoke above the scents of roasting meat and burning wood. The walls inside were crenellated and buttressed, furrowed with deep niches and open doorways leading into smaller rooms; the plain brown mud-bricks of the walls and columns were adorned with inlaid patterns made by plugs of colored clay, red and black and pale dots forming triangles and lozenges and bands of zigzagging lightning. At the end of the shrine, in the largest of the niches, stood a huge statue of painted stone: Inanna, Queen of Heaven, robed in pale blue linen and standing on the back of a gilded lion, with a star of gold blazing over the diadem on her brow. On either side of her stood two palm trees, hanging heavy with ripe fruit; it took a moment for Akalla to realize that the fronds of the trees had been carved from wood and painted, and the bunches of dates, though real enough, hung from their branches by hooks. The voices still rose and fell, and through gaps in the walls Akalla could catch glimpses of the singers, and hear the plinking of the lyres that accompanied them, but for the rest, he seemed to be alone.

"What are you doing here?" a deep voice husked behind him. "This is not a time for the people to come in: the singers and their accompanists have much to do before they are ready to sing the *tigi*-hymns at the wedding of Inanna and Gilgamesh, and it is not for those who do not belong to the temple to listen to them when it is not time."

Akalla turned, to find himself looking down upon the long silver-gray hair of a wizened little man—but a man who stood like an eagle upon the crag, his proud beak tilted upward to catch the wind. The old man was robed in white linen with bands of scarlet and purple upon it, and over his thin chest shone a great pale silver-gold disk that sparkled with clear and black stones. Unable to speak, the trapper did as he had done before: he pulled his father's seal out and handed it to the priest.

The priest turned it over and over in his fingers, biting thoughtfully at his lip. "It has been long since I last saw this seal," he mused. Deep as it was, his voice did not ring: Akalla could hear the years of dust in his throat, the throat of a man who had breathed the hot winds of the desert through much traveling, and spoken so often that the music of his voice-box had worn away. The old man handed the seal back. "Yes: you must be the son of Gunidu, once chief shepherd in this temple. You have some of his look, though it is clear that you follow a rougher trade, and far indeed from Erech. What brings the son back to his father's stead, after so many years have passed?"

"Great lord," Akalla said, for he did not know the priest's rank, "my father sent me here. For I have seen a wonder, and he sent me to tell the lord Gilgamesh of it and ask him for . . . for . . ." Akalla's throat stopped again. How could he say to this man—this awesome, terrifying, little dry date-husk of a priest—what counsel his father had given him? Now it seemed to him like the worst of folly that he had not fled in silence from the watering hole where the wild man and his lions had stood, kept his silence through the night and turned to seek another hunting ground in the morning. He knew that the gods took terrible revenge on those who did not show them fit respect: what would their priests and priestesses do for their sake?

The prickling behind Akalla's eyes burned harshly, the first stinging of salt tears eating away at eyelids already beginning to ache from the shrine's thick smoke. He stared hard at the priest, the little man's figure blurring and wavering in his sight like the thousand thousand flames from the oil-lamps, doubling and starring in his tear-glazed eyes.

The priest's small hand, dry and rough as a leather glove left three years without oil, closed on Akalla's wrist. "Come this way," he said. "You are tired, and I hear the thirst and hunger in your voice; but the milk is already being brought from the sheepfold; the fat of the ox our Ensi sacrificed as he made ready to give his justice has been prepared for the goddess, and its meat is now full-cooked. Inanna, who is clothed in pleasure and love, in whose lips are sweetness, wishes none to go hungry in her house—least of all one who has seen a wonder fit for the hearing of the Ensi. Truly I should be no longer En of her shrine if I did not tend her children as she willed."

There was no surprise left in Akalla, but the dull shock seemed to thud into his belly: the man he spoke to was indeed the En, the high priest of Erech, of whom Gilgamesh alone was the equal. And yet that holiest of men was leading Akalla down the steps of the platform-shrine, to the cluster of buildings whose windows now shone with light; and now he was seating the trapper on a chair of polished cedarwood by a small ivory-topped table, with a lion-skin beneath his feet, and calling a slave to bring water to wash with, food, and drink. Akalla settled himself uncomfortably on the seat: in all his settlement, only Puzur-ili, the village's chief man, had a chair, and he only sat in that for the greatest assemblies.

"You may rest a little," the En said, "for Gilgamesh must finish his work before I call him to us, however long ago his patience for the task may have run out." The old man sat down at the other side of the table, leaning his wrinkled brown elbows against the smooth ivory and resting his chin in his palms. Akalla could not meet his gaze for too long; instead he glanced about the room. The legs of the chair on which he sat were carved into delicately hooved ibex-legs; the arms of the larger chair on the other side of the room finished in gilded bulls' heads with lapis eyes, horns, and forelocks, and its back decorated with inlaid designs of glimmering shell. On the floor lay several lion-skins, manes dark as a sudden rush of river-water over their tawny pelts. The slave entered with a bowl of water and a linen cloth: Akalla absently patted the dust from his face and hands, still looking about in amazement.

The walls were painted with scenes that at first Akalla could not put a name to: a man in the simple kilt of a shepherd approaching a cloaked woman; the woman lying upon the ground as if dead while the man sat upon a high throne with a host of people gathered before his feet, paying her no attention; the woman rising with seven dark shadows behind her; the man changing into a gazelle, hiding among the sheep until dragged forth by the shadows, then falling dead beneath the blows of their weapons; and, lastly, the woman exalted upon the throne with a star upon her brow and a lion at her feet—Inanna, the goddess triumphant over . . . her beloved husband Dumuzi, Akalla thought, and smiled for sheer relief, for the tale was coming back to him as his gaze plodded through the pictures again. Inanna had wed Dumuzi and gone to the underworld, but he had exalted himself instead of mourning. When she came back with the *gallas* dogging her heels, seeking another to take her place in Erishkegal's grim kingdom, Dumuzi had begged her brother Utu to turn him into a gazelle so that he might flee, but wherever he went, the *gallas* followed, until at last they brought him forth and slew him. Yes, Akalla remembered the story well enough—but now he frowned: he knew of Inanna and Dumuzi, yet the old priest had spoken of the wedding of Inanna and Gilgamesh. Still, he did not want to seem foolish by asking more, and now the food was set before him: a neat pile of ox-meat cubes well-spiced with cumin and sweetened with honey, sitting on a heap of cooked and buttered wheat-grains like the shrine atop its platform, and the whole resting on a thick platter of bread, served on a plate of fine bronze, and beside it a silver cup of sheep's milk, warm and smooth in his hand.

"Now we shall see," the old priest said, rising to his feet. "Stay here, and eat in peace: we shall soon be back."

As soon as the last scribe—still pecking notes down on his tablet—stood to go and the doors of the Court of Judgment closed behind the last petitioners, Gilgamesh handed his stave of office to his body-slave and sighed with relief. He lifted the ceramic water-bowl and poured it over his head, heedless of how the splashing torrent ran along the arms of his chair and soaked the carnelian-reds and heaven-blues of the finely woven carpet beneath his feet to agate and lapis darkness. Enatarzi was already at his elbow with a tall, fluted gold cup; the straw that poked forth from its depths was pure gold inlaid with triangles of lapis lazuli, but Gilgamesh cared only about the rich, mellow scent rising from the beer within. He seized the cup, draining the beer in a single slow draught, and held it out for the slave to refill.

"And that is a whole day wasted, when I had hoped to be done by noon, and training my men halfway through the day," Gilgamesh complained. "Do the people of Erech have nothing better to do than argue about who owns which goat and what sheep, or what is clearly specified in a bill of sale?"

"It matters a great deal to them, Ensi," Enatarzi answered calmly, blinking his wide black eyes. Like many eunuchs, he outlined them with dark paint so they would look larger yet, though he was far too old and fat to think of drawing men's gazes still. "To those who have little, a goat means as much as half Erech to you. As for training your men, have I not heard you say before that if they do not rise early in the cool of the morning, there is little time to swing sword and shield before the heat of the day will overcome them?"

"True enough," Gilgamesh owned. "Still, there are many men who might see to the courts well enough without me, while I am the only Lugal of Erech; and if Kish comes upon us when we are unprepared, instead of our setting about them at our leisure, the poor folk of Erech will have far more to worry about than troubles that bleat and baa."

"And yet you are Ensi," said Enatarzi stolidly. "But the day's work is done: you may drink your beer in peace while your food is fetched, or I will send for musicians, or your wife-priestesses."

"Food is enough for now," Gilgamesh answered. "And I will think more of a piece of bread and a hunk of cheese or a few strips of dried fish, if they arrive quickly, than I will of the finest cooking in Erech, if it is slow in reaching me."

"At once, Ensi." Enatarzi bustled off; Gilgamesh stretched his legs out with another sigh and drank a swallow of beer. This day's judging had chafed at him more than usual: the cases had seemed pettier and the plaintiffs more combative than ever, shrill women and angry men shrieking at one another so that he had twice been forced to crash his stave of office down and shout for silence. The heat had risen toward the end of the day, so that keeping his eyes open had been like trying to stare into the heart of a sand dune in the middle of summer, and Enatarzi's best efforts at fanning had not been able to keep the big black flies from swarming to his sweat like drunkards to an open jar of beer. But it was over now, the gods be thanked, and tomorrow he could go back to his army with a clear heart.

Gilgamesh did not turn when he heard the door opening behind him. It was only when he heard the two sets of footsteps on the hard brick floor—one shuffling, one lifting high and treading lightly—that he looked to see who it was.

The En and Shamhatu stood behind him, their faces grave. Both were wearing simple clothing, white linen with colored bands; Shamhatu's necklace was a plain one of small carnelian and gold beads strung between leaves of lapis, and her dark hair was not covered by one of the great diadems, but hung loose and smooth as a polished flow of wood, the red highlights gleaming from it like oiled cedar. This eased Gilgamesh's heart a little, for they were not dressed to come before him as En and Inanna, but only as the overseers of the temple.

"What is it you want?" Gilgamesh asked. "I have just now finished giving judgment, and not yet washed or eaten."

The En glanced at the wet locks of hair plastered against Gilgamesh's neck, then down to the fading stain of water on the rug. "If you have not washed, then the Buranun must be flooding out of season," his deep voice said dryly. "As for eating, a meal awaits you in the *gipar*—together with a guest who will hold your interest."

His tiredness and hunger forgotten, Gilgamesh leapt up at once; only his swiftness of hand let him catch the toppling golden cup before it had spilled more than a mouthful of beer onto the rug. The gold drinking straw rang against its sides, clattering softly to a halt, as Gilgamesh demanded, "Who? What manner of man have you found?"

"Softly, Gilgamesh," Shamhatu said. "Our guest is a simple trapper from west of the Buranun. He says that he has seen a wonder, and that his father told him to speak with you."

Gilgamesh's hands unclenched slowly, as though he were unwillingly loosening his grasp to give over his chariot-asses' reins. "Take me to him, then. I will hear what he has to say, so long as I may eat while I listen."

When the En guided them into his house, the trapper was in the priest's front room, sitting bolt upright in a cedar chair, back well away from the chair-back and hands in his lap as though he feared that his sweat might profane the very wood of his seat. Before him was an empty platter of bronze with only a few crumbs on it. His hair was short-cropped, but not shaven; his skin was tanned dark as old leather, tight over sharply lined muscles. Though he bore no marks of true deformity, his forehead sloped back farther than most, and the heavy ridges over his eyes gave him an oxlike look of stupidity; his mouth was slightly open as well, as though his tongue were too thick for his jaw. Gilgamesh gazed on him a moment, feeling the bitterness gathering like drops of gall in his stomach. This man will tell me a wonder? he thought. It is as like to be a tale of a sheep walking east instead of west as anything worth the hearing.

The trapper rose and slumped into a prostration in almost the same motion, as though he feared to stand upright before the king. Now Gilgamesh watched him a little more closely: for, stupid as the man looked, he moved with the smooth grace of one who had long since mastered his body.

"Rise and sit," Gilgamesh said. "I am told that you have a tale for me."

"Ensi . . . Lugal . . ." the trapper stuttered, sputtering an odd little whistle around the sides of his tongue.

"You need have no fear," Gilgamesh told him as one of the priest's slaves came in with a plate of food; then, aside to the slave, "Bring date-wine for me, and for this man as well, I can see that he needs it." The slave was back in a few moments, carefully bearing a silver platter with four tall bronze cups on it. Gilgamesh took a generous swallow of his own, letting its sweet warmth wash out through his body, then waved the trapper to go on.

"I was in the mountains . . . there is a man who has come from the mountains," the trapper stuttered. Gilgamesh felt the muscles of his stomach tightening as he bent forward, waiting for the next words. "I think . . . he is the mightiest in the land, his strength is as mighty as the shooting star of An. All the time, he goes over the mountains; he is always jostling at the watering place with the animals, and plants his feet opposite the watering place. I was afraid . . . I was afraid, so I did not go up to him. He filled in the pits I had dug, he . . . he wrenched out my traps that I had spread, loosed from my grasp the wild animals. He does not let me make my rounds in the wilderness. I saw him standing among the lions, and I was afraid, for he seemed like a lion himself. He stood among the lions . . . he stood among the young lions who have manes but no prides, and he bore a mane of gold himself."

The breath hissed out from between Gilgamesh's teeth. His heart was throbbing with a pounding urgency, beating in his ears like the drums of the temple, and he tightened his hands on the bull-heads that tipped his chair's arms until their lapis horns bit into his palms.

"Who is this man? Where did he come from, and how long has he walked the wilderness?"

"Ensi, I do not know," the trapper answered; Gilgamesh could see the tears welling in his eyes. "Only that he came from the mountains, and goes about with the animals: I saw him standing among the lions, and his footprints in the herds of gazelles, where he had torn up the grass with the gazelles. He was not one of the black-headed folk of Sumer; his mane was gold, and a pelt of gold grew upon him. He is the mightiest of men, the mightiest I have ever seen but for yourself: perhaps he was a little shorter, perhaps a little heavier of bone, but elsewise a match for Gilgamesh, Gilgamesh . . ." The trapper paused as if remembering a lesson. ". . . two-thirds god and one-third man."

Gilgamesh forced himself to lean back in his chair, to breathe deeply and loosen his muscles as he would if he were circling a dangerous foe with blade in hand. The lamp-shadowed friezes on the wall across from him seemed to mock him: Dumuzi, half rearing with shock, his callused shepherd's hands turning into the dainty forehooves of a gazelle and his sandled feet into the slight rear hooves; the dark *gallas* dragging him away from the sheep, forsaken by Inanna and abandoned to Erishkegal—and, lastly, Inanna sitting upon Dumuzi's throne, the gold star that crowned her diadem wrought in real gold, gleaming and flickering with the light from the oil-lamps, with the rippled gold of her lion's mane below shattering the same brightness and casting it about like sunlight on fast-flowing water. Before Inanna sat Shamhatu, her painted eyes dark against the smooth pale oval of her face. She smiled, and said, "Gilgamesh, why not leave your place for a little while, and go with this trapper? So long as you are back in time to ready yourself for your wedding to Inanna, the city elders can govern well enough for a little while: did they not do so for the fifteen years before you took up the stave of office?"

Shamhatu, Gilgamesh thought, why do you tempt me with the words my own heart is speaking, when you have always urged me to duty before—the more pointless and tedious, the better? Then a clearer thought came to him: if he were to go away for five moons, the army he had fought and scrabbled to dig out of the mud-flats and palm-groves and long green fields around Erech would melt back into their homes, most of the young men glad enough to turn from sword to plough, from army-mates to sweethearts. This was the best time of year for training,

now that the sun's heat was cooling a little; it was the only time of year
when a Lugal might lead his men out to war and hope for victory.

And yet . . . and yet . . . two weeks, perhaps a moon; that would not
do his army too much harm, and the prize to be won!

Gilgamesh looked into his cup, tilting it gently. The sticky dark wine
sloshed thickly, still more than halfway up the side: though it was strong,
the wine was not to blame for the whirling buzz of thoughts in his head.
He was about to speak again, to ask the trapper how far away this wild
man was and when he had last been seen, when Shamhatu's low voice
sounded through the room.

"Gilgamesh, it is well that you should go: the gods do not send their
dreams for nothing."

The Ensi's back snapped upright, a single flash of white burning
before his eyes with the hot shock that ran through his heart. Dimly, Gilgamesh felt the wine spilling onto his knuckles as he struggled for breath.

My mother told you, he thought. She told you my dream, and you . . .
you both wanted me to loose three-fourths of my army from their ranks,
to write the tribute to Kish into the lists forever. Only a fool dares the
gods—but the plots of priestesses and priests are another matter.

"Tell me more of this wild man," Gilgamesh said between his teeth.
Even in the lamplight, he could see the trapper pale beneath his tan;
when the man spoke, his sputter was back. "He . . . he . . . he . . . lord,
look to a lion . . . this lion under my feet. He . . . he . . . had a mane, and
gold hair grew all over him, and it seemed that the lions thought him the
strongest in the pride. There were no lionesses, it was a pride of young
bachelors. My father . . . my father said that if he scented a female, he
would leave the pack, as young lions do when they win their way into a
pride."

Gilgamesh looked at Shamhatu again. A gleam of the light off the
gilded mane of Inanna's lion shone on the curve of her cheek like a
brush-mark of gold powder; though he could not read her thoughts in
her face, he knew that she must see the slow smile growing on his own.

"If he scented a female . . ." he said musingly. "Surely such a man was
sent by the gods: but who knows whether he will be a gentle rising of the
river to water our crops, or a flood that leaves our fields a barren mass of

salted slime? The strength of the gods alone is too much for simple men to face, else why would Inanna have brought us priestship and rulership as first among the *me?*" Gilgamesh felt his grin growing wider as he spoke. "Yet once we lived as wild men, knowing none of those things which are needful for civilization. And so it seems to me—truly the gods must know it—that before the wild man comes to Erech, Inanna must bear the *me* to him: the knowledge of En and gods and rulers, shrine and shepherdship and exalted women, truth and battle-standard and weapon . . . and sexual intercourse, that gift of hers to turn the bachelor lion who is the pride's foe into the mated lion who is the pride's defender."

The Ensi rose from his chair, taking Shamhatu's slender hand in his. She stood without argument; holding her like this, Gilgamesh could feel the faint trembling in her bones, her fluttering pulse and quickening breaths. For a moment a qualm seized him: she was a priestess, raised in the temple from a foundling, and had never known a man who did not worship the gift she offered. More, she was small and slight even for a woman; could she, indeed, bear the strength of the wild man if he flung himself on her without care? And as for his lions, how could they be trusted not to tear her to pieces, whatever the man did? For a moment, Gilgamesh was ready to wrap his arms about Shamhatu like the walls of a city, protecting her from the beasts without.

Then the priestess looked up into Gilgamesh's eyes, with the cool, deep-seated gaze that had always annoyed him—as though his thoughts were scratched on the back of his skull for her to read through his pupils. "I dare it," Shamhatu whispered, so softly that only he could hear. "No priestess shall meet this wild man but I myself: there is more way than one for a woman to match the strength of a man, however roused he may be."

Gilgamesh led her before the trapper, setting her hand into his. "Go, trapper, bring the priestess Shamhatu with you. When the animals are drinking at the watering hole, let her take off her robe and show the wild man that she is a woman. When he sees her, he will draw near to her, and his animals, who grew up in his wilderness, will forsake him."

The trapper only stared at his own hand, at his thick dark fingers locked about Shamhatu's slim pale ones. "Mighty is Gilgamesh, Ensi of Erech . . . two-thirds god and one-third man," he murmured.

"Care for her well," Gilgamesh instructed him. "Remember that she is the chief priestess of Inanna, through whose body the goddess takes flesh. Eat when she is hungry, drink when she is thirsty, rest when she is tired, for she has grown up in the temple all her life, and is not used to the rough living of trapper or herder." He saw the twitching of Shamhatu's mouth, and his earlier pangs flooded back: if she began to weep now, he thought, he would order her to stay, and send an older and stronger woman in her place. But Shamhatu mastered herself, curving her lips into a smile.

"You need not fear for me," she said. "I shall see that we are well-provisioned, and I have no doubt that good Akalla will care for me properly."

Gilgamesh swallowed the lump in his own throat. "Then it is set: in place of the wild man of the mountains, you will bring me a champion fit to fight beside me in war and sit beside me in peace. Inanna be your strength, and I trust in her to bring you back safely in time to prepare yourself for the wedding." Or not, he added to himself: if the wild man kept Shamhatu in the wilderness a moon or two beyond the New Year's feast, it would not be his own eyes that were reddened with weeping. "O En, this is truly a wonder you have made known to me: have you more to say?"

The En's mouth cracked into a rare grin, his brown stubs of teeth glistening in the lamplight. "Who can contest the wisdom of the Ensi Gilgamesh on his day of judgment? Surely the gods have set him in his seat, exalted above all men of Erech, and their sagacity pours from his mouth like honey from the date. But you have the look of one who is tired, and the chill of night comes on swiftly. You had best go home, for there is much to be done in the temple before Shamhatu sets off on her journey."

Gilgamesh looked down at the little man, who had no more strength in his body than a dried palm-frond, and yet who could dismiss him so casually. The priest's dark eyes stared back up at him, and Gilgamesh saw how they crinkled at the corners with mirth, though the grin had gone as quickly as it came.

"I shall go, then. Gods keep you, and peace upon you."

En and priestess echoed the blessing; the trapper sat frozen as a rabbit in one of his own snares, but that mattered little to Gilgamesh.

With the sun long down, the wind had begun to chill in earnest: it would soon be winter. Yet Gilgamesh did not walk directly from the *gipar* to his own chambers, even to fetch a cloak: instead, still bare-chested, he paced steadily to the western gate, ignoring the streams of folk stumbling out of his way with muttered gasps. The guards did not speak as he passed through, looking out over the Buranun. The broad river rippled slowly along in the moonlight; a small fish jumped, and Gilgamesh heard the croak of a frog a little farther off. Over the river lay a wide stretch of flat fields sprouting with winter crops broken here and there by groves of palms and tamarisks; above, in the star-glittering sky, blazed the pathway of the gods, a stream of milk flowing from Inanna's jug. Gilgamesh found himself looking up at the constellations, naming them each to himself as he had done the night before every battle, their steady bright shapes as calming and solid as the braided gold wire wrapping the hilt of his sword.

Suddenly his dream came back to him again—the great star dropping fiery from heaven, the shooting star of An—and tears flooded to his eyes. He had lain alone, thinking on his war-plans and gazing at the sky, before his battles, and it had not bothered him then. But now it seemed to him that he was like a slave in the quarries who carries a great burden for so long he forgets its weight, knowing only that he must walk with head bent to the side, one shoulder tilted down and one up—then sets the basket of stone down for a short rest, and finds when he must heft it anew that it is too heavy for him to bear.

"Was I a fool, to send Shamhatu when I should have gone myself?" he whispered. "Have I lost the gift of the gods?"

But Gilgamesh remembered the rest of the dreams as well: the shooting star had fallen in Erech itself, the axe lying . . . at the gate of his wedding chamber. Whether through wisdom or foolishness, pride or good sense, he had done what was set forth for him. He could no longer hope that Shamhatu would stay away until after the New Year's feast, but he could wait in hope for what her return would bring.

• • •

THE EN CALLED for one of his slaves to show Akalla to those sleeping quarters reserved for honored guests of the temple. After the trapper had left, he settled himself in his seat again, gazing at Shamhatu. The priestess met his eyes as calmly as she could, although she could feel the trembling running through all her limbs—half fear, half excitement, the two quivering feelings blended together like the soft gold and hard silver beaten into a single plate of electrum. Still the En said nothing, and Shamhatu began to wonder: had she done wrong, her clumsiness in speaking of Gilgamesh's dreams turning him away from the very path he was to take? She did not dare voice her thoughts to the old man's ancient eyes, gleaming out of the darkness like chips of obsidian set in the death-mask of a forgotten king, but it was growing harder and harder for her to remain still.

A light tapping sounded at the door of the *gipar*. Shamhatu sighed silently with relief, standing and pacing smoothly over to open it. It was the priestess Rimsat-Ninsun, flanked by torch-bearing guards, their bitumen flares hissing and crackling against the cooling night. She wore her full regalia, but her brown eyes were clear with earthly sight: the might of the goddess was not upon her at this moment.

"Greetings, daughter," Rimsat-Ninsun said, closing the door in the faces of her stolid guardsmen. "What news? You must have spoken with Gilgamesh already, else there would be more folk here."

"Aye, we have spoken with him," the old En said, his dark eyes glinting as their corners crinkled. "The gods work with swiftness: who can fathom their thoughts, or plumb their wisdom's depth? The one of whom Gilgamesh dreamed, the companion you prophesied, has already stridden forth on the earth. And this I did not tell you, for I deemed it better that no ears should hear of it but ours: the trapper who saw him, and brought the news to us, is the son of Gunidu . . . that Gunidu who was once chief shepherd in this temple."

Rimsat-Ninsun drew in a deep hiss of breath, her eyes widening. Shamhatu felt the little hairs along her spine prickling up against her linen gown. There was some great matter here, of which she knew nothing; she had never been told more than that Gunidu was chief shepherd and bidding fair to become more, when one day, about a year before the death of Lugalbanda, he had suddenly walked away into the wilderness, and had not been heard from again. Shamhatu listened eagerly to hear what the Old Woman would say; but Rimsat-Ninsun answered only, "Who can fathom the thoughts of the gods, indeed? Surely none of us could have seen what lay in their minds, those twenty years ago: but they are wise with foresight, and their plans are beyond confounding. Tell me more."

The En and Shamhatu together recounted the words of the trapper; how Gilgamesh had refused to go himself to see the wild man, though the longing was clear on his face, and how Shamhatu had—half chosen, half been ordered—to go and tame the stranger with Inanna's might.

"Tame him, indeed," Rimsat-Ninsun murmured. "And more than that: it is well that there are five moons yet before the sacred Marriage must take place. For it is not enough that Gilgamesh's trusted companion should be brought in from the wilds. He must also be taught to act like a man. It is no little task that you have taken on yourself, to teach a grown man all that a child of five already knows by nature."

The Shamhatu thought with dark horror of one of the temple servants: a man near as beautiful as Gilgamesh, with green-brown eyes and a soft tangle of deep brown hair and clear fine features that often had him sitting as model for the temple painters—who had been given to the temple of Inanna as a child for his beauty, before it could be seen that he would never have more wit than a five-year-old. Now he was carefully set to sweeping floors in the temple; he could not be sent for water, for he could not remember not to spill it out of the buckets when it grew heavy, nor could he be trusted to help in the kitchens, where he might put meat straight into the fire to see the pretty flames. Shamhatu was no better at guiding his work than she was at tending children: though, like all the young women of the temple, she had taken her turn with the foundlings she had not enjoyed the work, nor done it well.

"Yet I must do it," she answered. "It must be done, and the task cannot be entrusted to a lesser priestess, when the hands of the gods are so clear."

"And more," the En said, "he must be taught to love the city, and to love, as well as know, all the *me* of civilization that Inanna brought to Erech. Even as the wild man must be tamed for Gilgamesh's sake, so, looking with new eyes upon all that Gilgamesh takes for granted, he will tame the Ensi as well."

The Shamhatu nodded. She would have to take a great deal with her: lyre and gaming board, fine metalwork and scented oils, and all the insignias that showed her as priestess and goddess in one. She would need a tent as well, for there was no telling how far from human dwellings she would have to roam before she found the wild man—from her days of herding the temple sheep, she knew that a lion could be pacing stealthily alongside the herd one night and two days' walk away by the next.

"All of this I will do, if I may take what I need and go as befits a priestess."

The En frowned. "You may take what you need, surely enough: but the trapper must be guard enough for you. He seems to be a man who can care for himself in the wilderness, and when you went out with the herds, you thought yourself safe enough with bow and staff."

That was true enough: Shamhatu had spent many nights wrapped tightly in a wool cloak among her sheep, waiting for the cough of a lion or the dark slinking shadows of wolves in the moonlight. It was beyond imagination, how little Gilgamesh really knew of the temple life, though he should have been nearly as familiar with it as she—wherefore she had struggled desperately not to laugh in his face as he urged the trapper to care for her as one too gently reared to bear life beyond the temple-city's bounds. Yet the journey she would have to go on now was another matter, with more perils than beasts along its way. "When I went out with the herds, I did not bear the jewels of Inanna, nor did I go far beyond the walls of Erech. The trapper said that the wild man came from the mountains; I would sooner face lions than bandits."

"I think that you can trust in Gunidu's son, though he has the face of a fool: the witless do not live long in the wilderness, let alone well. As for guards: I would have this matter kept a secret until the time has come. It will be told in Erech only that you have retreated to the goddess' fastness to purify and prepare yourself for the wedding. Only we three, and Gil-

gamesh, shall know otherwise. And because it must be so, you and the
trapper will leave well before dawn tomorrow morning, to avoid the eyes
of day."

The Shamhatu opened her mouth to argue further, then closed it
again. The En was right, for wonders of the gods always began delicate
as new-lit embers: before saying, "Look, we have a flame!" it was well to
make sure that the little coal had been fed into a fire strong enough to be
fanned, rather than put out, by the wind. The more so since the matter
touched so closely on Gilgamesh's rule and the temple's might: if the
wild man were to save Erech without destroying it first, it would be well
to keep mad rumors about him unspoken.

"So it shall be," she said. "Then we have much to do, for the sooner I
leave, the better it will be. Let us rouse the priests and priestesses before
they fall too deeply asleep, and read the omen of the liver for the one
that Inanna will have standing in my stead while I am gone—to take my
place, if I do not come back," Shamhatu added.

Once she had given her orders, she went straight to her bath—the
holy bath of Inanna's chosen priestess, which she did not have to share
with the other temple-folk. In a house a little farther from the chief
shrine, the rest of the priests and priestesses would be gathering, taking
their turns at drawing water from the well and pouring it into the great
tubs so that they could be properly cleansed—laughing, perhaps, or perhaps silent in anticipation of what could be so important as to call them
out to purify themselves at this hour of the night, readying for a ritual
that no one had scheduled or expected. But Shamhatu had her own well;
her tub was made of pale tamarisk and ruddy cedarwood, and a great fire
burned in the corner of the chamber where the slim young eunuch
Atab—a *gala*-priest himself, one of the temple's best soloists—was
already heating buckets of water to boiling point, ready to pour into the
cold bath until it was near blood-warm. His own short dark hair was
already sleek and spike-edged with water: he must have taken his own
bath swiftly indeed, in order to be cleansed and ready to assist her with
hers.

It was with the greatest pleasure that Shamhatu stripped off her linen
dress: soaked with cold sweat, the fabric clung to her back like the

embrace of the *lilitu*, the night-hag. Atab bent gracefully to untie her sandals; the mat of braided rushes was comfortably rough beneath her bare feet. She stretched, standing on tiptoes with back arched and breasts thrust outward for a moment before climbing over the side of the tub and sliding into the welcoming water. Atab gave her a handful of fresh tamarisk leaves to scrub herself with before pouring another hot bucketful slowly into the tub; the sweet, sharp scent of the leaves rose up with the steam, mingling pleasantly with the heavier temple-smell of frankincense and sweet flag. The Shamhatu began to speak the words of purification: behind her, Atab opened his mouth, the unearthly pureness of his wordless voice rising as a high counterpart to her low prayer.

"I bathe in the pure stream, the water brought forth from the pure well. If my feet have trodden upon uncleanness, I cleanse them of it; if my hands have touched uncleanness, I cleanse them of it; if uncleanness has come upon my head . . ." Here Shamhatu lifted a great, dripping double handful of water, pouring it over her hair, then arched her neck and leaned her head back until she could feel the bath's warmth creeping up her forehead. ". . . I cleanse myself of it. O Inanna," she went on, scrubbing her breasts with the tamarisk leaves until her plum-dark nipples crinkled tight, "purify my heart with holiness, and make me clean in your sight. Cleanse my womb where the blood flows forth, like the womb of a maiden ewe without spot, a young cow of the purest breed, a white-pelted jenny-ass without a single black hair. Cleanse my back of the gazes of the envious, and wash off the touch of the unholy: be the gateways of my body cleansed, that nothing which is not holy may pass within them or issue from them. Cleanse my flesh and soul, that I may be a spotless garment for the goddess, a cloak without rent or tatter, whose white fringes are stained by no mud . . ."

When Shamhatu rose from the bath, Atab stood ready with a towel of rough linen, drying her as she stood dripping on the reed mat. His touch was gentle, almost a caress upon her breasts and thighs, but she could read nothing in his fine-boned face—save, perhaps, that shadow of sadness at the back of his eyes which she had seen in other eunuchs. And yet he had chosen the cutting himself, for he had had the best voice as a boy that had been heard in some time, and knew that, barring acci-

dent or some great stroke of ill fortune, he would be chief among the
*gala*-priests someday. Although many eunuchs served in the temple of
Inanna, few were clipped against their will: there were always those to
whom power, or beauty, or love of the gods, was worth more than pos-
terity.

Including myself, Shamhatu thought. But now was no time for such
thoughts. Shamhatu wrapped a dry felt shawl around her body and
picked up her sandals by the strings, dangling them loosely in her hand
as she padded barefoot back to her own chamber. The lamps were
freshly filled and lit, the smell of their oil strong in the room; Inanna's
dress of pale blue linen was already laid out across her bed beside a fresh
white breechcloth, and the glimmering flames' reflections from the gold
and carnelian and lapis of the diadem and jewelry that adorned the stone
statue of the goddess in the corner seemed to beckon to Shamhatu.
Carefully she put on the breechcloth and wrapped the dress about her,
taking the girdle of agates from the hips of the goddess and fastening it
around her own. As she lifted each piece of jewelry from the statue and
put it on herself—she could feel the power of Inanna pouring into her
like pure water into a fresh-scrubbed cistern; the flames of the oil-lamps
seemed to burn more brightly, a rainbow of half-seen colors flickering
around the edges of their pure yellow glow, and it seemed to her that she
could hear all the whispering sounds of the night outside. Last of all, she
reverently raised the great crown from the goddess' stone head: heavy as
it was, she held it up for a moment to gaze upon it. In the front shone a
great gold star—and it was solid gold: Shamhatu's neck knew the weight
of it well. Tamarisk leaves of gold dangled all around it; swaying back
and forth as she moved, their tips would brush against her forehead just
above the eyebrows. The band between star and leaves was carven beads
of lapis lazuli—date-clusters and tamarisk branches, the heads of sheep
and oxen—interspersed with little glimmering beads of gold: it was the
crown of the Queen of Heaven, showing her star brightest among all the
stars, and the wealth she showered upon the earth.

Slowly Shamhatu lowered the crown onto her own head. At first—as
always—it seemed crushingly heavy, as though she truly sought to take
the weight of all the heavens onto her own neck. But then the tingle of

power ran through all her nerves, raising her head and stiffening her spine, so that she felt the crown no more than she felt the weight of her own skull. Now Inanna was upon her, indeed: it was the might of the goddess lifting her hand to open the door, the eyes of the goddess gazing out through the windows in Shamhatu's skull, and the goddess Inanna who felt the rustle of fringed blue linen against Shamhatu's bare legs as she strode out of the house and up the path that led to the shrine on top of its platform.

The priests and priestesses were all gathered in the temple, lined up along the walls of the central hallway-room that led from the doorway to the statue of Inanna. *Guda* and *gala*; the *ishib*-priests who poured the libations; *nindingir* and *lumah* and *mah*, each with their own duties—trance-priests and sacrifice-priests, readers of dreams and omens; those who went out among the folk of Erech to cleanse houses of death or sickness and to lay blessings where they were needed, and those who never set foot outside the temple-city: the hall was crowded indeed, but all stepped aside as Inanna walked past, that none might stain the fringe of the goddess' garment with their touch of clay.

Inanna reached the statue—her own image, mirrored in stone as a human face might be reflected in water—and turned. Her mouth fell open: the voice that issued from it rang through the shrine like a gong of bronze. "Hear me, my people! The Shamhatu of Inanna's temple is called away: she must withdraw from Erech, to make ready for the marriage. Bring to me a ewe without spot, for in her place must stand another: another must speak for me at the feasts of the new moon and the holy times, another must give my blessing to my people."

The En, now clad in the plain woolen kilt of a shepherd, but with the stone-studded electrum breast-plate of his office still gleaming brightly over his withered ribs, came forth from one of the side rooms, leading an unshorn white ewe whose fluffy wool gleamed from washing and combing. Beside him, towering over the little old man like a date palm over a stalk of barley, walked the sacrificial priest Urgigir, chief reader of the sacred livers. When they had halted before Inanna, she stepped from her place, walking slowly around the shrine and pointing her finger at her chosen maidens.

The twenty-one maidens crowded up behind the En and Urgigir, rustling and murmuring as the sacrificial priest scratched at his clay tablet, marking their names to correspond with the divisions of the prophetic liver. Now Inanna saw the women as human shapes no longer, but as a gathering of shadows, each bearing a greater or lesser flame within the cloudy haze of flesh that wrapped her. One burned brighter than the rest, flaring brighter yet as Inanna gazed at her; seeing this, the goddess stepped forth, laying her hand upon the side of the sheep. The ewe's rich brown eyes rolled in fear a moment, then her eyelids sank, her mind already drawing into a dream of green pastures and cool water.

Inanna moved back as one of the *ishib*'s stepped forward with a bowl of lapis lazuli in his hands, kneeling down before the sheep. A second sacrificial priest came to assist Urgigir, straddling the ewe's back and easing her down to lie on the floor. Urgigir crouched: his knife-edge flashed golden, then gleamed carnelian. The blood bubbled up from the throat of the sheep, her severed windpipe still sucking air for a few moments: but the stroke had been too keen and swift for her to feel any pain, and now she was already drifting off to sleep.

When no more blood dribbled into the *ishib*'s bowl, and no more bubbles rose in the deep red slash gaping through the bloodied wool, Urgigir nodded. The two sacrificial priests turned the ewe over, her legs flopping limply, and Urgigir began, with the greatest of care, to slice delicately through skin and abdominal muscle until the sheep's guts bulged free. Urgigir cut a flap free from her side, his assistant holding it back, and reached into the crimson darkness with his knife again.

A moment, and the liver was free, cradled in the sacrificial priest's big hands. In all the temple, there was no breath to be heard but Inanna's as Urgigir walked over to the mud-brick table between the goddess and her stone reflection, laying the liver out upon it and wiping away the blood with a clean piece of white felt before peering closely at it.

"The goddess has made her choice," Urgigir cried, his strong bass voice booming out through the shrine. "Behold, we are blessed, for the liver shines glossy and clean; surely the favor of the goddess is with us, and Shamhatu given leave to retreat and ready herself. Geme-Tirash, trance-priestess, come forward!"

Now Inanna could see the young woman who stepped before the table: pale skin and hazel eyes, a cloud of curly dark hair above plumply solid shoulders. The En dipped his finger in the libation bowl, marking her forehead; their mouths moved, but Inanna could no longer hear the words. She swayed aside to let the new temple-priestess take her place before the stone Inanna; since Shamhatu was not giving up her seat, she did not take the diadem from her head, the earrings from her ears, or the girdle from her waist, but only walked slowly down the middle of the shrine, out into the clean cool night air.

Shamhatu did not remember walking back to her own dwelling, nor did she remember disrobing; but when she came to herself, she lay sprawled naked across her bed, and the statue of Inanna wore all her gems once more. She was exhausted, dripping in sweat as though she had never bathed that day; she felt like a jenny-ass ridden to dropping point. Still, she forced herself to sit up and take a few dates from the bowl on her bedside table. As she slowly chewed their sticky-sweet flesh, she could feel a little strength returning to her, and she knew she would need it: there was much to be done if she was to be ready to leave before dawn.

THE WAGON THAT rolled out of Erech beneath the bright light of Inanna's star drew little attention from the gate-guards. It was sturdy and heaped high with goods beneath a woolen blanket, but plain: the wagon of some merchant from up-country—perhaps one who brought melons or wheat into the city from the farms around and fine leather-work, woodwork, and weaving from the city to the more outlying regions—who had a fair way to go that morning and wished to put as much as possible of his traveling behind him before the heat of the day began to slow his donkeys and scorch his head. The merchant walked beside the wagon with the lead ass' nose-ring in his hand; his wife sat atop it, with the reins in her hand. Their cloaks were both up, hiding their faces from the chill of the early morning air. The wife leaned down to hand the gate-guard their toll: a small ring of silver, one-tenth of a shekel. He hefted it, nodded, and gestured them through with his torch.

Once safely away from the gate-guards, Shamhatu let the cloak-fold covering her face fall aside, and Akalla did likewise. Her heart was pounding hard, as though passing through the gates unknown were a crime instead of the decree of herself, the En, and Rimsat-Ninsun—the three chief priests in the city, whose words only Gilgamesh might challenge. "We did it," she said softly.

"Easier that way than coming in." Akalla paused for a moment, and Shamhatu saw his mouth moving as though he were chewing on a tough melon-rind before he spoke again. "Where do we go now, Divine Lady? The boat that brought me across is too small for this wagon, and we have left the ferry-place well behind us."

"There is a ford some way upstream, where the herdsmen of the temple drive their animals across the river. If we make good haste, we shall be long gone by the time the first sheep's nose pokes outside the city walls."

They made good speed that day, passing from the palm groves and marshy vine-fields nearest the Buranun to the long flat stretches of stubble, crisscrossed by canals, where the wheat and barley had been gathered in. When the sun was a little past the height of the sky and the flies began biting more fiercely at their sweat, Akalla raised the Shamhatu's tent so she could sleep safely in the shade, himself curling up in the shadow outside her door. When they arose in the late afternoon, with a slight breeze already easing the heat, they drank a few sips of the water Shamhatu had brought with them in the wagon and went on.

As Akalla had promised, they reached the watering hole before the last ruddy glow of the sunset had faded from the western sky, when Inanna's bright star was the only one to be seen. Shamhatu murmured her evening prayers to the goddess even as she helped Akalla to refill their waterskins before the animals could muddy the pool, then unharnessed and watered the braying asses. Afterward, Akalla set to raising her tent again, but Shamhatu dipped a square of linen into the watering hole and, as best she could, set to cleaning the dirt of the road off her face and hands. Cleansed as best as she could be, the priestess drained a little beer from one of her goatskins into the miniature cup of lapis that she carried with her for offerings, pouring it out onto the dry ground for Inanna, then making a second offering of water to the goddess' brother,

Utu, god of the sun. Songs would be ringing out from the shrine now; in Erech, had Shamhatu been outside with her sweat clotting dust into mud on her skin all day, Atab, or one of the other priests, would already have readied her bath for her. And there would have been food waiting: perhaps tail-strips from a fat-tailed sheep, the crispy brown skin still popping from the heat, dripping richness onto the bread below, or fish stuffed with garlic and basted with butter and beer; perhaps there would have been pork smeared with date-syrup or honey and roasted, or seethed in date-wine. But here she was with only hard bread and dried meat, still grimy and stinking, her white linen shift streaked with dirt and sweat; and no chance for her to turn back, or to bathe until she reached the village. *In this condition, I shall teach the wild man of the me—when I am barely in a state to call myself civilized?* she wondered.

Akalla was crouching down by the edge of the waterhole, staring at a long track that was barely a shadow against the dark earth. "If I may, Divine Lady, I will go and set snares for the conies, so that we may have fresh meat in the morning. You need not . . . need have no fear of bandits: no men have passed this way for days. I will light the fire first."

"Go set your snares," Shamhatu said. "I can light the fire myself." She had brought coals, carefully banked, in a box of thick clay; it was the work of moments to add shredded dry palm leaves until the flames flared, then tamarisk twigs and sticks. Once the fire was going well, she poured herself a jar of beer, the welcome drink slipping smoothly up her silver straw and down her dry throat. If this was harsher and dirtier than temple life, she thought, reclining on the rug that Akalla had spread before the flap of her tent, at least it was far better than herding sheep, with the stink and bleating of the animals all about her and the ever-present need to watch and listen for wild beasts. So far from the city, the stars seemed very bright, the constellations glimmering against the lapis sky; the wide milky sweep of the heavens' Buranun flowed shining between its dark shores. Inanna's star shone fairest, not too far from Engishgalanna, the greatest of the moving stars, and both close to the fixed star called the Lugal; and that was a good sign. Yet the Scorpion was climbing upward: the Shamhatu frowned, for that had never been a constellation that boded well, and she was not sure what it should mean, that the dark beast should leap so quickly to her sight, its night-black carapace laid over the skeleton of stars glimmering faintly from its innards.

The temple's storehouses had not done badly by Shamhatu: there was good smoked fish and meat, and pork skins roasted to dry crackling in their own fat as well as cheese and bread and several jars of dates packed in their own honey. Akalla ate slowly and carefully, glancing at the Shamhatu before each mouthful as though to make sure she would not stop him. She, for her part, was careful not to stare at him or make him meet her eyes: his awe was proper, but it did not behoove her to frighten or embarass him further. Only when he had finished his second jar of beer, and seemed a little more at ease, did Shamhatu address the trapper again.

"Your father is a long way from Erech, for one who might have lived well on temple-lands."

Even in the bright starlight, Shamhatu could not see whether Akalla was blushing, but he looked down into the beer as he spoke and his voice was muffled. "He chose to live where we do, Divine Lady. I have never traveled so far before."

"Do you know why he chose to leave?" The question was out of Shamhatu's mouth before she could stop it, and she could feel her own furious blush against the cooling night air. She had meant to creep up on the matter by single steps, so as not to frighten Akalla; but, though her habit of blurting out her thoughts had grown less in the three years she had been Inanna's chief priestess, it was not wholly uprooted.

"No, Divine Lady," Akalla answered, his voice more muffled yet. "Save that my mother died; my father has always told me that my mother died near to my birth, as women often do, and he has not gone to Erech since. He is still faithful to the goddess," the trapper answered quickly. "We have a shrine in our village, only a little shrine, but it does for us, and my father makes the sacrifices for the village there every season, and leads the blessings at the new moon. He can even read the liver to tell the shepherds when storm and bandits and bad luck are coming, and he predicted it when I was stung by a scorpion and came near to losing my left hand. He is still faithful to the goddess."

Shamhatu nodded slowly. If Gunidu were overcome with grief, it would explain why he had left the temple and the city. But the temple's lands stretched far and wide, and a good servant of the goddess could expect a fine portion to work and profit from, especially one who had held such an important post: Gunidu would not have needed to go so far into the wastelands to leave his memories behind. Indeed, it must have been hard for him, with a dead wife and an infant son to care for—why should he have chosen to make his life harder, by living on the fringes of Erech's rule where only the hungriest of farmers and shepherds, or men like this trapper, half wild himself, were able to scrabble out a bare existence?

But she would get little more out of Akalla: it seemed that he could only speak so long on a single topic before his thoughts wore into a rut and he began to fluster and repeat himself. Instead, Shamhatu said gently, "Akalla, are you married?"

Now he did jump, his beer-jar spilling out to soak the woolen kilt girded up between his legs. "Yes, Divine Lady! I am married, my wife . . . my, my, my wife, Innashagga, my wife, is waiting for me. I will do what the goddess commands, but . . ." The trapper's dark eyes shone liquid in the starlight as he stared at her, frozen as a bird trapped in the gaze of a snake.

She felt the laughter bubbling up from deep within her, forced it down with a strength of will only the harsh training given to Inanna's chief priestess could have imbued in her. Poor man; he thought that she was calling him to her bed, and feared it, when in truth she had only meant to put him at ease . . .

And yet the thought was not so funny: Inanna's lovers had been many, nor did the goddess refuse the worker to accept the king. Dumuzi himself had been shepherd as well as ruler; Inanna had called to Ishullanu, the tender of dates, as well, and many other men, both high and low, for all were warp and weft of the city of Erech, and even Ensi or Lugal must not scorn to bear the first basket of dirt away on his own shoulder when a new temple was built. It seemed to Shamhatu now that she gazed at the trapper with Inanna's sight and saw—not the fool who had stumbled and stuttered his way through Erech, but a man simple and wise as the beasts he hunted, now in his own land where there was little need for speech and much for understanding. The starlight smoothed the coarse lines of Akalla's face, setting off the movements of his muscular chest and shoulders, the cording of his forearms as he picked uncomfortably at the rug's fringe. Nor did Inanna scorn her beasts: lion and stallion she had loved, it was said; the lion lay under her feet, and her brilliant star shone above the wilderness.

Yet the warm tingling within Shamhatu's loins was not the rush of ferocious desire, the devouring lust of Inanna for her chosen men. It was, rather, a more familiar feeling: the love of the priestess for her people, the blessing and help that the gift of the goddess bestowed upon those who needed it.

"Do you have children?" she asked.

Akalla shook his head, his wide eyes still fixed on hers. "We have only been married a year, Divine Lady. My wife is waiting for me, she is still young, my wife Innashagga."

Shamhatu reached out slowly—carefully, as if reaching to stroke the old lion that had dwelt in Inanna's shrine when she was a child. Not releasing Akalla's gaze, she reached slowly between his legs. His testicles were warm through the folds of shaggy wool; it seemed to her indeed as though she were caressing the testicles of a beast in their furry sac. She could feel the heat flowing up through her body, out through her arm and hand, feel the stiffening of his penis against her gentle grasp. Now the goddess would do as she willed; Shamhatu waited, to hear the words that would come from her own mouth.

"Save this seed carefully, for it is blessed," the familiar low voice said. "Spill it not till you reach your wife's side. Sons lie within—strong sons, to help you in your work while you are strong, and care for you in your old age. Though your father fled, he bears no curse: I say that your seed is clean."

Then Shamhatu felt her hand withdrawing from Akalla's groin, and the touch of Inanna withdrawing from her. The tears were dripping over the rim of Akalla's eyes now; their lids closed a moment, scattering a shower of bright drops to be lost in the dark patterns of the rug.

"Thank you, Divine Lady," he whispered. "Thank you."

She did not know what to say: though she had brought the blessings of the goddess to men many times before, it had always been within the temple, after the making of the proper sacrifices and offerings of silver and precious stones by men who knew full well how Inanna would heal their woes.

"You serve Inanna even now, while you care for me; you do the work of the gods, in bringing me to the wild man. The oxen who tread the grain are not starved in the midst of the fresh barley; so the gods are kind to their servants on this earth. But I am weary now," she added, "and will sleep. Wake me at midnight, so that I may watch in my turn: you will be of little use tomorrow if you are too sleepy to remember the way."

"I am used to sitting awake at night, Divine Lady," Akalla protested, but Shamhatu shook her head.

"You will wake me at midnight. I so command it."

The trapper bowed his dark head. "Divine Lady, it shall be done."

THE PRIESTESS AND the trapper traveled on for two more nights, the land growing steadily browner and drier around them. Once in a great while they would pass a flock of sheep or goats browsing on the sparse grasses, or see a herd of gazelles or ibex in the distance. Between the food and drink Shamhatu had brought and the small beasts and birds that Akalla trapped in the evenings and early mornings, they were well-fed, but Shamhatu was beginning to long desperately for a bath: her skin felt like a garment of sticky wool laid over her body, itchy with filth, and her hair was matted and dull with dust.

They came to Akalla's village a little before sunset: a sprawling little collection of mud huts around a well shadowed by a few palm trees, the dusty pathways between the houses littered with dried dung. A mangy dog slunk around the corner of a house and barked sharply at them once, then crept away, sparse-haired tail curled down between its legs. As the wagon rolled through the village, Shamhatu saw the doors cracking open, the glints of eyes and teeth within and the whispering of voices rising to a louder buzz as the wagon passed.

"You mentioned that there was a shrine to Inanna here," Shamhatu said softly.

"Yes, Divine Lady—a small shrine, with few fine things, but tended well: we give the goddess what we can."

"Can you take me there? I should like to bathe before I meet anyone."

Akalla looked at her blankly. "At the shrine, Divine Lady?"

"Is there no bath at the shrine?"

"Oh, no. We wash our faces and hands well enough before we enter, though," he added hastily. "We would not come unclean before the goddess."

"Then take me to the public bath, if you will: I am not so foolish as to value keeping the secrets of my body above cleanliness."

Akalla sighed. "Divine Lady, there is no public bath here. We have only the water from the well. Let me take you home, and my family and I will bring you plenty of water, all the water we can, so that you can cleanse yourself." He looked up at her, his eyes dark and liquid as the gaze of an unfairly whipped ox. Shamhatu rubbed her temples. She was tired, filthy, and hot, and had little graciousness left in her; but what she had would have to do, lest she insult the hospitality of her host.

"That will do very well," she said. "It is kind of you."

Akalla's house was a mud-brick hut, smaller than most, but well-built, crumbling only a little at the edges where storm and wind had scoured it. An old man sat outside in the reddening sunlight, his felted shawl pulled tightly around the whipcord muscles of his shoulders. As Shamhatu climbed down from the wagon, the old man got to his feet, coming forward to salute her properly with one knee on the ground and his forehead brushing lightly against the earth before he rose again.

"Greetings, Divine Lady, mouth of the Queen of Heaven," he said. Though cracking a little around the edges, his voice was full and strong, a rich tenor in which Shamhatu could still hear the remnants of temple-training.

"And greetings to you, Gunidu, once chief shepherd of the Queen of Heaven."

"Did my son care for you properly in your journey across the desert, Divine Lady? If I could have, I should have sent more worthy men to accompany you, that you might be fittingly known and praised by the folk along the way: surely it is a sad thing that the priestess of Inanna have in her retinue only a simple trapper."

"Your son is a strong man and a trapper of great gifts, worthy in all his errands. Truly the goddess has blessed you, to have such a staff to lean upon in your old age."

Gunidu's lips twisted in an odd little half smile. "Truly she blessed me with him, indeed. But come, Divine Lady, you have traveled far, and will wish to wash the dust of the road from yourself. Though we have not enough water for ourselves to bathe often, we are making ready a bath for you, and there is fresh goat-milk to soothe your throat, while my son and I tend to your beasts."

"That is kindly offered, and I thank you for it," Shamhatu said. Gunidu opened the door and she stepped over the threshold, blinking until her eyes adjusted to the dim light within. No oil-lamps burned in the house, though one sat lumpy and ugly on the middle of the table; their light came from a flickering, sputtering fire of dried dung in the middle of the floor. Against the wall was a long clay trough—a trough for watering asses, now pressed into service as her bathtub, Shamhatu realized with some dismay. Though it was clear that they had scrubbed it as clean as possible, a certain odor of donkey still hung about it, mingling with the stink of the dung fire and the lingering smell of unwashed bodies.

Gunidu followed the Shamhatu in, pouring her a draught of milk from the lopsided jug on the table. Shamhatu squatted upon a mat of woven reeds and drank gratefully, trying to compose herself: she had never been so far from Erech, nor seen a village so poor within the lands claimed by the city. The old man sat and watched her for a moment, his gaze cool and inquisitive, but Shamhatu could think of nothing else to say to him and he did not address her again.

A small, plump woman walked into the house bearing a jug of water, followed by two taller women who stared openly at Shamhatu as they emptied the jugs into the trough. They paused by the door a moment before going out, clearly waiting for something. For a moment Shamhatu struggled frantically to understand what they wanted—would she have to pay them for the water?—then she realized that she was likely to be the first priestess of Inanna they had ever seen, and they would want her blessing. Although she had never felt more like an exhausted worker and less like a priestess in her life, she stretched out her hand, murmuring a few words. The women smiled, showing her broken teeth and gaping gums; their right shoulders seemed curiously deformed as well, as though years of ceaselessly turning the quernstones had worked upon their bodies like the potter's hands on clay. They seemed likely to stay longer, but the little woman said, "Hurry back to the well: there will be time later, and the Divine Lady must have her bath. Divine Lady, do not fear, there will be more water coming for you, for half the village is gathered about the well, all vying for the honor of helping you." She swept the other two away, still chattering.

"My son's wife, Innashagga," Gunidu said softly. "A good woman, for all she has not quickened yet; but she is very young still. Now I shall go to help my son see to your beasts and the unpacking of your wagon. If there is anything you desire, you have only to say so, and we shall do our best to make it yours."

*I want a warm bath in a proper tub, not a cold dunking in a donkey trough,* the Shamhatu thought. But that, she knew, would be rude and ungrateful to speak, impossible to do, so she only smiled and said, "I thank you greatly for your care. Truly, it is better to be a guest in a small hut where hospitality is offered from the heart, than to lodge with the mightiest in the land when there is no friendship given."

The bevies of women were coming in faster now, each pouring out a jug of water and then standing for the priestess' blessing. Shamhatu could hear the sounds of murmuring outside the door of the hut as they walked back—tones of wonder and awe, mixed with consuming curiosity: why should the chief priestess of Erech have come here? Did the temple want something of Gunidu; had the priestess come to fetch him back? Or had that fool Akalla offended someone in some way; were the gods angry over something? Perhaps the priestess herself was going into exile; they had heard that she and the Ensi Gilgamesh were often at odds ... There would be similar murmurings in Erech itself, she knew, when it was seen that the priestess presiding over the next festival of the new moon was a different woman, though no lamentations had been decreed for a high priestess' death. But one learned when to listen to such voices, and when to ignore them, and now was a time to ignore them: by the New Year, if all went well, everything would be set to rights again.

Even when the trough was full to overflowing, the women with their jugs kept coming in, circling around the inside of the little house as though they were looking for somewhere else to pour their water as they eyed with wonder the things Akalla was bearing in from the wagon— gilded lyre and clay tablets, bright-dyed rugs to spread over the plain squares of woven reeds on the floor, large sealed jars of beer and smaller pots of figs in honey and dates, bags of dried plums and pears, and bags that rustled and clinked with the heavy sound of gold. Although Shamhatu was growing more eager even for the cold and donkey-scented water in her makeshift tub, they would not leave her alone, and she knew that she had no right to bar the door of her host's house, nor could she simply tell them to go away when they reached out toward her so.

At last Gunidu came back. The old shepherd glanced at the women moving about his house, eyed Shamhatu for a moment, then clapped his hands sharply together. "Good women, we thank you for your help, but the priestess has traveled a long way and is tired. Let her bless you now, then leave her alone, that she may refresh herself: she has done us a great kindness in coming all the way from Erech, but even the best-bred of jenny-asses will drop when she is ridden too far."

Shamhatu stretched out her tired hand again and spoke the blessings once more in a voice that was beginning to crack with exhaustion. The women murmured their shy thanks, then, mercifully, fluttered out the door like a flock of turtledoves, leaving the little house quiet.

"Do you wish to bathe alone, or shall I call Innashagga in to attend you?"

"I shall bathe alone," Shamhatu answered firmly. Gunidu nodded, leading his son out and closing the door firmly behind him.

Shamhatu stripped off her shift: though linen was almost as hard to stain as it was to dye, it would take much washing before the garment was clean enough to wear again. Shivering, she lowered her naked body into the donkey trough, the cold water spilling over the side in little rivulets, and began to scrub her hair and body vigorously. She wished for a handful of tamarisk twigs or cleansing herbs, but she knew that if they could be had here, Gunidu would have offered them to her.

When she was done bathing, she was chilled to the bone and smelled slightly of the donkey trough, but she felt lighter by several mina-weights with all the dirt washed off. She put on a fresh dress, enjoying the pleasant warmth of the soft clean wool against her skin, then drew an ivory comb from one of her bags and sat down by the fire, tugging its tines through her thick mass of tangled hair. It was some time before she remembered that Gunidu and his family were still outside, waiting for her to finish bathing; guiltily, she hurried over to open the door and let them know that she was through.

The food Innashagga offered was as plain as the house itself: millet porridge, strengthened with flakes of dried meat. Without spices, the food seemed bland and tasteless, but Shamhatu was hungry, and ate accordingly, though she was careful not to ask for her bowl to be refilled before everyone else had gotten their full shares, as she knew that Gunidu's family would go without to feed her.

The old shepherd leaned back against the wall letting loose a long, resonant belch. Shamhatu patted her stomach, trying to raise a small burp of her own in praise of the food. Innashagga smiled at her shyly, averting her eyes even as Shamhatu met her gaze. "You provide well for a weary traveler," the priestess murmured. "Blessings upon your house."

"Our house is blessed by your presence, Divine Lady," the smaller woman answered, tugging nervously at a strand of the black braid wound around her head. "I know you are used to far better; I beg you to forgive our poor home."

"After my travels, I promise you, it is the finest of resting places." Shamhatu looked around the house. With the unloading of her wagon, it had already changed from a hovel into a comfortable small room: her rugs on the floor, her lyre gleaming upon a chair, her jars of food and drink stacked against the wall . . .

"But it must have been a dreadful journey for you? I have never been to Erech, I was born and raised in this village here, but I have heard about the glittering walls and the temples paved with gold. Can you tell me about the city? And the Ensi Gilgamesh, I have heard that the heads of other men do not reach to his shoulders, that he is stronger and more handsome than any man living, two-thirds god and one-third man."

"All that is true," Shamhatu answered gravely when Innashagga paused for breath. "And I will be glad to tell you of Erech later, as much as you wish to know—but I am tired now, and I think we must rise early, if we are to be ready to track the wild man."

"We must, indeed," Akalla said. "No telling how far he has gone. But I can go out tomorrow and try to track him, to save you some trouble."

"No. I shall come with you: I feel it in my heart that I shall meet him soon. Yet now you shall lead me to the shrine here, so that I may make my prayers to the goddess this evening and be ready to leave by the first light of dawn."

The crude little clay lamp in Akalla's hand as he led Shamhatu through the village burned with a heavy stench of sesame oil mixed with goat fat, its greasy black smoke blowing into her face now and again. It was far from the fine imported olive oil of the temple, scented with precious resins, but Shamhatu had already seen that even such a lamp was a luxury to the trapper. Like the rest of the houses in the village, Inanna's shrine was made of baked mud-bricks and thatched with palm-fronds that whispered in the light breeze. Within, all was dark; as they entered, Shamhatu heard a faint scuttling over the hard dirt floor, and was glad that she could see no better.

Inanna's statue stood at the end of the shrine with a table of heaped mud-bricks before her, as in Erech. But here, the bowls before the goddess, though neatly made, were plain clay instead of hollowed stone or inlaid wood; no bright paint adorned the stone carving or the smoke-darkened walls, and the only scents within were charred sheep-dung, burning fat, and a whiff of cheap perfume that the lowest tavern-girl in Erech would have been ashamed to wear. The statue itself was as crudely worked as the offering-bowls: a tall lump of rough limestone, half-shaped to hint at ponderous breasts and wide buttocks, with eyes and mouth barely a hint in the gray blankness of the face. Her necklace was made of painted clay and shells; her crown a rough clay diadem studded with smooth pebbles of dull black and green and blue-gray, matching the rude lumpen carving of the goddess herself. Only on the forehead had the carver taken more trouble. There, a clearly incised mark stood— a double-pointed arch, which seemed oddly familiar to Shamhatu, though she could not name it.

Flustered, she spoke before she thought. "What is that sign upon the forehead of the goddess?" Shamhatu asked, and even as she did, the words formed in her mind: as well to ask a donkey or ox as Akalla.

"It's . . . Divine Lady, my father says . . . The folk here call it the Gates of Death and Life, but no one knows why."

"The Gates of Death and Life," Shamhatu mused. Yet it was the Lady of the Underworld, Erishkegal, who ruled over the gateways of death, and set her doorkeeper to keep the laws there; life was the kingdom of Inanna. "Leave me be, if you can find your way back without a lamp. I would speak to the goddess alone, and do not know for how long."

"As you wish, Divine Lady. But I shall wait outside for you."

When Akalla was gone, Shamhatu stepped closer to the statue, running her hands over the curves of the goddess' breasts and hips, then, in spite of the chill, pressing her own body against the statue until her own warmth had seeped into the stone and the invisible mark of her embrace was no longer cold beneath her palm. It was not so rough as she had thought: many years and much touching had worn down all the edges, and the same passage of time had eroded Inanna's face to blank stone. Yet the mark on her forehead was newly cut—no: Shamhatu's questing fingers, brushing over the rock as if lifting a lock of hair from the face of a lover, found old edges, signs of older marks. It must have been carved again and again over the years, wearing itself deeper in the stone even as its meaning flaked and crumbled from memory.

"The days of humankind are short in this earth," Shamhatu murmured. "To each the gods declare a time, and to each an end . . . O Inanna, cleanse me with the waters of your blessing, for I go to do your work . . ."

TIRED AS SHE was, Shamhatu lay awake that night, staring into the blackness of the ceiling and listening to the rustling of the insects and little reptiles through the bundles of palm fronds that thatched the house. Her bed, heaped high with her own rugs and blankets, was clean and comfortable enough, but the unfamiliar stink of the house, especially after sleeping in a tent beneath the open sky for three nights, weighed heavily upon her. As well . . .

Yes: to herself she could admit it, she was frightened. Frightened and a little excited: it would be something new, to lie with the golden-pelted lion of a man Akalla had described—to lie with any man who did not come to her in fear and reverence of the goddess, but simply flung himself upon her in desire, would be fascinating enough. Shamhatu had hoped sometimes, lying by herself in her quarters at the temple, that Gilgamesh would not be so much in awe at the marriage that he would not crush her to him, or let her feel all his strength and fierceness as he took her. Such a man would the wild man be: like a storm over the desert, the Buranun and Idiglat flowing together in their flood tide! She wriggled slightly, feeling the beginnings of a pleasant tingle in her loins.

*And yet storm and flood can both kill a land*, Shamhatu reminded herself, *leaving what was once a fertile field reduced to a barren slime of salty mire where nothing more may grow.* And a wild man as large and strong as Gilgamesh himself could, if he chose, rend her to pieces; if he dwelt among the lions, he must feed upon their food, and who knew whether he might not see her as a tender sheep rather than a lioness? More: the gods had given him a lion's golden pelt, and the great dogs as companions—might he not also have the claws and fangs of a lion, to tear her to death even as they coupled? Even the tamest of lions, raised by hand within Erech's walls, must have its fangs and claws filed blunt or cut out, lest the gentlest kneading of its loving paws rip through the flesh of the humans who tended it; and this wild man would be no more like a tame lion than the fiercest of Gilgamesh's picked soldiers was like a temple eunuch.

Shamhatu curled herself up beneath the blankets: the night seemed colder than it had been. Yet she could not change the decrees of the gods, nor turn back when she had come all this way. "The morning will bring what it will bring," she murmured to herself. "The feet of Inanna rest on the back of the lion, and her brow is crowned with a star . . ."

• • •

THEY AWOKE EARLY, as Shamhatu had planned. The water from the donkey trough was no cleaner than it had been the night before, but she only needed to wash her hands and face before she slowly began to garb herself in breechcloth and blue linen gown, with girdle about her hips and bracelets on her hands and feet, Inanna's necklace around her throat and the great star-crown of the goddess resting upon her head. Now, fully clad in the regalia of Inanna, she stepped out to gaze at the brightness of the goddess' star shining through the clear blue light of dawn.

"Inanna, sailing in your Boat of Heaven," Shamhatu murmured. "Laden with the *me*, those holy gifts of mankind, given you by Enki when the blessed beer made him glad—Inanna, battling the monsters of the water for the sake of Erech's people, bringing the *me* to your city. Inanna, from Erech I have come with a full-laden wain, as you came full-laden from Eridu; I bring the *me* to the wilderness and the wild man, as you brought them to Erech, and in my lap he shall learn what it is to be a man among humankind."

She did not hear Akalla come out of the door behind her, nor know that he was there until he stepped in front of her, clearing his throat apologetically. "Ah . . . Divine Lady," he muttered. "I don't, I don't think . . ." He stopped with a spluttering little whistle, licked his lips, and tried again. "Divine Lady, we go out to find the wild man today?"

"Yes."

"Divine Lady, it will be a long walk over harsh trails, much of it in the heat of the sun: we may have to go up into the mountains, where the pathways are rocky and the going hard. Do you, do you mean to wear . . . ?"

Shamhatu's heart clenched with cold shock; it felt as though a rotten melon had burst in her chest. Of course, she could not wear the goddess' regalia while tracking the wild man: the crown would weight her head down, the bracelets shackle her wrists and ankles, and, if they found him and her sprang upon her, whether as lover or slayer, he would surely tear girdle and dress asunder.

"Of course not," Shamhatu answered slowly. "I merely put it on to ask the goddess' favor. Give me a little while, and I shall be ready to walk."

She stumbled back into the house, stunned as though a heavy beam had struck her head. To take off the garb of Inanna when she had most need of the goddess to stand forth within her skin, to willingly deprive herself of all the tools of a priestess' power when she had only that power to meet the wild man with . . . it was madness, foolishness, and yet even Akalla could see that it was more foolish yet to go roaming in the wilderness dressed as if she were about to lead the rites in Erech.

Slowly, her fingers numb, Shamhatu lifted the star-crown from her head and unbound her hair. As she did, half in trance, she heard herself beginning to whisper the words of Inanna's Descent: the goddess' passage through seven gates leading down to the dreary kingdom of Erishkegal—the way to the Netherworld, the land of no return. When the time was right in the temple, she would sing them, with the deep bass of the sacrifice-priest Urgigir answering her; now, her voice was no more than a low murmur, and she could not hide the fear in it from herself.

*"Enter, my lady, that the Netherworld may rejoice over thee,*
*That the palace of the Land of No Return may be glad at thy presence."*
*When the first door he had made her enter,*
*He stripped and took away the great crown on her head.*

"Why, O Gatekeeper, did you take the great crown from my head?" Shamhatu murmured.

*"Enter, my lady, thus are the rules of the Mistress of the Netherworld."*
*When the second door he had made her enter,*
*He stripped and took away the pendants on her ears.*

"Why, O Gatekeeper, did you take the pendants on my ears?"
*"Enter, my lady, thus are the rules of the Mistress of the Netherworld . . ."*
"Why, O Gatekeeper, did you take the chains around my neck?"
*"Enter, my lady, thus are the rules of the Mistress of the Netherworld . . ."*
"Why, O Gatekeeper, did you take the ornaments on my breast?"
*"Enter, my lady, thus are the rules of the Mistress of the Netherworld . . ."*

"Why, O Gatekeeper, did you take the girdle of birthstones on my hips?"

*"Enter, my lady, thus are the rules of the Mistress of the Netherworld . . ."*

"Why, O Gatekeeper, did you take the bracelets round my hands and feet?"

*"Enter, my lady, thus are the rules of the Mistress of the Netherworld . . ."*

"Why, O Gatekeeper, did you take the breechcloth on my body?"

*"Enter, my lady, thus are the rules of the Mistress of the Netherworld . . ."*

The crown of rule and the earrings of pride; the chains of strength and the breast-ornaments of abundance; the girdle of will and the bracelets of craft; and, last of all, the breechcloth that guarded modesty and all things of the body: these, Inanna had given up one by one to pass through the gates of death, until she stood naked before the dreadful gaze of Erishkegal, Mistress of the Netherworld, to be hung on a stake as a corpse. Now Shamhatu stood likewise naked; it seemed to her that she could glimpse, as from afar, the face of Erishkegal, sallow and pale as a cut-down tamarisk, with lips black as a bruised reed, and she shivered.

But neither Inanna nor Erishkegal was holding back the sun; it was already lighter within the little hut, and Shamhatu could no more go naked than fully jeweled as a priestess. She put on a simple long gown of gray wool, throwing a fringed shawl of white wool over it to keep her warm while the sun was rising, and to protect her head when Utu reached his height.

"I am ready," Shamhatu said to Akalla. Firmly she grasped the ring-headed staff that would serve her both as her one sign of the goddess and her walking stick, and stepped outside. "Let us go."

THEY SET OFF on foot: Shamhatu had thought of taking the wagon and pitching her tent at first, but Akalla asked her to think about stalking lions from a wain. If they found the wild man, and he could not be brought back to the village at once, Akalla would come back with wagon and tent when Shamhatu was sure that he would not run away.

The rising sun cast trailing streaks of pink light over the cold sky, slowly brightening the long stretch of scrubby grass and rocks beneath. Shamhatu heard the scampering of small animals; once, they startled a covey of quail that rose into the air, whirring softly, and scattered in front of them. The priestess wondered whether, if he had not been burdened by the rolled covering and stakes of his simple tent and three days' food for the two of them, Akalla could have netted the birds. But the trapper's dumb-ox face was still: if he regretted the lost catch, there was no way to tell.

Chilly as the dawn was, and though the pace Akalla set was gentle, Shamhatu soon found herself warming enough from the labor of walking with her bedroll on her back that she was able to fold her warm shawl aside and let the cool breezes play through her hair and stroke along her bare right shoulder. The paths were rougher here than in the sweet green lands between the twin rivers Buranun and Idiglat: the ground dry and hard as bone left to weather in the desert, unwatered by any kindly floods for years upon years, more years than Shamhatu could count ... perhaps since the Great Flood of Utnapishti, when the Heavenly Gods sent the waters to destroy humanity. Although the hardened leather soles of her sandals seemed to jar against the hardened earth as though she walked on solid rock, Shamhatu paid it little mind as she gazed up at the stark sweep of the stony hills, then down at the tiny fragility of flowers struggling white through the baked-clay soil. The gray-green edges of the straggling strands of grass seemed unnaturally sharp in the clear cold morning air; Shamhatu's blood seemed to hum in her limbs as she walked, and now and again it seemed to her that glimmers of light flickered in the corners of her eyes. She wondered if Gilgamesh felt thus, riding to battle in his onager-drawn chariot—his gaze keener, the scents of wind and dry grass keener in his nose, the touch of his clothing rougher upon his skin, as though everything within him strove to capture the last moments of life in a frieze of sharp-carved stone and glittering inlay, and yet reached forward for the sword-edged moment to come.

High above the plain, a single black speck soared in lazy circles through the brightening sky. Shamhatu could not tell whether it was an eagle seeking hot blood or a vulture seeking cold carrion. The little hairs on the back of her neck rose and crawled at the omen: either the best of birds or the worst, the soaring and noble bird of Enlil or Erishkegal's corpse-eating demon. She knew that she could ask Akalla, who knew all the ways of the wilderness—but it would make little difference: she could not turn back, whether the gods had chosen to raise her up with their blessings or to have her torn to pieces by the beast-man of the wilds.

Though Shamhatu was strong and fit from practicing temple dances daily, her breath was coming a little faster by the time the two of them had nearly reached the crest of the hill. Akalla looked down, shaking his head.

"They have not crossed this way again," he said. "This was where I first found his tracks among the lions'—you can see traces yet, though the wind has eaten them."

Shamhatu obediently bent to follow his pointing finger with her gaze, but saw no more than a few blurred depressions in the dirt. The ball and toes of a large man's foot, or the blunt paw-marks of a lion: she could not tell which, would never have seen them in the dust if Akalla had not pointed to them.

The trapper straightened, a sigh hissing out of his mouth like wind through the rocks. His heavy-ridged brows and hanging mouth did not hide his thoughts: Shamhatu had seen the same relieved disappointment on the faces of many men in the temple when told they would not be set to couple with Inanna in her full glory but would receive her blessings in a quieter manner within the shrine. The wild man, she thought again, would have no fear, she would not have to spend the night hopefully plying her skills to raise his courage for the goddess' gift . . .

Shamhatu started as Akalla grasped her wrist, steering her skillfully away from the low tumble of rocks she had been about to walk through. Retrieving her arm from his clasp, she was about to speak sharply when his murmur cut her off.

"Divine Lady, that is a dwelling of serpents—see you the holes there beneath the rocks, and the marks of their writhing in the dust all about?

They may still be sluggish, but the day is warming quickly, and you should take no chances."

"I thank you," Shamhatu answered, the blood rising to heat her face. Wary of both scorpions and snakes, she walked more carefully thereafter, watching where she trod so as to overturn no stones.

After a time, Shamhatu had to raise her white shawl over her bare shoulder and head again: the sun was burning down more fiercely, the crown of her dark head catching and holding its heat as though she wore a copper burning-bowl for a cap, and a pink flush was already showing through the pale olive skin of her shoulder. The sweat trickled between her shoulder blades, itchy against her wool gown, and the far-off horizon was beginning to shimmer with heat. Even burdened as he was, Akalla strode on ahead of her as though the sun's fire merely glanced off the deep bronze of his shoulders and chest, though a light dew of sweat already burnished the play of his muscles. Had she not assured him earlier in the journey that she needed no special cosseting, Shamhatu would have asked the trapper to slow his steps; as it was, she grasped her ring-headed staff more tightly and hurried to catch up with him.

The sun had reached his height when at last Akalla stopped beside a watering hole. Although it was neither large nor deep—if Shamhatu waded in, she would not be wet above the waist even in the deepest part—its waters were clear. The pool was ringed with a few scrawny reeds and a green fringe of soft grass stretching from its edge into the dry earth beyond. The grass itself was trampled and muddied in places, and even Shamhatu could clearly see the spoor of different beasts: smaller and larger hoof-marks, the small paw-pads of wolves and the larger ones, wide as the span of a man's hand, of lions . . . and, among all the rest, two clear human tracks so large that Shamhatu might have put both her feet into one.

As Shamhatu stared at them, her knees began to tremble and she could feel her hand shaking on the staff. "He's here?" she whispered to Akalla.

"Those tracks are more than a day old," Akalla answered. "It is a good sign, though: he was here, and he has come here more than once. Now we have only to wait."

"How long?"

The trapper shrugged. "Maybe until evening, perhaps two or three days. If he has not come within four, we shall have to follow him."

Shamhatu did not let her dismay show; after a moment, Akalla went on. "Let us raise the tent a little way from the waterhole, beyond those rocks. There, we can wait without taking harm from the sun, and will not be so likely to frighten the wild man when he comes upon us."

"Us frighten him? I should think a man who lives among the lions and wild beasts would fear nothing."

"He is as a beast himself; and even a lion may feel himself warned when he hears the footsteps of a man, or catches human scent on the breeze."

Shamhatu did not argue further, but set to helping the trapper raise the little tent. After they had eaten and drunk from the waterhole, Akalla suggested that she lie down inside, as it was best to sleep during the hottest part of the day, and he would keep watch. "Though," he added, "it is less likely that the lions will come now. The beasts are wise: they, too, sleep when Utu pours out his full strength on the plain."

Though Shamhatu had meant to stay awake, the heat soaking into her tired muscles quickly lulled her into a doze, then sleep. She did not open her eyes again until a cool breeze brushed against her face; looking out the tent-flap, she saw that the western sky was already glowing with streaks of red-orange like lamplight shining through a fine carnelian, and the pale blue bowl above darkening to lapis in the east. Akalla crouched by the tent-flap, his finger to his lips, though he shook his head in answer to Shamhatu's eager gaze.

Carefully the two of them crept up behind the rocks to look at the watering hole. To Shamhatu's delight, a whole herd of gazelles jostled about it like a great confection of date syrup folded into cream, their delicate little hooves sinking deep into the muddy grass, gentle dark eyes rolling at each other as they butted for a place at the watering hole or dropped their heads to tear at the grasses. She had often seen the small carcasses carried in on the poles of the temple's hunters, but never gone far enough into the plains to watch a living herd. Now she could feel the smile spreading over her face: so lithe they were, so beautiful, like little wind-spirits given flesh!

"The wind is with us," Akalla murmured almost soundlessly in her ear. "If the gods will, we shall dine well this night." He dropped again, crawling carefully to the edge of the rocks, then nocking an arrow to his bow. Crouching, he drew, the muscles of his arm and shoulder leaping out in sharp relief. Then Shamhatu heard the singing hiss through the air, followed by a dull thump. The herd of gazelles whirled, running with a fleet speed that had them lost in the dimming light almost before Shamhatu could blink; but she had seen one droop behind and fall, almost out of sight.

Akalla rose to his feet. "A long shot, but a good one," he said with satisfaction. "Can you start a fire while I fetch and butcher it?"

Shamhatu set to turning the drill; by the time the first smoke was curling up from the wood, Akalla was back, the small body flung over his shoulders with its head drooping down his back. He had already pulled the arrow out, but Shamhatu could see the dark stain spreading slowly just behind the gazelle's shoulder.

"If the wolves and hyenas do not get them in the night, we can set the entrails and bones out tomorrow, and they may draw the lions," Akalla told her as he made the first slit down the gazelle's cream-colored belly. For a moment it pained Shamhatu, to think of how it had jostled at the watering hole, thirsty and innocent of its beauty. But the entrails tumbled out the dark wound like those of a sheep . . . And sheep, Shamhatu thought, are holy—we call ourselves Erech of the Sheepfold, for that is Inanna's temple: the ruler of the city is meant to be its good shepherd, and its people his sheep, cared for in their lives and given to slaughter only at need. Though the gazelle had not been raised in the fold, nonetheless it must feed Akalla and Shamhatu; though the wild man was not raised in the fold, nonetheless he must be brought to stand by Gilgamesh . . .

"Not too many worms," Akalla said. "A few in the bowels, and a few little sores in the hide with fly-eggs starting to hatch, but the liver and heart are clean. It will make a good meal."

IN THE NIGHT, Shamhatu heard the howling of the wolves and the rough barking laugh of hyenas; she and Akalla rose before the dawn, taking their place behind the rocks to see who would come to the watering hole in the early morning. But the pond lay still and quiet beneath the rising sun, reflecting unrippled brightness when the sun was at full height. Now and then Shamhatu would glance sideways at Akalla to see if his blocky face showed any signs of dismay or flagging hopes, but he sat patient and stolid as ever beneath the broiling rays of mid-afternoon, seemingly content in his waiting.

The sun was lowering again when Akalla suddenly froze in his place, tapping Shamhatu softly on the shoulder. "They come," he whispered. "Ready yourself."

Shamhatu peered in the direction he pointed, far out upon the plain. At first she thought she saw only a rippling of the thin grasses here and there; then the sleek tawny shapes took form like images suddenly springing to the mind's eye from the roiling river mist. Breathing deeply as she crawled back toward the tent, she tried to calm herself. As she had learned in the temple, she raised her dress, untied her breechcloth and squatted outside to empty her bladder. Instead of putting the breech-cloth on again, when she was safely inside she cast it away, squatting again and reaching down between her legs. Though a faint dew of antic-ipation was already moistening her, she was still tight with fear, and there was little chance of the wild man taking time to coax her gates open and her well into flowing. "He is here, Shamhatu," she murmured to herself as she anointed her inner parts with scented oil, gently circling her finger within herself to ease the clenched muscles. "Prepare to embrace him; open your legs, show him your beauty. Do not hold back, take his breath from him. He will draw near you when he sees you; take off your robe and spread it, he will mount you; let this beast-man know what a woman is! The animals who grew up in his wilderness will become strange to him, and he will grunt and murmur upon you with desire."

When she came out again, Akalla was crouching outside. "Now they are drinking," he murmured. "Now, Divine Lady . . ." His words seemed to stick in his throat like a date-seed lodging sideways. Shamhatu leaned over and kissed him on his forehead, then rose to her feet and walked out from behind the rocks.

Before her, calf-deep in water, the wild man straightened to look at her. He had been drinking like a beast with his mouth in the pool; water streamed from his long golden hair and beard, running in rivulets down the broad expanse of his gold-pelted chest to pearl in the rough hairs of the shrunken gazelle-hide tied about his waist. Looking at him, Shamhatu gasped for breath. She could feel the moist slipperiness of the oils between her legs, the wool of her dress rasping against her nipples as she breathed. Then a cold dagger of terror slipped through her, for one of the lions, a huge dark-maned beast with shadowy markings on its forehead, raised its head with an odd mewling growl, and the huge slit-pupiled eyes were gazing straight at her.

The wild man turned, raising his arms so that he towered over the lions behind him, and let out a deep howl that seemed to ring from the darkening bowl of the sky. Shamhatu's heart fluttered in her chest; she could see the flaking stripes of blood down his back and arms. The lions could tear him, they could tear her . . . but he growled again, stepping forward as though to grapple with the dark-maned lion, and the great dogs turned away, slipping into the wilderness like ghosts.

Now the wild man turned back to Shamhatu, his green-brown gaze meeting hers. She wet her lips and reached for her belt, unclasping it and letting it fall, then slowly pulled her dress off and laid it on the hard ground. Standing naked before him, she cupped one hand beneath each breast, offering them to him as she moved her hips in one of the sinuous temple dances. Nostrils flaring, the wild man paced slowly forward until he stood almost at arm's length—well within arm's length for him: his sheer mass dwarfed her, as though she stood in the shadow of Inanna's great raised shrine. Shamhatu flung her head back to look up into his eyes, breathing deeply and opening her legs a little.

The wild man's huge hands closed upon her wrists, holding her still. His knees bent; his head lowered, his wet beard tickling her nipples as he nuzzled her neck and chest. Then he dipped down, forcing his head roughly between her legs. A soft little growl came from his throat as he breathed in her scent; then he turned Shamhatu around and pushed her roughly to her knees, his forehead pressing·against her neck until her shoulders dropped. She thought wildly of beasts mating, this lion-man . . . *dear Inanna, male lions have spiky*—She cried out in pain as his teeth closed in the back of her neck, but did not forget her training. As the bruising proddings of his hard staff against her buttocks grew more urgent, Shamhatu arched her back, squirming until she felt the tip where it should be and thrusting herself onto him before he could make another misguided stab. Stubbornly she clenched him within herself as he moved, though each thrust from his powerful thighs threatened to fling her forward onto her face; it was not long before his hips shuddered hard against hers and she felt the hot river of seed gushing forth inside her.

The wild man withdrew and rolled off Shamhatu. She lay back, panting as she rubbed the back of her neck—at least he had not broken the skin, though she would be bruised for weeks. He leaned over to nuzzle at her breasts again, butting his head against her side. With the first flush of fear over, Shamhatu could look at him more closely. His body was magnificent, well-shaped and hugely muscled—very like Gilgamesh, indeed, though hairy and rough-hewn where the Ensi was clean-shaven, groomed, and oiled. He also stank of long-unwashed man and old blood; at least the half-rotten gazelle-hide had fallen off as he thrust at her, and he was not trying to put it on again. This close, she could see that his long golden hair and beard were streaked with filth and full of mats and burrs, like the wool of a mountain sheep, and the marks the lion-claws had left on him ranged from light grazes to a few deep slashes in the heavy muscles of his back, which ought to be washed and bandaged to keep them from catching rot.

"Can you speak?" Shamhatu said.

The wild man's eyes—green oddly mingled with brownish-gold, like streaks of tarnish over copper—met hers, but she could see no thought in them: it was the sound, not the words, that had made him look up. Yet she kept talking, her voice as soothing as she could make it. "I am the Shamhatu of Inanna, the priestess of her temple. The Ensi Gilgamesh sent me to you, for he had heard tales of you . . . of your wonderful strength, of your marvelous fierceness, of how you ran with the gazelles in your fleetness, and stood alongside the lions in your wildness . . ."

Shamhatu had not been speaking long before the wild man reached for her again, picking her up and turning her over. Knowing what to expect, she was better readied this time: she took little notice of his teeth fastening in the skin of her neck, and was able to reach back between her legs to steer him into harbor.

THE WILD MAN stayed with Shamhatu all through the night and the next day, always within arm's reach of her. Although none of his couplings were long, she had never heard of a man who could spill his seed and revive again so often: he would roll away from her and snore for a few minutes, then reach for her again. It had been difficult at first to lure him into the little tent, which she had only accomplished by crouching inside with her rump wantonly raised toward him; to her surprise, however, it had been easy to teach him only to relieve himself outside, and he had the cat's trick of scraping earth over the mess when he was done.

It was late afternoon of the next day, shadows stretching long over the rough ground in the reddish light of the setting sun, when the wild man lifted his head toward some sound that Shamhatu could not hear, springing lightly to his feet and walking out of the tent. Half curious, half worried, Shamhatu followed him. The faint bray of an ass came to her from a distance, and she realized that Akalla was coming back with her wain. She sighed in relief: now she would have the things of civilization, to teach the wild man the *me*, and something more to eat than the last pieces of half-raw, half-burnt gazelle that his voracious hunger had left her.

The wain rumbled into view at the top of one of the eastern hills, paused a moment as though Akalla were trying to choose the safest path down, then started again, the asses picking their way among the rocks with delicate, careful steps. Watching them, Shamhatu did not notice the grimace that pulled the wild man's lips back to bare his teeth; it was only when the low growl rolled from his throat that she turned, and then it was too late.

The wild man ran over the plain as swiftly as a gazelle, moving with a smooth beauty that would have broken Shamhatu's heart if she had not been so afraid for the trapper. The asses brayed and tried to run in opposite directions; one of the wain's wheels ground to a halt against a large rock. As the wild man leapt up on the wagon, Akalla leapt down, turning tail and running without a single backward glance; Shamhatu saw the pale flash of his kilt as he disappeared over the crest of the hill. The wild man stopped there, silhouetted against the darkening eastern sky for a moment as he watched the other man go, then turned back to the donkeys, reaching toward the tangled harness at the neck of the right-hand one. Shamhatu raised her eyebrows: had he worked with animals before he went wild? But then she saw his hands close and tighten, heard the frantic braying of the other ass and saw how the hooves were scrabbling, back buckling beneath his hold. She began to run toward them, but it was already too late for the donkey the wild man had grabbed first: his powerful hands had crushed its throat as surely as the jaws of a lion.

Now he was reaching for the other, but Shamhatu shouted, "No! Don't!" The words meant nothing to him, she knew, but the sharp sound of her voice caught him, spinning him around to look at her. She held her hands up, palms forward, and shook her head sternly; he held his own hands up with the sad look of a little boy about to be caned by his elder school-brother. Shamhatu closed the distance between them, reaching out to the terrified donkey as it struggled against its yoke. After a little time, it stilled, letting her stroke the coarse hair of its neck and scratch behind its twitching ears. The wild man watched for a moment as she unharnessed the beast and turned it loose to run toward the watering hole, then he crouched down by the carcass of the dead ass, grasping one of its legs and turning and twisting it until Shamhatu heard the cracking of bone and cartilage, then bending to bite through the hide so he could wrench the leg free.

"Enjoy that," Shamhatu said to the wild man. "Very soon, you'll have some useful work to do. You can help me drag this down there and set up the tent." He would have to learn how to help: Shamhatu and the single donkey would not be able to get the wain down by themselves, and though Shamhatu thought she could put up the large tent by herself, the wild man's strength would be helpful indeed.

He grinned up at her, his mouth ringed with blood, and red streaks running down through the dirty gold of his matted beard. He would have the breath of a predator that night, too, Shamhatu thought with a sigh; but bad breath was one of the lesser ills that the priestesses of Inanna learned to ignore when they brought the goddess' blessing. She shook her head, shoving at the rock that had blocked the wheel until it shifted out of the way. Lifting the empty yoke onto her right shoulder and pretending to pull, she sank down when the weight became truly too much for her strength.

The wild man was watching Shamhatu's movements carefully, but she could not tell whether there was more behind his green-brown eyes than the curiosity of a cat watching a mongoose until he uncoiled lithely and grasped the other side of the yoke. The wagon's wheels began to roll; Shamhatu got out of the way, walking on the other side of the wild man and praising him as he pulled her wain slowly down the side of the hill and toward the little tent.

"That's very good," she said encouragingly. "Yes . . . very clever, very good." If he could not understand the words, she was sure that the tone of her voice made a difference to him, as it would with a hound or pack-ass. "You need a name," Shamhatu mused aloud. "I shall call you Enkidu, do you like that? Enkidu?" The wild man dropped the yoke from his shoulders, smiling down at her. "Enkidu?" she repeated.

Enkidu reached for her again, but Shamhatu slipped away from his grasp, running lightly into the tent. He was learning, if slowly, that beneath the sky was no longer the place to couple, any more than the tent was the place to relieve himself. By the time he had followed Shamhatu in, she was already laying on her back with her knees upraised, applying oil to herself with her left hand and holding her right hand over her throat—though her palm was becoming swollen and sore with bruises, letting him bite that was better, she thought, than having him chew on her neck.

When they were done, Shamhatu let him go after the carcass of the dead donkey while she struggled to put her larger tent up herself. By the time she had finished, Enkidu's belly was already bulging with the tremendous amount of meat he had gobbled, and his long golden eyelashes were beginning to droop sleepily. It was full dark by the time Shamhatu had finished the job of butchering what was left, hanging it on a pole above her smoky little dung-fire in hopes that it would dry rather than rotting—if Akalla could not come to her with food, they might need every bite. The other ass nosed uneasily around the edge of the makeshift camp, clearly afraid of Enkidu, yet unwilling to leave the fresh green grasses ringing the watering hole.

"Hush, little one, have no fear," Shamhatu murmured to it as she roasted a piece of its earlier comrade on the long charred stick that served her as a spit. A sizzle of fat fell into the fireplace, flaring in a stream of greasy black smoke—the temple fed its beasts well.

After she had eaten, Shamhatu climbed up into the wagon, listing its contents to herself by touch in the darkness. There, three jars of beer—that could stay where it was: the last thing she needed was for Enkidu to be drunk as well as wild. Food and gaming boards, the rest of her oils and jewelry . . .

Strings rang softly under her fingers; carefully the priestess felt along the taut wires to the frame of her lyre, lifting it up. The tuning had gone out, but the tone was still good. Carefully she carried it back to the tent, sitting outside and twisting the little pegs until the octave and its intervals rang clear and bright, each note seated in its proper place once more. Then, watching Enkidu where he lay curled in his sleep and snoring softly, she began to play and sing a lullaby.

ENKIDU WOULD EAT dried fish and meat, and Shamhatu sometimes saw him tearing up and devouring the grasses at the edge of the water-hole, but he scorned bread and cheese, however often he saw Shamhatu eating them herself. She talked to him constantly, and he loved to hear her sing, lying on the ground with his great hairy head in her lap as she plucked the strings of the lyre, and sometimes making a rumbling noise almost like a purr as he kneaded her thighs with his huge hands. Eventually, though by the time she succeeded her right hand was so swollen and bruised that she could barely plink out melodies with it, she had managed to train Enkidu not to bite when he coupled with her, and to slow the urgent pushing of his hips so that he could serve her for more than a few moments at a time. Still, she saw no more in his eyes than in the gaze of a trained animal; and more and more often, in that week as the half-moon waxed toward full, she began to doubt whether he would ever come to humanity.

Akalla appeared in the distance every day, a small figure on a far-off hill. He did not dare to come closer, for if he did, Enkidu would growl and roar and chase him away; but he always left some fresh food for them, most often new-caught birds and milk. Enkidu would slap Shamhatu's hand away if she reached for food before he was finished eating, and Shamhatu did not press him: the first blow had nearly broken her wrist.

Now the wild man lay lazing in the sun: he had devoured the little birds Akalla had brought, then flung himself upon Shamhatu, and was almost asleep in the grass, his head pillowed on the spill of golden hair flowing out around it. Shamhatu fetched her lyre from the tent and began to plink upon it—no tune, just a fall of random notes that seemed to glitter like an upward flight of larks in the warm air.

Enkidu raised his head from the grass, staring at her. For the first time since he had flung himself upon her by the watering hole, Shamhatu shivered at his gaze: it was the same fierce, single-minded glare that he fixed upon Akalla's birds before ripping their wings off and gnawing the flesh from their bones. She slowed her plinking, then stopped, in case the music had set him off in some way.

In a single bound Enkidu closed the distance between them, grasping both of her hands painfully in one of his own and pressing them to the lyre as he growled softly. Shamhatu began to play again, watching him from the corner of her eye. The wild man did not seem enraged, but her music did not seem to soothe him, either.

It was several moments before Enkidu reached out to her again—

brushing his thick black nails over her mouth, then her throat, as he growled and muttered. Shamhatu had listened to the little noises he made for so long that his guttural moans took some time to form into shapes in her ears.

"Sss . . . sing," Enkidu growled. "Sing."

The lyre rocked as Shamhatu set it abruptly down; only a swift movement kept it from toppling. Instead of singing, she wrapped her arms around the lion-man's thick neck, kissing him squarely on the mouth. "Enkidu!"

"Enkidu?" he repeated, struggling to wrap his mouth around the sounds. "Enkidu?"

"That's you." She laid her palm on his chest, stroking the thick tendrils of curly golden hair. "Enkidu. Enkidu."

He touched his own chest. "Enkidu," he said, and nodded. "I am . . . I am . . ."

"You are a man," Shamhatu said softly; and as she spoke, she could hear the voice of Inanna ringing through her. "You are a man, knowing life and death and the gods; you are a man, heir to the *me* that Inanna brought to Erech from Eridu, that her people might become civilized, even as you have been—a beast no more, but a man, like unto the gods in knowledge. Enkidu."

"Enkidu," he repeated softly. Now, for the first time, Shamhatu saw a human look in Enkidu's eyes as he stood up and gazed around—and it was a terrible look, full of despair and fear. "Enkidu!" he shouted, and ran from the waterhole, his feet skimming over the desert until Shamhatu could see him no more.

She stared after him until her eyes watered and burned with bitter tears, like salty waters rising over the rich fields. "What have I done?" Shamhatu asked herself. "Inanna, what have I done?"

After a time, Shamhatu sat down again, picking up the lyre and beginning to plink at it idly as the sun rose to hang at his height, then began his long way down. It was mid-afternoon by the time that Enkidu came walking back to the watering hole, his back slumped.

Shamhatu ran joyfully to him, heedless of the rank blanket of odors hanging about him. He folded her in his great embrace, holding her more gently than before; though she expected him to push her down and take her, he only let her go after a few moments. Then, to her surprise, he dropped to his knees before her, pressing his head against her belly.

"Seeing me," Enkidu said softly, with the tears welling in his eyes, "the gazelles ran away and scattered. The beasts of the wilderness fled from my body. I tried to rise up, but my body pulled back; my knees froze; the animals have all turned from me. I have grown weak, and my running is not as it was before."

"And yet you speak," the Shamhatu answered. Strange as it seemed, she did not wonder how the words could suddenly flow so freely from him. She knew that the gods had shaped him, forming his mind in wholeness like a clay vessel—left empty for a little while, now filled at once with the flowing liquid of language, a second, smaller miracle to follow that which had created him. "If you have lost the gifts of the beast, you have gained the gifts of the man, and the gods have given them to you in full flower." She bent down to Enkidu, taking his hands in hers and raising him to his feet again, then brushing his tangled beard aside to kiss the hollow of his throat. "Enkidu, you are beautiful, you have become like a god. Why should you run about the wilderness with the wild beasts? Come with me, and in time I shall bring you into Erech the Sheepfold, the holy temple, the dwelling-place of An and Inanna—the place of Gilgamesh, who is wise to perfection, but struts his power over his people like a wild bull."

Enkidu moved his heavy head slowly; Shamhatu could see the thoughts grinding behind his eyes like the great millstones of the temple granaries, and waited silently to hear what he would say.

"I will go," he answered. "You have made me a man; I must follow you to the holy temple, the dwelling-place of An and Inanna. Where Gilgamesh dwells, wise to perfection, but strutting his power like a wild bull—I shall call to him; I shall shout with all my might." Then his jaws tightened, his shoulders swelled, and he went on in a voice that rang from Shamhatu's ears, "Let me shout out in Erech: 'I am the mighty one!' Lead me in and I will change the way of things: he whose strength is mightiest is he who is born in the wilderness."

Shamhatu answered softly, though her bowels trembled within her at his words, "Come, we shall go, so that he may see your face. I shall lead you to Gilgamesh—I know where he shall be. You shall look about, Enkidu, inside Erech the Sheepfold, where the folk stand proud in wide belts and every day is a day for some festival, where the lyre and the drum play all the time, where the women of the temple and tavern stand about prettily, breathing the strength of their beauty and glowing with it, full of laughter, and the sheets are spread on the couch of night." She swayed as she spoke, chanting as she had learned to do in the temple; and it seemed to her that Enkidu's face eased, the corners of his lids beginning to droop like a child's. "Enkidu, full of life's strength: I shall show you Gilgamesh, the man of joy and woe. You shall look upon him, gaze upon his face: in manhood he is beautiful, and in manhood well-gifted, and his body glows with the strength of his beauty. He is stronger than you, even when he sleeps not by day or night: you must drive away thoughts which are wrong. As for Gilgamesh, the god Utu loves him. An of the heavens, Enlil of the storms, and Enki Word-Ruler have enlarged his mind—even before you came from the mountains, within the heart of Erech, Gilgamesh saw you in dreams."

Shamhatu took off the shawl of white wool that covered her head and shoulders from the sun, wrapping it around Enkidu's middle and tying it so that it somewhat resembled a man's kilt. "When you are among people, you will go clothed: a beast may be naked, but not a man. Now we will eat, and sleep together again this night, and when Akalla comes in the morning, you shall call out greetings to him, and bid him come to help us with the wain, for with one of the asses dead, we shall all need to work to get it back to his village."

Enkidu turned his gaze to the remaining donkey, which stood placidly chewing on a mouthful of reeds from the edge of the watering hole, then to the tangled dump of bones at the edge of their camp. "I . . . It was prey," he said suddenly. "I killed it, just as I killed when I ran with the lions."

"Yes, Enkidu, you killed it. But you are no longer a lion among lions, and will not kill again without good reason. The asses belong to the temple of Inanna; I will have to buy another one from the people of Akalla's village, and it is likely that Gilgamesh will pay the temple back in time."

"Pay . . . back?" Enkidu's eyes clouded, then brightened with tears. "Did I do something wrong?"

"Not wrong for a lion, as you were, but wrong for a man, as you are. Harm done must always be repaid, else there would be no order in the universe."

Enkidu bent down, picking up one of the asses' long leg-bones. He had snapped it for the marrow, chewing it up and licking the rich meat out; now the splintered bone was clean and dry, with only a few little insects crawling about within it. "Can I repay?"

"Gilgamesh sent me; he will pay the temple. Yet you will repay, for one ass alone cannot drag the wagon: you will have a chance to walk with the yoke on your shoulders in place of the one you slew."

Enkidu nodded. "That is right," he said, and it seemed to Shamhatu that she heard a warm tinge of satisfaction in his voice. "Now will you play and sing for me?"

Shamhatu picked up her lyre again as Enkidu sat down beside her, stretching out and resting his head on her thigh as he had done before speech came to him. To her surprise, she felt the tears prickling behind her eyelids again as she began to pluck the strings: she had not thought that she would miss the beast, but there must have been something about the simple trust and love the great dog of a man had placed in her— something Shamhatu knew she would not have again, for Enkidu would not forget that she had made him human. Though he might have the best of the bargain, he would remember what he had lost; and remember, too, that the choice had not been given to him.

*But no child that lives escapes growing up,* Shamhatu thought, *and few who are grown would give their wisdom to be children again.* Enkidu would not flee into the wilds, but come instead to Erech the Sheepfold. She struck a strong chord on the lyre and pulled her breath deep into her gut, opening her mouth to sing the words that Enkidu had heard over and over, and now would understand for the first time.

"Queen of all the *me*, glowing light,
Life-giving woman, beloved of An and Urash,
Priestess of An, much bejeweled,

Who loves the life-giving crown,
Who grasps the seven *me* in her hand.
My queen, you are the guardian of all the great *me*,
You have lifted the *me*, have tied the *me* to your hands,
Have gathered the *me*, pressed them to your breasts . . ."

The morning sunlight shone warm through Enkidu's eyelids, calling him from the scattered dreams of his sleep. He shifted, turning over so that the light was no longer in his face; but even as the vague images of his thought shaped themselves into words in his head, he found himself awakening. Enkidu stretched, rolling and turning, and a faded memory came to him: sleeping among the lions, safely surrounded by the musky scent of the bachelor-pride and the great warm bodies nestling against him in the cold of the night . . .

But the scents in here were sweeter, the oils Shamhatu rubbed on her skin blending with the delicious scent of her sex, overlaid with his own mating-musk—the scent of the pride-king, as he was. Enkidu rose to his feet, his penis already swelling with new desire for his queen.

Shamhatu was outside, kneeling by the watering hole and lifting great dripping double handfuls of water to pour over her long hair and bare back, then scrubbing her skin with a cloth. Pacing silently up behind her, Enkidu bent down to scoop her up.

Shamhatu did not struggle in his arms, but her gaze was sharp and firm. "Put me down, Enkidu. We cannot make love now: we must wait for Akalla to come, so that he may know that it is safe for him to come near and guide us back to his village."

Enkidu frowned, setting Shamhatu on her feet again. It seemed to him that two voices spoke at once in his head. One was the voice of Shamhatu, speaking plain truth—for without Enkidu's greetings, Akalla would surely drop his offerings and flee. But the other, a deeper voice, seemed to growl to him that there was food enough here, and the female was willing to breed: why should he leave, or share his good life with another male? Torn between the two, a soft rumble came from his throat; he could feel the hot blood beginning to seep back into his body, his confusion drowning out the hum of his desire.

Shamhatu shook back her heavy dark curtain of wet hair, glimmering drops flying from it like a swarm of tiny dragonflies. Her fingertips brushed gently over the front of Enkidu's makeshift kilt; he stood still, waiting to see what she would do.

"My love, you will find that a fig is sweetest when you have waited long for its ripening. Tonight you shall be bathed, and fed upon the food of humankind; then we shall sleep together in a real bed, beneath a thatched roof, and you shall learn more of how humans make love—of slower and more lasting pleasure, rather than the quick spurts of a lion; of the arts of caressing and kissing, and tending to your partner's desires. But there is much to be done between now and then: that, too, is the nature of being a man."

Enkidu sighed, turning his gaze away from Shamhatu's dark eyes to the stony hills rising against the blue sky. A small bird fluttered up and away in fright, then another, singing out their little cries of alarm. "Akalla comes," he said. "Let us go to meet him."

The two of them made their way toward the hill, Shamhatu leading Enkidu by the hand. As soon as the trapper's dark head appeared above the rocks, Enkidu cried out, "Come down, Akalla! You shall be safe here; I shall not seek to drive you away from my watering hole or my queen."

Akalla stopped where he was for a moment, staring. Then his shoulders and chest came into view; flung over his back was a net bag with the carcasses of a few small birds and a rock-rabbit in it. The trapper approached Enkidu slowly, and Enkidu could smell the sharp stink of fear upon him. That was as it should be, Enkidu thought: the other man's head did not come past his own chin, and though Akalla's shoulders were broad for his height, they seemed no more than half as wide as Enkidu's own. Enkidu felt the roar building in his chest, rumbling up into his throat—a cry of pride and power, ready to cow the little man before him. Yet Shamhatu had spoken, and he must trust in her, for she had the wisdom to make a beast into a man. And so, as the priestess had taught him, he reached out to grasp Akalla's forearm in greeting, though he could as easily have snapped the other man's bones in his grasp.

"Today we shall go back to the village, as soon as the wagon is packed," Shamhatu said. Akalla looked from the bones and scraps of rotting hide that had once been an ass to the living donkey nibbling grass beside the waterhole. "Enkidu," she added firmly, "will help to pull the wain."

Pulling the wagon was little work for Enkidu, though now and again he would raise his head sadly to look at the land about him—the heat shimmering over the patches of scrubby grass; a lizard, brown and dry as a dead leaf, scuttling over the face of a rock; the dark shape of a bird soaring through the blue sky above them. It would be better to curl up and sleep in the shade now; but if sleep were not on him and he were traveling alone, he would have turned from the path a hundred times to pounce on some small creature or merely sit and stare, taking in the dusty bluish haze of the wide horizon and the little sounds of rustling grasses and scuttling insects. Yet Shamhatu and Akalla had said that, if they walked steadily on and only stopped to rest for a short time when the day's heat was at its height, they should reach the village by sundown; and that seemed to be desired by both of them, so Enkidu could say nothing against it.

By the time the sun was half hidden behind the low ridge of the western hills, the village—a squat dark lump of square houses—lay before the three travelers. Around it were several fenced pastures; the shepherds were just now leading their sheep in from grazing, calling to the flocks now and again or striking an erring lamb lightly with their crooks. The hairs prickled up on the back of Enkidu's neck as he looked at it: though sheep were fine prey, rich with good fat and blood, the pride had always turned away from places such as this, away from the thick musty scents of the tall creatures with their shouting and strange weapons. Yet he could hear the light lilt of happiness in Shamhatu's voice as she called out to him, "There it is, Enkidu! Are you ready to go as a man among men?"

"I am ready," he called back, quickening his own steps to match those of the ass yoked beside him.

The people of the village were already coming forth from their houses as the wain rolled along the last stretch of road, staring wide-eyed at the newcomers. They seemed very small to Enkidu—few taller than Akalla, none as large as himself. Yet the smells that curled dark from the houses were beginning to make Enkidu's mouth water: meat scorched by fire as Shamhatu scorched hers, mixed with sharper and more pungent scents like the strong grasses that sometimes grew near the watering holes. He wanted to turn aside, to go into one of the houses, take his share of food and sit beside the fire where Shamhatu could sing to him, but when he looked back questioningly at her, she shook her head.

"Keep going, Enkidu. Akalla's house is only a little farther."

But we are here now, Enkidu thought, and one house seems no better than another. Several of the houses had goats tethered outside, chewing aimlessly at the dry stubble, and a few had an ass—not like the one that walked beside Enkidu: smaller, drab-colored beasts that rolled their eyes wickedly at him as the wain passed. At last Shamhatu called him to halt, and he let the yoke fall from his shoulders, looking at the hut she had chosen.

"Here, Enkidu," she said. "This is where we shall stay." She leaped lightly down from the wagon, taking him by the hand and leading him toward the door. A little bat swooped low over the roof in a jerky, chittering arc, barely visible in the darkening air; the door opened, and a small woman looked out, staring at Enkidu in wonder. She was shorter than Shamhatu, and plumper; instead of flowing free, her hair was wrapped about her head in a plaited coil, and she wore a necklace of painted clay beads instead of the bright stones that Shamhatu sometimes strung about her neck. Enkidu sniffed, breathing in her scent—the rich sweetness of a female, overlaid with a thin veil of smoke and curdled milk and strong grasses. He glanced back at Akalla, but the smaller man made no move to challenge him: either this was not the trapper's queen, or he would not fight to keep her.

Enkidu reached out to the little woman, one hand closing on the soft firmness of her breast and the other on the rounded curve of her rump. He smiled at her; he could already feel the pleasant swelling and throbbing ache in his groin, and knew that he was ready to take her as soon as they passed inside. The woman's eyes widened and she gasped, the sudden sharpness of fear rising through the heady mix of odors that hung about her.

"Enkidu!" Shamhatu snapped. "Let go of her! This is Akalla's wife . . . and, even if she were not, you are not to grab a woman like that until she tells you that you may."

Enkidu unhappily let go of the pliant flesh beneath his hands, and the woman scuttled backward into the house, out of reach, her mouth working silently. Akalla's lips were pressed together into a thin pale line, his hands closing tightly upon the shaft of his bow; Enkidu was ready to take him on, but Shamhatu was frowning and shaking her head. A strange pang went through his body, bringing the hot drops of saltwater to burn the insides of his eyelids.

"Have I done wrong?" Enkidu asked plaintively. "Must I repay?"

Shamhatu's gaze softened and she reached out to stroke his forearm. "You have done no wrong; but you must apologize to Innashagga, and promise not to touch her so again."

Enkidu looked at the little woman. Her eyes flickered up to meet his gaze, dark and nervous as the eyes of a gazelle at the watering hole. "I am sorry," he said, as Shamhatu had taught him. "I will not . . . will not touch you again without your leave."

Behind him, Enkidu could hear Akalla's soft breath of relief. Innashagga stepped a little closer, though she was still more than an arm's length away. "Then be welcome to our house, man from the wilderness." Her nostrils widened as Enkidu bent to creep through the doorway, the tips of the dried palm-fronds scratching lightly over his shoulders like a hundred long fingernails. "Divine Lady," the little woman said to Shamhatu, "shall I call the women of the village to bring water for a bath?"

"That would be well-done, indeed," Shamhatu answered gravely. "But I think it would be well for us to eat while the bath is being readied, for we have walked a long road this day, with little rest."

Enkidu stared about the inside of the house. It was not like Shamhatu's tent, as he had thought it would be. The fire was inside a little clay-house of its own, from which the smoke rose to drift about the roof and seep out through the bundles of dried palm-fronds. Before the fire squatted a little old man, his dark gaze bright through the smoky air of the hut. Beyond that was a great trough of clay, big enough that

Enkidu could have sat in it comfortably, if not stretched to his full length. On the floor were bowls and flat rounds of clay topped by flat white rounds of something that Enkidu could not name, but which smelled a little bit like grass-seed in the sun.

Shamhatu squatted down by the hearth, opposite the old man. Akalla came into the hut, bearing a large clay jar, and sat beside her. Enkidu hesitated a moment, but finally copied their movements.

"Civilized people," the Shamhatu said, "sit down thus when they are prepared to eat. Remember that you must use only your right hand for eating, because the left is unclean."

Enkidu looked down at his hands. The left seemed no worse than the right, though he could scent a faint pleasant pungency to it. The lions would have sniffed at the sharp fragrance in delight, but Shamhatu had told him that piss and shit were foul and unclean, and that he must take care not to insult anyone by offering them the hand he used to clean himself with, nor offend them by using it at meals.

Akalla's wife moved the jar her husband had brought in to sit in the middle of the circle, handing each person there a straw. Enkidu looked puzzled at it, wondering what he should do—it seemed too dry to be good for eating. But first the Shamhatu, then the old man and Akalla, leaned forward, dipping one end of the straw into the jar and sucking on the other.

"Come, Enkidu," the Shamhatu said brightly. "If you are to be a man, you must learn to eat bread and drink beer—eat the food, as you must to live, and drink the beer, as is the custom of the land."

Enkidu sniffed at the jar. The liquid within smelled like the grasses of a stagnant watering hole, bubbling with rot. Yet he had drunk worse when thirsty, so he lowered his own straw into the clay jug as the others had done, sucking as if the dry stalk were the nipple of a wild cow.

The beer did not taste as foul as Enkidu had thought it might: there was sweetness as well as bitterness in it, and it slid easily across his tongue, kindling a warm glow in his stomach when he had swallowed. He sucked harder at the straw, until he breathed in a little of the drink and began to cough and splutter. The Shamhatu patted him on the back, laughing.

"Many youths have done worse the first time they drink," she said.

"But now you should have some bread, lest you become drunken too quickly." She handed him one of the flat white rounds.

Enkidu squinted at it a moment, then took it, biting in and chewing. It tasted bland, with neither the salt of blood nor the fresh sweetness of grass, and it lumped oddly in his mouth, but he was able to wash it down with another draught of beer.

By the time they had finished the meal, Enkidu was feeling quite pleasant, loose and relaxed in all his limbs as though he basked in the sun beside a clear watering hole. He had eaten cheese made from milk, and roasted garlic smeared upon the rounds of bread, and the Shamhatu had brought out dates and figs in sweet syrup afterward. He did not know how much of the beer he had drunk, but saw several jars taken away empty, and had to walk outside several times to piss a dark stain onto the dry mud-brick wall of the house. The Shamhatu petted him and praised him; the women who walked in to pour their pitchers of water into the great clay trough made much of him, and even Innashagga no longer stared at him so fearfully.

Enkidu reached out, pawing gently at the fold of wool covering the Shamhatu's left shoulder. "Can we make love now?"

The Shamhatu giggled, pushing his hand away. She, too, was merry; laughing, she had told him that such was the way of beer. "First, my love, we are going to have a bath, and wash the wilderness from your golden pelt." She got to her feet. "Good people . . . can you leave us alone for a little?"

When Akalla and his family had left the house, the Shamhatu helped Enkidu to untie the shawl she had fastened about his waist, then slipped her own dress off, easily dodging his clumsy grab. "Not yet, my darling." She pointed at the trough. "In."

Enkidu stepped into the trough and sat down. The water was comfortably cool, soothing the hundred little itches and prickles of his skin. The Shamhatu got in beside him, a cloth and a comb in her hand. Moistening the cloth, she began to splash and rub him like a lioness grooming a cub. Now and again she would tug at a mat or a clump where something sticky had clotted in his hair, and he would hiss slightly; but for that, this bathing was pleasant to Enkidu.

At last the Shamhatu, shivering, stood up, brushing the water from her skin and reaching for a dry piece of linen to wipe herself off with. She grimaced at the dark streaks left on the cloth. "Such filthy water . . . I wish we could wash again in cleaner, but we cannot ask the women to fill this bath twice in one evening. Come, Enkidu."

Enkidu stood obediently as she wiped him dry, sniffing carefully. "Better . . . but you still smell a little wild," she decided. "Sit down and drink a little more beer while I blend an oil to anoint you."

The Shamhatu rummaged among her clay jars, pouring and stirring. Enkidu smiled at the familiar scents that had meant her tent and her open thighs to him; he had thought they were part of her own odor, but now he could see that they came from the golden oils that she smoothed onto her body. When she had finished blending to her satisfaction, she came to stand behind him, pressing her breasts against his shoulder blades. "Stay there . . . don't move, Enkidu," the Shamhatu ordered in a low soft purr. Her scented hands moved upon his shoulders and the back of his neck, smoothing the oil in even as her firm stroking kneaded and softened his muscles. Enkidu's eyes half closed as he leaned back against her, letting her hands creep down to rub the oil into the glisten- ing golden tangle of hair on his chest. He was aroused again, though not with the pounding urgency he had felt earlier; the pleasure of her touch seemed to stroke softly through his body, lifting him to meet her. After a little time, Enkidu lay back on the bench so the Shamhatu could rub and oil his stomach and thighs, her hands circling over his throbbing groin now and again, but never lingering long.

At last Enkidu said, "We shall make love now," and the Shamhatu did not demur, but smiled at him. "So we shall. No, stay there . . . aaah!" She lifted her lithe body up, palms resting on Enkidu's chest, and low- ered herself onto him. Enkidu grasped her and began to move his hips vigorously, thrusting as deeply as he could into the moist velvety haven sheathing him. "Slower, Enkidu: if you spill too fast, you will do me no good. Here, is this not better . . . ?" The Shamhatu raised and lowered herself slowly, her warm clutch caressing him with tingling, languorous pleasure. "You may stroke my breasts as well; women like to have their breasts stroked, when the time and the man are right." Enkidu reached up to caress the soft little globes, feeling her nipples hard against his palms. He wanted to grab her and thrust harder again, but now he understood that doing so would end what he was feeling—this slow swelling rise of ecstasy in his blood, now beginning to spill from both their mouths in moans and little cries as she slowly guided him up the fiery peak to the heavens.

At last the priestess threw her head back, her breasts lifted toward the ceiling, the ends of her long hair brushing against Enkidu's thighs. Enkidu felt her tightening around him, her firm grip pulsing unbearably before it loosened again. With a shout, he let himself go, pumping his hips hard against her until light burst behind his eyes and the seed exploded from his body.

Still holding him within her, the Shamhatu slumped over Enkidu's chest, her dark hair fanning out to mingle with his own hair and beard. Her breath was coming fast, the pupils of her eyes dilated; but her lips were curved in sleepy satisfaction. Gently she kissed his mouth. "You are learning well, my love. If you can remember not to grab women without asking their leave, I do not think that you will be lonely in Erech."

Enkidu sighed, holding her close to him. Her warmth was good, like the small body of a gazelle curled against him, and soon he was asleep.

ENKIDU WOKE IN darkness, choking on the smoke and the human scents pressing against his chest. For a moment he struggled in sudden fear, until the calm breathing of the Shamhatu beside him, the soft whispering snores of Innashagga murmuring between the deeper breaths of Akalla and the old man's whistling lungs, reminded him that he was a man among men and no longer a beast in the wild. Yet the habits of the lions were still with him: having napped well for a little time, his limbs were strong with wakefulness again. He stood, stretching. Remembering that humans went clothed, he reached down to grasp Shamhatu's soft wool garment, tying it about his waist before he went out.

A dog barked before one of the houses, rushing at Enkidu. He did nothing, but when the thin cur met his gaze it pulled up, slinking away with tail between its legs. It seemed to him that everyone else in the village was sleeping or dead—the goats curled up into lumps of wool, their owners silent and lightless within their mud-brick walls. Yet something drew him onward . . . not quite a scent, not quite a sound; a sort of humming through the soles of his feet as he walked to the heart of the village, where a few scraggly palm trees swayed black and spiky against the faint glimmer of moonlight.

Not knowing why, Enkidu turned aside before he reached the well and its ring of palms, ending up instead before the woven-grass door of one of the largest huts. He pulled it aside and stepped in.

The blackness within seemed darker than a nighttime cave; Enkidu stood on the threshold, poised on the balls of his feet to run or fight. But nothing happened, and so he carefully stepped in. One pace, two paces . . . Nothing lived in here: the only smells in his nostrils were rancid sheep fat, overlaid with the fresh scent of new-broken reeds and the faint stench of rotting flowers—and that other thing, the spoor he had followed. Though the Shamhatu had told him that men always walked upright, Enkidu dropped to all fours, sniffing as he cast about him to see what he could find.

Rustling through the reeds, it was not long before his forehead brushed against a curve of stone. He rose to his knees as his hands followed the shape up, stroking the swelling lines—the lines of a woman's body, warming beneath his hands, save for the necklace about her throat, whose clay beads seemed to chill to polished stone as he touched them. A soft sigh seemed to breathe from her; then Enkidu saw the first light kindling in the corner of his eye, the tiny flame of an oil-lamp, bright and pure in the darkness. Its gleam caught the gold that shone above the woman's brows—the great eight-pointed golden star in its setting of lapis beads strung on gold wire. More lights were kindling about him, like the stars slowly glowing into the evening sky; he no longer smelled the rank sheep fat and rotting flowers, but only sweet oils and musk. The hangings on the walls gleamed with silk and glittering threads of silver and gold, and the ceiling rose high above his head, supported by great columns of inlaid lapis and pearly shell.

"Enkidu," the woman breathed. Enkidu looked up at her. It seemed to him that he looked upon the Shamhatu, but she was arrayed as he had never seen her, glowing all over with the bright shine of gold and the dark gleam of lapis beneath the great starry diadem on her head. Coils of gold traced out her breasts beneath her gown of pale blue linen, and a girdle of smoldering agates ringed her hips, its intricately wrought clasp dangling down toward the dark triangle that showed faint through the sheer fabric. Her eyes were huge and black, deep pools with the stars of lamplight glittering from them. She reached out a slender hand, laying it upon his head, and her touch thrilled all through his body. "Enkidu, my lion, strong as a wild bull. Aruru made you in the wilderness; of silence you were born; Ninurta endowed you with strength. One by one I have brought the *me* to you, as to Erech so long ago. What is true returns: though the priests change places, the rites are wrought as before, and the strength of the world is reborn."

"Why?" Enkidu whispered. "These are great wonders you have shown me—but I know little and you wish much . . ." He bowed his head before her, for he could no longer meet her sky-dark gaze.

"All that you may learn will come to you, my lion. For now it is enough to know . . . I have called you to be my champion, to guard my bridal bed. The shepherd of Erech drives his sheep until they drop; the great bull tramples those who bring him fodder, and treads on the growing grain. And thus, hearing them cry out, the gods shaped you in the wilderness, from the dust of the desert, from the bones of lion and man. As we made all things living at the beginning of days, so we shaped you whole and grown in answer to the prayers of Erech, and my priestess opened the way that I might fill your ready mind with speech and knowledge. I have brought you to be a rebuke to the shepherd, and a yoke for the bull; I have brought you to share the shepherd's night-watches, and to strive at the bull's side, that he may learn his heart and care for his flock, that he may know the worth of the grain on which he has grown so strong. Though you do not understand now, my lion, my feet shall rest upon your back and my star guide you: you shall be my champion, and guard my bridal bed."

Enkidu felt Inanna's hand brushing over his eyes, soft as the flutter of a moth's wing in the shadow of an oil-lamp. Suddenly he was tired, bonelessly weary. He slid to the floor before her feet, his eyes closing against his will as he sank into the warm clouds of heaped rugs, and then was asleep.

WHEN ENKIDU AWOKE again, there was light shining painfully against his eyelids, and he heard the rough voices of men calling to each other, and smelled the heavy reek of garlic and cheese that seemed to seep from the pores of everyone in the village.

"Look! Here he is . . . here in the shrine."

"Sleeping before the feet of the goddess!"

"How did he come here? Do even beasts from the wild know of worship?" one whispered, and an older, drier voice answered, "I think the Shamhatu need no longer fear that he will fly from her. But you, Ilshu, perhaps you should fear for your place as guardian of the shrine, unless you hold it true that skill in wrestling far outweighs strength and size."

Enkidu opened his eyes, squinting against the dazzling morning sun and the shadows that stood in the doorway. Old Gunidu was there, leaning on his shepherd's crook, together with three younger men. Most of the folk of the village still looked alike to Enkidu, but one of the young men was bigger than the rest—bigger than anyone else he had seen here, though smaller than he; his nose was more straight than curved, and his thick black beard was trimmed close to his chin. Now the large man rubbed a hand over his shaven brown scalp, stepping forward.

"Ho, you," he said. His voice was calm, but Enkidu could still whiff his faint acrid undertone of fear. "What are you doing at the feet of Inanna? Do you seek to become the guardian of her shrine?"

Enkidu stood, stretching. Ilshu's brown eyes measured him carefully, like a lion watching a herd of ibex to see which faltered or limped, which might run more slowly or fall more easily. The night had faded in Enkidu's thoughts already, no clearer to him than any of the days when he had run in the wild, without words to fix sights and sounds and happenings in his brain; but, as when reminded of those days, a bubble of memory rose slowly in his brain, bursting to release what he had heard.

"I shall be her champion," he said slowly, the words strange and sweet as beer on his tongue, "and guard her bridal bed."

One of the other young men sucked in air through his teeth; Gunidu smiled a little crooked smile, but Enkidu could see the blood rushing swiftly beneath Ilshu's sun-bronzed skin, and the dark vein throbbing its jagged path along the side of his head.

"You must win it, if you want it," Ilshu grated through clenched jaws. "Do you know the rules of wrestling in the holy place?"

Enkidu shook his head.

"Learn them, then." Ilshu turned to one of his comrades, a small and lightly built man. "Each fixes his hands on the other's belt . . . like this: if one lets go, he is judged the loser. Then, when the priest or priestess gives the sign, each strives to cast the other down, by strength or skill. See!"

Ilshu tightened his grasp, his shoulders bunching as though to lift his partner bodily from the floor, but the smaller man squirmed close, hooking a leg behind Ilshu's. The big man's knee buckled; his body slewed to the side in a quick turn that whirled his partner through the air to land flat on his back with Ilshu kneeling triumphantly over him. "See!" Ilshu repeated with a grin, barely breathing hard. "I am the best wrestler in three villages; I have held the championship of this shrine for five years—longer than Gilgamesh has held it at the temple in Erech, and I have never shirked my duty afterward."

Gunidu's crook flashed out, landing sharply on Ilshu's back. "Do not speak such words! Least of all in the holy shrine of Inanna: whether there be truth in them or not, the goddess will not gaze well upon those who speak ill of her young suitor in Erech the Sheepfold."

Ilshu's face darkened again, but he said nothing to Gunidu as he released his defeated opponent and stood. "So, Enkidu. Are you ready to wrestle with me now . . . if someone will lend you a belt?"

"Wait," Gunidu said. "I know that garment he has wrapped around his waist, and I know that the Divine Lady will not be pleased if her shift is stained or torn. I shall fetch fitting clothes for him, and bring her back here, that Inanna's priestess may be pleased by the sight of the young bulls wrestling before her. As for you, Ilshu, gaze well upon the goddess, that you may strive for love of her, rather than anger or wounded pride, which are not fit offerings at her shrine: Inanna has pride enough for all, and, should her wrath be roused, anger as well."

"I hear your counsel, Shepherd," Ilshu answered in a more chastened voice. He turned to the statue at the end of the shrine, first sinking to his knees, then prostrating himself.

In the light of day, Inanna's beads were painted clay again, her stone face blank save for the double arch graven on her forehead. Enkidu stared at the sign, his brow furrowing: he had seen that mark before, those two sharp arches sharing a single pillar, but he could not think where or when. Only a vague memory of dark markings against gold, of warmth in the cold desert night . . . He gazed at it as the murmuring crowd gathered outside the shrine, until his eyes and head began to swim, until the door swung to, leaving the shrine in dusky twilight and he heard Shamhatu's voice.

"Come, Enkidu, let me dress you properly, that you may do battle for Inanna's sake."

Enkidu went to her, gazing down as she untied her shift from his waist and replaced it with a fringed kilt and belt like those the other men wore. He had seen Shamhatu last night, and yet not Shamhatu: for last night her crown had seemed to tower into the heavens and the strength of the goddess had overwhelmed him; and now, though she wore the same gold and lapis diadem, the same bracelets and breast-ornaments and girdle of stones, she seemed small and delicate beside him again, and it was he who looked down upon her. Yet, goddess or woman, she was lovely to look upon, the burnished-red gleams in her long dark hair and her great eyes and the fragile collarbones and pale skin showing where her dress left her right shoulder bare. His nostrils flared as he scented her musk: he could tell that she was ready to make love again . . . and that the winner of the wrestling match would have her.

"So Inanna sets her men against each other, to test which is the strongest," the Shamhatu murmured breathlessly. "Go forth to battle, my lion." She stepped forward, standing beside the statue of the goddess: roughly carved stone and fine-boned woman were of a height.

Ilshu rose from the floor, brushing bits of reed from his short beard and straightening his kilt. "Are you ready, wild man?" he asked softly.

"I am ready," Enkidu answered.

The two of them trod seven broad paces from where statue and priestess said, then turned to face each other. Ilshu reached out to grip Enkidu's belt; Enkidu gripped Ilshu's likewise.

"Begin," the Shamhatu said.

At first Ilshu hardly seemed to be doing anything: light pushes and tugs, as though testing Enkidu's strength and balance, no more. Then he moved suddenly to the side, extending a leg behind Enkidu and crouching down as he thrust his hip out and twisted. Caught by surprise, Enkidu was barely able to wrench away before the other could knock him off his feet; it was only by chance that his hands held their grip.

The Shamhatu gasped, hand going to her mouth; Enkidu tossed back his head, roaring. Ilshu's body seemed no heavier than a rock-rabbit's in his hands as he heaved the other from his feet. Desperately Ilshu locked his legs about Enkidu's knees, striving to bring the bigger man down with him; Enkidu brought his right knee up sharply, breaking the hold even as the blow thudded hard into Ilshu's thigh. The dark-bearded wrestler cried out; Enkidu slammed him sharply to the ground. Slowly Ilshu's hold on Enkidu's belt loosened, his fingers uncurling and arms falling.

Enkidu could hear the soft murmurs from the crowd outside. "Did you see? . . . Ilshu down . . ." Then, even through his roar of triumph, he heard the more sobering words, "Is he dead?"

For a moment Enkidu stood unsteadily, the flush of red lust over the body of his fallen foe battling with the darker cold of shame—that shame he had felt first at Shamhatu's words when she said, "Harm done must always be repaid," and he knew that he had done wrong. *I have killed him*, he thought: *I have done ill within the shrine, and am not fit to serve the goddess, or live among men.* Though Enkidu wanted to flee, or at least curl up and hide his face from the folk who stood gathered outside, he forced himself to bend down over Ilshu's body, listening carefully.

The wrestler was still breathing, a soft hiss rasping through his lungs.

Hearing the sound, Enkidu felt the weight of the yoke fall from his shoulders. And yet Ilshu was not moving, or speaking: would he die soon?

"Aside, let me see to him," the Shamhatu ordered. Enkidu yielded his place to her, watching as she crouched down beside the fallen man, peeling back his eyelids to stare intently into his eyes, then prodding and poking along his body. Ilshu's hand twitched, then his foot. Enkidu heard him groan softly, and his eyes fluttered open.

The Shamhatu straightened up, brushing her hands off. "His head will recover in a day or two, though he must be careful to drink no beer until his pupils are the same size again," she said to the two young men who had come in with Ilshu. "Two of his ribs are broken as well—if you bring me cloth, I shall bind them properly for him. Then take him home and put him to bed; give him plenty of milk and cheese, which help bones in healing, and see that he rests well for a week or so."

"What of our flocks, Divine Lady?" the larger of the two men asked. "Even as he was the guardian of the shrine, so Ilshu is also the guardian of the sheep, for no one kept the night watches better than he, nor drove the lions and wolves more fiercely from our flocks."

Now Enkidu spoke before the Shamhatu could answer, the breath of relief driving his words. "I shall watch in Ilshu's place until he is well, to repay the harm I have done him: I meant only to beat him, not to break his bones. I shall take his place while it must be filled."

Groaning, Ilshu tried to raise himself up. Enkidu stretched out his hand; the wrestler took it, levering himself into a sitting position. "I thank you," Ilshu muttered. "You did not need to make that offer; I have hurt men worse before in holy wrestling, for that is the chance we all take when we offer our bodies to the goddess."

"Yet it seems right to me," Enkidu answered.

Ilshu's friends helped him up, supporting him from either side as he walked to the door of the shrine. Gunidu followed him, pausing a moment to look backward and smile before he closed the door, leaving Enkidu and the Shamhatu alone.

She looked up at Enkidu, opening her arms to him. "You are a lion become a shepherd, and a beast become a wise man," she said tenderly.

"Now come, my champion: lift the diadem from my head, the necklace from my throat; undo the girdle at my hips, and take the dress from my body, for I am yours, and you are Inanna's."

WHEN ENKIDU AND the Shamhatu had fed and rested, she took him out to the village men again. He passed the afternoon in learning to shoot the bow, cast and thrust with the spear, twirling the staff as men did to frighten away the smaller wild beasts. The Shamhatu kissed him farewell at sunset, and Gunidu pointed the way for him to where the flocks were grazing peacefully beneath the reddening sky and the herder who had watched through the day stood ready to be relieved—to come back to his hut, eat his bread and drink his beer and roll himself in his blanket or warm himself in the tender arms of his wife.

THE SHAMHATU WATCHED Enkidu go, the light of the setting sun glinting red as burnished copper from his long mane of golden curls, then turned back toward Gunidu's house. Although Innashagga would never have asked, the Shamhatu helped willingly with the meal, keeping the oven stoked and turning the flat rounds of bread on the curved top of the hot clay beehive while Akalla's wife went out to milk the nanny-goat. Akalla had made a fine catch of thrushes that morning: some he sold, but some he kept for his own family to roast, so that they ate well that evening, teeth crunching through the tiny bird-bones. If this was not the fare Shamhatu had been used to as chief priestess, it was better than that she had gotten as child or young worker in the temple, and she was well-content to stand beside Innashagga scouring the bowls when the meal was done. Afterward, they sat about together drinking the last of the Shamhatu's beer—she would have to send to the temple for more supplies if they were to stay here much longer, she thought. The Shamhatu sang and played the lyre; in between times, Gunidu told stories, until the eyes of Akalla and Innashagga began to droop, and at last they begged leave to curl up in their bed.

The Shamhatu and Gunidu sat quietly for a little time, until they heard Akalla's deep breathing and Innashagga's softer breaths settle into the rhythmic, quiet snores of early nighttime. But after a while the

Shamhatu said softly, "Gunidu, your name is still spoken with honor in the house of Inanna. If you would return to Erech with me, there would be more for you than a pair of goats and a hut in this desert land."

"I left for good reason, and stayed away for good reason. I have more than a pair of goats and a hut: I have my son, and more moons will bring me grandchildren."

"The life of a hunter is hard here, so far from the river. Down by the Buranun are wildfowl in flocks, fat and tender from the rich grasses; wild boars dwell in the swamplands, and fish fill the river. A skilled trapper is ever in need at Inanna's temple, for the goddess has many bowls to fill."

Gunidu turned his face away from her, the great beak of his profile shadowy against the dying embers. The Shamhatu could not see the look in his eyes. "Hard my son's life may be, but at least he has it."

"Tell me more."

The old shepherd sat silent.

The Shamhatu quietly wiped her damp palms on her woolen shift; as she brushed a strand of hair from her face, she realized that her hands were shaking. Yet she went on: as priestess, she had learned that what was hidden was often most worth knowing. "There are folk who remember," she murmured. "The old En still lives, and Rimsat-Ninsun, the city's Old Woman, was alive when you fled. They recognized your seal, and remembered you: I might yet learn something from them."

Still Gunidu said nothing, his wrinkled eyelid rolling slowly across the dark gleam of his eye like a turtle blinking. The Shamhatu might almost have thought him asleep, save that even in the dimness, she could see the cords of muscle tight beneath his sun-withered skin. At last he shuddered, relaxing as though a sleeping draught were seeping through his body, and spoke.

"The sheep were dying," he said, his voice falling into the half chant of the temple storytellers. "It was during the days of ploughing after the Buranun's flooding when there was a great sickness among the sheep, that fell worse upon the ewes and lambs, and we were sore afraid. Neither the flocks of the temple, nor the flocks of the Ensi, nor the flocks of the poor, were spared: Erech the Sheepfold had become Erech, Graveyard of Sheep. And because the blessing of the goddess had left us, we prayed and burned precious oils; we offered oil and incense, honey and good butter. And at last we sacrificed one of the few sheep that yet stayed healthy—a strong ram, with glossy fleece and a good temper, ever a favorite of mine: I wept to see him die. Yet his death brought us an answer: though Lugalbanda had gone to Inanna's bed at the New Year only a little time before, the goddess wished to take a husband again. And because I was the chief shepherd of her temple—I stood in his place, in fear and pride and hope, for if my flocks were not saved, Lugalbanda's flocks would follow them down to Erishkegal's dusty lands."

Gunidu sighed, sucking the last of the beer noisily out of the bottom of his jug. "So she came to me, Inanna, star-crowned and glorious, the Queen of Heaven. She brought me her blessings; I emptied my seed into her, and she filled me again with her power. And in the morning I walked among the ewes that lay on their sides, and the lambs with yellow phlegm bubbling from their nostrils. I laid my hands upon them, and slowly they began to mend, and no more sickened. But she who was the Shamhatu in those days . . . she began to cast up her food in the mornings, and her waist thickened until her girdle of birthstones must be worn high between breasts and belly. Whether she forgot to take the brew, or it was not made strong enough, or whether the power of the goddess was so great as to overcome it, no one knows: but it was clear that she was carrying a child, and clear to me that it was my own. Though the child of the goddess has no mother, he may yet take his father's inheritance, just as Gilgamesh has become Ensi and Lugal after Lugalbanda, and I rejoiced that a son of mine would herd Inanna's sheep, or a daughter of mine walk through her temple in fine linen."

"But it did not happen so," the Shamhatu murmured softly.

"It did not happen so. The child was born on a night of high winds, when the palm trees lashed the sky like an overseer flogging a slave to death, and the voices of the *lilitu* and the lost souls of the *gidims* and all the demons of the air cried about the rooftops. In the temple of Rimsat-Ninsun the child was born, for the Shamhatu had not carried it easily those last days. I was not allowed within, but I sat by the back door, that haunted night, holding my cloak about me lest the wind tear it away, and waited with the cold and fear in my bones.

"It was near dawn," he went on, "when the door opened. I leapt in terror, for I had almost fallen asleep. But behind the door was old Bau—does she still live? She had a wrapped bundle in her arms. 'Do not cry out,' she warned me. 'They have told me to destroy the child, and that he bears the curse that was on the sheep. But I have seen curses, and I have seen worse births, and I tell you that this babe is clean.'

"I pulled aside a fold of the cloth, and though she had told me not to cry out, I gasped all the same. The babe was covered with dark hair like an ape, nose and chin pushing forth as a muzzle and forehead sloping straight back. It was wrinkled and ugly, more so than newborns are wont to be, and for a moment I was sure that it would be right for old Bau to destroy it. But she shook her head again. 'I have seen babes covered with hair before: it will fall out after some days. The face is squashed, for the Shamhatu's passage is narrower than most, but that, too, will right itself in time. I give you your son, Gunidu, and your choice: take him down to the Buranun's shore and set him among the reeds for crocodile and river-horse to eat, or bear him far from here, to a place where no one knows your name.'

"And so I made my choice. I took what I had, and stole from the city. A trader's caravan brought me to this village, where no one knew my name and the folk seldom remembered to change the reeds on the floor of Inanna's shrine; and here I stopped, and here I have stayed."

Gunidu paused again, tilting his empty beer-jar as though he hoped to see a last drop of drink within it, then setting it down with the care of an old man who had drunk more than his wont. "Yet my son's birth was a ill-omen . . . for the Shamhatu. That beautiful and kind woman, Lugalbanda came to her bed for the marriage again at the next New Year. And again the brew did not stop her from bearing—but Lugal-banda was a greater man than I, a giant in size and thew; and the passage that nearly crushed Akalla, Gilgamesh burst asunder." The Shamhatu reached out to lay her hand on the old man's shoulder. The muscle beneath her palm jumped like the flank of a startled donkey, then eased again. "Bau gave you good advice," she said softly. "Truly none can fathom the ways of the gods: for without Akalla's sight, we should not have found Enkidu, and it is in my mind that he is a tool with which the

Powers of Heaven will accomplish much." Both of them, she thought—for already a thought was blossoming darkly in her mind: if a substitute, also the son of Inanna, were given in Gilgamesh's place, might he not stave off the dark prophecy of Gilgamesh's ascension, and buy the king's life with his own?

"Truly it is so," Gunidu agreed. He stood, hitching up his kilt and walking stiffly toward the door. "It is late, and my body weakens as I grow older. I will not come back to Erech with you yet . . . but I shall think on it."

The Shamhatu followed him out, for she, too, had drunk more than a little beer. Lying in her bed a few moments later, she tried to think more on the story Gunidu had told her, but instead her thoughts turned to Enkidu . . . wrapped in wool, with a man's weapons in his hands, out guarding the sheep from those who had been his kinsmen . . .

ENKIDU SAT ALONE under the far hard gleams of the stars, with a flap of the wool cloak raised over his head, watching hard through the cold moonlight for the slinking gray shadows and listening for the bleats of a sheep trapped by wolves, or the bubbling death-breaths of prey with its throat crushed by a lion's jaws. Though now and again his head nodded into a lion's nap, he was always able to jerk himself awake again, remembering that he was a man. Then the tears came to his eyes, cold in the moonlight—and he did not know whether he wept for pacing the hills, or whether it was the warm huts of the village, where each curled against their most beloved, that stung his lids with salt. Yet the night air tasted clean in his lungs, with no dusting of burning dung; and yet it was good to hold the smooth wood of spear and bow-shaft, knowing that with it he bore the weight of human trust, warm as the cloak that wrapped his shoulders.

That night, Enkidu heard nothing and saw nothing, save the moon's light white on the backs of the sheep and the shadows of the rocks black as water. He came back in the morning's ruddy brightness to give the watch to the next man before tumbling into his bed, sleepy as he had never been.

When Ilshu was well enough to come out among the sheep again, still

Enkidu kept the night's watch. None could drive off the wolves and frighten the hyenas as easily as he; and he had closed with several lions—two had run, one graced the bottom of Shamhatu's tent, and the fourth now served Enkidu as a cloak better than any the sheep could weave. For that, the shepherds asked if he would stay, and when he said that he would, they lifted him upon the shoulders of four men and poured beer into his mouth until he snored on his bench. Shamhatu waited patiently in the village: it was she who had first counseled him to stay if he might, to grow accustomed to the simple things of the village folk before they came to Erech. She helped to grind the grain and bake the bread with the other women, and spent much time at cutting and stitching, for her hands were finer than theirs and her fingers more skilled.

So it was that when the winter's watch was over, and their wain had rumbled over the desert until the walls of Erech the Sheepfold stood high above the plain, it was a garment made by the Shamhatu's own hands that Enkidu wore: a kilt cut from her own best linens, not simply fringed to drain off water in a rainstorm and distract the Evil Eye as were the kilts of the village men, but made with frond upon frond, upon frond, waving from waist to floor like the overlapping leaves of a palm tree whose roots reached into a well. Shamhatu tied it upon him with careful hands, straightening the dry-skin head of the lion that arched over Enkidu's own to protect him from the sun and fluffing the golden curls of his own mane to mingle them into the golden mane of the great cat. The air was moist, here by the river: if Shamhatu had not told him so long of the great Buranun and its twin the Idiglat, he should already have run off to drink his belly-full, lest the abundance sink into the earth again before he could reach it. The ground burst with such soft green grasses that Enkidu yearned to leap down and tear at them, as he had done among the gazelles, but when he gazed at them with his mouth open, Shamhatu popped a sweet date into it.

"Now you must hold firm, my hero, and remember that you are a man," she murmured to him as he chewed. "There will be a great crush of people within, for they gather in the streets for the New Year. They will reach up to you, tug at the lowest fronds of your kilt and pull at the tail that drapes down behind you, for each brush of their fingers against your linen is precious. Do not fear, and do not strike out at any."

"I shall not," Enkidu promised, staring up at the high sheer cliffs of mud-brick. "Shamhatu, is that truly made of the same earth as bowls and houses? How can it hold under its own weight? Is it burned like bowls?"

"Because it is strong," Shamhatu answered. "If you truly wish to know more, when the New Year's feast is over, I shall ask one of the temple masons to speak with you."

Two men with spears stood at either side of the great gate; but when Shamhatu raised her crowned head above the rim of the wagon, they leapt aside, calling, "Great is the Queen of Heaven, Inanna of the Sheep-fold!"

Others on the street caught the cry, raising it up until it seemed to Enkidu that his skull was caught within the singing wood of Shamhatu's lyre, ringing and echoing from back to front. His head was dizzy with the scent of so many people, of date-honey and beer and garlic and sesame oil and the new-bloomed flowers they tossed into the air to shower over the wain and crush aromatically beneath the asses' feet. As Shamhatu had told him, he stood at the front of the wagon, and did not flinch at the hands that brushed along the lower fronds of his kilt, that stroked at his calves and tugged at the dark gold tuft of the tail hanging behind him.

Then one young man, in a linen kilt as many-fronded as Enkidu's own, but dyed the gold of ripe grain, leaped up upon the wain, and Shamhatu tugged at the reins, bringing the donkeys to a sharp stop. It seemed to Enkidu that his eyes cleared as he saw her dark gaze settle upon the youth's light figure, and yet the boy did not smell like a man grown. So Enkidu growled, "Shamhatu, who is this man? Why has he come here? Speak his name."

The young man turned, bowing to Enkidu so that his head almost brushed the tops of his feet. When he spoke, his voice rang high above the murmurs of the crowd, a clear note like the ringing of bronze on bronze. "They have called me to a wedding, as is the custom of the land. For the choice of brides, I have heaped up tasty delights for the marriage on the holy platter. For the Ensi of Wide-Marketed Erech, the veil of the folk is open to choice; for Gilgamesh, Ensi of Wide-Marketed Erech, the veil of the folk is open for choosing. He will mate with the destined wife, and let husband follow after. This is ordered by the counsel of An; from the cutting of the Ensi's umbilical cord, it has been destined for him."

"You spoke of Gilgamesh to me before," Enkidu said to Shamhatu, and he felt the blood rising into his face. "I shall go to meet him."

Shamhatu smiled, waiting for Enkidu to jump down from the wain and then stretching out her hand. Enkidu did not know what she was waiting for until the young man in the fine kilt gestured broadly; then, though he had seen her climb down with ease before, he reached up to steady her with his arm. A gasping murmur went through the crowd as they backed away to give the couple space.

"A little shorter than Gilgamesh . . . but broader-boned; he is a man holding power . . . sucked the milk of wild cattle, surely . . . a clashing of weapons in Erech, I see it with no doubt."

Enkidu paid it no mind, the mutterings of these little people: it seemed to him like the whispering of reeds, for Shamhatu stood there beside him, and took his arm and pressed her hip against his thigh, gazing up at him. Even when they fell down before him, when the crowd pressed close enough that they must stop and the soft wet touch of lips kissed his sandaled feet, it was little to him: he had his queen, and he would defend her against any.

GILGAMESH SAT BY himself in his house, waiting with little patience as the last embers of the sunset burned out. He had gone to the temple baths to be purified before the break of day, and stepped through incense-strewn fires until his kilt was golden with smoke, reeking sweet with the scents of frankincense and myrrh and sweet flag root; then been mewed up alone here at dawn, with only Enatarzi—no man and no woman therefore fit to attend him—to see to his needs. This one night, though everyone in Erech the Sheepfold rejoiced, husbands lying with their wives and bachelors with their lovers or tavern women and lesser priestesses, Gilgamesh alone would share his bed with none but the smooth linen sheets—for he was the Bridegroom, the Young Man of Erech, as his father had been before him.

And yet he suffered this at Shamhatu's will, and that was hard to bear, that this was her price for the needs of his war. Like Dumuzi, the gazelle bound in the sheepfold; like Lugalbanda, lost to madness in the wilderness: though it was the Young Man of Erech who spoke the laws and led the troops, it was Erech's Maid who made him pay her for his power. Gilgamesh thought of the prophecy of his ascension—his death at the will of the gods—and gritted his teeth, reaching for the gold straw that hung crooked from the lip of his beer-jar. It seemed to him that he could feel the noose tightening about him, like the cords of a fowler's snare; and it seemed hard, that he might ease his mind to no one—not even the old En, though the holy man might have had words for this night.

*And yet I sucked in this knowledge with my mother's milk,* Gilgamesh thought: *what need of other counsel have I? Gilgamesh, two-thirds god and one-third man . . .*

The thought did not comfort him. Though the beer was smooth and old, sweet with the honey of dates behind its rich malt, it did not wash the bitter rime from the back of his throat as he heard the swelling harmonies of the *tigi*-hymns, voices and lutes, ringing out from the shrine above his dwelling. Shamhatu stood up there, hailed as Inanna and no doubt drinking in every moment, while whatever stout peasant lad or trained temple wrestler she had chosen to stand against him was stretching and writhing and oiling his muscles for the morning—Enatarzi had told him that she had come back safely with a champion, but nothing more, and his hopes of the wild man had long since faded in these months with no word from the desert.

"And yet," Gilgamesh said to himself, "and yet . . ." He took another draught of beer, to wash the mud from the chiseled rock taking form in his mind. Though the Young Man of Erech was betrothed to the Young Maid, he thought slowly, yet Gilgamesh the Ensi held and used that right, to try every maid on her bridal eve . . .

"This I will do," Gilgamesh murmured. "To hold my place before the priestess' pride . . . his I shall do. I am no gazelle, to be driven to the sheepfold; no lion, to be lured into the pit, nor songbird to limp with a broken wing."

He settled back, the warmth of determination whelming the warmth of beer about his heart. He needed only to sit and wait . . . a little time, until he heard the clattering of sandals descending the stairs of the temple platform like the clapping wings of a dove-flock taking flight . . . a little time after that, until the women had time to sponge the sweat of ritual from Shamhatu's sides, anoint her, and sing the first hymns of the bridal bed to her . . . and then he could go.

So he waited, until the dull echo of the last footsteps on clay had died down and no more pale yellow oil-flames gleamed through the windows of the holy city, save for the one faint glow in the En's window. One of the old priest's slim slick-furred cats sat there, black against the light; then it leapt down, after a mouse or bug. Gilgamesh ducked his head as he crept beneath the window, moved up the stairs as silently as if he were treading through the damp river-reeds after a wounded boar. He walked carefully across the square platform before the shrine—the temple's marketplace, now empty and still beneath the black sky, where during the daytime the vendors of sheep and doves, oil and incense and milk, jostled to sell their wares to those who came to make sacrifice to Inanna.

The door swung open as Gilgamesh came near; a deep bass, rough with the accents of the countryside, rumbled, "You may not come here: this is the wedding bed of Inanna, where she waits for her groom." The shadow that stood against the dim flickering light of the single lamp at the end of the shrine was huge and squat, swollen in the darkness to a shadow near Gilgamesh's own size.

And there was something in the voice that angered Gilgamesh, so that he answered, "Who says that I may not? I am the Ensi Gilgamesh, and maid or matron, the woman who waits for her bridegroom must come to me first, for none can stand against me in my wrath!"

"Think you so?" the shadow murmured. "Then you shall learn differently, for I am the champion of Inanna, the guardian of her bedchamber; and it is against you that she called me to defend her, shepherd who eats his own flocks."

Gilgamesh let loose a roar of anger and reached for his sword. But before the scabbard was a huge hairy hand, and another grasping at the other side of his belt. As he had learned since a youth, without thought, he reached for the belt of the other; and Shamhatu's voice, cool from the darkness, said, "Begin."

Gilgamesh heaved—and it seemed to him that he was heaving at a rock too great to lift; and he gasped as the great hands pulled his belt up sharply beneath his ribs, striving to lift him with brute strength in turn, as no one ever had. Caught by surprise, he felt his left foot leave the floor, and he knew he was done . . . but in that moment, he felt the faintest flicker of hesitation, and launched himself forward with all the strength of his right leg, catching the other hard with his shoulder. He heard the surprised grunt and tightened his grasp, crouching as he had learned to do when he was younger and faced men no smaller than himself.

The shadow before him shoved in turn, the bull-rush driving him back into the door; Gilgamesh felt the mud-bricks crumbling beneath his back as the wall trembled, the door-posts giving under the blow. His foe was roaring like a lion; Gilgamesh bellowed in return, bracing himself and heaving. As the first shock faded, he moved more smoothly, testing the other's strength and balance with sudden, careful lunges, then moving into a tight embrace, the thick curls of his foe's chest-hair scraping rough across his own shaven skin and the other's strong musk in his nostrils. Only a flicker of shadows warned him as the other man butted up with his forehead, driving it in a blow that would have shattered Gilgamesh's nose and mouth had the Ensi not jerked aside and ducked, wrenching his enemy's body aside in the same movement. A villager's trick, which Gilgamesh would not have known save for his captain of the guard . . . and yet in that moment, he knew how to fight. Falling back and loosening his hands as much as he could without risking the loss of his grip, Gilgamesh let a soft grunt rise from his guts, breathing hard as though he had spent all his strength.

The hairy man rushed forward, as Gilgamesh had thought he would, holding back none of his force. His hands still tight on the other's belt, Gilgamesh sidestepped and went down on one knee, tucking his head in lest a flying limb strike his face.

The big man somersaulted over the Ensi's outstretched knee, his hold on Gilgamesh's belt breaking as he landed hard on the ground. He lay

there, breathing softly as though stunned, and all the anger leaked from
Gilgamesh like water flowing from a broken jar.

Slowly Gilgamesh's foe raised himself on one elbow. The lamplight
flickered nearer, and in its pure glow Gilgamesh saw his eyes, green-
brown as the rich river-land sprouting after a flood, and the golden curls
of his long hair and beard flowing into the oil-gleaming pelt that covered
his muscular body. The Ensi caught his breath, staring as the stranger
licked his bloodied lips and murmured painfully, "Ninsun, the wild cow
of the cattlefields, your mother—she bore you a man without match.
Your head is raised above other men's; Enlil Storm-God has granted you
kingship over the people."

Gilgamesh felt the hot tears coming to his eyes, and he reached to
stroke the other's shoulder. "Who are you? From where did you come?"

"I am Enkidu, born in the wilderness. The priestess, the Shamhatu,
found me and made me a man; she brought me to Erech to guard her, but
I have failed before your strength, for it is as she told me it would be."

"Enkidu," Gilgamesh breathed. "You have no match, you are mighty
as the shooting star of An. I dreamed about you, with none to cut your
shaggy hair, born in the wilderness, with none to stand against you." He
laid his hand upon Enkidu's shoulder, the warm hide with its soft curls
of hair like the pelt of a noble hunting dog, and felt the shaking of the
other man's body. For a moment they sat so; then Enkidu surged forward, grasping Gilgamesh hard about the chest so that they lay beating
heart to beating heart. Gilgamesh embraced the other in turn, rejoicing
in the strength he felt, the strong hard muscles and the clean smell of
sweat, Enkidu's body against his own.

"Let us be friends," he said. "There are none as mighty as we in the
land, and none to match us save each other."

He would have spoken more, but Enkidu pressed his mouth against
his own, his lips soft as the stroking of a duck's wingfeather beneath the
hairs of his beard. Gilgamesh felt the blood pounding in his head, his
groin swelling hard beneath his kilt to press against Enkidu's thighs.

"Be friends, indeed," Shamhatu's voice murmured softly. Both of
them looked up, startled at the light as children caught stealing dates
from their mother's hoard in the darkness. But Shamhatu only smiled

beneath her gold-sparkling crown, setting her lamp on the floor and reaching a hand to each of them. Though her strength alone could hardly have lifted Gilgamesh's arm, it seemed to him that his body rose like featherdown in her grasp, and he and Enkidu followed her willingly.

Behind the wall, the bridal chamber was lit with a dazzling dance of oil-lamps, their flames leaping in the wind of the three who passed there. Oil and wine and bread stood on the table of inlaid ebony beside the bed; the sheets were turned back, and flower-petals strewn upon them.

"Gilgamesh, though you came for a bride, you found a friend," Shamhatu said. "Enkidu, though you defended a queen, you won a friend. Embrace and be joyful, for Inanna smiles upon you, and your gladness this night shall bring Erech the Sheepfold life."

One by one Shamhatu blew out the lamps, her measured tread about the room echoing Gilgamesh's heartbeat, and the heartbeat of Enkidu beneath it. Gilgamesh nuzzled into Enkidu's beard like a lamb into its mother's wool, seeking the sweetness beneath the warm curls, then kissed his lips hungrily until Enkidu's breath came soft and quick against his cheek and he felt the clasp of Enkidu's arms tighten strong about him.

THE SHAMHATU LEFT Gilgamesh and Enkidu embracing, walking alone down the steps from the shrine. The exaltation that had filled her as she watched them wrestling was already sinking from her heart, leaving her empty and drained.

"For Gilgamesh, a friend and companion," she murmured. "But for me?" Back among the familiar sights and scents, the night noisy with the songs and laughter rising from the streets outside the Eanna, it seemed to her that she was more alone than ever, and her body ached with unslaked desire. Before Enkidu, she had never spent the night with a man, nor known the same man more than once; she had never been able to eat with a lover, nor sit and sing to him as the fire burned low. And she knew—bitter as wormwood, harsh and deeply painful as the swelling of a scorpion's sting—that unless the gods gave her another miracle, she would never do so again, for only Gilgamesh could be the lover of Inanna's chosen. It had not surprised her when she saw Gilgamesh and Enkidu turning to each other, for, from the moment their

hands met each other's belts, she had felt them cleaving together like two
pieces of glowing metal as the solder suddenly liquefied to flow bright
between them. But what brought the tears to her eyes was the realization
that, whether Enkidu desired her or not, she could never come to him
again. For she was the Shamhatu, forbidden love of her own, and as her
duty had brought her to Enkidu, so it must, inexorably, bar her from
him. And it was unfair, most cruel and unfair, that, while she had undergone the long journey through the wilderness and the waiting in the
desert, it was Gilgamesh who gained—she felt like a slave who, having
tended a grove of palm trees in thirst and filth through the summer's
heat, and climbed, battered and torn, to pick the fruit, must then deliver
them untasted to a careless master.

Wrapped thus in her thoughts, the Shamhatu did not notice where
she went until she collided with another walker. Soft flesh beneath a
half-askew linen dress, a breath of expensive perfumes; stepping back
quickly to keep her balance, the Shamhatu saw that she had run into
Shubad. Lit by the bright moon, the singer's large dark eyes were wide
open, and the Shamhatu could see her swiftly smoothing the look of
anger from her face as she realized whom she was about to berate.

"How is it with Gilgamesh?" Shubad asked. Even speaking softly, her
high soprano voice was beautifully mellow, pure as the glinting of sunlight off gold. "You are come swiftly from the shrine."

"Gilgamesh—" The Shamhatu coughed the crackling of tears from
her voice, started again. "Gilgamesh is still within. The gods have given
us a miracle, though not the one we looked for."

"Did he refuse you again, and within the shrine?"

The Shamhatu looked closely at the other woman's face. Though the
dark paint lining Shubad's eyes was smudged, the faint blush of passion
fading from her cheeks, the *gala*-priestess nevertheless contrived to look
innocent, as if she had only now come from her bath of purification.

"He did not come to refuse me."

"But still he did—O Shamhatu, it is well-known that he has kept
away from you, and this is a sorrow throughout Erech."

"What is that to you?" the Shamhatu asked roughly. "You sing the
part of Inanna, who is never refused by Dumuzi, and you are envied by

all the women who sing in the temple, as well as many of the eunuchs. Why should you concern yourself with other things?"

"I sing the part of Inanna," Shubad answered. "And therefore a thought has come to me. A bull that will not service one cow may well mount another; if Gilgamesh will not husband the goddess through one priestess, why not another? He is," and she smiled lazily, as if remembering a moment of pleasure, "not the most difficult of men to bring to bed."

The sharp blow of the Shamhatu's palm across her cheek snapped the *gala*-priestess' head to the side. Shubad stumbled back, her hand going up to cover the red mark on her face and the tears standing out bright in her eyes.

"You dare—" the singer hissed, abruptly biting her words back as she remembered once more to whom she was speaking. "I only meant to offer help, for both your sake and Erech's."

"Your help is not needed," the Shamhatu replied, the words cold pebbles in her mouth. "Go back to your lover, if you can remember who he is, and leave those things which are not for you alone."

"I am not the only one to think this, nor the first. Think you on it, for it may well be the worse for you if you do not."

Shubad turned and stalked away before the Shamhatu could reply to her. The priestess stared after the other woman until her shape had misted into the shadow of the *gipar*. The hot anger had felt good in her chest, drowning her pain for a moment, but it was chilling now, letting the sorrow flood back. If Shubad spoke from more than thwarted pride and hurt—was it all to be counted worthless, her striving to live up to the demands of her office? Nothing, that she brought the gift of Inanna to old men and ugly, or fair young men who could never give love to the woman, only the goddess? Nothing, that she must surrender Enkidu, though she knew now what she had not known before—what it was to love and be beloved, what it was to be treasured and cherished by one man for herself?

The Shamhatu looked up at the dark door of the shrine. Within, Gilgamesh and Enkidu would still be embracing. If she went up there now, stripped away her dress and crept naked and warm between them, what would happen? Would the marriage be consummated at last, with the arms of her dear lion about her as well?

But though her thighs tightened and her breath grew quicker at the thought, the Shamhatu knew that she could not do that. She had left the wedding chamber, and, though her mind squirmed and struggled for justification, her duty toward Enkidu was done. It remained only for her to hope and pray that her sacrifice was to some purpose, that the lion-man would do what neither she nor the En nor any other could, and ready Gilgamesh to come at last to Inanna's bed.

# 4

Innashagga stood by the well in the cool of the lowering evening, beneath the dusky shade of a palm tree, waiting her turn to dip down her jug and draw out her family's water. The feasting of the New Year had finished yesterday: now Akalla hunted again, the men pulled the plough through the dusty fields or tended their flocks, and their wives baked ordinary bread with no chopped dates or honey mixed into the flat rounds of dough. Innashagga wondered idly how things had gone in Erech—what had happened when the Shamhatu led Enkidu through the city gates like a tame lion on a lead, what sort of marvels had befallen when the Ensi Gilgamesh was brought to the bed of Inanna? With ploughing season upon them, it might be some time before their village heard news from the city.

An elbow jostled Innashagga rudely as she stepped forward to the well. "Hold back, there," Ninbanda said, her soft voice taking on the sharpness of souring milk. Surprised, Innashagga turned to look at her friend. The other woman's sun-browned face was set and hard; she passed her free hand quickly over her hair, as though to sweep back the frizzy tendrils escaping from the braid coiled about her skull.

"What is wrong?" Innashagga asked.

"The Shamhatu is no longer in your house, so you have no need to put yourself forward at the well anymore. She and her daily bath have gone back to Erech, and you have no feast-food to cook for her and her wild man."

The other women had stopped in their water-drawing, turning to look at Ninbanda and Innashagga. Though the afternoon's warmth still lingered, Innashagga felt the sweat springing cold on her forehead and back, a chill that neither the last reddening sunlight nor her tufted woolen shawl could ease.

"It was only good luck that brought her blessing to my house rather than any other, and have not all felt that blessing? Do not our lambs stand and suck in good health, with fewer sheep lost to sickness or wolf and lion this year than any other in memory, and does not the well's water flow more strongly?"

"Thanks be to Inanna," Ninbanda answered swiftly. "And none would deny the Shamhatu her rights: it was an honor to us all to serve her. But you are not she, and have no right to force yourself by us when you wish to get water for yourself."

"The rest of us are thirsty as well," Shubad added. The old woman glared piercingly down at Innashagga from beneath the wrinkled folds of her drooping eyelids. "Wait your turn and let others go first. Then you will get that which is fit for you, now that you no longer have the Shamhatu to serve—for all you had a string of gold and lapis beads hanging from your neck at the New Year's feast."

"But for Gunidu's sake—" Innashagga protested weakly.

"We do not speak of him." Shubad snapped her toothless lips tightly together. "Only of you."

The other women moved together, quietly closing ranks against her. Innashagga wanted to weep: she did not know what she had done, to deserve this from women who had sat spinning beside her in the evening's shade, who had made every excuse they could to step over her threshold and gawk at the Shamhatu's golden adornments and the fair, massive figure of Enkidu, often while nibbling at the cakes she had made from the fine emmet meal and date-honey or sipping at the aged beer the priestess had brought with her from Erech. She would have gone home straight away, but the harsh words from women who had been her friends, and the row of backs turned against her like a hedge of thorns, would not keep Akalla and Gunidu from needing water. And so

Innashagga waited, silent and unmoving, until the last of the other women had filled her jugs and drifted away.

The water was a little muddy, but not so bad as it often was for the last woman to the well: truly, as Innashagga had said herself, Inanna had blessed their village for their care of the Shamhatu. As she hefted the heavy clay vessel onto her shoulder, she thought it would be ungrateful of her to think that she had not been blessed as well, for had it not truly been a delight to have that radiant woman beneath her roof, eating beside her hearth and playing on the glittering lyre? And she and Akalla had made love to the accompaniment of the soft grunting of the Shamhatu and her lion-man; she had felt the blessings spilling warm into her womb like rain on the thirsty dust, and known, with all her heart, that if she were not barren, that this time she must have gotten a child—a child that might even now be growing in her womb, though it would be two weeks yet before she knew for certain. That time had been like touching a dream, like guesting for a little while in the sun-gleaming cedar forests of Dilmun, the Land of the Living. Even now, in the night, she would take the little string of gold and lapis beads the Shamhatu had given her from its hiding place between the wooden frame of her bed and the fleeces that softened it and run her fingers over the necklace, treasuring the cool bright smoothness beneath her touch as proof that those days had been real, that something fair and wonderful had passed through her house, leaving the jeweled strand behind as a bird might drop a feather in flight.

"And therefore," Innashagga said to herself, sick at heart, "are they envious of me. And I will have to drink muddy water like a wild mare, and crawl like a serpent to eat dust before them, until they feel me to be fully humbled again."

It seemed to her then that the jug of water had grown too heavy for her to bear. She set it down, turning her gaze past the palm-thatched huts toward the low black range of hills against the red western horizon. The house-swallows were already flittering out, swooping and diving through the cooling air; far away, Innashagga heard the *ri-di-ik ri-di-ik* cry of a shepherd-bird.

"My god," she whispered, "Enlil, Father, who begot mankind, I lift up my face like an innocent ewe . . . in pity, hear my groan. Inanna of the Sheepfold, would you neglect me, leave me unprotected, like a sheep with no shepherd—would you leave me unguided? Tears, lament, anguish and sorrow are lodged within me, suffering overwhelms me like one who does naught but weep . . ."

Innashagga's throat closed off then, and she stood silent. A burst of soft laughter came from inside one hut, the high giggles of children rising above the deeper mirth of man and woman. That was the house of Ilshu, who had taken up his duties as the guardian of the village shrine again, now that Enkidu was gone; for a bitter moment she wondered if he was laughing because his wife had told him of the scene at the well. At another time, Innashagga might have knocked on their door-pins to see if she could borrow or trade for a small jug of beer, but now she could not bring herself to lift her hand. Heaving her water-jar to her shoulder, she made her way home.

Akalla was already in from his hunting; the fresh skins of three rock-rabbits were hanging beside the door to dry. He would have cast the offal far away from the house, as was his usual custom, lest it bring vultures or wild dogs to their doorstep. But seeing the hides eased Innashagga's burden a little, for she knew now that all she would have to do for dinner was chop a few onions and her last turnip in with the fresh meat, then set the stew to cooking while she milked the goat; and a stew with three rabbits would feed them for a long time, or she could trade one for—

*Muddy water and a kick in the teeth,* she thought, and at that Innashagga could feel her face crumpling, the tears streaming hot down her cheeks as a deep racking sob broke forth from her throat. Carefully she set the water-jug down lest she break it, for a good clay jar of that size did not come cheap, and then she let herself cry in earnest. The village that bore her, that was her warm fold where she had always thought to find shelter for herself and someday her lambs—*may it please Inanna;* she crossed her hands instinctively over her womb—had cast her out into the cold wind now. She was a stranger in the place of her birth, worse off than a paint-eyed wanderer come across the desert from the Black Land or a black-skinned man traveling from Meluhha, who, though far away from home, would be greeted with wonder and curiosity . . .

Blinded by her weeping, Innashagga did not see the man who came up to her until his strong arms wrapped about her shoulders, holding her to himself. "My little one, my turtledove," Akalla's deep thick voice murmured, "why do you cry, when I have had good hunting?"

Innashagga only turned her head to the side, weeping against the warmth of his bare chest as he stroked her coiled hair until her sobs dried and hiccupped to a stop. "What has happened to you?" Akalla asked again. He lifted up her water-jug easily, carrying it inside for her. "Has someone done you wrong?"

"The women at the well . . . oh, I know not how—"

"But I can guess," Gunidu interrupted softly. The old man squatted by the hearth, his copper knife flashing now and again as he jointed the last rock-rabbit; the pale pieces of the other two already lay heaped in Innashagga's good cooking bowl, on a bed of finely chopped onions. "A slave who becomes an overseer may fare well or ill; but if he is set again to weeding lettuces with his fellows, no good can come to him. Is that not so?"

Innashagga only nodded, not trusting her own tongue.

"Believe me," Gunidu said, his low voice gentle, "I know well what things can come to pass when one is lifted up for a while, whether by ambition or chance: it came to pass often in the temple of Inanna. He is lucky who has a comrade in adversity, but thrice lucky who has one that will stay a friend through both ill fortune and good. The women spoke unkindly to you at the well, and our stew will be mixed with a little mud—because the Shamhatu gave us fine emmet-meal to bake cakes with, and you wore such beads to the New Year's rites as an artisan's wife in Erech might wear, am I not right?"

Innashagga nodded again.

"Even I have felt the cold breeze," Gunidu said musingly. "It was well enough for me to be the man from the city here, because I came quietly and asked little; it was well enough for me to lead the rites, and a pride to the village—and had the Shamhatu stayed but two nights, it would have been a joy to all. But when bearing water for her bath each day turned from a new blessing to an old burden, when the women saw how neatly and swiftly hands not roughened from their work could sew, and marked how easily her shawl of fine white wool fell over her straight shoulders, when their own brown garments hang crooked on shoulders uneven from long quern-grinding . . . they could not speak against her, but all they felt then is now your fault, for she is so far above them that there is nothing they could say, but you ate cakes of dust-fine meal and date-honey as you sat every night listening to her songs, and now you are eating bread of rough-cracked barley and drinking goat's milk and well-water again. Am I not right?"

"You are wise, Father," Innashagga said, her voice shaking. "But tell me—how is this the will of the gods, that a blessing turn to a curse?"

Gunidu set down his knife, laying the half-dismembered rock-rabbit to the side. "The sages say—a word righteous and straightforward—that never has a faultless child been born to its mother, nor a workman without sin lived in any age. In the sight of the gods, we are little worthy. We are all doomed to death, we creatures that Nammu shaped from the clay beyond the abyss; though the goddess Ninhursag worked above, and the mighty ones aided in our fashioning, that we not shame them, yet clay must fall back to clay in the end, and we shall never match their splendor nor their wisdom, for it is not ordained for us that we do so. Yet I am not sure that the blessing the Shamhatu brought to our family has indeed turned to a curse—has it done so, my dear daughter?"

"I . . . I think so," Innashagga answered. Now, Gunidu's dark eyes seemed to glow like coals: she could not turn her gaze from them, and it seemed to her that she could almost see a bluish halo of fire crackling around him in the shadow of the hut as he lifted an empty hand toward her.

"Oh, but I think not," he said, and the power in his voice washed the cracking of his age away like clean water washing the dust from fresh dates. "For I will tell you now, I have been thinking on this since before the Shamhatu withdrew from us. For many years I feared to go back to

Erech—you have no need to know why—but now it is both safe and well for us. For I will have a pension from the temple of Inanna, and a small house on temple lands; you need not turn the quern until you hold one arm lower than the other, and our family will be full of gladness within Erech the Sheepfold. And a small house there," Gunidu added, "is better than the best of homes here: we will have several rooms, and a little courtyard, perhaps with a fish-pool and a few palm trees of our own."

Innashagga's heart clenched painfully within her ribs as she listened to him. *But to leave all I have known, and never stand at the well with my friends again* . . . she thought, and then the remembrance of that day flooded in upon her again, and she was hard put to choke back her sobs.

"But . . . Father, you are, you are . . . Father, you are wise," Akalla stammered. "Father, I . . . I . . . I am a huntsman, a trapper of beasts. What . . . what . . . Father, no animals in city!"

Gunidu reached out, spidery fingers gently stroking his son's thick wrist. "My son, I was a shepherd—but I was the chief shepherd, and I sat with the priests when they spoke of wages and numbers of temple-workers. The trappers and huntsmen of the temple always got their share, be sure; and one of your skill has no doubt of a place and good pay. Down by the Buranun are ducks and geese and wild boar; lions and wolves threaten the flocks of Erech as surely as they threaten those of our village, and the priests are as glad as any to eat a good roast of gazelle, I can promise you that."

"A house with rooms in it, and a fish-pool of our own," Innashagga mused. *A place where I could wear the necklace the Shamhatu gave me in the streets every day, and no one to look ill at it* . . . And she thought, too, of the endless round of the quernstones, and the shooting pains in the sinews of her shoulders at the end of each day's grinding. "But . . . could we take our goat? She is such a good milker, and . . ." *And I think, I hope, there is a child in my womb; and if I milk scantily, or late, as many women with a first babe do, I do not want to have to beg or hope to buy its food—my child's life should not rest on so little!*

"We can take the goat, indeed . . . unless," and Gunidu's age-singed eyebrows lowered a little, "we must sell her to buy cart and donkeys. For though our possessions are few enough, we cannot bear them on our backs to Erech, and we must also have food and water to get all of us there alive."

Innashagga looked at her water-jug, whose lip stood a little above her knee, then at her good cooking pot, and around at the wooden bed-frames, their fleeces and blankets. None of those things had come cheaply: the water-jug had been her inheritance and wedding-present at once from her mother, who had died of a sudden fever a few days before the marriage-feast; they had gone without cheese and meat for a week to buy the cooking pot, and as for the bed-frames—what any wood but the cracking pithwood of palm was worth, well, ten milking goats would not have matched what they must have cost: Innashagga only knew that Gunidu had owned the cypress one when she married Akalla, and bought the one of beech with the last of what he had brought from Erech and carefully saved through his years of raising a growing son.

"If we must sell her, then we must," Innashagga said sadly. In truth, though most of her married life had been a struggle to keep the creature out of the onions, she had grown fond of the silky-furred nanny whose milk flowed as regularly as the water into the village well, and had often bought them what they could not make or grow for themselves. *But she is a good milker, well-known here,* Innashagga comforted herself, *and will not be slaughtered for meat if her new owner can help it.* "But you are right, my father: we should go to Erech."

Gunidu sat with chin on fist, turning his gaze to his son. Akalla dropped his gaze, lowering his heavy head. After a moment he murmured, "I will go to Erech with you."

"Then so it is spoken, my children." Gunidu's words seemed to Innashagga to come a little faster, a little lighter, like the hooves of a donkey scenting his home-pen and knowing how near would come the easing of his burden. "And so we shall go."

Innashagga knew that the decision should have lightened her thoughts as well, but it was she who lay awake beside the stolidly snoring bulk of Akalla, tossing and turning beneath the rustling palm-leaves above her. Instead of lulling her, the soft susurration of the lizards and insects creeping through the dry blades seemed to run along her nerves, tightening her muscles against each other and catching against the smooth flow of her thoughts, sending the ripples off into wild whirlpools. *What if I am with child, how then shall we manage? . . . Yet if Gunidu has a pension from the great temple of Inanna, how shall we want? . . . But he has been long away; he is wise, but even the wise do not know all. What if the temple no longer gives pensions, or they are not as great as he supposes?* She laid her hands over her belly once more, but felt only her own warm curve: Nanna Moon-Lord would have dwindled into the dark realm of Erishkegal and come back three or four times more before her child, if there was one, began to swell and squirm within her.

*O Inanna,* she prayed, *if you have given me a child's birth, then bless its life as well—please, do not give me hope only to see my babe die because I have no milk and we have sold the goat! Though Gunidu—and he is a true sage, well-learned in your ways, and knowing more about the ways of the gods than I—says that none is without fault, I hope that I have not earned such punishment. Please, dear goddess, who brings ewes and nanny-goats to fruitfulness and spared so many lambs and kids this year, give me the same blessing as they have. I will graze on poor soil if I must, as long as the child in my womb comes to life and holds it.*

Then Innashagga knew what she must do. Akalla slept on quietly as she reached beneath the soft sheep-fells of their bed, feeling down to the woven reed-mat strung between the wooden poles until her touch met the smooth beads of the necklace the Shamhatu had given her. Gold and lapis from Harahi—that would surely buy a good donkey-cart, to take herself and her family and all their belongings to Erech. One tear splashed warm onto the cold polished beads; but Innashagga had already wept enough that night, and what the gods had given—something too good for a simple village-woman—would be enough to carry them safe into Erech the Sheepfold, when their own fold had failed them.

So IT WAS that Innashagga made her way, in the early hours of the day after she had folded the night-cooking beans into bread for her husband and his father, to the house of the village's chief man, Puzur-ili; and around her neck was the strand that the Shamhatu had given her, glittering dark and bright in the light of the rising sun. She stood chill in the morning dew, waiting for Puzur-ili to lift the mat of woven palm that lay across the doorway of his house, ready to draw back if it were his wife who came out first to draw water from the well.

But it was Puzur-ili who came out first after all, his blocky shoulders brushing against the prickly mat as he lowered his shaven head to push through it; and so Innashagga stepped forward carefully.

"Please, mighty man . . ."

Puzur-ili shook his head heavily as if to shake off the buzzing of flies, not pausing.

"Puzur-ili! I would speak with you!"

Slowly he turned to her, grasping the dark curls of his beard. "What have you to say, woman?"

"I would buy your donkey-cart," Innashagga answered, her heart beating hard against her ribs. She would have turned and fled then, but she thought, though it was far too early, that she felt the movement of her child within her bowels, and so she could only stand her ground. She lifted the strand of beads about her neck and thought that she saw its glitter reflecting in the deep brown pool of his eyes. *For my child, and Akalla, I would give far more*, she reminded herself.

"You would, would you?" he said. "And what is it worth, this cart that draws our fleeces and meat to market?"

"What is it worth?"

"The life and health of our village . . . how can a price be set upon it?"

Innashagga lifted the beads a little higher, though it seemed to her that she tugged upon the great veins of her heart with that string.

"A price? I have a good price to offer, and I know what these are worth."

Puzur-ili took one step, lifting a blocky brown arm. His fingers closed upon the strand, holding it tightly so that Innashagga felt like a bitch upon a lead. "Do you, indeed? How long until these could buy us what we need?"

"Not long," Innashagga choked. "For the flood tide is over, and the traders will be coming out from Erech soon, to make their way across the desert to the Black Land; and I have seen them drive the high-bred donkeys, and those rough ones that feed on our low grasses, before them every year."

"But the donkeys, and the cart, or the good wood to build one—ah, you do not know what that is worth; you are lucky to have one nanny-goat, for the pittance that your husband's shooting can bring. Nor is the favor of the Shamhatu worth much, so far from Erech; I have already taken the many complaints that your behavior while she was your guest has brought, and she will not protect you."

"Mighty man," Innashagga said, almost weeping, "I offer you the best that has been seen in this village in my memory. I did not wear these beads to the New Year's feast out of vainglory, but only because they were given me as blessing, and I know that Inanna loves beauty. But I know that they are enough to buy a donkey-cart, and that is as fair as may be. Mighty man, I know also that the blessing of the goddess has brought strife to our village, and you do not wish to see that among the sheep in your fold."

"That is so," Puzur-ili said, his voice softening. "And so, though it is little enough for what you want, I shall be willing to sell you my donkey-cart—for Inanna's sake, I shall sell it for that trinket you wear." He held out his hand, spitting in it so she might mingle her spittle with his and seal the bargain. Innashagga coughed twice, trying to bring the water to her mouth.

"Sell it for what?" Gunidu's quiet deep voice broke in over Inna-shagga's shoulder.

Innashagga whirled even as she heard him, but she did not miss the inward hiss of breath through Puzur-ili's teeth.

"Away, old man," the chief man said. "The woman and I have sealed a bargain"—and he held his palm up, the frothy spittle glittering in the sun's new light.

"I saw you spit. She did not."

Then Puzur-ili's face darkened beneath the browning of his many days in the light, and his heavy shoulders swelled. "And what is it to you? What belongs to a woman is hers, and she may conduct her business as she will."

"I was the chief shepherd in Inanna's temple," Gunidu said mildly, "and will fare back to the temple soon, with my wife and kin. And a shepherd does not sit quietly when he sees a good kid-bearing ewe menaced, whether it is by a lion—or a fool who would shear her fleece when the winter winds threaten. Now, what is it you claim your donkey-cart is worth?"

Puzur-ili showed his teeth, tightening his fists against the thick brown swell of his chest muscles. "As a favor to Akalla's wife, since ill-feeling has come to this village over her, I was willing to take that glittering bauble about her neck, even though it is not worth so much. But if you interfere, old man, I shall insist on rights to your dung-thick little hut and your dry-uddered old nanny as well, or you may stay here and starve."

"You are a liar, a false man, and have no right to rule even this small village," Gunidu answered, his voice still calm. "You know full well that two of the beads on Innashagga's neck would buy your donkey-cart and half this village; I came from Erech, and since then have not seen either lapis or gold here, save for that which the Shamhatu brought with her. We are in no hurry, for my son's meat feeds much of the village, especially now, when few crops have sprouted and last year's are used up. Seek to starve us, fool, and it will not be our family who goes hungry.

"And furthermore," Gunidu added, and though his voice was still even, it seemed to Innashagga that she could hear it sharpening like a copper blade beneath a file, "Inanna has blessed you so far. But I—I, who was the shepherd at her temple—I can tell you what will take place when you seek to bargain unfairly for a gift of the Shamhatu." Then the old man raised his fists, thumb thrust through them; and it seemed to Innashagga that she saw him rise against the new sun until he was taller than Enkidu, his morning shadow falling across Puzur-ili. "Like a bandit who plunders a city, your works shall bring destruction on this village. Your words forge great axes of destruction, and they shall lay these huts neck to ground, like a man killed in battle. Nothing and no one shall escape the arm of your foolishness; the acres shall bring forth no grain, the ewes no lambs, the goats no kids, the palms no dates. You piss in your one well, and the water shall sink away beneath it. Those who sleep on the roof shall die on the roof, and those who sleep inside shall not be brought to burial: the people here shall droop helplessly with hunger, too weak to herd or reap or hunt, and the barley shall dry into stones in the dust. Enlil shall cut you off from the day, and Inanna from the bright light of her evening star."

Puzur-ili's mouth opened and closed. Then he straightened himself, pulling his backbone tight so that only a little of his browned belly lapped over his kilt, and said, "Gunidu, you misjudge me. I care only—"

"For your profit," Gunidu said. He stepped forward, his forefinger blurring; and Puzur-ili doubled over, choking. "I know how you have gotten so fat; and I know what would happen to my daughter's necklace if she gave it to you, as she would from a good heart. But you are not dealing with a good-hearted village-woman or a thick-tongued hunter, you are dealing with the man who was Inanna's chief shepherd, and has faced worse boars than you in the marshy shallows of the Buranun. Now I tell you: one lapis bead and one of gold from that necklace will pay for your donkey-cart and enough food to see us safe to Erech, and if I had not learned to love this village and this land, I should strike a single bead with a hammer and leave you with the shards of half of it for the same. But I say now: we shall give you those two beads, and half of that shall go to the shrine here—and believe me, I shall send temple-men back to see how it is kept in half a year's time."

Now Puzur-ili braced his back against the wood of his door-frame, straightening. "Inanna gives her blessing," he gritted out. "Those two beads, and rights to what you leave behind, and you may have my donkey-cart."

Gunidu grasped his slimy hand palm-up, hawked, and spat into it, then closed his own thin-knuckled fist over it.

"So we have sworn, before the gods!" Gunidu called, and it seemed to Innashagga that his cracked old voice echoed from the far-off hills.

"Now, Innashagga, untie your strand and give this man his price, for the sooner we begin to load, the sooner we may turn the donkeys' heads toward Erech."

Innashagga sat down on the hard earth, spreading out her skirt, for her hands were shaking so badly that she did not trust them to safely untie the knot that the fine fingers of the priestess had tied. And, indeed, when she had gotten the tight-spun linen free, the dark and bright beads scattered; but only one small piece of polished lapis bounced from the weave of her wool, and she pounced upon it before it had stopped spinning on the dust.

"This is your price," she said shakily, holding up one lapis and one gold bead. "And may Inanna see that you have what is right for it . . . and no more."

Puzur-ili snapped up the beads like a goat chomping a single blade of grass from dry ground. "So it is," he said. "And go swiftly from here, for you have caused enough trouble—a thornbush where we thought a lettuce grew, a barren goat where we thought to see a good ewe."

Innashagga made no reply, for she was too busy gathering the little beads from the weave of her gray-brown skirt and counting them, as she had done so many times in the quiet of the night. But again Gunidu spoke for her.

"We shall go swiftly enough, and with us shall go the blessing the Shamhatu brought, for it is clear how all of you valued the priestess— when you treated those who served her with pure hearts thus."

Then Innashagga had found all of her remaining beads, clenching them in her fist. She nodded and rose, standing behind Gunidu until Puzur-ili ducked his shaven head, until he and his hired man drove out the two gray donkeys with their cart rolling behind them.

THE SHAMHATU SAT in one of the quiet alcoves in the temple, considering. At last she clapped her hands. It was not long before one of the boys cleaning the shrine left off his work, handing his long-handled brush to another and hurrying to see what the high priestess desired.

"Bring Geme-Tirash to me," she said. He bowed low and hurried off.

When the trance-priestess appeared, the Shamhatu did not wait for her to kneel or give greetings. "Come closer," she said. "I must speak with you."

"What is it you wish, Divine Lady?" Geme-Tirash asked.

The Shamhatu studied her closely for a moment. After the New Year's feast, the trance-priestess had gone quietly back to her work, never showing any sign that she regretted stepping down from the Shamhatu's place, or that she wished that things could have gone otherwise. Nor—and she had been one of those that the Shamhatu had watched most closely—had she seemed to be one of those who whispered with Shubad, murmuring echoes of the words the singer had spoken on that night. If anything, Geme-Tirash had become more reserved, even more reticent to put herself and her visions forth to the Shamhatu, as if she feared that the least indication of forwardness might lead others to think that she desired to sit in the throne at Inanna's feet. But now . . .

"I saw your face at the dawn hymns to Inanna," the Shamhatu said. "You seemed rapt, as you do when a trance falls over you, but afterward you were shivering, and there was a look of fear upon you. What did you see? Was it more than the exaltation of the hymn and the cool of the morning?"

"It was," Geme-Tirash said, her voice soft. "I did not come to you, for . . ."

*For you feared my mistrust and anger,* the Shamhatu finished silently for her. By now everyone in the temple knew that she had struck Shubad. She had heard rebukes from the En and Urgigir, Shibtum and Elulu; she had seen how some of the lesser temple-folk looked slant-eyed at her; but none of them cut like this half-spoken reproach.

"You need not fear me," the Shamhatu told her, careful to keep her voice gentle. "You have always been faithful to the temple, and to those who serve Inanna. Will you tell your vision?"

Geme-Tirash looked away from the Shamhatu, into the flame of the oil-lamp burning in the small wall-niche. She began to sway back and forth; her voice dropped into the low half-chant of trance. The Shamhatu listened to her, her unease growing. At last she cut the other priestess off with a swift motion of her hand.

"Go to Gilgamesh," she said. "Before the vision leaves you, go at once into the Court of Judgment, and speak these words where all there may hear and witness. If any question, tell them that you are there at my order. You have done well."

GILGAMESH SAT IN his place at the head of the Court of Judgment, turning the polished wood of his stave of office about idly in his fingers as the next plaintiff and defender stood up to swear their oaths in the view of the small gilded image of Inanna standing on her ebony-inlaid table in front of the Ensi. Beside him sat Enkidu, his large hand resting warm on Gilgamesh's. The day was already growing hot, sweat sheening the bare shoulders and chests of the judges beneath the warm breeze blowing through the open doors, and a few of the younger men were beginning to shift restlessly where they squatted upon the floor. But it was amazing, Gilgamesh thought, looking fondly at Enkidu, how well the wild man bore the endless tedium of complaint and countercomplaint, his green eyes widening and narrowing as he listened to the words of each case as if he followed the spoor of a gazelle herd.

With an effort Gilgamesh wrenched his thought back to the matter before the court. One Urbargara had rented the donkey of Ludingirra; through a moment of appalling ill-luck or through careless neglect— depending on whether Urbargara or Ludingirra was speaking, the beast had broken its tether, and, in its brief dash for freedom, managed to fall and break both forelegs, so that it could only be slaughtered. Urbargara's claim was simply that he had seen to the donkey as well as anyone could, and was therefore not responsible for its death, particularly as the lead it had snapped was the one provided by Ludingirra. Ludingirra wanted the full price for his donkey, and Urbargara could not pay it save by selling himself into slavery.

The two men were both talking at once when Gilgamesh raised his staff to silence them. "The Ensi has heard your case. The law is clear: he who rents another's animal and allows harm to come to it is liable for that harm. The price of an ass in Erech is . . ." He glanced to the side, along the judges seated there, until his gaze met Naram-Sin's.

"Twenty-five shekels of silver," the older man said. "The price of an untrained laborer is twenty."

"Have you family?" Gilgamesh asked Urbargara. The man shook his head mutely, his liquid dark eyes staring up at Gilgamesh in appeal. Had he children, he could have sold two to make up the debt, but having none . . . "So be it. Let Urbargara be sold into slavery; the proceeds, or the slave himself if so desired, going to Ludingirra in compensation for his donkey."

Gilgamesh raised his staff and was about to bring it down to seal the sentence when he felt Enkidu's hand tighten on his own.

"Why is a man's life worth less than the life of an ass?" the wild man asked, his deep voice almost childishly clear.

Gilgamesh blinked, but it was Naram-Sin who answered. "Because, nobly favored of the gods, that is the price set on man and ass in the marketplace."

"Could this man not earn enough to repay his debt in a lifetime?"

"No doubt he could, in a year or two, but those are not the laws of Erech." Naram-Sin smiled into his beard, passing his palm over the gleaming round of his shaven skull.

"Why can he not work for Ludingirra for that time, then, instead of giving a lifetime's labor for the price of two years?"

Naram-Sin stared at him, mouth open, and Gilgamesh knew that he had never seen the old fellow so dumbfounded. He felt the bellow of laughter rumbling up from his own belly and let it go, ringing and building through the court. Tears flowed freely over Urbargara's stubbled cheeks; Ludingirra only frowned silently.

"That is just," Gilgamesh said, still laughing. "Thus is my lion from the wilderness, whose good sense and open heart can confound the wise men of Erech, fit to be Ensi beside me. Let it be as you have said, my Enkidu: Urbargara shall labor as a bondsman until his debt is paid— thus he shall buy himself free, and that better law shall stand in place of the worse. Urbargara and Ludingirra, go forth!" He brought down the staff, and was rewarded by Enkidu's brilliant smile through the golden curls of his beard. Gilgamesh did not turn his gaze away from his lover's green eyes as he went on, droning the rote words to open the next case. "Let a new claimant and defendant come before the eyes of Inanna, Queen of Heaven and Keeper of Erech the Sheepfold . . ."

But instead of the next pair in the row stepping before the small gilded image, there was a rustling by the doors at the back of the hall. Gilgamesh saw the common folk who were standing there give way before the woman who walked in. It was not—he noted with a soft, but heartfelt, sigh of relief—Shamhatu. Instead this was one of the trance-priestesses of the temple, the young woman who had served in Shamhatu's place while the head priestess was in the desert. Her name . . . Gilgamesh struggled to remember. He had bedded her twice, could recall the voluptuous softness of her pale breasts and the freckles sprinkled over them as clearly as he could see the smooth powerful curves of Enkidu's chest beneath his curly golden pelt now, but he could not recall her name. *Wait: Geme-something . . . Geme-Tirash! That was it.* The trance-priestess was dressed in a simple shift of white linen trimmed with blue-dyed wool, and her dark curly hair fell free, but around her neck was a sevenfold golden chain, and another glittering strand was tied about her plump waist.

As Geme-Tirash got closer, Gilgamesh could see that her eyes were wide, their hazel irises nearly drowned by the darkness within, and a prickle of danger iced his spine. It was not likely to be a good sign when a trance-priestess came abruptly and unannounced into the Court of Judgment: there must be some tidings from the temple important enough that he needed to hear it straight away.

Geme-Tirash's mouth opened, and a strange sound issued from it, a birdlike shriek that set the hair of Gilgamesh's head tingling. Beside him Enkidu seemed to be crouching in his chair, the great muscles of his shoulders bunching as though he were about to spring forward and seize the priestess. "Gilgamesh, Ensi and Lugal of Erech, protector of Inanna's folk and ruler over the black-headed people!" Geme-Tirash cried. "Behold, I lay down to sleep in the heat of the day, and there a vision came to me. I saw a scorpion lurking beneath the rock that turns under the Ensi's sandal; I saw a snake coiled in the shadows at the side of the path where the Ensi walks, and the Shamhatu sent me to tell you of it. There is treachery by your side, and treachery about you: though you tread in the sun, its shadow falls across your way, and I fear that it seeks your death. The boar of Kish roars before you, but it is not that threat which speaks its name that you need fear: the snake seeks out and devours both wild goat and wild bull. Gilgamesh, making ready for war: Gilgamesh, Ensi and Lugal, two-thirds god and one-third man—beware!"

Enkidu was on his feet in a moment, his fists bunched tight as he roared, "What danger threatens Gilgamesh? Make it known to me, and I will make an end of it!"

But Geme-Tirash only slumped where she stood. Her lids drooped down, and when she opened her eyes again, her swollen pupils had shrunk back into themselves. For all the heat, she was shivering now, and Gilgamesh quickly lay down his staff and stood to wrap his discarded cloak about her shoulders.

"I do not know," she whispered, "only that it is treachery of some sort . . . Gilgamesh, someone you trust, have reason to think you can trust, is working toward your destruction even now."

*Shamhatu?* Gilgamesh thought. Surely she could not be so mad . . . save that if he were dead, the city would be ruled by the houses of elders and men, acting together as a council as they had done while he grew to manhood, and the Shamhatu would stand as the chief single figure to speak in Erech.

But no: Shamhatu must have given Geme-Tirash permission to warn him—had done, for Geme-Tirash had said that Shamhatu sent her. Who, then, could . . . ?

"Lady, I shall defend him," Enkidu said, putting his own arm about Gilgamesh's shoulders. Beneath the warmth of the embrace, Gilgamesh could feel the shivering deep within his friend's powerful body, as though Enkidu were responding to the chill Gilgamesh felt. Yet that thought, in turn, strengthened and heartened Gilgamesh: how could ill befall him when he had Enkidu by his side?

"Stay close to him," murmured Geme-Tirash. "And be wary . . ." She straightened her back again, letting the borrowed cloak drop from her shoulders and handing it to Gilgamesh. Two older women, temple servants, stood at the entrance to the hall: the moment Geme-Tirash had passed out between the carved wooden doors, they were beside her, supporting her away.

Enkidu held Gilgamesh tightly to himself for a moment, his rich, musky scent warm in Gilgamesh's nostrils. Their eyes met for a moment, and it seemed to Gilgamesh that the light in Enkidu's green gaze, the brightness of his tawny curls and beard, together made up something so precious that he hardly dared breathe, lest he shatter the moment.

Naram-Sin coughed dryly. "Your loyalty does you credit, Enkidu: I am sure all here feel much the same. But, my Ensi, the warning seems to be well-given." Indeed, Naram-Sin's face was as pale as Gilgamesh's own felt, and Gilgamesh could see the older man's silver water-cup shaking a little in his hand: it had not only been Gilgamesh and Enkidu stricken by the trance-priestess' awe-full words. "Agga," he went on, "is not known only for his strength on the battlefield, but for his wisdom—and cunning—when dealing with strong enemies. Now I would say that it would be prudent and sensible for you never to go without a guard of picked men, whether you are training your soldiers or overseeing the building of the siege-walls—or doing the many other things that you do. Without you, after all, we have no war against Agga: Gilgamesh is both the chariot and the high-bred donkey stallion drawing it in this war—is that not so?" He tugged at the curls of his beard, and Gilgamesh realized that Naram-Sin was not speaking to him, but to the other judges gathered there.

"That is so," "It is true," and similar soft murmurs of agreement came from the rows of seated men.

"A guard," Naram-Sin went on smoothly, "which could be made up of some of your best young men, my Ensi . . . say, your commanders of sixty. With more than two hundred of them to choose from, a watch could be safely kept over you at all times; and you would have more time to observe them, to see who is worthy of advancement and who is not fit for his place. I know that Ishbi-Erra would be glad to volunteer; I am sure the same is true for all the other men in your army, for they all know your worth."

Gilgamesh opened his mouth to answer that he needed no guard except Enkidu, but the judges were already nodding in agreement with Naram-Sin's words. Enkidu's wide forehead was creased, his golden eyebrows drawn together as though deeply pondering the matter.

"My Enkidu," said Gilgamesh, "what do you think of this matter? Shall we be chained to a guard and safe, or roam as freely as we please and take the risks as they come?"

Enkidu made a soft rumbling sound in his throat, and his fingers flexed like great claws. "I do not know," he said at last. "The priestess seemed wise, and her words true. And if any harm should come to you, my own . . ." As though only just remembering it was there, he grasped the hilt of the new sword hanging at his belt. "Even the strong can be overcome, if they are taken by surprise, or by enough foes. I do not think a guard will stop us from doing as we like—and I do not yet know the ways of Erech well enough to protect you from . . ."

*Poison in my cup, perhaps?* Gilgamesh thought. *Or an arrow shot from hiding, from a bow behind a door or on a rooftop near the temple . . .* Assassinations happened now and again in Erech: sometimes the killer was caught, perhaps even forced to give the name of the man who had hired him, and sometimes he escaped—but the best justice dealt out to the slayer always came too late for the slain.

"It is not a bad plan," Gilgamesh admitted reluctantly. "And perhaps it must be so. Enatarzi!"

The plump body-slave stepped forward at once. "My Ensi?"

"Send a runner to Ur-Lamma. He should be told of this decision, and should pick twelve of the commanders of sixty as my guard—and let Ishbi-Erra be among them: we shall see if he is worthy of the trust his father-in-law places in him. And bring beer for Enkidu and myself, for the day grows warmer and we have several judgments yet to pass."

"As you command, O Ensi uplifted by the gods."

The beer and the guardsmen arrived at almost the same time. Gilgamesh looked around at the faces of the chosen twelve, calling their names to his mind; the effort was almost enough to distract him from how his hand was trembling on the cool fluted surface of the gold cup he held, how the lapis-inlaid straw clinked against the rim like the jingling of bells in a *tigi*-hymn. Enkidu was looking about at the guard likewise, his nostrils flaring as if he sought to catch and learn the scent of each man. The sweet beer was cold in Gilgamesh's dry throat, washing away the dust gathered there, so that he could say, "You have been told of your duty, and why you must do it?"

Each man nodded in turn as the Ensi met his eyes for a moment.

"Good. Say nothing of it to any other. The less of this that goes beyond the walls of this room, the better for all—for Erech's sake, and your own. Do all here understand me?" Gilgamesh added, rising to his feet and raising his voice so that it cracked like a whip of lightning across the sky.

A chorus of murmurs rustled behind his words; a host of respectfully averted heads met his gaze as it swept about the hall.

"So be it, then. Bring on the next case."

But Gilgamesh found that the words swept and eddied about him like the waters of a river sweeping about an unmoving rock. It seemed to him that Geme-Tirash's words had set up a great wall around his mind, holding out all beyond his skull so that his own thoughts could only ally or turn against themselves like the dwellers in a city long-besieged. He nodded or shook his head as the faces of those about him seemed to bid, speaking when spoken to and saying, "Let it be so," when judgment was passed. But ever-rehearsing in his mind were all the subtle ways that death might come—a poisoned cup, an arrow in the back, a brick dropped from the top of his rising wall—and an answer to each, what he and his guards must do, lest the war be ended and Kish victorious over Erech before sword ever touched on sword. Several times Gilgamesh rose to pass water, grateful for the short respite from the mumbling voices around him; but where once he had drained his bladder alone, two guards stood in front of the door, listening with care to the sound of urine splashing into the copper pot, and watching more carefully yet as one of the palace slaves came near enough to lift the vessel by its two ram's-head handles and carry it away.

At last the brightness shining through the hall's doors began to deepen into twilight, the warm breezes cooling swiftly. Thankfully, it was time for Gilgamesh to bring down his stave of office seven times to mark the end of the court—the blow, muted by the carpet beneath his feet, was no more than a whisper of a thud, but it sufficed. Petitioners and onlookers filed out; the judges and elders rose from the floor, tossing light cloaks about their bare shoulders against the evening's chill before kneeling briefly before the gilded image of Inanna and making their own departures.

Enkidu turned to Gilgamesh, taking the stave of gold-twined cedar from his hand and giving it over to Enatarzi. "You are tired, beloved friend," Enkidu rumbled, "and we have not eaten since before noonday. Let us go to our chamber, where we may feed and rest."

"Let us, indeed," Gilgamesh said. "Enatarzi, see that food awaits us there." He clasped Enkidu's hand, glad to feel the warmth and strength—the old calluses from running in the wild, and the new from swinging a sword and laying bricks; the hard white streaks where the claw-tips of the lions had scored his flesh in play, marks that would have crippled any man save the one made by the gods to be the lions' companion. Gilgamesh smiled, his resurgent joy washing away all thoughts of the trance-priestess' warning for a moment as the two of them walked toward the doors of the Court of Judgment together.

But then three of the guards hurried to walk before them, three behind, and three to each side, like hunting dogs pacing about a chariot; and Gilgamesh bit off the curse beneath his breath. *My guards indeed—as the gallas were Inanna's,* he thought bitterly. He and Enkidu would not go out and roister through the taverns that night; he did not even know if he would be given leave to summon any of his handmaidens, the votary women called the priestesses of Gilgamesh, to their bed if they desired, for which could surely be given full trust when a man had lost himself in her loins?

By the time they had reached his chamber, Gilgamesh was shaking again, and he did not know how much was fury and how much fear— fear of betrayal, fury that he must fear so, and that others must stand guard to keep him safe, when he knew that none save Enkidu was his match. But he was able to keep his voice calm as he said, "You men must wait outside the doors here, for within this chamber, surely I am safe, and Enkidu will not leave my side."

"And what of your body-slaves and servants?" Ishbi-Erra asked. "Which of them can we trust alone with you?"

"Enatarzi has been with me since my earliest days: him you may trust even when Enkidu and I are both locked in sleep. As for the rest—while either of us wakes, I need fear no man."

Ishbi-Erra bowed his head and stepped to the door, gesturing the other guards to leave with him. But the others stayed where they were until Gilgamesh waved them on.

As soon as the door swung shut on its pins, Gilgamesh and Enkidu clasped each other hard, embracing as if they were wrestling, save that each sought to steady the other's balance and hold him up, rather than to cast him down. Gilgamesh felt the tightness in his chest easing—a tightness he had not recognized until that moment, as if he had swallowed frog-spawn unknowing and whiled thus, unaware of what grew within him until he spewed up the full-grown frog. Enkidu's green eyes glimmered like polished agates in the clear sweet flickering of the oil-lamps; the soft curls of his golden beard brushed Gilgamesh's lips.

"No harm will come to you," Enkidu breathed, a raspy murmur halfway between a purr and a growl. "Not while I live."

They held each other like that a moment, until a knock sounded on the door and Enatarzi entered with two steaming plates. Slices of goosemeat glazed with date-honey, arranged like flower-petals upon a heap of fine emmet-groats, with a small cluster of dates at the center of each— Gilgamesh's mouth began to water as Enatarzi set the platters down, his stomach suddenly churning with hunger.

"My Ensi, Master Enkidu—I saw these plates readied for you myself, and brought them here with my own hands. Now, if you will, I shall taste of them first to be sure that they are clean."

"No, I shall taste," Enkidu argued. "I can smell unclean water or fouled meat from thirty paces: can I not smell unclean food? And it is better that the stronger should risk danger than the weaker."

*And what does that make me?* Gilgamesh thought, a sudden flash of anger heating his brow. But he held his tongue, for he knew that they spoke only out of love, and fear of the priestess' prophecy.

"But if there is ill in the food," Enatarzi said smoothly, "then it will strike me down more swiftly than it would strike you, and thereby be safer for Gilgamesh; if it is a slow poison, the sooner I begin to succumb, the likelier it is that the Ensi can be saved. And I am only an old eunuch, of little loss to Erech, whereas the two of you are the city's pride. One does not tether one's best ram in the field to lure a lion close enough to spear; one sets out the oldest and mangiest sheep in the flock." The eunuch's painted eyes closed, then opened again, very slowly, a blink of deep reptilian satisfaction, like a lizard half asleep on a wall in the sun.

It seemed to Gilgamesh for a moment that Enkidu was about to say something more. But then his lover inclined his head toward Enatarzi, lids shuttering the green gleam of his gaze for a moment. "You are right," murmured Enkidu. "Taste, then."

Enatarzi lifted a sliver of goose-meat from each platter, chewing slowly and swallowing. He followed that with one date from each, then, instead of using either of the silver-handled carnelian spoons upon the plates, drew his own copper spoon from the pouch at his waist to take two small scoops of the emmet-groats.

"The taste seems clean," he said. "But we must wait a little time, to be sure . . ."

"How long?" Gilgamesh demanded. "I have heard that some poisons can take days to show their teeth—by the time we are sure that this food is clean, it will not only be cold but half rotten, and cast to the dogs in the street as well. Should I die of certain starvation as a defense against a chance of poison? But I want my dinner now, not at midnight."

"Patience, Ensi," Enatarzi counseled. "Only a little time, and then we will know at least that it is not a swift-acting poison."

The eunuch's face did not pale, nor did he grasp at his belly; and at last he said, "You may eat safe from any swift venom, at least. If I fall ill in the night, I shall send for you at once. But now I shall leave and fetch you drink—the good wine will be best with this dish, I think. Be sure, I shall taste it at the source."

"I am sure you shall," Gilgamesh answered, at last able to grin at his slave. "Taste away . . . but bring it quickly, for the food is growing colder, and we thirst."

Yet, though his cooks must have worked mightily, Gilgamesh barely tasted the rich meat: even washed down by the sweet resinous wine, the goose's succulence seemed dry at the back of his throat; the thin honey glaze seemed sticky and cloying, and the soft buttered emmet-groats might have been a pile of sand. Enkidu ate carefully, as he always did, licking his lips and wiping his right hand between each bite, as if he feared that a drop of grease might dribble down his chin or his fingers leave a stain somewhere. Yet slowly as he brought the food to his mouth, he was still finished before Gilgamesh had eaten even half of his own.

"Your appetite is good, my friend," Gilgamesh said. He tasted the dark bitter stain of envy at the back of his throat even as he spoke, but Enkidu seemed to shrug it off without marking anything odd.

"Why should it not be? The food is good, there is enough of it, and we ate little earlier." Enkidu laid his hand lightly on Gilgamesh's shoulder. "But your body is tightening on itself, and so is your stomach, I think. Is this always the way among human folk, to fear the whispers of a foe you would not tremble to meet face-to-face?"

"The shadow always looms larger than the man," Gilgamesh admitted ruefully. "Agga the Lugal I do not fear, for I know him: I know his strength, and the strength of his army may be measured and met. But it is another thing to be able to trust no cup of water nor plate of food— to look at the man who trims my hair and wonder where his keen bronze razor will pass next. And if I find one spy, how do I know that three more do not lurk behind him? It is when I do not know how to fight or even what I fight—it is the fear of what may be, and what I do not know. I think that is always the way among human folk. Perhaps," Gilgamesh added, and now he knew that he had drunk too much of the wine, for the tart taste of terebinth resin was still in his mouth, and the words rushed out like water from a broken irrigation canal, "the Shamhatu did you no great favor when she brought you from the world of lions to the world of men."

Enkidu stood, moving behind Gilgamesh and kneading at his shoulders. The man from the wilderness had kept his nails filed back and blunted, but they still bit lightly into Gilgamesh's skin with a welcome pain, distracting his thoughts from the knotting in his stomach even as his beloved's touch worked through and soothed his tight muscles.

"I could wish for nothing better than to be here," Enkidu murmured. "I am always with you, ready to stand by you. And yet . . ." His voice choked still, and Gilgamesh could only guess at what thoughts or images might be showing now behind his green eyes . . . the sudden rush of the lion from behind the rock at the watering hole and the gazelle's slim red bones after, or perhaps the black wings of the vultures circling and rocking lower, down to where the long golden shape lay with fangs bared against its maned death-mask, and the last blood drying brown around the spear-wound in its side.

Enkidu's touch grew softer until it was barely a caress, blunted nails stroking lightly over Gilgamesh's back like the rough tongue of a great cat. Gilgamesh sighed, arching against him, then rose and caught Enkidu's hands in his own, holding tight so that he would not shame himself by beginning to tremble.

"You are always with me, indeed," he answered. "And it is only with you . . ."

Enkidu came easily into Gilgamesh's embrace, his warm strong musky scent rising to fill Gilgamesh's nostrils. Gratefully, Gilgamesh tightened his arms around his beloved, burying his face in Enkidu's great curly mane even as Enkidu nuzzled at the curve of his shoulder, making small soft growling sounds deep in his throat. Now his need was more urgent than any thought of Agga, washing away the sick traitorous tremors in the pit of his stomach like strong heated date-wine washing away the trembling of the frostiest winter night's cold.

Later, the two of them lay in the bed together, legs and arms lightly intertwined. Little drops of sweat rolled slowly down Gilgamesh's chest and back like the tracing of delicate fingertips on his skin, cooling as they trickled. Gilgamesh's right collarbone ached a little; he touched it, and a sharp pain shot out.

"You bit me," he said, half teasingly, half chidingly.

Even in the flickering of the oil lamps, Gilgamesh could see Enkidu's fair skin redden beneath his beard; it seemed to him that he felt a sudden leap of heat from his beloved's body.

"I did not mean to," said Enkidu unhappily. "Shamhatu taught me that I must not . . . but I, I . . ." It seemed to Gilgamesh that Enkidu was struggling to say something he had never learned the words for, or never shaped into thought before. Now he felt ashamed that he had spoken, but he could not help, only tighten his grip until Enkidu finished, "I forgot."

"You did no harm," Gilgamesh assured him. "We have done more to each other in wrestling." But that was not true, either, for Gilgamesh's muscles and sinews were as sore as they had been after their first bout, when they had wrestled with strength enough to rend each other limb from limb, had either been only a little weaker. Still, despite the aches and the keener pain from the bite on his collarbone, a delicious lassitude was beginning to flow through Gilgamesh's body. Although he knew they had cried out loudly enough for their voices to pierce through the mud-brick walls like the sound of a ram's horn from the height of the platform-shrine, and that surely his guards had heard each moan, he did not care. Now it was enough to see the glint of Enkidu's eyes, to feel the heavy warmth of Enkidu's thigh across his won, and breathe in the scent of their coupling mixed with the spicy fragrance of fine oils and the lingering, mouthwatering richness of the honey-glazed goose. Soon Enatarzi would come creeping in with tall cups of cooled beer to quench their thirst, for though a eunuch, he knew well what Gilgamesh wanted after making love in the summer's rising heat, and that, too, would be well; but for now, Gilgamesh had all he needed.

He leaned forward to kiss Enkidu again, their lips meeting tenderly. *It is odd,* he mused to himself, *how lovers can be all things to each other . . . from lust-*

*maddened beasts rutting, to petal softly brushing petal . . . and yet what more could one want than such a friend?*

THE SOFT KNOCK on the door broke through the ragged edges of Agga's drowsing dreams like a fist smashing through dried palm leaves, jolting him into sudden wakefulness. The Ensi of Kish drew a deep breath, then another, before he heaved his bulk from the bed and paced noiseless, barefoot and naked, through the darkness to the door. The wooden pins squeaked slightly in their holes as he drew it aside.

Before him, the high cheekbones of his narrow face flaring in his lamp's light like the wings of a dropping vulture, stood the chief agent who brought word back and forth from Erech. The folk there, and through most of Kish, knew him only as Gimil the Peddler: his short silver hair and puff of a silver beard had kept him from being drafted to build Gilgamesh's wall, and the many times he had passed through Erech's gate with pearls and jasper and other precious things in his pack, and come out again with finely crafted things and the best weaving of Erech's women, had lulled round after round of guards to let him pass by again and again. So he was one of only three who Agga had been able to keep active during Erech's latest preparations for war—and now the most valuable, for it was he who kept Agga in touch with a certain special agent within the city.

Agga nodded and stepped out, closing the door behind him. His queen slept; it was well that she stayed asleep, for he was one of those men who held it best for their wives not to know all their dealings. Her silent faith in him and in the gods of Kish was enough—let it not be shaken by seeing all the scaffolding that went to uphold his achievements.

Silently Agga led Gimil through the corridors of his palace. It was late, indeed: all the oil-lamps standing in the wall-niches had burned down, leaving only the flickering glimmer behind the Ensi's shoulder to light his way.

The night wind whispered over the walls of the inner courtyard at the palace's heart, cool upon Agga's naked body. The two men skirted the large fish-pond that gave back their lamp's light and the pale glimmer of the moon above in a broken gleam of spreading ripples, walking beneath the shadow of the gently bending palm trees and the fronds of tamarisk, black against the moonlit sky. Here, beneath the light of Ninurta's star—the bright star of the war-god, glinting as a light from the holy weapon Shar-ur, with which Ninurta slew the demon Asag in ancient times—Agga knew that he could speak with clear thoughts. Enlil's mighty son had blessed him before in many battles, and he had made sacrifice in return; he would make another sacrifice tomorrow, for though he knew his army to be the greater by far, there was always that disturbing prophecy, or threat, at the back of his mind . . .

"How goes your trading for stones?" Agga said without preamble. Even here, it was well to be safe, for none knew when foes might be lurking in the darkness, or when the gods might see fit to turn the least stumble into a grievous fall.

"Several have come to me, but few are clear or of unblemished color."

Agga settled himself down upon one of the courtyard's smooth diorite benches, the stone's touch soothingly cold against his massive buttocks and thighs. He gestured Gimil to sit as well, and the agent did, setting the lamp down between his feet.

"Our stone is in its bezel," Gimil went on.

"That is well. Why have you been unable to find clearer ones in trade?"

"For the sake of the difficult hunting in the place from which I have come. You have heard that the young lion of the marshlands has found a twin, shadowing him in waking and sleeping."

"All men have heard that. What more is there to say?"

"The Lady of the Evening Star has not yet chosen to tread the lion beneath her feet. Instead she called a warning before the hunter could close—and now the young lion is ringed by twelve mastiffs, and they watch him carefully, lest any harm come to him."

"Twelve mastiffs," Agga said. He rubbed at his shaven chin, the stubble prickly beneath the slight sheen of scented oil. So: the temple of Inanna had found something out, whether by spies or sorcery, and had put the wind up Gilgamesh. The full body of guards would not make matters easier.

"Aye. The fiercest of them is named Ishbi-Erra, and I have heard that he has a keen wish to better himself in the eyes of his master, and his position and that of his breed thereby. I do not think this hound will be swayed from his purpose, whatever befall."

Agga nodded slowly. "It is well to know the nature of a hound. *If he lives*"—and here the Ensi of Kish sharpened his voice, only a little, but enough— "no doubt his master will reward him well."

Gimil rose from the bench and bent down before Agga, brushing his forehead against the brick of the pathway. "There is no more to report, O Ensi, save that the wall of the house is still rising swiftly, and those who wager upon donkey races still reckon the numbers at five to three, or perhaps a little better."

"So it is." Agga rose himself. "Light me back to my chamber, and see the steward on your way out; he will pay you as is fitting for the wares you have brought."

When Gimil had gone away, Agga lay on top of the linen coverlet next to his softly breathing queen. Her profile was black against the darkness in the chamber, like a far-off mountain range seen against faint starlight: sharp nose sloping down into a tangle of curls, sharp chin sloping down to the softness of her throat, the high curve of her bosom below, rising and falling in an even sea-swell. Slowly he turned the massive ring of silver and carnelian on his right forefinger, around and around, as he pondered on the words his agent had brought. In his youth, Agga thought, he would not have wasted such time seeking to bring the war to an end before it had begun . . . ten years since, or even five, he would have torn down Erech's siege-wall before it was high enough to withstand a child's arrows, and smashed Gilgamesh's army before the young upstart could ever recruit three men to his own five.

But that was before the trance-priest came to Agga from Inanna's temple in Kish, where the Queen of Heaven held her sovereignty over the mighty ones, just as Kish held its sovereignty over all the city-states of Sumer, as the gods had decreed. The trance-priest had long hair, braided and bound like a woman's, and wore a little crown of gold leaves and lapis beads; his nails had been long and gleaming, and his hips had moved sinuously beneath the fringe of his shawl as he walked. It had been three years ago when he had come to Agga alone, as the Ensi rose steaming from his bath of cleansing at the eve of the new moon's feast. The voice that whispered from the trance-priest's mouth was high and childish, crawling along Agga's spine, and though his breath was sweet with mint and cardamom, it had seemed to Agga that he could smell the cold and dust and decay of the grave beneath it.

"Agga of Kish, woe to your city," the trance-priest had murmured. "Woe to your city, woe to your line. For Kish shall be cast down someday, and Erech exalted; gold and silver, tin and lapis, diorite from the Black Land and carnelian from Meluhha, shall flow from north to south; you shall bring the mighty cedars of Dilmun down from the mountains, only to delight the gates and temples of Erech. Your kin shall be yoked donkeys, where the wild bulls of Erech run free. Who once served shall rule, who once ruled shall serve—beware the turning wheel, Agga of Kish! For one of Dumuzi's line shall break the power of Kish, and take to Erech all glory!"

Then the trance-priest had turned and left, leaving Agga gaping after him, dripping and stunned. The Ensi of Kish had never seen him again, nor heard his name, search as he might through the temples. In another case, Agga might have called the priests and priestesses out to find the speaker, then had him tested by the magical means that would confirm or deny his vision—but the risk was too great that the trance-priest's ominous words might spread beyond the narrow borders of Agga's own hearing. So he was left to wonder; and so, though Agga had five men to each of Gilgamesh's three, and thrice the wealth to equip and feed them, the Ensi of Kish yet strove to destroy Dumuzi's heir before the war began—lest the gods find matter for grim jest. For this much was certain: if Gilgamesh were let off the tribute, he would smell the blood of Kish, and Agga himself knew that an army whose opponent had already proven his fear would swell like yeast-bread on a warm day.

*Yet the stone is in the bezel,* Agga reminded himself. His man was in place: for all his guards, even the lion-man from the wild, the knife of Gilgamesh's slayer was but a pace from the young warrior's throat.

Not comforted as he should have been by the agent's words, but less racked with worry than before, Agga closed his eyes. He had long since learned the art of sleep at need; now he forced the air deeply in, deeply out of his lungs until his body eased of its own will, slowly yawning down into the soft darkness.

INNASHAGGA STARED IN wonder at the walls of Erech, rising above the horizon like mountains. The outer wall was unfinished; she could see the shapes of men, black as tiny ants, crawling over the half-built towers and ridges, loading and unloading the baskets going slowly up and down along the wall, or bending to the work of laying their bricks. Beside his daughter-in-law, Gunidu whistled silently.

"That is a mighty fortification, indeed," he said. "All the tales we have heard of Gilgamesh's war must be true: even a young and rash Ensi does not raise such defensive walls on a whim. My guess is that life has not been easy in Erech this past year, if Gilgamesh has kept so many men working on the wall and has them there yet—even now, with the rivers ready to rise and cover the fields."

"It has gone up quickly," Akalla added, looking back at the two sitting in the cart as he led the donkey onward. "When I went to the city, it was an outer wall of painted bricks that I saw. Now that wall is hidden away."

"Well, so many workers must eat, and that bodes all the better for your shooting," Gunidu said cheerfully. It seemed to Innashagga that the sight of the city had infused new life into the old man's drying veins, filling the sags of his wrinkled brown cheeks with fresh blood and burnishing his eyes to a new dark gleam. "The temple's storehouses must be well-stocked, too, if so many can be spared from the field after harvest, when the ground must be broken before the sun bakes it into a great mud-brick."

The closer to Erech they came, the more awesome its size seemed to Innashagga. The walls rose higher than palm trees and seemed nearly an arm's length thick: she could not conceive of the force it would take to bring them down. *Truly, Gilgamesh makes Erech a safe sheepfold,* she thought, laying her hands protectively over her belly. *Little one, I shall be glad to be within those walls, where you and I shall both be safe.* And yet with each breath, she had to pass her hand over her brow; it seemed to her that the air was thick with water, as the water with earth, and that the sweat beaded from the air onto her skin.

The river-crossing was hard: the Buranun was coming into its flood tide, and the turnip-shaped boat of hide-covered reeds had to make three trips—one for the cart, one for the donkey, and one for the humans. It swung about sickeningly in the river, anchored only by the old ferryman's frail grip on his punting pole. The skinny graybeard laughed toothlessly when he saw Innashagga's fright.

"Thinking I'm too old to be piloting this thing, aren't you?" he cackled. "Yar, I've been boating on the Buranun since Dumuzi's time . . . near old enough to have sailed through the Flood on Utnapishti's ark!" He held the pole one-handed a moment, patting Innashagga lightly on the shoulder. "Don't you worry, now. It's true, most of the time my son does the heavy punting. But he's working half-days on Gilgamesh's wall now, and training for a soldier the rest of the time, like all the strong young men in Erech." He glanced over at Akalla. "Is that why you've come? Hoping to make something of yourself in the army?"

Akalla shook his head, spreading his hands. "I'm . . . a hunter. Only hunt beasts, not . . . Shoot, or trap, beasts to eat."

Innashagga could almost feel her husband's tongue thickening as he spoke, as it did whenever his thoughts were too large to get out of his mouth at once, but she could finish for him. "He is a slayer of animals, not of men."

The old man cackled again. "Better think about that some more, young fellow. You'll have to hunt like no one's ever hunted before to get out of the army. My son, now, he thought he'd never hold anything more dangerous than a punting pole or net-handle in his hands, but now he's got a bow and a spear and a new kilt from the Lugal, and my, you should see how he strides around!"

The boat bumped shore; the ferryman got out, wading through the reeds to pull it in and make it fast. "Here you are, you and your donkey-cart all—told you no one would steal it. Inanna bless you, and good luck to you in the city."

Akalla hitched up the donkey again; Innashagga and Gunidu climbed into the cart, and the hunter took the reins, leading the ass on the pathway to Erech's main gate.

Two tall men stood to either side of the gateway. Innashagga tried not to gawk, but the guards' shiny bronze helms and wristlets dazzled her eyes, so that she could hardly see past them to the thronging crowd of people inside.

"Names and business," one of them said to Akalla. His voice was bored and flat, but there was a hardness to it that made Innashagga's stomach squirm a little.

Akalla gulped convulsively a couple of times. "I—I'm Akalla . . . Akalla the hunter. These are, these are . . . this is, my wife Innashagga and . . . and my father Gunidu. We're here, we came to . . . want to live in the city," he said in a final rush of relief.

The guard nodded. "Well, you came at a good time: Erech needs men, so you have a job already. Follow Entemena here. He'll show you to the workers' quarters and get you started. Half-days on the wall, half-days training to carry a spear: that's the way it goes in Gilgamesh's army."

"But—but . . ." Then Akalla's words seemed to swell like yeasty dough, sticking and clogging in his throat. Innashagga could say nothing, breathless at the soldier's orders; but Gunidu stepped forward, drawing an agate cylinder from his belt-pouch.

"We are under the protection of the temple of Inanna," he said, his old voice deepening. "Do you recognize this, man?"

The soldier peered closely at the seal. "I recognize it, yes. Nobody is drafting you, good temple-man. You may pass on your way, but he"— he jerked a thumb at Akalla—"lacks any proof of exemption and owns a good strong back. If you claim it's so, we'll mark him down as belonging to the levy of men from the temple, since that's still running short. You can take the woman with you as well, if she doesn't mind being separated from her husband awhile, instead of living with the rest of the wives and children."

"Oh, but I do mind!" Innashagga cried out passionately. She could not reach her husband from her place in the cart, but she stretched out her hand toward him. "Where Akalla goes, I shall go with him. But must you have him for such work, when he is a skilled huntsman?"

"The wall and the spear, that's what strong young men do in Erech now," the guard said stolidly. "Lodgings with the rest of the workers and their families, millet porridge from the temple of Inanna, fish or meat stew two evenings a week, a new soldier's kilt, and pay at unskilled-labor wages: that's what they get for it. No exceptions—even Gilgamesh and Enkidu take a hand at laying bricks now and again."

Gunidu looked at Innashagga, then at his son. It seemed to Innashagga that she could see the strain within him, a cord stretched from both ends. Private quarters, perhaps the little house promised by his pension . . . but separated from Akalla and Innashagga, knowing that they were alone without his guidance in the city.

"In any case, I shall go with them," Gunidu replied, his voice firm. "Show us the way to the workers' quarters."

When Innashagga saw where they would be living, she had to bite back tears. The workers' quarters were nothing more than a mass of hastily cast-up reed huts outside the city walls, some of them already leaning over precariously. Outside, a large group of men—perhaps a hundred or so—were drilling with their spears, marching and jabbing; within one of the huts, a baby wailed, and Innashagga could hear the harsh tones of a woman's voice, though she could make out no words. A mongoose scampered out beneath the reed mat that hung over another doorway, its long body an undulating brown flicker through the grass.

"Three families to a hut—that one over there, they've got space for one more," the guard who had guided them said. "Men get their food free, but you're responsible for feeding the rest of the family by yourself. Pay's once a week, and if you get a craving for fish, there's always the river. You can set traps if you like, but there's a lot of hungry people around, so I won't promise that whatever you snare will stay in the snare long enough for you to eat it. Once you've settled in, report to your commander of sixty—that's Enannatum, drilling the men over there—and he'll write down when you started work and tell you what to do.

Remember, around here everyone except the other fresh fish outranks you, so speak respectful and be obedient. Understand?"

"I understand," Akalla answered.

The guard jerked his thumb. "That way, fellow. Work starts as soon as you get here; let the women worry about the rest."

Innashagga watched silently as the guard herded Akalla off, his broad shoulders slumping under the shadow of the spear. *O, my man, my man,* her heart cried within her. *What will you do without me, in this strange place?*

She dashed the sweat from her brow. Her draped sleeves were already stained from wiping, but the heavy dew of the river seemed to drip from her forehead again and again, even as she tied the donkey to the peeled stake before the mud-brick hut.

"I have seen worse," Gunidu murmured to her. "Let us go in."

As they passed from the bright sunshine to the duskiness beneath the palm-thatch, Innashagga saw two women within. One lounged heavy upon her woven-reed seat, buttocks dripping down over the edges like fat in the fire; the other waited, drawn thinly upon herself like a mongoose drawing back to pounce upon a snake.

Neither arose: the lids of the fat woman narrowed, the eyes of the thin woman widened, as though discovering an unwelcome secret.

"Who are you?" the fat woman purred. "Where have you come from; why have you come here?"

It seemed to Innashagga as though she was stripped naked before the other's keen gaze—the veil from her head, the clay beads from her ears, the lapis and gold chain from her neck, the stone beads from her breast, the rope girdle from her hips, and the breechcloth from her loins. Yet she answered, as well as she could, "I am Innashagga, the wife of Akalla the Huntsman, and I am come here for my husband's sake, because I will not leave him while I live!"

The fat woman smiled. The hand she held out was dainty in spite of the thick-swollen arm that bore it, her nails sanded smooth and clean. "Then be welcome here, Innashagga," she said, her touch such a faint caress that Innashagga might have thought a breath of wind had passed along her forearm. "For we all are come here for our husbands' sakes, where women of better sense might be serving beer in the taverns in the cool of the evening, lying with lusty young swains at night and sleeping all through the heat of the day—"

"Whore!" the thin woman broke in.

The fat woman passed her hand through her dark henna-reddened ringlets and grinned. "Nay, you mock me, for a whore is a professional talent, whereas I merely wait for the one man who paid my price . . . and believe me, to rent is better for the one who means to go elsewhere later than to lease, and to lease is a better bargain than to sell, but I am a canny businesswoman, and so I made well sure that my man bought for life! But here, it is the Ensi who provides our home, so I must show the new maid and the old fellow their place. And you must haul your belongings out of it, for we were told when we came here that another family was like to be lodged with us."

"My husband is a fine artisan!" the thin woman flared. Now Innashagga took note that her garment was of the very finest-spun wool, dyed a deep flame-red; this was a woman before whom she would have dropped her head to the floor, had she ever passed through the village. "I bear it well enough that you, baker-wife, share this room; but what of this wild jenny-ass, her hair dulled with the desert dust, and that old palm-husk who rustles along behind her? Have we not suffered enough for Erech, that my husband toils all day and those who should serve us are set to work beside us?"

The fat woman heaved herself from her seat, setting her plump neat hands upon the tangled mass of metal beside her. "Aye, it may be you have suffered," she said. "But others have suffered more. I have seen sons die beneath the metal wheels of the great, and still I will not turn down what comes to me from my brother's share in the casting pits where the molten bronze burned his bones, for I still have children that must be fed, and if he lived, I know what he would say to me. So cease your honking, marsh-heron, and haul your possessions into your side of the hut. Now tell me, countrywoman, where did you come from, and why in the names of all the great gods were you stupid enough to come to Erech now?"

For the first time, Innashagga's words fled down her throat like tadpoles down the throat of a mother frog. Now she felt the dust that choked in Akalla's throat whenever he tried to speak: for she could not tell this woman of the Shamhatu or Enkidu . . . how she would laugh, to hear a wild jenny-ass from the desert claim that the great ones of Erech had spoken with her! And so she said only, "We left our village, for the land was dry, and my husband the huntsman would find better game here."

"Fools again!" The fat woman laughed, her belly quivering like wheat porridge on the flame. "I see that I must take you in and tell you how things are here. Do not mind that mangy bitch." She cast a suddenly cold-lidded glance at the thin woman who sat blowing the coals to brightness beneath their gray ash-veil. "She thinks well of herself with her fine dress, as you may do for the sake of what hangs about your neck, but here in the camp of those who build Gilgamesh's wall, she who has food is queen and the rest may bite their finery till they starve of it!"

Innashagga raised her hand to her throat without thinking, the little beads of lapis and gold sliding smoothly beneath her fingers. She glanced at Gunidu, waiting for him to speak, but the old man only sat silent, his legs crossed beneath the gray wool of his kilt and his eyes empty as obsidian from faraway lands, the dark mirroring glass waiting for an image to flash across its shiny black pool.

"But Gilgamesh has decreed that he will have us here," she answered stoutly. "I see that his men have already set place and worth for all of us alike, and I am sure that this will be upheld whenever his guards are called."

The fat woman's spittle hissed in the cooking fire; the thin woman only scowled, and Innashagga marked the golden beetle-shape hanging in the hollow of her throat—a shape that the traders from the Black Land always bore, albeit in cheap blue-glazed clay where she wore ruddy gold.

"For the sake of our Ensi, whose will shows forth the wisdom of the gods," the fat woman finally allowed. "Think yourself welcome, you and the little dried turd you drag behind you."

Then, though Innashagga's temper was slow to rouse, she saw her nails tearing out the other woman's eyeballs, tears of thick fat dripping down her cheeks from empty sockets. She knew that Akalla need fear no woman, but for a female tongue to speak such defilement against the good Gunidu, once Inanna's shepherd . . . that burned like a whip of nettles, cut like a thistle-bed!

"For your sake, dear Inanna," Innashagga whispered, "let this game end!" She was so tired that she barely had the strength to hold back the tears pressing hot against her eyes; in another moment, she knew, she would either weep or scream.

"When your husband gets his pay," the fat woman went on, "give him enough for a pot of beer and keep the rest carefully where he can't get it, else he'll spend it all. A builder's wages: that's enough for any man, and a gods-cursed sight more than my useless bastard brought home before Gilgamesh's men snagged him for the army. Now, you lazy skinny she-mule," she added to the artisan's wife, "move aside: we knew we'd be lucky to share two by two, and you've no right to whine of a third." She turned back to Innashagga. "And if you snore all night, you stupid country jenny-ass, I'll stab you myself before ever the Ensi's spies, or even the vultures, get here. But now, get your arse and the skinny arse of that played-out weed behind you into my hut, and you can trust the safety of whatever's here. Because, by Enlil's help, I'll gnaw the bones of any bastard whoreson who comes near my hut or within fifty paces of my asses' lines, and may the High Ones roast my bones if I lie, rotten bitch though I may be!"

Innashagga gulped thick spittle, her ears burning. She had never heard a woman speak thus, for this was not how women spoke. She did not know whether this woman meant to be her friend or her foe, but each of the rough words thrust a cold barb through her belly . . . where, the goddesses be kind and the silence from her womb at the moon's dark witness, a child should grow . . .

But the big woman's arm was already draping around her shoulders, shielding her behind a warm veil of drooping fat and the soft hot smell of a mother breeding milk. Innashagga wanted, for a second, to turn into her welcoming darkness, even as the woman's deep voice purred, "Ah, don't be afraid of me, I'm just an old ewe with a loud bleat. Now, you want a little food and a little milk and a lot of sleep; and you'll have it, too."

Then there was the hard rim of the clay cup tipping over, spilling the warm creamy stream of milk into her mouth; and the sweetness of bread, the coarse grains grinding between her teeth. Innashagga chewed eagerly, though her eyelids were already closing, the colors behind them streaming bright against the dun mud-bricks of the rough hovel.

"You weren't so kind to me," a voice said sharply, and a softer, lower one murmured, "You only walked from Erech, and who should care? . . . But hush, she is sleeping, poor worn lamb from the hills. Leave her be."

Innashagga jerked awake to the sharp pinch at her thigh, opening her eyes to darkness. The thin woman's shadow loomed high above the fire-flickering shadows on the jagged thatch, while Gunidu lay still as a lizard lurking for its prey, and the great belly of the other woman sagged up and down, up and down, in her half-made bed—for none of the men had come back that night.

Then a dreadful cold fear closed upon Innashagga, like the claw of the night-bird *lilitu* tightening upon her guts. And she whispered to the darkness and the shadow darkening her, "Do you not fear?"

No answer came, and the silence emboldened her. And she murmured again, "Do you not fear? The men must have gone out in the night, since they are not here—you did not come here for your own sake, but you must have a loved one. Do you not fear for him?"

The blow stung across Innashagga's face; an edge cut her lip, the bitterness of bronze aching beneath the bright pain of blood. But the tall thin shadow beside her did not speak, and nor did she.

Presently that shadow lowered, lying down. Innashagga heard the rustling of woolen blankets, and pulled her own blankets up more tightly about her shoulders, until at last her shivering ceased and she slept.

THE SUN BURNED hot on Gilgamesh's head as he walked along his growing wall, his basket of mud-bricks balanced easily on his right shoulder. Though it unbalanced him a little, its weight was comforting, its weight and the heat of the rivulets of sweat running down his back to soak into the plain worker's kilt he wore. When his eyes flicked carefully to the side, he could see Enkidu, likewise burdened and simply clad, as though the two of them were only workmen on the wall—but ahead of them marched six soldiers with bows over their shoulders, and a like band followed behind, their spears upraised as though the glittering bronze points could hold off the danger of the priestess' warning, dropping like a storm-cloud from the high mountains. Fenced about by his guards, watched as closely as a prisoner, Gilgamesh found comfort in the strain of balancing the heavy basket of bricks, even in the ache beginning to grow in his back and neck from the lopsided weight he bore.

But it was also a relief to come to the end of the wall, where he could carefully set the basket down for the hands of the masons to empty it. *The price of being the strongest,* Gilgamesh thought, *is always having to show it:* no other man in Erech could have carried full baskets as large as theirs. Beside him, Enkidu grinned as he likewise unburdened himself. The heavy muscles of his abdomen stood out sharply beneath his pelt of golden hair as he stretched and arched his back; his fair skin was red from heat and work, dewy trickles of sweat dripping into his eyebrows and beard. "Only a few hundred more basket-loads until the wall is built?" Enkidu said.

Gilgamesh laughed, reaching out to tug lightly on the other man's thick tawny braid. "No doubt we could build it all by ourselves, given enough time. But it is as well that we don't have to: when would we be able to go to the taverns for beer?"

Enkidu looked up at the wall. Men on the ground handed mud-bricks up to men on ladders, who spread mud mortar with their trowels and carefully set the bricks in it, one by one. "It is a fine craft the builders have," he said, "to shape the earth and build it up until it becomes a mountain to hide behind or a cave to dwell in. I am glad to be helping."

Gilgamesh blinked. Mud-bricks were mud-bricks: few could afford or would bother to build in stone, but the little oblongs of baked clay served for almost everything better than a fisher's little hut or the hastily thrown-up reed houses where the workers and those of their women who would not leave their husbands stayed; everything from a simple stonemason's house to the great temple of Inanna. And yet Enkidu was right, that it was all earth, only shaped by human hands . . .

"Well, your help is good to have," Gilgamesh said. He glanced up at the burning yellow-white orb of the sun. "Now Utu sits in the middle of his judgment hall, or will very soon, and we should soon hear the ram's horn blowing the signal for rest and lunch. And those who have worked on the wall this morning will need training as soldiers this afternoon . . . shall we go somewhere cool for food and drink and rest?"

"That would be well," Enkidu agreed.

Arm in arm they rounded the wall, heading back toward the main gates of Erech. Suddenly Enkidu stopped sharply, head lifted and nostrils flared.

"What is it?" Gilgamesh asked. The soldiers walking in front of them already had bows nocked; those behind had lowered their spears, spreading out in a semicircle around Gilgamesh and Enkidu.

"There is no danger," Enkidu said, a strange sharp edge to his voice. "These men may get back from us."

*He is as tired of these guards as I,* Gilgamesh thought. *It was not fair of me to yoke them to him as well, when it is his nature to run free; perhaps—*

But Enkidu went on: "See that man—there?" He pointed to the back of one of the basket-carriers—a strong fellow, his broad shoulders deeply bronzed as though he had spent many years in outdoor labor. "That is Akalla the hunter, who brought Shamhatu to me, and thus me to you, and who let us stay in his house while I learned to be a man. I should like to speak with him again, and find how matters are with his family, who were kind to me."

Gilgamesh thought of the man who had come to him with news of the wild wanderer roaming among the lions—tangled tongue, oxen-stupidity; why should Enkidu wish to speak with him? Yet Enkidu sat through his own court cases and his arguments with counselors who, for all their smooth tongues, often seemed little brighter than the half-witted hunter. Could he not do the same for his friend?

"Well enough," Gilgamesh said. "Perhaps he would like to eat with us. You two"—he pointed at a pair of the bow-wielding guards—"go bring that man to us."

The two young commanders eased their arrows away from their strings, but did not put them back in the quiver. Lithely they trotted to either side of the basket-carrier; Gilgamesh heard Ishbi-Erra's sharp voice saying, "Put that down, man: you have been summoned by the Ensi."

Akalla heaved the basket from his shoulder, nearly overbalancing in his haste. One brick toppled out, breaking on the ground, but he recovered before more could spill. Gilgamesh saw the huntsman's coarse face go white beneath his deep tan as he glanced from side to side, at the bows in the hands of Gilgamesh's guards.

"Have no fear," Gilgamesh called out, pitching his voice so that it would carry easily to Akalla's ears. "We do not mean you harm, but honor, for the sake of the kindness you showed to Enkidu when he was a stranger in your home."

Akalla bowed low, his forehead almost brushing the dust. "Great Ensi," he stammered. "Noble one, uplifted, uplifted by the gods . . ." His tongue seemed to fail him then; his eyes rolled wildly, and he scrubbed his palm over his sweat-spiked cap of short black hair. Then he glanced back guiltily, to where another man was already picking up his basket. "I am sorry, Ensi, I did not mean to break your brick."

"There are many bricks," Gilgamesh said, as reassuringly as he could, "but I have only one Enkidu, and he remembers you well. Again, for the sake of the kindness you showed to him in your house, now that you are in Erech, will you come and eat with us?"

Akalla bobbed his head. "I—I . . . you are, too . . . If it, it is your will, you who are exalted above all men by the gods."

Enkidu reached out and patted him on the shoulder. "You need not speak so," he began. Ishbi-Erra hissed disapprovingly, and Enkidu blinked, looking at Gilgamesh. "Need he?"

Gilgamesh smiled. He had not tried to teach Enkidu any formal terms of address, for even had the rich array of titles and phrases left the wild man less confused, it eased the Ensi's heart to have one mouth that was never veiled from him by a cloud of flattering or pious words. "He need only call me Ensi or Lugal, as the rest of my soldiers and workmen do. If all the men in the army," he added a little more loudly, sensing by the tight set of his bodyguards' shoulders and the dark sideways glances flashing between them, "spoke to me as peasants before the court of the Ensi, Agga would be stripping the temple of Inanna before the message that his army was coming had been delivered in full." There: several of the young commanders-of-sixty who took it in turn to guard him were fonder of title and rank than was good for them, but a small dose of sense, Gilgamesh thought, might serve to dim their pride a little—not to mention, indeed, watching the Ensi and Enkidu eat and drink with a man who seemed to be no more than a half-witted worker: the low were as much a part of the army as the high, and a commander who could not remember that had no business leading men.

"And we shall go," Gilgamesh went on, "to that tavern beside the gate which is called the Ram's Horn, for I know that their cheese is fresh and their beer strong, and the innkeeper's daughter well worth looking on besides."

"But, my Ensi—" one of the other guards began.

Gilgamesh cut him off by chopping his hand through the air, then gesturing to Enkidu and Akalla with a wide wave of his arm. "Come, let us go."

He took off at a trot, Enkidu pacing easily by his right side, and Akalla, after a moment of standing like a temple ram with the felling blow just landed between his horns, catching up and easily matching him at the left. Behind, Gilgamesh could hear the panting as the guards struggled to catch up; for their sake, he fell back a little, so that the two in front could outdistance him a little and thereby know that they did their duty. And yet his fists clenched: must every step remind him of what might lurk before him, when all his life he had only needed to escape what might wait behind?

But he pulled up at the low mud-brick building where a ram's curling horn hung over the reed door-screen, and passed in between the two guards who already stood within, waiting at either side of the door so that no blow from the sudden shadows might surprise their Ensi's light-dazzled eyes.

Gilgamesh squatted in an empty place on the floor, the mud-bricks cool and rough beneath his knees. Enkidu settled in beside him, but Akalla stood, his hands twisting at the hem of his girded-up kilt until Gilgamesh gestured him to sit as well. The innkeeper's daughter was there in a moment, kneeling so that the fringe of ruddy hair over her forehead swept the dusty floor.

"Most noble one, exalted of the gods, blessed of Inanna and protector of Erech the Sheepfold," she said in a single breath, "what may I bring to please you?"

"Beer and cheese and bread," Gilgamesh answered. He reached out to take her small hand in his. Beyond the calluses of her work, it was very soft and smooth, as though she soaked it in buttermilk each night. For a moment he looked up into her dark eyes: lacking the finely ground cosmetics of higher-born women, she had smudged charcoal from the oven lightly over her eyelids, and her sweat had streaked it a little. He smiled. "What more might a man want?"

Although sun and work had dusked her skin, Gilgamesh could see the crimson blood coming to her cheeks as she glanced away from his gaze; but even so, her hand tightened on his. "Whatever the Ensi . . ." For a moment her eyes flickered sideways to Enkidu. ". . . and his beloved companion desire, we shall do our best to provide it here, though the Ram's Horn is but a humble tavern, and little worthy of the presence of the great."

Gilgamesh let go of her hand, but caressed her cheek a moment. "You are still within Erech the Sheepfold," he said softly, "and where else should the shepherd be found? But go quickly, maiden, and fetch our food and drink, lest we faint from sun and labor."

The innkeeper's daughter—what was her name?—scampered away hurriedly. Enkidu's head turned, his gaze following her, and Gilgamesh laughed.

"See, I told you that she was worth looking upon."

"Aye," Enkidu rumbled, "and her scent is right." He smiled, tossing his thick fair braid back from his shoulders. "If we mate with her tonight . . ." Enkidu stopped for a moment, as he often did. His eyes dimmed to the blank sheen of green agate; Gilgamesh had seen this before, and thought that he must be trying to bring the thoughts of the lion into the words of the man. He waited patiently until his beloved's gaze cleared, and Enkidu smiled. "If we mate with her tonight, she will make cubs, and she is young and well-favored and strong. Is that not good? For you . . ." Enkidu paused again. "You are king of the pack, and I am your close friend. But out first queen has given us no children yet, and surely there must be others?"

Gilgamesh gulped, silent himself for a few breaths' time. *Shamhatu*, he thought, *what else did you forget to teach?* Before him, he saw stretching out the great desert of customs and ways, the high mountain of Inanna's terrace-shrine hemming him away from the marriage of an ordinary man, even as it freed him to love as he would—*a green valley, but a narrow one; and what slaughterer awaits the ram at its end?* Enkidu might marry the maid, but for him to be tied to a tavern wench simply because he had gotten a child on her . . . ? And yet, how could he explain the deep gorge that lay between common and noble, especially when it was the Ensi's duty to bridge that ravine, or at least to seem to do so?

"There shall be, in time," he said. "But . . ."

Enkidu's eyes met Gilgamesh's, and his own words failed him. How, indeed, to tell a lion that he should not mate with every willing female he came upon . . . how many of the women they had gladly shared might already bear Enkidu's seed, or his own?

Gilgamesh wrapped his arm around Enkidu's shoulders, bent to whisper in his ear, nuzzling close into the sweat-warm curls of fair hair. "If you want her, you may have her," he murmured. "I must take care, for . . ." He did not finish the thought.

Enkidu embraced him briefly in turn—it was too warm, and both of them too sweaty and heated with work on the wall, to cling closer. "I would not leave you, my friend," he answered. "There will be time for us to find queens and raise our cubs later, when we have won our . . . city . . . safe."

Gilgamesh nodded and closed his eyes, trying to hide his tears. *Who but a lion, to be my friend?* he thought. *To Enkidu, I am forever no more than a pride leader . . . he is nothing but my friend, Shamhatu a lioness whom the two of us may share, and Agga the leader of a rival pack.* For a moment his gut twisted within him . . . longing or envy, he did not know which; but Enkidu's hand still rested on his shoulder, and he could only dip his head in thanks to the gods who had shaped his friend and brought him in from the free wilderness to the writhing pit of men, so that Gilgamesh could see his own way out.

When Gilgamesh opened his eyes again, though, it was not Enkidu upon whom he looked, but the blocky blank face of the huntsman Akalla, silent as a gelded donkey beneath the yoke; and Gilgamesh remembered why they had come here together.

Again, though, it was Enkidu who saved him, speaking before Gilgamesh could shape the words beneath the reed of his tongue.

"I am glad to see you here, my friend Akalla," Enkidu said. "I was happy in your home, and did not hope to see you again."

Akalla blinked rapidly; and where before Gilgamesh had only seen stupidity in the dark liquid depths of his brown eyes, now, knowing Enkidu's struggles, he could see how the hunter fought to shape words from the wet clay of his brain, and believe that Akalla's skull was not an empty well, but one in which the water lay very deep.

"We must, we must leave our village," Akalla stammered. "When you left, all was not, was not . . . it was not the same."

Enkidu reached across the table, laying his great hand across Akalla's. A shaft of sunlight through the open door glimmered bright on the little golden hairs of his arm; then one of Gilgamesh's guards shifted, his shadow cutting off the light. "Did any harm come to you?" he murmured. "Did any work you ill?"

"No, not me, none . . . Only fewer, fewer wanted game, and my wife, she—"

"But you are here now," Gilgamesh interposed swiftly. "Your wife, where is she?"

"My Ensi, she is in the reed huts outside the city walls, with the other wives of the builders, where the law has driven them—" Akalla stopped, hand flying to his mouth and eyes flaring open so that Gilgamesh could see the white rim all around his dark irises like fat about a sheep's liver. "I did not mean, my Ensi—"

"You may speak freely," Gilgamesh said. "I take no offense: I know why I did what needed to be done, and that many would not be glad of it."

"And Gunidu?" asked Enkidu. "Is he with Innashagga, or has he gone up to Inanna?"

"He, the guards at the gate, they . . . they said he could choose, and he, he . . . with Innashagga, in the hut," Akalla stammered finally.

"I shall see that they are called in," Gilgamesh said gently. "It will not do for the Ensi's chief huntsman to work upon the wall, nor for his wife and kinsman to while in the builders' reed huts."

He waited a moment for his words to sink in, but Akalla only stared at him with the slow patience of one used to waiting for a stag's shoulder to show clearly among the rustling reeds at the watering hole.

"Henceforth," Gilgamesh went on at last, "you shall be my chief huntsman, for you brought in the rarest and most beloved of all game: the fierce lion of Erech, who shares my bedchamber and guards me in my sleep. What more can you say to that?"

Akalla only squatted there with his mouth opening and closing; it seemed to Gilgamesh that his words had burst around the man's ears like a thunderclap, deafening him as they silenced his voice. It was well that the innkeeper's daughter bent to set their mugs before them at that moment, for then he could lean forward, closing Akalla's fingers about the cool clay cup and lifting it toward the huntsman's mouth.

"Drink, man," he said, "for I think that you need it."

Akalla's throat convulsed as he drank, and Gilgamesh and Enkidu matched him draught for draught. The beer was sweet, heavy with the taste of dates, for Gilgamesh had drunk more than once at the Ram's Horn, and he knew that they took care to have the best there for him. But it would go swiftly to the huntsman's head; and there, Gilgamesh knew, it would either loosen his tongue or bind it past speech.

Yet, as the cool sweet draught swept down his own throat, Gilgamesh found that it was his own tongue loosened from the dust of the day's labor, and himself who spoke easily, saying, "While the Buranun floods, there will be no fighting, and the walls will rise swiftly enough without my help. Akalla, I desire to go hunting for a few days, before the waters fall back and Agga's troops come marching. Enkidu and I . . . and my guards," he added, the bitumen-dark stain of bitterness at the back of his throat, "and you to guide us. We may ride out to the place you choose, and thereafter we shall trust your tracking."

Enkidu's eyes closed, his white teeth showing through his golden beard; and though Gilgamesh was not touching him, he could feel the delighted relief surging through the body of his beloved, mirrored in his own. *Yes, this is right,* he thought . . . *or else the gods betrayed me when they sent me Enkidu, and then it must be time for me to die.*

"I—I—shall be glad, my Ensi," Akalla stammered. "If only, if only . . ." Then his mouth worked soundlessly, as though his tongue had swollen to choke his throat.

Gilgamesh could only look at him, then look away, lest his gaze be at fault. But from the corner of his eye he could see how Enkidu lay his arm across the huntsman's deep brown shoulders, hear the soft wordless rumble that came from his friend's throat. For a moment a sharp pang shot through him—a pang that he could not put a name to—and then Enkidu spoke.

"He fears for his own queen and the little one in her womb. We must see to them first, and then he will hunt well."

*How did you know?* Gilgamesh thought. And he did not speak the words, but then Enkidu was touching him, his blunted nails stroking down the Ensi's sweat-sheened back, and he knew that it was the same gift by which Enkidu knew all his own thoughts: some blending of scent and sight and feeling, just as a lion could tell a weak gazelle from a strong one where a man could never see a hair's difference.

"Then it shall be so, Ishbi-Erra!" he called.

The young man was before him before he had drawn another breath. Gilgamesh gazed at him a moment. *I misjudged him, perhaps . . .* Sululi had deserved a more loving husband, a man who desired her for more than her father's wealth; and yet, he had heard, Ishbi-Erra had given her a strong son within nine months of the wedding, and when the young woman went out, she was always decked in the finest linen and jewels of gold and carnelian beyond what folk thought Ishbi-Erra's means could support. *And so many weddings made for wealth or state end in love . . . what more could I want for her, poor thing?*

"My Lugal," Ishbi-Erra answered breathlessly. "How may I serve the exalted of the gods, the defender of Erech?"

"Go to the reed huts of the builders and find . . ." Gilgamesh glanced at Enkidu.

"Innashagga and Gunidu."

"The kinsfolk of Akalla the Huntsman. Bring them to the temple-town, and tell the steward there that they are to have their own home, as fine as can be found, for they are the wife and father-in-law of the Ensi's chief huntsman."

Ishbi-Erra turned, barking orders to another of the guards. Gilgamesh waited until he was done, then went on, "And see to it that my chariot is readied, and hunting gear for three. Tomorrow, Akalla, Enkidu, and I shall hunt for stag."

"And what of your guard?" Ishbi-Erra stammered. "We must follow you, for there are many dangers in the wilderness."

Gilgamesh frowned. "Fewer than in Erech the Sheepfold, it would seem: if my foes are not advised by the gods, they will have no way of knowing where I have gone. But if you must," he added, "have chariots readied for yourselves, so that you may follow behind in case of some mischance."

"As you command, O Lugal, blessed of Inanna and exalted of Enlil," Ishbi-Erra replied.

Gilgamesh breathed deeply, forcing himself to relax as he drank another draught of the sweet beer. His limbs were shaking with tightness, as if he were an untrained youth who had nerved himself up to fight one stronger and more skilled. *Yet I am well used to battle, and to arguing with those who tell me what the Ensi should not do. Why should a few orders given to a young guard have come so hard from my mouth?* But he could already see the lightening in Enkidu's green eyes, the little line of worry vanishing from between his beloved's thick golden brows. They had spent long enough together in Gilgamesh's home, among counselors and priests and political advisers; was it not fit that they go out to Enkidu's for a time, with no worse companions than lions and wolves and wild dogs? The relief surged through Gilgamesh's veins at the thought, too strong for him to deny it: he knew that the strain of waiting and watching for the boats and clouds of dust from the North, compounded by the newer shadows in the darkness and the unending nearness of his guards, had been slowly but surely pressing him down. But now there would be release from his prison, at least for a little time, and he and Enkidu could fling themselves back into the war with new strength and fresh joy . . .

The serving-girl had come and gone, setting down the food while Gilgamesh spoke. He bit into the slice of goat's cheese, savoring the nutty taste and the chewiness of the rind a moment before following it with a mouthful of the flat bread on which it lay.

"I am very glad of this," Enkidu said softly, and Gilgamesh needed to hear no more.

But Ishbi-Erra leaned closer to him. "My Ensi, exalted of the gods—there is something more that I would say to you, and it must be said in private."

Gilgamesh looked at him suspiciously, but the young man's eyes held steady on his own. Though he little wished to be alone with anyone save Enkidu, he could read only frank worry on Ishbi-Erra's narrow face. *And if he wishes to do me harm, it is his body against mine,* Gilgamesh told himself.

"Let it be so. Enkidu, Akalla—leave us a moment."

Enkidu frowned, but did not argue as he rose, walking across the room with the huntsman.

"Now you may speak," Gilgamesh told Ishbi-Erra. "What is it that you must say?"

"My Ensi, I have a glimmering of the direction from which your danger may come, though I do not yet know what may be done."

Gilgamesh gripped Ishbi-Erra's shoulder, easing off only when he felt the bones move beneath his hands and saw the other's face pale. "Tell me!"

"My Ensi—though you work beside the folk of the temple every day, as befits the great powers of the city, it is also truly said that the temple serves only the gods, not the Ensi."

Gilgamesh's jaw tightened. He had heard those words before: as a child, when he had been told that he must not do . . . something or other, he had forgotten what . . . within the shrine, he had boldly declared that when *he* was Ensi, things would be different. And the face of the Shamhatu had crumpled, and she had lifted him to her lap, rocking him softly, and murmured, *My son, my son. Do not think so, or speak so, else your days in the land will not be long. The temple serves the gods, not the Ensi, and if the gods turn against you, so will the folk of the Eanna.*

"What is it that you think? Have you heard something that I have not?"

"My Ensi . . ." Ishbi-Erra swallowed hard. "There is a woman of the temple that I know very well. She has told me that the Shamhatu thinks ill of you, because you have not come to her. Since your ascension, she has failed to bring you to Inanna's bed, and thus her own place is shaky. This she knows, and thus she holds that you are a stumbling block in the way of her power. If you were not Ensi, but some other could take your place . . ."

"Then he would come to her, and she would be confirmed forever," Gilgamesh went on slowly. "But it was the Shamhatu who sent the trance-priestess to warn me. Why would she do that, if she were the source of the danger? Would she not simply strike in the darkness?"

"Who would suspect her now?" Ishbi-Erra countered. "The one who seems most concerned for your safety—who would guess that she had dropped poison into your drink?"

"Have you proof of this? Can you tell me the name of your informant?" His lover—but the two of them had been discreet enough that no rumor had mentioned her name.

Ishbi-Erra's eyes dropped. "Without sure proof, it would only endanger her if I spoke her name."

"And you have none."

"Not yet—no. But I had to tell you this, that you might be wary."

Gilgamesh nodded. The guard's words troubled his heart, nearly as much as the prophecy itself had. The Shamhatu might disagree with all he said or did, might work as strongly as she could to thwart his plans when they did not match her own . . . but treason? Murder? Till now he would have sworn that those things could never enter her heart. Yet Ishbi-Erra's words were spoken, and Gilgamesh knew that he would never be able to cleanse the stain of suspicion wholly from his heart.

"Then it is as well," he said, "that we mean to leave the city for a time." One less thing to fear, at least for a little while—a short ease from a burden that he had not borne a few moments ago.

THE SHAMHATU SAT upon her bed, sipping slowly at her goat's milk. Though she drank through a silver straw, and her cup was made of thin slabs of lapis set into a framework of silver, when there was no one to watch her, she could still dip her little finger in and run it around the rim to scoop up the little blobs of cream left on the cup and suck them off like a child of eleven. One of her few silly pleasures, in that short time she had to herself when the day's heat became choking within the shrine on top of the platform and almost all the priests and priestesses retired to cooler grounds . . . Thankfully, her room was one of the best-set in the temple-city, with a window open to the river's cool breeze, but not to the direct light of the sun; and the carefully carven screen of thin cedar across it let light and air in, while keeping all but the smallest flies out.

She turned the octagonal cone of silver and lapis around and around, watching the streaks of white cream swirl on the slightly darker milk. That and a few dates would see her through the rest of the afternoon, until the evening's cool brought her appetite back; absently she picked one of the sticky fruits up and chewed at it, washing its sweetness down with another mouthful of milk. The random flowings of the cream whirled like clouds, drawing her eye into patterns . . . a wheel flying clear; something like a donkey's head, its neck twisting downward from the mass and falling away . . .

Shamhatu frowned, gazing more closely; but the shapes had gone, leaving her with only the disquieting taste in the back of her mouth, like the first hint of taint left by milk just starting to go bad. Yet the milk in her cup was good—she wiped the light dew of sweat from her brow and sipped again to prove it to herself.

Setting down her cup, Shamhatu drew up her legs, crossing them beneath her as she turned to stare at the gem-bedecked statue of Inanna in the corner. Even in the heat of the day, it seemed to Shamhatu that the goddess was cloaked in her heavenly shawl of evening: her gold diadem and breast-coils did not dazzle, but gleamed richly from the corner's shadows, the deep colors of her agate girdle promising a stronger fire beneath.

Shamhatu fixed her eyes upon the eight-pointed gold star of Inanna's crown, letting its rays draw her gaze in to the center.

"Praise to the goddess, greatest of the goddesses," she sang in a soft whisper. The ritual words filled her skull like the singing of the *tigi*-hymns filling the goddess' shrine, drowning out the sound of her own thoughts.

> "Revere the mistress of the peoples, most awesome of heaven's
>       gods.
> Praise to Inanna, greatest of the goddesses,
> Revere the queen of women, most awesome of heaven's gods.
> For she is clothed with pleasure and love,
> She is laden with life-strength, voluptuousness and charm.
> The goddess, with her there is counsel,
> She holds the fate of everything in her hand.
> Who can be equal to her greatness?
> Strong, exalted, splendid are her decrees.
> Inanna—who can be equal to her greatness?
> Strong, exalted, splendid are her decrees . . ."

Yet even as she sang, other words rose unbidden in the back of Shamhatu's mind, and it seemed that her gaze slipped away from the brightness of Inanna's star to the darkness behind the goddess' stone shape. *I saw a scorpion lurking beneath the rock that turns under the Ensi's sandal; I saw a snake coiled in the shadows beside the path where the Ensi walks,* Geme-Tirash's voice whispered in the dim recesses of Shamhatu's skull. Though the priestess had sung the hymn to Inanna from her childhood, the words fled from her now like river-mist before the stormwind, and she found that she was hugging herself and shaking, even as the afternoon-sweat rolled down her back.

"What is this threat, Inanna?" she whispered, "that it can turn my mind from your greatness, or make my trust in your strength tremble? What evil is it that I fear?"

Shamhatu took a deep breath, then another, until her heartbeats slowed. As she looked upon the statue of the goddess, another litany came to her mind, as old and well-known, but of sorrow instead of praise: *crown, ear-pendants, neck-chains, breast-ornaments, birthstone-girdle, bracelets and anklets, breechcloth . . . Enter, my lady, thus are the rules of the Mistress of the Netherworld . . .*

"I fear Gilgamesh's death," she answered herself. There it was, the horror that seized her: the thought of his loud voice stilled, his proud head laid low. For though he was two-thirds god and one-third man, he, too, could die—would die, must die in time. *For to each man is a day of death appointed, though he be high-born or low, good or evil, joyful or sorrowful in his days. None can escape the decree of the gods, though he flee to the mountain's height or the desert's end: Erishkegal prepares a place for each, and her gatekeeper knows the hour of their coming, before the living heart is stilled.*

"And how would it be for Erech," Shamhatu whispered to herself, "if the line of Dumuzi, beloved of Inanna, were to pass from it—and leave the New Year's wedding unmade? Surely it would not be long before her favor would leave Erech as well, before the *gala*-priests no longer sang hymns in her shrine, the augurs no longer read the livers of the sacrificial sheep and the sheepfold itself was given to the wind . . . by the hand," she added unwillingly, "of Agga of Kish."

But with Gilgamesh dead, there would be no war: Erech could send her surrender, and tribute to Kish, and all things would be as they had before. A new Ensi could be chosen: Shusuen, perhaps, for he was of the En's holy line, and, as chief scribe, already knew all the doings of Erech's rulers. Or—a stranger thought came to her—one lived who was also a child of Inanna and her shepherd. The Ensi's crown could be placed upon Akalla's head, the En's medallion around his neck, and if he knew nothing of rule and could not learn, well, the city's Elders and the Eanna had ruled well enough for the child Gilgamesh. They could do the same for Akalla, while he did all the gods required for Erech.

But she thought of the huntsman, so at home in the wilderness, so lost within the *gipar*. Could he grow used to sitting on a throne and drinking from a gold cup—with the whole of Erech laughing behind his back, because the Ensi could not read or speak without stammering? Inanna might accept him with love, but who else would give Akalla more than praise to his face, and scorn outside his hearing. And little Innashagga: she might delight in the fine clothes and jewelry she would receive, but what would she say when the votive-wives were presented to Akalla? Shusuen would be a far better choice, but still . . . for all his foolishness, what would Erech be without Gilgamesh?

The Shamhatu rose and knelt, pressing her forehead to the floor before Inanna's stone feet. "O, my goddess," she prayed, "shepherdess of Erech the Sheepfold, who cares for the city as each man's personal god cares for him, mother to all Erech's children, bride to Erech's mighty men . . . do not let us fall! For now that war is upon us, only Gilgamesh can win it, if you fight beside him and strengthen his host. Queen of Heaven, Lady of Battle, who sent your warning to our Ensi, who led Enkidu in to guard his side and his back—protect him now, for all our sakes!" Her tears dropped hot to the floor, darkening the fine weave of the sky-blue rug on which she knelt.

GILGAMESH AND ENKIDU rose before dawn, going out into the cool air beneath the glittering light of Inanna's star. A few folk were already stirring in the streets of the temple-city: a young herder leading his flock of sheep toward the gate, a baker bearing her high-heaped basket of flat loaves on her head. A faint light gleamed from the door of the shrine atop the platform—either Shamhatu or the En would be in there, doing the early morning reverences to Inanna's light.

Gilgamesh's chariot was already outside the stables, the four harnessed onagers twitching their ears and stamping their hooves restlessly. Akalla stood next to it, fumbling uneasily with the silver-embossed quiver strap crossing his chest—as Gilgamesh had ordered, it was the Ensi's gear that had been brought out for all three of them. Some of the

guards stood by their own chariots; others were busy harnessing up donkeys from Gilgamesh's stables.

Enkidu leapt easily into the Ensi's chariot, taking up the onagers'
reins. The stubborn beasts tossed their heads against the pull, then lowered them again. Half wild themselves, though raised and trained from
foals, they had learned quickly that it did little good to struggle against
the man from the wilderness, and Enkidu was set in his desire that he
would drive Gilgamesh's chariot while his friend did battle. Gilgamesh
followed him, bracing his leg against the side while he strapped on his
own hunting gear.

"Akalla, will you come up with us?" Gilgamesh said. "It is easier to
ride than to walk."

But the huntsman shook his head. "I have never ridden in . . . in a
chariot, my Ensi." He gestured silently at the thin boards Gilgamesh and
Enkidu stood on, at the open back, then at the restless onagers harnessed
before it. "I fear I would, I would . . ."

*Fall out*, Gilgamesh supplied silently for him. He shook his head.
"Well, as you will. When we get out into the field, it will be your task to
flush the game, anyway. Are we ready?"

Enkidu smiled. "More than ready. The game is at the watering holes
now: perhaps if we go swiftly, we can get there before it flees."

Gilgamesh looked at him startled—surely Enkidu knew how far they
had to travel before coming to the best hunting lands? But then Enkidu
laughed, and Gilgamesh realized that his friend meant to jest with him.
And so he laughed as well, even as the reins jingled against their silver
ring and the four onagers surged forward, their hooves pounding up a
cloud of cool dust from the dry street. Behind them, the guards were
shouting to each other, "Hurry!" "Get going!" "Cover him!"

Enkidu swerved the chariot to one side, narrowly missing a small
child that had wandered into the road. It swung dangerously, two of the
great flat wheels lifting from the ground, but Enkidu swayed his weight,
his strength throwing it back down to tear ruts in the road with new
force as they hurtled toward the city gates.

Gilgamesh saw a brief cold flash of bronze—a helm or a spear-point,
he could not tell—before plunging beneath the dark chill shadow of his

wall. Then they were out and thundering down the road, the onagers lowering their heads and plunging forward as if trampling their way into the host of the foe. Gilgamesh threw his own head back, hair streaming behind him in the wind of their driving, and shouted out a wordless battle-cry, even as Enkidu roared beside him. Drawing his sword, Gilgamesh laid about at the cool dawn air, chopping down, at last, the phantoms and hidden devils that had haunted the dark corners of his nights and whispered behind his back in the pressing heat of the day.

When at last the hard-breathing onagers slowed to a walk, beads of sweat were dripping hot and salty down Gilgamesh's face, beginning to chill on his chest and back. He sheathed his sword, smiling a little shamefacedly at Enkidu.

"It is good practice for the charge against Agga," Gilgamesh said.

Enkidu laid one warm hand on Gilgamesh's bare shoulder. "It is good to run and be free," he answered.

Behind them Erech's walls were beginning to show dark against the growing light of dawn; and in that rising blue light, Gilgamesh could see the shapes of the other chariots against the road. Even good racing donkeys were not as swift as onagers, but they were tireless. His guards would be catching up with him soon. For a moment he had to stifle the twisting urge to tell Enkidu to drive away, over the fields, leave their set path altogether and see if they might escape. But that, Gilgamesh knew, was foolishness: his own mind turning back on him like a snake caught by the tail, or a scorpion by the head.

"It is good to be free," he said. "But we should pull up and wait for a little, lest we leave all our companions behind."

Enkidu tugged the onagers to a stop. They stood there until the first donkey-chariot—Akalla trotting by its side—was nearly abreast, then Enkidu urged their beasts into a walk again, so that Gilgamesh seemed to ride stately in the lead of his procession.

All through the morning they rode through the dry fields. Only the rising waters flowing fast through the irrigation canals—the waters that had lain flat and brown less than half a month ago—showed that the flood tide of the Buranun was near. It would not be long before the waters had risen and drawn back, before the green shoots of barley and beans and cabbages showed above the drying mud—and the armies began to march. Yet the inundation was safety for a little time, and delay in battle: a water-bounded moment of peace for Gilgamesh. Above, a hawk circled, lazy as a feather floating on the breeze.

As the sun rose, the sky burned brighter—a burnished bowl of tin, reflecting Utu's growing heat back upon the earth. Gilgamesh called a halt at noon, and the men rested and ate beneath the rustling shade of a grove of palm trees. Their food was simple: hard-baked bread spread with sheep's cheese, washed down with rough young beer. After they had eaten, Gilgamesh stretched himself full-length on the scruffy dry grass under the palm trees, his head on Enkidu's lap, as the guards drew lots on who should sleep and who should watch during the midday heat.

In the evening, the hunting party stopped at an inn by the side of the road—a plain mud-brick building, with a bunch of dates and a sheaf of dried barley hanging outside its door to show that food and drink could be had inside. Gilgamesh had stayed there before on his way to his hunting grounds: he knew that there was water and stabling enough for their beasts, that the beer was good, and that there was enough space inside for all of them to sleep comfortably, with Enkidu and himself in a room of their own where none of the guard would jostle or nag them.

"Why do you sigh?" Enkidu asked curiously. "Is something wrong with this inn?"

"I have often come here surrounded by young men of high birth, riding in chariots with bows ready to draw and loose upon game," Gilgamesh answered, his voice low. "And their company has never been onerous to me before."

Enkidu only put his arm about his friend's shoulder, as if he knew Gilgamesh understood the answer to his own complaint already. "It will be good to hear Akalla talk of tomorrow's hunt," Enkidu said. "Have you marked how he cast about and trotted around us, already seeking out footprints and spoors? Truly, he is as fine a huntsman as you could hope to see."

Gilgamesh smiled, a little of his real delight in the chase coming back to him like the first drops of springtime water coursing through the canal-veins of the dry earth. "And what have you seen, my friend?" Gilgamesh asked. "Or scented—I did not watch Akalla, but it seemed to me that some message came to you on the wind more than once."

"There are deer not far from here: I caught that scent clearly, one or another time. Lions as well—the shepherds must guard their sheep with care." Enkidu paused, his gaze dimming as though he turned it inward, staring at a memory of his own. Was he drawing back what he had learned that afternoon in the language he knew before the Shamhatu had come to him, the language of scent and spoor? Gilgamesh did not know; he only knew that he was glad when at last Enkidu's broad shoulders shrugged and he finished with, "Nothing more . . . nothing fit for our hunting, or fighting."

"Well, if there are deer about, we shall find what we came for easily enough." Gilgamesh ducked his head to pass beneath the dates and barley, pushing the inn's door open.

As always, it was darker within than without, the little oil-lamps on the low tables that stood in rows along the benches flickering in the gloom. The inn's common room was almost empty, only one old man and one old woman pushing clicking ceramic tiles around the tabletop between them. As he saw them, the old man rose to his feet, then dropped slowly, with ponderous dignity, to his knees.

"Be welcome ever, Ensi of Erech, exalted to the heavens by Anu, beloved and cherished of Inanna, shepherd of Erech the Sheepfold," he said.

Gilgamesh nodded, gesturing him to rise. "It gladdens me to come to this house. The blessings of the gods be upon it. Now bring beer for myself and my company—bring it swiftly, for we have traveled far today, and thirst greatly."

The innkeeper and his wife hurried out of the common room. Gilgamesh and Enkidu settled themselves upon the floor; Akalla sat beside them, and the guards ranged themselves about. It was only a few moments before a younger woman came in, bearing a large jug with two wooden straws sticking out of it against the curve of her hip. This she set down before Gilgamesh and Enkidu as the older couple set about serving the guards, saying, "The blessings of Ninkasi, who bakes the sprouting barley with lofty shovel, who pours the fragrant malt into the drinking vessel, be with you. Though this be but coarse-husked beer, it is the best we have: may it gladden your hearts and lift your voices to song."

"Praised be Ninkasi, gracious lady-who-fills-the-mouth," Gilgamesh answered. "And thanks to the bearer of her holy drink." He smiled at the woman, and her olive skin darkened, her hands fluttering like doves about her face. She was not so young—though the oil lights smoothed the little creases about her eyes and softened the henna-red stranded through her dark hair, Gilgamesh guessed her at ten or fifteen years older than himself—yet the curves of her wide hips and the sway of her breasts beneath her shawl were comely enough. Perhaps she would come to bed with him tonight, or with Enkidu . . .

"Your forgiveness, exalted one of the gods," Ishbi-Erra cut in, "but one of us must taste this draught first. Even here . . ."

Staring coolly at the young man, Enkidu drew one of the straws to his mouth. Gilgamesh counted three long breaths before his friend lifted the jar and shook it. The beer gurgled within: Enkidu had half drained it in a single draught.

"The only harm in this beer," Enkidu said slowly, "is, maybe a thick head in the morning. You may trust me for that."

The tavern-woman had stepped back, fingers to her mouth, at Ishbi-Erra's words. Now Gilgamesh could hear her breath of relief, even as Ishbi-Erra bowed low, saying, "Your forgiveness, Lion of Erech. I seek only to make sure of the Ensi's safety."

And I would rather have an enemy by my side than such a friend, Gilgamesh thought. But such words he could not speak aloud: much care was called for when faulting a soldier for zeal overspringing the moment's need. Instead he said, "I am sure that the food and drink are safe here. But lest we should be crept up on in the night, Ishbi-Erra, take two of the other men and go through the rooms, seeing which is most secure and where you guards can rest and keep your watches around us."

Ishbi-Erra saluted and moved off. Gilgamesh turned to the tavern-woman again. "Bring food for all of us as well, whatever you have and deem most fitting."

"O noblest of rulers," she said, her hands fluttering about her face again, "there is little ready. We can make you a dish of roast partridges stuffed with dates, but that will take some time, and to feed all your men as well, we have only a common stew of lentils and fish and onions."

"If you have bread to serve with it, that will do well enough," Gilgamesh answered. "And bring more beer."

The room Ishbi-Erra chose for them had only one door, easily guarded by a single man. There was a large window open into the courtyard around which the inn was built, but three guards already stood outside there by the time Gilgamesh and Enkidu went to bed. They rested comfortably enough on the inn's couches, and woke gladly when Akalla came in to whisper to them that dawn was not far away.

THE MORNING WAS fresh and cool, a light dew upon the grasses and shrubs. They were coming into a more jagged and hilly land now—a land with boulders behind which wild sheep could hide or lions lurk, bushes and low trees among which red and fallow deer could conceal themselves. The tracks were uneven, rocks jarring hard against the great flat wheels of the chariots, but that mattered little to Gilgamesh. His onagers were more surefooted and walked more quickly over the unkempt pathways than the donkeys of the others; following Akalla's swift, flowing tread, it was not long before Gilgamesh's chariot passed out of sight of his guards every time he rounded a bend or swerved past a copse of trees.

The huntsman walked with his head lowered, casting about from side to side as though he were sniffing out the animals' tracks as well as looking for them. Now and again he would look up and nod; and then Gilgamesh would see, springing forth in the dust as though newly pecked by a scribe's reed pen, the sharp-marked hoofprints of a deer. Other times he would shake his head a little: then it might be for the little rounded pads of a single fox, or—once—the scuffled mess where a pack of jackals had passed over the trail. Enkidu, meanwhile, sniffed at the wind as he drove, turning his great golden head this way and that. Sometimes his nostrils would flare, his green eyes narrowing or widening, but Gilgamesh could not begin to guess what he smelled.

They had come to something of a flat clearing, well ahead of the rest, when Akalla stopped, stooping for a moment. He held up his hand, opening it to show a little pellet of deer dung resting there like an agate bead in the palm of a merchant. "Warm," he whispered. "Stand. Be ready."

Gilgamesh nocked an arrow in his bow; Enkidu stood still, the reins dangling lightly from his hand like whip's lashes ready to be flicked into action. As Akalla ghosted into the trees, Enkidu turned his head slightly, and Gilgamesh thought that he must be following hunter and deer by sound or smell or whatever lion's instinct he still bore beneath his gold-pinned cloak.

Then Gilgamesh heard the branches cracking like dry palm leaves in a fire, crashing toward them. As Akalla's wordless cry whooped the deer in their direction, he drew his bow—its power thrumming through his arms like the blow of sword meeting sword—holding it steady for the moment when the deer would burst out of the trees.

For a second Gilgamesh saw the great stag sharp against the budding trunks—muscles sliding beneath the deep copper-brown hide, velvety antlers branching high above its back like a trail of torch-flames in the wind, the gleam of a single dark rolling eye. Then, as though it felt the heavy swing of his arrow's point, it turned, leaping forward and away into the trees . . . only for its tail to flash a little farther up the path.

"Keep to its side!" Gilgamesh roared to Akalla, even as the onagers sprang forward, charging along the winding pathway. The chariot lurched alarmingly, leaping to one side or the other as its wheels struck rocks; only Enkidu's strength and Gilgamesh's lifetime of learning to fight from the vehicle kept it from tipping over. They were racing along the side of a hill now, the trees a little below them. Gilgamesh's arms were beginning to ache, but he kept the bow at three-quarters' draw, for he knew there would be only a heartbeat's time for shooting.

Suddenly the stag was there, ahead of them at the edge of the trees. Gilgamesh leaned to shoot—and the twang of his bow became a dreadful rending crack beneath his feet, throwing him violently sideways even as the edge of the chariot flew up to meet him, flinging him back the other way. He kicked out hard with both feet, turning his fall into a leap. Hitting the rocky ground hard, he rolled, fetching up . . . against Enkidu, who sat on the ground as if half stunned, staring at the wreckage of the chariot.

The front axle had broken, the right wheel flying off. All of the hunting weapons were scattered about—most shattered, a few still whole. Gilgamesh's double-spouted beer-bag of white goatskin lay bleeding the last of its contents into the ground: one of its mouths had spewed forth its stopper under the force of the crash. Two of the onagers lay kicking on the ground, moaning the horrible moans of donkeys with broken legs; the other two were dead, their heads twisted half around by the reins. Gilgamesh saw at once that if it had not been for Enkidu's strength forcing them over, the chariot would have toppled down the hill, rolling over its riders as it went—he and Enkidu would be lying broken like cheap pottery dolls, as the onagers lay now, dead or hoping to be.

There was nothing to be done for the beasts save cut their throats quickly, and that Gilgamesh did, trusting in the quick slice of the knife to steady his shaking hands as he stabbed the bronze blade in and jerked it out swiftly through windpipe and great blood vessels. Once, twice: the hot red flows pooled fast into dark mud as the bubbling breaths slowed and quieted.

Enkidu had risen to his feet; now he was crouched over the wreckage of the chariot. In his palm lay the silver rein-ring. The little gold onager that had crested it was bent to one side, a long ear broken off. Yet it was something else he stared at—it was the two broken pieces of wood that had been the front axle.

"Gilgamesh," Enkidu said quietly, "this did not happen by chance. The axle-pole was thinned down, the hub loosened. They were meant to break."

Gilgamesh did not want to look over, but the horror of it drew his gaze like the shreds of a hyena-eaten corpse by the roadside, forcing him to see where the axle had been broken—filed a little narrower and stained dark again to match the rest of the wood, with one thin-sawed notch that had been filled in with bitumen. He spat out a mouthful of thick, gummy saliva, then drew his breath to shout for Akalla.

But the huntsman was already running from the forest, face flushed deep red and chest heaving as though he were about to founder like an overdriven ass. "Ensi," he gasped, when he was closer. "Ensi, your arrow—missed the stag, wounded the leopard waiting for it. Chariot falling startled it off, else . . . sprang up almost at my feet, I would have—"

Gilgamesh sprang to his feet. "How bad was the wound? Where did it go?"

"A deep graze along the shoulder—farther into the woods, that way." Akalla pointed.

They had brought lion-spears: Gilgamesh cast about the ground until he found three unbroken in the wreckage. He handed one to each of his companions, shouldered the other himself. "We must go after it," he stated. "A wounded leopard is a danger to all, and this one will not lie down to die if we leave it be. Come, Akalla, show us the way: then I will take its charge, and you two stand ready to help if there is need."

Akalla had already gotten his breath back—he was no weak man, Gilgamesh thought—and now he started off down the hill at a slow lope, Gilgamesh and Enkidu following. Gilgamesh's mind whirled with thought as they went, following the spoor of padded paw-prints and blood-drops spattered here and there upon the budding leaves. The fiercest if not the strongest of cats, leopards, rare even in the mountains, were seen very seldom in these lands—what sign of the gods was it, that a leopard should lurk at the same spot where treachery had nearly taken himself and Enkidu both? And yet the one danger had fended off the other: had it surprised them as they butchered the stag, or caught Akalla as he drove it, at least one man would surely have died that day.

Gilgamesh's hands tightened on his spear as he half saw, half felt the great muscles of Enkidu's shoulders stiffening.

"Close," Akalla whispered. "Very close." He touched a finger to the dry ground, brought it up with a smear of wet blood across the pad. "He may come to us. Angry."

The three of them froze there, spears at the ready. Gilgamesh's eyes flickered about: dappled sunlight shaping sinuous patterns through the branches of the trees, dappled leaves rustling sinuous movement through the bushes, dappled shadows shaping sinuous patterns across the ground . . . His own breath, silent as he could make it, still hissed harsh in his ears; he could hear his blood thrumming through his veins, his heart beating like a war-drum sounding from a besieging army's encampment at night. His spear seemed weightless as a willow-wand, brought to life by its own death-dealing power and ready to spring at the breast of the prey. Holding the hard smoothness of the wooden shaft in a light grip, he waited for two, then three, endless breaths.

Suddenly Enkidu's eyes widened. Even as his friend whirled, Gilgamesh whipped his own spear about and crouched, bracing its butt on the ground to take the charge. The leopard leapt forth in a sudden flash of sunlight and shadow, its snarl ripping through the air. Its body struck the spear with a blow that almost knocked Gilgamesh sprawling: its front claws ripped the air not a cubit from his face; the narrowed eyes glared yellow around a gray rim; black lips drew back from white fangs, pink mouth breathed the hot stench of carrion and blood toward him like the smoke of Erishkegal's temple . . .

"Back!" Enkidu shouted. His own spear went in even as the leopard coiled around Gilgamesh's, as, without thought, Gilgamesh flung himself backward. The scythe-sharp claws of the hind feet lashed through the air so close that the wind of their passing brushed Gilgamesh's chest; he rolled back behind the deadly swing, leaping to his feet again. Three spears crossed in the leopard's chest now: it kicked once again, but weakly. With a final lift of its head, it bared its teeth again at its slayers. Then a cough bubbled blood between the white fangs. The head dropped, the great spotted paws twitched a few times more, and the leopard lay still.

Gilgamesh bowed down to stroke the leopard's head. The gash along its shoulder had been long, but not deep: they were lucky it had bled as long as it had, to give them such a clear trail. Already the flies were beginning to blacken the leopard's wounds to new spots in its hide, buzzing over the blood as though it were the sweetest of oils burning in the temple. He sighed, a deep peaceful weariness dropping over his body like a heavy cloak. The beer was lost, and there was no water in sight, so that the pouring of libations would have to wait; nor had any of the musicians who accompanied his great hunts come along, to ring bells and play flutes over the body of the prey. But though his throat was dry and rough, Gilgamesh could still sing the hunter's song of praise to

Shakkan over the dead leopard; and as he began, Akalla's thirst-rasping voice joined in as well, with Enkidu's deep bass purring wordlessly below them, holding the tune together.

"Shakkan, shepherd of the wild beasts,
Shakkan, who gives the wild beasts life,
All praise to thee, to thy holy name . . .
The gazelles flock around thee, swift upon the grasslands,
The bears roar thy name, mighty in the mountains,
The lions adore thee, and the deer sing thy praise.
Thanks be to thee, keeper of the wilderness,
Thanks be to thee, towering in the wilds.
Who is like to thee, shepherd of the hunted?
Wild bull and elephant, they all honor thee.
Who hears the voice of the animals, who gives them food for
    their needs,
Who hears the call of the hunters, who gives them prey for their
    needs.
Praised be thee, Shakkan! Shepherd of the beasts,
Praised be thee, Shakkan! Praised thy holy name . . ."

The ritual song trailed down into Enkidu's deep hum. For a moment the three men stared wordlessly down at their prey—the mighty body of gold, studded with onyx and beaded with darkening carnelian, its mottled spots like writing telling unreadable secrets. A noble beast, fit quarry for a ruler born of the gods: and Gilgamesh himself might have lain there, the top of his head torn off by foreclaws and fangs or his guts spilled out by the terrible coiling kick of the leopard's hind legs, save for those who stood by him and the lot of life he bore.

"Fate is a cloth which hangs over me," he whispered, before he bent to draw his spear out.

"We have hunted well," Enkidu said. "Should we not go to water now? I am thirsty."

Gilgamesh thought of going back—thought of his guards about his broken chariot, and the words he would hear when they returned. Already he seemed to hear their calls, crying like far-off ravens over the dead. Let them cry a little longer, he thought: for all their care, they could not ward me well enough. If I must have watchers, this will serve as a lesson to them—that what they must watch for is stealth, not the sort of attack a simple band of soldiers might ward off.

"If you know where there is water, I would gladly go to it," he answered. "And there we can skin the leopard and wash ourselves, as well as drinking."

Enkidu smiled. "It is not far. I can smell it—that way, not a far walk."

The other two pulled their spears out of the leopard, and with one of the shafts they fashioned a makeshift carrying-pole. Gilgamesh and Akalla bore it between them, for it was as heavy as a large-grown man, and Enkidu went ahead to show them the path. Soon they were out of the trees again, onto a rolling plain of grass and tufted shrubs; and there, as Enkidu had said, was the watering hole, ringed by green bushes.

The water was clear and sweet, a cool draught sinking down Gilgamesh's throat as fast as his two hands could cup it, while Enkidu leaned over to lap straight from the pool. Dealing with the leopard was a simple business, since they only had to skin it and take the teeth, not butcher it for food. It saddened Gilgamesh a little, to see the glorious gold and black hide laying on the grass, while the long body it had clothed lay naked and pitiable with its fierce paws and fangs cut away, weaponless and ready for the jackals or hyenas to rend it at their pleasure. "How swiftly you have fallen, mighty one," he whispered. "And yet the gods send us all death and life at their will: I thank Shakkan that it was you and not myself who died this day."

Gilgamesh started as Enkidu laid a hand on his shoulder. "Come, wash with me," Enkidu said. "The Shamhatu told me that I should always wash before and after any great doings, for the soul is washed with the body."

"The Shamhatu . . ." Gilgamesh started. But Enkidu was right: it was fit for him to cleanse himself now, just as if he had ridden forth to hunt as Ensi with priests and attendants and musicians by his side. While

Akalla carefully rubbed himself clean, Gilgamesh and Enkidu stripped off their sword-belts and kilts, kneeling by the side of the watering hole and casting great double handfuls of water to trickle cold and welcome over each other's bodies, rills and rivulets cutting channels through the sweat and grime until their skin tingled with cleanness.

Gilgamesh put an arm around Enkidu's shoulders, and they lay back together, letting Utu's heat slowly dry the beads of water from chests and stomachs and thighs. It was good to lie thus: it felt to Gilgamesh as if the sun god were spreading his light over them personally, Utu's warm strength slowly soothing away the day's aches and restoring their own might.

"Ensi . . ." Akalla said hesitantly. "Ensi, I . . . the leopard, the smell of blood and body, won't it bring . . . I think, lions come here, tracks are not all that old."

Gilgamesh felt the soft sigh shuddering through Enkidu's chest, and for a moment his heart twanged in his breast like an ill-tuned lyre string. *If the lions should come, and call him back to the wilderness . . .* But yet there was nothing he could say, save, "Enkidu, what is your mind on the matter? Should we go back now, or may we rest here?"

Enkidu lifted his head slightly, green eyes slitted against the sun. "There are no lions near us yet, though one has been here not long ago and is likely to come back to the scent. But are we not a strong pack ourselves? What have we to fear, if we choose to wait for him?" Then, as if he knew, he turned to kiss Gilgamesh lightly on the mouth. And that stilled all the little doubts quivering cold in Gilgamesh's guts; and so he was glad to let his limbs ease again, and fall asleep.

Yet Gilgamesh awoke to Enkidu whispering in his ear, "Now the lion comes. Let me greet him." Though his limbs ached to act, Gilgamesh lay still as he opened his eyes, gazing about for the tawny shape slinking over the plain. He could see nothing; and so he carefully sat up, reaching for his spear. Enkidu was already crouched down, though he had no weapon in his hand. The muscles stood out sharply beneath the golden pelt on his back—so, too, did the many white scars he had gotten from lions' claws in play.

Gilgamesh drew in his breath sharply as he saw the pale ripple among the grasses, for now he was sure that he knew what Enkidu meant to do. And there was something far worse than Enkidu running back to the wilds: and that was Enkidu rent by a beast like those who had been his brothers. He poised himself, ready to rush and stab. From the corner of his eye he could see Akalla doing the same.

The lion slunk low, disappeared behind a bush. Then, suddenly, it was almost upon them, standing only a few rods away. Its mane bristled huge about its hunching shoulders; its snarl started as a low growl, rising to a full-throated roar. Gilgamesh braced his spear, waiting.

Enkidu rose to his hind legs, shaking his mass of tawny hair so that it tumbled about his own shoulders and pawing at the air. His deep bellow matched the lion's; but Gilgamesh could see him starting to smile.

The lion's tufted tail lashed as it dropped its head, then suddenly made a sideways rush at Enkidu. Enkidu dodged, charging in to hit it low with his shoulder. The lion rolled to grapple with its claws, snarling horribly, and bright blood sprang out along Enkidu's back as the two of them rolled over and over on the ground. Gilgamesh watched with his spear poised for a terrible moment—though the lion was killing Enkidu, he could not trust that a thrust would strike through one and not the other, and he could not bear to know that he had slain his beloved. His horrified glance flickered over to Akalla, who stood white-faced with his own spear raised, the weapon trembling in his hand.

Then the sound beneath the lion's snarls reached Gilgamesh's ears. Enkidu was not crying out in pain, but laughing—and now Gilgamesh could see that the lion's claws were more than half pulled back, Enkidu's wounds not the gaping, bone-deep slashes he had thought he had seen, but only long scratches. His knees sagged; only the shaft of his spear still braced him upright. Awed, he watched his lover wrestle the lion, forcing the great beast over to get an arm about its throat in a neck-breaking hold. Then the two, lion and man, broke, the lion shaking its shaggy mane and rubbing its cheek against Enkidu nearly hard enough to knock him over. Enkidu reached down, scratching between and behind its ears, and Gilgamesh noticed that it was oddly marked: two dark joined arches on its forehead, like the markings of the old En's shorthaired cats from the Black Land.

Enkidu's face shone like polished gold, gleaming with sweat and bliss, when he looked up to meet Gilgamesh's eyes. "One of my friends has not forgotten me—though the pack fled from me, he has come back!" Enkidu cried joyfully. "Let him feed on our kill, for he is hungry, and we have no use for the meat."

Gilgamesh and Akalla stepped away as the lion sprang growling upon the carcass of the leopard, tearing it open and reddening his muzzle among the entrails. Enkidu, too, moved back a little to let the lion have a free space to feed. Gilgamesh picked up his cloak and carefully walked around to stand beside him, dabbing at the little rivulets of blood running down his back: there would be fresh scars to go with the old ones.

"Lions are rough playmates," Gilgamesh murmured. The lion was ripping away great mouthfuls of meat now, gulping them down with starving abandon.

"And so have we been sometimes," Enkidu answered. "O Gilgamesh, how could I wish for more than to be with you and my wild kin together? Blessed be Inanna and Shakkan, who have made it so."

Gilgamesh's heart could not but kindle with his friend's joy, and he felt the smile spreading across his own face. "Blessed be they, indeed."

The sun was halfway down the western horizon by the time the lion had finished his meal and lay, full-bellied, lazily licking at a bone. Meanwhile, Enkidu had rolled up the leopard's hide—growling at the lion and raising a hand to show that this was his own share—and the three men had dressed themselves. Yet, though they were ready to leave, the lion would not move, though Enkidu called to him and rubbed against him. At last Enkidu sighed and said, "He must come or stay as he wills. It is good to have seen him once again," then turned and began walking along the path by which they had come.

The three of them were already to the spot where they had slain the leopard when they heard the rustle in the bushes and saw the great maned head thrusting out ahead of them. "He will come," Enkidu murmured. "Perhaps as far as the walls of Erech . . ."

Gilgamesh thought for a moment of the chained lions at Erech's gate. Yet this was no slave, but a friend: he knew that Enkidu would as soon have worn chains about his own neck as see his companion bound. But what place for a lion, so close to the city? Though lions were supposed to be the Ensi's game alone, he knew full well that any shepherd would kill one nearing his flock—and what of the sheep devoured, if orders came to leave this lion in peace, for fear of the Ensi's revenge? For a moment Gilgamesh's mind shaped the image of the lion pacing freely through Erech, even into the temple of Inanna . . . the *gala*-priests screaming musically as they lifted their kilts to run, the sacrifice-priests tripping over their offering bowls in their haste to escape, Shamhatu herself shrieking and fleeing like any maiden startled in the marketplace . . . and he had to stifle a laugh.

The chariot-wreckage had been cleared up when they got back: one guard stood alone at the site of the crash, bow and arrow at the ready. Gilgamesh saw him before they came out of the trees, and shouted, "Rejoice! The chariot was broken, but we are well—and have had good hunting!"

The guard—it was Ishbi-Erra—started violently, the arrow dropping from his hand. His narrow face twisted with shock, then broke into an expression of joy.

"Praise be to the gods!" he called back as Gilgamesh, Enkidu, and Akalla hurried up to meet him.

"Where are my other men?" Gilgamesh asked.

"Some have gone back to the inn with the precious things from your chariot; others are searching for you . . . I did not wish to leave this place, for I hoped that you might return."

"That is well-done," Gilgamesh said. But Ishbi-Erra did not meet his gaze; he was staring behind Gilgamesh, and his mouth was open in what might have been fear, or awe. The hairs prickled upon the back of the Ensi's neck as he heard the faint rumbling of the lion's growl. "Do not be afraid," Gilgamesh murmured to his guard. "The lion is a friend of Enkidu's, and he has fed well today already. If you do not fear him, he will do you no harm. Now call in the other guards, and let us return, for we hunters are hungry."

Ishbi-Erra lifted the bone whistle that hung on a chain about his neck and let loose three piercing blasts. Others answered: two, three, four, singing out of the depths of the forest like shrill-voiced birds.

By the time they had reached the inn again, it was full dark. The light of the oil-lamps within glowed cheerily through the open door; but Gilgamesh could see the shadows of his guards slumped against the warm brightness, no hand moving to tear at bread or lift cup to mouth. Gilgamesh strode in ahead of the others, letting the men who sat there get a good look at him. For a moment they were silent, then they sent up a lusty shout.

"I am well; we are all unhurt," Gilgamesh said as the cheer died down. "If a cowardly whittled axle-pole is the worst threat Agga has to offer me, then indeed we have nothing to fear from him."

"We should not have let you ride so far ahead," said Birhurturre, the eldest of the young men in Gilgamesh's guard. He pulled ruefully at the black curls of his beard; his dark gaze was downcast, as though he feared to meet Gilgamesh's eyes. "We came to guard you from harm, not to send you into it."

Gilgamesh leaned down to clap Birhurturre's shoulder. "You could have done nothing, even were you right beside me when the axle-pole broke. The assassin must have known that I was well-watched, and chose his means accordingly. Now—"

He broke off his words as he saw the eyes of his men widening. Though he knew what he would see, he turned his head to follow their gazes. Enkidu stood shadowed in the doorway, with his lion beside him. The great cat's head was raised to sniff the air, his tufted tail lashing, and a single pang of fear shot through Gilgamesh's heart—what if the lion turned from the threshold, and Enkidu walked away with him?

One paw lifted, set down silently again, then another. Suddenly the lion was prowling through the room, between the men who sat frozen in the lamplight like a gathering of statues in a temple long left to the wilderness.

A choked voice broke the stillness: the cracked voice of the inn's owner. "That beast—what is it doing in my tavern?"

"Peace," Enkidu rumbled. "He is uneasy beneath a roof, that is all." He followed the lion in, murmuring something too soft for Gilgamesh to hear. But even in the flickering yellow flames of the oil-lamps, the Ensi could see the death-paleness of fear on the tavernkeeper's face, mirrored by the whiteness of his own guards, and he knew that he must speak.

"Come, my friends," Gilgamesh said softly. "There is a courtyard farther within, and it is a warm night. Let us sit there and eat, where none will be disturbed."

Enkidu nodded. He followed Gilgamesh through to the courtyard, the lion pacing behind him. The two men settled down with their backs to the wall beneath the window of the room where Gilgamesh had slept the previous night; the lion wandered the yard for a few moments before settling down with his head on his paws near Enkidu's feet, a few arms' lengths away from the Ensi.

Gilgamesh reached out to put his arm about Enkidu's shoulders. The lion raised his muzzle and growled.

"He does not know you yet," Enkidu apologized. "He must come to believe that you are one of the pride, before he trusts you too near to me. It will not take much time," he added, and Gilgamesh heard a faint pleading note in his voice, sour as the taste of yeast in bread left to rise too long. "He has only to see . . ."

Is that so? Gilgamesh thought bitterly. With war upon us, with both our lives nearly broken today by an assassin's trick; and the whim of a beast can still take you from me? But he could not say that, lest he destroy Enkidu's joy in the lion's companionship, or drive him back to the wilderness—the Ensi was old enough to know that nothing would destroy love faster than the words: *choose, the other or me.*

"I hope that it is so," Gilgamesh answered. Even thus, he could not keep the bitterness off his tongue, and he saw the hurt on Enkidu's face, his mouth twisting for a moment like a broken-backed snake beneath the moon-paled curls of his beard. "No, I am sure it will be," he hastened to add. "Did he not choose to follow you, and is he not here beneath the stars with us?"

Ishbi-Erra came out quietly, bearing platters of cheese and bread; came out again with cups of drink. "I have tasted it for you, and seen that the tavernkeeper had some of each dish as well," he told the Ensi. "You may eat and drink without fear."

Thirsty as he was, Gilgamesh almost choked on the first mouthful he drank, for it was strong date-wine instead of beer, its sweet glow burning up from his empty stomach. And yet it stilled the shaking in his hands, which he had not noticed until that moment—the shock of spilling from his broken chariot at full speed, perhaps, waiting to fall upon him just as the aftermath of battle seemed to wait for him until the corpses were cooling on the field and the victory-beer streaming into his golden cup. He drank again, a good deep draught, and then began to devour the salty cheese, tearing at the wheaten bread with his teeth between mouthfuls.

The two of them sat talking quietly, comfortable in the warm night. And yet the lion growled whenever Gilgamesh reached out for Enkidu; and that troubled the Ensi's heart even beneath his lover's reassuring words and the thickening blanket of the date-wine on his senses. But at last Gilgamesh felt his eyes drooping and the yawns stretching his throat, and he had to say, "Will you come to bed now?"

The moon was down; Enkidu's face was only a pale blur in the starlight, so that Gilgamesh could not see his expression.

"I should . . ." Enkidu murmured. "I should stay out here with the lion, for until he is used to the houses of men, he will feel strange and alone. He might leave, which he will if he must, but I fear more that he might forget why he is here, and do some harm."

Even though his feet swayed beneath him so that he must brace himself against the wall, Gilgamesh knew that Enkidu was right in what he said. And yet it seemed as though another single word would bring the tears spilling from his eyes like beer frothing over the rim of a cup; and when Enkidu reached down to stroke the lion's mane, it seemed that he was tugging against something in Gilgamesh's chest, something that stretched and tore like a muscle pulled beyond the bounds of its strength.

"We will guard you together," Enkidu said, pointing up at the low window. "Sleep, beloved friend: you need fear nothing, while I am with you."

Gilgamesh leaned forward as to kiss Enkidu, but the growl warned him back again. One hand on the wall to steady himself, he made his way back inside and past the guard on his door, stumbling onto his bed even as his eyes closed in unconsciousness.

ENKIDU SAT AWAKE for a long time, listening to the soft snoring from Gilgamesh's window as he looked up at the stars. He knew their wheeling patterns well, far better than he knew their names—there was so much to learn, so much of the wisdom of men, and the noisy words that spun around and around in his head until they finally flashed into shape, showing him another piece of mystery unveiled. Out here, with his pride-brother lying silent by his side, feeling the warm breeze caressing his face and the stinging of the cuts the lion's claws had left on his back, it was almost possible for him to feel that nothing had changed, that he still roamed the wilderness without words or thought. But what had lodged in his head would not leave him, and the space where Gilgamesh had leaned against the wall was empty, terrifyingly empty. Enkidu had drunk only a sip of the wine, for it was a thing of men, and the lion would not recognize the smell; yet it seemed to him that the odd melancholy coming over him was very like what he had felt once or twice when drinking late in the taverns of Erech with Gilgamesh and thinking on the clean air of the wilds and the taste of the grasses by the watering holes.

"O my beloved friend," Enkidu murmured to the lion, "we have traveled a very long way, both you and I—along the ways of men, along far tracks. Were you driven out, or did you choose to go?" He stretched his legs out along the ground, and the other's warm body rolled up against him. "I have found one I love, the great king-lion, my Gilgamesh. I am part of his pride; the whole of Erech is part of his pride. Each of them, all the craftsmen who labor, the scribes who peck on their clay tablets, the priestesses and priests who sing to the gods, they are all part of him, as I am." Almost without his noticing, Enkidu's voice had dropped into the soft purr that he had made while sleeping among the lions, the bachelor pride spread out in the warmth of the sun or curled together in the coolness of the night. Yet his words came easily, as they seldom did among men, when he so feared to err or speak amiss. "I do not know if I have been tamed or freed, if the ways of men are tools in my hands, as it seems when I learn something new, or chains upon my wrists, as it seems when I cannot master them. But I know that when Gilgamesh is threatened, I would die to defend him; when he leaves my side, I am alone; and when he touches me, he is all that I desire. O beloved friend, would you come within the walls of Erech with me, and accompany him there? For his sake, though I did not know it, I left the steppes; for his sake, I seek out the wonders of his people, for they are joyful to me in his light, and I wish to bring the same brightness to him . . ."

Enkidu could speak no more, but he could see the lion's tawny eyes glowing in the darkness as the great head rubbed against his leg, and for a moment he felt wholly at peace, wholly at home. Then the lion's ears pricked up, his long body springing from liquid rest to coiled tension. At the same time, Enkidu heard the scrape of the door within, the soft noise shocking through his body. Soundlessly he rolled over into a crouch, lifting his head to look into the dark room.

The faint shaft of starlight through the window glinted bronze and sharp, keen as the sudden scent of fear flooding into his nostrils. Enkidu leapt, but the lion moved more swiftly, his startling roar ending in a man's scream that rose higher and higher with the sound of a body beating against walls and floor. Enkidu found himself roaring, too, shouting out for Gilgamesh's guards even as he stood, sword drawn, over the sleeping body in the bed.

The door banged open; the light of torches streamed in to show the loops of pale intestine dangling from the twitching body in the lion's jaws, the spatters of blood shining blackly everywhere and the bronze dagger gleaming on the floor by the bed. Three of the guards stood outside, staring in shock. Behind them was Akalla, bow drawn and arrow nocked—aimed at the lion.

"Do not shoot!" Enkidu shouted at the huntsman. "He is protecting Gilgamesh."

"The Ensi!" Birhurturre said. "Is he harmed?"

Enkidu sheathed his sword and bent down to feel Gilgamesh's body. Still warm, breathing deep, heart beating evenly—no sign of a wound, but for all the noise, and even when Enkidu shook his shoulder lightly, Gilgamesh did not seem to waken. Suddenly suspicious, Enkidu bent down to smell his breath. It was heavy with the sweetness of date-wine, but there was something more beneath it: musky, a little acrid, not a scent Enkidu knew; and it had not been in the first cup of wine. Only when he himself had stopped drinking . . . and only Ishbi-Erra would have known, for it was he who kept bringing the salty food and refilling Gilgamesh's cup . . .

"I think he was . . . was drugged," Enkidu said shakily. "To make him sleep." He bent down, picking up the assassin's dagger. "So he could be killed."

Birhurturre lifted his torch higher. Its light shone down on Ishbi-Erra's agonized face. The guard's lips were still moving a little, a slight pulse of breath showing in his chest; but the lion had torn his right arm half off and ripped his guts out. Even now, beneath the light of the flame, the lion sank his teeth deeper into the place where Ishbi-Erra's shoulder joined his neck. The body spasmed and then went limp; the lion growled, crouching over his prey.

Birhurturre's face contorted, the heat of rage darkening his high-boned cheeks. "Ishbi-Erra, so careful of the Ensi that he put shame to us all," he snarled, his voice low and deadly. "Ishbi-Erra, the faithful one, who waited for Gilgamesh's return while others sought after bodies and chariot-pieces . . . and who could he have meant to blame for failing in the watch but you, still a stranger in the land with the strangeness of your beast beside you? Second best, and more than a little stupid, after the broken chariot failed, but it could yet have worked, in the confusion over the Ensi's death, and with Agga sending his agents into the very heart of Erech. Mighty are the ways of Inanna," Birhurturre added, his tone softening into awe as he stared down at the feeding lion, "who knows all the inmost hearts of men, who judges and passes judgment while mortals stand blind. A fit end for the traitor; but I do not think he acted alone. I knew Ishbi-Erra, and I do not think he could have conceived of these plans by himself, or sought to carry them out without backing."

"Who—" Enkidu began to ask.

"Let the Ensi speak of it when he wakens," Birhurturre answered bleakly. "I have my guesses, but he has the might of law. Is it safe to leave him here, with your lion still feeding?"

"Safer than anywhere," Enkidu said; there was no doubt in his heart. "Yet he should not waken to the sight of death. Time to tell him, when he has thrown off the drug."

"Yes . . . that is wise."

Enkidu bent to lift Gilgamesh, bedclothes and all. The other man's body was heavy even for his strength, thick arms falling limply over Enkidu's shoulders as he carried Gilgamesh through the door. Enkidu could not keep from shuddering at the feeling: it was too like lifting the corpse of a freshly slain animal, warmth still in the flesh but all the sinews flopping unstrung. Yet Gilgamesh was breathing, his heart beating still, and once he seemed to murmur something softly.

"I wish that we had one of the Eanna-folk with us," Birhurturre mused. "They know the way of poisons and drugs better than soldiers like ourselves ever will. Yet it seems to me that if Ishbi-Erra meant to stab the Ensi, whatever he fed him will do him no harm. He must have thought that, by making a show of being taster and cup-bearer, he could get the drug into the drink, but not a poison. And he was right, too!" Another spasm of anger passed across the man's face; Enkidu could smell his bitter sweat.

"Ishbi-Erra is dead," said Enkidu, "and Gilgamesh is not."

"But for you . . ."

"We all guard him. You watch the door, and I shall sit inside. If the lion comes, let him in, for he means Gilgamesh only well."

Akalla lowered his bow slowly as Enkidu passed, heavy brows furrowing. "Can I, can I . . . what should I do?"

Birhurturre touched his shoulder. "You can only watch and wait until the Ensi awakens. None of us can do more."

GILGAMESH'S AWAKENING FELT like swimming slowly upward through dank mud, his head pounding harder as he grew closer to the light. He could hear voices . . . no: a voice, softly whispering, "Gilgamesh, are you awake? Can you hear me?" Then a cool hand laid upon his forehead; a damp rag wiping the sweat from his face even as the brightness stabbed painfully through his closed eyelids. He moaned and tried to turn over, but strong arms were holding him fast. "Gilgamesh, wake up. Drink this."

Gilgamesh opened his mouth for the straw, sucking hard at it. The cool water ran down into his parched throat, soaking into his body like rain into a field of sun-cracked mud. "Enkidu?" he whispered.

"It's all right, Gilgamesh. I'm here."

"What . . . what happened?" Gilgamesh forced his eyes to slit open. A wave of dizziness ran through him as he tried to sit up, and he had to fall back again. "I remember . . ." Drinking, yes, he had gotten drunk; but he had been drunk before, with no more than a slight headache and thirst the next day. And it vaguely seemed to him that he had heard shouting, something desperate through the thick fog of his sleep, but too distant to rouse him.

"You were drugged. Ishbi-Erra tried to kill you. The lion got him."

Now, heedless of the dizzy buzzing behind his eyes and the throbbing ache through his skull, Gilgamesh did manage to struggle up into a sitting position. "He tried to kill me?"

"He put you to sleep with something in the wine. He meant to stab you. O beloved friend—you were asleep for two nights and a day, and hardly moved. We feared to carry you back to the city before you awoke."

"Help me up."

With Enkidu's arm around him, Gilgamesh was able to get to his feet. His body ached all through; his stomach twisted, and he was afraid he would spill out the precious water again. Yet his mind was already racing, his heart beginning to pound painfully in his chest. "Ishbi-Erra did not do this alone. Now I see the plot: Naram-Sin planned this all along, setting the scorpion in the folds of my garment. We must start off for Erech now, and hold the judgment tomorrow—quickly, before rumors spread and my city's heart for war be lost."

Enkidu shook his head. "You are the king-lion. Wait a day and rest; let none smell you when you are weak."

Gilgamesh would have argued further, but his legs sagged from beneath him. Enkidu caught him, bearing him up and back to the bed.

"Then send one of my guards to the city with a message. Tell the Shamhatu of what has happened, and let Naram-Sin and whatever is left of his family be taken into custody. We shall hold the judgment as soon as I get back."

"It is well. It shall be done." Enkidu bent to kiss him; Gilgamesh closed his eyes gratefully beneath the gentle caress.

GILGAMESH SLEPT MOST of that day as well, only waking to drink the clean water Enkidu brought him and to nibble at a few pieces of bread;

but by the next morning his head was clear and he was ready to rise and go, with only a couple of halts along the way. The lights of Erech burned clear through the dusk by the time Gilgamesh and his little band rode in through the city gates, with the lion padding behind. Gilgamesh could not keep from glancing back now and again, but the great dog walked stealthily through the streets, a tawny shadow in the deepening gloom, and did not turn aside even as they passed the market-booth where a heavy countrywoman was loading her cages of squawking ducks into a small wagon, though her donkeys shifted and brayed fearfully at the lion's passing.

The door of the Court of Judgment was open; Gilgamesh had sent Birhurturre ahead when he first saw Erech's walls rising above the plain, to summon the judges and order that Naram-Sin be brought forth. Because his legs were still weak, he let Enkidu lift him down from the chariot, but then gestured his friend's helping arm away, straightening his back and lengthening his stride through sheer force of will.

Enatarzi was waiting at the door with Gilgamesh's staff of office; the Ensi curled his fingers about the polished wood, lifting it as he walked to his seat behind Inanna's image. The words he had learned young came easily to his mouth, although his sight was beginning to spin from exertion and the last lees of the drug in his body.

"Enlil, whose command is far-reaching, whose word is holy,
The lord whose judgment is unchangeable, who forever sets
    destinies,
Inanna, proud queen of the earth-gods, highest among the heaven-
    gods,
Receiver of the *me* from the God of Wisdom,
Queenship and godship placed into your hands,
Sitting in majesty on your high throne,
Gaze on us here: bestow judgment and wisdom,
Bestow your mighty decrees, that your wills be wrought on earth!"

Seven times Gilgamesh's stave thudded softly against the floor, and a soft sigh went up from those gathered there. Gilgamesh sank gratefully into his seat, and only then did he look at the prisoners who stood on the left side of the room. The little bristles stood up from Naram-Sin's shaven scalp; his long beard was disheveled and matted, and instead of a fine fronded kilt, he wore a simple skirt of wool. His hands were not bound, but the grim face of the guard who stood behind him with spear-point set at his heart seemed enough to fetter any prisoner.

Then Gilgamesh drew in his breath hard. For instead of the sons or colleagues he had expected to see at Naram-Sin's side, only one person stood: the young woman Sululi, with a babe in her arms. Motherhood had rounded her angular body, curving out the plain dress she had been given; even without the chance to wash or oil her skin, her face gleamed golden in the lamplight, and instead of meeting Gilgamesh's eyes, she was murmuring to the child she held, trying to soothe its fretful moans. Now he remembered the orders he had given—for Naram-Sin and his family to be taken—and knew that in his rage and the dullness of the drug, he had forgotten that Sululi was the nearest kin to both his would-be assassin and the man who had set him by the Ensi's side. He glanced at the Shamhatu, who sat in her own chair at the right side of Inanna's image with a small double-headed axe in her lap, but her eyes were dark as chips of obsidian, staring beyond the prisoners at Enkidu and the lion waiting by the doorway. Angry, Gilgamesh turned his face from her, striking the staff of judgment on the floor again.

"Bring Naram-Sin forth," Gilgamesh called. "Birhurturre, come forth as well: let the tale be told, let the case be heard."

The guard marched Naram-Sin forward. The older man's face was set and hard, clenched as though he strove to hold back bitter vomit. Yet his voice was clear as he said, "O Ensi beloved of the gods, I do not know why you have brought me here like this, when—Inanna knows it—I have sought only to work for the good of Erech. What has befallen, when a nobleman is treated as a slave, and the faithful as a traitor?"

"I shall tell you what has befallen!" Birhurturre burst out, before Gilgamesh could intervene. "Your son-in-law Ishbi-Erra sought twice to murder the Ensi, and only Inanna's will saved him. Now he is dead, slain in his deed; now he is eating clay and drinking dust, enslaved in Erishke-gal's dark realm forever, as well he ought to be!"

"Hold, Birhurturre," Gilgamesh said, as calmly as he could—though in truth his own bones were trembling beneath his flesh, with rage and the renewed shock of knowing how close he had come to death, not once, but at least twice and perhaps thrice. "Let both of you take your oaths, before Inanna and the Shamhatu; let this go forth according to the law."

Naram-Sin stepped forward, laying his hand on the small table before Inanna's image. The words of the oath came easily from his mouth—he had long sat as a judge in Gilgamesh's court.

"Inanna, Honored Counselor, Queen of Heaven, Joy of An! You render a cruel judgment against the evildoer, you destroy the wicked. You look with kindly gaze upon the straightforward, you give him your blessing. Hear the truth of my words: I swear that there is no lie in them."

He moved back, and Birhurturre took his place. The guard's speech as he took the oath stumbled once or twice, but his fierce gaze did not shift from the statue's gold.

"Now tell your tale," Gilgamesh said. "Tell simply what happened, and what you saw."

Birhurturre recounted his story again. A soft susurration of gasps rose from the lines of men squatting on either side of the hall as he told of how the lion had fallen upon Ishbi-Erra; it might have been little believed, Gilgamesh thought, but for Enkidu standing there with his arms crossed over his massive chest and the great beast lying beside him, eyes half closed and mane draping over his bare feet.

"And all who were there will tell you the same," Birhurturre ended. "Ask Enkidu, or Singashid, or any of Gilgamesh's guards: we all saw." He dropped to his knees before Gilgamesh, lowering his head as though to offer his neck to the axe in token of his truth, until the Ensi gestured him to rise and waved him back.

"If this is true," Naram-Sin said, his voice pitched to carry easily through the hall, "why yet should I have been taken so? I did not watch my son-in-law each moment; though he dwelt in my house, not being able to afford a home of his own while he toiled as a conscript in Gilgamesh's army, he conducted his own affairs. It was he who spoke to the traders about my daughter's weaving after the marriage; it was he who saw to the things of their marriage, as pleased him best, while I tended to my own business."

"That is not true," the Shamhatu said flatly. Then Gilgamesh heard the sparks in her voice bright as fire glittering on gold, and he knew that her anger was roused. "True in words, perhaps, but not true in deed. Sululi is among the finest weavers in the city, as you know, for each year you have paid your temple-fees with her work, and last year the same. The business you tended to was indeed your own, as you have said, for your daughter and son-in-law dwelt in your household. And do you not think that we know who deals in exports of the best weaving, when so much of the Eanna and its business is supported by the same skill? You have never ceased to see Sululi's crafts sold, nor sent abroad—even to Kish, from whence payment aplenty came back to you."

"There has been no ban on trade with Kish, and all those cities that lie between us," Naram-Sin answered. "Yet it was only my name that was used since Sululi's wedding, since the traders were used to coming to my house for her works. She and her husband were the ones who dealt with them, and what either of them might have done, I cannot say. I have done only what was best for my family, and for Erech."

The Shamhatu leaned forward, the lapis-beaded fronds of her shawl clinking together as she gripped tightly at the haft of her little axe. Light gleamed from the tight skin over her delicate cheekbones, and her voice sang taut as a mooring-rope tugged by the flood as she went on. "There was found in your house, in one of your private chambers, a shattered tablet. Much of it had been ground near to dust beneath a heel—but a part of the seal-mark survived, and the seal-mark was that of Agga of Kish. Now deny that if you may; but your slaves have already given the names of those who came to your door, by day or night, and we know the whereabouts of each: what is hidden to men is yet open to the all-seeing eyes of Anu and Enlil and Inanna, and from the Eanna's heights they gaze down over Erech. And Sululi will, I think, give voice on her own, as best she knows how to. As to what is best for Erech . . ."

"I trust that Sululi will follow in the ways of her father and her husband, as she always has," Naram-Sin said calmly. Suddenly, before anyone could cry out or move to stop him, he had whirled, grabbing his guard's spear—not to wrest it away from the younger man, but to guide the thrust that was already sinking into his flesh, pulling the bronze blade deep into his chest. He staggered back, blood already spilling over his lips to redden the silver strands of his beard. As he fell, he pursed his mouth, spitting blood toward Gilgamesh's feet. Then his cheeks pulled back into a smile, or a death-grimace—there was no way to know—and he lay limp upon the floor.

"I have seen men heart-stabbed in battle," Gilgamesh murmured, "and they seldom went so easily."

"He wished to die," the Shamhatu answered, her voice just as soft. Then it hardened to the ring of bronze on bronze. "It will not go so easily with him in the Netherworld."

"So it is done," Gilgamesh said. He could feel the weariness in his bones now, weakening him as a day of fighting or hunting had never done. "The assassin and his patron have found their ends; we have only to deal with Agga now."

"No." It was another of the older judges who spoke, Girbubu. Silver-haired and quiet, he seldom raised his voice in council, but now he stood upright. A gold ring glittered from his finger as he stretched his hand out toward Sululi. "Ensi, most blessed and exalted one, there is still the matter of the woman. What we have heard leaves me in doubt that she is wholly innocent in this matter, and we will not leave this court until justice has been fully done. One of the guilty has been slain, one slain himself: the case has not been heard out."

Gilgamesh breathed deeply, trying to steady himself. He beckoned Sululi forward and she came, kneeling awkwardly before him with her child still in her arms. She gazed steadily up at him, her wide frightened eyes murky and dark as mud-puddles in the moonlight. For a moment she half lifted her babe, as in supplication, then clutched the infant to herself again. It let out a little frightened cry, like the squeaking of a wheel beneath a great weight, but stilled as she stroked the dark fluff on its skull and breathed something soft to it.

"Take the oath," Shamhatu said kindly to her.

Still kneeling, Sululi reached out. Her hand trembled on the inlaid wood as she whispered the same words her father and Birhurturre had spoken; afterward, she murmured something else too quietly for Gilgamesh to hear.

"Is it not usual," Girbubu asked, treading into the center of the room to look down on Sululi, "for skilled weavers to sell the work of their hands themselves, and to deal themselves with the traders who buy their work and sell them the skeins of linen and wool that they must use? Is it not the way of our city, that a woman holds property in her own right, and disposes of it herself?"

"It is," Sululi admitted in a whisper.

"And did you do this?"

"I chose the threads and wool myself, for only I could choose them. My father oversaw the selling, for he said I could not bargain well enough, and he dealt with paying those from whom I bought."

"From whom did you buy, and whom did you sell?"

"I know only those I bought from. I can give you their names; they were . . ." She went on with a list; Gilgamesh saw his scribe frowning, pecking hard at his clay tablet as though it were drying beneath his reed.

"Did you speak to them alone?"

"Only with my father, my husband, or my maidservants by my side; it would not have been fitting . . ."

"And your father and husband are dead, and cannot gainsay your word now."

Sululi shook her head mutely. She did not glance back at the body that lay cooling behind her, but Gilgamesh could see the trembling of her shoulders, and the slight gulping in her long throat.

"What fine weaving and buying of good stuffs did you do after your wedding?" the Shamhatu broke in.

"Little," Sululi admitted. "My maidservants who spin the dyed wool and warp my looms were all busy, set to weaving soldiers' kilts to meet the Eanna's quota for the war. And they told me that we had less money, for—"

"For Ishbi-Erra had only the pay of a commander of sixty in the army," the Shamhatu said. "The whip that drove him is not hard to see, nor is that which drove your father."

Sululi's breath shuddered into her lungs with a soft gasp. She shook her head, her golden leaf-earrings—earrings that he had sent her, Gilgamesh realized—jingling with a soft chime. And yet he remembered the fine garb in which Ishbi-Erra had clad her; and the memory of white linen and red carnelian shone differently in his eyes, newly revealed in the bitter light of the young man's rivalry—*for a rival who never guessed that Ishbi-Erra was striving against him,* Gilgamesh thought. He shivered: a shadow stretched great by the sun's light could easily twist into a monster.

"And you," Girbubu pursued. "What of you?"

"I never . . . I would never have worked to harm the Ensi. I knew nothing of this. Had I known . . ."

"What?"

"That they sought Gilgamesh's life. I would have . . ."

"You would have done what?" the old judge asked. "Which would you have betrayed?"

"Enough of this!" Gilgamesh shouted, pushing himself to his feet with his staff. "There is no proof against this woman: her only fault is the household in which she dwelt."

"The only proof of her innocence," Girbubu went on, not flinching before the Ensi's gaze, "is her own word. When your life is at stake, my Ensi, and on that life depends the hope of our city against the armies of Kish, that is not enough."

"What more do you want?" Gilgamesh demanded.

"There are none here who can vouch for Sululi—few who have seen her beyond the walls of her father's house. Nor, no matter how you search, will you be able to find a free-born witness who can speak for her truth."

For a moment the courtroom was silent, the only sound the scratching of the scribe's reed-point upon his tablet. Then Enkidu's voice rumbled through it.

"I will vouch for her. I will be her witness, and hold myself responsible for her deeds."

Girbubu turned toward the doorway, facing Enkidu's as he strode in. "What knowledge do you have?" he asked, his voice cracking in surprise like a youth's. "How do you know what she has or has not done?"

"I know well enough," Enkidu said, but his step was already faltering.

"And how shall you hold yourself responsible for her, save that you take her as wife and keep her by you?"

"Then I shall do that?" For a moment Enkidu's eyes—clear green in his shadowed face—met Gilgamesh's across the courtroom. Gilgamesh's heart clenched within him: *O my love, will I lose you to her?* But he remembered how Sululi had trembled beneath him, near as frightened by his touch as she seemed now, kneeling before him with her life balancing on axe-edge. *Enkidu and I have shared women before,* he thought, and, *Can I deny her now? I do not doubt that Enkidu is right . . .*

He nodded.

"I shall," Enkidu said.

Gilgamesh thumped his staff upon the floor. "It has been spoken. Let Enkidu take Sululi into his care, and his household, as wife, and by his word be she cleared of her menfolk's crimes. Before Inanna, and Enlil, and An, I declare this court at an end." He raised the stave again, brought it down—seven blows and it was finished. Yet no one rose: they were still staring at the door, where the lion stood on the threshold, lashing his tail.

Gilgamesh walked over to Enkidu. "They are afraid," he whispered. "Go out, for a little while, until they have left."

Enkidu leaned over to brush his lips swiftly against Gilgamesh's, then turned to leave. Not until their shapes had vanished into the night did the first of the judges rise to take his leave, the others following.

"Rise, Sululi," the Shamhatu said gently, reaching out to the woman who still knelt upon the floor. "You and your child shall come to the Eanna with me, and I shall see to it that you are readied for your wedding. You need have no more fear."

"Thank you," Sululi answered. Gilgamesh saw that her teeth had bitten a white crescent into her narrow lip. "And thank you, my Ensi. Believe me, I—"

"I know." Gilgamesh touched Sululi's head, the thick coil of her dark braid soft as new-combed wool beneath his fingers. "I know." He turned to the Shamhatu. "The wedding should be tomorrow—and quietly held, for this is not a story for the city to hear, so close upon the brink of war. Or perhaps ever," he added, glancing sharply at the scribe Shusuen who stood at his left shoulder.

Shusuen lowered his dark lashes, veiling his blue eyes. "Ensi, you know you may trust in me. Have I not written your deeds truly since the gods anointed you upon your seat?"

Gilgamesh rested his hand lightly upon the young man's shoulder, the narrow bones sharp beneath the warm skin. "I know. And if that tablet should fall and be broken—no harm would come of it."

"Accidents sometimes happen," answered Shusuen, bowing.

The Shamhatu took Sululi by the hand to lead her out; the scribe followed after them, and Enatarzi joined him at the door.

His legs trembling beneath him, Gilgamesh stood alone in the Court of Judgment, waiting in the guttering light of the oil-lamps until he heard the soft tread he knew best. The lion had gone—he knew not where, but he trusted that all would be well, else Enkidu would not have left it. With two steps he crossed the space between them, flinging his arms about Enkidu. His beloved's wide chest was hard and warm against his body; he could feel Enkidu's heart leap and settle into a steady beat, matching his own.

"Enkidu," he said softly, "you did not have to . . ."

"Did you not want me to?"

"I did. And yet—why? To take on a wife and child, only to save their lives?"

"There was no stink of guilt on her, as there was on the man. Only fear, and sorrow, and her nursing milk. Is that not right?"

"It must be."

"And did you not know . . . I thought you knew . . ." Now Enkidu's voice was bewildered, as often when Gilgamesh did not see all he saw.

"Knew what?"

"The little one . . . he is yours. He smells like you. I could not mistake it. And your child is mine, and a child of our pride."

Gilgamesh gasped, his lungs fighting for air against the tightening of his heart. A child lately born, nine months since the wedding . . . when he had been Sululi's first man.

"My son, and I did not know it," he breathed. "I could have condemned him, to death or to sale as a slave."

"You could not," Enkidu answered, his voice warm and comforting as a blanket of thick wool against the night-cold of the desert. "For you would not have let him die unjustly." His hand stroked lightly along the fronds of Gilgamesh's kilt, kindling a familiar warmth. "Come, my beloved. The night grows late, and dawn will rise soon enough."

Arms about each other, Gilgamesh and Enkidu left the Court of Judgment—walking toward their room, where Enatarzi had already kindled the lamps and turned down the scented bed-linens as though to welcome a bridal couple to their chamber.

## 5

Enatarzi came early to wake Gilgamesh and Enkidu, lighting the oil-lamps in their room with a long reed taper. The coolness of morning still lay damp in the air, chilling Gilgamesh's skin as he pushed the light woolen blanket back. Enkidu still lay sleeping, head cushioned on the heavy muscles of one arm. His mouth was slightly open, breath stirring a tawny tendril of beard; his tanned skin glowed softly as polished cedar in the warm light. Gilgamesh reached out, stroking a finger down the strong curve of Enkidu's neck. The other man yawned deeply, turning his head, and his pale eyelashes fluttered open.

"Awaken," Gilgamesh said, smiling. "This is your wedding-day, and you must wash yourself before you see your bride."

"My . . . ah!" The drowsiness of sleep faded from Enkidu's face like the morning ribbons of river-mist before a high wind. "What must I do?"

"So eager to be married, and yet you did not know?" Gilgamesh mocked him gently. But when Enkidu's gaze lowered, a little flush of shame warmed the Ensi's cheeks, for he knew how keenly Enkidu felt his ignorance of the ways of men. "But you have had no need to know before. It is a simple thing. First you and I shall bathe—bride and groom always have their friends beside them."

"Will any others be with us?"

"Whoever you would like."

Enkidu's eyes shuttered closed for a moment, as though he were turning his gaze inward upon himself. He scratched absently underneath his chin, then nodded.

"I should like to have Akalla and his father Gunidu there. They are friends to me."

"As you wish, beloved. I shall send word to them straightaway. Meanwhile, in the shrine, Sululi will be bathing as well, and adorning herself with her finest clothes and ornaments, to make herself ready for you. Then we will meet the bride's party. The two of you will sign the contract of marriage, and declare yourself wed; the bridal songs will be sung for you, and we shall have a fine feast together before you take her to your bed. And then I know well that you know what to do; and so does she, for I taught her myself."

Enkidu's strong teeth gleamed in a smile. "Will you come to the bed as well? Surely she is yours already."

Gilgamesh caught his breath, an old lesson echoing through his head. *The male lion kills his rival, and his rival's cubs as well, that he may get new ones upon the queen at once.* He knew by the furrowing of Enkidu's tawny brows that something must have shown upon his face, and hastened to pour out words, trying to wash his thoughts away. "No, I should not. It was for hate of me that her father and husband died; if I came to her bed today . . ." He stopped, shook his head, ended lamely. "I think it would cause her unneeded pain."

Enkidu's gold-maned head moved slowly, as though he drowsed over prey. He wrapped an arm around Gilgamesh's shoulders, holding him tight for a moment. "That is the way of men. You are kind to her. I will be kind, too."

"I know you will." Gilgamesh embraced Enkidu in turn. "Come, let me call Enatarzi back to summon—" He blinked as though he had suddenly stepped from a dark room into blinding sunlight, as another thought struck him. "Enkidu, where is your lion?"

"He went to the *gipar*-courtyard last night, and they gave him a sheep. If he has not left, he is still there. But I think he sleeps, for he was very weary. Lions do not make long marches in a day."

"Oh."

THE WOMEN WERE already gathered in the shrine atop the terrace when the men arrived: Shamhatu, Sululi, and another woman Gilgamesh did not recognize, as well as three of the temple-maids. Shamhatu was simply clad in a robe of white linen with a necklace of figured electrum; her companion, little and plump as a turtledove, wore a gown of pale wool that trailed on the floor beneath her rounded belly and a strand of lapis and gold beads about her neck. But Sululi's hair was bound up in a golden filigree of wire vines and date-clusters; above her milk-rounded breasts gleamed a great amethyst flanked by two silver lions, which Gilgamesh had sent to her after their night together. Black paint rimmed the edges of her eyes, hiding any redness or swelling that might have shown a night of sleepless tears, and her hands were folded calmly above the clasp of her girdle. One of the temple-maids was carrying Sululi's child; the babe slept quietly, a milky bubble dripping from its open mouth. Three *gala*-priests stood on the men's side beside Gilgamesh's scribe, whose slender hands held a damp clay tablet.

When Enkidu and his companions had reached the others, Shamhatu stepped forward. "I will speak for the bride. She has read the contract of wedding, and agrees to its terms, signed by her seal. Gilgamesh, read it to Enkidu."

It was a blunt beginning, but with no families there to trade boasts and pleasantries and festive words—and given how the wedding had come about, that was well enough. Gilgamesh took the tablet from his scribe's hands and read it out. It began simply enough: listing Sululi's inheritance and the dowry she brought, stating her rights to her property and Enkidu's to his own, and mentioning Enkidu's adoption of her child as a condition of the wedding. Then, however, it had been added that Sululi should sell her father's house and dwell in the Eanna, as a weaver of the temple, and that Enkidu should see to all her outside doings until such time as the temple saw fit to set her free. Beneath, as the Shamhatu had said, was marked a simple seal-design; a woman's emblems, spindle and loom and the two looped reed-bundles of Inanna.

Enkidu frowned; the rounded muscles of his chest swelled as his hands clenched before his belt. For a moment his eyes seemed to glint more golden, like sunlight flashing from the surface of a watering hole.

Gilgamesh set his teeth tightly, barring his own tongue from speech, but his thoughts cried out, *Enkidu, it must be thus! Think on how we came here, and what will become of her and my child if all does not go well with us!*

At last the ridges of Enkidu's shoulders loosened. He drew from his belt-pouch the lapis cylinder-seal Gilgamesh had had made for him and rolled it along the bottom of the tablet, leaving the neatly raised images of tiny lions and wrestlers, hunting scenes and chariots, behind in the damp clay.

"Sululi, before Inanna and Erech, is Enkidu your husband?"

"Enkidu is my husband," Sululi answered, her voice low and clear.

"Enkidu, before Inanna and Erech, is Sululi your wife, and her child yours?"

"Sululi is my wife, and her child mine." Enkidu reached out, touching Sululi on the shoulder. She turned to the temple-maid who held the babe, taking it and handing it over to him. Cradled in his massive arms, Gilgamesh's son was almost hidden from sight; but then Gilgamesh heard the child's gurgling coo of laughter, and saw the tiny arm reach up to tug Enkidu's beard. Something prickled against the back of Gilgamesh's own eyes like a scattering of wind-blown dust, and his ribs tightened warmly, as though Enkidu's strong embrace pressed them inward. *My son . . . my beloved . . .*

The temple-maids began to sing, their three voices rising in sweet harmony. It was one of the old bridal songs, more than familiar to Gilgamesh's ears—had he not heard it at every New Year's feast, among the songs of Inanna and Dumuzi?

"He has sprouted, he has burgeoned,
He is lettuce planted by the water,
He is the one my womb loves best.

My well-stocked garden of the plain,
My barley growing high in its furrow,
My apple tree, bearing fruit to its crown,
He is lettuce planted by the water."

And the *gala*-priests, two deep-voiced and one soprano, answered,

"O Lady, your breast is your field,
Sweetest Lady, your breast is your field.
Your broad field pours out plants,
Your broad field pours out grain.
Water flows from on high for your servant,
Bread flows from on high for your servant.
Pour it out for me, my sweet lady,
I will drink all you offer."

And the women sang,

"My honey-man, my honey-man sweetens me always,
My lord, my honey-man of the gods,
He is the one my womb loves best.
His hand is honey—"

Suddenly, the sound of sandals slapping on mud-bricks outside and a man's harsh, deep panting broke through the women's voices. One faltered on, "His foot is honey, he sweetens . . ." before she, too, fell silent, turning to face the newcomer.

Shamhatu whirled like a startled lizard, her mouth opening in a grimace of anger, but Gilgamesh held up his hand to halt her words as the runner slowed to enter the shrine. He blinked at the shadow against the door's brightness, blinked away the blackness falling over his sight as his guts clenched, recognizing the stocky figure of his general Ur-Lamma.

The wheezy bellows of the elder man's breath was the only sound within the shrine as Ur-Lamma walked swiftly toward the wedding party. The old general's face burned red from his run, the fringe of hair around his bald pate dripping lank and dark with sweat and his grizzled beard streaming back over his shoulders. Though Ur-Lamma was not young, he was as fit as any of his men: he must have run hard from the farthest gate.

"Lugal," he panted. "Shield of Erech the Sheepfold, exalted of the gods . . . forgive me for coming here without leave, but you must know.

Our scouts have just gotten back: Agga's armies are on the way, not more than two days from our walls."

"How many?"

"The harvest time must have slowed him. It is smaller than we feared, not more than three men to our four, although he has summoned not only the men of Kish, but those of the other cities beneath his domain, even Nippur."

"And not all of those may look to Kish's gain, or fight for him with full hearts . . ." Gilgamesh mused. If there were a way to exploit any weakness between Kish and his subject-states . . . "Still, in battle, the foe is the man standing before you, and the friend is the man at your side." He thought for a moment.

"Call in the builders' women and children from their huts," Gilgamesh commanded, "and summon all the men to the northern gate. Enkidu—the wedding is completed, save for the songs and feasting, and that we can do at a better time. Come, my friend. Agga has moved more swiftly than we thought. No doubt he hopes to take us by surprise. But now let the peaceful tools be put aside for the violence of battle, let the battle weapons come back to your side, let them bring about fear and terror. When he comes, fear of me will fall upon him, his judgment will be confounded, his counsel will be dissipated."

"Judgment and counsel, indeed," the Shamhatu said. Her face was white, save for two spots high on her cheekbones that glowed like fresh brands. "Agga must have been marching already—while you left your war to go hunting."

"Reproach me for it later—if we live!" Gilgamesh snapped. His fists clenched tightly; he opened them again, thinking, *Remember who is truly your foe now!*

Enkidu passed the baby gently back to Sululi. "Take good care of him," he said, then, to Gilgamesh, "I am ready. Let us go."

The two of them followed Ur-Lamma out. Gilgamesh paused for a moment by the side of Birhurturre, who stood guarding the door. "Did you hear those words?" He hardly needed to ask: Birhurturre's wiry frame was already quivering with alertness, like a coursing hound ready to be loosed upon his prey. A bead of sweat trickled down from the bronze rim of his helmet, tracing a shining snail-path beside the thin curved sweep of his nose.

"I heard, Lugal."

"Henceforth, I will need less guarding. Go to the stables and see to the readying of a chariot for me. Sad, that my best onagers were killed . . ."

"The gods see to things as they will, my Lugal," Birhurturre answered. "But there are good beasts for you yet, and none can handle them like Enkidu."

"True enough. Go, and we will meet you there."

Gilgamesh and Enkidu went hurrying down to the room in the *gipar* where their armor and gear were kept. They laced each other's hauberks of leather covered with glittering bronze, then lifted the heavy bronze breast- and back-plates over each other's heads, tying them firmly on. Gilgamesh's helmet was gilded bronze, figured with hair-curls and crested with feathers; there had been no time to have a matching one made for Enkidu, but his golden hair and beard streamed out beautifully beneath the polished bronze of his plain helm. Briefly they kissed, the metal rims of their helmets grinding hard against each other, then took up their weapons. Enkidu had his sword and a heavy mace hanging from the loops of his arms-belt; Gilgamesh had sword and axe, as well as bow and quiver over his back and a bundle of narrow throwing-spears—the weapons he would use from his war-chariot as Enkidu drove. In the battle itself, there would be a few spare axes in the chariot, for though bronze was harder than copper, its edge dulled easily, and the harder weapon was little good when its edge bedded and stuck in the metal of the softer, as bronze would.

Birhurturre was waiting by the stables when they got there, the reins of the chariot in his hands. The wain was plainer than the one Gilgamesh had thought to drive for the battle, adorned only by a simple silver rein-ring, but the onagers stamped their feet and tossed their heads, braying with fine eagerness. Gilgamesh and Enkidu mounted up, and Birhurturre handed Enkidu the reins.

"Off to your command, now," Gilgamesh said to the young officer. "They should be gathering at the northern gate. Take them to secure the river-gate, that none may pass in or out: Agga may mean to outflank us and make an attack there."

"I shall see to it. May Inanna strengthen us, and Enlil judge well for us, my Lugal," Birhurturre said, bowing.

Gilgamesh and Enkidu rode slowly through the city. As they passed, the noisy bustle of Erech, the shouting of the street-vendors and the voices of the folk who stood talking in the roadways, died down into a whispering susurration: there was no one in the city who did not know what it meant when the Lugal put on his war-gear, when his golden helmet burned with fiery sunlight and the battle-axe hung by his side. Gilgamesh had heard this soft humming of voices before, when he rode out on his campaigns against Ur and Eridu, Larsa and Ubaid: the sound tightening like the sinews of a hand clenched on the sword-hilt, the murmurs sinking about him and rising before and behind, as though the onagers trotted along the furrow between two waves. But now it was different: not the warm hum of bees, but the sharper buzzing of flies, whirring black wings and jittering nervous through the wind. For now it was Erech the Sheepfold herself who must hold fast against the invader, and Gilgamesh's gilded helm shone not with the pride of conquest to come, but as a beacon that must not sink or fail, lest Erech be broken and her folk put to sword and chain—and a beacon borne on the head of a man who, though he be two-thirds god and only one-third man, could still fall to arrow or spear or sword.

Yet Gilgamesh had little doubt. He still had the better ground, the better-trained troops, and if the worst befell, Erech's wall would hold fast. But it was true that Agga's army, though smaller than they had feared when news of his growing wrath and alliances had come to them over the months after Gilgamesh's challenge, was still larger than they had thought when the younger men had refuted the cautious words of their elders and given assent to battle. Their words still rang in the Ensi's head with the sound of the onagers' hooves on the hard-packed dirt road: "Of those who stand, those who sit, those who have been raised with the sons of kings, those who press the donkey's thigh, who has their spirit? Do not bow down to the house of Kish, let us smite it with weapons. Erech, the handiwork of the gods, Eanna, the house rising up to heaven—it is the great gods who have shaped its parts, its mighty walls touching the clouds, its lofty dwelling place established by Anu. You have cared for it—you, king and hero, conqueror, prince beloved by Anu. How should you fear Kish's coming? That army is small, its rear totters, its men hold not high their eyes."

*Did we dare the gods?* Gilgamesh wondered. He turned his mind from that thought, as though reining an unbroken onager in beside its chariot-mates. If it were so, Erech were lost already; and if he believed it so, the same would befall. No: the great ones of heaven had strengthened the hearts of his men, and if time and hard work had worn the gilt of their first enthusiasm off to show the dull bronze of gripes and complaints, the thought of battle before them must give the men of Erech a new luster, to dazzle and confound their foes. Thus Gilgamesh grinned as he rode, whooping now and again and tossing a throwing-spear whirling into the air, only to catch it neatly behind the blade as Enkidu urged the chariot suddenly forward to meet the weapon's path. Ahead he could hear the brazen roar of the trumpets sounding to summon the officers to Erech's main gate, and their cry sent a shivering thrill down his spine.

The gate was a whirl of mad activity when Gilgamesh got there, the women and children of the builders hurrying inside with their bundles of possessions and the men hastily arming themselves and gathering into their phalanxes. Ur-Lamma stood on top of the wall, gesturing with his carven general's staff and occasionally shouting an order, though even his battle-trained bellow was largely lost in the noise. Gilgamesh was pleased to see how quickly the ranks were forming up: the discipline of the many months training and working on the wall was showing now. *If I could keep this army standing,* he thought for a moment. But of course there was no way for any Lugal to hold more than a small military force in full battle-readiness: he had strained the reserves of Erech to the limit this year between the missed planting and the breaking down of her trade as craftsmen and merchants were drafted and set to work as builders and soldiers. Still, the next time he had a need to call up his force . . .

Then he put the thought from his mind: enough time to think about future battles when he had won this one. He dismounted, waiting for Enkidu to leap down lightly behind him and hand the reins to one of the young soldiers who stood waiting by the gate for his phalanx's call to fall in. The two of them made their way to the top of the wall, joining Ur-Lamma.

The old general's helmet was pushed back, a trickle of sweat running down from the rim of beaten copper. "What now, Lugal?" he asked, his voice cracking hoarsely.

"Once the army is ordered, we should summon the commanders of six hundred to the Court of Judgment. I would speak to them." The last plans to be made, the selection of units to deploy, signals to be gone over . . . and it still seemed to Gilgamesh odd that, even expecting himself to be assassinated and Erech in chaos, so old and wily a bull as Agga should have set out with a force smaller than what Gilgamesh knew he could command. It was not for this that he had built the great siege-wall, not for this that he had pressed the men of Erech into their arduous service. "Have the scouts been sent out yet? I will want news of Agga's every move, for he may yet have some trick planned."

"I sent them as soon as I got word of his approach," Ur-Lamma answered.

"And what of Akalla?" Enkidu asked. "Would the hunter not be best as a messenger over wild country? He is used to both running and hiding, and will travel as fast as any of our scouts; I have seen him."

Ur-Lamma turned to look at him, rubbing a finger thoughtfully along his craggy nose. "He would, yes," the old general said thoughtfully. "That will be well-done."

Gilgamesh smiled, feeling the warm glow that always came over him when Enkidu showed his wisdom. *The wisdom of the lion*, he thought, looking fondly at the golden and bronze figure of his beloved. The bright sunlight caught the glints of yellow around Enkidu's pupils, a tracery of gold filaments radiating out through crystal green. He was about to add his own praise when he heard the distant sound of a roar cutting clearly through the bustle below.

Enkidu raised his head, listening, then breathed deeply and opened his mouth. The sound of his answering roar was shockingly loud, even from his broad chest: Gilgamesh's ears rang with the echo for several seconds afterward.

"What was that?" Ur-Lamma asked breathlessly.

"My pride-brother has awoken, and wonders where I am. It may be that he is confused by the city—but perhaps he will be coming here."

Gilgamesh looked down at the swarm of humanity below them, the polished helmets and the bare dark heads. Even if the lion only meant to find Enkidu, he would stampede the flock of women and children at the gate.

"I think we had best go to the *gipar* before that happens. There will be time enough later for him to walk the walls of Erech." And what a sign that would be for the battle, to put heart in his soldiers and take it out of Agga's: Inanna's beast, the living favor of the goddess, standing upon their ramparts!

THE FINE WEATHER did not hold: two days later, when the first scouts arrived at dawn with the breathless news that Agga's army would be in sight by noon, a light rain was drizzling down from the dull gray sky, soaking the plains around Erech into fields of sodden mud. Gilgamesh and Enkidu were already on the wall with a small band of officers when they heard of the approach. At once Gilgamesh seized the bronze trumpet that hung about his neck, blowing the signal to form into phalanxes. There would hardly be time for much speech before marching; but Ur-Lamma had often told him that a short address before a battle was better than a long-winded one, and he had found that to be so before.

"Men of Erech!" he cried out when the troops were mustered before him. "The time is short, the foe draws near. Forth to battle, to win our freedom from Kish. We have the greater army; we will not lose. Know that the names of those who fall bravely will be remembered and their families cared for, while those who live shall have great glory. Forward—for Inanna and Erech!"

"For Inanna and Erech!" the cry went up, roaring back along the ranks as those who were close enough to hear repeated Gilgamesh's words to those behind them. The banners were lifted, flying the eight-pointed star of the goddess; the signal horns sounded, shivering through the dank air, and the troops began to march. Gilgamesh and Enkidu climbed down hastily, mounting into their chariot, and Enkidu urged the onagers forward to take their place at the head of the Lugal's band of picked warriors, just behind the archers and slingers. Ur-Lamma remained on the wall, where he would be able to see the course of the fight and send messengers to Gilgamesh; below him waited the ranks of reserve troops, who would march forward to replace the fallen—or cover a fighting retreat.

"Are you ready for battle?" Gilgamesh asked Enkidu as they rode forward.

Enkidu grinned. "How should I not be? The wait for it seemed very long to me—for I am eager to meet Agga face-to-face." For a moment it seemed to Gilgamesh as though he could see the lion's fangs beneath Enkidu's mane of golden beard. It was not often that Enkidu showed the fierceness of the beast, but now Gilgamesh could almost smell it on him, the heavy, musky scent of the male going to defend his pride. It was a comforting smell, for Gilgamesh knew that, though the best warriors in Erech were ranged behind his chariot, he could have no stronger protector in battle than his beloved.

The clouds shielded the sun from their sight, but Gilgamesh judged that it was nearly noonday when he heard the first faint blowing of a strange signal horn, and their own answering to say that Agga's army neared. The slingers trotted forward, setting up their baskets filled with heavy balls of baked clay; the archers unslung their weapons from their shoulders, drawing their bowstrings from pouches of oiled leather. From the vantage of his chariot's height, even though his unit was back at the very edge of arrow-range, he was one of the first to see the ranks of men marching stolidly over the horizon, and ready to blow the signal to attack as soon as he judged them close enough. Agga's own chariot was, Gilgamesh thought, at the very rear: he could see the banner raised above it, and the dull gleam of gilded bronze beneath a plume of white ostrich feathers. Of course, the older man would be commanding from the rear—as well as the safest place, it would be the best vantage for marking his troops' movements, just as Ur-Lamma was doing for Erech. Still, it was disappointing to be so far from the man who . . . *tried to assassinate me*, Gilgamesh thought. His guts clenched tight with anger, the heat of it swelling through his body, unstoppable and powerful as the Buranun rising into full flood. Beside him, he heard Enkidu's soft growl, and saw the shining in the eyes of the men ranked about him as they nocked arrows or hefted their casting-spears.

"My bow will stretch, ready to shoot like a raging serpent," Gilgamesh murmured to himself. "The barbed arrows will flash before me like lightning, like flying bats they will speed into the mouth of battle. Slingstones will rain down on my foes, the heavy clay will fall thuddingly on them like hard stones. I will cut them down with my throwing-spears and shields like locusts . . ."

The ranks of Kish's army opened to let a single man through—a tall, slender young man, as far as Gilgamesh could tell at that distance, armored, like himself, but wearing no helmet; his long hair fell in gleaming dark ringlets over his bronze shoulder-plates. He bore the banner of Ninurta's weapon Shar-Ur, emblem of Kish's military power, and his high voice rang clearly through the air. Gilgamesh guessed that this messenger would be one of the folk from Ninurta's temple.

"Gilgamesh of Erech!" he called out. "Agga of Kish demands to know why you are gathered here in force, after refusing Kish the rightful tribute which she has received for generations."

"Agga may know by this army that Erech is free, and will pay no tribute. What Agga wants he must come and take—if he has the bravery to meet us upon the field, after the assassin he sent to drug me in the dark has failed."

"Will you hold parley? Or will you call the wrath of Ninurta upon yourself and your city? He who slew the great demon with the weapon whose sign I bear, he will not deal lightly with you if you dare his judgment. He who, like Irra, has perfected heroship, dragon with the hands of a lion, the claws of an eagle, the great lord of Enlil: he is endowed with might, he vanquishes the houses of the rebellious. When his heart is seized with anger, he spits venom like a snake; he is the toothed axe that uproots the evil land, and the arrow that breaks up the rebellious land."

"Inanna, Queen of Heaven, Lady of Lions, fights for her city, and her weapons are not light," Gilgamesh answered. "Her frightful cry, falling from the heavens, devours its victims; her quivering hand makes the midday heat hover over the sea, and her nighttime stalking of the heavens chills the land with its dark breeze. In the van of battle, all is struck down before her, and she is all-devouring in her power: none can stand before her awesome face, or soothe her angry heart. If Agga will not retreat, he, and you, and all who stand beside you, will feel them. Now say to Agga that there will be no parley, not with a coward who enlists traitors to do what he cannot do himself. Flee, or fight: that is all the answer you will get from Erech."

The cheer that went up from the men around Gilgamesh drowned out the young priest's next words, but Gilgamesh saw him close his hand and make a casting gesture as though throwing an invisible spear. For a moment a shiver ran over Gilgamesh's skin like a sudden shower of cool rain, and he thought, *Should I have begged for the Shamhatu's blessing before coming forth to fight?* But he was Gilgamesh, two-thirds god and one-third man, and he was sure that the Ninurta-priest's curse would not bite on him; and anyway, it was too late now.

The priest stood for a moment, watching them, then turned his back and walked back into the ranks. Gilgamesh waited. To him, this was always the hardest moment of the battle, these nerve-shredding minutes when his muscles ached to fight, to feel the onagers leaping forward and the war-bow thrumming in his hand, yet he knew that he must hold himself back and wait for the foe to come to him. But at last the signal-horn sounded from the rear of Agga's army, and the host of Kish moved forward. It had begun to rain.

The first volley from Agga's men fell a little short, shot-balls and arrows thumping harmlessly into the mud in front of Gilgamesh's front rank. Gilgamesh blew the signal for his men to hold fire: they would wait for the foe to come to them. Slowly the men of Kish moved forward. When Gilgamesh judged them close enough, he let fly with his own shaft.

Barbed arrow went whirring over the heads of his own archers and slingers, taking a slinger on the other side neatly through the throat. Like a host of black bees following a single scout, the arrows of Erech sang into the air, followed a few seconds later by the heavier hum of the slings. Agga's men returned fire; Gilgamesh heard the dull thump of arrows and shot striking flesh in front of him, the first cries rising up as the battlefield stink of blood and death began to swirl into the damp breeze, mingling with the scattered showers of rain.

Volley followed upon volley, the barbed arrows tearing into bodies and the shot-balls striking to crush bone. The slingers—most of them simple men, with the least war-training—suffered worst: the least valuable members of the army, they also wore the least armor. The archers fared much better, for many of them were covered by shield-bearers and they were also somewhat protected by the loose ranks of slingers ranged before them. From his chariot, Gilgamesh could see that he held the advantage, and shouted his men on.

When a heavier gust of rain struck him in the face, however, he could tell that the bowstrings would not keep their strength too much longer. His own arrows were already beginning to fall short of marks that they should have struck, and those of others likewise. That simple good luck dropped one right in front of his chariot, which might well have stuck in his flesh. Now, he judged, it was time to move in.

Gilgamesh raised his horn, blowing the signal for the bulk of the slingers and archers to move back, taking as many of the wounded as they could, while his phalanxes marched forward under the remaining covering fire. Agga's trumpet answered faintly from across the field. *To his advantage not to lose too many of them, if he means to besiege,* Gilgamesh thought. But his army was already moving on, and now the casting-spear leapt from his hand, winging its way forward to sink through a foeman's thick leather armor and deep into his guts. Now Gilgamesh drew his battle-axe in one hand, lifting it into the air as he cast a second spear, and shouted on his column of picked men as Enkidu urged the onagers into a gallop. To hammer into Agga's army, that was his plan; to strike fast and hard at the center, letting Agga know that Gilgamesh was coming for him.

The chariot hit something that thudded beneath its wheels. Gilgamesh heard the scream, but barely noticed it. Now he was truly caught up in the roaring joy of battle, swinging his axe at the men below him while Enkidu deftly guided the onagers here and there. One blow cleaved neatly through a man's broad shoulder: he saw the bearded mouth wide open, eyes staring in shock beneath bushy eyebrows, for just a second before the spray of blood hit him in the face. He spat the bright salty taste out, blinking hard to clear his eyes. Another man was coming at the chariot with a battle-axe, and Enkidu swerved hard, leaning out to clout him one-handed with his mace, bursting his skull in a fan of blood and brains.

Some of the neat phalanxes were broken now, men swarming over the field, but others were holding—too many, Gilgamesh realized dimly in a clear moment before three warriors converged on the chariot. Then he was too busy fighting to think. A mace grazed the side of his knee, dropping him down into a low stagger; the edge of a copper axe hissed over his ribs, grazing the bronze plate with a rough scraping sound that jarred through his head. He shouted wordlessly, whirling his own weapon about to slice through the arm-joint of the first man, catching the other through the neck on the backhand swing. Panting, he wiped more blood from his face and glanced swiftly about him.

They're fighting to hold, he realized—to delay us. Why?

Another clash, weapon on weapon. The short copper sword bent, Gilgamesh's bronze axe-edge biting deeply into it. The Ensi swept the other man's weapon from his hand, bringing the encumbered axe around to cave in his foe's helmet with its back. He dropped the weapon—no time to wrench the half wreath of copper from its edge, and the keen bronze was already growing dull—and snatched up another. *Something is wrong . . . does Ur-Lamma see it yet?*

Then Gilgamesh heard the sound that chilled his heart, the notes of the trumpet arching over the field like a bright-bladed spear. It was the signal for a fighting retreat, sounding from the walls of Erech.

*Agga has tricked us,* he realized dimly as his men gathered tightly in about him and they began to beat their way backward. The phalanxes of Erech were drawing in, tightening their formations as they had drilled so often; slowly the army began to beat its way back toward the walls of the city, where their remaining reserves were waiting to cover them.

Gilgamesh and his picked troop held the rear until they reached the safety of the two reserve wings, which folded in around them. Ur-Lamma was still on the wall; Gilgamesh signaled Enkidu to speed the tired onagers as swiftly as he might. As they passed through the gate, he leapt from the chariot—and stumbled with a gasp of pain: that grazing mace-blow had given him more hurt than he had felt, in the thick of battle. In a limping run, he made his way up the stairs to the top of the wall, rushing to his general.

"What is it?" he demanded breathlessly. "What has Agga done?"

Now he noticed the tall figure of the huntsman Akalla standing behind Ur-Lamma, sweat streaming down his bronzed face like rivulets of tears. Ur-Lamma gestured as though the man should speak; Akalla's mouth opened, his thick tongue moved, but no words came out.

"He just got back with the news—gods know how he made it through," Ur-Lamma said, his voice rough as wind-blasted bark. "This force was only a decoy. Agga sent most of his army downstream. They had just disembarked when Akalla saw them—look you, there on the horizon."

Gilgamesh strained his eyes, trying to pierce the gray veil of drizzle. Suddenly, like the hypnotically patterned mosaic on the temple-walls breaking into its hundreds of embedded clay-pieces before dazzled eyes, he saw the dark shadow at the farthest line of sight resolving into movement and shapes. "If they had held us just a little longer . . ."

"Agga would have cut us to pieces," Ur-Lamma said. The general looked up, holding his Lugal's eyes for a moment. His own gaze was deeply shadowed, black circles about his sunken eyes; beneath the streaks of sweat and grime, his face was gray as stone-dust. "I—"

Suddenly the word broke into a gasp. Ur-Lamma doubled over across the parapet, toppling. Gilgamesh leapt to grab him before he could pitch from the wall. Ur-Lamma screamed in his arms, a throat-tearing bellow of agony that ripped through Gilgamesh's ears like the barbs of a hunting-javelin. An abrupt gout of bright blood choked the sound in the general's throat, and Gilgamesh realized in horror that the stabbing prickle against his own wrist, where he held Ur-Lamma, was the butt of a war-arrow which his grasp was driving deeper. As gently as he could, he laid the older man down on the wall, taking his helmet off.

"Rest easy. Easy, Ur-Lamma, we'll have you safely to the temple. They can heal you . . ." But Gilgamesh knew he lied: the arrow had driven in only a little below Ur-Lamma's breastbone, a lucky shot that had slid between the bronze plates of his armor. He would die, soon if he were fortunate, and he knew it as well as Gilgamesh did.

Ur-Lamma struggled up to one elbow, his face twisting as the arrow's barbs twisted within his body. His mouth moved beneath the blood that matted his beard; he spat blood again, struggling to speak.

"I . . . I failed you."

Then Ur-Lamma's arm collapsed beneath his own weight, as though that admission were too much for him to bear. Gilgamesh propped his head up on his own lap.

"You did not fail me, Ur-Lamma," he said gently. "You did all you could. A man may work with no more than he knows. And . . ." *I think the arrow was aimed at me,* Gilgamesh was about to say, but his tongue seemed to swell in his mouth, as though he were as speech-halt as Akalla.

Blood drooled from Ur-Lamma's mouth. A single bursting bubble was his only reply. Then Gilgamesh felt the older man's neck sagging, saw the dark eyes already beginning to glaze, and knew that Ur-Lamma was dead.

Painfully Gilgamesh crept along the wall, taking care to keep his head below the parapet. His senses seemed insanely clear: for all the shouting and tumult below, he could still hear the sound of Akalla crawling behind him, hands and feet rustling dustily along the hard-baked clay. As they reached the stair, a horn sounded—a deeper horn than the bat-tle-trumpets, its voice stilling the clattering and cries for a moment. The gates of Erech had closed.

Gilgamesh paused for a moment, looking back at the huntsman. He could feel his knee swelling painfully against the straps holding on his greaves, but he knew that in a moment he must climb down the stairs and show himself unwounded and hale, putting what heart he could into his surviving men and walking among those of the wounded who had managed to drag themselves or be carried off the field. He breathed deeply, gathering his strength, then dragged the back of his hand across his face to smear away the slick of blood and sweat and drizzle.

"What . . . what now, Ensi?" Akalla stammered. "I did not . . . did not mean to bring ill."

Gilgamesh reached back to lay a hand on the huntsman's bare shoulder, feeling the hard muscle quiver and jump beneath the rough-chilled skin.

"You did not bring ill. You saved the men of Erech. Without your word—and your bravery in hastening through the fight," Gilgamesh added quickly, for he had just noticed the many gashes and bruises marring the huntsman's chest and shoulders, the trickles of blood draining away in the rain, "we should have been lost altogether. As it is . . . we wait.

"Now come," he went on, trying to force cheer into his voice like the froth of new beer into a narrow-necked jug. "There is much yet to do, for the war is not over. But as for you, go to the temple and tell the Shamhatu what has befallen, and that I said that those who yet live owe their lives to you. She will tend your wounds, and see that you are rewarded well, as you deserve."

Akalla bent forward, touching his head to the bricks. "My Ensi, you are . . . you are too good to me. I do not deserve . . ."

"You do, and well. Go."

Akalla scrambled past Gilgamesh, glancing back once as if to reassure himself of what had just passed, that it was not a glittering dream of water against dry sands. Then he hurried down the stairs. There was a deep gash just beneath his left shoulderblade, still weeping blood. One of the gods must love him, for him to have come through alive, Gilgamesh thought. One of the gods . . .

He put away the thought. There would be time to deal with the gods later, while the siege lasted, time enough for the priests and priestesses to sing their hymns and the smoke of the offerings to curl up from the high-stepped temple hill to the sky. Now he was Lugal, and he had his men to tend to before anything: that was enough for now.

THE SIEGE, and the rains, went on—it seemed to Gilgamesh that they had lasted a year, though he knew it was only a count of eleven days. After he had made his rounds, the half-true assurances dripping like the melting sweetness of locust-bread in his mouth, he had finally gone to the old En to see about his knee. The old man's fingers, thin and gentle as the bending green twigs of fresh-cut tamarisk, had probed it to this side and that as Gilgamesh bit back a hiss of pain. Finally he had straightened, three of his shorthaired cats weaving dappled shadows about his skinny ankles.

"You will heal from this blow," he had said. "I learned in the Black Land how to make a salve for it. But I must warn you . . ."

"What? Warn me of what?" Gilgamesh had asked, his voice sharp with the rising pain in his leg and his steadily growing worry.

"It may never be as strong again. Henceforth, you must be careful of it. It will always weaken you a little, and pain you as you age. You should not walk on it for a fortnight, though I know that you must."

"I must, indeed. And it will not weaken me. See to it well."

The old En had only sighed, and gone to mix the foul-smelling salve. A cat had leaped on Gilgamesh's lap as the priest did his work; he had been about to push it off, when the almond-shaped green eyes met his, and he heard the deep rumbling purr—so like Enkidu's. He had stroked it instead, thinking, *Little lion, little lion, how may you be so untroubled, when the foe stands at your city's very gates?* And for that moment he had envied it.

Yet, when the En offered him a potion to ease the pain in his leg, he had waved it away so roughly that a spattering of the precious liquid was dashed on the floor, dark teardrops sinking in to stain the rug's white weave. "I have no need of that. And I must keep my head clear, for none but the gods and Agga himself may know when Kish will choose to storm the gates."

"Pain and exhaustion will dull your wits as surely as any drug," the En had replied quietly. "Rest, as much as you can, and I shall do my duties as you do yours."

So now Gilgamesh lay awake in the dark, the knee's throbbing sending its drum-messages of pain up his thigh to grate against his hipbone. Had he been able to rest, it might have healed by now, but each day's rounds, about the city and up and down the wall, strained it freshly, so that it was little better now than it had been the morning after the battle. Beside him, Enkidu snored softly, his broad back's warmth the sole comfort against the shivers that now and again took Gilgamesh's body by storm as the two memories twined and grafted in his mind: the En's soft murmur—*It will always weaken you*—and Ur-Lamma's hoarse cough. *I . . .*

*I failed you.* Outside, Agga's drums beat on, a steady pulse through the night, like the pulse of Erech's blood leaking out through a great vein—as Agga must have meant it; it could not have eased his own men's sleep.

"We are not," Gilgamesh whispered to himself, "we cannot, be fated to always fail. There must be something of us strong enough to stand."

Beside the bed, something stirred softly: Enkidu's lion rose to his feet, padding back and forth. The beast had been restless all night, now prowling out into the corridor, now rubbing against the corner of the bed with a soft chuffing sound. This time, however, Gilgamesh could see the tautness of the long pale shape against the dark; the low growl, he felt in his bones as much as heard, and at once Enkidu was sitting up beside him, turning his head this way and that as though listening to something beyond Gilgamesh's hearing.

"What—" Gilgamesh began, but Enkidu cut him off with a sudden movement of his hand. The shock of it hit Gilgamesh like the flat of a cold bronze blade in the face, and he was still, his mouth gaping open.

"Something is wrong," Enkidu whispered. "Wait . . ."

The lion's roar was deafening in the small room, as though they were trapped inside the bell of a roaring trumpet. The sound faded a little from Gilgamesh's ringing ears, then seemed to rise again, going on and on. He rubbed the sides of his head, trying to drive the strange echo away, when the lion roared once more, then padded swiftly from the room.

"What is it?" Gilgamesh gasped again.

"The lions," Enkidu answered. "Can't you hear them?"

And Gilgamesh could: the roaring was growing louder and louder, with no breaks between, as though a single huge cat were giving voice to the endless, earth-shaking sound. Against his will, the hairs were prickling up all over his body, springing up in answer to the deep alarm that quaked, below thought or self-rule, through his bowels. Though he was Ensi, though he was safely inside Erech's walls, he could not keep himself from glancing about nervously through the darkness, and clenched his fists to keep his hands from shaking.

"Why?" Gilgamesh asked. Now, though they were within the Eanna's house, at the heart of the city, he had to raise his voice to hear himself.

The shadow of Enkidu's golden head drooped in the darkness. "Once . . . once I would have known. Now I know only—they roar for men to hear their voices, because something has happened. I must go," he said suddenly, and darted away, after his lion.

Gilgamesh sat shaken in bed, not knowing whether to follow or stay. Yet Enkidu would not have left him, and so he leapt up, running heedless of the shocks of pain that each step sent up his injured leg.

Stepping outside was like stepping into the heart of a great thunderstorm, the torrents of sound beating against him in great waves. Gilgamesh tried to peer through the darkness, strain his eyes through the unseen drizzle that was already running over his naked body in chill sheets, but he could see nothing, hear nothing except the overwhelming, endless roaring. He was shaking hard now, his breath coming in fast silent gasps as though he had been fighting, and his bowels quivered and spasmed within him.

"Yet I am within," he said fiercely to himself—though, deafened, his voice sounded only within his skull. "And the lion is the guardian of Erech!"

Gilgamesh thought then on how Agga's men must feel, encamped on the open plain with the roar of the lions about them shaking the earth. The thought strengthened his heart like one of the En's warming, bitter cordials, and his lips pulled back to bare his teeth in a smile.

"The lions roar for Erech," he added. Though the trembling in his limbs eased only a little, he felt a new strength flowing into them with the terrifying sound; though something deep within him still gibbered out its need to flee from the roaring dark, he knew that he would not go within while the lions' call was still raised.

After a little time, Gilgamesh's knee began to buckle beneath him, and then he leaned back to prop himself up against the wet roughness of the mud-brick wall.

THE SHAMHATU SQUATTED alone on her soft-spun rug of white wool, staring at the flame of the oil-lamp on the cedar table before her. The light glowed from the polished wood in streaks of pale gold and deep red, a calm and orderly counterpoint to the far-off throbbing of Agga's drums. She tried to open her gaze, to let herself sink into the still point of fire, but she could not. In order to cleanse herself, she had carefully bathed all the blood and stink of three days' tending the wounded from her body—every one of the temple-folk had been set to that duty, from the smallest shepherd-boy carrying baskets of bandages to the Shamhatu herself, trimming torn flesh with a keen small knife and pulling sinew-threaded needles through rent skin until her fingers were blistered and bleeding. She had soaked in the sweet scents of tamarisk and spikenard and sweet flag until the water cooled, while Atab sang softly to her; she had rubbed her body with the oils of sesame and frankincense. And yet, though learning to loose her own heart and find the gods' peace at the heart of the flame had been one of her first lessons as priestess, her hands still trembled like a flame in the wind, her thoughts gusting here and there uncontrollably.

Gilgamesh's foolishness, Gilgamesh's rashness . . . they had brought the enemy whose drums pulsed ceaselessly through the air, brought the arrows and axes to Erech's gates. Already Agga was building his siege-weapons, and soon a greater drumming would be heard on the walls of the Sheepfold, the rams raised to thrust their way into Inanna's unwilling vulva as the barbed arrows sang their message of death back and forth from the walls. And yet how could she call, full-hearted, the goddess' blessing on a stupid war, raised for no reason but Gilgamesh's pride?

"I could ask him to give in now," she whispered. But she knew her words were futile, no more than the rustling of wind through dry palm leaves. Agga had brought too many men, come too far in harvesttime. He meant more than to claim his tribute: he meant to punish, to show all of Sumer what happened to those cities, however great, who defied the overlordship of Kish. He must mean to restock his own lost harvest with the granaries of Erech, to pay his own expenses with Erech's wealth, and replace his lost men with the enslaved labor of Erech's citizens.

*Too late, too late*, the Shamhatu thought. *When the bellwether is a fool, how may the flock be saved?* And who better than she herself to know how Inanna could be harsh as well as kind? Even the smallest child serving in the temple had felt a bundle of reeds, bound like the two in the goddess' hands, striking stingingly against bare palm or bare leg as a reminder that Inanna held the power of chastisement as well as fruitfulness; speaking with the goddess' voice, words crueler than any blow had come from the Shamhatu's own mouth.

"Inanna fastened on Dumuzi the eye of death," she murmured. "She spoke against him the word of wrath, she uttered against him the cry of guilt—'Take him! Take Dumuzi away!'" And had it not been Inanna who spoke against humankind in the assembly of gods, when the great flood was decreed to sweep over the earth? Though she might have regretted it later, when she saw the bodies of men floating like the bloated corpses of fish upon the sea, Inanna had decreed it. She could do the same for Erech, if she so chose, bringing Agga's host to fall upon the city like the waves of floodwaters . . .

Yet Gilgamesh, thought the Shamhatu, had not come to Inanna's bridal bed as summoned; whatever the goddess would have of him was not fully ripe—if she had not given up on him, and his city, altogether.

*As well she might!* the Shamhatu said to herself. Her breathing had grown ragged; she strove to calm it again, gazing at the single point of flame before her and forcing her ribs to rise and fall in an even motion. But it was the glittering behind it that drew her eyes: the thousand tiny lights reflecting from the spiral breast-ornaments of gold upon Inanna's statue, the girdle of agates, the golden necklace and rings, and, most of all, the bright and dark gleaming of gold and lapis from the goddess' great crown.

*What are you, that you should judge for me?* the black hollows of stone beneath Inanna's brows seemed to ask her. *What is your wisdom set against mine, that you should think to guess my will for Erech?*

"Nothing," the Shamhatu whispered. She wanted to bow her head, flatten her face against the floor, but the carven shadows of the goddess' face held her gaze.

"And yet," she went on, "and yet I must call upon you for Erech, and see to your affairs here, for human hands must steer human steeds, though the gods say where the chariot shall roll and what befalls it." She wanted to be silent then, but Inanna's stone stillness drew the words irresistibly from her; she found herself yielding her thoughts like a well yielding its water, helpless to resist the bucket drawing out all it held. "But how can I call upon you with a whole heart, to bless an endeavor in which I see only foolishness and harm? How can I call you to bless an Ensi who will not do his duty by you, and who leaves your sheep shorn to the winter wind, for the sake of his own pride?"

*Better shorn and shivering than slaughtered, with the walls of the sheepfold shattered and the wind sighing empty through it,* the goddess' silence seemed to answer her.

Now the Shamhatu did bow her head in shame, her cheeks stinging with warmth as though struck with a bundle of reeds. "Forgive my weakness, mighty Queen of Heaven. Am I unworthy of your gifts, of the way you raised me up, to sing your exaltations and speak with your voice? Truly, humans are as worms in the dust before you, short-lived, foolish, and soon to die."

*You are as I shaped you,* the still voice replied. *Does the clay question the potter, or dare to judge his work? Soften your heart, and let me shape you still.*

The Shamhatu raised her gaze again, meeting the unfathomable darkness that hid the statue's wide eyes. The oil-lamp's brightness gilded Inanna's cheekbones, light radiating out from flame and gold breast-ornaments in a dazzling fan. It seemed to Shamhatu that the fire was growing, that she could hear its roaring, deep and strong as the voice of a lion. The sound in her head rose and fell and rose again, growing louder and louder, till she could no longer hear her breathing or her heartbeat or even her own gasp of awe through the thunder that filled her skull.

"Take me as you will, my goddess," she said soundlessly. The floor seemed to be shaking beneath her feet with the sound, like the roaring of a hundred lions, which overwhelmed her. "I am yours, to do your will." The first wave of dizziness rose over her, darkening her sight to a blackness swarming with sparks of lightless color; she felt herself toppling sideways, and knew no more.

GILGAMESH WAS NOT sure when he first noticed the light from the door to the shrine at the top of the temple hill. It was only slowly that the brightness in the corner of his eye drew his whole gaze, so that even through the thunderous roaring of the lions, he found his head turning in wonder. At first he thought that the temple-folk must be lighting a great bonfire in answer to the roaring, but the light spilled out of the open door, brighter and brighter, until he was sure that no flame was burning there.

It was then that he thought he must be dreaming, for he saw something moving at the heart of the brightness. He blinked dazzled eyes, for the shining shape was coming down the hill toward him. The figure of a woman, armed for war in helm and bronze-plate armor, with axe in one hand and mace in the other—yet her face was shadowed as if by a warrior's beard, and by her side walked a lion, its mane a dizzying cascade of fire. Now and again the great cat lifted its head and roared, and then it seemed as though the sound that shook the night all issued from that one lion's throat.

"Inanna," he murmured, and drew himself up straighter, though his knee quivered with pain and threatened to buckle beneath him. He would meet her, Gilgamesh thought, whatever the cost; he would face the goddess and not turn away from her burning gaze, for she was arrayed for battle, and her choice now would be Erech's life or death.

Yet, though the words were ready in his throat, the brilliant figure of the goddess passed straight by him, without turning her head or seeming to mark that he was there. Deafened by the lions, half blinded by her brightness, Gilgamesh stared after Inanna, trying to blink away all the burning afterimages that shimmered against his vision so that he could see her clearly. But she walked on, her roaring lion beside her, and he knew bitterly that he could not run after her to ask the questions that gathered in his mind like flies to spilled honey: if she would not speak to him now, he could not tug at the hem of her garment to beg audience. Though his heart hammered madly against his ribs and the breath was choking in his lungs, Gilgamesh forced himself back, settling once more against the wall to wait.

The night seemed endless to him, the circling of the stars hidden by the rain-fringed cloak of black clouds, and all sense of thought and time driven away by the endless roar that still rose over Erech. But at last the first graying came in the east; the long roar stuttered, breaking here and there, until only two or three lions still answered one another across the plain. Gilgamesh rubbed the gritty sleep from his eyes, knowing that he must soon rest. Still, he waited until he saw the two shapes, broad-shouldered man and shaggy-maned cat, pacing along the road in the growing light.

"Enkidu," Gilgamesh said, his voice too tired to bear up the gladness and relief springing in his heart. "Are all things well? How is it with the lions?"

Enkidu hurried to him, enfolding him in a rain-wet embrace. The fairer man was soaked to the skin, his golden hair tarnished darker by the water and dripping tiny droplets from the point of each curl. His skin was chill, but Gilgamesh could feel the warmth within, and the powerful beating of his heart.

"My beloved," Enkidu rasped, his voice worn to a whisper. "This much I know: that somehow the laws of men and lions here have been broken. I do not know how, for my pride was far from Erech's walls, and each place has its own silent treaties between hunters—whether men know it or not."

"The laws of men and lions . . ." Gilgamesh mused. He knew of only one such law about Erech: that the lion was the Ensi's game alone. And that, he would not say to Enkidu.

Enkidu put his arm around Gilgamesh's shoulders, tilting his head up a little to kiss Gilgamesh softly on the lips. "Come, beloved. Let us sleep while we may."

Gilgamesh let Enkidu lead him back to their chamber, the lion following behind. He did not yet want to speak of what he had seen—even now, in the day, the burning image of the goddess in her war-gear seemed like a fevered dream of the night. He knew it would be fairest to tell his love of it, trading vision for knowledge, and yet he could not set it into words enough to make it clear. Instead he nestled beneath the blankets with Enkidu, and let sleep come to him at last: if anything new came to pass outside Erech's walls, he would be awoken at once.

THE EN WAS not in the shrine for the sunrise hymns to Inanna. Instead, when the rite was done, one of the temple-children came to the Shamhatu to tell her that he wished to see her in his chambers. When she entered, the old man was squatting by his fire with three cats curled beside him, holding a clay tablet and a thin rolled leaf. He looked up at her and smiled, a small grim smile.

"We have received two messages. This from Agga"—he held up the tablet—"and this from Ninurta's En in Kish, brought by one of the temple-doves."

The Shamhatu drew in her breath. The secret of how the great temples sent messages one to another was one known only to the highest of the priests and priestesses: the En of each city, and one or two trusted companions. The message-doves were not used lightly, or often; since she had been Shamhatu, she had sent only three of the little rolled papers to her fellow shrines rather than going by the usual means of couriers and priests sent to discuss matters of importance. She reached out for the thin cylinder of leaf, unrolling it carefully to read the words marked upon its surface. There were no greetings, no prayers: only the briefest thoughts could be sent tied to the dove's leg, lest the bird be hampered in its flight and fall victim to hawks or other perils of the way.

*Agga oversteps. We need good harvest. Ninurta no longer stands with him.*

The Shamhatu read the message thrice, though there could be no mistaking its meaning. She could feel the smile dawning on her face—not a smile of victory yet, for Agga was unlikely to back down, and his army was still a great force to reckon with.

"Now, before you think on that, read this quickly," the En said, handing her the clay tablet. The Shamhatu scanned it, hissing through her teeth in disbelief.

"Agga oversteps, indeed," she whispered. "How dare he? No wonder the lions roared last night! No wonder . . ." When the roaring began, driven by the ceaseless, earth-shattering sound, she had decked herself in the regalia of Inanna. Silently, she walked through the streets and along the walls of Erech, heedless of danger from arrows or slingshots, and knowing that her steps were not her own, for the goddess walked in her priestess' skin, drove her whither she would.

"The time has come to act," she said firmly. "If Inanna is with us, and Ninurta no longer strengthens Agga—then we must strike now, before the siege weakens us too greatly to do more. Let us call Gilgamesh to us, that he and we together may devise a plan of attack."

The En's wrinkled eyelids drooped for a moment, as though he were deep in thought. "We should call Gilgamesh to us, aye. But before we do, we should have a plan set and ready to offer him. With or without the help of the gods, simply charging Agga's army with our remaining forces will do us little good. The stronger may use strength alone; the weaker needs guile, and that Gilgamesh lacks. It is for you and I to give it to him."

GILGAMESH AND ENKIDU slept till almost noon, then arose and ate hastily, going along the walls to hearten the men of Erech and see how matters stood with Agga's troops after that night. The beating of the drums had stopped, but the rows of tents and men still stood drawn up as they had been, the long boats moored by the river's shore, and in the new stillness Gilgamesh could hear the hammering as Agga's engineers beat together their siege weaponry. Nearer to him, however, were the whispers that ran ahead and behind, whispers of awe and fear. "The roaring of the lions . . . not since before Dumuzi's day . . . just come off watch, but I heard . . . told me Inanna walked the street . . . shat myself when the roaring started, I tell you . . ." Gilgamesh could not help but notice how the men, soldiers he had sparred with and builders he had carried bricks beside, turned their faces away from his gaze and Enkidu's. He had felt this before, this sense that, even while walking on hard mud-brick beside other men, he yet stood on a dizzying height, aloft and alone, looking down at them with the long clear gaze of a falcon. This exaltation, this cold brightness of his sight, seemed to him to be that which was godly within him; and borne up on that wind, it seemed to him that the tide had turned for Erech and he must strike quickly.

*But how?* Gilgamesh mused to himself. He could see Agga's tent, far to the rear of his armies. The scarlet banner flapped in the rain-laden breeze, bright against the dull mud and clouds; no sign showed that the ruler of Kish might be daunted. His men were still too many, and the besieged were safest behind their walls. *If I could only reach Agga, meet him face-to-face . . .*

A sharp pang from his knee reminded Gilgamesh that he had been standing too long, but he could not afford to show it. Instead he draped an arm about Enkidu's shoulders, and Enkidu moved in a little closer to bear up his weight.

Gilgamesh did not hear the footfalls behind him, but the sudden silence told him that someone of importance was coming. Slowly and carefully he turned to see. It was one of the temple-folk, a young man whose glossy black curls shed the rain like polished stone.

The youth bowed gracefully, bending his lithe body to brush his forehead against the damp clay bricks of the wall-path. "Ensi, most noble one, exalted of the gods," he said musically. "I am sent by the En to call you to him, for he has tidings that you must hear. You will find him with the Shamhatu, in the house where the women of the Eanna do their weaving."

Gilgamesh raised an eyebrow. "A strange place for me to be summoned to, but I shall come. Tell the En to await me."

"As you will, beloved of Inanna." The temple-youth rose and departed, his damp white cloak swishing against his bare calves.

THE EN AND the Shamhatu were not alone in the weaving-house. Sululi was also there, pulling thick tufts of cream-colored wool through the web on her loom with a little bronze hook. Beside her squatted the woman who had been at her wedding, watching carefully; Akalla, his wounds now bound, sat nearby, dangling the fronds of his new kilt in front of Sululi's son, who crawled gurgling on the floor.

Gilgamesh sank down onto the thick rug in front of the En and the Shamhatu, glad of the chance to rest his leg. The Shamhatu's oval face was very pale, as though she had slept no better than he; her hair was pulled back into a simple knot, and only a few faint traces of paint showed around her puffy eyes.

"What is it?" Gilgamesh asked bluntly. "Why have you called me here? If there is news, should it not be for us alone?"

"Sululi weaves for Enkidu," the Shamhatu answered. "She weaves a cloak that will keep him safe in the thickness of the fight, with the blessings of Inanna—her thanks-gift for her life, and a wedding-gift for her new husband. Do not grudge her the right to hear the dangers he will face, for that will make her weaving stronger."

Gilgamesh looked at the young woman bent over her loom—the line of her long nose, the strong jaw with a little plumpness of flesh beneath, the low arch of her wide cheekbones. Sululi did not glance up, only kept tugging at the shaggy tufts of wool, and her lips moved to shape words that Gilgamesh could not hear. It seemed to the Ensi as though he could feel the bronze hook yanking at his own heart, the more so when he saw Enkidu's gaze fixed warmly on the child at Akalla's feet—*my son*. Truly, Gilgamesh thought, he could not be jealous of either—not when Sululi had borne his child, and Enkidu seldom left his side by day or night— and yet there was something about the scene that sent a strange pang through him.

The En waved a thin hand. "Be calm," he said. "You will need to be, for this is not a time for rashness." His wrinkled face was set, impassive. Gilgamesh could read no thoughts behind the polished jet chips of his eyes, but the hairs were already prickling up along the Ensi's arms and back.

"What is it?" Gilgamesh demanded again.

The En picked up the clay tablet that lay beside him. "We have received this message from Agga. 'To Gilgamesh, Ensi of Erech, from Agga, Ensi of Kish, greetings. Your city is besieged, your army outnumbered, and you cannot hold out much longer. As is my right, I call upon you again to recognize the age-old sovereignty of Kish, granted to my forefathers by the mighty ones of heaven in early times and upheld by the will of the eternal, all-powerful gods. As token of this sovereignty, I have set my men to the slaying of the lions of Erech, which formerly you had kept as your own game, the sign of your own power of rulership so far as Inanna allowed you to hold it: by this I take it from you. Three maned and five unmaned hides already hang by my tent: hear this and be abashed! By the might of Ninurta, beneath the banner of Shar-Ur, so it is written.' Agga has signed it with his own seal."

Gilgamesh was on his feet before the En had finished reading, axe firmly gripped in his hand. The pain flaring in his knee now seemed a burning goad driving him on, ready to rear up and cut down the one who had offended him. Enkidu's green eyes widened in sudden understanding, and Gilgamesh heard his beloved's soft growling gasp. The baby at

Akalla's feet began to cry, and Sululi put down her hook, hurrying over to pick her son up and nestle him against her milk-swollen breasts.

The En uncrossed his scrawny legs, shifting into a more comfortable kneeling position. "Be calm, I said. Other news has come to me as well. I know what came to pass last night, for I sat tending the lamps in the shrine. I heard and saw all. And I am now told that, for these deeds, Ninurta no longer stands behind Agga. Cities may march to war, but matters often go differently in the councils of the gods, and rulers who forget this"— a slight smile seemed to pull the En's withered lips tight against his teeth—"are lost. Sit down."

Unwillingly, Gilgamesh sat again. It seemed to him that he could feel the thin barb sliding in beneath the old priest's pious words, but he could not protest, lest he prove beyond a doubt that the point had been aimed at him. Enkidu took his hand in his own, and Gilgamesh held tightly to him, trying to bank the leaping fires of his fury into the slower, long-burning coals of the anger that would strengthen his hand and heart against his foes.

"A frontal assault will not serve," he mused. And the thought that had troubled him earlier came back, buzzing like a fly within the walls of his skull. "But if I could somehow reach Agga . . ."

"Agga's men are already shaken, and I do not doubt that he is as well," the Shamhatu said. Her voice seemed oddly quiet, as though the creamy milk she sipped through her silver straw had coated her throat to soften the usual sharpness of her words. "If they can be distracted long enough— distracted and awed, to weaken their hearts and cloud their minds—"

"Is that not the duty of the temple?" Gilgamesh snapped.

The En's brow furrowed, and his eyelids drooped a moment, but he said only, "Indeed it is. And a plan comes to my mind, though Gilgamesh would have to show himself upon the walls while others went forth among the foe."

"That I shall not do," Gilgamesh answered. "Should it be written that I, Ensi and Lugal, held back from the forefront of battle?"

"Is it your name you care for?" the Shamhatu asked, her voice still gentle. "Or is it that you wish to meet Agga face-to-face, to wreak your revenge on him yourself?"

Taken aback, Gilgamesh was silent for a moment. "Both are true," he said at last. "And this as well: how should my men trust in me, if I sent others in my place at such a time? If I am not sure enough to dare the greatest dangers myself, who will dare them for me?"

"I shall," Enkidu answered at once. "You are the Ensi; what is Erech without you?"

Gilgamesh reached out to stroke Enkidu's shoulder. "My beloved, you surely shall not go into danger while I remain behind. Both of us will go, or neither."

"Will you hear my plan first, and make your choices after?" the En asked.

Gilgamesh nodded. "I will hear it."

"You shall send a man you trust to Agga as a messenger—a strong man, who you know can bear whatever Agga does. Then, at dusk, you shall walk along the walls where all of Agga's army may see you. While they are so distracted, and believing attack unlikely, a band of your best warriors shall slip from one of the smaller gates, creeping two by two through Agga's camp, and fall upon him in his tent. When he is captured, then you may unleash your army, for his will be in confusion."

Gilgamesh frowned, rubbing the tightness from his temples. "It is a good plan. And yet I do not like it, for it should be myself who takes Agga in his tent. If there were one who could take my place upon the wall . . ."

"But who should take your place?" the En questioned reasonably. "If Agga has never seen you, he has at least heard your fame. There is not a man in Erech who is your like—and, as the gods are with us, the sight of you will confound Agga and his men with awe."

The Shamhatu leaned forward, almond-shaped eyes flickering about the room. "I think there is one who may take the place of Gilgamesh upon the wall, who may rightfully bear the might of the gods before the sight of our foes." She arose, walking gracefully over to Akalla and brushing a hand over his close-cropped hair. "Let Akalla be disguised with wig and beard, and decked out in the gold helm and bronze armor of the Lugal—let him bear Gilgamesh's mighty axe in one hand, and his mace in the other. I myself will call upon Inanna to lay upon him for a time that awe which belongs to Gilgamesh; I will anoint him with honey and oil, and feed him upon the offerings of honey and butter which are given daily to the Ensi."

The En's eyes narrowed, his wrinkled lips tightening. "Heir to the sheepfolds of Erech . . ." he murmured. "Yes: that may be done."

Akalla's mouth moved soundlessly; he glanced wildly from side to side, like a stag realizing himself trapped by the hunters. "I . . . I . . ." he finally stammered. "I cannot, that . . . that cannot be right."

"You can," the Shamhatu said, and her voice seemed to ring oddly loud and deep in the small room. "You can, and must. You have done much, but Inanna is not through with you yet—as she was not through with your father, though the Eanna's shepherd fled to the wilderness. Do not question, for this is as it must be. You have only to trust in me, and walk along the wall. Do you trust me?"

"I . . . I . . ." Akalla licked his lips nervously, giving a little dry cough. "You are, you are the Shamhatu. Surely all must trust you."

Gilgamesh stifled his reply, making only a small snort: this was not the time or place to bicker. Instead he said, "You may trust her, indeed. And know that it is my will as well, that you should take my place before the foe, so that I may go to meet him face-to-face."

Akalla bent forward, touching his forehead to the floor. "I shall do whatever you wish, my Ensi. That is as it must be."

"Good," said the Shamhatu. "Go forth, Gilgamesh. Send out your man and ready your troops: this should be done while the eyes of the gods are still upon us, and Inanna walking beside us, before the terror of the night has passed from Agga and his men. Hurry at your weaving, Sululi, for Enkidu will need his cloak this evening. Come with me, Akalla, and I shall cleanse and prepare you for what you must do. Innashagga . . ." She turned to the little pregnant woman, who squatted wringing her hands and staring white-faced at Akalla. ". . . have no fear. Your husband will not be in danger as he walks the walls, no matter how many arrows fly from beneath the curved arches of Agga's siege-shields. Gilgamesh's own shield-bearers shall walk before and behind him, and be sure that no harm comes to him. We shall bring him back to you whole, and safe, and blessed sevenfold for what he has done for Erech."

"I thank you, my lady," Innashagga whispered. She did not raise her eyes to the Shamhatu, but her palms pressed flat against her belly, as though to reassure the child within.

" 'The mountain who paid not tribute to Inanna,' " the En chanted softly, his voice rough and husky, but still true, " 'vegetation became unclean to it; she burnt down its great gates, and its rivers ran with blood, its folk had nothing to drink. Its troops were led off willingly before her, its armies disbanded willingly before her . . . Against the city that said not "Yours is the land," she promised her holy word, turned away from it, and kept afar from its womb. Its woman spoke not of love with her husband, whispered not tenderly with him in the deep night, revealed not to him the holiness of her heart.' Innashagga, the goddess has blessed you both, even in the defense of her city: you have nothing to fear."

Innashagga did not speak again, but rose and went to her husband, flinging her arms about him and kissing him as though she sought to breathe air back into drowned lungs.

But for all her soothing words, the Shamhatu found it hard to look Akalla in the eyes as she scrubbed him with tamarisk branches and rubbed him with scented oils. It was not unknown in the cities of Sumer that when the omens predicted an Ensi's death, another man might be raised up and hailed before the gods for a short time—and then slain, that the prophecy be fulfilled and the life of the Ensi saved at once. If she had not dwelled with Akalla and Innashagga for those months, she could have made the choice easily. Akalla was nothing to Erech, save a diversion for Gilgamesh: she could have ordered his exaltation and death in the place of Lugalbanda's son as easily as she ordered the sacrifice of sheep and cattle, and provided for his wife as the Eanna provided for their lambs. Yet for her hand to bring this good man, who had done so well by her, to his death, and little Innashagga to a widow's weeping . . .

And yet she remembered Queen Sheep, that gentle ewe, who had died that she might be named as high priestess of Erech. Sheep were raised for the sake of men, and men for the sake of the gods, and that could not be denied, however worthy or beloved the beast. With the greatest care, the Shamhatu fastened the long fronded kilt about Akalla's waist.

"Kubaba, Gilgamesh's votive-wife, will come soon," she said. "She brings the offerings made to the Ensi, butter and honey and oil. When you eat of these, you will become as Gilgamesh, and for a time you will also be the Ensi of Erech—do you understand?"

But Akalla's deep-set eyes did not brighten, nor was there any understanding on his heavy-jawed face. "I . . . I do not know, Divine Lady. You say that I must only walk along the wall . . ."

*It is well that you are innocent,* the Shamhatu thought sadly. *You will go without fear—and if the gods take you, to fulfill the prophecy, it will be swift for you. Huntsman, you are the quarry now, but neither you nor I will know whether a greater hunter waits hidden until you come back safe—or her arrow finds your heart.*

"That is all you must do. The gods will see to the rest."

WHEN THE SUN had just sunk behind the western walls of Erech, Gilgamesh, Enkidu, and those soldiers of the Ensi's phalanx who had survived the first battle in fighting condition—thirty-three left now, out of the sixty who had marched out that morning—stood gathered at the hidden gate in the eastern wall. The evening shadows stretched long and blue over them; though cloaks hid the bright plates of their armor, the cold still seeped through the bronze, so that there and there Gilgamesh saw a man trying to hide a shiver.

It had been Birhurturre who volunteered to go to Agga: Gilgamesh had only to say a few words—"My heroes with darkened faces, whoever of you has heart, let him arise, I would have him go to Agga"—and the young man had leapt up at once, answering, "I shall go to Agga. His judgment will be confounded, his counsel will be dissipated." And so he had gone out as planned, and Gilgamesh had seen the army parting around the guards who took custody of him, opening an aisle along to the tent of Agga—then nothing thereafter. *A brave man,* Gilgamesh thought. *Brave—and still trying to atone for Ishbi-Erra, as though he could have guessed better than Enkidu or I, for all I have told him that he did not fail me.* Now Birhurturre was entirely at the mercy of a foe in whose deeds there had been nothing but ill; and yet he had leapt at the chance to deliver himself into Agga's hands for his Ensi's sake.

*Not long now, Birhurturre,* Gilgamesh shaped the words silently with his lips, as though he could send them to the young man in the enemy's camp. *Hold fast.*

"He will do well," Enkidu said, moving closer so that his shoulder rubbed against Gilgamesh. "I know it."

Enkidu's golden hair and beard were hidden by folds of the huge tufted cloak Sululi had made for him; yet it seemed to Gilgamesh that, muffled in the shaggy golden-cream garment, his beloved seemed more of a lion than ever.

"Almost time to go," Gilgamesh answered. He lifted a corner of the thick cloak, drawing his lover in for a last kiss. Enkidu's mouth was sweet, perfumed by coriander and spikenard and honey from the little cakes they had eaten just before arming themselves for this venture.

The warmth of the kiss lingered on Gilgamesh's lips as he turned to call his troops to order. Now Akalla should be mounting the wall at the north; now it was time to go, creeping out under the shadow of Erech the Sheepfold. The En had muttered his prayers and spells over them to hide them from the eyes of Agga's troops, and there was nothing left but to trust in their own skill and strength. *And the will of the gods:* Gilgamesh heard the dry voice of the En in his skull, as he had heard it so many times during his schooling in the temple. He shook his head, as if to dislodge a stubborn fly, and gave the signal to begin.

Two by two the men walked silently out through the little door. On the other side, it led into a thicket of thornbushes, which could be passed through only by a path known to few. Gilgamesh and Enkidu came last—now stooping, now crawling on hands and knees, stopping every few steps to listen for the sound of an alarm being raised. But no alarm came, and at last they stood free in the shadows, ready to go among Agga's army.

They stepped forth boldly then, for any furtiveness would only have proven them strangers. After the first nervous tremors had passed off, it was easy for Gilgamesh to relax as they walked through Agga's camp. Almost too easy: the smell of pork and barley stew cooking, the sound of men sucking ale through straws and belching or breaking wind, the snatches of overheard conversation—"What in Nergal's name are those pigsuckers playing at? . . . When this is over and I get home, I'll . . . And you should have seen that barmaid I had on the way through Nippur! Breasts like melons, an arse like . . ."—Gilgamesh had heard them all before on his own campaigns, when he had led the battles against other cities, shooting upward from beneath the curved rim of a great siege-shield to see the defenders topple from their walls, waiting for the gates to burst under the attack of Erech and his own soldiers to flood in like ants hastening to spilled date-juice. Only the sharper northern accents and the pangs that jolted through his knee now and again kept him reminded that the past few days had been more than the fading memory of a bad dream, that he was not going among his own men to share their fire and food, but walking through the camp of Kish with his face half muffled in a cloak, daring capture and death on a single turn of fate—*or the gods' will*—in order to come to Agga's tent. And, though the rough soldiers' songs were the same, others were different: it was not Inanna whose battle-hymn rose up from a group to the right, but Ninurta.

"Ruler, when you came on the enemy, you scattered him like
  rushes,
You meted out to him the harsh measures of loss and death.
Lord Ninurta, when you came on the enemy, you scattered him
  like rushes,
You meted out to him the harsh measures of loss and death.

Ruler, of the house of the foe you are his adversary,
Of the city, you are his enemy.
Lord Ninurta, of the house of the foe you are his adversary,
Of the city, you are his enemy.

Ruler, of the house of the contentious and disobedient, you are
  his adversary,
Of their city, you are the enemy . . ."

Yet the remembered ease of many other nights like this loosened Gilgamesh's limbs, kept him walking naturally and nodding to the men who nodded to him. *A good thing, as well, that Agga has the men of other cities in his army,* Gilgamesh thought: any slight strangeness of the warriors of Erech, in dress or manner, could be more easily overlooked thus. As well, he noticed the dark hollows under the eyes of many of the men, and how they glanced nervously about themselves even as they laughed and talked in loud voices. The lions had gotten their message through, whether Agga's soldiers understood it or not. *They are no longer sure of themselves,* Gilgamesh thought, and smiled to himself.

As they passed around to the north, the conversations around them became fewer and more scattered, dying down to low mutters, so that the faint sound of a massed choir singing could be heard from Erech.

*Inanna is known by her heaven-like height, she is known by her earthlike breath,*
*She is known by her destruction of rebel lands, massacring their people, devouring*
*    their dead like a dog.*
*She is known by her fierce countenance, she is known by her flashing eyes, she is*
*known by her many triumphs . . .*

But it was not until Gilgamesh heard the soft gasps and saw the heads turning around him that he looked back up at Erech's walls.

For a moment he, too, stood gaping in awe. The figure who walked there was haloed in fire, the last rays of the setting sun shining ruddy-gold from his helmet. Long ringlets of blue-black hair curled beneath its glowing rim, and his blue-black beard shone like polished lapis. His mighty chest gleamed bronze above the edge of the parapet; the keen edge of the axe in his left hand glittered bloody with crimson light, while the mace in his right rose black and deadly as the head of a serpent. Gilgamesh's knees weakened beneath him, as though his own strength had been drawn from him to cast the glowing shadow of himself upon Erech's wall.

"Gilgamesh," he gasped, and others around him took up the word, until his name became no more than the hissing murmur of wind through reeds all about him.

Enkidu took his hand, holding it tightly. "Gilgamesh," he whispered back: not a gasp of awe, like all the rest, but an affirmation. With that, Gilgamesh was able to turn his head away from the man who walked the wall in his place.

The soldiers who stared up at Erech's wall might have been struck blind and deaf by what they saw; Gilgamesh and Enkidu passed between them as easily as walking through a grove of palm trees, through to the center of the army where Agga's tent stood with the lion-skins stretched on drying-frames all about it. The guards before its flap were heavily cloaked, their faces hidden, and Gilgamesh smiled to himself again: he had guessed that the guard would change at sunset, and that it would be easy for his men to take their places.

The tent-flap rustled, and Gilgamesh and Enkidu stepped aside into the darkness as it opened. Two guards came out, each holding one of Birhurturre's arms. Even in the fading light, Gilgamesh could see the black trickles of blood running from the young man's swollen mouth, and mark how his eyes were slitted within the puffy flesh of rising bruises. He forced the hiss of anger down from his throat into his belly, even as the deep voice issued from within the tent, "Slave, is that man your Ensi?"

Birhurturre coughed, spitting out a dark mouthful of blood; but though his voice was weak, Gilgamesh still heard the cymbal-clear ring of triumph in his words. "That man is indeed my Ensi."

Gilgamesh nodded to Enkidu, lifting a hand to sign to his own men. Two pairs of Gilgamesh's warriors took the guards who held Birhurturre from behind, one striking while the other leapt to silence the dying man and catch his sagging body.

"Raise the signal," Gilgamesh whispered as he and Enkidu brushed past, sweeping into Agga's tent.

Agga sat cross-legged on a fine black-patterned crimson rug with a dish of meat finely chopped with sweet-scented herbs in front of him, oil-lamps burning to either side of him as though he were in his own chambers in Kish. His head and face were shaven, and the silver stubble gleamed in the wavering light of the lamps. Agga was a bigger man than Gilgamesh had expected, bull-broad shoulders and mighty chest sagging down into a heavy swell of fat over the edge of his fronded kilt. A cape of leopard skins hung down his back, and his belt was ornamented with plates of electrum and gold; the gold rings on his fingers clinked as he reached for the axe that lay on the ground beside him. Gilgamesh put his foot on the axe, then kicked it out of Agga's reach.

Faster than Gilgamesh could have expected from a man of his bulk,

Agga was rising, lashing upward with his gold-hilted dagger in a wicked disembowling stroke. Gilgamesh flung himself back; his knee buckled under him, and the thrust that should have taken him in the throat ripped the fold of wool over his head, the knife's bronze edge shrieking across his helmet. Gilgamesh grabbed Agga's knife-hand by the wrist, jerking downward and turning to block the other man's knee with his thigh even as he slammed an elbow into Agga's solar plexus, then twisted back to drive his fist into the side of his enemy's jaw. The knife tumbled from Agga's hand, winking in the light of the oil-lamps, and was lost in the shadows on the tent's floor.

At once Enkidu was behind the Ensi of Kish, binding his wrists with a jagged strip sliced from his own rug and slapping a fist over his mouth so that he could not cry out. Gilgamesh heard the high sound of the trumpets blowing—his own signal horns, sounding from the great gates of Erech—the shouting and clashing of weapons, and the voice outside bellowing, "Hold! We have your Ensi!" His picked warriors would have surrounded the tent, ready to defend it from any who might come to Agga's aid; now, and he felt it as a sudden springing lightness in his heart, Gilgamesh knew that the war was won.

He bent down, staring straight into Agga's eyes as the other ruler struggled to suck gasps of air in through his nose. "To whom have the gods given sovereignty now?" Gilgamesh asked. "You thought to assassinate me in my own stronghold; behold, I have you captured now in yours. Enkidu, let him speak."

Enkidu took his hand from Agga's mouth, kicking the heavier man behind the knee as he jerked backward on the makeshift bonds. Agga's broad rump thudded down upon his ravaged rug; the thump drove the air from his lungs again. His face was red with heat and anger, sweat streaming into the deep creases of his brow and dripping from his bushy silver eyebrows. The leopard-skin cape was twisted over his left shoulder, its gold pin digging into the roll of fat at his neck.

"How dare you treat the Ensi of Kish thus?" he blustered after a few moments. "You and your minion, sneaking in the night to lay hands on me . . . I suppose one could expect no better from an upstart like you, who knows nothing of the duties and dignity of an Ensi."

Gilgamesh strove to calm his voice, though his body was still shaking with elated anger. At Agga's last words, his hands had balled themselves into fists; he forced them open, reminding himself that his enemy was already beaten and bound. "As for sneaking in the night, you know more of it than I, paymaster of assassins. And the duties and dignity of an Ensi—you forsook them when you set your men to slaying my lions, and dared the gods thereby. Your judgment is confounded, your army in confusion, and my men are cutting yours to pieces even now: a headless snake has better guidance than your soldiers. Now all that is left is for you to give me your surrender."

"And what then? I suppose you think you can conquer Kish, and set your own dynasty in the place of mine as the rulers of all the land?"

For a moment the thought tempted Gilgamesh. With Agga in his hands, if he marched north now . . . But he knew, with certainty real as the stabbing pains shooting up from his injured knee, that for now Erech's might would just suffice to keep her freedom: he had strained his city to her limits, and nearly beyond.

"Although my hair is not silver yet, I am wiser than you," he answered. "I seek to hold what is mine in peace and freedom—I am no greedy dog, to devour more than my stomach will hold, only to cast it up again at once. Call your priest and a scribe, for I will have this sworn and written: that Erech owes no tribute nor submission to Kish, but the ruler of Erech holds sovereignty over all southern paths of the land . . . and I over you, as long as you are within the lands of my dominion. I will have it sworn, and written, and signed with your own seal."

"I will not sign."

"Consider," said Gilgamesh mildly, "how your men handled my messenger Birhurturre, who came out to you under a banner of truce. Or better yet, consider the lions whose skins are stretched outside. There are lions within Erech as well, some tame and some . . . not so tame. And if all else fails, consider this: you came here with a great advantage in men, having prepared your attack cleverly; you drove us back behind Erech's walls. And yet the lions roared, and your soldiers were daunted, their heads failing and their hearts drooping; and we are here and free within your tent, while you are bound and at our mercy." Ignoring the shooting pain in his knee, Gilgamesh crouched down, sinking his fingers deep into the padding of oiled fat covering the heavy muscles of Agga's shoulders as he forced the other Ensi to look into his eyes. "You will swear, and sign, for fate has overcome you. The gods have delivered you unto me, and you live or die—or suffer—at my choice. Which is it to be, Agga of Kish?"

Agga closed his eyes a moment. The breath hissed slowly from his lungs, and he seemed to sink into himself like a wineskin leaking to emptiness.

"I will sign."

"A wise choice. Now summon priest and scribe."

"How shall I do that? Will you unbind me?" Agga asked sarcastically. "The priest of Ninurta—and he will do for a scribe as well—does not dance attendance on my every move."

"I shall fetch him," Enkidu broke in. "Where is he?"

Agga jerked his head toward the rear of the tent. "His tent is behind mine. If he has not fled, he will be there now, raising his prayers, for all the good they do."

Enkidu slipped out, a pale shaggy shadow against the darkness. It seemed only moments before he was back, followed by the young man who had spoken to Gilgamesh before the first battle. The priest held clay tablet and reed in his hands; his fine-boned face was very calm, his dark eyes huge and liquid in the glimmering light of the oil-lamps.

"Ninurta has spoken in the assembly of the gods," he said to Agga, "and the assembly of the gods has made its decision. Victory is not ours. Accept that, for what men can stand against the powers of heaven, or question their wisdom?"

Agga's face darkened again, but he said only, "Write what you must."

"Unbind my Ensi's hands," the young priest told Gilgamesh. "Let him find his seal."

"And who are you to command me?"

"I am the priest of Ninurta. And this matter has passed from the hands of mortal men."

Gilgamesh drew his dagger, slicing through the strip of rug that bound Agga's wrists. The Ensi of Kish did not look at him, going instead to the polished chest of pale wood that stood beside his pallet of fine blankets and rummaging through it. Enkidu stood beside him, axe upraised as though to cut Agga down at the first hint that he might reach for a weapon. But the only thing Agga pulled from the chest was a cylinder-seal of gleaming green stone.

"Now speak your oath," the priest ordered his Ensi. "Before Ninurta, and Inanna, and all the mighty ones of heaven. Be sure that they hear you, and will deal more harshly with you than they have dealt today, if you fail."

"Whose side are you on?" Agga asked bitterly.

"I speak for the gods, who rule over all, Kish and Erech alike. Speak your oath." The priest set his reed to the damp clay, waiting for Agga to begin.

"I swear," the Ensi of Kish muttered, "before Ninurta, and Inanna, and all the mighty ones. That henceforth, Erech owes no tribute to Kish, and the ruler of Erech holds sovereignty over all the southern lands." Agga closed his mouth, glaring up at the priest.

"And?" Gilgamesh prompted.

"And," Agga growled reluctantly, "Gilgamesh holds sovereignty over me, so long as I am within the lands of his dominion."

The priest held the tablet out to Agga. Though he gripped it so tightly that the pads of his fingers sank into the damp clay, Agga rolled his seal over it and gave it back to the priest, who passed it to Gilgamesh.

Gilgamesh smiled. "Agga, my lieutenant, my captain—Agga, my army-general. Agga, you have filled with grain the fleeing bird. Agga, you have given me breath, you have given me life. Agga, you have brought the fugitive to your lap."

The priest nodded, brushing back a stray glossy ringlet from his high forehead. "Behold!" he cried, half singing. "Erech, the handiwork of the god, the great walls touching the sky, the lofty dwelling established by Anu. You have cared for it, Ensi and hero, conqueror, ruler beloved of Anu. Agga has set you free for the sake of Kish; before Utu, he has returned you the favor of former days. Gilgamesh, ruler of Erech, your praise is good."

"Now it is done," Gilgamesh said. "Agga, take your horn, go outside, and blow the signal for your men to surrender. There is no need for more to die. The war is over."

# 6

By the time the war was fifteen days past, Erech seemed almost as it had been before Gilgamesh had first pulled its young men from their trades and set them to work on his walls. The day was fine and hot; the marketplace was filled with its usual throng again, the hoarse voices of the sellers rising above the babble of conversation. "Melons! Buy my melons!" "Fresh garlic! Best in the city!" "Spring lambs! Young and tender!" But as Gilgamesh and Enkidu strolled through, Gilgamesh could see that the stalls of the fruit-sellers were not stacked half as high as they ought to be, while bread was selling at near twice the usual cost—the legacy of the half-spoiled harvest; even though the Eanna had given out a good quantity of grain from its vast reserves, bread and beer would not be cheap in the city until after the next harvest-season. Still, he could see the warm flush of Erech's victory in the smiles that flashed from the sun-browned faces of the merchants, hear it in the voices of the buyers even as they haggled over prices and quality. Enkidu stopped at one of the stalls, buying a small melon which he split in two with his knife, handing half to Gilgamesh. The two of them ate as they walked, sucking at the sweet slivers of cool green fruit.

At the far end of the marketplace a pair of stonemasons were busily chipping away at a large block of limestone—carving scenes of Erech's victory over Kish, to make a memorial where the kin of those who fell in the battle could come to pour their offerings of honey and butter and milk to the dead. Gilgamesh and Enkidu stood for a time, watching

them work. The masons' curled beards were white with stone-dust, and
the sweat trickled down the rippling muscles of their bronzed shoulders
and backs, but their chisels and hammers still rose and fell, leaping about
the carving with lively precision as it took shape beneath the ceaseless
tapping of their tools.

"It is a wonderful craft," Enkidu said. "What a fair gift of Enki and
Inanna it is, that men may make such pictures so that their deeds will be
remembered as long as stone stands."

"As long as stone stands . . ." Gilgamesh echoed. *And what on earth*, he
thought, *might be as enduring as stone?*

"How long does stone stand?" a cracked voice cackled behind them.
Gilgamesh whirled, his melon-rind falling into the dust as his hand
closed about the haft of the axe at his side; Enkidu was not a moment
behind him.

Before them was an old man, his matted gray hair and beard flowing
into the tangle of greasy rags wrapped about his body. He crouched
down, legs bent like a locust's, to look up into Gilgamesh's face with
eyes that skittered and jumped about so that it almost made Gilgamesh
dizzy to try and meet them.

"How long does stone stand?" the old man repeated. "Forever, or till
the winds wear it down, or a foe overthrows it; long in the making, a
moment to break." He leapt up in a peculiar sideways bound, twisting
his torso and head to skew his gaze up at Gilgamesh again.

"How long does a clay tablet last?" he asked the Ensi. "Forever, if it is
baked hard, unless a careless hand shatters it. Then all that was written is
lost, like the thoughts in a skull when its brains are spilled out."

Again he leapt, turning in the air so he landed with his back toward
them. Bending over, he looked upside down at Gilgamesh with his head
between his legs and hair straggling through the dust, brushing his gray
tangle of beard over the hem of his filthy bundle of garments. "How
long does a song last? Forever—unless it is forgotten. But Dumuzi was
Lugalbanda's father, and Lugalbanda your own, and yet whose name and
face do you know better, O Ensi?"

Once more he whirled and sprang up, and now that he stood straight-legged and face-to-face with Gilgamesh, the Ensi saw that the old man was a little taller than Enkidu—of a height with himself.

"How long will your name last, Ensi of Erech? Forever, unless it is forgotten. But many rulers win many battles, and the winds grind down all stone to dust in time. Why should men remember you?"

The old man laughed, a harsh high eerie sound like the call of a bird through the desert night. Suddenly he backflipped several times, whirling and leaping away in a swift series of strange contortions, and was gone into the crowd before Gilgamesh could move or speak.

Gilgamesh laid his hand on Enkidu's arm—to comfort himself, as much as reassure himself that he had not dreamed the scraggly shape and disturbing words that still seemed to echo through his ears. To his shock, he could feel a little tremor in the broad muscle of Enkidu's forearm, and his beloved's skin was cold.

"He troubled you," Gilgamesh said softly.

"He meant to trouble," Enkidu answered, equally quiet. "I do not know why he spoke as he did, but his words were not meant to bring peace to the heart. Still, I do not know if he meant you well or ill. Was he a priest, Gilgamesh?" Enkidu's green eyes looked up into Gilgamesh's own, wide and questioning.

"No priest that I have ever seen in this city. Nor is it the way of priests to dress like beggars, when they have the greater part of Erech's wealth at their command. A wandering madman, or acrobat, more like, though it was strange that he sought no reward."

"It may be so," Enkidu said. But his voice sounded hollow and distant, like a faint call from the depths of a cave. Gilgamesh squeezed his strong arm reassuringly.

"Come, my love. We have had little to eat today, and it may be that food and a pitcher of good beer will restore your spirits. There is no need to be downcast."

Yet, as they walked toward the inn, Gilgamesh could not shake the thoughts from his mind, the old man's strange questions and answers sounding oddly over his memories of the battlefield. The feeling of the arrow driving deeper into Ur-Lamma's body as he caught the general . . .

the moans of the wounded as he walked among them, trying to keep his swollen knee from giving way beneath his weight . . . and later, the dawn after his capture of Agga, when he looked down from the walls at the corpses floating in the river, turning over gently in the current like a convoy of sodden logs. . . . *How long will that memorial last?* he wondered. *How long, until the grandchildren or great-grandchildren of those who fell in the battle have forgotten to bring the offerings, to speak the names of men they never knew?* For the faces would fade even from living memory in time; the small details of life—of who ate garlic with every meal and who could not stand its taste, of whether a man kicked or caressed his dog, of how he stroked the hair of his wife when they lay together in the warm summer nights—all of that would be gone when those who had known them went down, in their turn, to the dark and dusty halls of Erishkegal, and it would make no difference, in a few generations, who had been remembered well by those who loved them or badly by those who hated.

But *I freed Erech from Kish,* Gilgamesh said to himself. *I will not be forgotten.* Yet the thought brought him little comfort.

The two of them paused outside the door of the inn for a moment, as though neither could quite bring himself to pull aside the hanging of woven palm-leaves. Several people were singing within; Gilgamesh heard his own name and smiled, stepping to the side so that he could listen for a moment without being seen if anyone else should pass in or out. The tune was familiar, a praise-song his scribe had written the day after the battle.

> "Hark, I will sing you the glories of Gilgamesh!
> Mighty his lance, striking foe's bodies in battle . . .
> Mightier still the lance he bears at home.
> In war he overthrew the men of Agga, they all fell before him,
> In peace he overthrows the barmaids of Erech!
> They all fall before him, he batters on their gates,
> His siege-engine breaks into every stronghold."

Enkidu was muffling a laugh. "The tune seems to have found different words," Gilgamesh said dryly, not sure whether to laugh or be outraged.

"Hark, I will sing you the glories of Gilgamesh!
The young men of Agga he overthrew in the field,
The young men of Erech he overthrows at home,
The delicate temple-youths, the strong soldier-lads,
They all fall before him, he batters on their gates,
His siege-engine breaks into every stronghold.

Hark, I will sing you the great deeds of Gilgamesh,
Mighty his lance, striking wherever he will.
I have heard that no daughter he leaves to her mother,
No son to his father—no sheep to her shepherd . . ."

Gilgamesh opened the door, stepping in. Without missing a beat, the singers shifted at once to the more familiar words of the praise-song as the Ensi knew it.

"Lo, his barbed arrows flew as bats at sunset,
Agga was confounded, all his host cast down . . ."

Gilgamesh shook his head ruefully, squatting down in an empty spot by the wall. The barmaid was there at once, setting a pitcher of beer with two straws between himself and Enkidu and telling him, in a breathless whisper, what food could be had at once and what cooked especially for the two of them.

"The roast lamb on bread will be enough for us, I think, if you bring it as quickly as you may," Gilgamesh said.

"At once, my Ensi." The maid hurried to the lamb that turned slowly on a spit over the fire, slicing a pair of generous portions from the tender haunch, then wrapping them in two warm breads from the middle of the heap that lay neatly over the rounded dome of her oven. The meat was succulent, flavored with coriander and mint; the chewy bread was soon soaked through with its juices, so that the ruddy dribbles were running down into Enkidu's beard, and Gilgamesh had to keep sucking his fingers clean. The three men and two women who stood singing in the corner had finished the first praise-hymn and started a second song to

Gilgamesh; and now the Ensi did have to smile, for the nervous glances they kept sending his way when they thought he was looking elsewhere made their first song seem far more comic to him.

"It would be a fine thing," Gilgamesh mused, "if the two of us could go out to do some great deed together—something that no one else could ever match."

"Shall we hunt together again?" Enkidu took a long pull of the beer, slurping noisily at his straw. "It was a good hunt we had, and will be more pleasant with no need for guards."

"There are many fierce beasts to be hunted, bear and plains-panther, wild boar and elephant," Gilgamesh said slowly. "It will be good to be out in the wilderness with you again. And yet . . ." There were few cylinder-seals of great men that did not show scenes of hunting where they were not marked with little images of triumphant battles; there was little to be remembered in that.

"And yet?" Enkidu prompted.

"And yet I should like to do something more worthy of us. For who has yet walked the earth that is our like? You are the only match for me, and I for you, and together there is none who can stand against us. We ought to . . ." His voice trailed off again, for he was not sure what more he could say. Vague plans, half formed, flashed about his head like the muted flash of lightning within black thunderclouds, showing neither shape nor path. *What have I done to be remembered?*

In the days after the war, Gilgamesh had thought often on what he should seek to do next. He had scratched campaign map after campaign map on clay tablets; he had called Shusuen to his side, and together, like boys with their gaming pieces, they had played out marches to the north, expeditions to the mountains of the east . . . all based on Shusuen's calculations of Erech's supplies and men in seven years' time of peace and good harvests, when the city had recovered. Shusuen had been careful to point out clearly to Gilgamesh that if there were another mighty power within marching distance who chose to come against them now, Erech would not even be able to defend itself, and further campaigns would be unthinkable for some years. Someday, Gilgamesh could ride out in his war-chariot again, in search of more triumphs to heap upon those he had won already—conqueror of all Sumer, in time, if he lived that long and his army did not fail him—but not now.

*If not war, what then?*

Rulers were builders as well as conquerors, and an Ensi's name would live on in the great shrines and halls he had commanded to be raised. But the coffers of Erech had been drained by the war, and besides, there was little of glory in the making of mud-bricks and the lifting of roofs. If he were to build, Gilgamesh knew it would have to be through some great doing, something no other could match.

As if the sun suddenly struck through the clouds, a bolt of light dazzled Gilgamesh's mind. There was one deed that would surely live forever, the making of its own memorial—a deed he could carry out with only the help of Enkidu and a few trusted men, if it could be carried out at all.

"I built Erech's wall for war, and it will stand a long time." Gilgamesh lifted the jug of beer, rolling the sweet-tasting straw from side to side in his mouth before sipping at the cool, malty liquid. "Now our battles are over, at least for a while; should I not build a gate for peace? To welcome traders in, to gladden the heart of Erech—to the joy of the gods, that they may look upon what we have wrought?"

"A good thing," Enkidu agreed. "But a great deed?"

Gilgamesh smiled. "The gate will be built all of cedar. We shall go to the great cedar forest, and there cut the trees we need."

"The cedar forest is guarded . . ."

"By the fierce creature Huwawa, who dwells there. We shall go there boldly—and if he comes against us, we shall slay him."

Even in the inn's dim lighting, Gilgamesh could see how Enkidu's fair skin paled, his golden brows drawing together.

"Even when I ran in the hills, ranging with the wild creatures, we knew of him," Enkidu said, his voice low. "To protect the cedar forest, Enlil set Huwawa as a terror to mortal men. Huwawa's roar is a flood, his mouth is fire, and his breath is death; from a hundred leagues away he can hear the least rustling in his forest. Who would go boldly there? Enlil set him as a terror to mortal men, and whoever goes down into the forest is frozen with fear. He never sleeps, and Enlil gave him a sevenfold awe with which to guard the cedars. Why do you wish to do this thing?"

Gilgamesh sighed, leaning forward to lay his hand upon Enkidu's chest. He could feel his friend's breath coming fast, the strong heart beating hard against Enkidu's thick ribs. "Who, my beloved, can ascend into the heavens? Only the gods can dwell forever in Utu's light; but the days of human beings are numbered, and what we achieve is as the wind. Now you seem to fear death, as you never did before—what has become of your bold strength? I will go in front of you, and your mouth may call out, 'Go on closer, do not be afraid!' Should I fall then, I will have established my fame: men will say forever that it was Gilgamesh who locked in battle with Huwawa the terrible, and afterward they will remember the child born in my house." He reached to stroke the soft curls along Enkidu's jaw, smoothing an unruly lock of golden hair back over one broad shoulder. "And you, my beloved, were born in the wilderness. The lion leapt up on you; you have experienced all without fear. But what I have heard this day grieves my heart. And so I will lift my hand and fell the cedars, I will make for myself a lasting name. Indeed, we shall soon go to order the weapons for this from the metalworkers, and watch ourselves while they are cast, for we shall need the strongest of weapons."

"We shall, indeed," Enkidu said heavily, "if we are to go into battle against Huwawa."

BUT IT WAS not to the metalworkers that Gilgamesh went first. Instead, with the old words of the stranger still buzzing in his head, he made his way alone to the rooms of his court scribe, Shusuen. The young man sat cross-legged on the floor, knee-length tunic askew and head bent as he pecked at a tablet of damp clay with his reed. Beside him sat one of the En's shorthaired cats, putting out a paw every now and again to bat at the moving length of stem—a gift from the old priest to his grandson.

Looking up, the scribe rose to his feet, bowing deeply to Gilgamesh. "What is it you wish of me, my Ensi?"

Gilgamesh sank down to the floor, gesturing for Shusuen to do likewise. "You have often chronicled my deeds," he began.

"As you know well, my Ensi."

"But you have done it from behind the city walls, from reports and tales of battle. Now I seek a greater adventure, and a tale that should be told by a witness of what no man has seen before."

Shusuen's eyes opened more widely; he leaned forward, resting his pointed chin on his fist. "What do you speak of, my Ensi?"

"I am going to do battle with Huwawa, the guardian of the holy cedar forest. Although you are no warrior, I wish you to come with me, so that you may tell a story which will live on—longer than the walls of Erech will stand. Yet," Gilgamesh added thoughtfully, "I would not force you to come, nor ask you to risk your life unwillingly or without great reward."

The young scribe's fair skin had paled further as Gilgamesh spoke, and it was a moment before he answered. "I must consult with my chief counselor," Shusuen said. "Remember: a mongoose is known for its actions, a cat—for its thoughts." He lifted up the cat, stroking its mottled back; the cat purred, staring up into his face. "What is your opinion, Basthotep?" he inquired of it, as seriously as if he were speaking to his great-grandfather. "What do you think of this venture?"

Shusuen cocked his head as if to listen to the cat, a lock of thick brown hair falling over his forehead. "Hmm. Basthotep says that it is indeed a dangerous undertaking, and that a sensible man would not risk it. Going against Huwawa is far too close to daring the gods for his taste, for he is a most pious cat. Still, he thinks that if you must go, then with your protection on the way . . . and a sufficient reward . . . Not for myself, of course, for I desire nothing more than to serve you, but Basthotep must have his proper payment."

Gilgamesh laughed. "And what does your cat think is a sufficient reward? A lifetime supply of milk and mice, perhaps? His share of the butter-offerings given to the temple?"

"Oh, that is not nearly enough for such a noble cat, descended from the temple-cats of the Black Land. Basthotep says that he wants . . . yes, little royal cat?" Shusuen bowed his head closer to the cat's again, then looked up sideways at Gilgamesh, blue eyes bright and a little smile on his finely chiseled lips. "He will require a chariot of his own, drawn by milk-white donkeys, with a parasol over it so that the suns of the journey will not scorch his tender fur, and the chariot should be adorned with gold and silver as well. And he will have to have a cup of gold to drink his milk from, and a fine silver plate for his meat, for his simple clay implements could easily break on the way. It is a hard life, he says, being the cat of a simple scribe, even though my great-grandmother did come from the Black Land as cat-tender for the En in his youth, and we live near the heart of the Eanna."

"An impudent and extravagant request, if a scribe had made it," Gilgamesh said, "but I have seen how well your grandfather's cats think of themselves. Tell the cat that his fee will be granted."

Shusuen blinked in surprise, lifting up the cat to look directly into its face. "Did you hear that, Basthotep? The Ensi has recognized your proper worth. Yes, he is a most wise and generous ruler, worthy of many lifetimes of remembrance, is he not? Surely there will be many fine songs sung about him."

Gilgamesh had risen and was almost to the doorway, but something about the scribe's last words made him look back. "Speaking of songs . . . I heard a most interesting song today, something that sounded very much like your work, although it was not, I am sure, one that has ever been sung in my hearing before."

"My Ensi!" Shusuen protested, spreading his hands in wounded innocence. "You know that I write only the truth as your scribe—and only so much of that as is fit to be written."

"Indeed," Gilgamesh said, trying hard to suppress his smile. "Well, there will be ample to keep your active wits occupied for a while, anyway. Now come with me, for Enkidu and I must summon a gathering of the elders of the city, to tell them of our plans and hear such advice as they may give."

THE SKY WAS darkening outside the door of Gilgamesh's judgment hall by the time the elders of Erech were all in their places; the young temple-maids and youths were carrying oil-lamps around the hall, their flickering lights deepening the craggy wrinkles of the old men's faces. The En sat in his place beside Gilgamesh, and his look was very grave, as though he had already heard the Ensi's plan and had time to shape all his doubts.

When he was sure that everyone was there, Gilgamesh rose to his feet, striking his staff of office against the floor. "Elders of Erech," he called out, "the gods have set a new plan in my thoughts, that after this war, there should be a time of peace for this city." From far down the hall, he could hear the breaths of relief; those men closer to him stifled their sighs, but he could see the aged faces softening. "I have built the city's siege-walls; now I shall adorn them with a great gate, holy and beautiful in the sight of all. And the gate shall be built of great cedar trees, from the forest of Huwawa—I shall travel there with my band of picked warriors, and if the guardian of the wood stands against us, we shall overcome him."

The babble of words rose up like a river in flood, cracked voices and strong striving against each other. "Why do you wish to . . . ? You are young, Gilgamesh, your heart runs away with you . . . Huwawa is terrible to look at . . . Forest runs for ten thousand leagues . . . Huwawa's roar is the deluge . . . mouth is fire . . . breath is doom . . . What you seek to do you know nothing about . . . No equal match, trying to stand against . . . Who is there that would go up to . . ."

"Silence!" Gilgamesh shouted, his cry cutting through the others as if he were shouting commands on the battlefield. He thumped his staff on the floor again, and gradually the voices of the elders stilled. "I have been warned of the dangers, and yet I am resolved to do this: Enkidu and I shall go together with my men. I ask for your advice and blessing, not for you to seek to daunt me."

The En rose to his feet, the glittering disk of electrum on his chest scattering bright sparks about the darkening room. He coughed several times before he spoke, and his voice seemed frailer than usual, though it still carried clearly through the hall.

"If you must go, then listen to words of wisdom. Do not trust wholly in your great strength, Gilgamesh: be sure that your eyes are wide and your blow certain. The one who goes in front guards his friend, and the one who knows the way keeps his companion safe—let Enkidu go before you as you march. He knows the way of the forest, to the cedars; he has seen battle, and understands warfare." The En's thin hand gestured outward, including all the old men who sat and watched in his next words. "Enkidu will watch over his friend, make the way safe for his companion, and will carry his body over all pitfalls. Enkidu . . ." The En's fingers brushed lightly over Enkidu's massive shoulders. ". . . we, in our assembly, entrust the Ensi to you; let you, in turn, bring him back to us again."

"May your god protect you," another old man's voice murmured in the stillness as the En sat again, and others echoed him. "May he lead you on the road safe; may he bring you back to the landing place at Erech."

"I thank you for your blessings," Gilgamesh said gravely. "I shall come back to you. Now, Enkidu, let us go to the great temple Egalmah, to the presence of Ninsun, the mighty ruler—Ninsun the wise, who knows all. She will lay out a wise path for our feet."

Enkidu seized Gilgamesh's hand in his warm grip, and the two of them went out beneath the glittering black gazes of the old men, into the cool evening air. The smells of garlic and onions, stewing meat and baking bread, wafted out over the streets together with the shrill voices of children at play—as if the war had been over for a lifetime, Gilgamesh thought; and he did not know whether he should feel comforted or melancholy at that.

RIMSAT-NINSUN SQUATTED on a pile of sheepskins in her little chamber behind the goddess' shrine, sipping at a small cup of beer through a silver straw. She was very tired, the age aching in her bones. Since the war's beginning, her shrine had been filled with the smoke of incense rising to the goddess as the women of Erech prayed for their menfolk—first for their safety, then, as the wounded were brought in and the lists of the dead made known, for their healing or for blessings in Erishkegal's halls. The altars of the shrine were heaped high with little images, of clay or gold, bronze or silver, as women could afford them: feet and hands and eyes, all the wounded pieces left from the war. Rimsat-Ninsun's ears still seemed to ring with the endless din of wailing prayers; her own feet were sore from days on end of standing to her duties, her voice worn to a whisper by leading the chants of the Old Woman's temple, and her hands blistered from grinding and mixing healing herbs for those whose wounds were festering. Now she could rest for a little time, but soon she would have to rise again, for though she was no longer the Shamhatu, the days of a priestess in her shrine were longer than those of any laborer. Even now she heard the creaking of the door-hinges, and set her cup down, rising with a sigh to see who had come in.

Though at first glimpse the two men were only shadows bulking high against the door's darkness, Rimsat-Ninsun recognized them at once. "My son and Enkidu," she said. "Be welcome in the Old Woman's shrine. What brings you to me this night?"

"My mother," Gilgamesh replied, "I am brought by my strength, for I must now make a long journey to the place of Huwawa. I shall face a battle about which I do not know; I am about to travel a road I cannot know, until I have gone and come back—until I have reached the forest of cedars, until I have destroyed the terrible Huwawa, and removed from the land whatever is baneful and hated by Utu."

Gilgamesh undid his belt; his fronded kilt dropped to the floor in a puddled froth of white linen, so that he stood naked in the shrine, his muscular body gleaming in the lamplight. "See, I take off my garment before you: I ask you to call to Utu on my behalf. I have spoken to the elders of the city about this, and the En has given me advice."

Rimsat-Ninsun closed her eyes, for the heavy smoke of incense in the shrine was beginning to sting them. At first the sense of Gilgamesh's words ran off her mind like heavy rain off hard-baked earth, sinking in only slowly. Then the last strength drained from her legs, so that she had to lean her back against the temple wall, staring at her son and his companion.

*He is certain in his mind,* she thought. *What can I do to sway him?* Then, *Nothing, for I know his thoughts. Once he is set, there is no turning him back—not for his own sake, or that of any other. Gilgamesh will only listen to Enkidu: gods who made them for each other, grant that Enkidu protect and advise him well!*

"I shall call to Utu for you," Rimsat-Ninsun said. "Since I know that you will not be turned aside, at least you shall not go unblessed."

She turned away, for she could no longer bear to look upon Gilgamesh. Whole and perfect in his strength as he was, the muscles rippling beneath his skin, she had lately seen too many strong young men
with their limbs gashed and torn, moaning with their guts spilling out,
or shaking and pale from the fever of infected wounds. *He is so precious to
me, so fair in his strength; mightier than his father Lugalbanda, he is the greatest war-
leader Erech has ever known. And yet he runs from danger to greater danger, like a wild
bull after a cow, seeking ever for what must overcome him in time* . . . These were evil
thoughts, which she knew she must turn away from her son—her hands
made an unconscious gesture of warding—let no gods or demons hear
them and be tempted to bring her fears to truth.

Rimsat-Ninsun went into her chamber again, stripping off the simple
white dress she wore and lifting the goddess' garment of deep blue over
her head. A wide breast-brooch of lapis set in silver and circlet to match;
then she rang a small cymbal to summon Bau.

"Bring me water for a libation, incense and coals," Rimsat-Ninsun
said to the ancient temple-woman when she appeared. "Summon to me
the Shamhatu and her women, the votaries of Gilgamesh, and make this
room ready as if it were a wedding chamber."

Rimsat-Ninsun's knees creaked beneath her as she climbed the steps
to the height of the shrine, the water in her carmelian bowl slopping
from side to side. Reaching the top, she paused for a few moments to
catch her breath before she turned her face eastward and knelt, sprin-
kling a handful of frankincense upon the coals in her little brazier. The
breeze caught the small curls of gray smoke, flinging them lost into the
night as she began to pray.

"Utu," Rimsat-Ninsun called, raising her hands up toward the dark
horizon where the god would rise at dawn, "why have you raised up my
son Gilgamesh thus? Why have you inflicted upon him this restless
heart?" She had to pause then, for the tears were streaming down her
face, splashing into the bowl of water, and for a little time she could get
no words out. "Now you have touched him," she went on at last, "so
that he must fare on a long journey, to the place of Huwawa—to face a
battle he cannot know about, to travel a road he cannot know, until the
day he goes and returns. On the day set as his limit, if he fears, may Aia

your bride remind you, and may she commend him to the watchmen of the night. Be with him in the mighty cedars, Utu, protector of men; let your light shine upon him, and on Enkidu his companion. Battle beside them, great god, until they have overcome Huwawa, until they have cleansed the land of whatever you find ill, and brought light to the cedar forest. As I call in the darkness, so be with them in the night, and watch over them ever, so that nothing that walks by dark or day do them harm."

Carefully Rimsat-Ninsun lifted the carnelian bowl, pouring out a stream of water to darken the clay bricks of the shrine's flat roof. It seemed to her that she felt a warm glow within her breast, like the glow of a far-off campfire brightening the heart of a traveler in the desert, and she could only hope that Utu had heard her prayer and would answer. She bowed her head in humbleness before the god and waited, but no other sign came to her: the sky was dark, the stars glimmering faintly above, and Utu would not turn back from his nightly journeying.

When she came down the stairs again, Rimsat-Ninsun found that the women had already prepared her room as she had instructed them. The floor was freshly strewn with sweet flag and tamarisk twigs, the coverlet pulled down and the lamps filled with fine oil. Kubaba, Enmebaragesi, and Peshtur stood beside the bed, all three arrayed as brides, in sheer dresses of fine linen with woven crowns of fresh green palm-leaves upon their heads.

"This is well," she said. "Now I shall bring Enkidu forth to you, for he, too, is the Ensi, and must be given your full blessing if he is to keep Gilgamesh safe through this long endeavor that Utu has set in his heart."

His eyes filled with the sight of Gilgamesh standing naked in the shrine beside him, half drunk with the scents of frankincense and sweet flag and the warm muskiness of his lover's body, Enkidu hardly noticed when the door opened again and Rimsat-Ninsun stepped out in her robe of deep blue, a golden pendant dangling from her hand. The priestess' husky voice was soft, but every word cut clearly through the sweet smoky air.

"Mighty Enkidu, you are not the child of my womb, but now I adopt you as my own—I, together with the votary-priestesses of Gilgamesh, his lovers and sisters." She stepped forward, reaching up, and Enkidu bent his head to allow her to place the pendant about his neck. "May the gods witness: I have taken Gilgamesh to Enkidu, Enkidu to Gilgamesh I have taken. Until he goes and returns, until he has reached the cedar forest, until he has killed the fierce Huwawa, be it a month or be it a year." She lifted Enkidu's hand, placing it in Gilgamesh's and wrapping her own slender fingers tightly about their larger clasp. "Come into the bridal chamber I have prepared for you, my son—come both of you, for you are one flesh, one spirit, one single man. Let the women take you, let the daughters of the gods make you great together."

Rimsat-Ninsun drew them forward, past the wooden statue of the goddess who stood gazing down at them and into the room behind the shrine where Gilgamesh's votive-wives waited. Though Enkidu had often sated himself with them, they seemed strange in the dim lamplight, as though he looked upon them for the first time—not only Gilgamesh's priestesses, but now his own as well. His manhood was already swelling hard beneath the kilt as Enmebaragesi and Peshtur came forward, each reaching out to stroke the golden pelt on his chest and shoulders with one hand as they caressed Gilgamesh's smooth body with the other. The Ensi's phallus was standing, jutting forth from the dark curls at the fork of his legs like a knobbed branch of polished cedarwood; Enkidu brushed his fingers lightly over it even as Peshtur unfastened his kilt, kneeling upon it and bending her head to take his own rod deep into the soft wetness of her mouth. Kubaba sat upon the bed, watching, a faint smile upon her lips as Enmebaragesi drew Gilgamesh closer. Gazing at his lover, Enkidu's heart was filled to overflowing with joy, and a soft moan of delight escaped his lips. Together, never to be parted: he knew that he could not ask for more, for all had now been given to him.

GILGAMESH AND ENKIDU arose before dawn on the morning of their departure. They dressed each other slowly, arranging the fronds of each other's kilts and pinning each other's cloaks on carefully, then helping one another with armor, and at last setting the helms on each other's heads. Gilgamesh could feel the faint tremble of anticipation in his lover's body, and a shiver went through his own flesh: though he had watched the casting of their great weapons himself, done a hundred things to ready for the journey, it was only now that the enormity of his plan rose before him.

"We shall go to the temple of Utu," Gilgamesh said, "and make our offerings there as he rises over the horizon: Utu, too, is a journeyer and a warrior." He reached out to stroke a strand of Enkidu's curly golden hair out of his face, then bent forward to brush his lips against Enkidu's.

"That is well," Enkidu said, "for we shall surely need his help."

Shusuen was already waiting for them outside. The scribe's thick hair was tied back with a strand of white linen; he wore a simple kilt and cloak, with no adornments or jewelry. His eyelids were a little puffy, as though the heaviness of sleep still lay upon them, but his blue eyes shone brightly, his face live with excitement. A leather traveling bag lay at his feet, and his cat was sitting upon it.

"Are we ready to depart?" he asked. "Basthotep's chariot—for which he thanks you most greatly, kind Ensi—is outside, with the asses already harnessed to it, and the others are gathering beside it."

"We go now to make our offerings to Utu," Gilgamesh answered. "You may come with us, if you wish, to hear our words and see what signs the god wishes to send us."

Utu's shrine was at the eastern side of the city, built high to catch the first rays of the rising sun. Gilgamesh and Enkidu, with Shusuen trailing behind them, did not go inside, but instead mounted the stairs by the side of the temple, climbing up to the flat roof. A priest was already standing there—a thick-bodied man in his middle years, with shaven head and long black beard. On the little table before him stood bowls of incense and water beside a small basin of glowing coals; he held a fragrant fan of dried cedar cuttings, the sharp edges of the twigs standing out clearly beneath the paling sky.

"Greetings, and welcome in Utu's holy name, my Ensi," the priest said, bowing low before them. "Have you come to make the dawn offering here?"

"We have, and to pray for our journey," Gilgamesh answered.

The priest nodded, a small smile of satisfaction curling beneath the thick tendrils of his beard. "So shall it be." He handed Gilgamesh the fan and stepped back.

Gilgamesh laid his helmet aside and sprinkled a pinch of scented resin on the coals, fanning the basin until the sweet gray smoke began to curl upward. Gazing eastward, over the green fields beyond Erech's wall, he fell silent for a moment. Below him, the city was beginning to come to life, a soft wordless babble of voices rising; far to the east, he saw the pale shapes of a flock of sheep making its way to the hills, with the darker figure of the shepherd in their midst and a gray dog running behind to keep the stragglers together. The sky was very bright now, sunrise gold fading to blue behind the few pink-tinged wisps of cloud scattered thinly across it. Gilgamesh stood so for a few breaths, then knelt, lifting his hands toward the sky.

"Utu," he murmured softly, "I go with my hands lifted in prayer. May all be well with my soul; bring me back safe to the harbor at Erech, and set your protection over me." As he spoke, Enkidu knelt down beside him; he said nothing, but his face was raised to the heavens, clear green gaze fixed on the brightening horizon and long golden hair streaming back to mingle with the shaggy pelt of his cloak. To his own surprise, Gilgamesh felt hot tears prickling at the back of his eyelids, and more words came unbidden to his throat. "I shall go down a road I have never walked, to fight a battle about which I do not know. And yet I should fare well, with joy in my heart. Enkidu is beside me, my friend and companion: together with Utu's light upon us, there is none mighty enough to overwhelm us." He rose, lifting a bowl of water and spilling it slowly out upon the shrine's roof in a glittering stream so that the drops splashed upon his feet; after a moment, Enkidu did likewise.

"Fare with us, Utu," Gilgamesh said. "In our going, in our fighting, in our returning to Erech—light our way, and stand beside us, until we have come home safe again."

As Shusuen had promised, the chariots were already massed outside the Eanna premises. Gilgamesh had gotten a new one made for himself after the pattern of the one he had lost in the assassination attempt; as for the scribe's, since it was truly owned by the cat, Gilgamesh had ordered silver cats set at each corner, and just as the sides of his own were decorated with scenes of the Ensi overcoming his foes, Basthotep's chariot was adorned with reliefs of the cat catching mice and rats and small birds. Behind the chariots of the warriors was a great wagon drawn by four oxen: if all went well, it would bring back the great cedar trunks for Gilgamesh's gate.

"Hail, my Ensi!" Birhurturre called from his place at the head of Gilgamesh's band. "Are we ready to depart?" The young warrior had recovered quickly from the beatings Agga's men had given him; only a few fading bruise-marks still showed yellow upon his face, and his movements were as supple and quick as ever—Gilgamesh had made sure of that before summoning him to this expedition.

"We are ready," Gilgamesh answered. "To the city gates: there I will have my weapons brought to me in the sight of the people of Erech, and the elders will bid me farewell."

Enkidu leapt up into the chariot, taking the reins, and Gilgamesh followed. With Basthotep cradled in his arms, Shusuen mounted into his own more carefully, settling beneath the shade of its canopy—the scribe's fair skin would be little more marred by the sun of the journey than by sitting beneath the roof of Gilgamesh's judgment hall. Some of the warriors had grumbled at that, claiming that Shusuen was too delicate to take on the long road where there might be fighting, and would only slow them down, but Gilgamesh had deafened himself to their protests. He would have his scribe beside him, to record all that took place when he went against Huwawa . . . and if the worst befell, Shusuen's tablets might outlast the warriors' bones.

The trumpet sounded; the onagers surged forth. The streets cleared ahead of them, the people surging back behind like a tidal wave, craning their necks and calling blessings or tossing flowers and fronds of palm leaves. Gilgamesh glanced about at their faces, swarthy and bearded or pale and smooth, and wondered what they were thinking. Some, there must be, who thought him mad and reckless, who might heave a sigh of relief if he never came back and the governance of Erech fell wholly to the Eanna again until Enkidu's adopted son and Gilgamesh's only heir grew to a man's age. Others, he suspected—the young men who cheered and whistled themselves hoarse, the maidens who leaned from the windows of the houses with flower-twined hair falling about their shoulders and wreaths of blossoms in their hands—must feel some stirring pride, that the Ensi of their city could dare more than any other man, faring from battle to greater battle with the light of victory still shining from his gilded helm.

"May you come back to Erech safely!" they called, over and over again. "May the gods bless you! May you smite Huwawa mightily!"

The thunder of their voices was like the roar of an army at Gilgamesh's back, bearing him up. He smiled and waved to them, taking care to catch the eye of this one or that one now and again, so that they might know that their words had not gone unheard, or unappreciated.

The old men of Erech were assembled at the city gates, decked out in their best clothes as though to preside at a holy feast. With the En stood the Shamhatu and several of her priestesses, and four muscular temple-men bearing the great weapons Gilgamesh had ordered. Rimsat-Ninsun waited beside them, her finely wrinkled face pale and stark in the morning light.

"Now let our weapons be lifted up to us," Gilgamesh said, calling out so he could be heard above the softening murmurs of the crowd. "These mighty weapons—they have been cast as Huwawa's bane, the hard bronze sharpened to spill his blood, and blessed with the favor of Utu and all the gods, to wipe out what is baneful in the land."

One by one the En handed the weapons up to Gilgamesh and Enkidu, his withered arms trembling with their weight. Two heavy swords with gold pommels; two huge axes, which would serve for striking both Huwawa and the cedars he guarded; quivers and bows; thus they were armed, and Gilgamesh lifted his axe to glitter in the sunlight before the sight of all Erech.

"Go forth, Gilgamesh," the En said, his words husking softly from his thin chest. "Do not trust wholly in your own strength. Keep a clear eye, guard yourself, and let Enkidu go before you, for he knows the road: the one who goes in front guards his companion. May Utu grant you your wish. What your mouth has said, may your eyes see—may Utu open the barred path for you, unclose the road for your steps, unlock the mountain for your foot. May the sendings of the night please you, and may your father Lugalbanda stand beside you to fulfill your wish. After the killing of Huwawa for which you have striven, wash your feet; at night when you stop to rest, dig a well, so that the water in your water-skin is always pure. Offer up cool water to Utu, and keep your father Lugalbanda always in your mind. Go, and may the god who keeps you safe stand beside you."

The Shamhatu then said, "You did not ask my counsel on this—but may it satisfy your restless heart at last, so that you are content to dwell in Erech when you return." To Gilgamesh's surprise, he could hear a faint choking in her throat as she spoke, and it seemed that the bright morning sunlight was dazzling tears in her eyes. She turned her face from him quickly, reaching up to lay her hand on Enkidu's for a moment. "Remember well what I have taught you," she murmured to him, "but do not forget the wisdom of the lion, for you will need it on the long ways to Huwawa's forest."

Looking down at the Shamhatu's delicate face, a memory suddenly jolted Gilgamesh. Naram-Sin's trial, and then the whirling excitement and horror of the war, had driven the thought from his mind—too long? Gilgamesh did not know; he knew only that he must warn her before he left, lest it be too late when he had returned. He laid a hand upon her fine-boned shoulder, gripping her carefully. At his touch, she half jerked away, then mastered herself.

"Shamhatu," he murmured, "before I leave, I must tell you this—I had no chance to before. Ishbi-Erra told me that . . ." He could not repeat the traitor's accusation to her face. "He said that there was a woman in the temple who spoke against you, who said folk muttered about you and your place was unsteady because—because I had not come to you. I think if you find his lover, you will find your foe within the Eanna."

As soon as Gilgamesh had spoken, he blinked in disbelief. Was it not what he wanted, to have a different woman in the Shamhatu's place? A woman who would not fight against his plans, who listened to the Ensi with respect and helped to make his way smooth? Had his hasty words not served only to thwart his own desires?

*But another woman would still be Inanna*, the dark cold voice whispered in the depths of his heart.

The Shamhatu nodded gravely. "I had guessed as much. And I thank you for the warning, and the proof. But you need not fear for me: what the gods have decreed is not for mortals to thwart. It is you who goes rushing into peril now. Gilgamesh—go well, and come back safely."

"Go well, and come back safely," Rimsat-Ninsun repeated. She said no more, but only stood gazing at her two sons in silence.

The moment stretched out, long and awkward. Then Enkidu tossed his head back. "Come, my friend! Since you must fight, let us be on our way. Make your heart fearless, and come with me, for I know where he lives, and the road Huwawa travels."

Gilgamesh raised his hand to signal to Birhurturre. The trumpet sounded again; the gates swung open, and they were on their way.

The Shamhatu was silent as she walked back to the Eanna, brooding on Gilgamesh's words. Ever since her altercation with Shubad at the New Year's feast, she had been more aware of the mutterings within the temple. Now and again she had chanced to overhear the cruel jokes, more pointed since Gilgamesh had taken up with Enkidu—rude jests that she might really wish for a herder with sheep-dung still on his feet, even suggestions that, since clearly Enkidu had one thing she lacked, she should carry a *naditum*'s pestle when next she tried to bring the Ensi to bed. But she had passed by in silence when such remarks had accidentally reached her ears, for she knew very well that like things were always said by lesser folk about those whom the gods had placed above them. The En's age, Urgigir's eye for pretty women and eunuchs, the woven rod of correction that Elulu always carried with him: she had made her own jokes about them before she became the Shamhatu and knew she could no longer mock her colleagues. Yet in the last months it had become harder for her to pretend she did not hear, to keep herself from descending in full wrath upon the offenders. Only the knowledge that she was already thought unmeasured and unjust enough for having slapped Shubad enabled her to hold her peace—but the jests rankled all the same.

And more worrying were the conversations that she did not hear: the whispers and mutters that stopped abruptly when her feet passed by, the sudden guilty and sideways glances that met her own. She had tried to put it down to the trials of the war, or to her own nervousness, making her see shadows in every corner, but she could do that no longer— Gilgamesh had seen to it.

"What shall I do?" the Shamhatu asked herself. "To whom shall I speak?"

It came to her that she could brace Shubad directly: accuse her of fomenting dissension in the temple, even, if it could be proven that she was Ishbi-Erra's lover, of having had some hand in the plot to assassinate Gilgamesh. But the thought did not last long. Though it was against custom, there was no law against questioning the Shamhatu, and as for the other—what could be proven now? Only that Shubad had known Ishbi-Erra well. Even if she had been a co-conspirator, the only two who could have told of her guilt were dead, and when Ishbi-Erra's own wife was pardoned . . .

Nor could she simply say to Shubad, "Get out: you are no longer of the Eanna," nor sway Elulu's decisions as to when and what the other woman might sing. Not without claiming a vision from Inanna: and she knew that she could not claim falsely, and if she did, when everyone knew of the quiet strife between herself and Shubad, her word would never be trusted again.

From the shrine's high doors floated the sound of a *tigi*-hymn. The choir rehearsal would be nearing its end now, freeing the temple again for those who wished to come and make offering; already a few folk were gathered on the steps. The Shamhatu's steps slowed, then stopped. There was at least one singer she could trust, one who could tell her how matters went with Shubad and those she sang and ate and talked with daily.

Keeping her face turned away from the gathering petitioners, the Shamhatu waited until the singing had stopped and the musicians came flooding out of the shrine doors.

"Atab," she called softly. The young eunuch turned, his great dark eyes liquid with surprise as she beckoned him over.

"What is it you wish, Divine Lady?"

"Come with me. I would speak with you in private."

They went back to the Shamhatu's own chambers. She settled on the edge of the bed; he squatted on the rug by her feet.

"Atab, you know that I have always trusted you with my bath and my person. Can I trust you with my thoughts now?"

"Always, Divine Lady. What is it that troubles your mind?"

"I have heard . . ." The words stuck in the Shamhatu's throat. She had spent so long beating her own thoughts down, forbidding herself to speak of her fears to any; it was as if she had been heaping up her own siege-wall about herself, and now found herself trapped within, with no gate built for escape. As if sensing her misgivings, Atab began to hum quietly, a gentle melody of soothing.

"Stop that!" the Shamhatu said sharply. Atab looked up at her, and she could see the hurt darkening his fine-boned face. "No, it is not you, but . . . I have heard . . . I was told . . ." She gathered herself, and the words came forth in a sudden rush, like a flood bursting through a crumbling dike. "I have heard that there are those in the temple who mutter against me, who say that I am not fit to hold my office because Gilgamesh has not come to Inanna's marriage-bed. And I think that I know who—"

"That mangy she-dog!" Atab burst out, his high voice sharpening to the sudden stab of an awl-point. "Forgive me for speaking so, Divine Lady, but I know exactly who is troubling you. It is Shubad, is it not?"

The Shamhatu nodded.

"Her arrogance is unbounded," the slim eunuch went on. "The *gala*-priests have known this for a long time, for once she had mastered the songs of Inanna, she went on to demand more and more of the best solos of the temple—flirting her hips and eyes at Elulu, that he might even choose her for pieces meant for the voices of eunuchs. And in the last months . . ." Atab's voice lowered; his eyes dropped, staring at the interlacing of his slender fingers in his lap. ". . . she has, indeed, spoken as you say, and with little restraint."

"And do many agree with her? Atab," the Shamhatu added as he opened his mouth to speak again, "tell me the truth, not what will comfort me. I must know; it will only harm me to be deceived."

"I do not think that many of the leaders of the temple do," Atab said slowly. "I once overheard Elulu tell her that her mouth made such a fine noise only because her head was empty, and she should spend her time on the pieces he had given her to sing, not on meddling with matters beyond her. But I must tell you, Divine Lady, that she is not without followers among those of lesser understanding."

The Shamhatu's face must have shown something of her feelings, for Atab's hand fluttered up to rest lightly on her knee. "Though we won the war, many are still dispirited, and folk will always complain when they have suffered hardship. Shubad's whisperings are but as a little coal, that may flare bright beneath the right gust of wind but will quickly burn itself out and grow cool again. Divine Lady, I am sure you have nothing to fear: her followers will quickly be abashed by you. You have done all Inanna demands, and if the Ensi will not fill his part, then it is upon his head."

The Shamhatu shivered. As if the moment had never passed, she could still hear Urgigir's deep voice grating out of Geme-Tirash's throat: *The omens are not good . . .* And those other dark words: *The Ensi of Erech is dead.* Without thought, as if she were a peasant warding off the Evil Eye, her hand formed a horned sign of aversion, index and little fingers out.

"Do not speak so! Not when the Ensi goes forth into unknown danger."

"May the gods turn ill away," Atab murmured mildly. His tone did not cheer the Shamhatu's heart: if those folk of the temple who were not turning against her had decided to set all the blame on Gilgamesh, how could Erech stand whole before the gods? But she did not say that to Atab, for it seemed to her that she could feel all her steady supports slipping away from beneath her feet like river-mud under a strong current, and she knew that she needed his loyalty unshaken.

"Only remember what you have said, my trusted one. And if you should hear whisperings, use your own tongue to answer them—and should what you hear be dire enough, bear the news to me."

"That I shall do, Divine Lady. I wish," Atab added, "that Shusuen had not gone with Gilgamesh. There is no one like to him in slaying treachery with mockery, and stilling wagging tongues with a swifter one—and of the many that Shubad has tried to seduce, he is among the few who had the sense to refuse."

"How do you know that?" the Shamhatu asked, trapped by her curiosity in spite of herself.

"Because she spat and moaned and cursed his name for more than a week, though she would not say why. And so I asked him, and he told me the words with which he had sent her away."

The Shamhatu would dearly have loved to ask, but she knew that her dignity could not stretch quite so far. She could only reply, "Well, since Shusuen is not here, you must do the best you may." But her heart was lightened by the news that the young scribe had been supporting her all along, even while remaining loyal to Gilgamesh.

EVEN WITH THE heavy wagon trailing them, the party made good speed; it was well before midday by the time Erech's walls had receded beyond the horizon. His heart light and his forebodings gone, Gilgamesh laughed aloud as they rode, and now and again found himself humming a few bars of song. Enkidu, too, seemed lighthearted, as though he had indeed put all his worries about Huwawa aside; he clucked cheerfully to the onagers, and reached out every so often to stroke Gilgamesh's thigh or the back of his hand.

"How is it with Sululi?" Gilgamesh asked, the thought coming to his mind suddenly as a startled bird flying up from the reeds. "She did not come to bid us farewell."

"I made my farewells to her last night," Enkidu answered. "She said that she could not bear to watch us ride out—I think it will be long," he added more sadly, "before she can look with a glad heart upon men armed for battle again. Though she seems happy otherwise; the Shamhatu has made her the chief weaver in the Eanna, so that she never lacks for the finest of wools and threads, and she has become close friends with Innashagga, whom she has taken as apprentice. And she was sorry to see me go, for I think I have become dear to her, but she blessed me, and sent her tenderest greetings for you . . . As for your son, he roared and shook his little fists as though he wished to ride with us. I think he has inherited all your strength of heart."

Gilgamesh smiled. "He is yours as well as mine. And he will be our heir someday, and Ensi of Erech. I wish," he went on reflectively, "that I had thought to go to her house last night, but there was so much that had to be done . . ."

"You can greet them well enough when we come back. And greetings are gladder than partings."

"True enough." Gilgamesh put an arm about his lover's shoulders, feeling the strong play of muscles beneath his touch as Enkidu guided the onagers on their way. "For nothing makes me gladder than greeting you at dawn each morning—and may we never have to part."

"Not while we live."

The words warmed Gilgamesh's heart; he sat well-content in the warm sunlight as they drove along.

Suddenly, without warning, a furious meow sounded from Shusuen's chariot, followed by a spate of hissing. The scribe's cat was standing on his lap, back arched as he stared into the distance.

"Soft, soft, Basthotep," Shusuen murmured, trying to stroke down the fur bristling along the cat's spine. "What is it? What do you see?"

Enkidu laughed, pointing along the line of the cat's gaze. For a moment Gilgamesh could make nothing out; then he saw the long tawny shapes slinking slowly along the heat-hazed plain. "My friend is out there," Enkidu said, "and your cat is challenging him for his queens, for he has caught the scent and thinks he has another tom like himself to fight."

"Ah, my brave little ruler," Shusuen said, lifting the spotted cat up. "Can you not see that the lion is many times your size? He would eat you in a gulp and not notice it, but you do not care, do you? You are a Gilgamesh among cats, and you would fight him anyway." Shusuen ducked his head, glancing at Gilgamesh. The scribe's lips were pressed together, hiding his smile, but Gilgamesh knew Shusuen's look of guilty amusement far too well.

"Are you trying to tell me something?"

"My Ensi"—and now Shusuen did smile—"who would presume to

give advice unasked to Gilgamesh, who is two-thirds god and only one-third man? I only compliment little Basthotep on his bravery, for what finer compliment could he have than being compared to you?"

Gilgamesh waved a hand dismissively. From their days in the Eanna's school together, he had long since learned that it was useless to try to match words with Shusuen; as well try to match the flickering of a lizard's tongue. "If you wish to keep your fine cat, you should hold his leash tightly tonight," he advised, and turned back to Enkidu. "Do you think your friend will come all the way to the cedar forest with us?"

"No, for he is pride-ruler now, and has queens and his own lands to look after. Still, it is good to see him, and it may be that he will come closer."

IT WAS NEARLY a month's ride before they caught sight of the mountains at last—the low peaks rising from the plains, with the greater crags arching up far behind them, blue as the cool shadows of evening. "The going will be slower from here on," said Enkidu. "We are still some way from the cedar forest, but it is time that we began to guard ourselves more carefully. And . . . I think you should make an offering to Utu tonight, for in the highlands we are closer to his hall."

A cold shiver went through Gilgamesh at Enkidu's words, though he did not know why. But he nodded soberly, and answered, "I shall do that."

So it was that, as the sun began to lower in the sky, Gilgamesh commanded his men to dig a westward-facing well, and took up a pick himself to dig beside them. With several strong men working, the digging went quickly; and to Gilgamesh's surprise, clear water began to trickle into the pit before it had reached the depth of a man's height. He filled his two-mouthed water bottle from it, then said to Birhurturre, "I am going to the peak of the crag. I wish to go alone—but watch carefully, lest I should need any aid."

"Aye, my Ensi," the young warrior answered. "I shall watch well; I shall not fail you." Looking into his wide dark eyes, Gilgamesh seemed to catch the thought, *as I did before.*

The Ensi laid a hand on Birhurturre's shoulder. "You proved yourself well worthy before Agga of Kish, when I put my trust in you." Though Birhurturre said nothing in return, Gilgamesh could feel the muscles easing beneath his touch, and knew that he had spoken rightly.

The mountain path was easy climbing, if rocky. The grasses and shrubs around it had been nibbled low to the ground; Gilgamesh saw the delicate cloven hoofprints of wild goats, and here and there a small nubbly pile of dried droppings. It crossed his mind that he should set some of the men to hunting here, for the fresh meat would be welcome after the many days of hard-baked bread and crumbly dried cheese. Though the sun still shone upon him, gilding the tops of the mountains with ruddy light, the air was cooling quickly, chilling the faint dew of sweat upon his brow and shoulders. A great bird of prey circled above, black against the pale sky—from where he stood, Gilgamesh could not tell whether it was an eagle or a vulture, only mark the lazy tilting of its wings through the air. He paused a moment to watch it, then climbed on again, until he stood upon the mountain's peak, looking down at the camp far below where his men toiled with their campfires and blankets. The wind sweeping down from the greater mountains beyond was colder up here, stroking his skin with a breath of winter so that the little hairs of his arms and shoulders bristled up in tiny bumpy ridges.

"Mountain," Gilgamesh breathed, shaking out a scattering of flour from the small bag he had brought with him, "bring me a dream, a good message from Utu. Utu, I stand near to the door of your hall, nearer to the gates of the cedar forest. I offer clear water from our well." He unstoppered his water bottle, scattering the bright drops in a circle around him. "I offer you flour milled from Erech's grain. Show me the way; give me rede of the help I should expect from you in my battle. And you, my father, Lugalbanda, who dwells among the gods—you who journeyed over the mountains in your time, whose faring-tales are still told, I call to you. Strength and sinew you gave me, Erech's mighty Ensi; stand with me now, for I travel hard ways, as you did, and have most need of those gifts your might fathered in me."

The bird above Gilgamesh—an eagle, he was sure of it now—had circled him again. Now it was flying straight toward the higher crag, until it sank into the shadow of a gorge and was gone. He waited a little longer, but the sun was lowering fast, and he knew he must hurry back to camp before the path grew dark.

The fires were already blazing below when Gilgamesh came among his men again, making his way to the campfire where Enkidu sat cross-legged, chewing on his evening ration of bread.

"I have made our bed ready," Enkidu said, "with a covering over it, for the night winds here are fierce. We should sleep early, for tomorrow's travel will be hard."

Gilgamesh opened his mouth to protest, but found a yawn stretching his jaws already. Suddenly it seemed to him that he was very tired, as though the cold breeze from the mountain had sucked his strength out with the heat from his body, and he realized that he was shivering. He squatted down next to Enkidu, close enough to feel his lover's warmth; and when he had finished his supper, Gilgamesh let the other man guide him to their nest of blankets.

"Lie down now," Enkidu told him, "and I shall keep your back warm."

Gilgamesh curled up tightly beneath the coverings, knees to chin, glad for the makeshift windbreak Enkidu had set up out of blankets and dried branches. He barely felt Enkidu climbing in behind him, for sleep was already pouring over him like a wave of dark poppy-syrup.

IT WAS BITTERLY cold and dark when Gilgamesh woke, the only warmth that of Enkidu's body curled against his back. His limbs were all locked into trembling stiffness, and for a moment he did not know where he was.

"Enkidu," he called softly. "Enkidu?"

"Gilgamesh?" came his lover's voice, blurred with sleep. "Gilgamesh, is all well?"

"My friend, didn't you call out to me? Why did I wake up? Did you not touch me? I am robbed of holy sleep." A violent wave of shivering ran through Gilgamesh's body, shaking him like a palm-frond in the stormwind. Enkidu reached out to him, holding him tight against his chest until the spasm had passed.

"Why am I trembling?" Gilgamesh asked wonderingly. "Did a god pass by? . . . Enkidu, I have dreamed."

"Tell me your dream," Enkidu murmured, his breath soft against Gilgamesh's ear.

"The dreams . . . they were disturbing. I dreamed that we were in a mountain gorge, and the peak towered high above us. Then it toppled and fell, rocks showering down—we were like flies before it."

"Ah," Enkidu sighed. Then, "The meaning of your dream comes to me. It is a good dream, I feel, and full of meaning. My friend, the mountain of your dream is Huwawa. It means that we will capture Huwawa, and kill him. We will bring him down, and cast his body into the wastelands. In the morning, there will be a good sign from Utu."

"How do you know this?"

"I know it . . ." Enkidu stopped, and for a little time Gilgamesh could hear only the quiet sound of his lover's breathing rustling through his own hair. "I know it as I was born in the wilderness, as I know the path to Huwawa's land—as I know how matters stand with the lions."

*But there are no lions in these peaks,* Gilgamesh thought. *Only wolves, and bears, and birds of prey.* Yet he was comforted a little, and so he spoke his second dream.

"When that dream was done, another came to me. I was wrestling with a wild bull of the wilderness; his bellow split the ground, and raised a cloud of dust into the sky. I sank to my knees in front of him; his grasp encircled my arm. Then a man appeared, and his face was shining so that I could not look at him. My tongue hung out and my temples throbbed, but he pulled me forth and gave me water to drink from his waterskin."

"The wild bull is not Huwawa, to whom we go," Enkidu answered. "The wild bull you saw is Utu, who guards us, who will hold our arms when we come to hardship. The one who gave you water to drink from his waterskin . . . He," said Enkidu, his voice now ringing firm with quiet sureness, "is Lugalbanda, your father and god, who brings honor to you. We shall join together to do the one thing, such a deed as has not yet been done, and death shall not diminish it."

"And yet," Gilgamesh sighed, "I had a third dream, and it disturbed me deeply. The heavens roared and the earth rumbled. Then . . ." He shivered again, remembering the vast black abyss where he had seemed to stand alone, with neither sound nor sight to strengthen him. ". . . it became deathly still, and darkness loomed. A bolt of lightning cracked, and a fire broke out. The clouds thickened above, and I saw it raining death. Then the white-hot glow faded and the fire went out, and everything that had been falling around turned to ask. Let us," he added suddenly, "go down into the plain where we can speak of this. The mountains suddenly seem too near to . . ."

"To Huwawa?" Enkidu asked gently. "But this, it seems to me, is the best of your dreams. Huwawa's roar is a flood, his mouth is fire, and his breath is death. In your dream you saw what no one has faced. Yet the glow faded and the fire went out, and the deadly rain turned to ash. We shall defeat Huwawa, and strip his seven cloaks of awe from him. In the morning, there shall be a good sign from Utu."

"And yet I dreamed again . . ." Gilgamesh stopped there, for what had passed in the night was already fading from his mind. "There were two more dreams, but I cannot remember them. Something of a man, many cubits tall—no, they are gone." He blinked hard against the darkness beneath their canopy, wishing that he could see the stars.

"These dreams are good," Enkidu purred, "and they bring comfort to my heart."

"And to mine," another voice broke in—Shusuen's dry, cultivated baritone. "Although Enkidu's readings are more comforting."

"Shusuen!" Gilgamesh burst out, sitting bolt upright. The icy air chilled his bare chest and shoulders at once, as though he had plunged into one of the cold mountain streams, but he hardly noticed, so angry was he. "How dare you come to spy on us?"

"Easy, be easy," the scribe answered. Now that his eyes were used to the dark, Gilgamesh could see the young man's faint bundled shadow outside their lean-to, his hands spread placatingly. "Basthotep trod on me and meowed, telling me that something of importance must be happening, and that therefore I must go to you. You brought me to record all, did you not? And what could be more worthy of remembering than the dreams of the Ensi on his way to a great battle? Would not any of the folk of the Eanna say the same?"

"We are the only folk of the Eanna here," Gilgamesh growled, but the wrath was already cooling in his breast. "Still, you may be right. Go back to sleep, and write these things down when morning comes."

"As you command, my Ensi." Shusuen rose, and Gilgamesh heard his feet crunching over the frosty pebbles outside as he walked away.

Gilgamesh lay down again, pulling the wool blankets tightly up around himself. "Do you suppose," he wondered aloud, "that Shusuen's cat really tells him these things? It is very convenient for him, that cat."

Enkidu's laugh rumbled softly through his great chest. "The cat is kin to the lion," he answered, "and Shusuen is the En's grandson. Who knows what it may tell him? Still, it was you who wished to have them by us, and they are not bad companions."

"It was, and they are not," Gilgamesh allowed. "Yet it annoys me to think Shusuen is creeping about when I do not expect him . . . I suppose I could put a belled collar about his neck, to warn us of when he is nearby."

Enkidu laughed again. "You could, but he is clever with his hands. I do not think it would stay on long. And he loves you well; I think he will write no ill of you."

"Save, perhaps, songs meant to be sung out of my hearing . . ."

They lay for a while, talking so of little things. Gilgamesh hardly noticed when sleep drifted over him again, nor did any more strange dreams disturb him before the brightness of dawn filtered through their coverings to awaken them.

THEIR RIDE THROUGH the mountains was quiet, with hardly the growling of a bear or the howling of a wolf to disturb them. The sound of sixty-three men in their chariots was enough to frighten away most of the wild beasts, and if any bands of outlaws lurked in the crags, they had sense enough to know they were overmatched and stay out of sight of Gilgamesh's company. Each night, Gilgamesh had a fresh well dug; each night he went up to make his offerings to Utu and Lugalbanda. The weather stayed bright and clear, the mountain breezes wafting fresh by day and biting cold by night, and that seemed sign enough of godly favor for most of his men.

On the sixth day, however, as they were nearing the plateau where they meant to camp for the night, a chilling yowl rose from the chariot behind Gilgamesh's. When the Ensi looked back, he saw that Shusuen's wain had stopped some fifty paces behind.

"Turn back," Gilgamesh said to Enkidu. The onagers danced and twisted, lifting their dainty hooves high over the stony mountain path; the flat wheels of the chariot ground over the rocks as it turned about, sending a harsh vibration up Gilgamesh's spine.

"What is amiss?" Gilgamesh called out to Shusuen as they drew closer. "Why have you stopped?"

The scribe's cat yowled again, a high eerie sound. It stood in Shusuen's lap with legs spread and tail bristling, claws digging hard into the scribe's thighs.

"Basthotep will go no farther," Shusuen answered. Gilgamesh could see the little drops of blood already staining the plain linen beneath the cat's paws; Shusuen's face was very pale, and his fine lips pressed tightly together. "I think that we must be close to the lands of Huwawa, for he is greatly afraid."

Gilgamesh glanced at Enkidu.

"We are not far," Enkidu said heavily. "Another two days with all our company—a day to the cedar forest, if we leave them behind and travel by ourselves. And I think we must, for the onagers will not go past the place where we meant to camp tonight. No beast would, for there begins the edge of Huwawa's first cloak of awe."

"You cannot stay here by yourself," Gilgamesh told Shusuen. "Calm your cat, and tell him that he need not go much farther. Besides—you cannot either camp here or turn back, for there is not room on the path for two chariots, and all the others are behind you."

Shusuen nodded. As Enkidu turned the chariot again, Gilgamesh heard the soft sound of the scribe speaking to his cat. He could not make out the words, but it was not long before he heard the plodding thud of the white donkeys' footfalls on the path behind him, and glanced back to see Shusuen's chariot moving again.

By the time they reached the plateau, all of the beasts were restless. Shifting from foot to foot as they slowed, and glancing about anxiously, like gazelles scenting the first hint of a lion's musk on the changing wind. It seemed to Gilgamesh, as well, that he could feel something odd thrumming through his bones, like the vibration of a horn too deep to hear. When the well had been dug and he had made his nightly offering, he called all his men to a single fire. Standing behind it, the faces he saw were veiled behind the flickering shadows and the wavering gauze of smoke that blew now over this man, now over that; it seemed to him as if only the shape of Enkidu beside him were solid, as though he were addressing an army of ghosts.

"My warriors," Gilgamesh said. The height of the crags behind him, the dizzying drops to either side, seemed to eat his voice as he spoke, until only the thinnest whisper remained. He breathed deeply, calling out in a full-throated roar like a lion's challenge.

"My warriors, you have traveled far with me. Now our asses fail before us; now we have come to the edge of Huwawa's awe. Ahead lies the cedar forest, and now I say this to you: you have come as far as you must. The battle ahead of us is not a war of many to many, but a combat of champions, for Enkidu and I to fight by ourselves. It is we two who must open the way to the cedar forest. You shall wait here, until we come back to you with news that the gate is open, the guardian slain, and the cedars free. We must go alone."

The warriors shifted restlessly as they squatted, and Gilgamesh realized that none would look him in the face—shadowed eyes turning away, bones standing out stark beneath suddenly paling skin. Birhurturre closed his eyes as if in pain, opening his mouth twice as if to speak, then shutting it again.

"None need fear to have failed me by this," Gilgamesh said, more gently. "This is my deed, and Enkidu's: you have all done your part."

"All but me," said Shusuen's voice from behind Gilgamesh. The scribe came forth, the firelight licking the shadows from his aristocratic cheekbones and delicate chin. "I shall follow you to the cedar forest—for you wished me to record the whole tale."

Gilgamesh stared at him in astonishment. The young man's narrow body was held taut, trembling faintly like a harp's wire string twisted suddenly tight, but his face was grave and resolute.

"You, least of all, should follow. You are no warrior—what should you do against Huwawa?"

"Nothing—on the field of battle when you go to smite him. But my weapon is the reed, and my shield the clay tablet; and when you battle for destiny, which is more than land or rulership, you cannot do without them."

To that, Gilgamesh could say nothing. Instead he spoke more quietly, so that his words would not carry to the others, and smiled to show that his heart was light. "And what of your cat? Surely this is not the advice he gives you?"

Shusuen did not smile in return, though his voice was easy. "Basthotep suggested that we might stay behind, for the journey has been long and he has been as faithful to you as a cat may be. But you asked me to tell a tale as a witness of what no man has seen before, and I said that I would—and the two of you should not go into battle alone, with none to bring aid or even cool water if you need it."

"I shall go as well," Birhurturre broke in. He was standing now, too, and Gilgamesh could see how his body shook beneath the thick swathing of his cloak. "I must not leave you . . ."

"You shall both go," Gilgamesh told them. "But no farther than the edge of the forest, where you may see all that happens. Birhurturre, I give my scribe into your care. Guard him well, and be sure that, whatever befalls, he reaches Erech in safety again, for to him I have trusted all."

"You are kind, my Ensi," Birhurturre said. Gilgamesh could see the tears swelling dark in his eyes, and waved him back to his place.

"Now sleep well and gather your strength, my men. Tomorrow we shall open the way; the day after, when we have overthrown Huwawa, you will have much to do in felling and trimming and loading trees, ready to bring the mighty cedars back and build the gates of Erech!"

One or two men started a cheer; a few others took it up, but it sank ragged and unfinished into the night. *It is well*, Gilgamesh thought, *that I do not need to drive them farther*. Though—he must admit it to himself, as he had been surprised into admitting before Utu's light, that he knew little of what Huwawa really was or what he must face in the battle—he was sure in his heart that sixty men would be no better able to overcome the forest's guardian than himself and Enkidu alone.

"That is so," Enkidu said, and Gilgamesh realized with a start that he had been speaking aloud. "And I think—I think we should go on tonight. Though the path in the darkness will be hard, it will be best if we meet Huwawa at dawn."

"So be it. Birhurturre, Shusuen—gather your bedrolls and some provisions, for we must be off."

As ENKIDU HAD predicted, the way through the night was not easy. Though the moon and stars cast some light on the path, the peaks above—black shadows in the darkness—blotted out much of the sky's brightness. Enkidu went before, for his feet seemed to find the way most easily. Gilgamesh kept hold of the hem of his lover's cloak, but behind, he could often hear the sounds of Birhurturre and Shusuen stumbling. The scribe's breath was coming hard before they had gone very far; the thinner air of the mountains was not easy for any of the plains-born men of Erech to breathe, but Shusuen, little used to hard labor, seemed to suffer worst of all. *I should not have let him come,* Gilgamesh thought, listening to the young man's gasping. *At least, I should have made him stay behind at the camp.* But even as he told himself that, he knew that nothing short of binding the scribe hand and foot would have held him back in the camp, once Shusuen had made up his mind to follow. Better, that he had come with Birhurturre to look after him, so that if he faltered and could go no farther, he would not be alone in the mountain's night. After they had gone some way, however, Gilgamesh could no longer bear to hear Shusuen's raspy breaths, and called a halt.

"Birhurturre, can you take Shusuen's load? The path is growing steeper, and he will need all his strength."

"I am all right," the scribe protested. "I need no help."

"The Ensi has spoken," Birhurturre said stolidly. "I am here to look after you, and that I will do."

Gilgamesh waited until the rustling of cloth and the sound of straps buckling and unbuckling had ceased, then nudged Enkidu to go on.

Mindful of the two behind them, Gilgamesh and Enkidu slowed their pace, walking more carefully over the rocky ground.

They went on until the moon was down, following the dark path under the faint light of the stars. Now, beneath the clear glittering sky, Gilgamesh began to feel the cold creeping into his bones like the first shivering of fear. And yet he was sweating inside his cloak, lungs beginning to burn and calves to ache from the endless effort of stepping over rock after rock, his feet feeling each step carefully lest he stumble and fall over a hidden stone or root. The black peaks of the mountains above loomed heavy and unseen, their craggy weight seeming to press against the travelers like the shield of an impossibly great foe, as though their stony, unmoving strength were in itself enough to bring down the antlike shapes crawling about their knees. And—Gilgamesh realized it with a shudder—they were wholly alone. No bear or wolf, no mouse darting through the leaves, no night-birds singing or fluttering above: the mountain path was wholly lifeless, save for the four men who walked it in the darkness.

At the thought, Gilgamesh found himself faltering, his legs suddenly daunted by the struggle of the next step. But Enkidu, alerted by the tug at his cloak, turned half around. "Do not be undone," he whispered. "It is not your weakness, but the strength of Huwawa you feel, barring men from the cedar forest—go on, fight against him!"

Like wood rasping against wood, his lover's words kindled a new strength in Gilgamesh. *Easier to face a foe . . .* he thought, and spoke aloud to the men behind him. "Come on: the battle has already begun, and you two are fighting it as well. To fight with Huwawa, we must first breach the walls he has set about himself; and that we do in this night's march."

Neither Birhurturre nor Shusuen said anything, but their footfalls seemed surer behind him, and Gilgamesh knew he had spoken well. Now, though the sense of oppression strengthened with each step, crushing stonily in his lungs with each breath, he knew its source, and battled against it—fighting as he had in his childhood, learning to wrestle from grown men whose oaken limbs were hard and immovable as the pillars of Erech's gates. He had never given up then, but had struggled and turned without ceasing, until he had won his freedom or found the twist to upset his foe. It was that strength, bronze-cast before the strength of his body, that he called on now: for he knew that the weakness in his limbs could not be simple bodily exhaustion from the march, else Shusuen would have dropped by the way long before, instead of toiling on doggedly behind him. Rather, it was a battle of the soul and will, where strength of limbs could not be trusted to bring victory. *I chose well. These are the best of men with me; indeed, an army could not do better.*

In time, they reached a small shrubby plateau, and here Enkidu called a halt. "Here we shall rest," he said. "There is time for sleep before dawn. Sleep well and fear nothing, for nothing comes so close outside the gates of the cedar forest, and Huwawa will not pass from within."

IT SEEMED TO Gilgamesh that he had hardly laid his head down when Enkidu was shaking him awake.

"Waken, my love," Enkidu called softly, his golden beard brushing against Gilgamesh's cheek. "Dawn is near, and we must go. We must hurry, to get there before Huwawa goes down into the forest, or hides himself in the thickets. At this hour, he is not wearing his seven cloaks of terror: one he will have on, but the other six are laid aside."

Gilgamesh flung off the blankets and leapt to his feet. The little bruises and stiffnesses of sleeping in armor seemed to drop from him like a leaden cloak with all the horrors of the night. His body felt fresh and strong, answering to him like the finest of racing chariots to the charioteer's light hand as he slung his shield across his back. "Let us go, then."

Birhurturre and Shusuen were just stirring, sitting up and blinking blearily at him. "You two, ready yourselves to follow us to the gate. From there you can see all that unfolds; you should have no need to go farther."

The pathway was easier to follow in the gray half-light; the little company quickly passed through the narrow gorge between the mountains as the sky brightened. Still, the way was very rocky, and Gilgamesh's gaze was most often fixed on the trail before his feet.

At last Enkidu turned, putting a hand on Gilgamesh's shoulder. His wide eyes were very bright in the rising dawn, green crystal shot through with little flickers of yellow lightning; his beard and his long hair that curled below his glittering bronze helmet shone like eddies of molten gold, and his shaggy cloak was tinged with sunrise-red light. "Now we have reached it," he breathed. "Look up."

Gilgamesh turned his gaze up to the slope arching high before him, and his heart stopped in his breast. Behind the two great pillars of jagged rock that flanked the trail, the cedars rose tall, carpeting the mountain with green nearly to its peak; to either side of the path, the crags sank away into a perilously steep and rocky ravine, its depths still shadowed in night's blackness. The scented wind that breathed down from the forest was sweet as temple smoke, but fresh and wild, stirring Gilgamesh's heart so that all his hairs lifted beneath his helmet.

"This is worth the journey, and the battle," Gilgamesh whispered. He turned to look at Shusuen and Birhurturre. The two young men stood staring up at the cedar forest, mouths and eyes wide in awe. "Now your faring ends, until we have slain Huwawa."

Shusuen blinked, stepping forward. "Utu and Lugalbanda fight beside you, my Ensi," he said. "This shall not be forgotten." He reached out, and Gilgamesh embraced him for a moment, feeling the trembling of the scribe's slender body in his own grasp. *So slight, to bear the burden of my immortality,* he thought; and yet Shusuen had weathered the night as well as any. He brushed his lips quickly over Shusuen's soft mouth, as though to seal the words, then let him go.

"Battle well, and come back safe," Birhurturre said simply: a soldier's farewell. The guard and the scribe dropped back a few paces, leaving Gilgamesh and Enkidu before the gate.

"I shall go first," Enkidu told Gilgamesh. "We do not know—" He did not finish the thought, but walked forward briskly, laying his palm against the nearest pillar of rock.

The faint cry Enkidu made was no louder than a cub's first whimper, but Gilgamesh rushed at once to his friend's side. Enkidu's face had gone sickly pale, gray beneath the golden tan. His limbs were locked and trembling, his eyes rolling so that only a flash of green showed from the whites, and his breath came hard and fast.

Gilgamesh grabbed him, easing him away from the pillar. "We must go in together," he said, almost gabbling in his haste to get the words out, to ease whatever fit had come over Enkidu. "One alone can do little, nor can strangers, but a slippery path is not feared by two who help each other; twice three single strands can be sliced through easily, but a three-ply rope cannot be cut. The mighty lion—two cubs can roll him over. Why, my friend, should we fear so wretchedly? We have crossed over all the mountains together, we have bested all that lay in front of us on our way to cut the cedar. My beloved, experienced in battle, well-used to fighting, you need not fear death. Let your voice bellow forth like the kettledrum; let the stiffness in your arms depart, and the paralysis of your legs go away. Take my hand, love, and we will go on together. Your heart should burn to do battle now—do not heed death, do not lose your courage, for I need you. The careful man watches from the side, but the one who goes before guards himself and saves his comrade, and together they win fame through their fighting."

As he spoke, the rolling of Enkidu's eyes subsided, and Gilgamesh felt the strong limbs loosen in his embrace. Though Enkidu was still gasping for air as though he had just come up from a deep dive, color tinged his face again. "My strength comes back to me. Now we may pass, and whatever is fated, shall befall us."

Together, hand grasping hand, they walked forward. A deep chill struck through Gilgamesh's bones as they passed between the pillars, but it was over in a heartbeat; then they stood in the warm sunlight, breathing in the scent of the cedars.

Slowly Gilgamesh's eyesight adjusted to the green shadows beneath the tall trees. The cedars spread so thickly that no ray of sunlight could pierce their canopy; only a thicket of ancient, knotted thornbushes and boxwood grew below them, and half of the twisted plants seemed dead. "Utu's light does not shine here," he said wonderingly. "There are no saplings."

"Nor are there any birds or beast—Huwawa keeps them far." And, indeed, there was no sound in the forest, save the rustling of the wind through the branches high above and their own voices, quiet beneath the sighing of the trees.

"It will be better if we fell some of the old cedars, that new ones may grow." Gilgamesh drew his axe and walked toward the nearest tree, and Enkidu followed. The sound of the bronze edges striking the wood rang through the forest like a great bell, like the sounding of the huge cymbals from Utu's shrine, calling the folk of Erech to stay their work at the beginning of a holy feast.

The axes bit quickly through the cedar's trunk, each blow releasing another wave of its rich spicy scent. It was not long before the tall tree began to sway, then to topple, its weight slowly breaking a path through the branches of the other trees. Suddenly, the green-fronded web holding it up gave way; the mighty cedar crashed to earth, the sound of its fall shuddering through the ground.

"We have done it!" Gilgamesh shouted, exultant. But Enkidu laid a hand upon his shoulder.

"Draw your sword, my beloved, and lift your shield. Huwawa comes."

Now the shaking of the ground was growing stronger; up at the mountain's peak, where the trees no longer grew, Gilgamesh saw a deep red glow beginning to brighten. He unslung his shield from his back, drawing his sword. For all their weight, the weapons felt light to his arms: he was ready to do battle.

Then the thunderous voice roared from above them, and the blast of hot wind from the peak scorched the scent of the cedars to a burning, acid stink. "Who has come to harm the trees on my mountain? Who has felled the cedars?"

"Do not speak to him!" Enkidu said, his own voice sounding thin and weak in the echoes of Huwawa's shout. "Do not listen to his words!"

The glow drew nearer, shining more balefully until the cedars seemed black and burnt in its light. Rays of red light were leaping forth from it, darting free about the forest like burning hares to flash nearer and nearer to the companions. Gilgamesh was ready to strike at them, but Enkidu cried, "We may hunt them down later, they will run in the grass like young birds when the mother is caught. First Huwawa—then his little ones, if we must."

Huwawa's deafening voice sounded again, echoing from the peaks about and the ravines below. "A *lilu*-demon and a fool should advise each other—but why have you come to me, Gilgamesh? Enkidu, you do not even know your father: better you should advise turtles who suck not their mother's milk. When you were still young, I saw you, and one breath would have drawn you into my belly. But now you have brought Gilgamesh into my presence, and stand here an enemy, a stranger. Gilgamesh, I shall rend your throat from neck! I shall feed your flesh to the screeching vulture, the vulture and the eagle!"

As the ruddy glare drew closer to them, Gilgamesh strained his burning eyes to see through it. In the midst of the brightness was a terrible shadow, as tall as the raised temples of Erech—the shape of a huge scorpion, crowned with the head of a man; and it was from his mouth that the dreadful rays of light issued, leaping forth with each word. But it was Huwawa's face that struck dread into Gilgamesh's heart, for it seemed to be a massed tangle of shiny pink bowels, writhing about eyes and mouth like a slimy nest of worms so that Gilgamesh's eye could fix on no feature, nor his gaze on any place to strike.

"My beloved," Gilgamesh murmured in horror, "Huwawa's face keeps . . . changing."

"Do not whine in fear, do not hide behind whimpering," Enkidu whispered back urgently. "The glowing metal of your blade was well-cast in the smith's channel, like the greatest of weapons it shall strike. Do not turn your feet away, do not turn your back! If you are horrified, strike all the harder."

Gilgamesh tightened his grip on sword and shield, willing strength into his arms. "Let us go forward!" he called, but Huwawa's voice was already drowning his out.

"I shall carry you off and cast you down from the sky! I shall smite you on the head, and drive you down into the dark earth!"

The huge scorpion-body reared, pincers lifted aloft and tail curling high above the monster's squirming face. Gilgamesh squinted his eyes to tight slits against the dazzling glare shining from Huwawa's mouth and ran forward, swinging his sword with all his strength. Quicker than he could see, the pincers slammed down, one catching his shield sideways to wrench the grip from his grasp and fling him hard to the ground. He rolled with the blow, coming to his feet and leaping sideways. Huwawa's barbed tail arched downward, slamming into the ground less than a man-length from him; the earth cracked open beneath the blow. But the barb was stuck in the ground for a heartbeat, and Gilgamesh and Enkidu struck at once, sword and axe splintering through the shiny black chitin and grating off one another within the soft flesh inside.

Huwawa's scream of agony deafened the air; the branches of the forest cracked beneath it, tree trunks splitting like green twigs in the hottest part of a smith's fire. His body coiled, segment grating on segment; his pincers clutched and snapped with a sound like the crashing of a city's gates. Nimbly, Gilgamesh and Enkidu leapt between them, a swift and terrifying dance about the giant black claws as they flashed through the baneful red glow that still burned from Huwawa's open mouth. Then one of the pincers closed on Enkidu's axe, grasping the weapon tight and flinging Enkidu from side to side like a rag doll in a child's careless grip.

Gilgamesh ran forward, leaping up to drive his sword with all his strength into the join at the base of the claw. Again Huwawa cried out; half the pincers drooped away from the cut, and Enkidu stumbled to his feet, his axe still firmly gripped in his hand. As the second claw stabbed across at Gilgamesh, Enkidu lifted his weapon two-handed, hewing down with blurring swiftness. The bronze rang on chitin, skidding gratingly, then bit into the segment-joint. A gout of stinking white fluid gushed out; the great pincers fell, severed cleanly from the monster's arm.

This time, Huwawa's cry was only a low moan. Slowly his body began to settle to the earth, the burning glow of his mouth dimming until it was no more than a dull coal at the back of his throat. Gilgamesh and Enkidu backed away, leaning breathless on each other as they hacked gobbets of tainted air from their chests.

"Now we shall hack off his head," Enkidu said.

But Huwawa uttered another sound, a soft and pitiful cry. Chin on the ground, he twisted his head sideways to meet Gilgamesh's gaze. The eyes within the pulsing pink coils of bowel were wide and brown, curiously soft human eyes, and great tears were welling within them.

"Gilgamesh," Huwawa moaned. "You are young yet, your mother gave birth to you, and you are the child of Rimsat-Ninsun. O son of

Erech's heart, Gilgamesh, it was Utu who roused you to this expedition: have you not won what he desired? Gilgamesh, let me live and heal, and I will be your servant—I will cut down as many trees as you command, I will guard cedar and myrtle wood for you, wood fine enough for your household."

Gilgamesh coughed and spat, trying to clear his head of the fumes he had breathed in during the fight. Only now, with the rushing madness of battle over, did he realize how dizzy he had grown: if he and Enkidu had fought much longer, he knew, they would surely have succumbed to Huwawa's deadly breath, even if he had never touched them with stinger or claws. And yet they had overcome the monster—would it not be better to make him serve than to slay him, as they had done with Agga?

"Beloved, do not listen to Huwawa!" Enkidu pleaded, and it seemed to Gilgamesh that he could hear a curiously urgent note in his lover's cracking voice. "He will heal, yes . . . and when that happens, though the caught bird go back to its place, though the captured man go back to his mother's bosom, you will not get back to the city of the mother who gave you birth."

But Huwawa turned his head to stare at Enkidu. Though the monster could barely muster a shadow of his earlier roar, Gilgamesh still felt his own arm moving, his sword lifting to a guard-position as he heard Huwawa's words.

"Enkidu, you know the rules of the forest . . . half beast and half man, you are aware of all things as Enlil ordered them. I should have carried you up and killed you at the gate, at the very entrance to the branches of my forest; I should have fed your flesh to the screaming vulture, the vulture and the eagle. So now, Enkidu, it is your turn to show mercy. Speak to Gilgamesh, tell him to spare my life."

Enkidu's helm had fallen off in the fight; his golden hair and beard were tangled about his face in a grimy cloud, and now he looked as wild and grim as he must have while running with the lions. But the knowledge of a man was in his eyes still, darkening his green gaze as he said, "Beloved, we have overcome Huwawa, guardian of the cedar forest. Grind him up, kill him, pulverize his body utterly, before the foremost god Enlil hears his cries for mercy and the gods be filled with rage against us. Enlil is in Nippur, Utu is in Sippar. Slay him now; then raise up an eternal monument, telling how Gilgamesh killed Huwawa."

Huwawa snarled, a low hiss that scorched through the air. Though the evil strength of his breath was gone, the venom of his hate was still enough to chill Gilgamesh's spine as the monster spoke. "Enkidu, may the gods show you no mercy. If I must die, I curse you with my death: let Enlil who made me, Enlil who set me here to guard the cedars, hear it! You two are one, you say, a two-plied rope: may the rope be unplied, may only one strand be left. May Enkidu not live the longer of the two, may he not tread the land any longer than his friend Gilgamesh!"

Enkidu grasped Gilgamesh's arm hard, his fingers tight against the bronze forearm-guard. "My beloved, I have been speaking, but you did not hear me. You heard only the curse of Huwawa."

"Lift your axe," Gilgamesh said. "We shall strike together."

They walked about Huwawa's great head, already slumped in defeat. At the neck-joint, pink flesh melted into black chiton; the knobbles of Huwawa's spine stood out like fist-sized rocks beneath the skin.

Gilgamesh nodded. The two blades struck together, biting in with a single solid *thunk.* Huwawa's back arched up, a near-soundless cry hissing from his mouth; the scorpion-legs spasmed, twitching like the limbs of a spider dropped into hot oil. Huwawa collapsed utterly, lying still for a breath's time. Then, without warning, he seemed to come to life again, arching and twisting. Gilgamesh and Enkidu ran, fleeing into the forest as the great body thrashed from side to side, battering against the trees. They heard the crashing of branches, the sound of cedar trunks splintering beneath the rending blows of Huwawa's death-spasms. But at last the twitching grew feebler; at last the scorpion-body lay still, the coils of the horrible face drooping.

"He is dead," Gilgamesh said, his voice dull and quite in his deafened ears. Then a rush of gladness swept through him, like a river rushing suddenly through an opened floodgate. "He is dead, and we are alive, my love!" He grasped Enkidu about the waist, swinging his lover's heavy body around in an awkward dance until Enkidu wrapped his arms firmly about Gilgamesh to bring them to a halt.

"We have done what no other could do," Enkidu agreed. "Now let us cut off Huwawa's head. We must pull out his entrails, even to his tongue, lest he heal again, and cast his body into the ravine."

"My love—do not let his words trouble you. The dying often speak ill. But Huwawa's time was done, and his curse had no power."

"I am not troubled," Enkidu said. His smile came bright through the dirt and sweat caked upon his face. "If one of us must die before the other . . . I would not wish to outlive you. But now let us call Birhurturre and Shusuen, and finish this task. We shall have much time to rejoice, for we have won the cedar forest, and will soon have the great trees brought home to the craftsmen of Erech. And it will be fair to see what they make of them."

7

Gilgamesh and his band stayed in the cedar forest for several weeks, choosing, felling, and trimming the trees for Erech's gate. At last, when they had carried enough great trunks down from the mountain to heap the wagon high, Gilgamesh decreed the work done.

"We shall drive the cedars down to the river," he said, "and there lash some together for a raft, that Enkidu and I and a few others—some ten or twelve of the guard, I think—may go ahead of the wain." He looked again at the head of Huwawa, lying by the shiny shell of the monster's corpse. Instead of rotting, the head had dried out, the pink coils of Huwawa's face shrinking into a tangle of deep brown crevasses, like a mask wrought from skeins of clay. Walking over to the man-high head, Gilgamesh knocked against it; it boomed hollowly, like a distant wooden drum.

"We shall pass through Nippur on the way to Erech," he thought aloud, "for there the watercourses meet. Enlil, who set Huwawa to guard the forest, sits in Nippur, where he is the city's god . . ."

"Do you mean that we should not go there?" Birhurturre asked. "My Ensi—do you fear that Enlil will be angry with us for slaying Huwawa?" His voice trembled a little, as though about to crack like a boy's; his dark eyes were wide as he looked up into Gilgamesh's face, and Gilgamesh remembered with a sudden shock, like the twitch of limbs wakening a sleeper from a half doze, that he was indeed the representative of the

Eanna on this journey—the only priest to whom his men could come with their fears and worries about the will of the gods. This was not what he had wanted. And yet he also knew that if he had asked another priest or priestess to come, the din of complaints and advice in his ear for the course of the journey would have been endless and intolerable. This had been his deed; his and Enkidu's. Though they had asked the blessings of Utu and Lugalbanda, it had been their own hands that carried the task out, their hands that had slain Huwawa and were now blistered from woodcutting and sweetly stained with the fresh sap of the cedars. This they had done, and it was something to be proclaimed and made great, not hidden from Enlil or any of the gods as though Huwawa's slayers were children in the Eanna's school who—as he and the Shamhatu had done once, as all the children did—had stolen honey from an offering-bowl and must try to wash the stickiness from their hands before their tutor caught them.

"Mighty and unfathomable are the ways of the gods, and of Enlil who separated heaven from earth," said Gilgamesh, just as the Eanna's tutors had taught him to. "What was Enlil's, we shall bring back to him, as token of our mighty deed: we shall bring Huwawa's head to Nippur, to Enlil's temple there. And if he pleases, it may hang before the shrine to show forth the terrors he can set on earth. What do you think, Shusuen?"

The scribe sat cross-legged beneath the shade of one of the spreading trees, teasing his cat with a twig. At Gilgamesh's question, he looked up brightly. "If showing his power is Enlil's intention, I would think it tactless to come before him and say, 'What you have set up, we can cast down!' And yet"—he gestured toward Huwawa's head—"it would be even more tactless to claim that as a trophy, and worst still to leave it lying in the wilderness, for it may be that even monsters need burial rites, and who should know what to do with Huwawa save Enlil and his priests? My advice is that we go to Nippur humbly, to ask the god's forgiveness for what we needed to do, and offer ourselves for purification, as his priests see fit. The gods do not look well on pride," Shusuen added thoughtfully. Now his fine-boned face was very grave, and his voice flat and cold as he went on. "Even the greatest of us is of little worth before them—who can measure his strength against the whirlwind, or wrestle the flooded river back to its bed?—and Enlil will not be amused if you seem to be daring his strength. It will be very bad for us, I think, if we pass through Nippur without holding that in mind."

Gilgamesh frowned, the thoughts rumbling inside his head like a thunderstorm far over the plain. It was not Shusuen's place to speak so to him, as though the scribe were the En or the Shamhatu; though he was one of the Eanna-folk, he was not consecrated as a mouthpiece of any deity. And Gilgamesh knew all the pious words and sayings of the temple as well as Shusuen: why should the scribe mouth them at him now like a sage speaking to a child, chewing on the dusty bones of past wisdom when he had done something far past the power of the dead to imagine or speak about? A light-mouthed scribe was troublesome enough, a self-righteous one unbearable, and if that was not a proverb, Gilgamesh thought, it should be. Yet he had asked Shusuen for his advice, and could not chide him for giving it.

"We shall take the head to Nippur," Gilgamesh said tightly, "and let Enlil judge as he will. For the deed is done and the cedars felled, for the lighting of the forest and the good of the black-headed people of Sumer."

THE SHAMHATU ENTERED the House of Knowledge on silent feet, as though she were still a child coming for her lessons. The largest building in the Eanna save for the *gipar*, the House of Knowledge had many rooms: some where the scribes read and wrote, some where the Eanna's children were taught, many where the fire-hardened tablets were stacked on shelves like dessicated loaves on the shelves of a long-deserted bakery. The Shamhatu could have sent a scribe to look for what she wanted, but she preferred to go herself, to breathe the dust of dry clay and the damp earthy smell of fresh tablets, to search open-eyed through the hard slabs, hoping that words she had forgotten or never known about would spring before her sight. After the privations of the war, Erech needed a good harvest that year, and the Shamhatu thought it would be well to make some additions to the rites blessing the sowing; with only three months to go before planting began, there was no time to waste if her changes were to be properly planned for, rehearsed, and performed. And besides, one room of the House of Knowledge was filled with tablets inscribed with the words to songs, a few of which might distract her mind from the duties of her office in those rare peaceful times when she could sit in her chamber and play on her lyre and sing softly to herself.

Making her way down the corridor, the Shamhatu caught the sound of hushed voices coming from one of the scholars' rooms. She paused without thought—eavesdropping was habit to the children of the Eanna, as surely as rising with the dawn hymn to the goddess.

"And if he does return?" one—a eunuch's pure alto—asked. "Do you think that will change anything? If he succeeds in this mad task, he will only be more sure that he can defy the gods."

"*He* has succeeded in all he has done thus far," a husky tenor replied. "It is she who has failed in her one task—and failed, as well, to rule the Eanna properly. Do not the writings of the wise warn against a servant becoming master? A harsh hand, a whimsical justice, and the duties of the office left undone: this, we might have expected when a shepherdess was lifted above her station, and rough hands better suited to dagging dung-clotted fleeces set to bear in golden cups to the great."

"Shubad should have had her face slapped long before," said the eunuch tartly. "Who knows what she truly said to the Shamhatu to provoke it? As for the Divine Lady, *she* has done everything that she should; it is the Ensi who has failed in his duty."

"If he has failed, it is her fault, for she ought to be his guide, not his goad. If she were cast out, and replaced by a woman who is better fit for the office, someone of breeding and beauty and talent—"

"If she were cast out?" the eunuch replied, his voice incredulous. "I say, rather, that she should ask Inanna to call the *gallas* of the Netherworld—to either drag him to her chamber that the marriage be consummated, or else to Erishkegal's, that Erech might have a ruler who cares more for the gods and his people than for his own pride."

Shamhatu could listen no more. She flung the reed mat away from the door-frame, storming in. The two young men, the eunuch singer Utuhegal and the purification-priest Erra-imitti, stared gaping at her, plump smooth face and narrow bearded one alike in astonishment. Remembering where she was, the Shamhatu kept her voice low, the words hissing from her mouth like darkened arrows. "Which of you should I accuse of treason?" she asked. "Which of you is guiltiest of turning his hand against those the gods have exalted?" Utuhegal's olive skin paled to a sickly green; Erra-imitti's cheeks flushed beneath his scraggly black beard. "Well? What have you to say for yourselves, that you have polluted the House of Knowledge with words that should not be spoken? What punishment do you deserve?"

Utuhegal dropped to his knees before her. "Divine Lady! I spoke as I should not have, for I am not among the wise—but only from love for the temple and Inanna, for we all fear what the Ensi's obduracy may bring, if the gods do not soften his heart upon his journey."

"Be that as it may," the Shamhatu replied crisply, "it is a matter for the gods, and for Gilgamesh and myself. But you should bring your heart to reverence for Erech's mighty shepherd, and let your foolish words be heard no more, lest they lead you to the execution block for treason. As for you . . ." She glared at Erra-imitti, waiting to see if the awe of her office would overcome him. At last he dropped his eyes and knelt before her as well—but slowly, slowly enough to be almost an insult: though it was the gesture he ought to make, there was no reverence in it. Almost she said, *Has Shubad drained all your sense from you through your rod?* But that would only play to him, and be another weapon in the hands of her foes.

"You who scorn the herding of the sheep of Erech," she said coldly, "have you forgotten that Dumuzi was a shepherd? Your impious words shall be noted in the temple annals, where it is written that Erra-imitti, purification-priest, was set to herding for a year, that he might purify his own mind and become fit to serve Inanna of the Sheepfold again."

The Shamhatu could see the muscles of Erra-imitti's slanted jaw tightening beneath their scanty black pelt, but he choked out, "Your wisdom is magnified by the gods, Divine Lady, and none may speak against your voice."

"It is so. You are dismissed."

For a time the Shamhatu stood alone in the room, breathing great draughts of the dusty air and waiting until she could trust herself to leave without any sign of her fury on her face. She was too upset to look for the tablets she had come seeking; instead, she went back to her chamber, taking out her lyre and angrily striking chords from the strings, chanting the fiercest battle-hymns she knew until the storm within her had abated somewhat.

THE JOURNEY DOWN the river was calm, but long. The fields to either side were baked by the ceaseless heat of the sun, dusty-dry furrows of brown running between the crisscrossing green stripes to either side of the irrigation canals. After the cool thin air of the mountains, the heat seemed more oppressive, so that Gilgamesh found himself throwing off even the lightest of coverings in the night, and awoke in the morning with his bedding soaked in sweat. The only shade was that beneath the two chariots of the Ensi and Shusuen, which had been loaded onto the raft with the finest of the cedar trunks; Shusuen spent the hot days sitting beneath his wagon's canopy with his cat curled asleep on his lap, and between stints of poling, the weary soldiers would often rest under the belly of Gilgamesh's chariot. Still, Gilgamesh thought as he dug his pole deep into the muddy water again and again, doing his share to send the raft more swiftly downstream, it was restful to be floating along so, in these few days of peace between their labor in the forest and the time when he must return to his duties as Ensi. Enkidu seemed to feel so as well; when he was not taking his turn at the raft-pole, he lay lazily stretched over the logs of the raft, naked except for a simple loincloth. His skin had darkened to match the ruddy cedarwood, and the summer sun had lightened his hair to the pale gold of electrum, the little curls tufted over his body gleaming bright as ripples on the river. Looking at him so, Gilgamesh wished that the two of them could simply sail on forever, free of all their worries and duties, just as Enkidu must have been while he ran with the lions. But Huwawa's head squatted wrinkled and brown near the prow of the raft, a constant reminder that their journey down the river was bounded by the felling of the cedars at the one end, by the gates of Erech at the other.

THE WATERS GREW more restless as the raft neared Nippur: there the river forked, and they would have to make their way through the meeting waterways to the Buranun's stream. More than once it crossed Gilgamesh's mind that they would not need to pass through the city to do that. They could simply punt around, never entering Nippur's gates, and bear Huwawa's head on—*as a gift for the Shamhatu?* Gilgamesh thought, smiling wryly to himself. Inanna and her priestess had been silent enough at his going. Perhaps because the journey and the battle were things of men, even in the realm of the gods; perhaps only because the Shamhatu knew that her authority was only over the temple of Inanna, and she had not thought herself to have the power to stay him or urge him on. As he had wished himself: he had done his deed free from her, and none save Enkidu and those who had marched with him could claim a part in his success.

As his mind turned to the Shamhatu again, Gilgamesh found himself uneasily remembering the warning he had given her at their parting. He had thought that Ishbi-Erra's words might simply have been a traitor's trick to distract his mind from the real threat, as indeed they had. But her answer had shown them true. There was trouble within the Eanna: even now the Shamhatu might fear as he had feared, the knife in the dark or the poison in the cup from someone whose trust in her had failed. Though jealousy and whispered gossip were the legacy of leadership, as surely as the Shamhatu's crown or Ensi's mace of office, he knew in his bones now, as he had not understood before, the danger that came when there was the slightest real foundation in which mistrust and dissatisfaction might twine their twisted roots.

*If I came to her, upon my return* . . . Gilgamesh thought. *Even if I came, not yet as En, but as any man making his offering for Inanna's blessing . . . would it not quiet those murmurs?* He had little to lose by doing so, and much to gain: he knew that for every finger that pointed blame at the Shamhatu in secret, there must be another pointing at him, and—he had to admit unhappily—with better reason. He had seen, in preparing for his campaigns, how the prospect of war yoked folk together, and he had also seen, when each was done and the winnings distributed, how swiftly those yokes fell apart. If the rift between himself and the Shamhatu had cracked so deeply through Erech, it was time to see to its healing, as far as he could. And, when he faced and defeated Huwawa, how could little Puabi—with or without the crown of the Queen of Heaven—be so terrible?

Now they were within sight of Nippur. Gilgamesh moved forward to stand beside Enkidu at the raft's makeshift tiller—a length of cedar, lashed in with braided strips of blanket. "We shall put in before the gate," he said. "How many men do you think it will take to carry Huwawa's head?"

Enkidu glanced at the thing beside them. The days in the sun had baked the deep folds of brown skin hard as clay, so that it looked more than ever like a man-sized mask; whatever stuff Enlil had shaped Huwawa's brains from in the earliest days, it had dried and sifted away like dust, leaving only the skull and its wrinkled casing.

"I can bear it myself," he answered slowly. "No other should have to."

Gilgamesh reached out to brush a trickle of gleaming sweat from Enkidu's shoulder. "Or has the right. Now put on your kilt, for we shall soon be coming before Nippur's En, the wife of Enlil, and she should not see us looking like simple rivermen."

They tied up the raft a little way from Nippur's walls. Since they had left the onagers and donkeys behind, the beasts being too difficult to bring on the long downstream journey, Gilgamesh, Enkidu, and Shusuen had to walk, rather than ride, up to Enlil's Gate; and, despite Gilgamesh's words, their clothes were simple, for it would not have been fitting for Enkidu and himself to wear their fine armor when they did not come for battle or negotiations of war.

The guards standing at the gate were bare-headed, their helmets on the ground at their feet; even in the wall's shadow, it was too hot for anyone to bear the weight of bronze armor for a full day. One of them lifted his spear slowly as the three men approached. Before he could ask who they were and what their business in the city was, Gilgamesh strode up to him, speaking loudly.

"You, fellow! Go to the temple of Enlil, and tell the priests to send a greeting party forth to us here, that we may be welcomed properly into Nippur."

The guard started, sleepy eyelids blinking suddenly wide and the muscles of his shoulders bunching as he reached for the axe at his belt. "Who are you, to speak so? The priest of Enlil are not to be troubled by common wayfarers, nor do the guards of Nippur take orders from wanderers on the road."

Gilgamesh stared coolly down at the man for a moment. A long-term soldier, he guessed: something in the set of the guard's muscles and the close crop of his black hair—short enough to keep out of his eyes, long enough to give an extra layer of padding beneath a helm—spoke of a lifetime in the field.

"I am Gilgamesh, Ensi of Erech; and with me are my friend Enkidu, of whom you have doubtless heard, and my scribe Shusuen. If you doubt my word, open your eyes and look closely at us—or at what Enkidu bears. For we have slain Huwawa, the guardian of the cedar forest, and we have come now to bring his head to the temple of Enlil. Will you go, or must we say to Nippur's En that we were denied the ceremony and courtesy befitting our rank by the stubbornness of a common guard?"

The guard looked at Gilgamesh and Enkidu, then his gaze turned upward to fix on Huwawa's face. The blood dropping from his face and his mouth working silently, he stumbled back several paces. "I . . . I will go," he stammered. "Wait here, if you will, Ensi, for I am not fit to welcome you to the city." He turned, running through the gate; his figure was quickly lost among the maze of streets within.

It was not long before they heard the chiming of small cymbals and the jingling of bells, a few moments more before the procession of temple-folk came into view—twelve maidens and twelve youths, clad in shifts and kilts of filmy white linen. The foremost two passed through the gates, kneeling gracefully before Gilgamesh and Enkidu. The maiden lifted up a fluted silver cup of beer with two golden straws; the youth held up an electrum platter of bread and salt.

"Welcome, Gilgamesh, Ensi of Erech," the maiden said, her voice low and musical. "While you come in peace, the temple of Enlil makes you welcome in Nippur, and gives greeting to Erech and Inanna through you. Eat and drink, and be our guests, you and your companions."

"Nippur is gracious," Gilgamesh answered. He lifted the cup from her hands, drinking deeply. The well-aged beer was less sweet than most, and stronger, slipping easily down his throat. He held the cup up for Enkidu to drink from, then gave it to Shusuen. When the scribe had drunk, Gilgamesh tore off a small piece of the bread, dipping it in the salt and eating it before giving another salted piece to Enkidu and passing the platter on to his scribe.

"Now, our honored guests, come with us," said the youth. "A bath and food are being readied for you three, for you must be weary and hungry after your journeying. The En waits; she will see you when you have refreshed yourselves."

Gilgamesh, Enkidu, and Shusuen passed in through the gates. The group of temple-folk arranged itself around them, escorting them through the streets. At this hour, in the full heat of the day, there were not many people outside—a few old men warming their aged bones in the sun outside the door of the tavern, a pair of beggars squatting in the shade by the door of a little shrine, two or three children playing a hopping game around triangles marked in the dust of the road. But the cymbals and bells sang their melodious warning just as if the young priests and priestesses were pressing their way through a throng: someone had, indeed, ordered that Gilgamesh and his companions be received with the fullest courtesy.

Entering the temple court, Gilgamesh saw that the shrine of Enlil was not set on a platform like the shrine if Inanna, but it was a mighty building nevertheless, stone and brickwork raised over two stories high. The outside was brilliantly whitewashed, dazzling in the sunlight. About the door were set limestone reliefs, showing the deeds of Enlil: the god separating heaven and earth, the god bringing forth herbs and trees in the land, the god breaking up the earth with his newly made pickaxe, creating human beings from the furrowed dust, the god bringing forth the flood to destroy all mankind save Utnapishti and his wife, escaping in their boat . . . It was not into the shrine itself that the young priestess led the three visitors, however, but into one of the buildings at the side. There, most of the floor was taken up by a great sunken bath, the waters of which steamed gentle and inviting, sweet with the scent of rushes and spikenard. Bronze razors and mirrors were laid out on a little table beside the bath, and three many-fronded kilts of good linen hung on the wall-hooks.

"Take your ease here, as long as you will," the maiden said to them. "Food and drink will be brought to you soon, that you may refresh yourself fully." She bowed low, nearly touching her forehead to the ground, and left.

Enkidu heaved his burden down by the door with a soft groan. Standing up, he stretched until Gilgamesh heard the vertebrae crackling in his back.

"Huwawa's head is no light load," he said. "I shall have more pity on the donkeys for their burdens hereafter."

"Come, lie in the bath and I shall rub your shoulders," Gilgamesh answered. "That may refresh you."

When the three of them had finished bathing, more of the temple-servants came in with tall flagons of beer and platters of bread and roast honeyed duck. They ate ravenously: the rich sweet wildfowl was very welcome after months of nothing but traveling rations and stringy mountain goats' flesh. At last the maiden who had welcomed them returned. Her plump lips curved in a smile as she looked upon the three men in their clothes, then at the empty plates.

"Are you ready to meet with Nippur's En now? She awaits you."

"Lead us to her," Gilgamesh answered. "We are ready."

Enkidu heaved Huwawa's head to his shoulders again, and the three of them—Enkidu crouching low to get through the doorways—followed the maiden out into the bright glare of the courtyard, on to the doors of Enlil's shrine.

The statue of the god rose high upon a white dais at the far end of the shrine, sitting enthroned with axe in one hand and the Table of Destinies, where all the fates of men were written, in the other. His huge staring eyes were inlaid with onyx and mother of pearl, his rippling hair and beard with lapis. About his feet were grouped smaller statues of the other gods: Gilgamesh recognized Inanna by her two bundles of reeds, while gilded rays streamed around Utu; Nanna stood upon the crescent of the moon, and Enki poured his waters from one pitcher into another. The woman who stood before Enlil was so still, her eyes so wide and dark against her powder-white skin, that Gilgamesh did not realize that she was a living being until she lifted her hand, her heavy breasts sagging away from the movement, and spoke to him.

"Greetings to you, Gilgamesh, Ensi of Erech, and to Inanna, Queen of Heaven," she said. Her voice was very deep, thrilling through the soles of Gilgamesh's feet; though she spoke softly, Gilgamesh could hear the leashed power within her lungs.

"Greetings to you, lady, En of Nippur, and to Enlil, first among the gods," Gilgamesh answered. "We have come down from the mountains, from the cedar forest in the Land of the Living; we have come to pay our respects in Enlil's shrine, and to bring back to him what is his. For we have slain Huwawa, the monster who guarded the forest, and here is his head, to do with as you will."

Enkidu walked forward, shrugging off his burden to ease it carefully down before her. The En's eyes widened until Gilgamesh could see the whites shining all around their black depths, and the soft hiss of her breath drawing in was the only sound in the shrine.

"How did you dare this thing?" she breathed. "How dared you flout the will of the god, who set Huwawa to guard; how did you pierce Huwawa's seven cloaks of splendor to overcome him?"

Before Gilgamesh could open his mouth to answer, Shusuen spoke, his dry baritone soft and scratchy after the En's powerful contralto. "Utu urged my Ensi on to the deed, and stood by his side as he fought: the sun's light revealed Huwawa where he stood, and the strength of Gilgamesh and Enkidu together overcame him. I, Shusuen the scribe, watched the fight, and I saw and heard all that came to pass."

"Silence!" the En commanded him, and now the full strength of her voice lashed out like a gust of rain-laden storm-wind. "Gilgamesh, speak! Why did you do this thing? How dared you flout the will of

Enlil, who wished that Huwawa guard the cedar forest until the end of time?"

"We were stronger than Huwawa, and he fell!" Gilgamesh shouted back. "Enlil did not hold us back, nor did he protect his servant. But we let light into the forest, that new trees may grow. Birds sing in the cedar branches now, and foxes run among the thornbushes below, and some of the mighty trees are on their way to Erech, to build a gate such as no man has seen before. That is what we have done, and cleared the land of a monster who was baleful in Utu's sight."

Then a strange prickling raised all the hairs along Gilgamesh's spine, as though a wave of ants was crawling unseen over his body. Enkidu made a low sound, half a growl and half a whine; Shusuen was silent, but Gilgamesh could see how his slender body trembled where he stood, as though he braced every muscle against the overpowering need to turn and flee. The En's mouth hung open, and the wordless tone pouring forth from it was almost too deep to hear, low enough to shake the temple's floor. Her shape was no longer that of a heavy middle-aged woman, but shawl and shadow blurred her figure to a tall boulder, a hollow stone with the wind moaning low through her open mouth.

*THE HOLY CEDARS WOULD HAVE LIVED FOREVER.* The great silent voice seemed to come from everywhere and nowhere at once; a fall of dust shivered from the temple's roof, glittering in slow eddies through the light shining in through the open door. *THE THORNS WOULD HAVE PASSED AWAY, AND THE CEDARS STOOD ALONE AS THE DWELLING OF THE LIVING GODS. MORTAL LIFE YOU BROUGHT TO THE FOREST, AND MORTAL DEATH, WHEN YOU SLEW HUWAWA. GILGAMESH, WHY DID YOU ACT THUS?*

Gilgamesh stood dumbstruck, unable to move or speak, yet the words formed in his mind like patches of yeast spreading on fermenting beer. *For glory that would live past death . . . For a name beyond any man's, that would outlast living memory . . . to be known and remembered, whatever befall . . . For pride and fear,* he thought unwillingly, the realization spewing up rackingly from his heart like a deep gout of vomit.

*AND YET YOU LAID HANDS ON HUWAWA, AND DESTROYED HIS NAME. BECAUSE YOU HAVE LAID HANDS ON HIM, BECAUSE YOU*

*HAVE DESTROYED HIS NAME, MAY YOUR FACES BE SCORCHED. MAY THE FOOD YOU EAT BE EATEN BY FIRE; MAY THE WATER YOU DRINK BE DRUNK BY FIRE.*

Shusuen was weeping softly, but Enkidu stood still as stone, hand resting on the head of the axe in his belt. Gilgamesh did not know if they heard the same words he did, or how the god might speak to them; but it seemed to him that he could feel Enlil's curse searing his heart like a rod of bronze heated to glowing red. And yet, dry as his mouth was, he managed to swallow, and then to speak aloud.

"Why should you curse us, when you gave no help to your guardian? We were near to losing our own lives then, and you might have struck us down easily enough. But you did not, and so I ask you for blessing now, here in your holy temple, in your city where your priestesses and priests welcomed us as guests."

When the god's voice vibrated through the temple again, it was softer, the rumbling of distant thunder. *SEVEN CLOAKS OF SPLENDOR I GAVE HUWAWA. SEVEN DIVINE RAYS I GIVE YOU; I LAY THEM UPON YOUR HEAD, TO BE YOUR PROTECTION AS YOU WANDER THROUGH THE WILDERNESS. YET MAN CANNOT ESCAPE DEATH, FOR DEATH IS IN EVERY DRAUGHT OF AIR YOU BREATHE, AND ALL THAT IS BORN MUST DIE. YOU, TOO, SHALL DIE, GILGAMESH: OF THAT YOU SHALL NEVER WIN FREE. THE BANE OF MAN WILL HAVE BUT SILENCE FOR YOU AS ANSWER; MAN'S DAY OF DARK-NESS SHALL ARRIVE FOR YOU. THE PLACE WHERE THE WAR-CRY IS SOUNDED AGAINST MANKIND SHALL COME FOR YOU. THE WAVE OF BLACKNESS THAT YOU CANNOT BREAST SHALL COME, THE BATTLE FROM WHICH THERE IS NO FLEEING SHALL COME, THE UNEQUAL FIGHT SHALL COME, AND YOU MAY NOT SHIELD YOURSELF FROM IT IN THE HEART OF YOUR PHALANX. YOUR FATE BEFITS AN ENSI, BUT IT IS NOT FOR LASTING LIFE.*

The sound died down, leaving only an echo like the humming of a far-off beehive in Gilgamesh's ears. Suddenly the En stumbled, pitch-ing forward. Gilgamesh and Enkidu sprang forth at once, just in time to catch her before she stretched her length on the floor-tiles. Though her breath came fast and her eyes rolled in her head, the priestess's body was heavy as a dead man in full armor, and the chill upon her flesh struck cold through her garments. Shusuen nudged his way between them, forcing the En's mouth open and wedging the smooth ivory hilt of his knife between her jaws to keep her from swallowing her tongue. Then the flock of young priests and priestesses was upon them, gently easing Gilgamesh and Enkidu away from the En's convulsing body and lifting her up. One wiped Shusuen's knife clean before handing it back to him, but the temple-folk paid the three companions no notice otherwise.

Soon Gilgamesh, Enkidu, and Shusuen stood alone in Enil's shrine. But now the air seemed dull and quiet; the flat inlaid eyes of the great throned statue seemed lusterless, and Gilgamesh knew that the god had passed from their presence.

"We may as well go," he said. "I think there is no more for us to do here."

Quietly they walked from the shrine, leaving the head of Huwawa where it lay. The path back to the gate was easy to find, and the sunlight had soon dried the chill sweat that lay upon their shoulders and backs.

"What did you hear?" Gilgamesh asked Enkidu when they were on their way down the river again. "Did Enlil speak to you?"

"I heard the roaring of the storm, and the bellowing of the wild bull. I heard no words—and yet I was afraid, for the god seemed angry . . . What did you hear, Gilgamesh?"

Gilgamesh bit his lip, for he was little willing to repeat Enlil's words, either the curses or the dubious blessing the god had laid upon him.

"The scales are even," he answered at last. "I think we can be content with what we have won."

And Gilgamesh left it at that. Though Shusuen spoke hardly at all that night, only sitting and caressing his cat in a distracted manner, Gilgamesh could not bring himself to ask the scribe what he had heard or seen, nor did he think Shusuen would tell him if he did. Only if Shusuen saw fit to write the matter down would any other know. And Gilgamesh knew that he could not sway the scribe to write or not write: he could only trust in what wisdom the young man had inherited from his grandfather to choose his words rightly, lest Enlil be further offended or an ill fate be brought closer.

SULULI AND INNASHAGGA sat together in Sululi's house, drinking sweet date-wine and spinning. It had been a long day at the weaving, for the women of the Eanna had been busy making soldiers' kilts for the last year, and there had been little time to replace worn or rent garments within the shrine itself. Sululi was bone-tired, the muscles of her back aching: it was hard work, bending down to set up the warps of the great looms, and yet she could trust no other to count and stretch the threads as exactingly as they must be set for her finest weaving. Innashagga was learning as quickly as she might, but she was still only an apprentice: hands accustomed to coarse yarn and simple wefts did not easily grow used to the delicate mingling of linen and wool that was required for the priestly robes of the Eanna. Yet the hard work was a balm better than any salve for the thoughts that worried at Sululi's mind at night: it had been months now since Gilgamesh and Enkidu had departed from Erech's gates, and no one could know whether they were even now traveling back with the cedars they had sought, or if their bones lay bleaching on a distant mountainside, prey to Huwawa or to some peril of the way.

*Enkidu,* Sululi thought, wetting her fingers from the little bowl at her side and stroking the fine fibers of the linen-wool mix down into the delicate twist of thread lengthening from her spindle. *Gods protect you—I love you so.* She had been afraid when he had first come to her, desperately so. Between the fresh-bleeding memory of her father's body lying on the floor of the judgment hall and the tales she had already heard of her husband's death beneath the fangs and claws of the lion, she had been hardly able to do more than sit and shiver since leaving the hall as Enkidu's betrothed, dependent on him for her life. And Enkidu's huge hairy golden body, scored with claw-marks old and new, had seemed more a beast's than a man's; she had feared that he would crush her, tear her to pieces in fury or break her neck in his ardor. Yet he had unbound her hair gently and stroked it, holding her as she shook until his warmth had eased her bone-deep cold, and not so much as tried to kiss her. And grateful for that, her fear had eased, until at last he left her and went to play with little Ur-Lugal, tickling the boy's stomach and laughing as Ur-Lugal's tiny fists clutched at his bright beard. Then Sululi had truly known that she had nothing to fear, for a man who could take such joy in another man's baby—and one he thought, as he must have then, to be the child of his foe—could never harm her. So she had gone to Enkidu and embraced him, and let his touch soothe away the dreadful shadows that haunted her, the loveless months of imprisonment in her marriage to Ishbi-Erra and their bloody and terrible climax in the trial before the pitiless gazes of Erech's elders. There was no falseness in him, she had learned since: he spoke whatever came into his heart, and all seemed open and good; if there was much of the wild yet in him, it was only in his innocence, in the endless delight he took in seeing all the crafts and learning of men. Fascinated by the drawing-out of thread by spindle, Enkidu had even asked Sululi to show him how to spin, and though she had warned him that he must not do it in public, since folk would think it unmanly, he spun as he sat with her in the evenings, and joyed greatly in seeing how the yarn took shape beneath his big fingers. Though Sululi knew his heart belonged first to Gilgamesh, it seemed to her that having a part of Enkidu's love was better than owning the whole soul of any other man. Even Gilgamesh himself—though the memory of her wedding-night, knowing that for a few hours the Ensi had found her beautiful and worthy of love, had sustained Sululi through the whole of her marriage to Ishbi-Erra—even he paled in her thoughts before Enkidu, for where Gilgamesh was a single brilliant flash of lightning, burning in the darkness for a brief unforgettable moment, Enkidu was the warm, long-glowing fire that no wind or rain could put out, utterly trustworthy, his innocent goodness beyond doubt.

And yet no seed of Enkidu's had quickened in Sululi's body, though he had come to her nearly every night since their wedding. She would have been glad to bear him a golden-haired son or daughter, a lion-child with a heart to match its father's fierce gentleness, but her womb still twinged in empty readiness at every full moon, and cramped and wept blood when Nanna hid his brightness from the night sky. Her son Ur-Lugal—child of the one sweet night she had spent with Gilgamesh, she was sure—was a great joy to her: she could not but laugh when he gurgled and reached out for a new toy, and the silly tears came to her eyes when he rolled over and struggled to crawl on limbs still too young to carry his weight. But her happiness would have been complete if she could have said to Enkidu before his departure, "I bear your child,"—and if he never came back from the cedar forest, Sululi knew that her sorrow would be magnified twelvefold by the emptiness of her body.

"What are you thinking?" Innashagga asked. "Mistress, there are tears in your eyes."

"You need not call me mistress," Sululi answered. "We are all folk of the Eanna, and is not your husband Gilgamesh's chief huntsman?"

"That is so, but you . . . As you will, but you still seem sad. Will you not tell me why, and see if I can ease your mind? I know I can do little more than prattle of the weather and what the women in the market have said, but it is hard if you cannot tell your sorrows to anyone."

"It is only . . ." Sululi reached down to the basket at her feet, picking up a great fluffy clump of the linen-wool blend and tugging out a little tuft, dampening her fingers again to smooth it onto the tuft at the end of the thread before she set her spindle to whirling again, the fibers drawing and tightening beneath her touch once more. "I cannot keep from thinking of Enkidu, for he must have been journeying long, and on a perilous way."

"I think of him often as well," Innashagga answered. "You know that he guested in our house with the Shamhatu for some time before he came to Erech. Ah, he was strange and wild when she led him to us. He could hardly speak the language of men; his pelt was matted and he stank like three goats, for he had never washed in his life. And yet he was quiet, and so careful, as though he feared to shatter our bones with his very touch—just as we feared he might, at first, for no one in the village had ever seen such a powerful man. But once he had learned a little more of human ways, he was the best of company. Better than she, for though she was gracious, she expected all the comforts of the city, fine food and a bath every night, but to him our coarse bread was the finest of meals, and the simplest necklace of smoothed agates seemed to him a grand jewel. It was so strange, to see Enkidu dressed in fine linen and sitting beside the Ensi, and yet he has not changed: our old hut, with its roof of dried palm leaves, was no less wondrous to him than all the splendors of the Eanna. He would have been content to dwell there, just as he is content to dwell here." Innashagga's dove-dark eyes dropped, and she laid a palm over the swollen burden of her belly, as though to shield the child within from any evil thoughts that might have come to her. "Gilgamesh is a fine man, and brave . . . but he is the Ensi. Enkidu is our friend, and still seems to me like one of us—if that is not too much for me to say of your husband, mistress."

"It is not," Sululi reassured her. "It is part of what I love in him. And so . . ." The words came hard, and now she could feel the tears glazing down her cheeks, burning like glass melted in the hottest of fires. "So I fear for him, though we were only wedded a little time. If Gilgamesh does not come back, it will be sorrowful, but the Ensi is the city and Inanna's bridegroom: too great to fully give or get love from any mortal— save, perhaps, one such as Enkidu, who is not awed by any of Gilgamesh's power. Yet if Enkidu does not come back, I do not know how I shall live."

"As women always have, mistress," Innashagga answered. "But do not fear. Enkidu shall come back: I feel it as some can feel the sweet water flowing beneath the ground, though they be in the middle of the desert."

Sululi put her spinning down, reaching out to embrace Innashagga carefully about the shoulders. "Thank you," she said, the words choking against her tongue. She coughed to clear the tears away, spoke again. "Thank you." She sipped carefully from her cup of date-wine, the silver straw cool in her mouth.

The two women sat silent for a moment. Sululi would have spoken again, pouring out her thoughts to Innashagga, but then she heard the throbbing beat of the great kettledrums, pulsing deep even through the walls of the house. Innashagga's eyes darted about, and the village woman pulled her shawl tightly about her shoulders.

"What is that, mistress?" she whispered. "Why do they beat the drums? Has war come upon us again?"

"It cannot," Sululi answered, striving to calm the heartbeat hammering against her ribs, the pulse beating hard in her throat. She swallowed hard, forcing herself to think. "A foe would have been seen long before reaching Erech's walls, and we would have been warned long since if war threatened . . . And yet this is not a feast-night, nor any holy day. Come, let us go outside. We are safe here within the bounds of the Eanna, and there may be one of the priests or priestesses who can tell us more."

She rose to her feet, stretching out a hand to help Innashagga up. The shorter woman rose clumsily, unbalanced by the rounded weight of her belly. Beneath the soft light of the oil-lamps, Sululi could see how pale Innashagga was. The memory of her own pregnancy was a sharp pang in the depths of her belly: how each disturbance had struck a cold note of terror shivering through her, how each harsh word from Ishbi-Erra or her father had set her trembling, afraid that any blow from a man's fist might harm the child within her past repair. And so she murmured again, her voice as soft as if she were lulling little Ur-Lugal to sleep, "We are safe here. You need fear nothing, my sister, little dove, my friend. Come, let us go, let us see what is happening."

Innashagga let Sululi take her small plump hand, leading her on. Warm as the night was, the village woman's fingers were cold beneath Sululi's longer ones, and again Sululi remembered how her hands and feet had always seemed half frozen in the last month before she gave birth, as though the child within her was wrapping all the warmth of her body tightly about itself.

Outside, the sound of the drums was louder, the beat growing steadily more urgent. High on the temple-mound, red firelight spilled from the door of Inanna's shrine, and Sululi could hear the high keening chant rising above the deep note of the kettledrums, although she could not make out the words.

"Up," Innashagga whispered, tugging at Sululi's hand. "Look up."

The night sky was achingly clear, the stars glittering clear as drops of ice against its blackness. At first Sululi did not know what Innashagga could have meant, for the constellations shone as they ought, the patterns she had learned as a little girl, sitting on her father's broad shoulders in the courtyard of his house. Then her roving glance fell upon the moon, and she sucked in her breath in horror. For last night she had seen Nanna's bright face nearing his full; she had gazed up wistfully, thinking of how she wished Enkidu was there with her, for all women knew that children were most easily conceived at the full of the moon, halfway between bleeding and bleeding. Yet now the moon was less than he had been, the shadow creeping slowly across his light: the eclipse, darkening heavenly light out of time and season, could bode only ill. And that ill, Sululi knew—she had been schooled enough to learn it—was a single clear and certain thing. Its dark counter-light showed the baleful gaze of the gods: somewhere beneath the darkening moon, an Ensi was doomed to death.

Now Sululi could hear the noise from the streets outside the Eanna, a jangling cacophony of bronze beating against bronze and the duller thudding of wood and clay. Spoons beating on pots, hammers on posts: whatever folk could find to make noise, to avert the evil omen, they banged as loudly as they could, shouting and singing above the din. She tugged on Innashagga's hand, trying to pull the other woman back toward the house so that they could grasp for their own cooking pots and wide spoons—anything they could beat, to drown the fear in noise and turn back the darkness. But Innashagga would not move, her feet sunk heavily in the ground; and the shrinking light of the moon showed her round pale face turned away from the eclipse.

"North," Innashagga whimpered. "Look north."

Sululi's head turned to follow her companion's gaze, and before she could stop herself, a small scream burst from her mouth. For there, amid the familiar shapes of the stars, a new one blazed hot blue-white, and behind it streamed a short bright tail, fanning out thinly across the black sky like a windswept trail of shining cloud.

"What is it?" Innashagga asked fearfully. "What does it betide?"

"It is a comet," Sululi answered. Breathing deeply, she grasped Innashagga's hand tight to stop her own from shaking. "As for what it betides . . . let us go up to the shrine where the drums are beating. If Inanna has word for the folk of Erech, she will speak there, and if we learn no more, at least we will be in the goddess' own hall, and shielded from all evil."

THE SHAMHATU STOOD beside the statue of Inanna, staring down at the thronged priests and priestesses, the dark mouths opening and closing in the pale faces as they raised their voices in the holy hymns against the blackness slowly creeping over the moon. The beat of the kettledrums throbbed through the temple like a great pulse, shivering up through her body and pounding in her head. She had seen the comet burning outside, casting its strange tailed light over Erech, and the sight had filled her heart with fear. Now she shook like a leaf in the stormwind: it was well that the rites against the ill omen of the eclipse had long since been written and learned, for her mind was too dazed to think. The En stood at the goddess' other side, the lines of his old face carved deeper by the flickering light of the fires within the shrine. For all that his expression showed, he could have been masked, but it seemed to the Shamhatu that she could read the thoughts within his age-worn skull.

*The death of an Ensi . . . The eclipse is a sign of death, the comet of turmoil and disaster. Have Gilgamesh's days come to an end? Does he lie dead in the cedar forest, prey to his own stubborn pride and foolishness at last?*

*He deserves it*, the Shamhatu thought in answer. A tear streaked hot down her cheek, and she dared not raise a hand to dash it away lest anyone notice that she wept. Had she not always seen this in Gilgamesh's headlong rushing, in his endless quest for something to overmatch his strength? *Fearing death, he runs the faster to embrace it.* For a moment the laughing faces of Gilgamesh and Enkidu together came to her, black hair mingling with fair like trails of dark cloud stretching across the golden sky of sunrise, and the tears dropped faster from her eyes. *Did Enkidu not deserve better from his love?*

The En moved a little closer to her, his words almost inaudible beneath the sounds of the singing and the hammering beat of the ket-tledrums. "At least there is an heir," he murmured. "Ur-Lugal is Enkidu's adopted son, and therefore Gilgamesh's as well ..." His voice trailed off: the Shamhatu knew that they had both guessed that the Ensi was the boy's father by deed as well as law. Yes, there was an heir, and the Eanna, together with the council of elders, would rule Erech until he reached manhood, just as they had while Gilgamesh was growing up. And the Shamhatu would become Rimsat-Ninsun, the Old Woman of Erech, and a new maiden take her place, though the goddess had never worn her flesh in the New Year's marriage feast.

"We do not know that the omen is meant for Gilgamesh," the Shamhatu whispered back, though she could feel the falseness of the words ringing dull through her bones like tin jingling off lead. "When the eclipse is driven away, we must make a sacrifice and read the sheep's liver to learn more."

The wait seemed endless, the hymns growing shriller and more grat-ing to the Shamhatu's ears as even the trained voices of the *tigi*-singers began to tire. She had lost all track of time when the cry went up from the watchers at the door, "The tide has turned! The moon comes back!" Her knees weakened in relief; she stiffened her legs to keep from falling as the new wave of songs began.

At last the voices lifted in the final hymn, the evening praise of Inanna, Queen of Heaven:

"My Lady, amazement of the land, lone star,
Brave one, shining forth first in the heavens—
All the lands fear her."

The offering-priests standing near the braziers cast incense onto the coals; a fresh cloud of sweet smoke rose up, filling the shrine, and the Shamhatu lifted up her voice in the chorus with the others.

*"My Lady looks in sweet wonder from heaven,*
*The people of Sumer parade before holy Inanna.*

In the pure places of the steppe, on the high roofs of the
    dwellings,
On the platforms of the city, we make offerings to her.
Piles of incense like sweet-scented cedar
Fine sheep, fat sheep, long-haired sheep,
Butter and cheese, dates and fruit of all kinds.

*My Lady looks in sweet wonder from heaven.*
*I sing your praises, holy Inanna.*

We purify the earth for Our Lady, we celebrate her in song,
We fill the table of the land with first fruits.
Dark beer and light beer we pour for her,
Dark beer, emmer beer, emmer beer for Our Lady.

*My Lady looks in sweet wonder from heaven,*
*The people of Sumer parade before holy Inanna.*

The *sagub*-vat and the *lamsari*-vat bubble over for her,
We prepare *gug*-bread in date-syrup for her,
Flour, honeyed flour, beer at dawn,
Wine and honey we pour for her at sunrise.

*My Lady looks in sweet wonder from heaven,*
*I sing your praises, holy Inanna.*

The gods and the people of Sumer go to her with food and drink,
They feed Inanna in the pure clean place.

*My Lady looks in sweet wonder from heaven,*
*The people of Sumer parade before holy Inanna.*
*Inanna, the Lady Ascending into Heaven, is radiant,*
*I sing your praises, holy Inanna,*
*The Lady Ascending into Heaven is radiant in the sky."*

The priests and priestesses filed out as they had gone in. The
Shamhatu moved from her place to follow the sacrificial priest Urgigir,
reaching up to tap him on the shoulder. He looked down at her for a

moment, eyes shadowed in the caves of their deep sockets and mouth set grimly beneath his close-cropped black beard.

"You wish to read the liver," he said quietly, "and you wish it to be done in private, lest more ill omens in the Ensi's absence cause a panic in the city."

"That is so," the Shamhatu admitted.

"There are omens that must be taken now, indeed. Wait here: I shall come back in a little time."

The fires had burned low when Urgigir returned to the shrine; the En already held a bowl of lapis, for he would take the place of the *ishib*-priest while the Shamhatu steadied the beast's shoulders. Urgigir led, indeed, a tethered ram, the beast's thick-wooled head hanging low beneath the weight of his heavy horns—but he was not alone. Behind him walked Shubad, dressed in a filmy dress of golden linen and adorned with glimmering gold and carnelian jewelry, and Geme-Tirash in a simple fringed white gown. The *gala*-priestess' eyes glinted red in the light from the brazier's coals, and the Shamhatu saw the white flash of Shubad's teeth for a second before she pressed her lips together again. Yet it was Geme-Tirash who unnerved the Shamhatu, for her eyes were wide and frightened, and now and again a chilly shiver rippled over the skin of her bare shoulder. What horror had she seen in the eclipse's black light?

Urgigir bowed low to the Shamhatu, then the En. "Divine Lady, Inanna's Bridegroom," he said formally. "Nanna has hidden his pale face this night, and a tailed star burns above Erech. By these signs do the gods show their displeasure to living men. And as above, so below: there is discord and strife in the Eanna, which none of us has escaped hearing. When the shepherd cannot herd his sheep, they are taken from him, if not by his master, then by lions and wolves. Therefore, I set to you this: that we read the omens not only for the Ensi's fate, but to see the gods' will for the holding of the office of Shamhatu."

The Shamhatu's heart slapped against her ribs, sending an icy shock shivering through her body. But the sacrificial priest's craggy face was stern, unyielding as a cliff in the winter's frost. She darted a glance at

Shubad: though the *gala*-priestess held herself almost expressionless, the Shamhatu could see the thwarted beginning of a triumphant smile twitching at the corner of her mouth.

*Has she seduced him?* the Shamhatu thought. Though Urgigir was known to be fond of all the pleasures of Inanna, her heart still sank at the suspicion that he could have betrayed his duty so. But he might not have realized that he was doing it, for Shubad could be persuasive as well as seductive.

"And I see you have brought your counselors with you," she said. "It is well that a trance-priestess be present for the reading of the omens; but what use do you find for a temple soloist?"

"Who else is there to choose for the duty?" Urgigir rumbled. "Geme-Tirash has held it once already, while Shubad is the voice of Inanna when each New Year's celebration is sung. We must give to the goddess the tool that suits her best."

"And she herself made that choice," the Shamhatu replied. Now her anger was rising, a warm and welcome tide; and above that a furious delight, that at last she could look her enemy in the face and speak the words that had been seething deep in her heart. "You read the liver yourself. Urgigir, you come with a serious charge: that I have presided badly over the Eanna, and displeased the goddess. I shall return charge for charge. Either from foolishness or malice, you have given ear to one of the chief sources of strife within the Eanna's walls, and magnified her wicked counsels. Now, when your mouth opens, it is Shubad who speaks through you. It is she who has whispered in the night and set discord among us; not content with the place of honor she holds among the *gala*-priestesses, she has sought to raise herself higher, and to set Inanna's crown upon her own head." She turned from Urgigir to Shubad. Meeting her gaze, the singer took a step backward. "And I know worse of you, Shubad. For you were Ishbi-Erra's lover, and held counsel with him even as he plotted to slay the Ensi. Did he promise you that when Gilgamesh fell, I could be set aside, that you might become the Shamhatu under Agga?"

"No!" Shubad cried. "I knew nothing of what he planned."

"But you were his lover, and you told him that the Eanna was divided—a weapon to his hand, that he used against Gilgamesh in turn. This I have from the Ensi's own lips: do you deny it?"

"It is easy to put words into the mouth of a dead man, and to accuse the gifted of ambition," Urgigir broke in. "But if Shubad spoke aloud what others were thinking, how does this make her guilty? What has she done?"

"She has sought to break what should hold, and to dishearten the Eanna! And by speaking to Ishbi-Erra of the temple's doings, however deep she may or may not have been in his plots, she laid us open to the scorn of Erech. Is this the woman you would see as Shamhatu, who would glorify herself at the Eanna's cost?"

Urgigir's thick black eyebrows wrinkled low in a frown, but he said nothing, and the Shamhatu knew that her thrust had struck home, as surely as if she had sheathed a sword to the hilt in his belly. And before Shubad could speak again to defend herself, Geme-Tirash's husky alto broke the silence.

"She has done more," the trance-priestess said quietly. The four others turned to stare at her, but she went on, her eyes fixed steadily on the statue of Inanna behind them. "I did not speak of it before, for it seemed unfitting and I feared to cause more trouble. But while you, Divine Lady, sought Enkidu in the wilderness, and I held your place here—" She coughed. "My days were not easy. Once beer was brought to me, but it was a hot day and I wanted only water. It was one of my friends who drank the beer in my place, and her body purged for a week, and she could not carry out her duties for two weeks after. The illness might have been chance—but I found that the holy implements of ritual were not where I had left them when I wanted them, so that I must continuously send others to fetch them, and appeared both clumsy and careless in my office, as you will surely remember. Then I drank only the clearest water, and I shook out my bedclothes at night for fear of scorpions."

"Did you find them?" the En asked.

"Twice, and other things: scattered dust, clippings from a black dog's pelt, a vulture's feather—things that felt unclean to me. And I

knew that someone wished me harm—and I marked that I was safe
while the singers were rehearsing in the shrine, or the soloists training
with their master. And I was never gladder than when I heard that the
Shamhatu had come to take up her burden again. I pray the goddess
never offers it to me." Tears pooled in Geme-Tirash's eyes, glimmering
dark in the low light. As she looked upon the other woman, the
Shamhatu felt the shame burning hot in her own face. For she had given
only suspicion and doubt where she should have offered friendship and
trust; and had she spoken to her earlier, perhaps the matter could have
been solved long ago.

"These accusations—they are without proof!" Shubad burst out. "Is
it jealousy that sets you against me now, Geme-Tirash, when we have
never spoken ill to each other? And yet all of you may try, but you still
cannot prove that I am guilty of anything, save having loved the wrong
man, and a man to whom Gilgamesh himself showed the greatest favor
before Ishbi-Erra betrayed him."

The five of them stood like that: Shubad's gaze darting from face to
face, Geme-Tirash quiet again, as though she had sunk into meditation,
Urgigir's face set grimly, and the En watching as if he looked upon a ritual play. The Shamhatu lifted her hand. Shubad did not cringe away, but
her shoulders tightened as though she expected a blow.

"That may be true," the Shamhatu said. "But we now . . . all of us,"
she added, with a significant glance at Urgigir, "know what you are, and
what you have done. Shubad, *gala*-priestess, you may keep your singing.
But be sure of this: that should you be caught in your whisperings once
more, you will be cast out of the Eanna. Count yourself lucky that only
we have heard the words spoken tonight—and content yourself with
what you have, or you will surely lose it. Now make your prostration to
the goddess, and go."

Even in defeat, Shubad's movements were more gracefully sinuous
than the Shamhatu could ever have matched. Urgigir gulped convulsively as his gaze flickered over her departing figure, and even in the dim
light the Shamhatu could see his knobbly cheekbones reddening above
his beard.

"Every man may be deceived once, Urgigir," the En said kindly. "Are you able to read the omens now, or will you choose another priest to do it this night?"

"No. No, I am able to do it. But let Geme-Tirash stay with us, that the gods may grant her understanding if my own fails."

"Inanna and Anu, Enlil and all gods," the En said softly, reaching out to lay his hand on the ram's head. "Make clear to us what the darkness is hiding; speak to us further of the omens, that we may be made wise. You who know all, who see all, who draw the cloth of fate across the faces of men—show us, we pray, what we must know, that your will be done in Erech."

He nodded, crouching down with the dark-gleaming stone bowl in his hands. Urgigir drew his knife and steadied the ram's head with his other hand, stabbing swiftly in behind the point of the sheep's jaw and jerking the blade out through its throat in a shower of firelit blood. Half severed, the ram's head lolled to the side. Its legs jerked, hooves lashing out blindly—one bruising-hard blow caught the Shamhatu's leg below the knee, but she did not loose her hold on the thick-fleeced shoulders. The sheep's open windpipe bubbled air and blood, its eyes dulling into the sleep of death.

The four of them waited until the last twitches of the sacrificial beast had passed away. Then, his big hands sure and precise even in the half darkness of the shrine, Urgigir opened its belly. The hot entrails still shivered a little beneath his hands as he carefully sliced the liver free, wiping the blood away with a fine cloth and bringing it over to an oil-lamp where he might look more closely at it. His craggy brows lowered as he stared at the slick dark organ, and the Shamhatu could hear the faint deep rumbling in his throat.

"The omens are not good," he said at last. "I fear that matters will go badly for Erech, and worse for Gilgamesh, if something is not done to avert them. The gods are displeased; there is wrath in the gazes they turn upon us. Enlil is displeased . . ."

The Shamhatu heard Geme-Tirash's sharp intake of breath, freezing herself as she remembered: the words of the trance-priestess' prophecy, from Gilgamesh's ascension. "What can we do?" she asked. "Is there any sign of help?"

"Inanna's star yet shows brightly, and she is the queen of this city. And . . . I was wrong to listen to Shubad. It is you who must call to her and ask her will. But the marriage must take place," Urgigir added softly, gazing down at the mass of slippery liver cradled in his wide palms. "We have gone without it too long."

The Shamhatu did not question him: there was more to being a sacrificial priest, and reading the will of the gods, than having memorized every sign and note scratched on the liver-shaped clay models the Eanna used for teaching the omens.

"I shall call to her this night. Thank you, my brother, for lending your skill."

"All as the gods will, though men be fools," Urgigir answered. He bent down to scoop up the body of the ram, holding it at arm's length as easily as a lesser man might hold a dried palm branch, and bore it from the shrine.

The Shamhatu and the En stood together for a time. At last the En said, "I shall leave this to you: this is a mystery into which I may not enter. May Inanna grant you wisdom, and bring her blessings again to Erech." He bowed low—the Shamhatu could hear the fragile bones of his spine crackling—set the bowl of sacrificial blood at Inanna's feet, and withdrew, Geme-Tirash following him.

Alone in the shrine with the goddess, the Shamhatu stood shivering. The heights of the temple were black as the darkness above the stars: the shadowed walls seemed to stretch up endlessly, reaching far past her sight. Below, the fires had dwindled to beds of coals, the little flames of the oil-lamps to sputter and fade as their wicks guttered.

"Inanna!" she cried out. "Where is he? Is he still alive?"

The face of the goddess, indistinct in the darkness as the weathered face of the image in the little village shrine, showed the Shamhatu nothing, and her own voice was thin and faint in her ears, as though she heard her words echoing across a great abyss. "My goddess, Queen of Heaven, show me . . . Why have you set this fear in my heart? My limbs tremble, there are tears in my eyes; I am overcome. Why have you set this fear in my heart? For Gilgamesh . . ." Now she was weeping freely, her slender frame racked by great sobs that tore through her like gusts of stormwind ripping the palm thatch from a fisher's hut. Her legs could no longer hold her; she dropped to her knees, staring up at Inanna through tear-blurred eyes. "Where is he?" she repeated. "Is he still alive?"

Then a dark thought came to the Shamhatu. Once she had anointed and exalted Akalla, that he could stand on the walls of Erech in Gilgamesh's stead, and she had wondered then if he might die for Gilgamesh as well. Now the omens spoke ill for the Ensi: the second half of the prophecy—*The Ensi of Erech is dead*—was yet to be fulfilled. But though the gods determined all destiny, it was also true that fruit could be warmed and watered and brought to ripeness where it would not grow on its own; and when doom was laid upon the Ensi, another man could bear the title until the ill-fate had run its course. If she told Akalla that it was needful, he would allow her to pour oil over him and set the horned cap on his head. He would never feel the blow that cut him down—and Gilgamesh would live, free of the shadow that had lain across him even in his exaltation.

But she would have to carry out the betrayal, knowing what it meant, as guilty of Akalla's death as if she had slit his throat in the desert. She would have to look Innashagga in the face and tell her what she had done, and why. And yet, if that were the only way to save Gilgamesh . . .

If—the Shamhatu's eyes shut tightly against her will, as though to block out a sight she could not bear—Gilgamesh were still alive. And that was what she did not know: were the tailed star and the eclipse prophecies of the Ensi's death, or announcements?

Now it seemed to the Shamhatu that she could remember every harsh word she had ever spoken to Gilgamesh since the two of them were children in the Eanna together; how she had criticized his every move, pressing him to go forth when he would hold back, to hold back when he would go on.

"But it was only," she whispered, "only because . . ." She could not say the words aloud; they stuck hard in her tear-swollen throat, finer and sharper than a fishbone.

"I wished him to be a good Ensi, to bring life and prosperity, justice and wisdom, to Erech, and the days of his holy rule to be long in the land. The onager takes the strongest of hands to drive it, but it is the best of steeds." The line came from her mouth as if by rote: she had learned it often enough. Yet it was not more; she cast about in her mind for what else she might say.

"I wished him to be the bridegroom of Inanna, to come to her bed at the feast of the New Year, to fulfill the promises given by his grandfather Dumuzi and his father Lugalbanda. The hardest bronze takes the longest filing, but holds the sharpest edge."

Still the goddess gazed impassively down at her priestess, and it seemed to the Shamhatu that she could read both pity and scorn in the shadowed face beneath the great golden diadem. The Shamhatu closed her eyes, her head whipping from side to side. She knew that she was pinned there like a fish on a gaff, like a serpent impaled on a barbed spear, and no matter how she thrashed about, there would be no escape. In despair she fell forward, hiding her face against the mud-brick floor, until the cry finally burst forth from her mouth.

"Because I love him!" The Shamhatu struck her fists on the floor, her wail rising up through the shrine. She did not know what feeling was shaking her so—anger or grief, relief or passion—it was too strong for her to name and too strong to bear, so that her limbs beat about wildly and the words howled forth from her throat against her will. "I love him, gods curse him, bless him—I love him!"

She wept and wailed so until her voice had worn to a whisper, until her exhausted body would no longer carry the violence raging through it. Then, whimpering softly, she curled like a child at the feet of the goddess, her back against the cold stone.

*I did not know.* The still thought was like a cool breath of breeze after the scorching-hot fury of a sandstorm. *I did not know how I loved him—not until now. I told myself I feared for Erech, or wished that Inanna's will be done, and all along . . .*

Now she knew what she would do if Gilgamesh still lived and came safely back to Erech. She would go to him and beg him, upon her knees if she must, to carry out the marriage: for his sake and her own, she would promise him whatever he wanted in return. Even if he desired another priestess as Shamhatu, even Shubad, she would give him his desire.

A strange clarity was stealing over the Shamhatu's mind and heart now: the calm clear brightness of the evening sky, lit by the pure gleam of Inanna's rising star. The words of the shrine's evening hymn came to her: *At the end of the day, the Radiant Star, the Great Light that fills the sky, the Lady of the Evening appears in the heavens . . . The men purify themselves, the women cleanse themselves . . .*

"Now, my goddess, I am naked before you," the Shamhatu whispered. "I have told you all: you have shown me the depths of my heart, and I have opened it all to you—I am here before you, an empty vessel of clay. Now, I beg that you fill me with your wisdom. What must I do? For Gilgamesh's sake, for my own—show me the way, Queen of Heaven, and enlighten me with your knowledge."

And now, at last, the Shamhatu heard the goddess' silent answer: not in words, but as a power that thrummed through her, bearing her up like a great wave. Helpless as a stick carried along by the flooding river, she found herself rising and going from the shrine to her own chamber. There, her hands moved of their own accord, stripping her rainment from her body, lifting the jewels of the goddess from the shrine to place over her nakedness: the belt of agates, cold about her hips, the chilly gold ornaments on her breast, the earrings tugging at her lobes, the heavy diadem on her head. All her senses seemed faint—sound muted, sight blurred, the feelings of her body a very long way from her. As if in a dream, her feet moved, carrying her forth again and onto the paths of the Eanna.

THE RAFT FLOATED down the river beneath the light of the stars and moon. Since they were so close to Erech, Gilgamesh had decreed that they should not pull in for the night, but continue on to the city. It was a little past nightfall when they first caught sight of the new tailed star, shining bright in the north.

"What is that?" Enkidu asked. "It is beautiful, but I have not seen it before."

"It must be a comet," Shusuen answered. "These strange stars are signs from the gods, and many have gone a lifetime without seeing one. It means . . ." The scribe paused, and even in the starlight Gilgamesh could see the shiver pass over his slender body. "It betides some happening of great moment. I have heard that they are often seen just before wars."

"Should we raise the army once more?" Gilgamesh wondered aloud, only half jesting.

Shusuen shook his head soberly. "Erech cannot afford another war. The last one brought us close enough to disaster—I know that better than any, for who is it that did the accounts for your army? Our provisions are low, and we lost too many of our forces in the battle with Agga. We can only hope that no one is marching against us, though that seems unlikely to me, since we have just beaten the largest army in Sumer, and Agga will not come against us again." He stroked the cat curled on his lap; the cat raised his head with a soft purring yawn, then laid it back down again. "See, Basthotep is of the same mind. If he, in his wisdom, sees no likely threat, why should you be worried?"

"Has the comet to do with Huwawa's death?" said Enkidu.

Shusuen pursed his lips, glancing up at the tailed star once more. "It could. Who, save the gods, knows what changes the freeing of the cedar forest may have wrought in our world?"

Gilgamesh thought that the scribe would say more, but Shusuen fell silent, staring at the sky. At last he spoke once more, his voice cold and distant. "Look at the moon."

The Ensi turned his gaze unwillingly away from the comet's blue-white brightness. For a moment he could not guess what Shusuen meant: then he saw, and sucked in a deep breath. A fingernail-edge of darkness had already crept across the swelling moon's brightness—the first shadow of the eclipse.

"The moon is darkening," Enkidu said wonderingly. "Why?"

The dry voice of the En came back to Gilgamesh, as he had heard it years ago, when the old priest sat enthroned with the youths and maidens of the Eanna squatting about his seat. *The gods show us their minds in many things; in all things, their power is displayed. In the liver of the sacrificial sheep, in the flights of birds, in strange births, in the movements of the heavens, we may read what they will tell us of their wills and their plans.* And there had followed the lists that they all had to learn, to write down and memorize and recite back; and hidden among the many omens, great and small was this: *The eclipse foretells the death of an Ensi.*

Shusuen's hand lifted and fell back, blood and expression draining from his face together until it shone as a pale cold mask in the slowly dimming moonlight. *He knows, as well,* Gilgamesh thought. He could not tell Enkidu the omen's truth: twice he opened his mouth to speak, and his tongue clove dryly to the roof of his mouth, even as Enlil's words sounded again in his head. *The bane of man will have but silence for you as answer; man's day of darkness shall arrive for you . . . The wave of blackness that you cannot breast shall come, the battle from which there is no fleeing shall come, the unequal fight shall come, and you may not shield yourself in the heart of your phalanx . . .*

The chill struck deeply into Gilgamesh's bones as he watched the darkness slowly creep across the moon, inexorable as the slow march of age against the body's strength, even as the tailed star grew brighter against the sky. Now, more than ever, he wished to be home in Erech, hailed as a hero with his long journey done. He reached down to stroke the rough cedar bark beneath his feet, and its touch brought him a little comfort: the shadow on the moon would rise and fall, but his cedar gate would stand for many lifetimes. And yet . . . and yet . . .

Enkidu put his arm about Gilgamesh's shoulders, and Gilgamesh could feel his own trembling against his friend's solidity. "You are troubled," Enkidu said. "Why?"

"The eclipse . . . is a bad omen," Gilgamesh answered him. "Often it betokens death." He bit the words off before his heart could betray him, before he could say more.

"We have faced death before," Enkidu reminded him. "Have no fear, beloved. I shall stand before you, so long as I live."

"Still, I would wish a better sign for our return to Erech."

"Shall we pull in here, and go on to the city tomorrow?" Shusuen asked. "If you think that would weaken the omen, we should do it."

"No. Tomorrow I shall go forth to tell the folk of Erech of our deeds, and I shall do that in the full splendor that befits an Ensi, which will take some time to ready. We shall enter the city tonight."

They tied up the raft just before the gate. Gilgamesh and Enkidu drew up their cloaks to muffle their faces, lest they be recognized. The moon was almost blinded now, but the streets of the city blazed with torches, clanged with the sound of pots and pans banging before every door as the people of Erech shouted and sang to drive the eclipse away. In the thronging streets, the two of them were able to pass unnoticed along the way to Eanna, following the sound of the great kettledrums that boomed out across the city below the faint keening wail of the shrine's hymns.

Gilgamesh and Enkidu did not go up to the shrine, for they were both filthy from the journey. Instead, they made their way to Gilgamesh's chamber, where a freshly lit oil-lamp burned sweetly beside the bed, as though he had only been out hunting for the day.

"Enatarzi!" Gilgamesh called. "Enatarzi, come to me!"

In a moment he heard the quick soft steps of the eunuch outside the door. Enatarzi was breathing hard as he stepped in, his plump shoulders slicked with sweat.

"Master!" he cried. "My Ensi, you are home! Praise be to Utu, who guarded you on the way, and praise to Inanna, who brought you back. I have waited here for you, and kept all clean and in readiness for your return. How fared your expedition? Did you achieve your goals?"

"We slew Huwawa and carried off the cedars," Gilgamesh replied. The triumph in his words was not as great as he had expected: the tiring length of the journey, and the fear that still lay coiled deep in his bones like a serpent in a night-chilled burrow, had tarnished the ecstasy of their achievement. Still, it was good to be able to speak so, and comforting to look down at the familiar, ringlet-framed face of his old servant. "But we have been traveling long, and must cleanse ourselves. Bring hot water and cloths, scented oils and fresh rainment for us, and food and drink afterward—but tell no one that we are here."

"As you command, beloved Ensi." Enatarzi bowed and withdrew.

Gilgamesh and Enkidu washed each other carefully, until the white linen cloths were black with the grime of their journey and their own skins were clean and glowing, then picked their way through the thick mats of each other's braids with the gold-inlaid ivory combs. Gilgamesh sighed, tossing his newly cleaned ringlets over his back. The hot water had eased all the muscles of his body, soothing away the little pains of all the small bruises and scrapes, and his skull, freed of the weight of tangles and dirt, felt several minas lighter. The linen kilt was soft against his legs; it was too warm for even a thin cloak, but the night air caressed his bare shoulders lightly as a lover's touch.

"It was a good journey," Enkidu said, "but it is good to be home again."

Gilgamesh could not but agree with him, and think that their home-coming was sweeter for this evening of peace. There would be time tomorrow to ride before the people of Erech in triumph; time to climb to the roofs of the temples and make their thanks-offering, to call out the best of Erech's carpenters and woodcarvers and set them to fashioning the great cedar gate. But now, for just a little while, they could enjoy the comforts of their own dwelling without waiting for a knock on the door-frame, for a summons to judgment hall or *gipar* or shrine to deal with some weighty manner. It seemed to him like those rare days in his childhood when he had been let off from school, freed from the endless rounds of reading and writing and learning rituals by rote and allowed to run through the streets of the city, spending his few rings of copper on cool melons or sweet dates as he pleased; and like the child he had been, he found himself untroubled by thoughts of what the next day would bring, only curious as to what good things Enatarzi would find to soothe the emptiness in his belly.

Even as he thought thus, Enatarzi stepped into the room again. The eunuch's hands were empty and his painted eyes wide, the whites shining in the dim light. His high voice shook as he said, "My Ensi, set your crown-cap on your head. The goddess of the city has come to you; even now she stands before the door, for she will speak to you alone."

Gilgamesh sprang to his feet, grasping Enatarzi's shoulders. His fingers sank into the soft flesh until the servant let out a frightened squeak. "Did you tell the Shamhatu that I had returned? I told you—"

"My Ensi, I said nothing to anyone! My Ensi, you're hurting me. She is at the door in her full glory, and she knew already that you had come—can anything be hidden from the eyes of the great gods?"

His heart racing, Gilgamesh let go of Enatarzi. The marks of his fingers stood out stark white on the eunuch's shoulders for a moment, then the blood flooded back in to darken them; he would be bruised tomorrow. "I am sorry," Gilgamesh said. For a moment he hesitated, torn, then hardened himself to speak again. "Enkidu, my love, go on to Sululi. She will be glad to see you this night, for she has waited long without word from you. Greet her from me, and little Ur-Lugal also."

Enkidu's face was troubled, but he did not speak, only leaned forward to kiss Gilgamesh softly on the mouth before he rose and padded from the room.

Gilgamesh opened the chest where his Ensi's regalia were kept. He wrapped the blue-trimmed robe of scarlet linen and wool about his shoulders, tying the golden sash around his waist; he took out the great diadem of gold figured with the shapes of lion and bull beneath its layered peak of overlapping horns and set it upon his head, and he armed himself with the Ensi's ceremonial mace, the smooth ivory of its hilt cool in his hand.

"Now I am ready," he said. "Tell her to come before me."

It was not long before Gilgamesh heard the footsteps in the hallway outside—not the deliberate pace of Inanna walking before Erech in her temple, but the swift light tread of a maiden hurrying to her lover. A chill ran over his skin, for faintly ringing in his ears, he could hear a woman's voice chanting: the words of Inanna to Dumuzi before their wedding, the snare of sweet song that had led Dumuzi in time to his death.

*"My vulva, the horn,*
*The Boat of Heaven,*

*Is full of eagerness like the young moon.*
*My untilled land lies fallow.*

*As for me, Inanna,*
*Who will plough my vulva?*
*Who will plough my high field?*
*Who will plough my wet ground?*

*As for me, the young woman,*
*Who will plough my vulva?*
*Who will station the ox there?*
*Who will plough my vulva?"*

Half entranced, a pulse of desire already rising between his legs, Gilgamesh felt his lips parting and his lungs drawing in breath. He knew
his part, long beaten into him in expectation of the day when he would
take his grandfather's place as husband and sacrifice; but with a fierce
effort of will, he bit his tongue until the blood flowed, locking his teeth
tight as siege-gates against the words that sounded in his head. *Great
Lady, the Ensi will plough your vulva . . . I, Dumuzi the Ensi, will plough your
vulva . . .*

"Inanna fastened on Dumuzi the eye of death," Gilgamesh whispered
to himself; and the blinded eye of the moon in eclipse came again to his
sight. "She spoke against him the word of wrath—*blazing from her mouth
like the comet'*—she uttered against him the cry of guilt: *'Take him! Take
Dumuzi away!'"*

She stepped in through the doorway, a gust of sweet wind blowing
around her with the scents of honey and sprouting earth, apples and
cedar incense and the freshness of lettuce planted by the water. The
oil-lamps burned brighter, filling the dim room with warm light;
Inanna's ornaments glittered upon her pale body, lapis and gold; the
agates settled upon the curve of her hips glowed softly, their arc
sweeping down over her smooth belly to brush against the glossy triangle of dark fleece between her legs, and two gold spirals lifted up the
globes of her breasts like apples offered by the fruiting tree. Her
mouth was coated with amber, her eyes painted wide and dark, and

upon her forehead the great star of her diadem glowed too brightly to look at. Her scent filled Gilgamesh's nostrils more strongly with each breath he took, inflaming his senses like a lion with a queen in heat, like a bull with a cow in season. His phallus was swollen hard with need; the seed ached in his balls, an underground river ready to spurt forth at her touch.

"I bathed for the wild bull," Inanna said softly, moving toward him. "I bathed for the shepherd Dumuzi, I sweetened my sides with ointment. He shaped my loins with his fair hands, he filled my lap with cream and milk. He stroked the hair of my loins, he watered my womb. He laid his hands on my holy vulva, he smoothed my dark boat with cream, he quickened my narrow boat with milk, he caressed me on the bed. Now I will caress my high priest on the bed, I will caress the faithful shepherd Dumuzi. I will caress his loins, the shepherdship of the land, I will decree a sweet fate for him."

Her body pressed hard against Gilgamesh's, slender and yielding; she turned her face up, dark eyes gazing into his own, and his limbs trembled with the fiery urgency roaring through him, so that he could not turn away from her. "Come, Gilgamesh, be my lover, grant your fruit to me. Be you my husband, and I will be your wife. I will have harnessed for you a chariot of lapis and gold, gold-wheeled, with horns of electrum; it will be harnessed with the great storming mountain onagers." She took his hand, placing it gently upon the soft curls between her legs. "Come into our house, into the sweet fragrance of cedar. And when you come in, the door-posts and throne-dais will kiss your feet. Kings, rulers, and princes will bend down before you, mountains and lands will yield their fruits to you. Your nannies will bear triplets, your ewes drop twins. Even burdened with full loads, your donkey will overtake the onager. Your chariot-steeds will bristle to gallow, your ox at the yoke will be matchless."

Dazzled and shaken by her nearness, his body already cleaving to her like the wings of a bird trapped in a sticky net, Gilgamesh stammered, "What must I give you, if I should take you as a wife? Would I give you oils for your body, and fine garments to clothe it? Would I give you bread and food—you who eat the food of the great gods, you who drink the wine of Ensi and temple? They pour libations for you, and you are clothed with the Great Garment. Ah, the gulf between us, if I take you in marriage!"

Yet Inanna moved against him, the nipples of her gold-wound breasts brushing unbearably over his skin, and he heard her voice taken up as if by a great chorus of women, the unearthly high singing sounding above her words. "Let the bed that rejoices the heart be prepared, let the bed that sweetens the loins be made ready! Let the bed of the Ensi be prepared, let the bed of queenship be made ready! Let the bed of the rulers be prepared!"

Grasping his hands in hers, Inanna drew Gilgamesh toward the bed that lay there in the chamber, its fresh scented linens smoothed down in readiness for his return. But the movement shattered the single glow of the star on her brow, its trembling light scattering droplets of brightness about the room, and suddenly Gilgamesh was able to wrench himself free of her, flinging himself across the chamber to rebound bruisingly from the wall as the mace clattered down from his hand. Staggering and panting, the taste of blood in his mouth, he spoke in a choking gasp. "You are a cooking fire that goes out in the cold, a half door that keeps out neither wind nor storm. You are a palace that crushes its brave defenders, a well whose lid falls in, pitch that blackens its bearer, a waterskin that soaks its drinker. You are limestone that crumbles in the wall, a battering ram that shatters in the land of the foe, a shoe that bites the owner's foot.'"

Inanna's mouth opened, and Gilgamesh could see the brightness within, but he went on heedless, the words spewing from his mouth like a torrent of froth from an uncorked jug of beer—the thoughts that had fermented within him ever since he had been old enough to learn of the fate of Dumuzi, of the place he was expected to take and the fate that came with it. "Which of your bridegrooms have you kept forever? Which of your little shepherds has always pleased you? See, I will recite the list of your lovers. Dumuzi, the lover of your youth—for him you ordained lamentations, year on year. You loved the bright little-shepherd bird; then you seized him and broke his wing, and he stands now in the forest crying, 'Kappi! My wing!' You loved the lion, full of strength and power, yet you dug for him pits, seven and seven. You loved the battle-glorious onager, yet you ordained for him whip and goad and halter, ordained that he should gallop seven and seven hours, ordained that he should roil the waters as he drinks, and drink from muddied waters; you ordained weeping for his mother Sululi. The shepherd, the master herder, him too you loved. Cakes baked in embers he gave you, and he daily slaughtered kids for you. Yet you struck him, turned him into a wolf, so that his own shepherds drive him away, and his dogs tear at his hide. You loved Ishullanu, your father's gardener. Every day he brought you baskets of dates, and each day he brightened your table. You lifted your eyes to him, and you went to him. 'My Ishullanu,' you said, 'let us pleasure in your strength; stretch out your hand to me, and touch my vulva!' Ishullanu said to you, 'What is it you want of me? Has my mother not baked, and I not eaten . . . should I eat the bread of bad faith and the food of curses? Should rushes be my only cover against the cold?' You heard his answer and struck him, you turned him into a frog, and made him live in the middle of his garden, where he may go neither up nor down. And now me: now it is me you love, and you will ordain my fate as you did with them."

Gilgamesh stood for a moment, glaring at her. The hot wind of anger that had roared through him had scorched him empty; his body felt like a shell of clay pulled fresh-baked from the oven. He did not have the strength to move or speak; he could only stand there as Inanna walked past, striding from his chamber. A gust of air blew in as she tore the hanging aside, snuffing the light of the oil-lamps. Slowly Gilgamesh's legs gave way beneath him; his back slid down the wall, and he sat shaking in the darkness.

AFTER SHUSUEN HAD seen Basthotep fed and settled purring comfortably upon his bed, and had carefully packed away all his tablets of notes from the journey, he went to the Eanna baths to cleanse himself. Even at this nighttime hour, the baths were full of temple-folk, washing and chatting loudly or murmuring in hushed voices of the twin omens of eclipse and comet. Not ready to talk with others yet, he kept to the shadows where his face would be hidden, content to wait on the fringes and listen. What the scribe heard spoken in soft voices disturbed him: there were none who did not think that the signs boded ill, and few who did not read them as promising a dark fate for Gilgamesh. And Shusuen knew well—as none should know better than a scribe, well-versed in the songs and tales of heroes as well as the keeping of records and accounts—that for folk to think and speak of bad omens was to bring them more than halfway into being, the more so when the matter in question was the subject of a great man's fame and health. Yet it was not time for him to argue or refute: those portions of the journey he published would do that better than his voice could, while those that he held back . . . would wait until whatever the gods had ordained for Gilgamesh had showed itself forth, until there was no fear that his own words could harm the Ensi.

But in spite of the hot water easing his body, in spite of the refreshing feeling of the steamy air against his fresh-shaven cheeks, Shusuen's heart was still full of trepidation. For as well as seeing the eclipse's strange darkness and the comet's strange light, the scribe also remembered what he had heard in Enlil's shrine: he could not forget it, for he had written it down before the shock of the god's voice could fade from him. There was no doubt in his mind that Gilgamesh would have a hard road ahead of him, and this could not bode well for Erech and her people. Shusuen knew that the gods were not lightly dared, that their favor was hard-won and easily lost. And so, when he had dried himself and put on fresh rainment, Shusuen went forth from the baths, stopping on the way to collect a pair of turtledoves as an offering. Though he was tired, he knew that he could not wait until morning, for throughout the journey, he had pushed himself beyond the limits of his body and nerves. Even now there was nothing holding him up save the last dregs of the urgency that had driven him throughout the quest; once he had lain down, he would not get up again easily, and, with all the dangers and strains safely past and gone, he was likely to lie in bed shivering for the next two or three days.

Shusuen did not turn his feet to the great raised shrine of Inanna, for the fires there had died down and the voices no longer sounded forth from the open door. Instead he went to the older shrine below its shadow, the eldest heart of the Eanna—the temple of An, lord of the sky, Inanna's mighty father. There, the rites had always been quieter, the priests and priestesses less full of themselves and less caught up in the business of governing the many threads of Erech's life that wove and knotted together in the Eanna; and after the endless days of going between Gilgamesh and Inanna's temple, of balancing the delicate shifting weight of politics and judgment even as he struggled to keep Gilgamesh from overturning them, Shusuen found this a relief. Although it was said in the hymns that Inanna had seized the Eanna from An, had feared not her father, but had changed the rites of holy An, altogether, that quietness was more to Shusuen's taste than the loud cries and pageantry of Inanna's shrine.

A rush-light burned at either side of An's altar; an offering-bowl of polished onyx filled with butter stood upon it, before the tall cap with seven superimposed pairs of horns meeting around it like the steps of a temple-platform—the headdress of divinity, the sign of the oldest god. No one was there, but the wicks had been freshly trimmed and the lights newly lit. The turtledoves cooed and cheeped sleepily as Shusuen carried their little wicker cage forward.

Prostrating himself before the altar, the scribe was about to speak when he heard the violent banging on the door-frame behind him. Muffling his face in his cloak, he moved swiftly to the side, hiding himself behind one of the tall mud-brick pillars.

The door blew open, an icy blast like the first gust of a storm sweeping through the warm still air of An's temple. The woman's harsh cry chilled Shusuen's bones, and his bowels quivered with fear as he gazed upon her. He knew the Shamhatu's face, yes, but she was transfigured by the awful, incandescent light burning forth from within her. Her naked body, adorned only by the jewels of Inanna, shone terribly before him, as though her oiled skin were bronze armor polished for battle, her eyes were black as bitumen about to burst into flame, and glowing tears streamed down from them. The scribe dropped to his knees, hiding his

face, but there was no hiding from her voice: it filled the temple, reverberating as if to sound from the depths of the seas to the sky above the
clouds, and he could not help but look up at her again.

"An, my father; Urash, my mother!" she cried out—and Shusuen had
no doubt that he was truly in the presence of Inanna. "Gilgamesh has
insulted me! He has spoken of bad faith, of my bad faith and my curses!"

Shusuen held his breath, listening. And then, as in the temple of
Enlil—though there was no mortal mouth from which sound might
issue—he heard the distant voice of the god rumbling, like thunder out
of a starlit sky.

*INANNA, RULER, WHAT TROUBLES YOU? DID YOU NOT PRO-
VOKE GILGAMESH YOURSELF? AND THUS HE SPOKE OF YOUR BAD
FAITH, YOUR BAD FAITH AND YOUR CURSES.*

Inanna strode forward to the altar, lifting one rush-light flame in each
hand. Wickless, without fuel, the two little fires burned in her palms as
she raised her hands above her head, showering their light down onto
her starry diadem.

"Father, make the Bull of Heaven for me! Let him slay Gilgamesh in
his own dwelling! If you do not give me the Bull of Heaven, I shall
smash in the Gates of the Netherworld. I shall break the door-posts and
knock down the doors, and I shall let the dead go up to eat the living.
And the dead shall outnumber the living!"

Though the goddess' mouth had stopped moving, her terrible words
still flew about the shrine, dark birds of sound flapping wildly until the
din rose to a scream of wordless fury—until, at last, An's great deep
voice calmed Inanna's cry again.

*IF YOU ASK THE BULL OF HEAVEN FROM ME, FOR SEVEN YEARS
THE LANDS OF ERECH SHALL HARVEST ONLY EMPTY HUSKS.
HAVE YOU STORED UP GRAIN FOR THE PEOPLE? HAVE YOU MADE
GRASSES GROW FOR THE BEASTS?*

"I have heaped grain in the granaries of the people," Inanna answered.
And Shusuen moaned softly, for he knew the truth of her words: she had
promised out the Eanna's seven-year stocks against famine—already
lower than they should have been, for the war and its aftermath had

already been chewing on that hoard—and brought on the very calamity against which they were stored to protect Erech's folk. "I made grasses grow for the beasts, so that they might eat through seven years of empty husks. I have stored up grain for the people, I have made grasses grow for the beasts."

*THEN I SHALL MAKE THE BULL OF HEAVEN FOR YOU, AND YOU MAY BRING IT TO HIM. ERECH IS YOUR OWN, TO DO WITH AS YOU WILL; IF YOU WISH TO THRESH IT TO CHAFF FOR THE BULL, THAT IS YOUR OWN AFFAIR, MY DAUGHTER. COME FORTH, AND I SHALL GIVE YOU THE BULL OF HEAVEN.*

With shocking suddenness, the light that burned from the Shamhatu's body shot upward, leaving Shusuen's eyes dazzled in the darkness. He barely heard the weak cry at the foot of the altar; but soft sobbing followed it, like gentle rain pattering down after a violent burst of lightning. Slowly he dragged his aching body across the floor, until his hand touched the Shamhatu's warm flesh. She was shivering all over, as though she had suddenly plunged into an icy mountain stream. Shusuen took his cloak off, wrapping it gently around her bare shoulders, and held her until her trembling eased.

"What happened?" he asked quietly. "Why did the goddess . . . ?"

The Shamhatu's voice was weak, her words coming out in little stammering bursts. "I . . . she came to me, and my body was not my own . . . She went to Gilgamesh as a bride . . . the marriage should have taken place, but he . . ." She coughed, sitting upright. The little cries and flapping of the turtledoves against their wicker cage were very loud in the sudden stillness, the only sound in An's shrine until the Shamhatu spoke again. "He turned away from her—he spoke of the lovers whom she had brought down. He turned away, and she left in wrath."

Shusuen closed his eyes, clenching his hands tight. He had feared this moment for a long time. For years he had watched Gilgamesh; long before Gilgamesh became Ensi, he had seen the youth's face go cold as the hymns of Dumuzi's terror-struck flight from death were sung, the tales of how Inanna had set the *galla*-demons of the Netherworld on his grandfather, that Dumuzi might take her place in Erishkegal's dark kingdom. And he had been witness to every wrangle between Gilgamesh and the temple, every harsh word spoken between the Ensi and the Shamhatu; he had early guessed at the tangled feelings that lay between them, like warp-threads knotted so that the weft might never weave smoothly across them. And now, for the goddess to come to Gilgamesh on this night of all nights, when eclipse and comet had scrawled the dread omen—*the death of an Ensi*—across the sky for all to read . . .

"The bronze-smith knows the mix of his metal, and temperatures and times are written on the apprentice's tablet, so that he should know when it will cast smoothly and when it will shatter in the casting," Shusuen said aloud, the words bitter as wormwood on his tongue. "The builder knows the strength of his stone, and the weight his walls will bear; it is he who takes the blame when they fail and fall. Do the gods, who shape us as the metalworker shapes bronze or the stonemason his rocks, know less than they, that they cannot guess what weight will break us?"

The delicate tendons of the Shamhatu's neck moved beneath Shusuen's touch as she shook her head. "I do not know," she answered. "I know only that she came, and he turned away, and now . . ."

"And now the Bull of Heaven is to be loosed, and the omens' promise made manifest."

But the Shamhatu was weeping again, great racking sobs, and Shusuen knew that it would be cruel to speak further to her: though she had had her part in the misbegotten building of the night, at the last she had been but a clay vessel for Inanna, bearing and pouring forth the godly wine she had been shaped and consecrated to hold.

"Come," he murmured to her. "It is done, and the gods have made their wills known. Now it is for us to measure and mete out the grain of the Eanna as we must do, that whatever becomes of Gilgamesh, Erech and her people shall survive. We shall go to bed, and tomorrow I shall order a full census of our storehouses."

Carefully Shusuen helped the Shamhatu to her feet. Even her slender weight was a heavy burden for him to bear now, but he supported her out of An's shrine, helping her along to her own chambers. She winced with pain as her hands touched the gold diadem on her head, and Shusuen remembered the flames burning in her palms.

"Let me see," he ordered her. Wordlessly, she opened his hands, showing him the two deep-charred marks. The scribe's breath hissed through his teeth as he looked at the burnt wounds.

"You should go to the En with those."

"No! No . . . not tonight." The Shamhatu bit her lip, lowering her gaze. "I do not wish to speak to anyone."

Shusuen sighed. He could well understand her feelings, for he felt the same. "At least I shall clean and bandage them for you."

He did that as best he could, trying not to hurt her, then helped her to take her jewels off and adorn the statue of the goddess with them again. "Now sleep, for we shall both need our rest against the morning."

The scribe rose, ready to leave, but the Shamhatu's soft cry called him back. "Shusuen . . . do not leave me. I am afraid, and I do not want to be alone, least of all . . ."

Shusuen saw her eyes flicker up to the stone statue of Inanna, radiant in her gems again, and he understood. "Give me one of your blankets, then, and I shall stay the night with you."

"I am sorry," the Shamhatu said brokenly. "I did not mean . . . this was not a burden that should have been laid upon you."

"I am Gilgamesh's scribe," Shusuen answered. "He called upon me to witness and write, as is my duty, and before that I was set to arrange the earthly affairs of Ensi and Eanna. If the gods walk among us, that does not release me from my office."

The Shamhatu stood, embracing him gratefully, then stretched up to brush her lips across his. "And yet a weaker man would have failed long before. Thank you, my friend, for keeping your trust."

"Always, my lady."

WHEN GILGAMESH COULD stand again, he tottered from his chamber, out into the warm air of the night. Between *gipar* and shrine, beneath the unearthly light of the tailed star that still shone across the sky, he made his way down to the house of Sululi. From the little window he could hear the sounds of Enkidu's growling, Sululi's soft moans, and he shut his eyes in pain. His loins ached in pain with the thwarting of the longing Inanna had set there, and he knew he could not bear to be touched again that night. So he waited until he heard Sululi's sharp cry, then Enkidu's deeper gasp, and waited still longer, until their breaths had stilled beneath his hearing, before he went around to knock on the door-frame.

Thankfully, it was Enkidu who answered—heavy-lidded, a piece of cloth wrapped hastily around his loins. Even in the dim starlight, Gilgamesh could see the troubled cloud falling over the face of his beloved as Enkidu looked upon him.

"What is wrong?" Enkidu asked quietly. "My love—what has befallen you?"

Gilgamesh could not answer, only clasped Enkidu in his arms, crushing his lover tightly to his chest.

"Will you come in, or shall I go back with you?"

"No! I . . . let me come in. I will stay here this night, if I may."

"Of course you may. Come in. You are shivering," Enkidu added wonderingly.

Gilgamesh let Enkidu lead him into the house and sit him down on the fine-woven woolen rug, sat quietly while Enkidu fetched a cup of beer with two straws, squatting beside him and lifting the cup to his mouth.

"What did she say to you? Was it about the sky?"

"It was . . ." Gilgamesh found himself choking, so that no sound could come out. He could open his mouth, he could move his tongue, but the voice behind the words was gone, as though Inanna's touch had torn out all the cords and sinews of his throat. He swallowed, tried to speak again—simply to speak the name of his lover, to let one word open the floodgates—but still nothing came from him.

For a moment a dreadful terror possessed him, so that he shivered and closed his eyes. Had Inanna struck him dumb forever—was it her curse that froze him so, that all the torments seething within him should never find voice?

"Gilgamesh, what is wrong?"

And yet he could not speak: the silence wrapped him like a cloak, like the cloth of fate drawn over his face. It seemed to grow thicker moment by moment, sifting over him like sand, and the longer it lasted, the more sure he became that he could not break it—that he would sit forever, an image carved in stone, while the voices about him grew more and more distant to his ears.

"Gilgamesh, my love . . ." Enkidu lifted a hand to him, but Gilgamesh felt his muscles hardening beneath the touch, as if to shut out the warmth of the other man's fingers on his shoulder. So he would sit someday, stone forever in shrine or *gipar*, distantly watching, hearing the clamor of temple-folk or the heart-weeping prayers at his feet like the faint buzzing of flies—alone, beyond pain or death, beyond all the voices that had shouted or wheedled all his life, demanding him to take up burden after burden without ceasing or easing.

"Gilgamesh, tell me. Gilgamesh . . . please."

Now Gilgamesh could hear the raw pain in his lover's soft voice, pain and fear—fear such as he had never heard from Enkidu. *He is afraid for me*, he thought. Though it felt as if he were lifting one of Erech's walls alone, he raised his hand from his thigh, stretching it out to grasp Enkidu's fingers in his own.

"Please," Enkidu said again, and the word wrenched at Gilgamesh's heart, squeezing out the blood like date-juice from a press.

"I . . ." he croaked. "She . . ." Then the walls of his throat burst, like the banks of an irrigation canal giving way beneath the flood, and he was telling Enkidu of all that had passed—and more, of the fear that had lived with him like an unseen servant through all his life, since he was old enough to know that Dumuzi had been his grandfather.

Enkidu sat and listened, clasping Gilgamesh's hand in both of his own. His pupils were dilated wide as a cat's in the dim flickering of the oil-lamps, and Gilgamesh could see his nostrils flaring and jaw clenching as the Ensi spoke. For a moment a terrible doubt came over him, and it made him shake all the more, his words stuttering to a halt.

*I should not have told him*, Gilgamesh thought. *He will think the less of me—he will forsake me, for was he not made by the gods and brought forth by the priestess of*

*Inanna?* In a moment all the words of worship Enkidu had spoken—all the words of wonder at the gifts of the gods, the way his lover had urged him to make offering when they were far beyond Erech and the forms and rites that had to be followed—came back to him, and his heart sickened with him.

But Enkidu was leaning forward, his fierce whisper filling Gilgamesh's ears. "She shall not take you!" he hissed. "My love, while I am with you, Inanna shall not be your death. The one who goes before wards his companion; I shall go before you, and stand between you and the goddess. We overcame Huwawa: surely we can overcome whatever else is set in our way. You are my life, and the sole reason I live, and I will not see ill befall you."

Gilgamesh's heart burst like a cloud split by lightning, filling his eyes with a storm of tears. He clasped Enkidu to him, drinking in the other man's nearness like a well of cool water in the middle of the dry desert. "My love, my love . . ." he murmured brokenly. "You are the only true joy of my life . . ."

# 8

The weather stayed hot long after it should have broken; when the autumn rains should have clouded the heavens, instead the sky stayed hot and bright as a bowl of burnished tin. The grain should have been sprouting, but each scorching day brought new life only to the worries in Shusuen's mind. He tossed and turned each night as the tailed star burned brighter and then faded slowly overhead, his thin linen sheets heavy and sweat-damp as thick woolen blankets, and each morning when he arose, barely able to drag himself from his sleepless bed, he looked up at the cloudless heights and saw the breath of the Bull of Heaven swirling across the burning blueness like heat-ripples rising from a fire.

The first sure sign came in the early autumn, when one of the temple's hireling-shepherds came to the *gipar* with a handful of dried sheeptendons sprouting from his gnarled fist like a child's bouquet of dying flowers.

"Exalted Scribe," he said to Shusuen, "keeper of the accounts of Inanna, I beg your hearing."

"Tell me what you have to say," Shusuen answered, though he hardly needed to ask. The tendons were proof enough of the death of the sheep, all the law required, and there were too many for the claim to be against a marauding lion or pack of wolves.

The shepherd fell on his face before Shusuen, his graying hair straggling out across the rug like a tangle of unwoven thread-ends. "Exalted

Scribe, they all died! I guided them as well as I could, but there was no grass, the grass and weeds were all dead, scorched away as if a fire had burned over the hills. I sought everywhere to find them food and water, but there was none . . . I was driving them back to the city, but they staggered and fell in their tracks, one by one. My poor sheep, I tended them, they all had names . . . I tried to feed them my bread, but there was not enough for each to have more than a bite. Even my own little ewe, she lasted the longest, because I shared my own food with her, but she died almost within sight of the city's canals. Exalted Scribe, I have brought all their tendons to prove it. I did not fail as their shepherd, but there was no more I could do."

"It is written," Shusuen answered. He reached down, taking the handful of dried tendons from the shepherd even as he helped the man to his feet. "Tell me, did you see or hear anything strange as you herded?"

"Only the low roar of the desert wind, like the bellowing of a bull in the distance," the shepherd answered. "The wind blew endlessly, like the breath of a furnace—you see how it has scorched me."

Shusuen looked more closely at him—shortsightedness was a gift in a scribe who must read and write the finest signs, but of little help in the things of everyday life. Indeed, the shepherd's face was scoured red over the deep wrinkled tan of a lifetime in the sun, as though he had stood too close to the heat of bronze melted for the casting.

"No blame falls upon you," Shusuen said at last. "I, Shusuen, the Eanna's scribe, have judged it."

He did not know what to tell the shepherd next. If a flock were lost to beasts or robbers, with a good herder truly blameless, the Eanna would reassign more sheep to him and send him out again; but Shusuen knew that to do that now would only be to cast seed upon rocky ground. Better to pull in as many herds as the irrigated land near the river would support without destroying those crops that could survive on the canals' water alone, and to order that the rest be slaughtered and their meat dried as soon as possible.

*And yet, who will believe me if I call for such harsh measures so soon?* Shusuen asked himself. *They will think that I take too much upon myself—perhaps even think that I seek to take Gilgamesh's place in time.* For he was the En's great-grandson, the only living descendant of the man who had fulfilled Inanna's marriage through the years while Lugalbanda, and then, in his turn, Gilgamesh, had grown up to take the part of the goddess' husband, and though Shusuen had no wish to stand before the people with the Ensi's diadem on his head or the En's medallion—which Gilgamesh should have taken already, as husband to the goddess of the city—about his neck, if . . .

But there was a simple answer to the question of who would believe him: the Shamhatu. Shusuen and the priestess together could force through whatever measures were needful for Erech's survival, and if that made both their positions shakier for a time, the passage of even a year beneath the breath of the Bull of Heaven would prove them right.

Shusuen was saved from having to speak by the arrival of one of the temple's messengers. The young woman bore a tablet in her hand and was out of breath; she tried to sink to her knees, but Shusuen cut her off with a small motion of his hand.

"Give it to me," he said.

In the last year and a half, the Eanna had needed to send to other cities for wool, since the demand for soldiers' gear had far outstripped their usual supplies and left them badly shorted afterward. The tablet had come from one of their chief sources in Ur, and now Shusuen read it with growing unease.

*From Lot of Ur, to the god-raised and holy priests of the Eanna of Erech, greetings and blessings. Regarding the wool which you ordered from me and for which you sent payment: I regret that I cannot supply it at the present time. My uncle Abram, who tends the flocks of our family outside the city walls, tells me that the grazing has grown suddenly scarce due to the drought, the like of which we have not seen in our lifetimes. He, and the other shepherds with whom we deal, must move farther away in order to preserve the animals which are their livelihood. Be sure that, as soon as matters improve, I will send the materials for which you have paid me. In the meantime, I trust that you will recognize the situation in which we find ourselves, and act accordingly, remembering the credit which I gave you last year in your times of hardship.*

*May your gods ever bless you, and bring better weather swiftly.*

The letter was signed with Lot's cylinder-seal—a pattern Shusuen knew well, for he had often sent correspondence to wrangle with the man over materials and prices. Lot had waited a month to be paid just before the war, and Shusuen had known at the time that he would never let Erech forget it . . . though the scribe had not expected the reckoning of reproach and excuse to come so quickly.

"Take care of this man," he said to the messenger. "Be sure that he is fed and housed during his stay in Erech the Sheepfold, and shown to the proper authorities regarding his flock, which was destroyed through no fault of his own. I must attend to this business at once."

Shusuen turned on his heel, walking away briskly. There was no time to lose: the breath of the Bull of Heaven had already claimed its first victims, whether anyone else was able to see it or not, and now he must act swiftly. Yet—and now his steps slowed and turned, like dry leaves suddenly caught in a contrary wind—he was not the first to deal with Erech in crisis. The gods had walked in the city within living memory, and one man had given up and taken the medallion of the En again and again, as Erech's Ensi was exalted and cast down at Inanna's will. It was to his great-grandfather that Shusuen went now for counsel: no man in the Sheepfold was wiser, or would be better able to see what was taking place.

The En was leading the midday observances in the shrine; Shusuen waited quietly by the door until the rites were done, reaching out from the shadows to tap the old man on the shoulder.

"Great-grandfather," he said, "I would speak with you alone."

"Come."

The Ensi led Shusuen down to his own chambers in the *gipar*. The shorthaired cats from the Black Land leapt down from shelves and beds as they entered, running to the En to weave about his ankles like a tabby-striped rug. The En bent down, stroking backs and scratching behind ears, and Shusuen squatted as well to tend to them.

"The care of the lions," the En murmured. "Did I ever tell you . . . when I left the Black Land with your great-grandmother, that was what the chief priest of Ra said to me."

"What?"

"He gave me the cats, and your great-grandmother to help care for them, as a sign of honor between priest and priest. And he said to me—ah, he was very old then, and I was very young, no older than you are now. 'My boy,' he said to me, 'you shall care for the lions, and be their protector.' I wondered what he meant by that, for I had always thought, as most folk do, that lions were nearest kin to wolves and dogs. But the longer I watched my cats, the closer to lions they seemed, until at last I wondered how anyone could think they were different creatures." The En scooped up a heavily pregnant queen, who draped over his shoulder, purring loudly and digging her claws into his skin as she regarded Shusuen with an indifferent golden stare. "But you have not come to me to talk of cats. I know Basthotep is well, for I saw him stalking very proudly through the *gipar*-halls with a mouse in his mouth this morning—if he has not eaten it, you are likely to find it on your pillow this evening."

"I have not come to talk of cats," Shusuen admitted as his great-grandfather squatted down beside him, dislodging the striped weight of the cat from his shoulder and easing her down to the rug. "I have come to talk of sheep, and bulls, and the fate of Erech the Sheepfold."

The En nodded slowly and thoughtfully. "Perhaps you should have come to me before, when the Shamhatu did. Yes: she has already told me of what passed between Inanna and Gilgamesh, as well as she could remember it, and of how Inanna called the Bull of Heaven against Erech. And now you see the Bull's first spoor—is it not so?"

"It is. Great-grandfather, I fear that Gilgamesh's doom is upon him, for no man can challenge the gods. And worse, I fear that he has dragged Erech down with him."

"Gilgamesh's doom . . ." the En echoed. His thin shoulders sagged, and Shusuen could see the weight of all his ninety-three years written deeply in the wrinkles that scored his face like lines of cryptic script scratched into a clay tablet. "Yes."

Shusuen stared at his great-grandfather, unable to believe the word so bluntly spoken. But the En's expression was one of certain sorrow and old resignation—the look of a man who had already led the funeral rites for two Ensis, and still conducted the *gala*-priests as they sang the yearly mourning for the friend of his youth, Dumuzi. "Is it already written, then?" he whispered. "Is Gilgamesh to die?"

"There is no doubt. The omens have all brought a single word, and Inanna called his death down upon him herself. Yes, he will die by the horns of the Bull of Heaven, and Erech will suffer for seven years. And you, great-grandson . . ."

"And I?"

"I am an old man, soon to die, and Gilgamesh's heir has not yet taken his first steps. Though Enkidu is wedded to Gilgamesh, and stands as Ensi beside him, he cannot rule alone—think you on it."

Shusuen did not need to, for the thought had already crossed his mind a hundred times since the eclipse had first darkened the moon. Enkidu's innocence of all that everyone else took for granted, his straightforward thoughts, his utter lack of subtlety or subterfuge . . . Beside Gilgamesh, Enkidu brought a new and welcome brightness to the Ensiship, enlivening the many years of law and tradition with his questions, like gold dust suddenly sifted over an ancient tablet. But alone . . .

*And who would guide him, if not his scribe?* the treacherous thought whispered in Shusuen's mind, like a snake hissing inside a thornbush. *A strong Ensi, yet one who is little-versed in the ways of men, and of Erech . . .* Though Enkidu had struggled to learn, he had not yet mastered the intricacies of reading, let alone writing: he would be wholly dependent upon Shusuen to tell him what was taking place, and what must be done. *I could rule unseen; I would have the power to order the affairs of Erech, and see that all things were done as they ought to be. The city would run better than it has ever done, for the one who knows most would have most power, as it ought to be . . .*

And yet the price for that would be Gilgamesh's death. Even as he thought on that, the tears prickled hot against the back of Shusuen's eyes. For Gilgamesh to walk no longer the halls of *gipar* and shrine . . . for his laughter to ring no more in the taverns of Erech, and the streets of the city to feel his step no longer, his dark ringlets not rippling down his powerful back as he strode purposefully from place to place, but carefully arranged about his death-pale face . . . His image carved in stone would be cold comfort for those who had known him living, who had felt the rays of his splendor warming them in life. Shusuen had long expected to outlive his Ensi, for if no illness or accident befell a scribe, he could expect to go on until old age at last overtook him, while Inanna would have her sacrifice in his course: battle or sickness or some fate unknowable by mortal men, Gilgamesh's fear of the goddess was rooted in the rich earth of good reason and history. Yet he had not expected doom to fall so soon, not wound so closely about the heels of Gilgamesh's latest triumphs like a clinging vine choking a fig tree.

*And what would become of Enkidu?* Shusuen asked himself. He knew that, though he would mourn, though the emptiness left in his heart by Gilgamesh's passing would never be filled, he could go on, the years of his life gradually enfolding the pain of loss like the wood of a tree thickening and gnarling about a bronze spike driven into its trunk. But Enkidu . . . Shusuen had watched the wild man with Gilgamesh long enough, seen how his green eyes lighted whenever he turned them upon his lover. Other men had other things to sustain them: Shusuen knew that, however his own heart should be broken, or the joys of his life slip away from him, his duties would still brace him like the great pillars holding up the roof of a shrine whether light and incense burned within, or all was dark and cold. But Enkidu had nothing save his love. Through the course of the journey, Shusuen had marked how the golden lion-man faded and drooped whenever he was parted from Gilgamesh. He had wanted to comfort him then, but he knew that there was nothing he could do, for he was not Gilgamesh. Though Enkidu was awed and excited by Shusuen's knowledge of writing and figures, and loved to play with Basthotep, rolling the cat over and tickling his spotted belly while Basthotep growled and meowed and attacked Enkidu's hand with his claws, Shusuen knew that matters could never go further than play and talk, for Enkidu's heart beat in Gilgamesh's breast, and the gods had shaped him for that one purpose.

*He would die. As surely as melons shrivel and die when the canal that waters them silts up and will no longer flow, Enkidu would die without Gilgamesh.*

The En waited patiently, watching his great-grandson. Though Shusuen was well-schooled in the art of hiding his thoughts from his face, the En had ninety-three years of reading a tabletful in the flicker of an eyelash, the twitch of a lip, or the flicking of a finger. Before the old man, Shusuen felt transparent as a thin sheet of polished alabaster, a child moving his first pieces in a long and hugely complex board-game.

"I . . ." Shusuen's tongue stopped in his mouth, caught between *I cannot do it* and *I must.*

"So I felt," the En said softly, "when the *gallas* first came for Dumuzi."

"But must we live it all over again? Is not once enough?"

"Never enough," the En answered. "The seasons change, year on year, and what happened before must happen again. Dumuzi goes to the Netherworld each year, and each year he returns—do you not think I mourn most keenly of all, I who knew and loved him, and rejoice most joyfully when I know that he has come back to Erech? Gilgamesh—the gods have granted me to know—will become, like his grandfather and father, a revered ghost: the Ensis of Erech will make sacrifice to him, and he will guide them in their final hours. Two-thirds god and one-third man: thus Gilgamesh is, and it is not for us to judge his fate, only to tend the folk of Erech the Sheepfold when the shepherd has fallen."

"And is there nothing I can do?" Shusuen asked desperately.

The En's voice was flat as the smack of wet clay upon a table. "Nothing. Ready yourself."

He turned his back, and Shusuen understood that the audience was over. Rebelliously, he waited a moment, stroking a few of the cats that writhed about him, before rising to his feet and leaving the En's chambers . . . *the chamber that would be his soon, if . . .*

THROUGH THE SCORCHING days, the Shamhatu avoided Gilgamesh: she hurried from his path when she saw him striding across the Eanna's courtyard, and when the Ensi took his place in the temple's ceremonies, she was always careful to linger before the altar afterward until sure that he was long gone. After what Inanna had done through her flesh, she could not face him, nor could she say to him, "It is the goddess, and not I, who came to you—it is she who has turned against you, not I!" And, knowing the fate that she had helped to bring upon Gilgamesh, she could not bear to look upon him for long. Soon, the dust would dull his bright eyes; the gleaming strength of his arms and shoulders, the breadth of his chest and the power of his legs . . . they would all fall away in death like a pot of damp clay collapsing inward under the potter's hands. Nor could she bear to go to the house where the women wove, lest she have to speak with Innashagga, whose husband she had planned to betray into sacrifice—and wished that she could, that Gilgamesh's fate could thus be averted. But that was no longer possible, for it was no longer the Ensi of Erech against whom the gods had turned in wrath, but Gilgamesh himself: the Bull of Heaven would find him, whether he stood crowned on the walls of Erech or fled in disguise to the sheepfold.

To push away the weight that bore her down more heavily through the crushing heat of each day, the Shamhatu flung herself into her work. She went over the rosters of the temple-folk, spending hours in conference with the head priests and priestesses responsible for each duty, inquiring about the performance of those below them in order to make sure that discipline and promotion were meted out properly. To Shusuen, she gave full authority over the coffers and stores of the Eanna; though Meskalamdug, the master of the treasury, grumbled exceedingly, he was an old man who seldom looked outside his lists and calculations, while Shusuen had taken it on himself to deal directly with all the reports and complaints coming in to the Eanna—and besides herself and the En, he was the only one who knew the gods' decree of seven years' devastation. If not comfort, her duties at least offered a certain numbness and distraction . . . save for one.

It was the old priestess Shibtum, responsible for all the priestesses and priests who brought Inanna's blessing to their worshipers with their bodies, who was also responsible for looking over the petitions from those who sought to lie with the goddess. She decided which were worthy of consideration by the Shamhatu herself, and presented a report on her choices. Though the rich and the mighty, as was the way of the world, made their way in more often, Shibtum was careful that now and again a common man, worker or herdsman or hunter, was allowed to come to the Shamhatu, lest it begin to be whispered by the folk of Erech that Inanna's representative loved only the great, and the Shamhatu trusted Shibtum's judgment greatly.

Though Shibtum was in her fifties, only her hands and the lines about her eyes showed it. There was a little more flesh upon her belly and hips than when she had trained the Shamhatu, but her hip-length hair was still glossy black, her ruddy cheeks smooth and lips full, and she moved with the grace of a woman who had been dancing before the gods for thirty years. While being trained, the Shamhatu had seen Shibtum lower herself backward till she lay full-length with only her hands and feet touching the floor. From that position she had undulated her hips, drawing a full-sized pestle inch by inch into herself, then pressed it slowly out again until she held only the head. Then she had raised herself again, settling down upon the pestle and lifting her legs to cross her feet behind her head, and shown her class how to twirl about a man's rod "like clay on a potter's wheel." The Shamhatu was a little in awe of her, as were all the priests and priestesses she had taught.

"Behold," Shibtum said, handing the Shamhatu a clay tablet. "Many men have come to the temple this morning, but I think you should see to this one yourself. He is a farmer, who cannot read or write; he paid one of our scribes to write out his petition, and I spoke with him myself."

The Shamhatu scanned the tablet quickly. Ibul-Il, farmer, had been wounded in the war and lost most of his harvest: now, because of the weather and the state of the baked ground, he feared for his autumn planting. He had brought what he had as offering, and prayed that Inanna would give him her ear for his troubles, and blessing.

"I will see him," she said. Then, dreading the answer, "Are there many such?"

"As many as we have priestesses to serve them. Not since the time before Lugalbanda's death have men flooded into the shrine like this. Divine Lady, today there were five or six petitions that, had they come singly in quieter times, I should have directed to your notice. If this keeps up . . ."

The Shamhatu felt herself clenching within, but she nodded. "I trust your judgment."

"Then, Divine Lady, if the need is great enough, may I call for the help of all those I have trained, whether they have gone to fulfill different duties or not?"

The Shamhatu cringed. The work of the temple . . . what would such an order do? But the offerings that were made would go into Inanna's coffers and storehouses, to strengthen their bulwarks against the horrors of the coming famine. "Do it."

The Shamhatu spent the rest of the day in dread. Since the night of the eclipse, she had put on her regalia as she must for the temple's rites, and called out the invocations of the goddess, but she had not been able to look her statue in the eyes, and struggled, as best she could, to block Inanna's touch from her. But now she must do the thing she feared: she must ask Inanna to wear her flesh again.

"And I cannot," the Shamhatu murmured as she readied herself for Ibul-Il. Though usually the preparations for the goddess' lovers were enjoyable, now she felt only uncomfortable twinges as she massaged the drops of scent into her breasts, and the act of oiling between her legs was simply the slicking of a tool, not a pleasurable promise of delights to come.

The farmer Ibul-Il was a handsome man, shoulders broad and muscular from his work in the field, short dark hair streaked red by many hours in the sun. The wound he had mentioned had healed cleanly, a jagged scar shining pink against the deep tan of his thick-muscled forearm. He did not dare to gaze straight at her, but the Shamhatu could see the trembling of joyous awe on his sunburned face, and feel the shivers of desire and fear that ran through his body as he knelt to kiss her. *Forgive me*, she thought, even as her voice said warmly, "Inanna calls you to her. Come to my garden . . ." *I have swindled you of the offering you made, and I betray your hope. Forgive me.*

Ibul-Il's first thrust was painful as no lovemaking had been since her first days as Shamhatu, his rod forcing its way through her clenched muscles. Remembering the control of her inner muscles she had learned from Shibtum, she forced her vulva to open to him; she met his thrust with the rolling of her own hips, and matched her breathing to his. When the feeling of Ibul-Il sliding in and out of her began to become uncomfortable, she grasped him harder in her, speeding the rhythm of her squeezes until at last he gasped and shuddered; then she contracted and cried out to match him.

Though the Shamhatu tried to listen to Ibul-Il's recounting of his troubles, her mind kept turning away: she could not bear to hear his trust when she knew herself false. But when he was done, and she must speak her lying blessings, she had to look into his honest, broad-boned face. At last, though she knew it was foolish, she drew off one of Inanna's rings from her finger. "Take this to the scribe Shusuen. Tell him that I have ordained that you should receive a gift from the coffers of the Eanna, that your family may live and thrive this year."

Painfully the Shamhatu listened to Ibul-Il's pouring-out of thanks, until at last he prostrated himself before her and left. She knew what she had done was stupid: the Eanna would need every shekel in its treasury in the year to come—and the six years after. They could not afford gifts to soothe her conscience. And yet . . . Ibul-Il's trust had reminded her of Enkidu in his innocence, or Akalla. She had led the one to the love that must soon break his heart; that she was not guilty of the other's death was only a matter of the gods' swiftness; and it meant much to her, though she could not say why, that Ibul-Il not be the worse for his dealings with her.

But the Shamhatu lay awake in the heat that night, turning restlessly in her sweat-soaked linens and staring into the darkness. When at last she slept, she dreamed that she was herding sheep again, but her flock had scattered and she was running without rest after this one, then that one, while all about her she heard the sound of lions and wolves ripping into the bodies of her lambs. She cried out when Atab shook her into wakefulness. During the day, the Shamhatu's eyelids drooped heavily through the daily litanies, and she longed for nothing but her bed, but when she lay down at night, she found her body struggling against rest, twitching and jerking as if to fight off the nightmares lowering over her sleep.

When she had passed several such nights, the Shamhatu went to the En for sleeping draughts. She slept then, but the nightmares grew worse, and it was harder for her to drag herself from their sodden grip in the mornings. And during the days, another burden was coming upon her. Though she was undertaking her duties without the help of the goddess—though the invocations stirred nothing within her, nor did Inanna's exaltations lift her up—the least things seemed to draw her into a trance, like deep mud sucking her under. The sight of her own curved face in the gleaming silver of a cup; the distant rhythm of the drums when the musicians were rehearsing in the shrine; even the sound of her own fingers plinking at the strings of her lyre, until she feared to lift the instrument; all brought the veil of darkening sparkles over her sight, the deep thrumming in her ears . . . and the sudden terror that her body would be taken from her again, her self cast aside without thought as Inanna worked her ruthless will through her. And every day, as if her own misery were not enough, the Shamhatu had to listen to the voice of another man who had made offering so that he might speak to the goddess of his troubles, and pretend that she could give him Inanna's blessing. It was working worse upon her than the strain of the war had: twice already, half-tranced and groggy from the lingering effects of the sleeping draught, she had given the wrong response in a litany. The En had covered for her, but she knew that sooner or later something would happen that he could not hide.

And perhaps, the Shamhatu thought, lying fretfully in her bed with the covers cast off in the heat, that would be best. To let Shubad have her way at last, to give her this wretched duty and be free . . . *Free to herd sheep, and watch them starve and die in the drought? Free to ply my trade in the taverns of Erech, where at least the men who came to me would believe I gave them no more than their sneeze of pleasure?* But she had made sure that Shubad would never hold her office—and stepping down, no matter who succeeded her, would not free her from the memory of what Inanna had used her to do. Nor did she believe it would release her from her nightmares, nor anchor her mind from floating unwillingly into trance. Only her death would do that.

Once the thought was upon her, the Shamhatu found it hard indeed to push away. If she died now—if she opened her wrists, or stole a vial of poison from the En's room, or leaped head-first from Erech's wall— she would no longer have to sit through the endless round of daily chants before Inanna, would not have to hear the cries of petitioners in the temple. Though the breath of the Bull of Heaven baked all Erech to a mud-brick, her skin would be cool and dry at last in the lands beneath the earth. She would no longer have to lie with strangers every day, listening to their desperation . . . and she would not have to see Gilgamesh die, only sit in Erishkegal's dark realm to await his coming.

Thus thinking, the Shamhatu arose and dressed herself. Although the stars were bright overhead, the moon was down. No one saw her passing through the Eanna, nor was she molested as she walked alone through the city streets and mounted to the top of Erech's wall. The plain was pale and empty in the starlight.

*Now I shall be free,* she thought. In Erishkegal's kingdom, she would not wear the starry diadem, nor bear any name other than the one she had set aside: she would simply be Puabi, one among the many ghosts in the halls of dust.

She pulled herself up onto the rampart, standing there at the edge. A strong gust of wind would have knocked her off, but no wind blew: there was only the hot still blanket of night air about her. *Now, just two steps and it will be over.*

The dry earth glimmered beneath her; it seemed to ripple in the heat, rising and falling like waves on the river. She could see nothing except its shimmering movement, hear only the high humming in her ears, the song of Erishkegal calling her. *She is sleeping, she is sleeping . . . Her holy shoulders no garment covers, no cloth drapes her holy breasts, the Mother of Birth and Death, who sleeps . . .*

Eyes and ears dazed, the Shamhatu stepped from the edge of the wall. She did not feel the rushing of air about her; her sight darkened, she waited for the earth to strike her, but her feet were moving, carrying her through the blackness . . . the blackness, lit by the glittering stars above. It was only then that she realized she was walking again through the streets of Erech: tranced, she had not leaped forward, but back, and her feet had carried her back on the path toward the Eanna.

"Am I not even to be allowed to die?" she asked despairingly. But no answer came.

Within the gates of the Eanna the Shamhatu's tread became more purposeful. Making her way to the House of Women, she went to the chamber Geme-Tirash shared with two other trance-priestesses.

"Geme-Tirash, awake!" she called softly. "It is I, the Shamhatu. Awake, and come with me."

In a few moments the trance-priestess appeared at the door, eyes heavy with sleep and curly dark hair disheveled. "What is it?" she asked anxiously. "Why do you need me?"

"I am troubled," the Shamhatu replied, "and I would speak with you."

She led the other woman back to her chamber, lighting the oil-lamps and squatting down on the rug beside her. "You have been trained as a trance-priestess since you came to the Eanna," the Shamhatu began, "and therefore you must know . . . you must know what to do when visions threaten to come to you unbidden and unwanted, for I have heard Ninkisalsi speak of novices he has had difficulty teaching this skill to."

"It is true, we learn how to shield our minds. But why should you have need of this? Are not your visions always holy, and your body given over for the use of Inanna?"

"It was," the Shamhatu said. Although her eyes were dry, dry as the plains about the city, her shoulders shook, and harsh sobs now tore up through her throat. Geme-Tirash reached out to her, putting her arms about the Shamhatu's shoulders and holding her gently until the racking tremors had eased.

"Tell me," the trance-priestess murmured. "Surely you know now that you can trust me . . ."

Her words sent a pang through the Shamhatu, thinking of the harm her years of mistrust had allowed to come to Geme-Tirash. But for that, she might not have been able to speak, yet with the goad of guilt pricking above her own burden of pain, her throat unlocked. She told Geme-Tirash of what had befallen between Inanna and Gilgamesh, and the loosing of the Bull of Heaven; she told her how the goddess no longer spoke through her priestess, and of her nightmares, and the torment of the trances that threatened constantly to seize her. And lastly, she told her of what had happened that night upon the walls of Erech.

"And so I wish to know how to make sure that my mind will stay my own long enough . . ."

Geme-Tirash clasped the Shamhatu's slim hands tightly between her own plump ones, and the Shamhatu saw that she was crying, the tear-trails glinting golden over the curves of her cheeks.

"Oh, no, Divine Lady," Geme-Tirash wept. "No, please! You must live, for no one in the Eanna could do what you do."

"I have failed at it, and brought ruin on Erech. And I no longer have faith in Inanna, or wish to serve her. The starry diadem should fall to you now, for you would wear it far better than I."

"No!" Geme-Tirash let go of the Shamhatu's hands, prostrating herself on the floor. "Divine Lady, I beg you! Please do not . . . go away, for my sake, if no other. I fear I would be chosen, and I know that I could not bear it. I was only able to endure before because I could hope each day that you would return before nightfall and free me. I will teach you how to shield your mind if you desire it, but only if you swear to me that you will stay, and live."

The Shamhatu caught Geme-Tirash's hands, raising her up to squat on her heels again. "It would not be the burden you think, if you held it in your own right," she said soothingly. "The En told me that the Shamhatu chooses her own duties, whether she wishes to be a ritual figure alone or rule the Eanna in truth as well as name."

"But she must always sit at the head of the temple, with all eyes on her. And . . . there are the men she must lie with as the goddess. It was bad enough then, when I knew it must end, and worse now, though all the women are saying that this flood should end soon."

"Now? But you are a trance-priestess. You do not mean . . ."

"Shibtum called me, because she had given me a little training as Shamhatu," Geme-Tirash admitted, wringing the hem of her dress in her hands. "But even when I can feel that Inanna is with me, I have no joy of it. I know I should not complain to you about it, since you have carried out the duties of your office for years—but I had never lain with men until I took your place, and when you returned, I hoped that I would never have to again." She wiped her eyes, snuffling. "I am sorry, Divine Lady. I did not mean to trouble you, when you have so many troubles of your own."

The Shamhatu stroked Geme-Tirash's head, smoothing the thick soft curls. "No, Geme-Tirash. I was sunk too deeply in my own troubles, with none to give me comfort, and you have eased my burden a little already." She moved closer to the other woman, leaning against the warm softness of her shoulder. Geme-Tirash turned her head to gaze into the Shamhatu's eyes, and her arm went about the Shamhatu's waist.

"If I may comfort you, I am glad," the trance-priestess said. Her eyes were wide, still shining with the last of her tears, and the Shamhatu was close enough to see the green flecks gleaming in her hazel irises. Geme-Tirash's breath was sweet as fresh water. She tilted her head back a little, mouth half open, and the Shamhatu found herself leaning closer until their lips met in a soft, melting kiss. Geme-Tirash's palm caressed her left breast, cupping it as if she held a sweet fruit; the Shamhatu reached out for her, feeling the warm weight of the trance priestess' heavy breast in her hand—touching her as she had not touched another woman since her days of training with Shibtum. A slow, sensual pleasure was beginning to steal through her, warm and relaxing as a long draught of date-wine, and she tightened her fingers slightly on Geme-Tirash's nipple as she caressed the other's petal-soft lips with her own. Geme-Tirash gasped, pulling the Shamhatu closer and stroking down along the curve of her hip, along the insides of her thighs. Carefully the two women undressed each other, caressing until the Shamhatu could feel the tingles of delight shivering all through her body and Geme-Tirash's breath came fast and soft. The Shamhatu did not realize that she was crying again until the tip of the trance-priestess' tongue licked the tears from her face, salt mingling with the sweetness of their kisses, but she embraced Geme-Tirash the more passionately, pulling her into the bed.

The Shamhatu and Geme-Tirash lay together for some time after they were done, the sweat slowly cooling and drying on their bodies. The Shamhatu would have liked for Geme-Tirash to stay with her, but that was impossible: eventually the trance-priestess had to rise and dress again. "Tomorrow I will start teaching you how to shield yourself," Geme-Tirash told her softly. "Until then, sleep well, and do not fear . . . and if you need me, call on me."

The Shamhatu lay awake for some time more, but she felt no need to move. She would have to live and go on now; she could not betray Geme-Tirash, as well as everyone else. The Eanna would go on, and if she no longer listened to Inanna, nor Inanna to her, there were plenty of other priestesses to do—whatever it was that would have to be done.

THOUGH THE DAYS should have cooled with winter's approach, they grew hotter instead. Gilgamesh soon learned to turn aside whenever he heard Shusuen's light tread in the passages, for he knew that the scribe would be seeking his seal to set upon another damp tablet that read, *The shepherd thus-and-so is not guilty of the death of his sheep . . . The will of the gods decreed that they should die from lack of food, because . . .*

And yet he could not avoid Shusuen completely, nor hide from the news his scribe bore him each day. Famine and poverty for the city, and for Sumer: Lot of Ur and all his family had faded into the desert with Erech's money, as had several of their other chief suppliers in other places when they could not meet the contracts they had been given. And now the rumors were growing stranger: the men who came, bedraggled and heartbroken, to the Eanna, told of a great bull, whose breath was the scorching furnace-wind, and whose hooves left huge crevasses in the dried land where he trod. The Bull of Heaven—Inanna's punishment for Erech, the drought that would last seven years without rain or respite: there was no escaping it, by night or day, for the unnatural heat baked the bricks of the *gipar* as hotly and thoroughly as it burned the lands around Erech. And though Gilgamesh had ordered the able-bodied men of the city to keep digging the canals anew, they silted more quickly than they could be shoveled clean, stopping the waters of the river in their tracks so that no plants could be sprinkled green in this season when they ought to be sprouting and burgeoning with life. The only thing that was growing, awesome in the gleaming beauty of its red- and cream-streaked wood, was the cedar gate of Erech: the craftsmen worked into the night, shaping and smoothing the timbers, carving upon them scenes of the victories of Gilgamesh and Enkidu.

Gilgamesh and Enkidu were sitting in the Court of Judgment, listening to yet one more shepherd who had come with the tendons of his dead sheep in a bag slung over his back—sheep who had died of hunger and thirst by the blocked canals, even after Shusuen had ordered the flocks to be drawn in and those who could not be fed to be slaughtered—when the messenger burst into the hall, running down its length to throw himself on his face before Gilgamesh.

"Ensi, I bring dread news: I pray, do not harm me! I have only come to tell you what I have seen."

"Rise, and tell me," Gilgamesh answered. "What have you seen?"

The messenger lifted himself from the floor, but kept his shaven head bowed, so that he did not look his Ensi in the eyes. "I have seen the Bull of Heaven, storming in his heat about the walls of Erech. He snorted, and a crevasse opened in the plain, so great that a hundred men could have been lost in it; he snorted again, and two hundred men could have fallen into the second crevasse. Now he strides about the banks of the Buranun, and as each hoof strikes the earth, the river runs muddier and another wave of silt washes into the canals. My Ensi, exalted of the gods, two-thirds god and one-third man—I have come to you, for no other may save us from the fierceness of the Bull."

Gilgamesh breathed in deeply, letting his breath out in a soft sigh. Now the time was upon him, the time to meet Inanna's revenge face-to-face. And yet he was sure in his safety, for Enkidu sat beside him, and he knew there was nothing that the two of them could not overcome.

"Come, Enkidu," he said. "Let us arm ourselves. We could not battle against sun and wind, nor would any edict force the Buranun to run clear and the canals to open, but if the Bull of Heaven has shown himself—him, we can overcome together, and cast him down as we overwhelmed Huwawa."

Enkidu rose, and smiled, and the look upon his face filled Gilgamesh's heart with strength. "Let us arm ourselves," Enkidu agreed, "and go forth to the Bull."

THE SHAMHATU SAT in her throne before Inanna, listening dully to the noontime chanting. Her strength was exhausted, for since she arose that morning, she had been struggling to keep her mind clear. She had used all the techniques for shielding herself that Geme-Tirash had taught her: she had made herself a wall of polished obsidian, distracting herself within by concentrating on the practical matters of the temple; and when she felt herself growing faint, she grasped the wooden arm of her chair, grounding herself in the roots of the tree it once was. Soon the rite would be over, and then she could eat; she could keep Atab by her, asking him for the gossip of the Eanna. And if she felt herself slipping away too badly, she could drink a sip of the draught the En had made for her—he had warned her against taking too much, or too often, but it would keep her mind clear.

Yet even as she thought that, a sudden wave of dizziness flowed over her, darkening her sight. The power was beating against her from Inanna's statue, overwhelming as a mighty river in flood, and she could not stand against it. Gasping as if she were drowning, the Shamhatu slumped down in her seat. The En reached out to catch her, but her arm pushed him away. Her legs gathered themselves under her; a voice cut through the singing—her own voice, ringing from her mouth against her fading will.

"You priestesses, come forth! Come with me to the walls of Erech, for my champion, the Bull of Heaven, is to do battle for my sake!"

GILGAMESH AND ENKIDU wore no armor, for lightness and speed would be of more worth in this combat than heavy protection. But Enkidu had his axe, and Gilgamesh his sword—the mighty weapons that had overcome Huwawa. And so they went forth from Erech's gates, treading carefully over the deep-cracked plain.

"I hear his snorting," Gilgamesh said. "Let us wait here—I think he will come to me."

The sound of the Bull's snorting grew louder, the hot wind scorching their faces. At last the huge golden shape showed against the horizon, lapis horns lowering as the Bull tossed his head.

"He knows his foes are here," Enkidu said.

The Bull snorted again; the burned earth cracked beneath his breath, huge dry furrows opening themselves under his plough of drought.

"Now, my love!" Gilgamesh cried. "Let us go forth to him."

The Bull turned toward them, trotting heavily forward. Gilgamesh laughed, for now the fears that had overcome him in the night, the sweat that had soaked his sheets and the cramping in muscles that could find no foe to fight against had a single shape: and his sword was light in his hand.

Beneath the Bull's breath, another huge crack opened in the plain. Enkidu stumbled and fell, sinking to his waist in the dry-baked earth. But even before Gilgamesh could cry out, Enkidu had leapt free again, springing toward the Bull. Like a lion springing upon his prey, Enkidu jumped upward, grasping the Bull of Heaven by the horns and somer-saulting over his head, balancing precariously on his back. The Bull's spittle spewed burning-hot over the plain like drops of molten gold; his tail lifted, and his dung scattered out behind him, fist-sized heaps of glowing bronze sinking deep into the earth.

"My friend!" Enkidu shouted. "We have made ourselves great—how shall we overcome him? I have seen his strength; I shall grasp his tail, and we shall share the kill; but you thrust your sword between nape and horns and skull."

With those words Enkidu slid backward, his hands sinking deep into the shining hide of the Bull's tail. The great beast bellowed, dropping his head to hook backward with his huge horns. In that moment of distrac-tion, Gilgamesh ran forward, leaping up with his sword grasped firmly in both hands. The tiny hollow between nape and horn and skull shone bright for him; he stabbed in with all his strength, wrenching his shoul-ders sideways to sever the Bull's spine.

The Bull of Heaven gave one last bellow, flinging his body sideways as if to crush his slayers in his fall. But Gilgamesh and Enkidu both leaped clear, dancing as they landed to keep their footing upon the cracked and shaking plain. Then the Bull's eyes rolled up; his hooves lashed out convulsively, beating at the empty air, and it was over.

Gilgamesh ran around to embrace Enkidu, clasping his lover close to him. "We have done it!" he gasped. "We have slain the Bull of Heaven. The rains will come again, the canals will open their watery mouths— Erech shall live, and all the fears of scribes and priests be set to naught."

And yet, even as he spoke, Gilgamesh heard the wailing rising high and unearthly from the city walls. Although he did not want to, his head turned and his eyes rolled upward to the parapet there, where the songs of mourning howled out over the dry earth.

"Inanna weeps . . ." Enkidu said uncertainly, staring upward.

"She may well, but we, my beloved—" And suddenly Gilgamesh was surprised by the words that sprang forth from his mouth. "Let us offer the heart of the Bull to the god who was true to us in our journeying. If

Inanna wishes us ill, her twin brother Utu wishes us well, and he deserves this gift."

And so Enkidu's axe broke through the great rib-bones of the Bull of Heaven, and Gilgamesh pulled out the heart—so huge that his two hands could not encompass its span, and still quivering with the life-strength of the Bull as he lifted it up to the burning sun. "Utu!" he called. "You who travel across the sky, bearded and long-armed: we have slain the Bull of Heaven, and give you his heart. Mighty god, shining and all-seeing, we make this offering to you. Take it and look well upon us; defend us in the councils of the gods, as we honor you in the affairs of men."

With that, Gilgamesh cast the Bull's heart upward with all his strength. The sun shone bright into his eyes, so that he had to blink as the dark organ reached its zenith; it seemed to him that the light flashed brilliantly, consuming the heart in a single flare, but he had to turn his gaze aside, so he could not see whether it had come down or not.

But the voices of the women rose higher in their song of mourning; and in the brilliant sunlight, Gilgamesh saw the Shamhatu standing upon the wall of Erech—the wall that he had built—with all the priestesses behind her, their curled hair streaming loose in mourning as they bewailed the death of the Bull of Heaven. And even as he and Enkidu sank down, squatting beside the corpse, Gilgamesh heard the voice of Inanna ringing forth over the plain.

"Woe unto Gilgamesh, who spoke ill unto me, who killed the Bull of Heaven!"

At that, Enkidu leapt up, grasping one of the Bull's mighty hind legs. His axe flashed down, severing sinew and joint, and Enkidu's muscles bunched as he flung the Bull's hindquarter up at the city walls. His face twisted into a mask of rage as he shouted, "If I could reach you, I would do the same to you! I would hang his guts over your arms."

Gilgamesh ran to Enkidu, grasping him from behind. He was not strong enough to pull down the other man's mighty arms, but Enkidu gave up at his touch, letting Gilgamesh hold him back.

"Hush, Enkidu," Gilgamesh said. "Hush. I am alive, I am here . . . let them moan as they will, for we are together."

Enkidu turned, holding Gilgamesh close. The thick hair of his body scratched softly against Gilgamesh's chest; the Ensi could feel Enkidu's heart beating hard beneath his heavy muscles.

"We are together, and we have slain the Bull of Heaven," Enkidu repeated softly. "Let us call the men of the city, let us celebrate what we have done."

Gilgamesh sent out the orders that a feast should be readied in the *gipar,* and to it he invited the men who had gone with him at the slaying of Huwawa, and as many of the other bright young soldiers who had fought in his war as his halls would hold: the Bull of Heaven would provide meat for them all. Then he called together the craftsmen of Erech, who sawed the lapis horns from the Bull and wondered at their beauty.

"Thirty minas of lapis lazuli in each," said the Eanna's chief worker of fine stone. The muscles of his shoulders bunched beneath the grizzled hair that grew thickly over his body as he lifted up one of the great horns, turning it this way and that in his broad-fingered, stubby hands. The lapis gleamed dark in the sunlight, sprinkled through with tiny glittering flecks of gold like a scattering of stars across the night sky. "Thirty minas, at least, and plated two fingers thick; and they will hold six measures of oil together, I would guess. What do you mean to do with these treasures you have won, my Ensi? Do you wish me to carve them, or take the stone and shape and set it?"

"I shall take these horns," Gilgamesh said thoughtfully, "and fill them with oil; I shall hang them up in the shrine of my ancestors, as an offering to my father Lugalbanda, who watches over me, that he who was Ensi shall know how well his son protects the city."

And this he did: he bore the horns to his bedchamber, which had been Lugalbanda's before him, and had brackets of bright silver set in the wall for them, and filled them with sweet-scented oil, so that their perfume filled the whole chamber.

"Lugalbanda," Gilgamesh said, "Enkidu and I have done what no others could do, nor any man alone. Even from the wrath of the gods— even from the Bull of Heaven, we have saved Erech. The rains shall come; the canals run free of mud, and the young plants sprout by the waterside again. Speak you to the great gods, in honor of what we have done."

Turning to leave, he nearly tripped over Shusuen, whose slender body was well-hidden in the shadows of the hallway.

"What are you doing here?" Gilgamesh asked. "Did you see the battle?"

"I stood on the walls of Erech beside the Shamhatu," Shusuen answered. "I saw all that came to pass, and all will be written down. You are unbelievable, Gilgamesh! Is there no dare that you will not take, or challenge that you will not meet, even if it is the gods who cast it down before you? And yet you have slain the Bull of Heaven—and I think you have bought Erech's freedom from hunger and debt, if the gods do not send another curse against us." The scribe's voice was soft, wondering, as though he did not yet dare to trust the promise of relief from his months-long burden of measuring stores and issuing orders and struggling to balance the Eanna's accounts against the threat of the seven-years' famine.

"Put on your finest clothes," Gilgamesh told Shusuen, "and prepare to go before the people. Enkidu and I will arm ourselves fully again, and ride through the streets in triumph; you shall ride in front in your own chariot, crying out the news that the Bull of Heaven is dead."

"That news is known already, for the priestesses of Inanna are bewailing it from the top of Erech's walls, and progressing all around the city as they mourn."

"Then we shall make it a progress of rejoicing. If the women mourn the fallen foe, let the men celebrate the victory!"

Gilgamesh and Enkidu dressed once more in the glittering gold and bronze of battle. Together they went to the great gate of the city, where the cedar-timbers stood half carved—where their woodcarvers were already sketching out the battle with the Bull of Heaven on the upper parts of the posts. The smell of cedar was rich in the air, its clean perfume sending Gilgamesh back sharply for a moment to the towering mountains, their green-carpeted slopes stretching high above his head and the fresh wind blowing down. The joy of swinging the glittering axe with all his strength, feeling it bite deep into the wood . . . the trickles of sweat down forehead and back, cooled by mountain air . . . the easy laughter of the men who worked with him, fearless before the drying head of Huwawa, and the endless pleasure of embracing Enkidu beneath the scented green boughs . . . But that was past, like a twig swept on the Buranun's flood. Only the great gleaming timbers still leaned against Erech's walls as proof of those days in the cedar forest, the enduring skeleton of a memory, with the smell of cedar rising around the huge wooden bones like offering-smoke.

The chariots were waiting there. Shusuen already sat in his, its canopy shading his fair skin from the hammering heat of the sun. As on their journey, his cat was crouched on his lap, seeming to care little about the noise of the priestesses wailing from the walls or the hammering and sawing of the butchers. Then, as Gilgamesh got closer, he saw that the cat was chewing on something—on a large scrap of bloody meat.

"Is the flesh of the Bull of Heaven to be fed to cats?" he asked Shusuen indignantly.

The scribe gestured gracefully with one long-fingered hand. "You gave orders that it should be prepared as a feast for the brave young men of Erech. How can you complain if one of the bravest, who came with you to the cedar forest, and gave you good advice on the way, prefers his portion rather less cooked?"

"That is wise," Enkidu said unexpectedly. "Bloody meat is the strongest."

Gilgamesh reached out to stroke his lover's bearded cheek beneath the bronze rim of his helmet. "Would you like some? You may eat freely, my love."

"Not for myself . . . I dwell within the city walls and eat cooked meat now. But I will claim a piece to set out for my friend the lion and his pride, for they are not far. Though they have taken shelter for the day, he roared to me last night."

"As you will, beloved. There is enough for lions and warriors both."

Gilgamesh helped Enkidu to cut off a share of meat for his wild comrades, setting it out beneath the sparse shade of a tamarisk tree. Then the two of them washed their hands in the Buranun, thin trails of the Bull's blood streaming into the brown water like little bright-dyed threads slowly weaving into a plain warp. Arms about each other's waists, Gilgamesh and Enkidu walked back to their chariot, mounting up. Shusuen urged his own wain on, shouting so that his voice would carry beneath the moaning wail of the priestesses on the city wall.

"Rejoice! Gilgamesh has slain the Bull of Heaven; Enkidu has slain the Bull of Heaven! Rejoice, for victory is given; the heroes of Erech are victorious! Rejoice in Huwawa's slayers, who overcame Agga of Kish; the mighty they have cast down, and they have defended the weak."

The people of Erech thronged thickly in the street, their cries nearly drowning out Shusuen's voice. Though there were no fresh flowers for them to throw, they lifted cups of beer and date-wine, raising offering-saucers of butter and oil and honey to Gilgamesh and Enkidu as they passed. Gilgamesh heard the strumming of lyres, the banging of drums and ringing clash of cymbals in the streets, and now and again the long note of a curled ram's horn blowing. The noise seemed to lift him up, the whole city gleaming golden in his sun-dazzled eyes, and the strength and joy swelled in his body, so that he cried out to the people of Erech, a great boast whose simple words seemed to encompass all Shusuen's praise-poems and songs of his deeds, all the carved reliefs of stone and wood and ivory, like a single drop of cedar oil awakening the whole vision of the for-est: "Who is the best-shaped of heroes? Who is the strongest of men? . . . Gilgamesh is the best-shaped of heroes! Enkidu is the strongest of men!"

So it was, already drunk and flushed with triumph, that Gilgamesh and Enkidu led the troop of young men into the great hall of the *gipar*. The vats of beer and wine already stood about the hall, their heady breath mingling with the scent of the dried rushes on the floor, sweet flag and spikenard giving up their perfume as the feet of the men crushed them. Plates of hot bread steamed on the long tables between bowls of butter and honey and platters of cheese, the offerings set out for the Ensi to be shared by his followers this day. The musicians were gathered behind the twin thrones of Gilgamesh and Enkidu, and as the two of them entered, the song of praise began.

"Hail to Gilgamesh: a hero from his mother's womb was he!
Hail to Enkidu, a mighty man from his day of birth!
Fierce-eyed lion, born of the plains,

Ruler of the four corners of the earth,
Trustworthy, lords of all the lands,
Herdsmen and shepherds of the black-haired people,
Son of Ninsun, open-jawed lion of Utu . . ."

Gilgamesh led his beloved to his throne, lifting off his helmet and taking the many-horned crown of the Ensi from Enatarzi to set on his head in its place. Hands filled their golden cup with date-wine, lifting morsels of bread and honey to their mouths, as the warriors crowded close with their congratulations.

The celebration lasted long into the night. Gilgamesh's cooks had roasted the Bull of Heaven with mustard seeds and honey; its flesh was surprisingly tender, rare and savory, so that everyone swore they had never eaten better. The empty vats of drink were carried away and fresh ones brought, until some of the young men were ready to stagger home, while others dozed away on the couches that had been set up in the hall. At last Gilgamesh and Enkidu, too, made their way to their chamber, embracing and rolling together on the bed in drunken delight as they stripped the clothes from each other's body. Enkidu's mouth was warm and sweet, rich with the tastes of the Bull's flesh and date-wine; his soft touching and murmuring were the finest of pleasures to Gilgamesh, until at last the two of them fell asleep, their limbs still twined together beneath the thin linen coverlet.

IT SEEMED TO Enkidu suddenly that he stood within a great hall, pillared like the shrine of Inanna, except that the pillars were of living cedarwood, inlaid with cones of gold and lapis and carnelian, and the light that shone from the roof was so splendid that he could not look upon it. Yet he was cold as he had never been, his bones shivering within his flesh, and his limbs were frozen with fear, as if he stood again before the gates guarded by the splendor of Huwawa. Before him, raised high upon a dais of gleaming white stone, were four thrones, and the men seated upon them were many times the height of human men, their faces hidden by the brightness that radiated from beneath their high horned crowns. One wore a robe the color of the blue-black night sky, and far-off stars glimmered in its folds; from the sleeves of the second streamed rivers of freshwater with little fish swimming along them; the thunder-gray robes of the third were wind-whipped, as though he were garbed in a storm; golden rays shone from the shoulders of the fourth, and he held a pruning-saw in his right hand. Slowly their names came to Enkidu, vibrating through the tumult and awe in his mind as he looked upon them. An, Enki, Enlil, and Utu: four of the greatest gods sat there at their council, in the hall of the heavens.

*Where is Inanna?* Enkidu wondered. *Should she not come among them?* And then, *Why am I here? Why have they summoned me?*

But the gods did not look upon him or speak to him. Their terrible glances fixed only upon each other, and beside them Enkidu felt insub-stantial and shadowy as a wisp of mist rising from a waterhole beneath the morning sun. When they spoke, their voices sounded through his body, shaking him so he feared he would be torn to pieces, but he could not speak to beg them cease, or lift a hand to beg their mercy.

*BECAUSE THEY HAVE SLAIN THE BULL OF HEAVEN,* said the sky-garbed An, *AND HUWAWA THEY HAVE SLAIN—FOR THAT REA-SON, THE ONE WHO STRIPPED THE MOUNTAIN OF ITS CEDAR MUST DIE.*

Enkidu would have cried out then, but no sound came from his lips. For if the gods deemed that Gilgamesh must die . . . He could not think beyond that, nor guess what might befall himself and Erech.

Yet Enlil lifted up his arm, his storm-robe swirling. He spoke with the bellow of a wild bull over the plains—the bellow Enkidu had heard in his shrine in Nippur, but now shaped into words by the human throat he wore.

*LET ENKIDU DIE,* he replied. *BUT GILGAMESH SHALL NOT DIE.*

Then Utu arose, standing before Enlil, and his light shattered into rainbow-beams across the other god's stormy darkness. His voice was bright and mellow as the sounding of a brass trumpet, a sudden warmth after the cold of An and Enlil's speech.

*WAS IT NOT BY MY ORDER THAT THEY SLEW THE BULL OF HEAVEN AND HUWAWA?* Utu argued. Could Enkidu have moved, he would have fallen on his knees before him—Inanna's brother, the protector who had gone before them in the wilderness; even now, Enkidu could see that Utu held the heart of the Bull of Heaven in his left hand, and the sight filled him with a sudden hope. *It was he who brought me here,* Enkidu thought, even as Utu said, SHOULD NOW INNOCENT *ENKIDU DIE?*

But Enlil turned toward him in anger, and the clouds of his robe swelled and streamed out as though the wind of his wrath were tearing them to tatters from within, dimming Utu's brightness.

*BECAUSE YOU TRAVELED DAILY WITH THEM AS A COMRADE—THIS DOES NOT FREE THEM FROM GUILT. YOU CANNOT SAVE THEM FROM WHAT WE DECREE HERE, NOR WILL INANNA STAND TO PROTECT THEM.*

Then it seemed to Enkidu that he was hurled suddenly away, falling through a great black void. He cried out, but he could not hear his own voice—until the scream jerked him awake, sitting bolt upright in the sweat-soaked bed with Gilgamesh beside him.

"Enkidu?" Gilgamesh cried out anxiously. "Enkidu, what is wrong?"

His lover's hand was very cool against Enkidu's forehead, soothing away the nauseating dizziness of heat that swept through him in great waves. The dripping linen sheet stank of sickness; Enkidu tore it from himself, casting it away, and the movement exhausted him so that he had to sink down in the bed again.

"My beloved," he said weakly, "why are the great gods in council? I dreamed . . ."

Slowly, tearing the words from his mouth like lengths of sinew stuck chokingly in his throat, Enkidu told Gilgamesh of his dream.

GILGAMESH LISTENED, STUNNED, to what Enkidu was saying. He could not believe it—and yet Enkidu's face was white and damp as long-soaked linen, his lover's skin burning like heated bronze beneath his touch.

"My brother, my dear brother," Gilgamesh choked, "why should they absolve me at the cost of my brother?"

"And now must I become a ghost?" Enkidu wondered feverishly. "To sit with the ghosts of the dead, to never see my dear brother again?"

Gilgamesh lay down beside him, his body comfortingly cool as he embraced Enkidu. "My beloved, why has your heart said such strange things—a true dream of great fear? Your limbs are still as one touched by a god; I fear the dream is true. For the living it brings sorrow, the dream causes the living to mourn. I will pray to the great gods, I will search for your god and turn to him. I will go to the father of the gods; I will go to Enlil and plead for you. I will make your statue of gold beyond measure . . ."

His voice trailed off. Yes, he had feared to lose Enkidu in battle, as warriors ever feared to lose their friends—but the words they spoke now were not like battle, where the fear of death could be put off by girding on armor, by lifting axe and sword and reminding themselves of their own strength against the foe. What could he now do against the sickness that shook his lover's body, save call Enatarzi to bring clean sheets and cool water to keep Enkidu covered and soothe away the worst of the fever burning through him?

"And send for the En," Gilgamesh said when the eunuch had finished rearranging the bed-linens. "Tell him to bring all of his medical tools, for Erech has more need of his healing skills now than it ever will."

It was not long before the En arrived, three of his striped cats writhing around his feet. As he looked at Enkidu—now resting quietly with a damp cloth across his forehead—his face grew graver.

"Do you hurt in any one place?" he asked.

"My body aches all over," Enkidu replied, and the soft unsureness of his lover's voice pressed against Gilgamesh's heart, for though Gilgamesh had seen Enkidu frightened before, he had never seen him so cast down.

The En bent over the bed, his fingers lightly probing Enkidu's body beneath the thin sheet. Enkidu groaned a little, and moved away from his touch; once or twice he reached out a hand, as if to beg the En to stop. "It hurts wherever you touch me," Enkidu murmured. "But there is no pain sharper than any other."

At last the En straightened up. "I cannot feel that any of his organs are distressed," he said to Gilgamesh. "A poultice will be of little use as yet . . . Have boiling water brought, and I shall make an infusion that may bring his fever down."

Gilgamesh caught at the old man's elbow, the bones sticklike and brittle beneath his hand. "What is the matter?" he demanded. "What is wrong, and how can you heal him?"

The En shook his head. "I do not know, save that he is fevered and much distressed. Keep him cool and comfortable, as best you may."

The old priest made his infusion, steeping dried leaves and seeds and a spoonful of pungent mashed root in the boiling water. He murmured over the thick-rimmed clay jug as the herbs floated in it—words in a language Gilgamesh did not know, perhaps the tongue of the Black Land. One of the cats leapt up onto the bed, sniffing at Enkidu's face and raising a plaintive cry; the other two joined it from the floor.

"They sense . . ." Enkidu whispered, but did not go on. But a cold serpent of dread coiled about Gilgamesh's heart, for he knew what his lover was thinking: that the cats sensed the truth of Enkidu's awful dream.

When the En was done, he stopped the jug and handed it to Gilgamesh. "Two spoonfuls of this, now and whenever his fever rises again. Call me if there is any change."

Tasting the medicine, Enkidu's nose wrinkled as if to spit it out, but he gagged it down, and Gilgamesh held up a cup of water for him so that he could wash the taste away. Enkidu coughed and swallowed, and Gilgamesh saw a little color coming back to his white cheeks.

"If yesterday I had known that this should befall . . ."

"Should we not have gone out to the Bull of Heaven?" Gilgamesh asked. "I would have gone out alone to meet him—or let Erech linger beneath his breath as long as I must, if it was needed for your sake."

Enkidu shook his head, and Gilgamesh could see that even the brushing of his disheveled hair against the pillow hurt him. "No. It is only that there are things I might have done, matters I might have seen to. I would have left the celebrations for a little time last night, to speak with Sululi and play with Ur-Lugal; I might have visited the house of Gunidu, to greet him and Akalla and Innashagga—I had always meant to give them gifts in thanks for guesting me for so long, but there were so many other things to do, and I never seemed to find a fit time. But I am glad we were together; it would have been unbearable to pass up the chance of our last night of joy."

"There will be time yet," Gilgamesh said desperately. "You will recover and be well; you will have all the time in the world with wife and child—and with me." He went on, telling Enkidu of his plans for the future: how he would order a house built in which he and Enkidu and Sululi and Ur-Lugal might live together; Enkidu might see to the choosing and carving of the reliefs that ornamented it himself, for Gilgamesh knew how such craftsmanship joyed him. He spoke of how there would be other children to play about their feet in the safety of the Eanna; of the hunting of the wild boar, which were growing fiercer and more numerous in the swamplands; of the festivals that were coming up in the next year, with all their music and pageantry . . . There would be much to do, with Enkidu by his side.

At last Enkidu's breathing slowed, slipping into sleep. Now and again he would turn as if, even in his slumbers, the aching of his body in any position crept deep enough to cover him, but presently he began to snore softly.

Gilgamesh watched him for a time, and then left the room. He went to demand one of the Eanna's sheep—easy enough to do, for there was a flock penned for the slaughter just outside the *gipar*. Though the sheep were thin, their sides covered with hanging scabs of matted wool, he took the best of the rams, leading it to the temple of An.

"I have brought this for a sacrifice," he said roughly to the pale-faced priest who greeted him at the door. "Bring to me what I need, then go, for I wish to be alone here."

With the sheep's hot blood covering his hands, the Ensi knelt, staring up at the overlapping pairs of horns adorning the high-rising cap upon the altar. Though the craftsmen of the shrines delighted in showing the gods as clearly as they might, fine-carved stone and wood bringing forth the might of divinity, that men might look upon it and be awed, An was too lofty and remote for such simple shapes: most felt that his power could be seen only in the overarching heavens, too high for mortals to gauge or fathom. Now Gilgamesh felt his resentment splashing forth, warm and steaming as the blood that had gushed from the ram's throat.

"It was you who did this!" he cried. "It was you who shaped the Bull of Heaven, whose mighty sinews and burning heat stemmed from you alone—why did you not hold to your decree that I should die, and leave Enkidu in peace after me?"

Yet no answer came. Gilgamesh had only the silence of the shrine, and the crowned altar with a still flame burning to either side. Was he of too little note to answer—or had, as he feared, the answer come already: the words written that no man could erase, scriven deep into the Tablet of Destinies that Enlil held and read forth?

After a time, Gilgamesh rose, going forth from the shrine: the priests and priestesses of An would tend to the body of his sacrifice. Now it was a bull he called for, white-pelted and high-horned, with four men to lead it forth to the shrine of Enlil.

This shrine was like the one in Nippur, though not one-half so great: Enlil's statue sat enthroned alone upon the dais, and the scents were less costly and penetrating. Since he could not offer up the bull alone, Gilgamesh did not dare to speak his prayers aloud, but the anger hummed through his arm as he swung the heavy mallet to jar crashingly between the bull's horns, stunning the great beast, and as he stabbed at the nape of the skull to sever its spine with a single blow—just as he had done with the Bull of Heaven—his cry rang out in silence.

*Enlil, all men must die—but why now, why thus? You decreed my death: was that not enough for you? Give us respite, that we may enjoy our lives.*

But the bull on the ground before Gilgamesh was only cooling meat, as if he had slain it for any of the butcher-shops in the city, instead of in the shrine of a god; its blood shone neither as offering nor as prayer, but only as a sticky mess darkening his bronze sword and staining the floor, with flies already beginning to buzz toward it. He cleaned his blade and sheathed it, going back to the Eanna.

Yet, though his worry for Enkidu hastened his footsteps, he found himself turning away from his own chambers, as if to avoid seeing once more the still figure of his lover in his painful sleep. *This I must do for him,* Gilgamesh told himself, as though to assuage the prickles of guilt tingling through his feet. *It will bring him joy.*

Sululi was with the weaving-women, as she was every day, guiding the warps and wefts of the others when her hands were not busy with her own loom. The huntsman's wife squatted on the floor watching, though the newborn babe nursing at her breast told why she was not working herself.

"Come," Gilgamesh said to her.

The blood dropped from Sululi's face, her cheeks suddenly sallow and pale as yellow clay. "What is wrong?" she asked softly. "Has some ill befallen?"

"Come," Gilgamesh said again, and she rose, following him without word or question until they were outside.

"Has something happened to Enkidu?" Sululi asked then. In the fear-tinged pleading of her voice, Gilgamesh heard the girl she had been on her wedding night; he thought unwillingly of all the pain he had caused her, and his tongue moved heavily in his mouth as he spoke.

"He is ill—very ill, but I hope he will recover. But he spoke of you, and I think he will be glad to have you beside him. Fetch such belongings as you need, and bring Ur-Lugal with you, and come to my chamber. I dare not move him, so you must stay with us."

"I will come—oh, gladly, for I would do anything for Enkidu! Only . . . how long do you think it will be? Has the En seen him, or any doctor?"

"The En has seen him. He does not know."

"I will come," Sululi repeated. "Tell him that we are coming."

Gilgamesh watched her go, her slim back straight as if she bore a basket of heavy bricks balanced upon the coiled pile of her black hair. Then he heard the shouting and turned, running as fast as he could, each step pumping the blood through his heart like searing venom.

"Lion!" someone cried. "A wild lion, within the Eanna! Fetch Gilgamesh, it is the Ensi's right alone . . ."

*To slay the lion,* Gilgamesh thought; but his feet turned first toward his own chamber, to be sure that Enkidu was well. *If he has died alone . . .*

But when he got there, Enkidu was still alive, though his breathing had sunk to a hoarse rasp. And beside him lay the lion: his old friend from the wild, the tabby-mark upon his forehead to prove that it was the same beast that had come back with them from the hunt.

Enkidu opened his eyes, reaching out as if to caress the lion's fur. His arm sank; his hand lay limply on the tawny golden pelt.

"This is strange," he said vaguely. "Lions leave the sick, to live or die by themselves . . . there is no room in the pack . . ."

"He loves you," Gilgamesh answered. "As we all do. Rest, my beloved. Sululi is coming, and our child with her. You shall not be left alone."

He leaned over to kiss Enkidu's lips—already cracking with fever, like mud below the burning sun. The lion made a soft noise; not a growl, more of a deep chirrup of greeting. Gilgamesh lifted the warm cloth from Enkidu's forehead, dampening it in the bowl of cool water and laying it back over him.

"Rest," he said again. "Rest, for you must get well."

BUT THE SECOND day Enkidu was no better. The En's potion no longer eased his fever, no matter how often Gilgamesh and Sululi spooned it into him; he could not move his legs at all, and he said that there was a painful prickling in his fingers and toes, as though he were walking upon thorns. Gilgamesh turned back the bedclothes, holding Enkidu's hands in his and stroking them gently. They seemed the same mighty hands that had wielded axe and spear so powerfully, handled the reins of his chariot with such light skill and joy: blunt-nailed and callused, with tiny curls of golden hair upon the backs—the same that had caressed him, their strength restrained to the gentle patting of a padded paw—and yet he could see the pain in Enkidu's face from the little invisible thorns piercing him, and it seemed worse because there was no sign of wounding or sickness visible upon hands or feet.

Furious, and more frightened, Gilgamesh sent out for the great physicians of Erech, calling them to the sickroom with promises of gold for whoever should succeed in healing Enkidu. One by one they came, dressed in their fine robes, shaven-headed or with luxurious torrents of ringlets. Each by each, casting nervous glances at the lion who lay asleep by the foot of the bed, they prodded at Enkidu's body until he moaned and tried to turn his face away. But Gilgamesh was firm with Enkidu: the physicians must look at him, for they would be able to help where the En had failed.

*And did he fail because he chose to?* The niggling thought went through Gilgamesh's mind as he waited outside in the corridor while yet another healer carried out his examinations of Enkidu's body. If the gods had spoken to him—or worse yet: what if the Eanna had decided that it was well for Enkidu to die, that the Ensi henceforth have nothing to turn his mind from the dull duties and heavy burdens of the Ensiship, no love to turn his face away from the deceptive promises of Inanna and toward the hope of life and such happiness as any simple man might know?

"They will not win," Gilgamesh said aloud, clenching his fists. Though the En, with the healing arts he had learned in the Black Land, was the most famed of physicians in Erech, there were others nearly as good, and more trustworthy: they would know of Enkidu's illness, and how to heal it.

"What are you speaking of?" Shusuen asked.

Gilgamesh whirled, his hand upraised in startlement as though to strike the scribe. Shusuen backed off a pace, bowing low; his cat scurried away from his feet as if it had suddenly roused a sleeping mastiff.

"That is none of your concern. Have you no duties, that you are here at this hour when you should be recording cases in the Court of Judgment?"

"And you—" Shusuen stopped—wisely, for Gilgamesh knew that he would have struck him if Shusuen had reproached him with his absence from the daily affairs of the city. "I have come looking for you, that I may fulfill my duties." His chin indicated the stack of clay tablets he held close to his chest. "These must have your seal upon them before the clay dries, that the decrees may be carried out."

"What are they? Another stack of shepherds whose flocks have died in the bad weather?"

"Shepherds, and merchants begging for time before they must fulfill their contracts, since the goods they need cannot be had this year—I have already weeded out the lazy and greedy; these are the ones which I have proven to be well-founded, whose petitions are worthy of granting. You have only to roll your seal upon them, and then I will leave you."

The last physician stepped out from under the door-frame, wiping something sticky from his plump fingers with a fine cloth of embroidered linen. He went down on one knee for a moment, heaving his corpulent little body up again with some difficulty.

"Ensi, exalted ruler of Erech, I have examined the patient thoroughly. It seems to me that the fault lies in his liver, and I have rubbed it with oil and crushed turtle-shell; I have made up a medicine of beer and pulverized pears, cucumber seeds and thyme, mixed with the oil of river bitumen, and that he is to drink twice a day. But his state is grievous, and his recovery may be long."

"Thank you for your services," Gilgamesh said coldly. The physician bowed and bustled off, the leather bag of remedies and tools over his shoulder swinging from side to side like a cow's full dugs as he hurried away. Gilgamesh was about to walk into the room, but Shusuen coughed lightly.

"Gilgamesh, your seal . . ."

Suddenly filled with unreasoning fury, Gilgamesh turned on the scribe, shouting in his face, "How dare you disturb me with these matters now!" He scrabbled in his belt-purse, pulling out the little cylinder of carved lapis, and cast it at Shusuen. With his mark so close, the violence of his arm threw his aim off. The seal bounced off the wall by the scribe's head, clattering down the hall until Shusuen's cat sprang from the shadows to pounce upon it. Shusuen ran to pick the seal up, and Gilgamesh turned his back on him, going in to Enkidu.

The air in the chamber was so thick that Gilgamesh could hardly breathe: to hide the stink of Enkidu's sickness and the musk of the lion, two of the physicians had burned aromatic incense, its heavy sweetness overlying the sharp smells of bitumen and scorching roots, resins and crushed seeds. Clay jars now lined the floor beside two walls, with a little tablet of instructions for use lying at the foot of each, as though the bedroom had become a doctor's whole store of remedies. White bandages wrapped Enkidu's chest and abdomen, hands and feet, and a different poultice stained each. The beads of sweat stood out sharply against his pale forehead, and his face twisted as he struggled to breathe. Suddenly he turned his head to the side, spewing out a thin blackish gout of vomit that splashed across the bed-linens and the floor.

Gilgamesh held Enkidu's head until he had finished, then wiped the bite from his lips and kissed him. Enkidu's mouth was bitter with the medicines that had been poured down him, his breath foul from sickness, but Gilgamesh did not turn away.

"Are you any better, my love?" he asked anxiously. "Are the poultices helping?"

"They burn against my skin. I do not know if that is good or bad."

"It must be good; I have heard it said that it is the healing power of the medicines that heats them."

"But . . ." Enkidu caught feebly at Gilgamesh's wrists with a bandaged hand. ". . . no more of the potions they left for me. They taste foul, and turn my stomach, and leave me feeling more dizzy and sick than before."

"Enkidu, my love . . ." Gilgamesh stroked back the sweat-damp hair from his lover's forehead. "Medicines are often hard to take, but you will be the better for them. Sululi has gone to the market to get fresh fruit, to cool your throat and nourish you a little, and when you have eaten that, it will be easier for you to keep your medicine down. And you must do that, beloved, for you must live."

WHEN SHUSUEN HAD signed and delivered the tablets, he went back to the chambers of the En. The old man was carefully grinding a mixture of fresh and dried herbs with a mortar and pestle; over the little fire in his room bubbled a pot of water, and two thin strips of precious papyrus from the Black Land lay upon his table, the red ink of the carefully drawn pictures slowly drying. Basthotep sniffed at the other cats, then began circling one of them, soft growls issuing from his throat.

"There will be a fight in a moment, if I am not mistaken," the En said. "My queen Nefereremkhet will soon be in heat, and the toms have been discussing the matter of who will breed with her all day, though the lady herself favors none of them as yet."

Shusuen bent down to scoop his cat up, but Basthotep squirmed out of his arms, running under the bed.

"But you have not come to breed cats, my great-grandson. From the look of your face, I think you have been with Gilgamesh and Enkidu."

"I have," Shusuen admitted. "And matters are not going well there."

"No. Enkidu is dying."

Shusuen stared at the old man, shocked at the fact so baldly stated. "He is ill," Shusuen stammered. "Gilgamesh has been calling in the physicians."

"Who have muttered over Enkidu, and poulticed him, and put medicines down his throat, and cannot say—if they are honest—what is wrong."

"I heard only the last, who thought that his liver was sick. But that is true."

"I am making a medicine that may bring him some relief. That is all we can do for Enkidu now: comfort him and ease his pain as best we may. Have you seen him?"

"I . . . no. No. I did not dare to ask Gilgamesh to let me in." For a moment images of others sick to death crossed Shusuen's mind: his mother, twisting and writhing in pain around the swollen crab-growth that had invaded her belly and eaten her alive from within; the young soldiers he had helped tend after the war, moaning for water as they burned with fever from their green-swollen wounds; an old priest of the Eanna dying of lung-fever, eyes bright as drops of water in the sunlight and his breath rattling like a loose wagon-wheel in his chest as he struggled for each gasp of air . . . He could not reconcile those images with the others that still lighted his heart, the sight of Enkidu standing tall and golden in Gilgamesh's chariot, or Enkidu leaning over his own shoulder as he wrote, green eyes rapt in fascination, and the nearness of his powerful body overwhelming and comforting as a great pillar of sandstone warmed by the sun. Shusuen did not want to see the lion-man lying on a bed of sickness, Enkidu's easy grin twisted to a grimace of agony and his muscular limbs weak against the illness raging through him. Shusuen had already mourned quietly for Gilgamesh since the night of the eclipse, readying his heart for what must surely come; when Gilgamesh and Enkidu had gone out against the Bull of Heaven, he had steeled himself to see the Ensi's blood sinking into the dry cracks of the plain. But this was a new pain, scoring bright across him as a knife-edge cutting freshly through a healing scar, and he was still reeling from the twin blows of *Enkidu is dying* and *Perhaps Gilgamesh will not die.*

"There is no doubt of it," the En said. He laid a hand upon Shusuen's shoulder. Even in the warmth of the chamber, the old man's touch was dry and cold, and Shusuen could feel that the En had grown more feeble in the past months. "I have seen my share of death. None of the friends of my youth live yet, save the one priest Menhotep in the Black Land—he has not yet answered my last letter, but travelers to and from that country grow less frequent, and if he were dead, I would know of it: I would have felt his passing. But all the rest—battle and sickness and age have all taken their share, and left none behind save myself. So it comes to pass with all men, and often those who seem mightiest are first to die, while those who are sickly in youth, and frail all their lives, may live on to see great-grandchildren: for the Tablet of Destinies does not often give clear signs as to the fate of any man, and the strength to run or fight or lift is not always the same as the strength to endure. And yet . . ."

"And yet?"

"We must mourn for Enkidu—and give thanks to the gods that the doom was not, as we feared earlier, laid upon Gilgamesh."

"You are relieved," Shusuen accused. But even as he spoke, the dreadful realization came to his mind, *I am, too.*

A younger man might have flinched at the words. The En did not even blink his wrinkled eyelids.

"I am relieved," he said quietly. "Chaos will not come to Erech; the city will recover from the blows that have been dealt to it. Enkidu brought us joy, but he did not, as we hoped, temper Gilgamesh's overreaching heart. Instead he dared the Ensi on to wild deed after wild deed—not by his own will, for his counsels were far more sensible than Gilgamesh's, but by his presence, and the results were the same. Erech will be quieter and sadder without Enkidu, but it is only in calm that she will steady, and, we may hope, Gilgamesh steady with her."

Still it shocked Shusuen, to hear Enkidu so calmly given up to death. But he could not deny the truth of the En's words.

"Now," the old priest went on, "this shall be ready in a little time. Perhaps if you are not too busy, you will do me the favor of bearing it to the chamber where Enkidu lies."

"I will do that," Shusuen said.

But first—for he had seen the rage that twisted Gilgamesh's face as the Ensi hurled the cylinder-seal at him, and felt his own death before him for a second—Shusuen called the chief physician of Erech, Ur-Gula, to his own chamber.

The doctor came quickly, for he had been called to attend Shusuen before, when the tightness in the scribe's lungs had halted his breathing like the owl-talons of a *lilitu*-demon closing about his chest. The penetrating scent of the poultice he made for Shusuen preceded him into the little room, like a breath of incense rising from the robes of a priest. Even looking upon him, Shusuen found himself breathing a little easier. Ur-Gula was a tall man in his late middle years, short silver hair brushed back from his high forehead; for all the heat, he still wore a dignified cloak of dark wool fastened at his shoulder with a little dog-headed electrum pin.

"You are troubled," Ur-Gula said as he entered, his kindly voice soft and deep. "I can hear that your lungs are tightening again, and you are very pale. It is well that you called for me before the fit grew worse."

"It is not—" Shusuen began, but the first wheezing in his lungs stopped his words.

Ur-Gula put a firm hand on the scribe's chest, pressing him down to the bed. "Lie down, and do not try to talk until the poultice has had a little time to take effect."

But the impatience to speak was squeezing his rib-bones tighter when they should have been loosening, until Shusuen had to wheeze out, "Honored physician, listen to me—I must speak to you."

Ur-Gula sighed resignedly, sitting down on the bed beside Shusuen. "What is it that has distressed you so?"

"You were with Enkidu earlier this morning. I know you must have been, for Gilgamesh would have summoned you first, before any of the others came."

The physician's dark eyes closed a moment, the furrowed line between his thick gray brows deepening. "I was indeed with Enkidu," he answered. "I looked over him as best I could, even with the lion lying by him and raising his head to growl whenever my touch caused Enkidu pain. I do not know what illness he suffers, for I have never seen its like before. I could recommend nothing but cool cloths and a decoction to keep his fever down—I dread," he added dryly, "to think what some of my colleagues may have done, in greater hopes of success."

"Is he dying?" Shusuen asked, a sudden desperate flash of hope convulsing his bowels. *The En could have been wrong, he is an old man.*

"It is not the part of a physician to tell such news to all who ask," Ur-Gula said gravely. "You, Gilgamesh's scribe, should know the virtue of confidentiality above all."

Shusuen tried to raise himself on his elbows, to protest his need to know, for the sake of all he must do, but Ur-Gula pressed him down again.

"Patience, young man. Yes, I will tell you. Enkidu is dying, and, save the gods lift their hand from him, there is nothing anyone can do."

"Did you tell Gilgamesh?"

The look of sadness on the physician's face deepened, like frost slowly cooling onto grass in the darkness of a winter morning. "Would you have dared?"

"No. And therefore I called you . . . therein lies my fear for you, you and all your colleagues. The Ensi is not himself. Already he is maddened with fear, like an elephant trapped in a pit, and therefore—"

The physician lifted his hand—strong and square, stained with the potions of his calling like a badge of office inked into the skin. "You need say no more. I shall leave for Nippur in the morning, and send the warning to the other physicians of this city. For it will not be long, I fear, before it is clear to Gilgamesh that there is nothing our arts can do for his friend. But as for you," he went on, "there is no reason why you may not live on for a good time, if you are more careful with yourself.

Do not force yourself to work too hard, which you have clearly been doing; keep yourself away from those things which quicken your heart and your breath too hard, and be sure that you get a full night's sleep for each day's passing. And whenever you feel your chest tightening, you must go at once to your chamber and lie down with one of the poultices that I shall leave for you, thinking of nothing that is not peaceful until the fit has passed. Will you promise me that?"

"I cannot," Shusuen said when his breath had eased enough to let him. "The care of the city's accounts is mine, and while Gilgamesh is indisposed, his care is mine as well, to make sure that he does nothing that will bring him greater sorrow later."

Ur-Gula shook his head. "I have seen one patient this morning that I shall surely lose, and another whose state is nearly as bad, though his body is sound. If you do not take better care, you risk death as surely as if you breathed each breath that issues from Enkidu's lungs. I have tended you since your childhood, and I do not wish to see you waste my work."

"I shall try to watch myself," Shusuen answered. "Yet I cannot forsake my duty for my health, any more than a soldier can leave his post because he sees the enemy approaching."

"Well, you know the risk you are taking, and I have done my best. Before I leave, I shall speak to the En as well, and tell him how to make your medicines, though he seems to know how to take care of himself no better than you. He should have passed the En's medallion to Gilgamesh when the Ensi was anointed, and devoted himself to quiet living thereafter."

But Shusuen would not speak of that matter, for it was not for those outside a few of the folk of the Eanna to know how Gilgamesh had refused to take his part as husband of Inanna, both Ensi and En, as his father and grandfather had been before him, and left the old man with a duty that his aged body no longer fit him to fulfill. And after a little time, Ur-Gula rose with another sigh.

"Rest here for a while more, and then you may go about your business again. And from all my heart—I think you, Exalted Scribe, for your warning, for I think you have saved my life as surely as I might ever have saved yours, or any man's."

· · ·

ENKIDU BORE THE poultices as well as he might, and let Gilgamesh
carefully slice the melons and lettuce that Sululi had brought back from
the market—poor wizened things that they were, for all the price that
she had paid for them; the cool fruits had suffered the worst from the
hot drought—and put the wet morsels between his parched lips, sucking
the sweet moisture down to ease his burning throat. And that soothed
Gilgamesh's heart a little, but when he tried to spoon more of the medicines into Enkidu's mouth, his lover turned his head away determinedly,
and the lion growled in warning.

"Is none of this helping you?" Gilgamesh asked. "Are not your pains
any less?"

"No. And . . . though my legs prickle and ache, they will not move."

"I shall put fresh poultices on you," Gilgamesh said. "It may be that
will help."

Enkidu's head moved against the pillow, a weak shake. "No. No.
Please, I cannot bear the stink. Even now, it turns my stomach. I know
the physicians meant to do me good," he added, his voice low, "but I
only feel the worse for all their trouble."

"What can I do?"

"Wipe these messes from me—I feel like a cub that has soiled himself—and do what you can to clear the air in the room. It grows harder
for me to breathe," Enkidu whispered. "I think clean air will be better."

At once Gilgamesh cut through the bandages, and wiped the oily
poultices away from Enkidu's feet and hands and body while Sululi
dropped her spinning to lift the woven door-screen, fanning the air with
a wide-spread cloak—the shaggy cloak, Gilgamesh noticed with a pang
of hope, that she had made to protect Enkidu during the war. It had
done its work well then; perhaps the prayers she had put into it would
help now? But already, as he dropped cloth after herb- and oil-stained
cloth by the bedside, replacing each with a fresh square of damp linen,
he could see how the fever was eating at Enkidu's body like a vulture, the
bones beginning to press up against the muscles that had knitted so
strongly across chest and abdomen, and the hard-edged flesh of his pow-

erful thighs sinking into sallow flabbiness under the thick golden hair that still grew brightly over them.

*Gods, why must I see this?* Gilgamesh asked himself. And answered, *Because I will not leave Enkidu, whatever passes from him: be it beauty or strength or youth, I will love him still. Even when we are both gray-haired bags of bones, sitting in the sun and bewailing the rash antics of Erech's youths, I shall love him no grain less.*

Finally Enkidu sighed, his head sagging back, and Gilgamesh pulled the coverlet gently up over him again. "There, my love," he said. "It will be better now . . . you will be better soon. Do you want us to let you sleep, or shall I call for musicians to gladden your rest?"

"I would see Ur-Lugal for a little, if I may. Let me see our son at play with his mother, and that will lighten my soul."

"Of course it will, for you shall see him at play for many years as he grows. Go, Sululi, and fetch Ur-Lugal. For I," Gilgamesh found himself admitting suddenly, "shall be glad to see him as well."

YET THE NEXT morning, Enkidu was worse than he had been before. Though he could not rise, he had gotten little sleep; and Gilgamesh and Sululi had gotten little more, dozing off only to be awakened by the rustling of bedclothes or Enkidu's soft moans as he tried to move his betraying body into a less painful position. Only the En's potion had given him a little relief, soothing the rattling of his lungs. Though Gilgamesh had spoken harshly to Shusuen when the scribe had brought it, and Sululi had feared that he would throw the clay jar against the wall, the Ensi had clutched it to himself like a breast-plate against the arrows of the foe, and carefully fed it to Enkidu whenever his fever raged too high. But now Sululi's husband was sleeping peacefully, and Gilgamesh had slipped from the room—to do his duties in shrine or hall, or to speak with his counselors: Sululi did not know which. She could only sit spinning, watching Enkidu as he slept, reaching down now and again to stroke the curly dark hair of Ur-Lugal as he lay dozing with his head nestled against her foot. Though she was desperately tired, she dared not close her eyes while Gilgamesh was gone, lest Enkidu should wake and need her. Instead she sang softly, a lullaby to both of them.

Though her low voice was not strong enough for her to sing in the shrine, its tone was clear and true, and Enkidu had always liked her to sing to him.

"In my song of joy, he will grow strong,
In my song of joy, he will grow large . . .
Sleep will fill your lap with emmer-wheat,
I will make sweet for you the little cheeses,
Those little cheeses that are healer of man,
The healer of man, the son of the lord Shulgi . . .

May the wife be your support, may the son be your lot,
May the winnowed barley be your bride,
The goddess Ashnan your ally.
May you have an eloquent god, may you achieve a reign of happy days,
May your feast make bright the forehead.

Lie you in your sleep, array the branches of your palm tree . . ."

So she was awake when Gilgamesh came back into the room, his long hair disarrayed and the color high in his cheeks. "How does he?" he asked quietly of her.

"As you can see: he sleeps still."

"We must let him sleep, then. I have given orders against those false physicians: the strength of his nature will heal him better than they could with all their herbs and poking and muttering. It is a wonder that any sick person has ever gotten well in Erech, tended by those poison-mongers."

"Hush," Sululi whispered. But Enkidu's eyelids were already fluttering, golden lashes untangling. For a moment he seemed like a child awakening and a sudden flare of hope awoke in her heart, like near-dead coals whipped up by the wind.

"My love, my love," Gilgamesh crooned, reaching over the sleeping form of the lion by the bed. "How are you feeling this morning?"

"No better," Enkidu croaked. He half raised himself on one elbow, then slipped back again. "My dreams were dark, although I cannot remember them."

"Let the morning light drive them from you, beloved; after all dark nights comes a day. I have been down to the gates of Erech. It will joy you, when you are well, to see how the cedars are rising. The finest work of our carpenters and carvers, folk will look upon them from afar and marvel upon us, who brought the cedars back from the Land of the Living."

But Enkidu frowned, his lips pulling back into a snarl. He raised himself again, arching his back and hitching his body up on his elbows; his head bent back, as though he were already gazing up at the great height of the cedar gates.

"You door of the woods, empty of understanding," he said, each breath hissing from his lungs with a soft rattle. "I admired your wood even from twenty leagues away, even before I looked upon the lofty cedars with my eyes; nothing could have been like to your wood in my sight. Your height is six dozen cubits, your breadth, two dozen; one cubit your thickness, your door-post, pivot-stone, and post-cap . . . I carried you down to Nippur. Had I known, O Gate, that it would come to this, and that this would be your gratefulness, I would have taken your planks and chopped them up. I would have lashed your planks into a raft, to float down the river forever. But yet, Gate, I smoothed your wood, and I brought you to Nippur. May a ruler who comes after me reject you, may the god who condemns me . . . may he remove my name, and set his own name there."

Sululi saw the tears swelling in Gilgamesh's eyes as Enkidu spoke, streaming unheeded down the Ensi's face, and closed her eyes so that she would not have to look anymore. It terrified her to the bone, as much as Enkidu's sickness herself, to see Gilgamesh weep thus, for if the Ensi, in all the pride and power of his mighty body, were so helpless, then who might be strong?

Disturbed by the sounds of the adult voices about him, Ur-Lugal awoke and began to wail as well. Though months ago Sululi had stopped weaning him—the moment Rimsat-Ninsun had told her, when she went to the temple to ask for help in getting another child, that nursing would often hold off pregnancy—now she lifted him to her breast, filling his mouth with the comfort of an empty nipple, and shrank as far into the corner as she could, hoping that Gilgamesh would not turn against her in his sorrow.

Gilgamesh knelt by the bed, reaching out to clasp Enkidu's hands in his as Enkidu sank exhausted into the bedclothes again. "Do not speak so," he said, still crying. "You are only tired, as comes with illness—when you are better, you will look upon the gate, and its beauty will bring you happiness again."

Yet Enkidu lay there pale, his golden hair and beard the only bright-ness around his face, like gold woven about alabaster. Sululi wanted to go to him and touch him, giving him silent comfort against the despair ringing in Gilgamesh's voice, but she did not dare to: the Ensi's muscu-lar back stood against her like a wall, keeping her from her husband. Only when Gilgamesh moved downward, turning back the coverlet to rub and caress Enkidu's feet, did she dare rise from her place and go to him, wetting and wringing the cloth that had fallen from his forehead to wash his face afresh, smoothing away the lines of pain that scored his sweat-beaded skin.

"Will you have some more of the Ensi's potion?" she asked him.

"No more. I am still muzzy with the last dose, and I am not so much worse . . ." Enkidu's voice trailed off as though the effort of his speech had utterly exhausted him, and between that and the fierce glare Gil-gamesh cast at her, Sululi was afraid to speak again.

ENKIDU LAY THUS in his pain, until day and night began to seem alike to him. His fever waxed and waned, the blisters on his lips swelling and bursting like bubbles in boiling mud so that blood and fluids trickled down from the deep cracks in his mouth whenever he opened it to eat or speak. Sometimes he burned with the heat until he could not remember where he was, and it seemed that he crawled end-lessly across a parched plain toward the faint green shimmer of a mirage waterhole. Other times he shivered with a cold that no blankets could ease, trying to burrow into the bed like an orphaned cub seeking out the shelter of frosted rocks in place of its mother's warm body.

Sometimes the prickling in his hands and feet was fierce and sharp, tearing at him like the needle-teeth of invisible fish; sometimes it was only a glimmering tingle, like blood flowing back into a sleeping limb. Early, when Enkidu had felt the little pangs in his feet, they had given him hope that he would be able to move his legs again, but as the prickling pain grew greater and they yet lay still and limp as the sprawled limbs of a half-eaten gazelle beneath the bedclothes, he began to realize that his legs might never bear his weight up. Not to run, or stand lightly balanced in Gilgamesh's chariot, never to walk the streets of Erech again by his lover's side, laughing and careless in their strength as they looked together upon the works of the city's crafts-men, the finely wrought leathers and metals and woods; not to stride into the taverns in search of beer and the plump laughing wenches who served it . . .

The tears came to Enkidu's eyes when he thought of it, whenever he forgot and tried to curl his feet under him or, half asleep, to draw his knees to his chest. Then, he could not turn away when Gilgamesh bent over to kiss the salty bitterness from his lids, but the touch of his beloved's mouth brushing cool and soft against his hot skin was another wound, reminding him, clear and harsh as desert crags standing high in the hard light of dawn, of all that he had lost and was yet to lose.

It was worse, those times that Gilgamesh went from the room, for he was sure to come back with something bright in his hands or on his tongue, as though Enkidu's life were a bird that he could lure back into the painful snare of his failing body. A great bow, inlaid with horn and figured ivory, with barbed fishing-arrows and broad-headed hunting-arrows, wrapped about in Gilgamesh's promises of the jour-ney they would take down the Buranun as soon as Enkidu was strong enough to enjoy it; a bowl-stand in the shape of a billy-goat standing on his hind legs with forehooves tangled in a thicket of gold, his fleecy coat rendered in hundreds of little pieces of deeply carved shell and lipis set in bitumen, and gleaming eyes made of onyx in mother-of-pearl; a silver rush-light holder, its pillar a rough-barked tree upheld by three lions who stretched upward, their claws sinking deep sharpening-scratches into the argent wood . . . All were things that would have filled Enkidu with delight and awe, thinking that the hands of men could work so carefully and finely, rendering the glimpses of a moment everlasting in wood and precious metal: of all the *me*, it had often seemed to him that craftsmanship was the gift rendering humans most like the gods. But now, caressing the smoothed lines and rounded figures brought him no joy, for the prickling in his fingers drowned out the silkiness of ivory and silver beneath his touch, and the weight of the gifts, even the lightest, was too much for his weakened arms to bear for more than a moment. And yet he had to feign happiness with the last of his strength, for even when his eyes ran blurry with pus, he could see the anxiety and sorrow on Gilgamesh's face, and knew how his lover strove to bring him gladness from the depths of his own terror.

Sululi was more comforting in her quietness: she sang softly, and stroked his forehead with cool cloths when his fever raged high, and spoke only now and then, of little things such as the weather and weaving and the prattled half-talk and clumsy steps of Ur-Lugal. And always the lion lay beside him, lifting his head now and again to butt against the bed-frame or run his tongue lightly across Enkidu's hand, the familiar scratchy pain of his lick driving away the little lightning-needles for a moment. If Enkidu wept when he heard the lion's soft growls, gnawing upon the haunches of stringy sheep that the servants brought in for him each day, it was only because the sound was the one thing that carried him forth from the foulness and sweat of his sickbed, a clean breath of the wilderness where he had run.

PERHAPS EIGHT OR nine days had passed when Enkidu awoke in the darkness. The oil-lamps had gone out, as had the rush-light in the stand Gilgamesh had given him, and however Enkidu strained his eyes against the blackness, there was no glimmer anywhere. He could hear Sululi breathing upon her pallet, and the soft little snores of Ur-Lugal beside her, the scents of woman and child and lion were clear even through the stink of his own sick body, like streaks of whole flesh still showing pink on the rotting white skin of a leper, but he could not hear or smell Gilgamesh there. Suddenly the darkness seemed horribly oppressive to Enkidu, as though the room had become a box without openings, trapping him like a moth shut within an airless chest.

"Sululi," he called out painfully, the name rattling in his lungs. "Sululi, are you awake?"

Sululi rose at once, the hem of her robe whispering against her ankles as she crossed the floor in a few swift steps. "I am. What can I do, beloved husband? Is your fever high again? Do you need more medicine, or wish any food?"

"Only light," Enkidu gasped. "It is too dark in here; light the lamps again, that I may see. This hour before dawn, between moon and sun, is always hardest."

Enkidu heard the soft hiss of Sululi's indrawn breath, the softer sigh and the sound of her swallowing hard.

"What is it?" he asked, a new horror beginning to creep through his laboring heart like a trail of ants winding through a rotten stump.

"Enkidu, my husband . . . the lights are all burning brightly, and the light of dawn is rising outside. Your eyes are open . . ."

"No."

Enkidu shut his eyelids tightly, opening them again. It made no difference: the featureless blackness still shrouded his face like a cloth draped over him, remorseless and without easing as the fetters of paralysis that bound his legs like ropes, the weight of his ribs crushing in like iron bands tightening about his lungs. Like a bird in a snare whose struggles only tightened the cords around its wings, like a fish lifted in a net, its gasps of air only hastening its dry drowning, he was trapped indeed.

The lion raised his head with a small questioning chuff, nosing against the bed-frame as if to nudge Enkidu awake, as he had often done when the long shadows of dawn stretched across the plains under the red-streaked sky. A day of running and hunting, of lying in the grass and wrestling with their playfully growling fellows—a day like all the others, without memory or thought, but only the knowledge of the fresh breeze ruffling their pelts and the sun warm on their lazily stretched bodies; the little sounds of the long waiting by the waterhole, letting bird and insect and rustling grass fade as they lifted patient noses for the scent of gazelle or ibex . . .

And now Enkidu was caged here, and would never find his freedom living: finding him in the wilderness, Akalla had brought him to this trap, as surely as if the hunter had dug a pit for him himself and wrapped the ropes about his body.

Remembering that, Enkidu's heart suddenly clenched with anger, a sudden pain shooting through his aching chest as the pus-thick tears poured forth from his eyes. "Utu," he rasped, "for my heart's sake I appeal to you, because of that trapper, that wretch, who did not let me find as much as my friend. May he not get enough to feed himself; make him lose his profit, weaken his power. May the path in front of him hate him, may the animals escape from him, keep the hunter from the fullness of his heart!"

Enkidu might have said more, but his words broke into a long spate of coughing, the foul sputum bursting painfully up from his chest to fly in gobbets from his mouth. Sululi's cloth was there in a moment, catching the worst of the thick spray and wiping his lips and chin clean after, as the spasm eased.

"Where is Gilgamesh?" Enkidu asked. And then, half fearing the answer, "When will he be back?" For the one blessing of the blindness, Enkidu knew, was that he would not have to look on Gilgamesh's face as his lover learned of it, as yet another brick was added to the siege-wall of hopeless desperation rising between them.

"He has gone to make sacrifice for you in the temples of the great gods, as he does every day: the blood of sheep and bullocks runs like water, and the dogs outside the shrines are growing fat on their bowels. If there is anything that will give him the least hope for you—"

"Can he not see that I am dying?" Enkidu cried out. "How could I live on like this, crippled and blind, like the most wretched of beggars in the marketplace? My body is nothing but pain, and the light has left my eyes."

"My love, my husband," Sululi murmured, and the sadness in her voice weighed upon Enkidu's chest like a heavy paw. "I know. I, too, would have you well and strong again, but where the gods have decreed—we can only hope for a merciful end. I love you greatly, for you have been the dearest joy of my life: the days of my happiness only began in the moment when you spoke to save me from execution. If the road of your illness leads at last to the earth, I shall mourn for you a year, and two, and three; I shall mourn for you, and miss you, every day that I draw breath, but I shall live on for the sake of our son and the work that must be done in the weaving-house of the temple, which no other can lead as well as I. But for Gilgamesh: he sees his own death made full in yours, though his body is strong and well. Your flesh is his own—what wonder that he cannot bear to believe what eyes and ears and all words tell him?"

*And so he shares in my blindness,* Enkidu thought. And in his weakness, he found that he was weeping again, thinking on his lover—wanting, now, Gilgamesh to get back from his sacrificing, for Gilgamesh to hold his wasting body in his powerful arms, the smooth breadth of his chest and the strength of his heartbeat a shield against the darkness.

Yet it was not Gilgamesh's tread that sounded in the hallway outside, but lighter, more hesitant footfalls—the tread of a woman, wrapped in a spicy, familiar scent. Enkidu turned his head to the side, coughing again as his empty stomach cramped with nausea: the least breath of incense was sickening to him, for too much had been burned already to cover the stink of his illness, like a mask of gold sinking onto the face of a long-rotten corpse.

And worse, to him, was the woman whose robes were steeped in the sweet smoke. She who had brought Enkidu out of the wilderness, given him speech and thought and all the torments of memory—she who had been his queen, her thighs flowing with honey and her breasts sleek as cream—she who had sought to steal Gilgamesh's life, she who had stood on the walls of Erech, mourning the Bull of Heaven and cursing its slayers . . . *What should she have come for now, save to gloat in the revenge of the gods?*

Now, at last, Enkidu's anger was unstoppered and he had a vessel upon which he could pour it. Though each breath sent rays of pain shooting through his body like the arching cloud of arrows in battle, he was able to cough out the black words festering in his lungs.

"Shamhatu! I shall speak your fate, a fate without end, that shall last forever. I shall curse you with a great curse; it shall rush like a throwing stick to strike you. May your hungers never be sated, may you never love a child of your own! May you never dwell in the chamber of young women; may dregs of beer stain your lovely breasts, and the drunkard's vomit soil your festal robes. May you never get treasures of bright alabaster; nor the shining silver, man's delight, be cast into your house. May the dust of the potter's crossroad be your dwelling, the wasteland your bed, the shadow of the city-wall your standing place. May thorns and briars tear the skin from your feet, may both drunk and sober strike your cheek in the city streets. May the lion roar at you, may the builder not seal the roof of your house, may owls nest in the cracks of your walls, where no feasts take place evermore—because of me: because, in my innocence, you sent the demon of paralysis against me."

If the Shamhatu replied to his harsh words, Enkidu could not hear her. The sound of his own wheezing lungs rose like a great wind in his ears, the irregular hammering of his heart beating like a door hanging loose in the storm-blast. And over that roaring, it seemed to him that he heard a voice speaking to him—the voice of Utu from his dreams, bright and steady as a shaft of sunlight through the gale.

*ENKIDU, WHY DO YOU CURSE THE SHAMHATU? SHE WHO GAVE YOU BREAD LIKE THAT OF THE GODS, SHE WHO GAVE YOU DRINK FIT FOR A RULER, SHE WHO DRESSED YOU IN FINE GAR-MENTS, AND GAVE YOU THE BEAUTIFUL GILGAMESH AS A COM-PANION? NOW GILGAMESH IS YOUR BELOVED BROTHER: HAS HE NOT MADE YOU LIE DOWN IN A GREAT BED, A COUCH OF HONOR, AND PLACED YOU IN THE SEAT OF EASE ON HIS LEFT HAND, WHERE THE RULERS OF THE WORLD KISS YOUR FEET? HE WILL MAKE THE PEOPLE OF ERECH WEEP FOR YOU, CAUSE THEM TO KEEN YOU. THE JOYOUS CITY WILL FILL WITH WOE FOR YOUR SAKE. AND AFTERWARD HE WILL BEAR THE SIGNS OF GRIEF ON HIS BODY, HE WILL DRESS IN THE SKIN OF A LION AND ROAM THE WILDERNESS.*

As Enkidu listened to the voice of the god, his agitated heart grew calm, its painful beating steadying to a slow aching pulse. A wave of shame swept over him in place of the furious anger, like rain pouring down to cool the air after the burning passage of a lightning bolt. He remembered each little kindness from their days in the desert and village—the bread cut and served by the Shamhatu's hands, the straw put into his mouth from her cup, the gentle scrubbing and oiling of his body—each making him more fit to come to Erech, to stand before Gilgamesh and lay his hands upon the Ensi's belt. Where would he have found a mate in the wilderness? Where would he have learned of joining souls in speech and touch, of the perfect happiness of knowing and speaking of love? If a short life and painful death were the price of his time with Gilgamesh . . . how was this worse than ending his days sprawled among the rocks, with the deep claw-gashes of a rival gone septic and rotten beneath the burning sun?

Abashed, Enkidu spoke again. Though his curse seemed to have torn through his throat like a blowfly ripping free of its brown pupa, his broken whisper sounded clearly over the breathing of the others in the room.

"Shamhatu, I shall speak your fate," he said again. "Let the mouth which has cursed you bless you. May you be set in your rightful place; may Ensis and nobles love you. Let the man one league away bite his lip in longing for you, let the one two leagues away shake out his hair in readiness for you. May the warrior not refuse you, but undo his buckle for you; may he offer up to you carnelian, lapis, and gold, and give you earrings of filigree, heaping up all his storehouse for you. May you enter the house of the gods, and even the mother of seven be abandoned for your sake."

The Shamhatu felt the tears dropping from her eyes, for his words of kindness were harder to bear than the harshness that had gone before. "Enkidu," she murmured, brushing her finger against his cheek. "I never meant for ill to befall you. I deserve your curse, and Inanna through me, for what we have done to you—you who were innocent and happy when I came upon you."

"Yet ill has befallen me, and cannot be turned aside. And still, I spoke wrongly to curse you—it was my pain and fear speaking through my mouth, demons whining through the rocks. I did not mean to wish that I had never come to Erech."

"Enkidu . . . my beloved lion—is there anything I may do for you? I have entreated the gods, but they will not listen; I have spoken to the En, but he says he has already stretched his arts to the utmost for you, and Gilgamesh has forbidden him to come near or speak to you."

"I wish that he could come near," Enkidu whispered. "For he is old, and soon to die himself—he has long looked down the road on which I must travel."

"I am sorry, Enkidu," the Shamhatu said. "For all that has happened—I am sorry."

"Do not be," he husked, the breath rattling in his lungs. "Only stay with me awhile."

She settled herself beside his bed, stroking the bright hair back from his sunken face. Behind her, Sululi's dress rustled softly: the other woman was rising, going from the room.

"Enkidu, my lion. I wish . . ." Now she could speak the truth to him, for there was no one else to hear. "I wish that you and I had stayed in the village and never come to Erech. Though all seemed bright then, it was ill-fated. You have lost your life, and I . . . I have lost all my trust in Inanna, and I no longer wish to be her priestess. She wore me like a cloak, and used me as a tool to destroy all that I love—I would have died myself, sooner than see what has come to pass."

Enkidu turned his face toward her, thick tears trickling from his blind eyes. "Do not speak so, Shamhatu. I do not wish to die with your sadness hanging over me. For all that has happened, I am glad that you brought me here. And was it not Inanna, through you, who gave me the *me* of speech and love and delight in all good things? Though I cursed her before the walls of Erech, I regret the words I spoke. And I regret . . ." He paused, coughing shudderingly. "I am sorry only that you never came to me again after we entered the city's walls. I would have liked to mate with you again."

"I wish I had, my lion." And the Shamhatu found herself weeping again. She had denied herself, and him, all that delight—and for what? Only for the office that she no longer wished to bear.

"I have heard—" Enkidu coughed again, a fit that went on longer. The Shamhatu wiped his cracked lips with a cloth, waiting patiently for him to speak again. "I have heard that you bring the blessing of Inanna to men who come to the shrine. Will you give it to me?"

Suddenly cold, the Shamhatu felt the blood dropping from her face. How could she deny Enkidu his wish—perhaps the last he might ever have of her? And yet, to open herself to Inanna once more, not even knowing whether the goddess would indeed offer blessing or curse the dying man . . .

"I will give you what I can," she answered. "I will give you my love, and hope that blessing will come with it."

As she drew the sheet back from Enkidu's body, the thought came to the Shamhatu that if Gilgamesh came in now, he might well slay her. But that would be as the gods willed it, and there were worse ways to die; if it might bring Enkidu comfort now, it was worth the risk. She bent, taking his soft rod in her mouth. It was fever-hot, but clean, and as she gently suckled, she could feel the head swelling and shaft growing in her mouth. She closed her eyes, willing herself to forget that Enkidu was dying, forget all her own sorrow and fear and remember how it had been when the two of them sported in Akalla's hut. And to the Shamhatu's surprise, a small tingle of anticipation began to swell in her loins. Thus they had played together, she and her lion-man, half drunk on beer and delighting in each other's bodies . . .

"Come into my garden, beloved," she whispered, drawing her fingers up and down Enkidu's thick shaft, circling the head of his penis until he caught his breath in pleasure. "The pomegranate is plucked for you, the sweet fig awaits." Lifting her skirts, the Shamhatu climbed onto Enkidu's bed, kneeling over him. Without conscious volition, she found herself murmuring the holy words, the words of Inanna to her lovers. "Behold, my vulva is the Boat of Heaven . . . I bring it to you, filled with the blessed *me*." The lips of her body parted smoothly and easily as she lowered herself onto Enkidu, taking him into her in a slow long caress. "Lie still, beloved, and let me delight in you," she purred, rocking gently upon him. "My tree growing by the water, my holy love . . ."

Careful even as her own desire grew not to lean her weight on him, or speed her rhythm too quickly for him, the Shamhatu moved upon

Enkidu's body, drawing him into her over and over again until the wasted muscles of his chest tightened and he gasped, spilling into her. Only then did she let her passion flower fully, tossing her head back and clenching her hands on empty air lest she cause him pain.

As the waves of pleasure ebbed slowly from her and Enkidu sank out of her, the Shamhatu realized that she felt very strange. She felt . . . as she had before the eclipse, when the touch of Inanna was exaltation, and a joyful heart when the goddess had withdrawn. *And if Enkidu can make his peace with Inanna now, and ask her blessing after all he has undergone, why should not I?*

She rose and carefully cleaned both of them, kissing Enkidu before she pulled the sheet back up.

"Thank you," Enkidu rasped.

"Thank you," she echoed. "You cannot know how much you have eased my sorrow. Enkidu—is there anything more I can do for you?"

"Bring me a cup of beer, if you will, and fetch your harp. I would drink, and listen to you sing, as I did in the village on the edge of the wilderness."

THOUGH HIS BLISTERED lips clung to the smooth gold straw, the beer was more welcome to Enkidu's throat than drink had been for days, and the Shamhatu's singing seemed to lift him from the enfolding darkness as surely as her touch had, words lighting the world within his mind.

> "While he was Ensi, freshwater flowed in the river,
> In the field grew rich grain, carp and fish filled all the sea.
> Old and young reeds sprouted in the canebrakes,
> Deer and wild goats filled the forest,
> In the plain grew the *mashgur*-tree.
> Honey and date-wine filled the watered gardens,
> In the Ensi's hall grew life . . ."

She was still singing when Gilgamesh came back, his heavy tread sounding like the beating of a drum beneath the harp's clear notes. The Shamhatu stopped in mid-line, and Enkidu heard the quick rustlings of her garments, like the sound of a doe casting about this way and that to see where she might flee.

"You!" Gilgamesh said. Beneath the damp scent of the clean water he had washed in, Enkidu could still smell the blood and smoke of the sacrifices he had made, clinging to him like bitumen-stains to the fingers of an inlay-craftsman. "What are you doing here?"

"I came to speak to Enkidu, and give him such comfort as I could. And he asked me to play and sing for him."

Gilgamesh's footsteps crossed the room quickly, and his hand caressed Enkidu's hair. "Does her music give you pleasure, my love?"

Enkidu nodded.

"Then you shall hear it. Play, Shamhatu: let your harp soothe us, as well as you are able to do something so pleasant and peaceful. And here, look what I have brought you. Is the wood—ebony from a land far to the south—not beautiful, and the inlay of cedar and carnelian not pleasing? Is . . . Enkidu?"

Painfully Enkidu moistened his lips. "Gilgamesh—I cannot see."

The low moan that issued from Gilgamesh's throat seemed to go on forever, an agony in Enkidu's ears. "Beloved, when did this happen?"

"I awoke, and all was dark."

"Why did you not send for me at once? I would have come straight back; I would not have left you. Oh, my love . . ." Gilgamesh knelt down, embracing Enkidu about the shoulders. Enkidu bit his tongue to keep from groaning, for his bones, now pressing against his sunken skin, felt raw beneath Gilgamesh's grip, as if they had been rasped to the marrow by a lion's tongue. But his need for the comfort of his lover's touch gave him the strength to bear it, and he said nothing when he heard the quick light footfalls of the Shamhatu stealing out of the room and away.

BECAUSE THE DAY was fine, Innashagga was in the courtyard of her family's house. Her son, Eannatum, lay upon a sheepskin rug by her side, kicking his feet and gurgling; Ur-Lugal, whose care she had taken over part of the time since Enkidu's illness began, had crawled to the edge of the fishpond, staring down at the flickers of silver among the water-weed and laughing at them. Gunidu was not there, for he had been called back into the service of the Eanna. Though he was too old to tend sheep any longer, he added his keen eyes and wisdom to those who were going over the temple's flocks, deciding which beasts should be slaughtered and which the shepherds should try to save.

"Are . . . are the babes well, my wife?" Akalla asked as he came out into the courtyard. His bare shoulders gleamed with beads of water, his close-cropped hair standing up in little damp spikes; he had come in from the hunting a little time ago, and gone at once to wash himself—a habit they had all picked up quickly under Sululi's tutelage. He had shaved freshly as well, only the faintest shadow of black stubble stippling his heavy jaw. Save that he was cleaner and better dressed, though, their sudden rise in the world had little affected Akalla: even his brief stint in the Ensi's place seemed to have slid from him like water from polished granite, leaving him the same stolid, quiet, skillful man he had always been.

"They are very well, my husband," Innashagga answered. The corners of her lips curved fondly as she reached down to tickle Eannatum's fat stomach, letting him grasp her forefinger in one tiny hand. "Will you grasp a bow thus when you are grown, my little one? Will you become the Ensi's chief huntsman after your father?"

Akalla smiled, squatting down so that Eannatum could grab his finger, too, even as he glanced swiftly at Ur-Lugal to make sure that the child was in no immediate danger of falling into the fishpond.

*How well-fit he is to be a father,* Innashagga thought. *What care when he touches the children, what delight he takes in them! Perhaps we shall have another soon—I shall ask it of Inanna.* It would not be extravagant to have the care of another child, she knew. Their fortunes had, it was true, dipped somewhat in the last months: with all the beasts that had to be slaughtered and eaten as soon as possible, even the high folk of the Eanna could little afford to freshen their palates with the flesh of wildfowl and game. But the Ensi's huntsman got a steady salary, whether he could augment it by extra sales or not; and Gunidu and even Innashagga herself were issued rations of food and goods from the temple for their work. *Yes, I shall ask it of Inanna.* Though Innashagga knew the goddess must be full to bursting with sacrifices of sheep and cattle, she herself could easily afford a fine bowl of myrrh and cedar chips for Inanna.

"They grow finely."

"Yes, both of them do. Our son shares our happiness—and Sululi's sorrow does not seem to have touched her child."

Akalla's thick lips tightened, heavy brows lowering over his eyes. "How does Enkidu? Did Sululi give you any news this morning when you went to fetch Ur-Lugal?"

"He was still sleeping, she said, but seemed no better."

"So there is little hope for him, then. That is sad."

"It is. Ur-Lugal!"

Sululi's son was now leaning precariously over the pond's rim, one chubby arm splashing in the water like a bear-cub trying to scoop out a fish. Innashagga rose to her feet at once, but Akalla was faster: in three strides, he had crossed the distance to the pool, sweeping Ur-Lugal up and carrying him back to the skin where Eannatum lay. Ur-Lugal began to howl, but Akalla jiggled him in his arms, murmuring, "Hush, hush, little Ensi. You shall catch fish in your time. Many fish, big fish, you shall catch fish. But now, no bigger than a fish yourself, you catch no fish."

Innashagga shaded her eyes, looking up at the sun. "It will soon be time to take him back to his mother. And I think . . ." An idea had been ripening slowly in her mind all day, like a melon swelling beneath the sunlight, and now her decision was coming to fullness. Although she had not been allowed into the sickroom, Sululi's condition had showed her all she needed to know of Enkidu's: the highborn woman's gaunt face, sallow skin hanging from her wide bones and deep bruise-purple circles beneath her eyes, the shaking in her hands as she gave her son over to her apprentice's care, promised that the one who lay within was near indeed to going down into the earth.

"We must go to Enkidu," she said firmly. "If we do not see him soon, we shall never see him again outside the halls of Erishkegal. And I would say my farewells to him before he goes much farther on the road to the Underworld, or passes through those dread portals from which the living cannot return."

Akalla chewed his lip thoughtfully, settling Ur-Lugal comfortably against one broad shoulder. "Is that wise, wife? Father said—"

"I know what he said." It was true, Gunidu had warned them—and her most particularly, since she must go to fetch and return Ur-Lugal from Sululi—about Gilgamesh's wild swings of mood. And did not all Erech know how he had ordered the arrest of those physicians who had failed to cure his beloved, his rage only thwarted by some chance or secret warning that had sent nearly all the doctors away from the city just in time to save them? "And yet I would see Enkidu. We shall take Father with us, if you think it safer."

Akalla's shoulders sagged a little. Though she could still see the doubt plain as a fresh scab across his heavy features, Innashagga knew that she had won the argument. She scooped her own son up in her arms, resting his weight against one hip. "Come, let us go."

GUNIDU WAS OUT with the other shepherds, going through a flock and pointing with his crook. His bald spot shone dark as polished mahogany, and the ropy muscles stood out sharply beneath his deep-tanned skin as he waved his sign of office. "That one, that one, and that one . . . no, seize him firmly. Of course his fleece is straggly: they are all straggly this winter, with the heat what it has been. But look at the muscles still under it! That is a hardy fellow, who will be a good father for another flock. Take them quickly now, and get them out of here before Gilgamesh comes to sacrifice more of the best sheep who ought to be kept alive for breeding. The rest of these—there is little hope that they will live, and no use wasting good grass and water on them with supplies to scarce. Tell the butchers to make them into mutton and salt them, as Shusuen has ordered."

The younger shepherds easily snagged the legs of the sheep Gunidu had pointed out with their own crooks, bringing the beasts down and dragging them away. The old man wiped his forehead with the back of his hand, dashing the sweat away. Only then did he limp over to join his son and daughter-in-law.

"How goes your work, Father?" Innashagga asked politely.

"Harder every day, and made three times as hard by the help of the exalted and god-beloved Ensi," Gunidu grumbled. "He has the eye to be Shepherd of Erech, indeed, for he can pick out the best beasts at a glance, and what does he do with them, when we need them most if we are to have any living sheep next year? He hauls them away to slit their throats in the shrines, like a watchdog turned wolf."

"Does he not know—" Innashagga began. Gunidu laid a silencing finger on his sunken lips, glancing this way and that, and she realized she had nearly spoken aloud the riskiest words that could be spoken in Erech these days: *Enkidu is dying.* With a surge of effort, as though she were wrenching a limb free from beneath a fallen rock, Innashagga turned her mind back to her purpose.

"Father," she said, "we are going to give Ur-Lugal back to his mother, and, for the sake of the time Enkidu spent in our house, and the favor that has been shown to us on his account, I wish us to greet him ourselves."

Gunidu's breath hissed through his teeth, and he leaned down heavily upon his ceremonial crook. "This is not wise. The Ensi is very protective of his beloved friend's rest."

"Nevertheless," Innashagga declared, "we shall ask to see Enkidu. If he is sleeping, we shall leave him be, but he will know that we have asked for him and are thinking of him. If he wakes, we may be able to bring him some cheer, for he was happy when he was among us."

Gunidu sighed again, shifting his weight from foot to foot. "The daughter is a man's salvation," he muttered, "and the daughter-in-law a man's demon." But there was no prickle in his tone—all dry leaves and no thorns—and Innashagga knew he would not refuse her.

ENATARZI LET THEM in without question, for he was used to Innashagga's coming and going with Ur-Lugal. Innashagga felt her footsteps slowing as she led her family closer to the chamber where Enkidu lay, as though they were treading on holy ground, approaching the great statue of Inanna in her shrine. It was indeed holy ground, Innashagga reminded herself with a small shiver, for did not everyone, even an ignorant village girl like herself, know that the bones of Lugalbanda were buried beneath the bed of his son, and the building itself stand as the ancestral shrine of the Ensis of Erech?

Even before reaching the door-posts, Innashagga could hear the harsh rattle of Enkidu's lungs above the low voices from within. Akalla's face was pale, Gunidu's hard-set as they stood there, waiting for Innashagga to gather her courage. At last she knocked.

It was not Sululi who came out, but Gilgamesh, thrusting the woven screen aside and stamping out into the passageway like a wounded bull. He, too, had grown thinner in the last days, noble cheekbones and chin knobby under the thick growth of beard-stubble, and the whites of his eyes were swollen and red. But the drawn pain on his face softened as he looked upon Sululi's son sleeping in Akalla's arms.

"Bring the child in," he said. "And Akalla, you come in as well, for we have a hunting trip to plan."

*Hunting?* Innashagga thought in shock. *How can he think of that, when his beloved lies dying?* But she held to her resolution, though her voice quivered like the cooing of a turtledove as she shyly asked, "If it please you, Ensi, may the rest of us also come in? I should like to speak with Enkidu, for the sake of the days when he guested in our house."

For a moment Gilgamesh hesitated, his fierce gaze turning away from her. It was not until the weak rasp came from inside—"Let them in, beloved"—that he lifted up the screen again, gesturing the little family through.

Once her eyes had adjusted to the lamplight within, Innashagga stood gaping with shock, staring at the bed. The figure that lay beneath the coverlet was little more than a scattering of bones, every line in the disheveled tangle of drawn sinews somehow speaking of near-unbearable pain. Though Innashagga had expected to see Enkidu pale and wasted, this was beyond what she could have guessed. The lion-man who had squatted before her hearth, stormed joyously through their village, and stood gleaming in bronze before the folk of Erech—now she could recognize him only by the clean bright curls about his face, like the golden hair and beard still shining about the sunken-fleshed skull of a sun-dried corpse. His green eyes still moved in their blackened sockets, but Innashagga could tell that they saw nothing, for though his head was cocked toward them to listen, his gaze rolled aimlessly as a child's round playing-stone on smooth tiles.

"Enkidu," Gilgamesh said, and now Innashagga could hear the forced gaiety in his voice, like the face of an aged barmaid painted brightly to make her a mockery of maidenhood for the New Year's feast. "Akalla the huntsman is here. Akalla, when Enkidu is well, we wish to go downriver to hunt. His new bow is finished—you see it there in the corner, beside his spear. It will do well for waterfowl and most game, though I wonder if it is strong enough for wild boar, or if we should expect to use spears for that hunting."

Innashagga tightened her grip on Eannatum, praying that her husband's lack of words would befriend, rather than betray, them. If Akalla spoke in his surprise, saying what Gilgamesh could least bear to hear . . . ?

But the huntsman only handed Ur-Lugal down to his mother, who squatted spinning with her back against the wall, and went to look at the bow. At Gilgamesh's nod, Akalla braced with his foot to string it quickly; the heavy muscles of his shoulders and back stood out in sharp relief as he struggled to bring it to full draw, then released the string slowly and unstrung it again.

"I would . . . would use that spear standing against the wall," Akalla said thoughtfully, gesturing at the great bronze-headed weapon. "But the bow is very strong, and a good hand and eye for it," he added, "Enkidu has. Yes. Yes . . . that is, it . . . it will do for wild boar, if it is well-aimed."

"Do you hear that, beloved?" Gilgamesh asked. "I told you that it would be."

"Yes," Enkidu whispered. "You did."

There was a brief silence, broken only by the wheezing of Enkidu's lungs. In the stillness, something moved near the floor, like the shifting of a golden boulder. Her eyes drawn to the motion, a dreadful chill of fear came over Innashagga. For by the bed lay a great maned lion: he had lifted his head, tawny eyes fixing upon her and her child, and his gaze froze her like a dove trapped by the mindless glare of a snake.

*But it must be safe*, Innashagga whispered to herself. *Else Sululi would hardly keep Ur-Lugal here beside her.*

"Akalla, come closer to me," Enkidu rattled. Slowly, his sandals scuffling across the floor, the huntsman made his way to the bed. Although Innashagga could hear the cost in his breathing, Enkidu lifted his hand slightly, and after a moment Akalla reached across the lion to grasp it.

"My friend . . . I am sorry."

Innashagga turned her face away to hide the tears. How often had the wild lion-man spoken those words in their house, whenever he, in his huge innocence, had broken or soiled something too delicate to bear up under his half-tamed strength? To hear their shadow now, twisted and weakened like Enkidu's own body, was nearly too much for her: she longed to run from the room, but she reminded herself that she had come to bid Enkidu farewell on his journey to the land of no return, and she would not leave without giving him her blessing.

"Sorry . . . for what?" Akalla asked, the puzzlement standing out clear in his thick-tongued voice.

"In my pain, I spoke wrongly. I cursed you for what was not your fault, but I wish only blessings for you."

Akalla's hands twisted together, the little muscles of his skull moving beneath their close-trimmed pelt of black hair. At last he said, "I have seen, have seen . . . animals in pain, many times. I have seen . . . they, they . . . anything will bite, or strike out, regardless of friend or foe, when hurt. You, you . . . no different, my friend. Think not of it."

"Yet I am sorry. I owe you only blessing and thanks, for you were my first hosts, and gave me the first roof that covered my head. I had always meant to do something for you . . ."

"And so you have," Innashagga said swiftly. "Because you recognized my husband and spoke to him, we live in a fine house now, and our lives are better than we could ever have dreamed. Enkidu, light of the plains, you have repaid our hospitality sevenfold and sevenfold again. Let no thought of us trouble you on your journeying, but go with a glad and clean heart."

Suddenly Gilgamesh whirled upon Innashagga like a dust-demon swooping upon a traveler. Beneath his furious gaze, her heart choked in her throat, and she tasted the bitter-salt spoor of her own death in her mouth.

"What do you mean by 'Enkidu's journeying'?" the Ensi demanded.

Though Innashagga's tongue had always wagged readily, now it lay limp as a piece of boiled meat behind her teeth. For a dreadful moment she knew that she would not be able to answer Gilgamesh without spitting the truth out, and then she would walk the dusty road down to the nether places of the earth before Enkidu did. But Eannatum opened his mouth, letting out a little gurgle; and her child's sound was the bubbling water that dampened Innashagga's dry throat then, letting her speak.

"Ensi, exalted one of Erech, you spoke of a hunting trip, when Enkidu is well." She could think of no more to say, but Gilgamesh's nostrils flared as he drew breath sharply, and it was as if she could see him seizing upon the half-spun thread of her words as though they were warp-yarn strong enough to support the heaviest weft.

"So I did. And it is settled that we will do that, Akalla? Before the New Year's feast, it should be."

"Yes, my Ensi," Akalla answered.

"Go, now," commanded Gilgamesh. "Enkidu is tired, and must rest."

"Goodbye," came the faint murmur from the bed.

The moment they had passed the door-posts, letting the tapestry-screen swing back behind them, Innashagga shoved Eannatum hard into his father's arms. She would have dropped him otherwise, for her legs were shaking so badly they could barely hold her up. With his free hand, Gunidu grabbed her arm, leaning heavily on his shepherd's crook as they limped swiftly away.

They did not speak until they were safely back in the courtyard of their own house, sitting in the cooling evening air. Surprisingly, it was Akalla who broke the silence, his voice strangely clear and flat.

"If I were hunting on the plain," he said, "and I saw an animal so ill, lion or wolf or hyena . . . only one thing I could do."

"Gilgamesh is doing his beloved no kindness," Gunidu agreed. "And yet, what else can he do but try to ease Enkidu's mind, and take his thoughts from his pain?"

*Let him die,* Innashagga thought. But she could not say that aloud. Though she had seen Enkidu and knew, still she—even here, even now—could not bring herself to so draw the eyes of the gods to Enkidu's sickbed. If it were Akalla who lay there, or—and she horned her fingers against the evil thought—Eannatum, could she thus resign herself to loss? Or would she cling as desperately as Gilgamesh, flailing and lashing out blindly at that which no mortal could overcome, even at the risk of destroying all around?

*Gods, be kind to me,* Innashagga prayed, a prayer wrung from the fervent depths of her heart. *Grant that I never have to find that out.*

GILGAMESH AWOKE TO the awful sound of cries from the bed. It was deep in the night: the lights had all burned out, leaving only the choking darkness and sickroom stench. Enkidu's groans became words, words that tore at him like the talons of a vulture.

"My beloved hates me," Enkidu moaned. "Once, while he spoke with me in Erech, I feared the battle with Huwawa, and he encouraged me. My friend who saved me in battle has abandoned me . . ."

Stumbling through the blackness, Gilgamesh hurried from his pallet to Enkidu's side, easing his body onto the sweat-clammy bed. "My beloved, my beloved, I have not abandoned you," he crooned. "Only see—touch me, I am here."

The bones of Enkidu's fingers, hot as though he had just set down a bronze pan of boiling water, closed upon Gilgamesh's arm. "You are here," he repeated. "My innards churn, lying here alone. My beloved, I had a dream in the night."

"You are not alone, for I am here. Tell me of the dream, beloved."

Enkidu tried to speak, but coughed instead, his lungs gurgling like those of a drowning man pulled from the river. Gilgamesh listened helplessly, until at last the spasms weakened and Enkidu was able to whisper, "The heavens groaned; the earth cried out, and I stood alone between them. A dark-faced man appeared before me, and his face was like that of the whirlwind-bird Imdugud. His hands were the paws of a lion, his nails the talons of an eagle. He seized me by the hair and over-came me. I struck him, but he leapt upward, and bore me down. He trampled me like a wild bull, his grasp encircled my body. I cried out, 'Help me, beloved!' But you did not save me, for you were afraid. Then he struck me and turned me into a dove, so that my arms were feathered like a bird's. He seized upon me and led me down to the house of dark-ness, the dwelling of Irkalla—to the house where one who goes in never comes out again, along the road of no return, to the house whose dwellers never see light. There, dust is their drink and their food is clay; their clothes are like birds' clothes, a garment of wings, and light cannot be seen—they dwell in darkness, and dust has settled deeply upon door and door-bolt."

Enkidu paused, his rattling lungs laboring for breath. Gilgamesh reached for the cup on the table beside the bed, wiping the gold straw clean and lifting it to Enkidu's mouth. Enkidu sucked weakly at it for a moment before going on.

"When I came into the house of dust," he gasped, "the holy crowns of rulers lay heaped on the earth, and wherever I listened, I heard of the bearers of crowns who ruled the land in early days. They were images of An and Enlil among men; now they served up cooked meats and baked foodstuffs, they poured cool water from skins. When I came into the house of dust, there sat the En who brings gods and men together, and the wailing priest of the funeral. There sat the *ishib*-priest of purifications and the *lumahhu*-priest of trances, there sat the anointed priests of the great gods. Etana, whom the eagle bore to heaven, sat there, and Shakkan of the beasts sat there. Erishkegal, queen of the Netherworld, sat there, and Beletseri, the scribe of the Netherworld knelt before her; she held a tablet, and was reading it aloud to Erishkegal. Erishkegal raised her head and . . . and looked straight at me."

Gilgamesh felt the movement in the wasted sinews of Enkidu's shoulders as his lover turned his head to the side. For all the heat radiating from his body, Enkidu was shivering hard, the sickly sweat-dew clammy on his skin. Gently Gilgamesh lifted the coverlet, sliding down so that Enkidu could feel the length of his body against his own, but careful not to cause his lover pain by pressing against him.

"She said, 'Who has brought this one here?' And the one who had seized upon me, the lion-pawed man with the talons of the eagle, answered, 'I have brought him.'

" 'Why did you bring him here?' Erishkegal asked. 'He is neither beast nor man: why is he here, in the dwellings of the Netherworld?'

"And he answered her, 'It was written in the Tablet of Destinies that the Ensi of Erech must die, for he has earned the wrath of the gods. Does this man not bear the Ensi's crown upon his head, and have the priestesses of the Ensi, the votary-priestesses of Gilgamesh, not made him great?' And it seemed to me that I wore your great horned cap, and held your staff in my hand, and she could not deny it. Again Erishkegal looked upon me, so that I could not move nor speak.

" 'The one who comes to the City of Darkness,' she said, 'must stay here. The one who receives the *me* of the Netherworld does not return; the grave does not open to spit the dead forth from the mouth of earth.' And Beletseri, the scribe who knelt before her, said, 'It is written thus, and the Anuna have judged it. Do not question: thus are the rules of the Mistress of the Netherworld.'

" 'To me,' said Erishkegal, 'the dead are the same. For no one goes forth from the underworld unmarked, and when I have readied a place, it must be filled: so Gilgamesh's seat here shall not be empty, however he whiles his days in the world above. Know, then, that the flood you cannot breast has come to sweep you away. Though the trance-priest sing and chant, writhing in his ecstasies, he cannot help you; though Gula be beseeched on her hound-flanked throne, she can bring you no healing, for the whirling storm has laid you low, and the mouth of earth has seized upon you. Only the portions of the dead shall be yours, mourning and wailing, and beer poured into the funeral cup, the pipe of clay draining into the earth.'

"And then, beloved . . ." Enkidu's voice had grown very faint. He struggled to turn toward his lover; Gilgamesh wrapped his arms carefully about him, feeling the hot bones of Enkidu's rib cage press into his own body. "Then I awoke. I, who went through every hardship with you, remember me, forget not all that I went through with you."

"This dream seems to promise ill," Gilgamesh said sorrowfully. "But it is a dream of fever, a mist-mirage that will melt away when the fever fades. Sleep, my love, and I shall stay with you: I shall not abandon you."

Slowly Enkidu's breathing softened to a harsh rattle. After a time it seemed to Gilgamesh that his beloved slept again, and he closed his own eyes, letting the wasted body in the bed beside him grow unreal in his mind as he remembered how it had felt to sleep next to Enkidu, curled against him and trusting in his strength.

When Gilgamesh awoke again, the lamps had been lit and the dawn was upon them. The room seemed strangely quiet, and for a moment he could not think why. Then he realized that the dreadful gurgling of Enkidu's lungs had stopped—Enkidu lay sleeping quietly, and lying beside him, Gilgamesh could tell that the fever had broken: his lover's body was no warmer than his own.

Gilgamesh drew a deep, shuddering breath of joy and relief. More carefully than he had gotten in, fearing to break the first peaceful rest Enkidu had gotten in days, he eased himself from the bed.

Yet his effort was of little use, for Ur-Lugal had already crawled out of the pallet he shared with his mother and was toddling toward Enkidu.

"Da-da?" the child asked. "Da-da?"

Then Gilgamesh heard a sound that struck through his heart like a sudden frost blighting new shoots. The lion had raised his head, staring at Ur-Lugal, and a deep growl was rumbling in his throat.

"No," Gilgamesh whispered. "Back, my son."

But Ur-Lugal took another faltering step, and in less than a heartbeat the tawny muscles had uncoiled to launch the cat-swift spring, the huge outstretched form filling the room.

Gilgamesh did not know how he moved so fast, nor how the spear came to his hand. But suddenly the hot blood was spattering into his face, his body wrenching violently from side to side as the claws raked his shoulders and thighs, as he struggled to hold the great beast pinned against the wall, the spear-point driven through the lion's flesh and into the bricks behind. Then the lion was sagging, and even his strength could not hold it up; but the claws no longer ripped out, and the furious fanged gape lolled open as the head drooped to one side.

Panting, Gilgamesh let go of the spear, staring down at the lion's bleeding corpse. "Why?" he whispered, his voice almost inaudible beneath Ur-Lugal's screaming, even as Sululi leapt up, shrieking, "Gilgamesh! Ur-Lugal! What has happened?"

Gilgamesh swept the child up in his arms, looking hastily over him. Ur-Lugal was bawling at the top of his lungs now, but there was no scratch upon him: Gilgamesh's lunge had driven the lion across the room before its claws could touch the boy. He was shaking so badly

that he feared he would drop his son, and so he gave Ur-Lugal over to
Sululi.

"The lion . . . went mad," he panted. Then, "Enkidu? Enkidu, did
you see . . . ? I had to, I could not let it . . ." Surely Enkidu could not
have slept, could not be asleep, with Ur-Lugal's wailing ringing off the
walls. But he lay there very still, and did not move his head or speak.

"He sleeps yet," Gilgamesh said wonderingly.

Sululi looked at him, then at the huge tawny corpse of the lion
sprawled out upon the floor. At last her gaze turned to Enkidu, and the
tears began to spill slowly from the rim of her dark eyes. Holding Ur-
Lugal against her hip, she walked over to the bed, reaching down to
touch Enkidu's forehead, then to pull back the coverlet and lay her hand
upon his sunken chest.

She shook her head, but said nothing.

"No," Gilgamesh whispered. "No." Then the great shout burst from
his mouth, the sound rising through the chamber like the flapping wings
of a whirlwind, beating against the walls and all within. "No!"

He leapt to Enkidu's side, embracing him about the shoulders and
lifting him up. But his lover's wasted flesh, no longer warmed by Gilgamesh's own heat, was already cooling, and his head rolled onto one
shoulder, mouth hanging open and eyelids slack.

"My beloved, what is this sleep that has taken hold of you? You have
grown dark, you do not hear me. You do not lift your head, your heart
does not beat beneath my touch."

With infinite care, Gilgamesh laid Enkidu down again. He could not
stop the keening flowing from his throat, the words of anguish ringing
out like the calling of prayers from the high-topped shrines of the city;
he paced about like a circling eagle, coming back to his lover's body
again and again like a lioness to the corpse of her cub.

"Enkidu, you were born of gazelle and onager, raised by creatures
with tails, and all the animals of the wide wilderness. Your roads up and
down to the cedar forest mourn you, their weeping does not end night
of day. The elders of broad Erech the Sheepfold mourn you, all the folk
who blessed us mourn you, the folk of mountains and hills mourn you.
The pastures weep, they mourn you as if they were your mother, cypress

and cedar wail over you. Bear and hyena, leopard and tiger, jackal and lion, wild bull, stag, and ibex: all the creatures of the plains mourn you. The holy river Ulaja, on whose banks we strolled, mourns you, and the pure Buranun, where we filled our waterskins and poured libations, mourns you. The men of Erech the Sheepfold, who we saw looking over the walls as we killed the Bull of Heaven, mourn you. May all who praised your name in Eridu bewail you, and those who have not yet exalted your name. May the woman who brought you food mourn you, the one who set butter before you and poured beer in your mouth; may the priestess who anointed you with sweet oils weep for you. The wife who placed a ring upon you . . . May the brothers go into mourning like sisters, and shear their hair in grief." Gilgamesh set his foot on the lion's corpse, pulling the spear loose, and grasped a handful of his own locks, sawing the thick hair roughly against the bloodied edge of the spear-point until it fell loose to the floor. He was weeping now like a woman, like a lamentation-priest, howling bitterly. There were not enough words in the world to give shape to his grief; it burst out of the words like a torrent of molten bronze shattering its clay mold.

"I shall weep for you in the wilderness . . . Enkidu was the axe at my side, the bow at my arm, sword at my waist, shield before me. My festive garment, sash over my loins—an evil has risen up and robbed me! Enkidu, swift mule, fleet onager of the mountain, panther of the plains, we joined together and went into the mountains, we caught and killed the Bull of Heaven, and brought down Huwawa who dwelt in the cedar forest. Now what is this sleep that has seized you? You have become dark, you do not hear me."

Still wailing, Gilgamesh pulled up the thin coverlet of linen, for he could not bear to see Enkidu's open eyes staring into darkness any longer, or the gaping opening of his mouth black inside its nest of golden curls. He covered Enkidu's face like a bride's, crouching over him as he wept.

After a time, Gilgamesh became aware that Sululi had crept from the room, taking Ur-Lugal with her. He stepped over the sprawled body of the lion—he could not bring himself to kick it, so he kicked the blankets of Sululi's pallet instead. A tuft of wool stuck from the disarrayed folds: the shaggy cloak she had woven for Enkidu.

Gilgamesh pulled it free, grasping it with both hands. He wanted to rend it in pieces, that false protection that had done Enkidu no good in his hours of pain, but the cloth was too strongly woven for that. At last, crying tearlessly in frustration, he wrapped it about his own shivering shoulders.

The chambers seemed very small to Gilgamesh now, cluttered with all the useless, precious objects he had brought in hopes of luring Enkidu's heart back to life—full, yet empty, like an offering-shrine from which the god had been stolen. The lapis horns of the Bull of Heaven still hung, dark and gleaming, above the shrouded shape on the bed: little good his gift to Lugalbanda had done! Gilgamesh lifted down one of the horns, the oil slopping over the side. Its sweetness had grown rancid in the last twelve days, and dead flies floated in it.

"Curse you!" the Ensi shouted, throwing the horn against the wall as hard as he could. It crashed resoundingly against the bricks, flinging a great wave of oil over the floor, but the thick blue stone did not shatter or crack. As Gilgamesh bent to pick it up again, his knee—the one that had been wounded in the first battle against Agga—gave way beneath him suddenly, so that he fell with a gasp of pain, grasping at his swelling leg. He must, he realized dully, have wrenched it again in his struggle with the lion. Gilgamesh did not have the strength to rise: he sat with the horn in his hands, turning its great weight over and over again. Beautiful without, its perfect blue-black polish dusted with gold, it now came to him how ugly it was within, knotted filth sheened over with oil and bugs, as though it had long since rotted away from inside. He sat like that and did not move, even when the men came in to bear the body of the lion silently away, turning their faces from their Ensi's gaze.

SHUSUEN STOOD OUTSIDE in the *gipar*-courtyard, checking a list of figures as he consulted with Gunidu. The old shepherd had been of the greatest help in the last months. Neither his wisdom nor his eye for the quality of sheep had been diminished, so far as Shusuen could tell, by his long exile; and with the huge flocks that had to be judged for slaughter or survival, the Eanna had had much need of his skills.

"I am told that the canals are already flowing more freely since the death of the Bull of Heaven," Shusuen said. "Therefore, I think we can afford—"

He stopped, for Gunidu was not listening to him, but staring at something behind him. Shusuen turned to look, to see what had drawn the shepherd's thoughts so quickly from their conversation.

Four of the Eanna's muscular servitors were walking out of the door that led to the Ensi's quarters. Between them they bore the maned golden body of a lion—the forehead-marked lion that had followed Enkidu. His four paws hung down limply; a few dark drops of blood still dribbled from the wound in his chest, staining the dust of the court-yard.

"He is dead," Shusuen said.

Gunidu nodded.

"And Gilgamesh—I must see to him."

The shepherd lifted his hand, placing it gently on Shusuen's shoulder as if to hold him back. "Will you disturb him in his grief?" he asked. "Think on it—the lion did not die of Enkidu's sickness."

Shusuen thought a moment, then cast his resolve anew. "Yet someone must see to the Ensi. I shall be ready to run if need be."

Gilgamesh sat on the floor, his back to the shrouded figure on the bed, cradling one of the heavy lapis horns of the Bull of Heaven in his arms. His hair was disarrayed, the locks that had rippled shiny down his back now matted and hacked about, and blood streaked his chest and thighs from a number of shallow gashes. *Did he do that to himself?* Shusuen thought, shocked. Then he remembered the lion, and sighed with relief: *if the Ensi had the strength to fight, he must be that much further from his own death.* But the reeds Gilgamesh sat in were filthy, strewn with drifts of black hair, stained with blood and soaked with old oil—one careless brush of a gar-ment or hand, knocking a lamp or rush-light over, would have set the whole room aflame in a heartbeat.

The Ensi did not look up when Shusuen came in, but the scribe could see the dark emptiness in his eyes, and his heart trembled within him. *If Gilgamesh had gone mad . . .*

"Gilgamesh. Gilgamesh, do you hear me?"

"I hear you," Gilgamesh replied dully. "Go away. There is nothing for you here, scribe. He did not die in battle. You have nothing more to write of."

Though his legs shook, Shusuen walked over to the chest where he knew the Ensi's regalia was kept. By law, the penalty for what he was about to do was death; but he knew if he were to be punished so, Gilgamesh would do it by his own hands now, and his choice would have nothing to do with the law.

The scribe reached in, drawing out the high cap of overlapping horns, and held it out before Gilgamesh's eyes. "I have an Ensi," he answered. "The Ensi of Erech, upon whose head this should rest now."

Gilgamesh set the Bull's horn down on the fouled rushes, pushing himself up against the wall. He was limping badly, his knee swollen red, but he took the cap from Shusuen's hands. Instead of putting it on his own head, however, he went to the bed, placing the ruler's headgear tenderly upon the pillow.

"The Ensi of Erech is dead. Go to the city walls and tell it so, scribe. But Enkidu shall lie here, and I shall stay with him."

"And who shall I say is his heir, unless it is the one already anointed upon the throne-dais of Erech?" Shusuen persisted. "Enkidu lies there, but Gilgamesh stands here, and the duties of the living do not end at death. Would you forsake Enkidu now, letting him go unguided and unprovisioned, unweaponed and unclothed to the Netherworld? He must have the funeral that befits him, and that cannot be done unless you come forth to purify yourself and perform the rites. I shall send the lamentation-priests for Enkidu—"

"You shall not!" Gilgamesh snapped, and suddenly light burned in his eyes, like lanterns flaring up in the depths of a moonless night. "Go away! Do as you will—but do not disturb us here again." He reached for the spear that leaned against the wall, but missed his grasp; as it clattered down, Shusuen saw that its head was dark with crusted blood. Before

Gilgamesh could bend to pick it up, the scribe had already bowed quickly and left.

Outside in the courtyard again, Shusuen's steps slowed to a walk. He would have to tell all the folk of the Eanna, assembling the lamentation-priests to go throughout the city and set Erech to mourning. The daily slaughters made sure that there would be no lack of meat for the funeral-feasting, but extra rations of grain would have to be drawn to bake bread, and he would call for offerings of milk and butter. The mourning-beer would be a problem, for, at Gilgamesh's command, he had already ordered the stores of drink to be opened for the celebration after the death of the Bull of Heaven, and even had there been time to brew more, there was not enough surplus grain that he would have chosen to risk taking what was needed from the storehouses. Though the Bull was dead, the waters of the canals flowing again, the Eanna's stocks were still far too low to risk extravagance, not now, not until they had another year or two of good harvests behind them. Shusuen would have to send to the taverns throughout the city, perhaps in exchange for a remittance of taxes for a time . . . yet he thought the cost there would not be too heavy, for even the meanest of tavernkeepers had no ill word to say about Enkidu, whatever they might have muttered about Gilgamesh beneath their breath. And he would have to call up the diggers and stone-workers, so that a proper burial chamber could be constructed, as befitted Enkidu. For it was true, what Gilgamesh had cried out in his grief: Enkidu had been as much the Ensi as Gilgamesh, and should remain so, in death as well as life. Though the figures were already adding themselves in Shusuen's mind, more quickly than his fingers could slide the beads back and forth on his scribe's counting-web, those costs he could not begrudge, even at the thought that the gold and silver might be better weighed out in buying grain from other cities.

*As for himself . . .*

Shusuen breathed deeply, testing his heart as a soldier might probe at a healing wound. He had already done his weeping in private, when the finality of Enkidu's death had made itself manifest to him. Now he felt only numb sorrow at the loss of the lion-man, and that was already over-spread by his burgeoning worry for Gilgamesh.

The scribe's steps quickened again, his mind made up. First he would find the Ensi's body-servant, to be sure that Gilgamesh's chambers were cleaned properly and his wounds tended before they festered—no, he would go to Birhurturre first, asking him to choose a few of the most trusted men in case the Ensi needed to be restrained. Then he would tell the En and the Shamhatu, if they had not heard the sorrowful news already; then he would see to arranging the details of the funeral. He still had Gilgamesh's cylinder-seal, so the Ensi could be left in peace for a day or two more, until he was actually needed to perform the rites, and by then—Shusuen could only pray—Gilgamesh must be calmer, must have accepted that Enkidu had gone down a road where he could not yet follow.

# 9

For seven days and seven nights the city of Erech mourned for Enkidu. The lamentation-priests wailed from the city walls and along the streets; those who had known him rent their garments and tore their hair. The hot weather had not yet broken, but the air was hazy and muggy, weighted with dampness and the threat of thunder to come. Gilgamesh stayed closeted in his chamber with the body, allowing no one in save Enatarzi, who brought him food and drink.

"Yes, he is eating and drinking," Enatarzi said to Shusuen. "And the wounds he got from the lion are healing cleanly, though I cannot say why, since he would not let me so much as wash the blood from his gashes. But he lies in the bed and clings to Enkidu's corpse; I have heard him speaking to the body as though he could coax him back to life. Yet . . ." The eunuch leaned closer, his breath soft against Shusuen's ear. "I think this cannot last much longer. Though the Ensi must have forgotten what clean air smells like, the stink has reached the hallway, and the flies . . ."

Shusuen grimaced. "It is as well that the burial chamber is near-done. Keep a close watch, and call me at once if there are any changes."

Yet the next morning, while crossing the *gipar*-courtyard at dawn with Basthotep pouncing at his heels, Shusuen caught sight of a huge shaggy figure emerging from the Ensi's door. For a moment, the faint morning light deceiving his shortsighted eyes, he could only think that a tame bear had somehow gotten loose in the city, wandering about into the

Eanna. Then he realized that the tufted pelt was too pale for a bear's, and his next blink resolved the shape into a man—wild-haired and unshaven, garments torn and disarrayed beneath the shaggy cloak, but still, recognizably, Gilgamesh.

"Shusuen!" Gilgamesh shouted. "Come to me!" His voice was hoarse and broken from weeping, like the cry of a vulture, but his words were clear.

Shusuen hurried to his Ensi's side, careless of the tightness beginning to wheeze in his chest as he ran. "Yes?"

"Have you tablet and reed with you? I have orders to give."

"Always, my Ensi."

"Let it be known that I decree this, and issue this call through the land. 'Artisan, metalworker, stone-worker, goldsmith! Create my friend, shape a statue of him. O my beloved, though your body of clay perishes, your shape shall not be lost to Erech, nor shall I cease to gaze upon your face. Of lapis shall be your chest, of gold your body, all the size of life, as you have always towered over other men, and the horns of the Bull of Heaven shall adorn you.' "

Dutifully Shusuen noted the words down, trying not to wrinkle his nose as he wrote. Close to, the charnel stink that clung to Gilgamesh overpowered the smell of his unwashed body; standing beside him was like standing by an open grave. Less fastidious than his human caretaker, Basthotep crept up to Gilgamesh, whiskers twitching in excitement as he rubbed against the Ensi's legs and purred, then stood on his hind legs to paw passionately at the filthy tatters of Gilgamesh's torn kilt and the end of his dangling belt. But Gilgamesh hardly seemed to notice: his gaze was already lifting to the eastern horizon, even as the high voice of a *gala-*priest rang out from the shrine above, chanting, not one of the songs of lamentation that had sounded above the city for the last week, but the familiar dawn-time praise of Inanna.

*Honored Counselor, Ornament of Heaven, Joy of An! When sweet sleep has ended in the bedchamber, you appear like bright daylight . . .*

"O Enkidu, my beloved," Gilgamesh murmured. "I had you recline on the great couch, on the couch of honor I let you recline."

*When all the lands and the people of Sumer assemble, those sleeping on the roofs and those sleeping by the walls, when they sing your praises, bringing their concerns to you, you study their words . . .*

"I had you sit in the place of ease upon my left, and the rulers of the world to kiss your feet. The people of Erech I had mourn over you, and the joyous people were filled with woe over you."

The full chorus came in now, the swelling song of gladness that had awakened Shusuen nearly every dawn of his life. Now it brought his heart a special easing, for it seemed to mark the end of the mourning for Enkidu, promising that life would return again to its daily round.

*My Lady looks in sweet wonder from heaven, the people of Sumer parade before the holy Inanna. Inanna, the Lady of the Morning is radiant. I sing your praises, holy Inanna. The Lady of the Morning is radiant on the horizon.*

"Have brought forth for me," Gilgamesh ordered, "the great offering-table of precious wood, a carnelian bowl of honey and a lapis bowl of cream, set out in the sight of Utu. Enkidu shall still receive the offerings of an Ensi as before, that none may forget, just as his body is to be dressed in the clothes of life, and washed with the sweet-scented oil."

"As you wish, my Ensi."

Gilgamesh turned away, but Basthotep's claws caught in a frayed strip of his kilt, so that he had to reach down to disentangle the cat. For a moment he hesitated, then picked Basthotep up. The cat purred louder, butting his tabby head against Gilgamesh and kneading the Ensi's cloak hard with his paws.

"What became of the lion's body?" Gilgamesh asked suddenly.

"My Ensi, I had the hide tanned for you, and the body we buried in Inanna's shrine, as seemed fittest for such a noble beast."

Gilgamesh's mouth worked, as though he were chewing over two answers at once, but he said only, "Bring the skin to me. I shall wear it after my beloved."

WRAPPED IN ENKIDU's cloak, with the lion-skin about his shoulders and Enkidu's bow and quiver slung over his back, his lover's axe in his belt, Gilgamesh limped forth into the streets of Erech when he had made his offering. He paid no attention to the people who stared after him, to the soft murmurs going before and behind him, no more than to the flies buzzing about his head. He knew only that he must walk, and if his knee stabbed a dagger of pain into his thigh with each step, then at least it drew a little corner of his mind from the aching of his heart. And yet it seemed to him as if Enkidu walked near, just out of sight—and yet that, too, was a torment, for he could not see or touch his lover, only feel the warmth of the lion's pelt about him and the coarse fur that he rubbed constantly between his fingers.

There, in that tavern—what was the barmaid's name? Gilgamesh could not remember, though her rounded face and crooked-toothed smile were clear in his memory, like the swelling of her breasts beneath his hands as she leaned back to lick Enkidu's bearded throat, giggling between the two of them. Enkidu had lingered often in that copper-smith's workshop, asking the burly man endless questions about his craft, which the smith answered patiently, never missing a single hammer-tap as he spoke. That fruit-merchant's stand—there were no melons there now, only strings of dried onions and garlic.

At last Gilgamesh came to the middle of the city square, where his war memorial had been raised, its stone freezing the scenes of battle, of Enkidu driving the chariot in which Gilgamesh stood with axe uplifted and the bodies of the foe falling about them. Looking upon it, fresh tears burned through the swollen channels of Gilgamesh's eyes.

"How foolish I was," he said softly, "to think that stone, or words, or memories, could make up for a lost life." The words he had spoken before the battle—*Know that those who fall bravely shall be remembered*—came back to him now, empty and stupid as the croaking of a crane in the reeds.

How many had died in that fight? How many women, their year of widowhood still not done, mourned yet for their beloved husbands, even as he mourned for Enkidu? *I risked our lives in the battle*, Gilgamesh thought, *because I did not believe we could die—because I did not know death, for all my battles before, nor could I guess at how it seizes upon the heart.*

"Was it worth it?" the Ensi asked himself, the words bitter as a crushed apricot-kernel on his tongue. For a thousand years of Erech's tribute to Kish would not buy back Enkidu's life: if it could, he would promise it at once, he would crawl on his belly before Agga and lick the old man's sandals. But a thousand years of tribute, or ten thousand, would not bring Enkidu back to him, nor compensate a single lover for the loss of a loved one. "Was it worth all those lives?"

*Was it worth one?*

And who could put a price on life, that one treasure that, once lost, could never be regained? What did it matter that there would be more wealth and pleasure in Erech with the tribute lifted and the war won? What were the wealth and pleasure of ten thousand, or a hundred thousand, when weighed against a single life? What was the worth of memory or bravery, praise or power, honor or tradition or the tales of mighty ancestors?

"Nothing," Gilgamesh whispered, "to one whose love is slain."

He turned on his heel and walked from that place, for he could no longer bear to stand there. Had he worn his sword, that weapon shaped only for slaying men, he would have broken it there, letting the glittering fragments refute the praise of his battle-glory. But he did not have it by him, and the monument reproached him, a memorial of his crimes carved in everlasting stone.

Ahead of Gilgamesh, the great gate of cedar reared high and gleaming against the mist-hazed sun, the ruddy wood shining rich and sweet in the morning light. The artisans must have worked doubly and triply hard, to have finished it so soon . . . He stood a moment, staring up at the gate. The scent of the cedar forest, the warm days floating down the river . . . *Enkidu's voice, already weak with sickness, croaking, "Had I known, O Gate, that it would come to this, and that this would be your gratefulness. I would have taken your planks and chopped them up . . ."*

Gilgamesh drew the axe from his belt, clenching his hand tightly about the smooth hilt. And yet he could not strike the carven wood, for Enkidu's image was graven there, speaking silently and forever to his own. Though he wished that he had never looked up upon the mighty peaks of the tree-carpeted mountains, that he had never set foot upon the road that led to the Land of the Living, Gilgamesh's arm would not raise, nor could he swing the axe in the long glittering arc that would end with its blade biting deep into the smooth cedarwood. After a little time, he put the weapon back and walked through the gate, heedless of the guards' voices that hailed him.

The Buranun flowed quietly, its green shores still speckled white with a few flocks of sheep. But Gilgamesh turned away from it, his back to Erech, his knee cracking painfully with every step. Behind him he heard the distant rumble of thunder through the heavy air. The weather was breaking at last: let it break, let the downpour flood behind him, for he no longer cared. Let Erech find another shepherd, until his son was grown, let priests and scribes and gods do as they pleased: he was done with the things of men.

DAY AFTER DAY, Gilgamesh made his way farther from the city, into the wastelands. His only waterskin was an old one some former traveler had cast away; he smeared its cracks with the fat of the animals he killed, so that the slow oozing through the leather would not leech the liquid away too quickly. The tatters of the kilt he had rent in his grieving soon tore and fell away from him in clumps like the wool of an unshorn sheep snagging on thorny branches, so that at last he had to wrap himself in the raw hides of hyena and ibex, deer and steppes-panther, replacing each skin with a new one whenever the chafing and stink grew too great for him to bear. The straps of his sandals had long since broken, and the soles of his feet had grown hard as horn, cracking like the hooves of a donkey that had long walked unattended over stony roads. He did not know where he was going, nor what he meant to do: the loss of Enkidu tormented him like the endless pain in his swollen knee, constant as the buzzing of flies about the bloodied stink of the skins he wore and the thirst for water that did not taste of pitch and old goat-hide.

Yet worse than all was the gnawing at his soul that made all the miseries of his body a mercy, a deserved punishment for his deeds. When Gilgamesh stood up in the morning, wrapping the half-rotted hides about himself, the rising sun echoed his dawn-time words to Enkidu at the gate of the cedar forest: *My beloved, experienced in battle, well-used to fighting, you need not fear death . . . Your heart should burn to do battle now—do not heed death, do not lose your courage, for I need you.* And to the silent reproach graven into his memory, he could answer only: I spoke thus, and killed my beloved. Could I not have been content with life and joy? It was fit that he stank: it seemed to him that his soul had grown fetid, the death he had brought on Enkidu rising from his own pores like the stench of stale alcohol from the skin of a drunk. He was tainted in himself, for all he sought to do led to the same end: the death of those who trusted him, who believed that they would help and support him, and gave their lives for such bad repayment. It was right that his knee swelled and ached, his body bearing the spoor of the battle that had sprung from his own pride and rashness. And Gilgamesh knew that it was well that he had left Erech, that he wandered here in the wild land of strangeness and death, for he was himself a curse upon all that he touched. Though a few might miss him for a time, or speak kindly of him once he was gone, it was better for him to be out here, nameless and faceless as a leper.

In time, Gilgamesh's path began to lead upward, into the rocky hills. The count of days had passed from his mind, but the coarse spotted hide of the hyena he had killed on the plain some time ago had grown slimy, its flesh-side beginning to turn green, and the footfalls of carrion-eaters were coming closer in the night. So he left it upon a rock, hiding himself behind a screen of thornbushes, and waited to see what wind and luck would bring him.

Surely enough, as the sun's light began to redden toward evening, a small bear came bumbling into the clearing, snuffling and casting about after the scent of rotting meat. Drawing the bow silently—although it was no longer easy for him to hold: the days of his mourning and wandering had eaten away at his strength like sunlight slowly withering fruit—Gilgamesh waited until the bear stood on its hind legs to look at the hide, reaching out a black-taloned paw to snag it. Then he let the arrow snap forth, to sink deep between the bear's ribs. The beast stood for a moment, pawing at the air like a man striking out against a foe, and then toppled, thick furry limbs jerking and writhing against the ground. When it had stopped moving, Gilgamesh tossed a pebble at its face. The little stone bounced off the bear's wet black nose, but it did not twitch. Nocking a second arrow to make sure, he crept closer.

The bear's eyes were already dull, flies gathering upon its lolling pink tongue. It was certainly dead, and so Gilgamesh grasped its warm paws, turning it upon its back to begin the job of butchery. As he skinned the bear, it became more difficult to look upon; naked, save for the wrinkled black snout and mitten-paws, it might almost have been the corpse of a short broad man. It was easy, as well—once he had sliced carefully through the layers of thick muscle over the abdomen so that the yellow fat came out with the smooth grayish coils of bowel—to picture his own belly slit open so with his knife, his own entrails, guts and dark liver and curl of stomach, laid out to the open air. Gilgamesh breathed deeply through his mouth, trying not to gag at the mingling of the butchering-odor with his own reek. To loathe himself just a little more, turning away from the sweet taste of living wind to the musty air below, and go to the joyless land . . . it was only fear that held his knife-hand to the bear's body and not to his own.

Though he could not rest for long, with the sunset glowing redder in the west and no fit drill to make a fire for the night, now and again Gilgamesh would stop to ease his eyes against the sky. And when he looked up from the bulging tangle of intestines that still quivered hot beneath his hands, he saw the eagle circling high above him.

"You shall have your share," he said to it. His voice, unused for these many days, was no more than the raspy growl of an old dog, but the sound of human words cheered him a little. "As Etana fed you after your days of starvation in the pit, your suffering of the serpent's revenge for devouring its young—I, too, shall feed you rich flesh. And will you bear me up to heaven as you bore him?"

The thought came over him in a dizzying rush, like drinking a pot of honey after days of starvation. In early days, it was said, the eagle had borne Etana up in search of the plant of birth, which grew only in the heavens, for the old king of Kish had gotten no heir. Though Etana's courage had failed him as the earth passed from view, nevertheless he was saved: he brought the plant back to Kish and by its power he begot a son named Balih, and lived for fifteen hundred and sixty years.

But although he had trodden in the heavens and eaten of the plant of birth, what lasting good had it done Etana? For Enkidu had seen him in the hall of dust, sitting among the dead and servant to Erishkegal, beneath the crown of the Queen of the Netherworld. The old king had avoided death's snares for a long time, true, but at last the noose of earth had closed about his foot, and he, like all men, had been dragged bird-fluttering down the road of no return.

"And I, too, shall I not die like Enkidu?" Gilgamesh asked himself despairingly. "Deep sorrow has sunken into my belly; I fear death, and now I roam the hills. Who, among men, may live forever? No dead man deserves death, for nothing can pay him back for the crime of stolen life; no living man deserves to mourn the dead, for nothing can recompense him for losing the beloved. And yet, all who live must die, and all loves end in mourning. And who, among men, may live forever?"

Though the question was bitter and rhetorical, even as he tugged carefully at the thin ligaments holding the bear's liver in its belly, hastening to cut the gall-bladder out before it got too dark to see and the rich meat was ruined, the answer crept upon Gilgamesh like the slowly growing light of dawn. For one man did indeed hold the gift of eternal life—one man and one woman, who had walked upon the earth as he walked now, and still trod the ground living. Utnapishti and his wife, sole survivors of the Great Flood, dwelling at the Mouth of All Rivers: they would have the answer to his questions. For the first time since he set out for Erech, a glimmer of light began to brighten in Gilgamesh's heart, like a single rush-light glowing small behind the altar of a great dark shrine.

"I will seize the road," Gilgamesh said, lifting his head. "I will go quickly to the house of Utnapishti, Ubaratutu's son, though I have arrived at the mountain-passes by night. From him I shall learn the secret of life, and bring it back to Erech. Then no lover need fear for the breath of a beloved, no parent for a child: those who walk at night need not fear the knife of the foot-pad, nor the soldier his foeman's axe; fear shall be ended with death, and all be safe and joyous. And I . . . perhaps I may atone thus for all I have done."

GILGAMESH MADE HIS night-nest beside the path, underneath Enkidu's shaggy cloak and the bear's slowly cooling hide, with his head pillowed on the rolled-up lion-skin. After a time, it seemed to him that he stood upon a promontory, a crag of rock jutting out above a great dark ocean beneath the star-glittering sky. Around him rose a chorus of voices, as though the rocks and sea themselves were singing.

"In the first days, in the very first days,
In the first nights, in the very first nights,
In the first years, in the very first years,
In the first days when all things needed were brought into being,
In the first days when all things needed were properly nourished,
When bread was baked in the shrines of the land,
And bread was tasted in the homes of the land,
When heaven had moved away from earth,
And earth was parted from heaven,
And the name of man was fixed;
When the Sky God, An, had carried off the heavens,
And the Air God, Enlil, had carried off the earth,
When the Queen of the Great Below, Erishkegal, was given the
       Netherworld as her domain,
He set sail, the Father set sail,
Enki, God of Wisdom, set sail for the Netherworld . . ."

The voices rose to the howling of the wind, whipping up the waves, and Gilgamesh saw a boat upon the sea, prow and stern curling high and proud. A long-bearded man stood behind the prow with a pole in his hand; upon his head was a tall cap, its layered rows of horns turned outward so their points curved up before and behind him like the branches of a tree. The winds blew harder, hurling glittering hailstones against the boat, small stones like a shower of silver above, huge stones seething up from the water to charge the keel like onrushing turtles below. The waves rose higher, devouring the bow of the boat in front like a pack of wolves and hammering against the stern behind with the mighty blows of lions; their froth dashed up against Gilgamesh's high crag, the fury of the storm blowing it into his eyes.

Gilgamesh blinked hard, wiping the pounding water from his eyes again and again. Slowly, through the blowing foam, something began to take shape before him—a pale-barked sapling, rooted on the riverbank where he now stood, its slender branches whipping about in the whirling wind that tore at its long green leaves. The wind was growing stronger, and the waters rising, eating the earth away from the sapling's roots.

Suddenly it toppled, falling into the river, and the white-laced torrent carried it away like a stick.

It seemed to Gilgamesh that he watched the little tree rising and falling, battered by the rushing flood; that he, somehow, was being swept downriver with it. But then he saw the woman standing by the river's bank, staring into the water and waiting. Her long dark hair was adorned with ornaments of gold, and a double string of little lapis beads hung upon her breast; her robe was pale blue linen, and she went barefoot. Her delicate oval face was like the Shamhatu's, but younger, more radiant, unmarked by the little lines of care or trouble that were already beginning to trace their first patterns around the priestess' eyes. Gracefully she bent, plucking the sapling from the river in a single swift motion.

"I shall bring this tree to Erech," she said. Her voice, too, was like the Shamhatu's, and yet it rang with overtones of sweet power that sent a thrill of delight and desire through Gilgamesh.

Then it seemed to him that he saw Inanna walking through the gates of Erech—the old gates, that had stood before the building of his siege-wall—with the tree in her hand, carrying it to the Eanna's courtyard. With her own slim hands she lifted trowel and shovel, digging out a hole and pouring the loosened soil again over the roots of the tree, then tamped all about it with her foot to settle the earth about it.

"How long will it be," the young Inanna asked, her sweet voice poignantly wistful as she turned her gaze upward to the heavens, "until I have a shining throne to sit upon? How long will it be, until I have a shining bed to lie upon?"

The little tree grew and sprouted beneath her gaze, and Gilgamesh felt the years passing. Five years, then ten: the tree grew huge and thick, but its bark did not split. Inanna looked upon it, smiling, seeing how its wood grew, as though she were already measuring throne and bed. But then Gilgamesh saw the flicker of darkness at the tree's foot, the gleaming slither of the serpent through its knotting roots. Inanna called to the snake, chanting it forth, but it would not be charmed; now and again its head darted through a root-loop, forked tongue tasting the air, and Inanna could do nothing.

And even as she bent and sang to the snake she could not charm, the clouds began to rush in overhead, their black flood overspilling the sky like a river bursting its banks. The wind tore the reed-thatch from the huts of Erech, flinging the bundles of dried grass through the air and scattering the little birds across the sky, tearing and tattering the leaves of the tree. The cries from the city streets were far-off and faint beneath its howling, and Inanna's tree bent and swayed, groaning as though it would be ripped up again. The dark clouds spread into a huge beating of eagle's wings, the torrential rain that poured from them spinning into hundreds of whirlwinds, each rending whatever lay in its path. Between the wings lowered a gigantic black lion's head, mouth gaping open to show fangs of flashing lightning; below dropped two great lightning-talons, each holding a lion-headed storm-chick—the monstrous Imdugud-bird and its young, which Lugalbanda had once met in the wilderness, whose likeness had dragged Enkidu down to the Netherworld. The great bird perched in the topmost branches, giving out an awful call; the whirlwinds of its flapping tore out leaves and twigs to stir into a nest and it settled its chicks within.

The Imdugud-bird slowly folded in its black wings, the sky clearing; the sun shone hot through the damp air again, wisps of mist seeping up from the streets of the storm-racked city. Inanna stared upward at it in distress, grasping thick locks of her hair and pulling at them with both fists. "Why have you come to nest in my tree, in my fine tree, that I plucked from the Buranun and set to grow in Erech? Why are you here?" she cried. But the bird only screech-yowled mockingly, its young making their own grating, scraping cries from beneath the wide shelter of its wings.

Then a second answered it: though it was broad daylight, the call was the mournful, unearthly *whoo, whoo* of the owl. And this chilled Gilgamesh's spine like the trailing of a cold finger down his back, tracing an icy line between his buttocks to his crotch—a lover's caress from a loathed one. The black owl swooped in from the desert: a woman's red-nippled breasts dangled from her feathered bosom, and behind her cruel beak, her face was that of a woman as well. Dark eyes heavily lined with kohl, red paint brightening her cheeks, she seemed like a portrait of Inanna painted by a clumsy artist, the heavy lines changing the goddess' young sensuality to leering lust.

Inanna whirled, her face whitening with wrath as she stared at the twisted half-twin hovering above her. "Lilitu! Get you gone, back to the wastelands and desert places which are your dwelling. The infants of Erech are not for you to seize upon, nor should you pass the city walls, or settle in my holy garden."

But the owl-woman swept down, her crooked claws clasping the wide bole of the tree above Inanna's head. She swung her breasts from side to side; her feathered tail lifted to show the rounding of her white buttocks, the black flash of her vulva, as her talons began to tear into the bark. "Here I shall make my home," she hooted. "Here, in this tree that you wished to have as throne and bed, shall I dwell, and you cannot drive me out. I shall have the young men of Erech as I please, and the infants shall I take as my own."

Inanna reached upward, grasping at her, but Lilitu was perched just above her reach. The owl-woman laughed mockingly, sinking her bed-hole deeper and deeper into the trunk. Then tears streamed down from Inanna's face as she implored the three of them, serpent and storm-bird and demon, to leave her tree, but they paid her no heed.

"Who will rid my tree of these creatures?" she asked despairingly. "Who will free my holy garden, and cleanse my holy city?"

Gilgamesh was about to speak, but a deep growling sound froze his bones, stopping the words in his mouth. Something heavy and clammy lay over him like a night-demon, something that stank of staling blood, and he saw only the dark that shrouded him.

The growl came again; Gilgamesh's body jerked upright, shaking, and his eyes opened to the faint starlight. It had been a dream, he thought in a sudden rush of relief. He lay beneath the skin of the bear he had slain that evening, all was well—save for the soft snarling and snuffling he could hear in the bushes where he had thrown the bones of the bear, a sound he knew; for had he not heard Enkidu's lion chewing just so upon the haunches of sheep beside the sickbed in those last dreadful days?

Yet though the noise had been comforting then, it filled his heart with fear now. Gilgamesh was not weaponed to face a lion; he had only bow and axe, and his arms were weaker than they had been. Holding his breath, he sat without twitching, only his eyes flickering about him until the bushes rustled again. Sparked by the sound, he cast the bearskin as far from him as he could, sprinting to a low tree that grew by the path and clambering up it, ignoring the agony that flared in his knee and the fiery scraping of rough bark upon his skin as he climbed.

The two lionesses burst from the thornbushes, pale shapes circling in the darkness. The eyes of one lit lambent green as she gazed up at him; her tail lashed, and she crouched to spring.

*Will it end so?* Gilgamesh wondered, grasping his axe in one hand and holding tight to the tree with the other. He would strike one good blow, at least: the lioness would not take her prey without paying for it.

But after a moment, her taut haunches eased and she stood again, sniffing the air, then followed her comrade to the bearskin lying in a dark heap where Gilgamesh had flung it. The two of them nosed at the skin, scratching and pawing at it for a little while, until they were sure that there was no meat on it, then slipped into the bushes again. But Gilgamesh waited where he was, shivering in the tree, until the sun had risen well into the morning sky and he was sure that he was alone again. Descending, he looked at the great gashes the lionesses' casual pawing had left in the bear's hide and shuddered, his hand passing over the fresh-healed scars on his shoulders and thighs.

"That I should fear lions," Gilgamesh said wonderingly, "that I should hear their sounds in the night and be afraid! I am not the man I was. And yet I shall press on to Utnapishti, for there will be an end to all my fears, and the sorrows of men." He picked up the tattered bearskin, wrapping and belting it about his loins, and set off again.

Though the night in the tree had inflamed his leg so that he had to stop before noon to cut a walking-staff, Gilgamesh did not let the pain of his limp slow him much, even as the trail grew higher and rockier. The lionesses had left him only a few scraps of bear-meat to scrape off the chewed and broken bones, but it was enough to sustain him through the day, its raw strength bloody in his mouth.

THIS NIGHT, WHEN Gilgamesh stopped to make his evening resting place, he chose a nest in the rocks above the path, where no wild beasts could come upon him in his sleep. Rest did not come easily to him that night, for he could not bend his swollen knee. The stones bit into his body, and the night air cut cold through the rents in the bear-hide that covered his calves and feet where Enkidu's tufted cloak did not reach. And yet, slowly, his eyes began to lighten with dawn; the howling of the wind shaped itself into words, the crying of a woman's voice, high and mellow as a golden flute above the cymbal-bright singing of the little morning birds.

"O Utu, my brother, leaving your royal bedchamber at the coming of dawn," she cried, "O Utu, in the days when destinies were decreed, when abundance overflowed in the land, when the Sky God took the heavens and the Air God the earth, when Erishkegal was given the Netherworld for her domain, the God of Wisdom, Father Enki, set sail for the Netherworld, and the Netherworld rose up and attacked him. At that time a tree, a single tree, grew by the banks of the Buranun. The South Wind pulled at its roots and ripped at its branches, until the waters of the Buranun carried it away. I plucked the tree from the river, I brought it to my holy garden, I tended the tree, waiting for my shining throne and bed. Then a serpent who could not be charmed made its nest in the root of the tree; the Imdugud-bird set his young in the branches of the tree, and the dark maid, the *lilitu*, built her home in the trunk. I wept—how I wept—but they would not leave my tree."

Yet though Inanna gazed upward, the light of the sun gilding the tear-streaks down her delicate face, it seemed that she received no answer. The folded black wings of the Imdugud-bird did not stir at the crown of the tree; Lilitu's hollow bed in the bole only rustled darkly, and the serpent slithered and writhed among the roots as before. For the whole day she waited thus, and through the night likewise, her hands raised in supplication.

At last Inanna turned her face from the newly dawning sky, and a little tingling shock went through Gilgamesh as her eyes met his. "O Gilgamesh, my brother," she said pleadingly, "in the days when destinies were decreed, when abundance overflowed in Sumer . . ."

A strange feeling of strength and lightness came over Gilgamesh as he listened to her plea. His armor was ready by his side, and he fastened it about his chest, the heavy bronze seeming weightless as a breast-plate of feathers. Lifting his great axe to his shoulder, he strode forth, entering Inanna's holy garden.

When the serpent's head darted forth again. Gilgamesh's axe flickered down. The edge cleaved the snake's skull into a neat fan of blood and bone-fragments; though its body thrashed among the roots, it would nest there no more. At the sound of the blow, the Imdugud-bird lifted its lion-head. Its wings rose, darkening the sky; a single gust of wind hammered down as it rose into the air, holding its chicks. From within the bole of the tree came a single dreadful screech: wood cracked and smashed within, a single trail of blood dribbling out along the bark. Like a blowfly creeping forth from a corpse, Lilitu slowly crept out of the dark hole she had hacked, spreading her wings to glide away on the wake of the storm, back to the desert wastelands.

Now Gilgamesh took the spade from Inanna's hands, digging about the great gnarled roots of the tree to loosen it. Huge as it was, it came easily from the ground, falling slowly to lie prostrate in the courtyard before Inanna's shrine. Birhurturre was there with him, an axe in his hand, and many of Gilgamesh's other young warriors; Shusuen was there, too, holding a planing-tool. And above their heads rose Enkidu's golden mane, his green eyes gleaming with delight. Gilgamesh ran to him, embracing him tightly— the broad-muscled back beneath his grip, the soft curls of fair hair against his chest, the sweet warmth of his lips and the caress of Enkidu's tongue on his mouth! It seemed as though a shadow had fallen away beneath the sun's brightness, a dark night-dream dispelled by the daylight into fading wisps of lost memory, and Gilgamesh might have clung there forever.

But there was much work to be done, and so together, as Inanna watched, they set to trimming the branches from the tree, stripping the rough bark from the trunk to lay bare the pale, gleaming flesh beneath. The wood split easily beneath the blows of the bronze blades, shining smooth under the strokes of Shusuen's planing-saw. With the edge of his axe, Gilgamesh notched the pieces to fit together; with its back, he tapped in the glistening gold nails.

"Behold, I have carved a throne for my holy sister from the trunk of the tree," he said, "and from the trunk of the tree, I have carved a bed for Inanna."

Inanna stepped forward, reaching down. Her fingers moved lightly about a coiled root and a straight branch, stripping them clean; ring and rod she held out to Gilgamesh.

"Behold, from the roots of the tree I have fashioned a *pukku* for my brother," her clear voice answered, "and from the crown of the tree I have fashioned a *mikku* for Gilgamesh, the hero of Erech."

Gilgamesh took the ring and rod, the holy regalia of the Ensi, from her. And in his hands they seemed to shift, until he held a shining drum and a bull-headed drumstick.

Now he was walking through the streets of Erech with Enkidu beside him, beating the drum, its compelling rhythm drawing the young men forth from their houses to follow him. In street and lane he made the *pukku* resound, for the siege-wall was rising slowly about the city, and Gilgamesh knew that war would soon be upon them. And where he went, under the light of the evening star the men crowded behind him; the women ran after their menfolk, mothers bringing bread to their sons and sisters bringing water to their brothers. The warriors shouted battle-cries, and the young men clamored with gladness, even though the throng was thinning as they dropped away one by one. But behind them the women wept, their wailing rising higher for the dead and the captives, bemoaning their losses and their widowhood.

Gilgamesh led his host around the city, back to his dwelling. Yet there, as he passed into his chamber, the cries of the women seemed louder, as though they issued from the walls. And beside his bed, a great dark hole, like an empty well without bottom, gaped in the tile floor where the body of his father Lugalbanda had lain. He leaned over to look at it, and the wood of *pukku* and *mikku* was suddenly oil-slick in his hands. Rod and ring, drumstick and drum, they shifted and twisted from his grasp, plunging gleaming into the black depths.

A cry of shock burst from Gilgamesh's throat. He lay full-length upon the floor, reaching down as far as he could, but his hand could not touch the holy items, nor could his foot find them. Sitting down at that gate, the empty black eye of the Netherworld, Gilgamesh wept, his face cold with paleness.

"O my *pukku*, my *mikku!*" he cried. "My *pukku* with lust irresistible, with dance-rhythm unrivaled—if only I had left my *pukku* in the wood-worker's house, if only it had been with the woodworker's wife, like the mother who bore me, the daughter of the woodworker beside me like my younger sister—my *pukku*, who will bring it up from the Nether-world? My *mikku*, who will bring it up from the Netherworld?"

Then Enkidu's arm was about Gilgamesh's shoulders, lifting him up. "My beloved," Enkidu whispered, "why do you weep? Why is your heart heavy? I shall bring your *pukku* up from the Netherworld, I shall bring your *mikku* up from the eye of the Netherworld."

Gilgamesh turned to meet Enkidu's embrace, the warm relief washing through his heart like the scented water of a purification-bath; yet behind it was a new trembling, at the thought of Enkidu descending into the black opening of his floor. "My dearest love," he answered, "if now you will go down to where the earth groans, I shall speak a word to you: take the secret thing I uncover, follow my advice." Now the knowledge seemed to bubble up in him like a stream of bitumen flowing black to the river's surface: he did not know from where it came, but he knew its truth, with all the certainty of a blade striking home.

"Do not put on a clean garment, lest it mark you as a foreigner. Do not anoint yourself with sweet-smelling oil from the beaker, lest at its scent they settle all about you. Do not cast the throwing stick in the Netherworld, for those the throwing stick strikes will turn and surround you. Carry not a stave in your hand, for the shades will flutter all around you. Tie no sandals on your feet, raise up no cry in the place where the earth cries out. Kiss not the beloved wife, nor strike the hated wife; kiss not the beloved child, nor strike the hated child, lest the song of the Netherworld tighten about you—the song for her who is sleeping, who is sleeping, for Erishkegal, mother of Ninazu, who is sleeping, whose holy shoulders no garment covers, whose holy breast no cloth drapes. This is my advice, if you must go down into the Netherworld . . ."

". . . THE NETHERWORLD," a harsh voice grated. The arm about Gil-gamesh's neck was not loving, but rough, and another hand was grasping for his wrist, bending it back. He cried out, twisting away, and felt the keen edge of a knife sliding across his shoulder. Gilgamesh tried to spring up, but his leg buckled beneath him; he rolled up onto his good knee instead, grasping for his belt-axe as he glanced hurriedly around. The light of the crescent moon showed him the shadowy shapes of three men, one turning Enkidu's bow over in his hands. The largest of the three, the knifeman who had seized him in his sleep, was coming straight for him, the point of the blade—held loosely underhanded—tracing tiny glittering circles in the darkness. *Foot-pads, outlaws, who meant to kill and rob.* The thought flashed through Gilgamesh's mind in a second, but they knew what they were about. The one who held Enkidu's bow had dropped it already rather than waste time stringing it; they were spreading out, flanking him.

In a heartbeat Gilgamesh had drawn the dagger from his belt and thrown it left-handed. Whistling through the air like an arrow, it struck low and off center, sinking into the knifeman's shoulder rather than his throat; but he cried out and dropped the blade. His back to a boulder, Gilgamesh heaved himself to his feet. He should not wait for them to circle him at their will, he knew—but with his betraying knee, he could not lunge in to attack.

The other two rushed in together, the axe of the taller raised, that of the shorter whistling in toward his waist. Gilgamesh turned his body hard into the high blow, bringing his left arm up under the stroke to strike his foe's wrist aside even as the same powerful twist drove his axe-hand down, chopping the weapon from the other man's hand. Reflexively he threw himself back from the tall outlaw's backhanded slice, all his weight behind the tip of his axe-head as it stabbed through the body of the man behind him. Gilgamesh jerked the axe free even as his knee gave beneath him again, swinging it in a wide arc. The robber's weapon passed above his head, its wind cold through Gilgamesh's hair even as his own blade bit solidly into the other man's thigh. A huge gout of hot blood spurted over Gilgamesh's face as he twisted the axe free, raising it barely in time to meet the other's falling blade. He did not try to block the downward force of the blow, only to deflect it inward, adding his own strength to smash the axe hard into the outlaw's groin. The tall man screamed and went down, but another blow slammed into Gilgamesh's back, knocking him forward. Rolling desperately away, Gilgamesh saw

that the knifeman held his weapon once more; though blood seeped
dark from the shoulder of his cloak, he was moving the arm freely, grin-
ning as he bore down on his fallen enemy.

"Come to me," Gilgamesh panted, pushing himself up onto one knee
once more, "and you shall surely die."

The knifeman paused, balancing lightly on the balls of his feet. "You
have it wrong, wild man." His empty hand flickered toward his belt and
out again. Gilgamesh dropped flat, facedown, lashing out desperately
with his axe. His blow swung short through the air; he was barely able to
turn to take the other's brutal kick on his shoulder instead of his face.
But the second kick he caught, grabbing the foot and twisting as he
pushed to bring the outlaw crashing down on his back. Snatching up his
axe again, Gilgamesh plunged forward over his foe's body in his second
of breathlessness, landing on the outlaw's chest with his full weight
behind the axe. The other man's ribs crunched in underneath him, his
body caving open under the blow.

Gilgamesh lay full-length across the robber as though embracing a
lover for a moment, the slain man's heart-blood soaking hot into his
cloak. Yet he could hear bubbling breathing behind him: one was not yet
dead. With the strength of his arms, he forced himself up, glancing about.

The outlaw he had gutted was moving, crawling slowly over the
ground. Gilgamesh picked up his bloodied axe again, standing painfully.
Now he could see that the wounded man was no threat to him, for his
entrails trailed behind, shining dark in the moonlight.

"Mercy," the dying man gasped. "Slay me quickly, for I am dead."

Gilgamesh looked down at him, and to his surprise his own eyes
began to fill with tears. This was an evil man, who would have killed him
in his sleep and had doubtless had his part in slaying and robbing many
other passersby, and yet . . .

The outlaw slumped upon the ground, something black spilling from
his mouth over his beard. He spat and spoke again. "My name is Girbubu. I fell in battle against you—grant me mercy."

Gilgamesh lifted his axe, but he could not bring it down; his heart
failed within him, staying his hand. To give yet another man over to
Erishkegal's dark kingdom, even as his blood cooled and sinews stiff-

ened from slaying his comrades: how could he fulfill that deed now, he who sought to bring back the knowledge of life?

Girbubu groaned, twisting his shoulders from side to side as though to relieve the intolerable agony of his bowels. "Mercy, I beg you! As you are human, do not make me suffer—let me die swiftly."

Suddenly, Gilgamesh found himself horribly reminded of Enkidu, moaning on his bed through his twelve days of dying, yet terrified by his dreams of death. "Mercy?" he said, his voice breaking beneath the strain. "Is not the worst moment of life better than hastening your footsteps down the road of no return?"

"No! Do it now, I beg you!"

Still wary of the other man's hands, lest they hold a weapon for one last desperate stab, Gilgamesh crouched down. His arm loosened; his axe fell. Girbubu's head dropped free, his stained lips moving for a second before his eyes rolled back in his skull.

"Three more dead," Gilgamesh murmured, straightening again. "Why?"

"Because they lurked in the night, to prey upon the weak and the sleeping," he answered himself.

And so does a lion, he replied silently to that. The lionesses would have had me last night, if they could; these men would have taken me tonight, and I slew them instead, because I was the better killer. Where does the difference lie?

Does lion prey on lion? Yes: the stronger drives out the weaker, takes his queens and destroys his cubs. What, then, is the difference between lion and man?

"I could have asked Enkidu," Gilgamesh whispered. "He, of all men, would have been able to tell me."

He bent over stiffly to pick up Enkidu's bow where the outlaw had dropped it, running his fingers thoughtfully over the figured ivory inlay. Whatever Enkidu had marveled at—crafts and writing, music and the administration of law—there lay the difference: the *me* of heaven, all that sought to know and shape the world, rather than merely living as part of it. And bound to that, the certain knowledge of death: Enkidu's twelve-day journey to the halls of dust, with the road of no return stretching, clearly seen, before him all the way. Going, open-eyed, down into the Netherworld . . .

Suddenly the realization burst upon Gilgamesh like a joyful blow to the face: held in abeyance by the battle, but not weakened or forgotten, his dream rushed back to him. Enkidu would go down to the Netherworld indeed, to retrieve what he, Gilgamesh had lost in his pride and foolishness—but he could come back! For Gilgamesh knew that his dreams were true: Enkidu lived even now, even on the verge of his descent, and, if the laws of the Netherworld were not flouted, would return to his beloved with *pukku* and *mikku*, the heart of the Ensiship that they shared. And then, with the knowledge of life in Gilgamesh's grasp, the secret he would win from Utnapishti . . . then there would be neither dying nor sorrow for them thereafter, but everlasting life in their love.

Slowly Gilgamesh dragged the bodies of the three dead outlaws close together, arranging them before his sleeping place—*my galla, my guard from the Netherworld.* If there were any others prowling the hills that night, men would see the corpses and be warned away, while wild beasts would feed on the dead before the living. He rolled up his lion-skin as a pillow again, and lay down, closing his hand on Enkidu's bow and hoping that his dreams would continue.

GILGAMESH DID NOT dream further that night, but the memory of the first dream held him up through the day's walking. Now and again the cut on his shoulder would open and bleed a little—it was deeper than he had thought at first—and the soreness of the fight was very stiff throughout his body, his knee as swollen and throbbing as when it was first injured. Yet whenever the pain grew too great for him to go on, he would lean on his stick and call to his mind Enkidu as he had seen him last: lion-strong, in the full flush of health, preparing himself to descend to the Netherworld for Gilgamesh's sake.

He walked on, making for the great twin mountains that rose above the other peaks like raised shrines above the roofs of Erech. Resting for the night in their foothills, he rose a little before dawn, his path brightened by the sunrise shining straight between the two crags.

As Gilgamesh came closer to the road between the mountains, a sense of dread and awe began to creep over him. He had felt this before: it was like the first splendor of Huwawa, the terror that fell upon those who approached the gate of the cedar forest. Unthinkingly he stretched out his hand, as if Enkidu would grasp it again, and though his beloved was not beside him, the gesture gave him courage.

The he saw the movement high upon the rocky slopes—the shiny black segments of two stinged tails curling up, the sideways scuttling of two huge insect-bodies, one creeping down each mountain. *Huwawa's kin,* Gilgamesh thought, appalled, *guarding the mountain gate . . .*

But, though alone, he was more resolute now. Enkidu had already gone before him: now he must not fail, lest, in his cowardice, he abandon his lover to the Netherworld and make Enkidu's dark dying-dream true. Though Gilgamesh could feel his face darkening at their dreadfulness, his sore limbs chilling and slowing like a lizard in the frost, he forced his way forward, each blow of his walking-staff against the ground sure and resolute as the knocking of his Ensi's scepter in the judgment hall.

The great scorpion-beings stopped on either side of the path, waiting and watching him. Though, like Huwawa, they had human heads the size of a man, their visages were not misshapen. The one to the left was bearded, long dark ringlets falling down around a noble, keen-eyed face, and upon his head he wore the god-cap of many-layered horns. The other was delicate-featured as a queen, her hair wrapped about her head in a thick coil of braids, adorned with pins of gold. Both of them stared upon Gilgamesh with a penetrating gaze, so that he could feel the power flowing steadily forth from their black eyes like a wind blowing against him—dark and chill as the mountain night, but with no foulness about it. Though their tails were curled up to strike, venom swelling at the barbed tips, Gilgamesh was no more fearful of the dreadful weapons than he would have been to see a guard lifting a spear at the gates of a city. Yet he felt impelled to stop, drawing himself up as straight as he might with the help of his stick and nodding to each as he would to a fellow ruler. *If I had known these beings before seeing Huwawa,* he could not help thinking, *I should have been three times as eager to slay the guardian of the cedar forest, who was to these as a leper to a whole man.*

The scorpion-man turned his head to the scorpion-woman and

spoke. His voice was deep and resonant as a kettledrum, but seemed muted, so that Gilgamesh felt his words more than heard them, shivering through the pebbles of the path.

"He who comes to us," the scorpion-man said, "his body is the flesh of gods."

"Two-thirds of him is god," the woman answered, her higher voice singing sweet through the thin mountain air, "and one-third human."

The scorpion-man looked down at Gilgamesh, inclining his huge head respectfully. "Why have you undertaken so long a journey?" he asked. "Why have you come here before us, to this place whose crossings are treacherous? I wish to penetrate your purpose: how your desires are set, I want to know. Noble one, exalted of Inanna and Enlil, I shall tell you of those who stand before you. Utu shaped us as his guardians; he set us to watch his road at the beginning of time, when An parted heaven from earth, and gave the Netherworld to Erishkegal. Here on the slopes of the mountain Mashu we guard Utu's gate to the *kur*, the door of his going down to the Netherworld and coming up from the Netherworld in his daily journeyings—in the goings and in the comings of Utu we guard him. Our terror is awesome, our glance is death, and our grim splendor is cast up the mountain's slope. Without our leave, you may not pass here: however far you have come, you must turn back to the lands of living men."

"Mighty guardian of Utu, blessed by the hand of the god," Gilgamesh answered, equally respectful, "I shall not turn back. I have come on account of my ancestor Utnapishti, who stands in the assembly of the gods, and was given eternal life. I have come to ask him about death and life."

A look of grave sadness came over the face of the scorpion-woman as she gazed into Gilgamesh's eyes. "Never. Gilgamesh," she said softly, "has there been a mortal man who could do that. No one has crossed the far path through the mountains. It is twelve double-hours, and dark throughout: the darkness is dense, and there is no light. To the going out of Utu, to the entering of Utu, we cause his brightness to go out, we cause his brightness to enter. No sound can be heard on that road, for the ways of the Netherworld are silent; no touching save the stones under your feet, no scent of herb or tree, no taste of water or bread. If you fail by the way there, no god or demon or man can save you. The darkness will hold you forever, far from the appointed halls of the dead where Erishkegal sits in state, where the great rulers of earth pour cool water for the gods, and a place is allotted to each of the fallen."

"No one has crossed the far path through the mountains," the scorpion-man echoed. "The wild way of the *kur* is not the feet of men. Gilgamesh of Erech, heed my words now, for I speak to you as a friend, and give the good advice of a counselor. Has not your pride led you before to do what you were told could not be done—and did that not bring you to bitter sorrow and sore weeping, to wandering in the wilderness, dressed in the skins of beasts?"

"And yet I cannot turn back. For I know that Enkidu walks the paths of the Netherworld, those dark and dangerous ways. Though his body has perished, he lives yet, and thus I must find the road to Utnapishti, and learn the wisdom of life, that Enkidu be returned to me. Though it be in deep sadness and pain, in cold or heat; though I gasp after breath, I will go on. Now—open the gate!"

The two scorpion-beings swung aside, lowering their tails and bowing their heads. "Go, Gilgamesh!" said the scorpion-man. "Fear not. The Mashu mountains I give to you, between the ranges you may pass freely. May your feet bear you in safety: the gate of the mountain is open to you."

"My thanks to you, noble ones," Gilgamesh replied. "Remember me to Utu, until I return again to the sunlit world."

Gilgamesh walked forward between the scorpion-beings, into the darkening shadow of the mountains. One step, and another, and another: and then, as they had warned him, all was black about him.

The darkness was suffocatingly empty: it seemed as though his eyes and ears were stopped with black dust, his body encased in it like a shroud. Gilgamesh could touch nothing, feel nothing but the stones grating beneath his hard bare soles—save for the pain that flared through his leg with each step and the throbbing score along his shoulder. His lungs strained, but, though he knew he must be breathing, he could taste no air. Yet, though his knee grew worse with every step, he did not dare to stop or rest: once begun, he knew, the road had to be walked to its end, and there was no turning back for him.

Twelve double-hours, the scorpion-woman had said. Yet Gilgamesh could not tell the passing of time as he walked through the darkness. He tried to count his footfalls . . . two hundred, three hundred, four hundred . . . but the numbers slipped away beneath his mind, so that he had to start over again and again.

After a while, sparks of lightless glimmering began to blossom before his eyes, like the afterimage of lightning against blinking lids. His ears hummed as well, like the humming of a deep empty vase, as though his body were trying desperately to fill the emptiness of the black road he walked, conjuring phantoms to grasp in place of the honest sounds and sights whose simple facts told him—before anything else—that he was alive.

Gilgamesh limped on, his feet following the road of black dust. He did not know how long he had been walking when, ahead of him, he saw the shaft of light piercing through the darkness from above. But the sight flowed into his starved eyes like fresh air into dust-choked lungs, and he hastened toward it.

As he reached the shaft of light—a single beam from above that shed no brightness around it—he was able to look up, to see that it stemmed from a man-sized opening in the dark, like a giant eye onto the world above. Gilgamesh could see the shadows above: the edge of a bed, the glimmer of a lapis curve upon a wall. It was his own chamber that he looked into, through the eye of the Netherworld; and there he saw the broad-shouldered shadow falling across the light, as Enkidu prepared for his descent.

*I shall be with him!* Gilgamesh thought joyfully. *I may guide him, stand by his side as he faces the terrors of the Netherworld, even as he guided and stood by me in the cedar forest.* Again he gazed on Enkidu, the golden beauty and strength of the lion-man undimmed by any shadow of sickness, and his body ached to embrace his lover, to hold him fast and safe.

Yet as Enkidu began to climb down the sunlit shaft, a cold edge of worry scored through the beating joy of Gilgamesh's heart. For Enkidu had not heeded the advice Gilgamesh had given, the warnings to hide those signs by which he might be known as a living man in the realm of death, or one who meant to come back from the land of no returning.

Enkidu had washed his body, and put on clean clothes. About his waist he had fastened a kilt of white linen, belted with a gleaming buckle of gold and carnelian. His shaggy cloak, its tufts freshly washed and brushed—Gilgamesh raised his hand wonderingly to its twin about his own shoulders, stiff with dried blood and filth—shone like the pelt of an ox bathed and combed for sacrifice at a festival. Stout sandals shielded Enkidu's feet, and he bore the crooked staff of the Ensi in one hand, a throwing stick in the other. His skin and golden curls shone, freshly rubbed with sweet-smelling oil, as if he were going to a feast, and the rustling of his garments sounded through the Netherworld like gusts of wind, each footfall landing with a clap of thunder.

"Enkidu!" Gilgamesh shouted. "You did not listen to me—why? Turn back, my love, before the *galla* come upon you, or the *gidim*, the restless ghosts, seize upon you. Take off your clean clothes and put on filthy rags; soil your body, take the sandals from your feet and lay down your staff. If you do not, they will see that you are alive."

But however loudly Gilgamesh cried out, running toward his beloved. Enkidu did not seem to hear him. His sandaled feet and the blows of his staff booming upon the pathway as though he trod on the skin of a great kettledrum. Enkidu began to walk upon the road of the dead. Gilgamesh came up beside him, calling into his ear; Enkidu did not turn his head, and when Gilgamesh reached out to stroke his body. Gilgamesh's hand seemed to pass over the broad curves of his golden-haired chest muscles like a mist whispering across stone, marked only by a slight chilling of the skin where his touch had passed.

"Enkidu!" Gilgamesh cried despairingly. Enkidu's green eyes were wide as a cat's in the darkness, and the golden threads radiating from the irises seemed to glow with light. He strode along easily: he could see well enough . . . everything but Gilgamesh. Gilgamesh's breast swelled with a dreadful cold sense of abandonment, like a skin filling with icy water. If Enkidu did not see him, could not look upon him; if his voice was nothing to his beloved's ears, if his touch drew no answer from his beloved's skin—what worse torment, than for Enkidu to be deaf and dumb and senseless to him, going into all the dangers of the Netherworld?

And now Gilgamesh could see the dark figures beginning to flutter about them, like bats at evening, swooping down to the little swarms of insects hovering about the riverbanks. *Gidim* and *galla, udug* and *mashkim, lilu* of the wastelands . . . the ghosts and spirits and demons of the underworld, the dead unsated by offerings and all the strange and unearthly beings who roamed the *kur*. Their shadows were misshapen in the dimness, but Gilgamesh heard the rustling of feathered wings and the flapping of leathery wings above, and the slither of scales against rocks below. A screech-owl cried out, her call rending the air; a wolf howled in answer, then another, the sound shivering through the dust about them.

Enkidu lifted his throwing stick, drawing back his hand. Gilgamesh grabbed his wrist, trying to stop him, but Enkidu's arm swung straight through his grasp, sending the stick on its wide arc. It struck one of the shadowy beings with a solid thump, and where it struck, the thing became more real to the sight—the shape of a lanky man with eagle-wings in place of his arms and a bear's paws for feet, lowering the wide bull-horns that grew from his sparse-haired temples. Enkidu cried out, and as the dark shapes fluttered closer, he hit out with the Ensi's staff. Yet each time he struck, another ghost grew more solid, and they crowded more closely around him, pressing and guiding him like hunting mastiffs herding a wild bull into a pit.

Drawing his axe, Gilgamesh stepped forward, standing between Enkidu and the shadows that swarmed about him. He struck, cleaving, and where his blade landed, the ghosts fell away in scatterings of black dust. Still Enkidu did not call out, or speak to him, but when Gilgamesh glanced back at his lover, he saw that Enkidu's brow was clearing, his fear of the inhabitants of the underworld dropping from him as they fell away, leaving him free to follow the road again.

Then something shimmered ahead of them, and Gilgamesh heard the soft sound of weeping, a hitching, muffled cry that he knew well—for had he not heard it too often in the darkness of Enkidu's sickroom, in the depths of the night, when the even rattling of his lover's lungs promised that he slept? Sululi was weeping, and Enkidu's head came up as he heard the sound, hastening forward.

*Why can he hear her, and not me?* Gilgamesh thought bitterly. Now he could see her: Sululi sat before them on the path, head bent low and thick black hair falling about her pale face as she cradled Ur-Lugal in her arms. *How have they come so swiftly to the Netherworld? Did the same sickness seize upon them?*

Gilgamesh ran toward Sululi and Ur-Lugal, but his leg hampered him from moving faster than a hobbling stumble. Enkidu, in the full of his strength, was swifter, sweeping down upon wife and child, leaving Gilgamesh trailing in his dusty wake.

"My wife!" Enkidu called. "My love, my dear child—weep not, I am here." And the new-wakening ache of jealousy warred with Gilgamesh's fear for his beloved: *He must not, he must not—he runs to embrace her, and not me; he sees them, and not me!*

But as Enkidu bent down, his powerful arms folding about Sululi and Ur-Lugal as though to sweep them up, they, too, misted away, so that his embrace closed on empty air. He stared down, unbelieving, at where they had been, then looked up into the blackness above.

"Why?" he asked, his deep voice clear and bewildered as a child's. "Why were you here in the Netherworld? Where have you gone?"

Only the shriek of the screech-owl answered him, calling from her far-off abodes in the dark wasteland. Enkidu squared his broad shoulders, walking on, and Gilgamesh hurried painfully to catch up with him.

The screech-owl hooted again, her wailing cry closer. Gilgamesh heard the rush of wings through the air, and braced himself, ready to fight off another swarming of shadows. *Enkidu, if only you had listened to me . . .*

But it was only one shape that flew about them, her own lurid light glimmering green about her form like the phosphorescence of rotting wood. The *lilitu* had come upon them, her heavy breasts swinging obscenely naked from her feathered body and her mouth stretched blackly open. In her talons she held a half-fledged owl-chick, quills prickling from the down about its human face and little claws ripping out at the still air.

To his horror, Gilgamesh recognized her features—different from the face he had seen on the owl-woman nesting in Inanna's tree. This *lilitu* bore the likeness of Sululi, her low cheekbones stretched into a broad mask of ugliness and her sallow skin weeping with red pustules beneath the thick whore-paint; and her chick's face was a twisted form of Ur-Lugal's, the boy's bright eyes squinted into beads of greedy cruelty above the beak that jutted out where nose and mouth should have been.

Enkidu cried out sharply, a roar of mingled disgust and rage, bringing up his staff to fend them off as they swept down upon him. The blow struck firmly, the loud crack of its landing resounding through the darkness.

Beneath the weight of the Ensi's staff, the bodies of the *lilitu* and her chick shattered like a thin-walled pot cast against a stone, their hollow shapes splintering away in a shower of jagged shards that fell to dust in the air, sifting down to become indistinguishable from the black dust of the roadway.

But the echoing sound of the blow did not die away, but rose instead, sounding all about Gilgamesh and Enkidu in a great groan, until it seemed that the earth was crying out above and below and around them. Enkidu's teeth were gritting, as though he struggled to hold back any sound of his own, but at last his lips parted and his own moan joined the cry of the earth.

As Enkidu opened his mouth, the groaning about them broke into words, a lamentation too deep and somber to spring from any human throat.

*SHE IS SLEEPING, SHE IS SLEEPING,*
*ERISHKEGAL, THE MOTHER OF NINAZU, IS SLEEPING.*
*HER HOLY SHOULDERS NO GARMENT COVERS.*
*NO CLOTH DRAPES HER HOLY BREAST.*
*SHE WHO SLEEPS, SHE WHO SLEEPS,*
*THE MOTHER OF BIRTH AND DEATH, WHO SLEEPS.*
*NO GARMENT COVERS HER CLEAN SHOULDERS.*
*HER BREAST, A STONE BOWL, DOES NOT GIVE SUCK.*

Enkidu's feet slowed and stopped as the cry of the earth came up around him, the song holding him fast. Black dust showered down over him like soil shoveled into a grave, darkening his hair and piling up in the shaggy weave of his cloak, clinging to the film of sweet oil upon his skin. Though Gilgamesh cried out and beat frantically at it with his hands, he could not move so much as a single speck, and still the dust kept falling, heaping higher around Enkidu as the light dimmed about them.

Gilgamesh stayed there, wailing, struggling to tear the earth away in the darkness. But there was nothing beneath his touch, nothing he could see in the blackness and nothing he could feel—nothing but the grating of the pathway's stones beneath the cracked and bleeding soles of his feet, the shooting agony of his leg and the throbbing of his wounded shoulder, and the rough wood of the walking stick in his grasp.

"I must go on!" he said to himself. "The Netherworld holds Enkidu fast: I shall never be able to free him if I do not win through."

Taking a firmer hold of his staff, Gilgamesh stumped forward. Though his feet were ready to give beneath him, he would not let himself fall. It was not for himself he walked now, but for Enkidu; and if he were weary, the weight of his own body as heavy a burden as if he carried his lover's corpse draped about his shoulders . . . that was as it was, and there was no help save to go on.

As when he had begun, Gilgamesh could see neither behind nor ahead of him. But heat flared up in his body, a burning fever spreading out from knee and shoulder, flaming in his face like the flaying rays of the summer sun, so that he felt the drops of sweat trickle down his cheeks to drip away into the darkness, lips cracking and throat parching in the heat radiating from within him: save for the blackness that he stumbled through, he might have been walking bareheaded through the desert in the full heat of summer.

That lasted for a time—how long, he did not know; the darkness was thick, with no light, and he could see neither behind nor ahead. But suddenly a gust of ice bit into Gilgamesh's face, freezing his sweat to a scum of salty rime that cracked away from his hair and his beard. Neither cloak nor bearskins shielded him against the cutting blade of the wind: it seemed to scour through his bones, frozen fingers running through his rib cage and between the joints of his spine, with the pain of his two wounds the only heat left in his body. His fingers and feet were numb—only the support his walking stick gave his leg told him that his frozen hand still held it—and when he blinked against the unbroken dark, thin scales of ice dropped away from his eyes.

Yet Gilgamesh went on, driven like a donkey with two goads pricking against his sides: the heart-joyful image of Enkidu, shining and whole, stepping through the door of the Netherworld on Gilgamesh's quest; and the constraining woe of the song of earth, settling dark about Enkidu to hold him fast. He should not stay trapped: while Gilgamesh could still move his limbs, whether they were dead with icy cold or alive with burning agony, he would not falter upon the road through the *kur*.

At last the bitter cold eased, leaving Gilgamesh trembling so hard that his staff kept threatening to give way beneath his shaking hand. It was still dark as before, and he could see nothing behind—but ahead, now, it seemed to him that the blackness was beginning to give way, that he could see the faintest sheen of gray against the darkness. As he walked, the light began to grow clearer, and he sighed deeply in relief. He must be near the end of the road now, as the scorpion-woman had told him: twelve-double-hours, and dark throughout its length.

And the sun was rising at last: far, far ahead, the dawn's brightness shimmered through a grove of gleaming leafed trees. Beyond them, beneath the lightening sky, the horizon stretched out lapis-blue, and against its darkness Gilgamesh could see the shape of a small building. There, he thought, someone must dwell: and whoever made their home in this place, beyond the path through the *kur*, would surely know the way for him to reach his goal—reach the dwelling of Utnapishti, at the mouth of all rivers. He was too weary and injured to hasten his steps, but he did not let them flag as he made his way toward the garden and the building beside it.

Tired and in pain as he was, Gilgamesh caught his breath in delight when he was close enough to see the garden clearly. It was ringed about with cedars as fair and fragrant as any that had grown in the holy forest, their sweet breath wafting through the air. On the bushes that grew between the trees, clusters of fruit glittered clear, berries of shining carnelian casting glimmers of red-orange light through the shadows of the leaves. A pool fountained up in the middle of the garden, a pillar of frothy white burbling and splashing back into the clean water. Beside it stood a tree hung with sea-bright stones, green and red and deep blue, that grew dangling from its golden twigs like precious carob-pods. Vines grew on pillars of silver: their leaves were lapis lazuli, spreading out above heavy bunches of deep blue lapis grapes.

Gilgamesh entered the garden and went to the tree by the pool, lifting his hand to pluck one of the fruits. It gave way, dropping into his palm: an apple of warm clear stone, glowing deep red in the sunlight. Tentatively he raised it to his mouth, testing his teeth against it. The juice spurted at once between his lips, sweeter and more refreshing than cool water in the depths of the desert, than date-wine after a battle. The heady wave of its taste rushed over him, the blood singing in his head so that he nearly fainted with delight as he devoured it.

The single ruby fruit was enough to slake both Gilgamesh's hunger and his thirst, easing the throbbing aches of his leg and shoulder. As its juice poured through his body, he felt it washing away his weariness, filling him with a tingling, thrilling rush of strength such as he had never felt—not standing in his chariot with axe uplifted as his onagers galloped forward; not climbing among the mountain cedars with the cold clean air sweet in his lungs, nor even when wrestling with Enkidu, feeling his lover's might as his own. He would gladly have stayed longer in that garden, watching the play of sunlight through the fountain and delighting in the sweet scent of the trees, the rainbow light of the precious fruits. But yet he knew that Enkidu waited for him in the Netherworld: how could his mouth take pleasure in the intoxicating juices of apple and berry when his love's mouth was stopped with dust; or his eyes enjoy the brightness of flowing water and shimmering stones when Enkidu saw only darkness? So he did not linger, but strode out of the garden, making for the building beside it. It was a tavern, he saw now— a tavern like any in Erech, made of mud-bricks and thatched, with a sheaf of barley and a clay cup hanging over the door.

A woman's low voice sang from within, clear and sultry through the scented air above the soft plinking of a harp. "My beloved, the delight of my eyes met me," she sang.

"We rejoiced together,
He took his pleasure of me,
He brought me into his house.

He laid me down on the fragrant honey-bed,
My sweet love, lying by my heart,
Tongue-playing, one by one,
My fair lover did so, fifty times—"


Her song broke off abruptly, her voice sharpening as she spoke. "That man is surely a murderer . . . where could he be going?"

As Gilgamesh headed for the open door, it closed in his face, and he heard the sound of a bolt sliding across it from within. He stopped, lifting his staff. Whoever the singer was, she could surely answer his questions: he had not come all this way to be barred by the fears of a woman.

"Tavernkeeper!" he called. "What have you seen that made you shut your door, shoot the lock, and bolt the gate?"

No answer came from within. Gilgamesh banged on the door, but still she did not reply. It could have been any tavern, shut after closing time, any surly woman refusing to open it for a weary traveler . . . but here, between the mountain path and the sea, beside the holy garden, matters must be different. Why should she, safe from outlaws and robbers in her fastness, shut him out before she could hear him speak?

Angry and frustrated, Gilgamesh kicked the door—though carefully, for he was still light-headed with the strength the fruit had given him, and he knew that he could easily shatter the heavy wood with too heavy a touch. "Let me in!" he shouted. "Or I will break your door, and smash the lock!"

"Who are you?" she replied. "Who are you that has come to me, dressed in animal skins and covered with old blood, stinking like a goat three weeks dead?"

"I am Gilgamesh!" he answered. "I, who killed the guardian Huwawa that lived in the cedar forest, who grappled with the Bull of Heaven and slew him, who met with lions in the mountain passes."

"If you are Gilgamesh, who has done all these things," the tavernkeeper said through her door, "then why are your cheeks wasted, your expression sunken? Why is your heart so wretched, your features so haggard? Why is there such sorrow deep within you; why do you look like one who has been traveling a long way, your face seared by cold and heat, and why do you roam the wilderness?"

"Tavernkeeper," Gilgamesh replied more gently, "should not my heart be wretched and my features haggard? Should there not be sorrow deep within me, and should I not look like one who has been traveling a long way, my face seared by cold and heat—should I not roam the wilderness? Enkidu, my friend, my beloved, who chased the onager and the panther of the plains, who overcame all with me, and climbed the mountains with me, and went through every hardship with me—" His throat choked; he swallowed hard, and spoke again. "The fate of mankind has overtaken him."

The bolt clicked back and the door swung open. The woman who stood within was short as a girl of ten or eleven years, her head barely reaching the middle of Gilgamesh's chest, but her body was rounded out in lusciously plump curves. The neck of her deep green gown was cut low so that when Gilgamesh looked down at her, he found himself gazing straight between the creamy slopes of her magnificently large and full breasts. She wore a necklace of buttery amber interspersed with patterned rounds of gold, and matching earrings hung from her ears; her hair flowed down her back in a shining auburn stream like polished mahogany. On her head was a golden circlet, holding down the wispy rust-colored veil over her face. Beneath the veil her blue eyes were very large, slanted at the corners above high cheekbones; her chin jutted out strongly beneath a firm little mouth.

"I am Siduri, the keeper of this tavern at the lip of the sea," she said. "Come in and refresh yourself, Gilgamesh, after your long travels."

Gilgamesh entered, ducking his head to keep from banging it into the low lintel. The rugs on the floor were thick and soft, woven with intricate golden and green patterns; her pot-stand was gold as well, as were her pots and the great vat of fermenting mash in the corner beside her little harp. Siduri poured out a cup of beer, gesturing him to sit.

Suddenly Gilgamesh became aware of how filthy he was, caked with the dirt and blood of his travel. With the toe of one grimy foot he pushed the corner of a fine rug aside, squatting upon the floor as he took the cup from her hands. The cool beer that flowed into his mouth through the gold straw was fresh with the scents of the fruit from her garden; his throat cleared and his thoughts opened as he drank.

"For seven days and seven nights," he said, "I mourned over Enkidu. I would not allow him to be buried until . . . until a maggot fell out of his nose. Then I was terrified by his appearance. I began to fear death, and to roam the wilderness, and thoughts of my beloved Enkidu lie heavy within me: therefore I roam the long trails through the wilderness. How can I stay silent? How can I be still, when my friend, whom I love, has turned to clay? For am I not like him? Will I not lie down, never to get up again?"

Something touched Gilgamesh's head, and he jerked away violently, his eyes wide in sudden horror. Then he realized that it was only Siduri's small hand stroking his hair, and he let her ease his head down to rest against her plump thigh.

"Gilgamesh, why do you wander?" she asked. "Even if you seek everywhere, you will not find the life you want. When the gods created mankind, they fixed death for mankind, and held back life in their own hands. Now, Gilgamesh, if you would be happy, let your belly be filled. Be joyful day and night, make a celebration of each day, dance in circles night and day. Let your clothes gleam with cleanness, let your head be cleaned, wash yourself with water. Attend to the little one who holds your hand, and let a wife delight in your embrace: this is the true task of mankind."

Siduri's wool-gowned thigh was pleasant and soft beneath the thick bristles of Gilgamesh's cheek, and she smelled of sweet myrtle and clean warm flesh. Her hand felt soothing, stroking his hair—and yet he jerked away from her, the beer splashing over the rim of the golden cup as he set it down.

"Tell me now, tavernkeeper," he said, "what is the way to Utnapishti? What are its landmarks? Give them to me! Tell the signs to me! If it is possible, I will cross the sea; I will roam the wilderness."

Siduri shook her head. "Gilgamesh," she said sternly, "there has never been any crossing, nor has anyone, from the beginning of days, been able to cross the sea. The only one who crosses the sea is Utu: apart from him, who may cross? The faring is painful, the way troublesome, and the Waters of Death stream across to bar its approaches. Gilgamesh, even if you cross the sea, what would you do when you arrive at the Waters of Death?"

Gilgamesh rose to his full height, staring down at the little woman and clenching his fists in mute frustration. She tossed her head back, looking him in the face as if daring him to lift a hand against her.

Suddenly his eyes burst, like clouds scarred by lightning. Gilgamesh's tears showered down, his shoulders shaken by great racking, coughing sobs.

"What do you want me to do?" Siduri asked irritably. "If there were a bridge, I would tell you of it, but there is none. It does not matter how far you have come or what your troubles are. Your way is at an end. You cannot go any farther."

Gilgamesh dashed the tears from his face with the backs of his fists. "Is there a boat? If there is any boat, I shall take it—I shall dare the Waters of Death, and fare as I must."

Siduri frowned. "Come with me."

She led him outside, pointing down the beach to a cove where dark trees lined the edge. "There dwells Urnashabi, the ferryman of Utnapishti. The Stone Things are with him, and he picks up the Urnu-snakes in the heart of the forest. If you can, cross with him. If not, turn back."

Siduri went back into the tavern. The door shut; Gilgamesh heard the bolt sliding across it again. After a few moments the harp-notes rang through the air once more, and he heard Siduri singing.

"My blossom-bearer, your allure was sweet,
My blossom-bearer in the apple orchard,
My bearer of fruit in the apple orchard . . ."

Gilgamesh walked down the beach, along the way Siduri had shown him. A boat lay moored in the cove, not a small boat, such as a fisher might use on the Buranun, but not as huge a boat as Gilgamesh would have expected for a long seafaring. But although its inside was very ordinary—a tight basketweave of bundled reeds caulked with pitch—it was lined on the outside with scarred gray stone. It had no raised prow or stern, only a small stone seat before and behind. For a moment it came to Gilgamesh that he might take the boat himself and set off; but he did not know how it might be poled or sailed, or even whether it would float for him.

Three trails led up the sand and into the pines. The middle one had been tracked by sandaled feet, but the ones to right and left were thick, dragging trenches through the sand, as though the walker had pulled something heavy along at either side. Gilgamesh followed them, tracing the spoor as white sand turned to sandy earth beneath the wide dark branches, then to soil.

As he heard the sounds of hissing and muttering ahead of him, he quickened his step a little. The tavernkeeper had spoken of snakes—he must, then, be nearing the presence of Urnashabi.

On either side of the pathway stood a stone statue in the likeness of a man, winged and kilted, holding a long forked pole and wearing a small pointed cap with horns projecting before and behind. Gilgamesh would have paid them little notice—but they suddenly moved, spreading their wings and whirling to block his way with their poles.

"You shall not pass," one said, its voice the deep grating of rock on rock. "Urnashabi lifts up the Urnu-snakes in the heart of the forest, and none may disturb him."

"I shall pass!" Gilgamesh answered. "I shall speak with him, for he shall ferry me over the waters, to the dwelling of Utnapishti."

"You shall not pass," the Stone Thing repeated, lifting its pole to aim the twin points at his chest.

Gilgamesh drew his axe, leaping forward beneath the clumsy swing of the stone pole. He did not aim with the edge: it would only shatter. Instead he turned the axe around to strike with the butt. One stone wing cracked away, then an arm, the pole dropping, to break in two on the ground. Evading the Stone Thing's clumsy, one-armed grip, Gilgamesh dodged in to deal with its comrade, hammering against it like a sculptor trying to shape granite that fought and writhed beneath the blows of his chisel.

"Break, curse you!" he panted through the ringing beating of axe-butt on stone—for he could feel the strength the fruit had given him draining away already, and his knee was starting to give way. "Break!"

And suddenly it did, the grasping hand shattering away in three pieces. Gilgamesh struck it once more, breaking away a huge shard of wing, before he realized that it was no longer moving. But something cold writhed against his feet, twisting against his ankles—a pair of black snakes, their forked tongues flickering out to test his skin. With a half-strangled yell of revulsion, Gilgamesh dropped his axe and reached down to grab each behind the head, ready to break their backs even as their bodies whipped about his arms.

"Hold," a soft voice called. "Open your hands—do not harm the snakes!"

Breathing hard, Gilgamesh forced himself to bend down again, opening his hands. The snakes flashed away through the fallen pine-needles and were gone. Looking carefully where he trod lest there be any more, Gilgamesh stepped away from the two half-broken statues.

The man who stood before him was ancient and gnarled, his gray-white hair spreading out over his back and down to his knees like a cloak of felted wool, and the matted tangle of his stained gray beard reaching down past his belt. The flesh of his face was thick, wrinkled like a dried fruit and deeply browned by the sun, but the black eyes that stared out at Gilgamesh were keen and bright, narrow with anger.

"Who are you?" the old man asked. "Your cheeks are wasted and your expression sunken—you look as though you have wandered a long way, your face seared by ice and heat. Why do you roam the wilderness, and what have you done here?"

"I am Gilgamesh, the friend of Enkidu. Should not my cheeks be wasted and my expression sunken—should I not look as though I have wandered a long way, my face seared by ice and heat? Enkidu, my friend whom I love, has been turned to clay, so I have been roaming long roads through the wilderness. Now, Urnashabi, what is the way to

Utnapishti? What are its landmarks? Give them to me, tell the signs to me. If it is possible, I will cross the sea; if it is possible, I will roam the wilderness."

Urnashabi walked over to the statues, running his hands over the jagged stone where Gilgamesh had broken their wings and arms, then looked down at the shattered poles and shook his head. His mouth was so sunken with age, hidden beneath his tangled beard, that Gilgamesh could not tell whether he was smiling or frowning, but his voice, when he spoke, was flat as that of a moneylender delivering a refusal.

"It is your own hands that have prevented the crossing, Gilgamesh. You have destroyed the Stone Things and have picked up the Urnu-snakes. The Stone Things are broken, the Urnu-snakes gone. Without them, we cannot cross the Waters of Death."

"And yet we must cross!" Gilgamesh cried. He did not wish to harm the ferryman, but he had to strike out; he picked up the axe again, turning it to aim another blow at the head of the nearest Stone Thing.

"Stop! You have harmed them enough. Know that it was they who protected me on the way across the Waters of Death: only their stone poles could withstand those waters, only their stone flesh reach over those waves to wield the poles. Thus, and only thus, was I able to make the journey to the house of Utnapishti, at the mouth of all rivers—only in the *magillu*-boat, whose life you have destroyed."

"I will dare it—" Gilgamesh began, but Urnashabi silenced him with a wave of his hand.

"Though your flesh is two-thirds god and one-third man, even so, you could not hold up against the Waters of Death: all that dies must fall prey to it. Then you would surely never find what you seek: folly, to ask for death when you would find life! And yet . . ."

The old man fell silent, looking up into the woven tracery of needles and branches above. He nodded once, sharp and decisive. "Gilgamesh, lift up that axe in your hand. Go down into the woods and cut poles of sixty cubits . . . hmm, three hundred of them. Strip them, paint bitumen on the sockets—you will find a place just down the shore where it flows up from the sand—and bring them to me."

Gilgamesh chopped trees all that day, and trimmed them through the night by the light of a few small torches he had borrowed from Urnashabi and stuck into the ground. When his strength flagged, he ate again of the fruit from Siduri's garden, and returned to his work renewed after each bite.

At last the three hundred poles were cut and trimmed, and Gilgamesh and Urnashabi loaded them into the boat, the long heap sticking out fore and aft so that the little vessel seemed to be merely a pile of logs.

"Now you must launch it," Urnashabi said. "I have not the strength by myself." He got into the boat and folded his arms across his mat of beard, waiting.

Gilgamesh put his shoulder to the granite throne at the boat's stern, digging his heels into the sand. For a moment he thought he would not be able to budge it . . . then slowly, very slowly, the *magillu*-boat began to move, groaning across the beach as though its stone keel scraped across a single great crystal.

One mighty heave, and then another, and another, straining all his sinews until he could hear them crackling against his bones. Even when the water lapped against Gilgamesh's knees, the boat did not float free, and he began to fear that without its stone steersmen it would be grounded forever by its own weight. Spurred on by that fear, he crouched down again, giving one last shove that tore through his weak knee like the blow of an axe—and the boat began to move, swinging about in the tide.

Urnashabi's boat went swiftly indeed, skimming through the waves so fast that none of the birds circling overhead could follow it. Gilgamesh had no way of guessing how far they had traveled, but it was nearing the evening of the third day when the boat suddenly slowed.

"Why is the boat slowing?" Gilgamesh asked. "What is wrong?"

"We have come to the Waters of Death," Urnashabi answered somberly. "Now we shall discover whether we may indeed pass . . . look out over the water, Gilgamesh."

Gilgamesh looked out, and could not take his eyes away from what lay before them. The sea was black and shiny as molten pitch, sluggish rainbow-slicked currents passing slowly across its face like the wriggling backs of great snakes, and ripples rose through the air like the shimmering curtains of heat rising from a campfire, bending low before the wind that blew over the ocean. The boat had stopped altogether at the edge of the Waters of Death: they sat becalmed there, like a chip of ivory inlaid in bitumen.

"Now, Gilgamesh," said Urnashabi, "hold yourself back, and take care. Take a punting-pole—but do not let your hand pass over the Waters of Death."

Gilgamesh lifted one of the great poles, swinging it around. Even before he let it slip into the water, the wood already looked half rotten, as though worms had eaten it for years. He pushed off once, and the boat slid forward over the slick black water. The pole was suddenly light in his hands, swinging free of the surface: the whole length that had entered the Waters of Death was gone, and the rot was creeping fast along the remaining stump, so that it crumbled away even as Gilgamesh stared at it.

"Drop it and take another," Urnashabi ordered. "As swiftly as you can: it is not good for living men to linger above the Waters of Death."

Gilgamesh punted with all his strength, and Urnashabi swung each new pole into his hands as quickly as the old was used up. Gilgamesh's shoulders soon ached with the strain, the burning sweat dripping into his eyes so that they stung and swelled with salt, but he did not dare stop to wipe his face.

And yet, by the time the last pole-stub had slipped from Gilgamesh's fingers into the dark liquid below, they were not within sight of land. He stared out before and behind and could see only the black flat sea, its shimmering ripples a dark reflection of the long horsetail clouds scudding across the sky.

"What shall we do now?" he asked.

Urnashabi shrugged. "We are becalmed on the Waters of Death. There is no way out. You may congratulate yourself, Gilgamesh, that in your end you have brought about my death—something neither man, nor time, nor fate had managed through the generations that I steered the *magillu*-boat."

The old man's tone was mocking and bitter at once, but Gilgamesh could see the despair sinking deep in his sharp eyes, like a flaw cracking dull through polished onyx. Urnashabi turned his back on his companion, facing forward to the featureless horizon. The wind blew his long hair and beard over the boat's prow-throne, just as it whipped Enkidu's shaggy cloak forward over Gilgamesh's shoulders.

"Wait!" Gilgamesh said. "We are not ready to die yet." He loosened his belt, peeling off the tattered bearskin, and stripped the cloak from his shoulders. Giving the bearskin to Urnashabi, he ordered, "Stand thus—hold it up with your arms raised, as I do with this cloak, and let the wings catch the wind. It blows strongly; its breath may yet bring us forth from these waters."

Without speaking, Urnashabi lifted the bearskin, its torn sides flapping in the breeze. The *magillu*-boat shuddered and lurched; then, as Gilgamesh raised the wings of Enkidu's cloak, it began to scud along like a silver ball rolled over a table of polished wood.

"We have done it!" Gilgamesh exulted. "We have won free!"

"We are not free yet," Urnashabi grumbled. But already Gilgamesh could see a faint blur between the black of the sea and the pale blue of the sky, the first fogged cloudbank-sight of land; and as they sped onward, the darkness beneath them began to thin like night thinning at the edge of dawn.

THE LAND THAT rose before them was pleasant and grassy, spider-webbed by blue streams flowing down over the hills. Apple trees grew here and there, their gnarled twigs budding pale green against gray-brown bark. With a start, Gilgamesh realized that he must have wandered throughout the winter: it would soon be time for the festival of the New Year. At home, in Erech, the En and the Shamhatu would be readying themselves to perform the wedding of Dumuzi and Inanna . . .

There was a man waiting on the beach, watching them. He was an ordinary man of middle years, slightly paunchy, with shaven head and close-cropped beard, wearing a simple kilt and cloak of brown wool. From his plain leather belt hung a pruning knife and a large pair of shears. Gilgamesh guessed that he must be another servant of

Utnapishti's—most likely a gardener, who had come out to greet the ferryman—and called out to him, "You! Help me with this boat!"

The serving-man waded out into the water, putting his shoulder to the stern-throne and shoving. Together, he and Gilgamesh managed to get the *magillu*-boat a few cubits more up the beach, nearly to the point where a stream of fresh water flowed clear into the ocean, before Urnashabi finally said, "Enough, enough. It will stay there."

The serving-man looked up and down at Gilgamesh, then at the boat. "Why have the Stone Things of the boat been smashed, and why does it carry one who is not its master?" he asked.

"I smashed them because they would have barred my way to Urnashabi," Gilgamesh replied, "and it carried me because I had need of the crossing. I must find Utnapishti, for I would speak to him—tell me the way, that I may go to him."

"Why do you seek Utnapishti?" the gardener asked as they walked up the beach, toward the small hut that stood at the edge of the stream. "Your cheeks are wasted and your expression sunken; you look as though you have traveled a long way, your face seared by ice and heat."

"And why should I not? I have been roaming long roads through the wilderness, because of my friend Enkidu." The words that had been echoing through Gilgamesh's mind since first he spilled them to Siduri came forth again, more bitterly poignant in this simple land before the budding apple trees and the little lettuce plants sprouting forth in their bed between hut and stream. The white goat tethered by the hut bleated, as if in sympathy, before lowering her head and beginning to chew the grass again; Gilgamesh noticed that her belly was swollen and her dugs hanging low. "My friend whom I love—Enkidu—has turned to clay. Am I not like him? Will I lie down someday, never to rise again? That is why I must go on, to see the far-off Utnapishti, about whom the tales are told. I circled through all the mountains, I crossed the treacherous mountains and the seas. That is why sleep has not mellowed my face, and why I have worn myself out with sleeplessness, why my body is racked by pain." As the other man's mild brown eyes gazed on him, Gilgamesh suddenly became aware of the tattered bear-hide that was his only garment beneath lion-skin and tufted cloak, as if he had unexpectedly found himself walking so unclad through the streets of Erech, and he hastened to explain before the servant could begin to think him mad. "I had not yet reached Siduri's dwelling before my clothes gave out. I killed bear and hyena, lion and panther, stag and ibex, the creeping things of the wilderness; I ate their flesh and covered myself with their skins. I lay down with animals, I slept in dirt and bitterness, Siduri barred her door when she saw me. I am unfortunate, and badly fated."

The serving-man picked up a pointed stick, bending over his young lettuce plants and prodding up the tinier green shoots of weeds that were beginning to spring up between them. He seemed unhurried, his face little troubled by Gilgamesh's words.

"Why, Gilgamesh, do you let yourself be consumed by sadness," he asked as he worked, "you who were created from the flesh of the gods and of mankind? Have you ever seen the fool at the New Year's feast? They place a throne in the Assembly for him, but to the fool they offer beer dregs instead of butter, bran and cheap flour mixed together like mud. He is clothed with a loincloth like a fronded kilt, and in place of a sash he wears the hide of a goat, because he does not have wisdom or rank, does not have words of counsel. Take care about it, Gilgamesh: though he is made to sit in the high place, the fool cannot change or hide his nature, nor hold his seat through the coursing of the feast. Though they have exalted him, they mock him, and he is twice the fool if he believes himself their master."

"An ill fate is set for some," Gilgamesh answered, "and Nanna bespoke mine on the night of the tailed star, when the shadow of the eclipse veiled his shining face."

The serving-man set down his stick and straightened up, brushing the dirt from his hands. He gestured Gilgamesh to come with him, following the little stone-edged path that led up to his apple orchard. The budding trees were all neatly pruned, with an occasional young sapling tied to a stake filling the gap where an older tree had been. The gardener walked among them, with Gilgamesh limping after. Here and there he would straighten a stake, or pull a bough downward to examine the buds for any signs of spot or sickness. "The gods are sleepless," he said, "and often troubled by restlessness. Yet the difference between gods and men was established long ago. You trouble yourself, Gilgamesh, for no reason, and your help is not easy to give to you. If Gilgamesh set himself up on a throne in the temple of the holy gods, what would he do?" The serving-man picked a little green worm from a twig, squashing it between his fingers and wiping his hand on his stained brown kilt. "The gods created all of mankind, and together they took counsel for his fate, but it is men who must live with what the gods have given them. Now, you are wearing yourself out through toil, filling your body with grief, and you are bringing your long lifetime to an early end.

"The offspring of mankind," he went on, squatting down to prod in the dirt about the roots of one of the young trees, "is snapped off like a reed in a canebrake. The fine youth and the lovely girl may be as close to death as the dotard and hag. No one can see the face of Death, no one can hear the voice of Death, yet still Death savagely snaps off mankind. And yet we are not the only perishable things in the world. Do we build a house to stand forever? Do we seal a contract to last forever? How long do brothers share an inheritance? And for how long," he added, standing and gesturing toward the running waters of the stream, "do dragonflies drift down the river? There has never been a face that could gaze upon the face of the sun; the sleeping and the dead are alike. The image of Death cannot be shown, yet it can be seen shadowy beneath the face of man and hero, throughout the days of their lives." The serving-man's voice had grown sad and grave. He reached up to one of the older trees, feeling along a branch to its joint before drawing his pruning knife and slicing through it. "Though I graft this wood to another root-stock," he added, "it will still bear the same apples as before. It will grow, and bear fruit, and die, as all my trees do in time, and I must replace it with another, for it cannot change the pattern to which the gods made it: I can graft it to stronger roots, but I cannot keep its fate from it. After Enlil had spoken the blessing, the great gods assembled, and Mammu, the mother of destinies, decreed destiny with them. They settle death and life: but as for death, its time is hidden, though the days of life are made plain."

Gilgamesh looked on the gardener again. An ordinary man, yes—hook-nosed, his shaven head browned by the sun, and hands callused and dirty from his work—but there was something in the remoteness of his brown eyes, the calmness of his speech, that seemed familiar. It struck Gilgamesh that he was very like the En, who had seen more than ninety years of life, as if nothing further could surprise or unsettle him. And he had spoken of replacing his trees—trees that lived the span of a long human life . . . *Now I have found him!* Gilgamesh thought savagely. *Now I will win the secret of life from him—I will wrest it by force if I have to.* He felt for the axe at his belt, but as his hand touched the haft, the strength fell away from it. Though he knew he could smash the older man's bones bare-handed, let alone overcoming him with a weapon, he understood now that battle would be useless here: Utnapishti would give up his knowledge of his free will, or not at all.

"I look upon you, Utnapishti," he said in wonder, "and your appearance is not strange, you are like me—you are no different from me! I came here resolved to fight with you if I must, yet my arm lies powerless over you. Tell me, how is it that you stand in the assembly of the gods, and that you have found life?"

Utnapishti turned the budding branch over in his hands, trimming the bark of its cut edge with his pruning shears before he answered. At last he said, "I will reveal a hidden thing to you, Gilgamesh, and tell you a secret of the gods. Set your ear toward me and listen—sit you down, for I see that you are weary."

Utnapishti squatted down beneath an old apple tree, its budding boughs casting a basket-weave of light and shadow over his face. Gilgamesh eased himself to the grass beside him. His knee was too swollen for him to squat, so he sat with legs sticking out in front of him, his back to the rough, sun-warmed tree trunk. He could hear the buzzing of the first bees, a pleasant hum behind the ancient man's soft voice.

"In Shurippak—I think you know the city, on the banks of the Buranun—the city was old, and the gods dwelt in it. And the hearts of the great gods were stirred to bring the Flood. Father An uttered the oath,

Enlil was the adviser, Ninurta the throne-bearer, Ennugi had charge of the canals; and clear-eyed Enki was there with them . . ."

As Utnapishti spoke, Gilgamesh could not turn his gaze from the other man's face. Utnapishti's soft brown eyes grew larger in his sight, drawing him in like whirlpools in a flood-muddied stream, until it seemed to him that he stood beside a wall of clay-caulked reeds, listening to the river whispering words through the grasses.

*Reed house, reed house! Wall, wall! Reed house, listen; wall, turn your ear to me. O man of Shurippak, O son of Ubaratutu, tear down the house and build a boat! Abandon your riches, and seek that which lives; scorn possessions, and hold to the living. Make all living things go up into your boat, the boat which you are to build. Let her measure be measured, length and breadth equal to each other, and roof her as the earth roofs the abzu, the great freshwater abyss.*

"My lord," Utnapishti's voice answered, "you have spoken your command; I heed, and shall do it. But what shall I say to the city, to the people and the elders?"

The river's rushing grew louder, a fresh flood of words pouring from it. *You may say this to them: "Enlil hates me, so that I cannot dwell in your city, nor set foot on the earth which is Enlil's. I shall go down to the abzu to live with my lord Enki, and he shall make richness rain down upon you, fowl in profusion, fish in abundance. He will bring you a wealth of harvest: bread will pour down upon you at dawn, and showers of wheat at sunset."*

"As dawn began to glow," Utnapishti continued, "my people assembled around me. The carpenter carried his hatchet, the reed-worker his flattening stone, the children carried the pitch, the weak carried what they could. I laid out the exterior on the fifth day, the size of a field. The walls were each ten times twelve cubits in height, the sides of its top of equal length, ten times twelve cubits each. I laid out the structure and drew all the plans. I gave it six decks, dividing it into seven levels, and divided the insides into nine parts. I drove plugs to keep out the water, I saw to the punting poles, I laid in what was necessary. Three times I poured three thousand six hundred gallons of raw bitumen into the kiln for the hull, and again for the inside. The basket-bearers brought thrice three thousand six hundred gallons of oil, apart from the oil which they consumed, and the oil, twice that, which the boatman stored away. I butchered oxen for the workers, and killed sheep every day. Ale, beer, oil, and wine I gave to the workmen as if it were a river, so they could celebrate as if it were the New Year's feast, and I anointed my hands with ointment.

"The ark was completed on the seventh day," he went on, and it seemed to Gilgamesh that he could see it—the great boat of bitumen-blackened reeds, high and square as a shrine, with its layered platforms within; the men straining against their poles to move it, sliding it slowly forward until the keel was two-thirds of the way into the Buranun. The gangplanks groaned beneath the weight of the beasts driven up into the boat, cattle and sheep, goats and donkeys and wild beasts; men carried baskets of gold and goods, and woven cages fluttering with birds, between the slow-moving pairs of animals.

The sky darkened and lightened again, and, as had been promised, loaves of bread began to pour from the heavens. The people danced in the city streets, gathering them up in great baskets and eating eagerly, rejoicing to the clouds that were already covering the sky, the misty veil hiding the sun. Gilgamesh wanted to cry out to them, but he was only a watcher, seeing something that had happened long ago: he was as powerless to warn or change as to move Utu's chariot in its courses.

The heavens grew darker and darker; but the torrent that poured down at evening was not water, but a rain of glistening wheat. Again Gilgamesh heard the sounds of rejoicing, the cries of drunkenness and pleasure. And the doors of the great boat closed.

"For the caulking of my boat," Utnapishti said, his voice very faint and faraway, "I gave Puzur-Amuri, the shipbuilder, my palace with all its goods . . ."

As dawn began to glow again, Gilgamesh saw the black cloud boiling up from the horizon, its seething turbulence lit from within by flashes of lightning. Great shapes flew about inside it: it seemed to him that he saw Ishkur standing on the back of his fire-breathing dragon, with the forked staff of lightning in his hand as he goaded the storm on; and before him went his ministers Shullat and Hanish, riding on wild bulls whose snorting cast great ropes of cloud across the sky. The ground cracked beneath it, the door-posts of the underworld opening, and Nergal came forth with curved sword and lion-headed staff in hand, the waters of the earth pouring forth in a torrent behind him. The land glowed with terrifying brightness, eerie blue flames flashing back and forth beneath the blackened sky: save for the continual flashing and hammering of the lightning, and the crackling of the strange unburning fires that glimmered over roofs and trees, there was no light. The earth shattered like a pot beneath the beating of the storm, the dikes of the river bursting in the Flood, so that the wind blew the waters over the ground like a huge tide rushing in over the city. Gilgamesh saw the roofs caving in beneath the weight of rain, the wild waves of the torrent washing walls from their foundations and overthrowing mighty boulders. The cries of the people below were lost in the thunder, the pounding rain and the roaring of the angry waters; their bodies were swept up like twigs in the swirling Flood, struggling helplessly after floating planks and the tangles of uprooted trees with their last strength before the water whirled them down.

Through the flashes of lightning that rent the blackness, Gilgamesh saw the great shapes flying upward like doves disturbed in their roosting, fluttering here and there amid the storm—even the shapes of the gods, overwhelmed and frightened by the Flood, rose and gathered above the clouds, crouching at the deep blue wall of the heavens like cowering dogs.

Inanna's hair was disarrayed, flying about her face in a wet tangle, and the tears streamed down her face with the pouring rain as she cried out, "The days of old are turned to clay, since I spoke evil in the assembly of the gods? How could I speak evil in the assembly of the gods? How could I cry out for the destruction of my people? I myself gave birth to my people—now they fill the sea like the children of fish!"

She wept, and the other gods wept with her. There was no one, Gilgamesh saw, to bring them food or drink; none to pour libations, to set out bowls of honey and beer, and no offering smoke to rise from the drowned shatters of the shrines.

"Six days and seven nights," Utnapishti said, "came the wind and Flood, the storm flattening the land. The Flood was pounding on the seventh day, the water was at war, struggling with itself like a woman laboring to give birth. Then the sea calmed, the storm fell still, the whirl-

wind and the Flood had ceased. I looked out at the day. Stillness had settled in, and all of humanity was turned to clay; the sea was flat as a great
roof. I opened a vent, and fresh light fell upon my face. I fell to my knees
and sat weeping, tears streaming down the sides of my nose. Then I
looked for a shore at the edge of the sea, and at twelve leagues I saw a tip
of land. The boat lodged firmly on the mountain Nimush; the mountain
seized the boat and held it fast.

"For seven days the mountain Nimush held the boat. On the seventh
day I sent off a dove, but it found no perch: it circled and came back to
me. I sent forth a swallow, but it found no perch: it circled and came
back to me. I sent forth a raven. It saw that the waters had receded: it ate,
circled around, turned, and did not come back to me."

As he spoke, Gilgamesh saw the waters draining away, leaving the
bloated corpses of men and beasts like sea-wrack on the side of the
mountain, and the black raven hopping from body to body, dipping its
beak into the water-swollen flesh. Then the birds fluttered forth from
the mouth of the ark in a great cloud, scattering against the sun, and the
men within the boat began to drive the beasts down the gangplank again,
blinking their tear-red eyes against the brightness of the day. But
Utnapishti took a ram by its lead, standing by the ark, beneath the peak
of the mountain that rose into the heavens like a great platform-shrine
of stone. There he and his wife kindled a fire, setting out seven and seven
vessels of figured gold and silver into which he poured beer and honey
and milk; into the coals they poured incense of dried reeds, cedar, and
myrtle, the sweet scent rising up into the cloudless sky. Lastly he cut the
throat of the ram, letting its blood stream upon the ground, then
expertly skinning and gutting it before he and his wife hung up the
haunches of steaming meat.

In the offering-smoke, Gilgamesh saw the misty shapes of the gods gathering around the top of the mountain, collecting around it like flies settling
on the sheep-sacrifice. The last to arrive was a goddess, great-breasted and
wide-hipped, her belly full with child and milk streaming from her nipples
beneath her deep blue necklace of carven lapis flies; there were streaks of
clay on her hands and her brown robe, as though she had just come from

making pots. It seemed to Gilgamesh that he recognized her at once as the goddess Nintun, mother and shaper of life from the earth.

Nintun closed her hand about the huge stone flies at her neck, lifting the lapis beads up. "You gods," she cried out, her voice low and powerful as the bellowing of a wild cow, "as surely as I shall not forget this lapis around my neck, may I be mindful of these evil days, and never forget them. You gods, approach the smoke of the offering; but Enlil may not approach the smoke of the offering, for without consideration he brought on the Flood, and numbered my people for annihilation."

As she spoke, a gust of wind swept over the mountaintop, the whirlwind whipping up the incense-smoke and spilling over several of the cups. Utnapishti fell flat upon his face before its fury, but the gods ranged themselves about, facing the gray-robed god who rode forward on his wild bull, axe uplifted in one hand and Tablet of Destinies in the other. The bull stomped and snorted with rage, lightning flickering from its nostrils as Enlil shouted, gesturing at the boat with his axe.

"Has life-breath escaped?" he demanded. "No man was meant to live through the devastation!"

It was the warrior-god Ninurta who stepped forward to answer him, face stern below his gleaming bronze helm. "Who but Enki could devise such a thing?" he asked. "Is it not he who knows the Word?"

Enlil turned on Enki, who sat with the rivers pouring from the sleeves of his robe. He did not rise, but spoke to Enlil from his throne. "You, valiant one, are the sage among the gods—how could you bring about the Flood without consideration? Punish the one who commits the crime; charge the offense to the offender alone, but be compassionate, lest mankind be cut off, and patient, lest they be killed. Instead of your bringing on the Flood, would that a lion had risen up to diminish the people—instead of your bringing on the Flood, would that a wolf and appeared to diminish the people—instead of your bringing on the Flood, would that famine had occurred to slay the land, and Erra of the Plague gone forth to ravage the land. It was not I who revealed the secret of the great gods: I only made a dream appear to Utnapishti, and he heard the secret of the gods. Now let us speak of him!"

Enlil gazed at the man and woman who lay before their spilled offering-vessels, cowering beside their boat against the wind. Slowly the gale stilled, and the god's angry face softened. He descended from the mountaintop to the ark, reaching down to take Utnapishti and his wife by the hands. Raising their trembling forms up, he made them kneel before him, touching them on the foreheads as he stood between them.

"Before this," he declared, his voice reverberating through the mountains, "Utnapishti has been human. Now let Utnapishti and his wife be transformed, let them become like us, the gods! Let Utnapishti dwell far away, at the Mouth of the Rivers."

The echoing of Enlil's voice faded from Gilgamesh's ears, his sight clearing again until he was looking upon Utnapishti's plain face, shadowed by the branches of the apple trees. "They took us far away," Utnapishti said, "and settled us at the Mouth of the Rivers. But as for you, Gilgamesh—who will call the gods to assembly for you, that you may find the life which you seek?"

He rose, and Gilgamesh followed him, his heart trembling with hope. "Sit here by the wall of my hut," Utnapishti told him. "You must not sleep for six days and seven nights."

Gilgamesh sat down, leaning his back against the dry wall of clay-plastered reeds. It would not be difficult to stay awake—not now, not in this pleasant place, when he had come so far through the greatest hardships and dangers. Yet life for himself would not be enough; would only be a torment alone. So it was that as Utnapishti walked away, Gilgamesh raised his gaze to the warm and cloudless sky.

"Enlil!" he called out softly. "Enlil, in your holy house in Nippur—in Ekur, the house of the mountains, I cry to you. Father Enlil, my *pukku* fell into the Netherworld, my *mikku* fell into the Netherworld. I sent Enkidu to bring them up, but the Netherworld holds him fast. Destiny did not seize him, the demon of plague did not seize him, the Netherworld holds him fast. The servants of unsparing Nergal did not seize him, but the cry of the earth caught hold of him; he did not fall in the battles of men, but the Netherworld holds him fast."

Yet the burnished tin bowl of the sky shone unchanged; no gust of wind blew to suggest that Enlil had heard, or would answer. Though the silence pressed despair upon Gilgamesh, he thought to himself: Enlil had decreed that Enkidu must die, Enlil who had shaped Huwawa and set him in his place, Enlil who had brought the Flood upon mankind. Though it was he who had given life to Utnapishti, it was only the rebukes of the other gods to which he had listened—he would not hear Gilgamesh, nor be swayed by his words or the desperate sorrow in his heart. Rather—and now it seemed to Gilgamesh that he had come closer to the advice Utnapishti had meant to give him—it was Enki to whom he should speak, calling the god's sweet waters to wash away the bitter salt of his weeping, and trusting in his mercy, which had saved human life upon the earth.

"Father Enki!" Gilgamesh murmured. "Father Enki, in your holy house in Eridu—in the *abzug*, the sea of fresh water beneath the roof of earth—I cry to you." Though his voice was beginning to choke with tears, he went on, forcing the words out from his heart through the clogged passageway of his throat, like blood pulsing out through the bandage over a wound.

"Father Enki, my *pukku* fell into the Netherworld, my *mikku* fell into the Netherworld. I sent Enkidu to bring them up, but the Netherworld holds him fast. Destiny did not seize him, the demon of plague did not seize him, the Netherworld holds him fast. The servants of unsparing Nergal did not seize him, but the cry of the earth caught hold of him; he did not fall in the battles of men, but the Netherworld holds him fast."

Gilgamesh waited, opening his heart as he stared out across the lapping waters of the sea, the green grass edging the beach and the still boughs of the apple orchard. Utnapishti had gone back to tending his trees, squatting down in the tangled shadows; the *magillu*-boat still lay on the strand, with new punting poles fixed in its sockets, but there was no sign of Urnashabi.

Then it seemed to Gilgamesh that he heard the little rushing noises of the stream by the hut growing louder, as though it bore the echoes of all the rivers of the world that flowed into it. Words arose from it, the far-off booming of a waterfall against the rocks, and the words filled Gilgamesh with a quiet overflowing gladness, like date-wine pouring into an empty cup.

*BRAVE UTU, WARRIOR AND HERO, SON OF NINGAL! OPEN NOW AN OPENING TO THE NETHERWORLD; RAISE ENKIDU'S GHOST FROM THE NETHERWORLD, THAT HE MAY TELL TO HIS BROTHER ALL THE WAYS OF THE NETHERWORLD.*

Gilgamesh held his breath as the sunlight brightened, a single shaft piercing down from the clear sky to strike the ground by his feet. The earth opened like an eye of darkness, the hole sinking away into the unknowable depths. His heart beating in his ears like a drum of summoning, Gilgamesh stared into the blackness, waiting for Enkidu to come forth.

At first he saw only a mist, as though a drop of oil had fallen into his eye, blurring the lens. But slowly—almost too slowly to bear—the blur grew stronger and more solid, until at last Enkidu stood naked before him, the gleam of burnished metal shining from his golden hair and the sunlight falling across his broad shoulders like a cloak. His green eyes were bright and clear as sunlit seawater, drowning Gilgamesh in their gladness.

Gilgamesh and Enkidu embraced as tightly as if they were wrestling, each clinging to the other with all his strength. Enkidu's kiss was bruising-sweet to Gilgamesh's mouth; their tongues sought each other, they breathed each other's breath, warm and alive. Gilgamesh felt himself hardening against Enkidu's solid hip, and let tufted cloak and lion-skin slip from his shoulders and bear-hide from his waist, his hands stroking down the powerful muscles of his lover's back as Enkidu caressed him in turn, his golden beard mingling with the dark growth matted upon Gilgamesh's cheeks and throat. Though Utnapishti was within sight, Gilgamesh did not care: he pulled Enkidu down to the soft grass with him, all pain forgotten, his whole body alive with delight in his beloved's nearness.

Gilgamesh cried out as he spent, a sharp cry rising above Enkidu's joyous roar. Sun-warmed sweat trickling down their backs, they lay holding each other for a little while, until their breathing slowed and their hearts beat evenly again.

"Tell me, beloved," Gilgamesh said after a time, "tell me what you saw in the Netherworld."

Enkidu shook his head, and Gilgamesh could see the shadow behind his eyes. "I will tell you, my love, but if I must tell you the ways of the Netherworld which I have seen, you will sit down and weep. There will be weeping enough for you."

Enkidu bent forward to kiss Gilgamesh before he spoke again. "My body, which gave your heart joy to touch—vermin eat it up like old clothes, and it is filled with dirt."

Gilgamesh turned his head away, grinding his face into the grass to shut out the memory. Enkidu's corpse fly-riddled, swollen, turning green beneath the golden hair . . . Yet he was here, and whole, sun-browned skin and fair pelt soft over his rippling muscles, eyes half shut against the brilliant sunlight like a lion dozing by the watering hole. Gilgamesh stroked the line between his lover's powerful chest-muscles with the tip of one finger, smoothing down the bright curls, and the familiar gesture of affection made it easier for him to speak again.

"What of the fates of men in the Netherworld?"

"I wandered everywhere, for I had no place in Erishkegal's halls, since I was not given to the tomb with proper rites. I was clothed as a living man, and could find no one to guest me; I hungered and thirsted, for I was given the offerings of a living man, which they still make for me in Erech, but which I could neither eat nor drink. It is the offerings given to the dead that help them in the Netherworld, the food and drink set out by their descendants that give them all the power and life and joy they may find there . . . The Shamhatu tried to explain it to me once, when we were in the village, but I could not understand her then, for I knew little of the worlds of men, and nothing of the Otherworld."

Gilgamesh thought back to the orders he had given, in the fevered madness of sorrow and guilt that had overtaken him after Enkidu's death, and closed his eyes with a shudder. "I am sorry, beloved," he said. "I only . . . I did not wish to give you up to death."

"I know," Enkidu answered, stroking Gilgamesh's back. "I know."

"What of the man with one son?" Gilgamesh asked to distract himself from the recurring image of his beloved wandering, lost and hungry, down all the dark and dusty roads of the Netherworld—abandoned by his own foolishness. "Have you seen him?"

"I have. He lies under the walls, weeping bitterly."

"What of the man with two sons?"

"He lives in a brick house and eats bread. The man with three sons drinks water out of waterskins filled from deep wells; the heart of the man with four sons rejoices. The man with five sons—like a good writer, scribe to the king, his hand is revealed, and he brings justice to the palace. The man with six sons feels pride like a man who guides the plough; the man with seven sons shines like a standard, blindingly bright."

"What of one who died a sudden death?" Gilgamesh inquired. "Have you seen him?"

"I have. He sleeps at night on a couch, and drinks pure water."

"What of Ur-Lamma, who was slain in battle? Have you seen him?"

"I have. His father raises his head, and his wife tends his body."

Gilgamesh nodded, and the thought brought him comfort. He would make offerings again to the old general when he came back to Erech, and thank him once more for all he had done. "What of Ishbi-Erra, whose corpse was thrown into the wasteland? Have you seen him?"

"I have. His spirit does not rest in the Netherworld."

Gilgamesh had expected more satisfaction from the answer, but his long wandering had muted his fury, dimming the little ice-coal of anger and remembered fear that Ishbi-Erra's name had been to his heart since the assassination attempt. *I might not pardon him from death, if he came before me now,* Gilgamesh thought. *But I would let him be buried, that even he might have his place in the halls of dust.*

"The one whose spirit has no one left alive to love him," Gilgamesh asked slowly, "have you seen him?"

"I have. The leftover pot, the scraps of bread thrown into the gutter— what no dead dog will eat, he eats." Enkidu's fair brows drew more closely over his eyes, and though he spoke no words of reproach, Gilgamesh felt them the more keenly: had he not refused to give his beloved what he would need in the Netherworld?

Gilgamesh caressed Enkidu's cheek, stroking the edge of his bright-curled beard. "But now it is over, my love. You have come back to the sunlit lands, and will live with me again."

Enkidu shook his head; his golden lashes fluttered and his eyes closed. "No. I was only given this little time with you, that I might tell you of the ways of the Netherworld. For I am dead, and you must go back to Erech as Ensi."

"No! No, my love!" Gilgamesh embraced Enkidu, holding him to himself as tightly as he could. "No, you are here at the Mouth of the Rivers, where Utnapishti lives forever. You have come back to me . . . how could I let you go again?"

"The destinies are set," Enkidu said, and already the deep rumble of his voice was beginning to fade, even as his body seemed to mist away from Gilgamesh's grasp. "I am dead, and you are alive . . . Farewell, my love."

"My love!" Gilgamesh cried out, his voice wrung with longing and despair. He tightened his arms, but there was nothing beneath them to hold; and when he looked for the dark opening in the ground, it had already closed, the grass-grown earth sealing the passage as though it had never been. "Enkidu, beloved . . ." He closed his eyes in despair, ready to sink down beside Enkidu.

Something touched Gilgamesh's shoulder, and he jerked violently. Utnapishti stood beside him, staring down with a look of remote and compassionate sadness.

"Are you awake?" Utnapishti asked.

"As soon as sleep was about to pour over me," Gilgamesh answered, struggling to his feet, "you touched me and aroused me."

"Look over here, Gilgamesh." Utnapishti pointed to a row of seven loaves, each with a mark on the wall above it. "Count the loaves, see what is marked on the wall. The first is dried out, the second is leathery, the third moist. The fourth has turned white, the fifth has gray mold on it, the sixth is stale, the seventh—as I put it down, you awoke."

Gilgamesh looked at the loaves in disbelief. They lay there, ranged from hard hollow shell to freshly steaming round: proof of his sleep, which he could not gainsay, and the final denial of his quest for life. *Are not the dead like the sleeping . . . ?* Even in this place of life, sleep had crept over him; even if he stayed here all his days, death would come to him in the same manner.

"O woe! What shall I do, Utnapishti? Where shall I go? A thief has stolen my flesh. Death dwells in the house where my bed is, and wherever I set foot, Death is there, too."

Utnapishti did not answer him. Instead he called to Urnashabi, who sat in his boat by the waters, gazing out over the sea.

"Urnashabi! Henceforth the harbor shall reject you, and the ferry-landing hate you. You have been coming to the shore, but the shore shall be denied to you from now on. The man you led here—matted hair covers his body, and animal skins have hidden his beautiful flesh. Take him, Urnashabi, and lead him to the washing place. Let him wash his filthy hair in water and become pure, let him cast his skins into the sea, let his body be moistened with fine oil, and the hair combed and tied on his head again. Let him wear a clean garment, the robe of life, so that he may go back to his city, and set off along his road. Let him put on an elder's robe, and let it not become spotted; let it be perfectly new."

Gilgamesh let the ferryman lead him down to where the stream flowed into the sea, wading in to his waist. He bent over, scrubbing at his hair in the clear water. Great mats floated away in hairy spider-tangles, the crusted blood and filth on his body flaking off beneath the gentle current. Unbuckling his belt, he unwrapped the stinking bearskin from his waist, letting the water carry it away like a dark mass of seaweed until it finally sank, bubbling down beneath the little waves. The scars of his journey shone sharp and red against his skin, the ridges of his ribs standing out along his chest. His seven days' sleep had healed the worst of the injury to his knee, but he could still feel it twinging when he moved, and was careful how he put weight upon it.

At last, feeling clean and light as a scoured gourd, Gilgamesh came back out of the water. Urnashabi was waiting there with a bowl of oil scented with spikenard and frankincense, and a new white garment, a robe woven of linen spun with wool like the ceremonial robes of the priests and elders. The fabric scratched lightly against his freshly washed body; he felt as though his cleansing had scraped away a layer of old skin to expose new underneath. Urnashabi handed him a comb, and he straightened his hair and bound it up, ready to set off on his journey again. He folded Enkidu's tufted cloak together with the lion-skin—he would give the cloak back with the death-offerings; though he did not know what he would do with the skin, he was not ready to abandon it—and, lastly, swung Enkidu's bow and quiver over his back.

"Are you ready to go?" Urnashabi asked. "Since the way of the sea is barred to me now, we shall go along the river. In time the Buranun, like all the rivers of the world, flows into this stream, and, if your strength does not fail, we shall pole up it to Erech."

"I am ready," Gilgamesh answered. They pushed the *magillu*-boat to the mouth of the little river and cast off, Gilgamesh poling upstream with steady thrusts.

They were not yet out of sight of the hut when Gilgamesh heard a woman's voice, carrying clear over the water. "Utnapishti, Gilgamesh has come here exhausted, worn-out with strain and toil. What have you given him as he returns to his land?"

Gilgamesh lifted the pole from the river-bottom, letting the boat slowly swing back toward the ocean. From his vision of the Flood, he recognized the woman who stood by Utnapishti as his wife: nearly as tall as her husband, her angular frame draped in a simple gray gown, and gray-black hair wound in a thick coil of braids around her head. She lifted her beaky nose, facing Utnapishti down. At last he nodded, gesturing them closer. Gilgamesh raised the punting pole, steering the boat back down the current until it came to shore by the hut.

"Gilgamesh," said Utnapishti, "you came here exhausted, worn-out with strain and toil. What can I give you as you return to your land?" He tugged at his short beard, looking slowly about himself, then met Gilgamesh's eyes again. "I will uncover a secret thing for you, Gilgamesh—I will tell you a secret of the gods. There is a plant whose roots go deep, like the boxthorn; its thorns will prick your hands like a bramble. If you can get that plant for yourself, you will become young again."

"Young again . . ." Gilgamesh echoed. The words seized him with a terrible longing. He remembered the fierce joy he had held in his strength, the sureness of his own power in which he had trusted. No more fear that his knee would betray him, buckling under him when he most needed it to hold; the weary weight of his wandering and mourning scoured from him like a crust of dirt from his skin, leaving him clean and whole of heart, untroubled by the leaden certainties that Enkidu's death and his journey had laden upon him. "Where is this plant? I would go and find it."

"Beneath the Mouth of all Rivers, you will find a passage leading down to the *abzu* beneath the earth—Enki's kingdom, that sweetest and freshest of all waters, where the deepest of all plants set their roots. There, in the very depths, you will find the herb you seek."

"I will do it."

Gilgamesh and Urnashabi moored the *magillu*-boat, and Gilgamesh went along the shore, looking for heavy stones. These he brought back to the boat, with twine to bind them firmly to his feet. He stripped himself, leaving only the plain leather belt and dagger around his waist, and balanced by the edge of the boat a moment, looking down into the waves.

The white sand of the shore dropped off swiftly where the stream flowed into the sea, the waters darkening green below. Far in the depths, he could see the gray-black shape of a large stone, edged by deeper black. Gilgamesh breathed deeply, several times, as though he could fill the storehouses of his body with air like grain kept back from good harvests.

One last breath and he was over the side, the stones on his feet dragging him swiftly down through the ocean. Its taste in his mouth was salt mingled with sweet; he could see clearly through the water, the purple- and green-fronded waving of the weeds and the darting of little brown fish at the corner of his eye. Gilgamesh's lungs were already aching when the stones settled on the ocean floor, but he had strained them far harder, training for battle, and he paid no attention to the pounding in his head.

As he had guessed, the man-sized boulder stood in the mouth of a channel into the darkness. Swinging his body awkwardly through the water, Gilgamesh shoved his shoulder against it, rocking it back and forth until at last it edged to the side and he could squeeze by. It was hard swimming, making his way against the stream flowing out through the conduit: he could see nothing, only feel the smooth stone walls bumping against his shoulders now and then, the mossy stone of the floor slippery beneath his hands as he pulled himself along. He did not dare to be afraid, for he knew that he could not hold his breath too much longer; and if he let his heart hammer with fear, or his lungs begin to strain harder in his chest, it would suck the last of air from his body like a *lilitu* sucking an infant's blood. He would die there, seeking renewal, like a child dying even as its mother forced it through the passage of her body . . .

No: he would come again to Erech with the plant in his hand. The old En would eat of it, and renew his sunken flesh, to preside in the shrine of Inanna for another seventy years or more; Rimsat-Ninsun would eat of it, praising her son as her wrinkled breasts grew firm and her age-worn face smoothed itself. The elders of Erech would no longer sit and mutter, chiding the young for their rashness, but would leap forward boldly, hunting and riding in their chariots again.

As Gilgamesh strengthened himself thus with his thoughts, the stone floor of the channel suddenly dropped away beneath his hands. Without hesitation—for he knew that if he hesitated a moment, he would fail— he swung his weighted feet over the conduit's lip, letting himself drop into the dark waters.

It seemed to Gilgamesh that he fell a very long time, plunging into unimaginable depths. But though his lungs ached, they were not yet bursting when his feet struck the ledge. He reached down carefully.

The thorns sank deep into his hand, biting in like the fangs of a snake to send a chilling pain up his arm. The nape of his neck and back of his head prickled up with the shock, and a silent bubble of air escaped from his lungs. But Gilgamesh held tight to the plant embedded in his flesh, pulling it from its moorings with a single jerk. As swiftly as he could, he drew his dagger and cut the twine that bound the stones to his feet, kicking powerfully off from the ledge and swimming upward. Now bright spots were beginning to blossom behind his eyelids, his head to spin and grow dizzy; but the water sucked him upward, into the passageway, shooting him along. The brightness of the sea dazzled his eyes as he forced himself out past the boulder. He struggled upward, overtaking the stream of clear bubbles that burst from his lungs.

At last Gilgamesh's head broke the surface. Gasping for air, he lay there in the rocking waves, kicking weakly and letting the current carry him back toward the boat. The salt burned his hand where the thorns of the plant had pierced him, little trails of blood curling away through the clear water. But the plant itself . . . It was a rich, deep green, its leaves frilled into hundreds of little leaflets, each tipped by a sharp thorn. Its root shone white, forked like a mandrake's. The herb was beautiful to look upon, but it was its scent, the dizzying sweetness that filled Gilgamesh's head and heart with strength even as he breathed it in, that told him that he had truly found what he sought.

Climbing over the side of the boat, Gilgamesh held the plant up in triumph, the tiny rivulets of blood and water running down his wrist from its leaves. "Urnashabi," he said quietly, "this is the plant of openings, by which a man can get life within. I will bring it to Erech the Sheepfold; I will give it to the elders to eat, and they will divide the plant among them. Its name is, the Old Man Shall Be Made Young. I, too, will eat it, and become again what I was in my youth."

Urnashabi only grunted, chewing on a piece of his long beard and spitting a few hairs over the side. "If you are ready to go to Erech, pick up the punting pole."

THE STREAM BROADENED as they punted up it, other branches flowing away from it like rootlets from a taproot. Urnashabi pointed out each to Gilgamesh, the turning points for the great rivers of the world. By the time the sun was low in the west, they had reached the fork for the Buranun. The river's banks were green the lettuces sprouting along the wet sides of the canals and the vines beginning to spring up and run along the ground.

"We shall stop here for the night," Urnashabi said. "We are closer than you think to Erech—we shall get there in the morning."

They stopped and made camp by the shore, lighting a fire and breaking out the provisions, goat-cheese and milk, bread and dried apples, that Utnapishti had sent with them. Gilgamesh found himself very hungry, eagerly devouring the soft cheese and flaky bread. He had not tasted such food since leaving Erech, he realized: there had been neither meal nor baking oven in the wilderness, only the tough gamy meat of his wild prey.

When Gilgamesh had eaten, he rose and walked about the campsite. It was on an open plain, where no one could approach without warning them; if Urnashabi was right about their closeness to Erech, there would be little fear of an attack by robbers in the night, in any case. Beside their bedrolls was a small pool of clear water, its sky-mirroring surface rippled by the flowing of the underground stream that fed it.

Though Gilgamesh's robe was unstained by his day's labor, he had sweated mightily, poling the *magillu*-boat up the river in the sunlight; his skin itched with salt, and his muscles were sore. If he were to go into Erech tomorrow, Gilgamesh thought, he should be freshly bathed and shaven—bearing the plant of renewal to his city, he should not appear as a weary wanderer, but as an Ensi in his full pride.

So thinking, Gilgamesh stripped off his robe and laid it carefully over a bush. When his feet began to sink in the marshy grasses around the pool's edge, he stopped, crouched, and sprang in. The pond was deeper than he had expected, its waters cool and soothing. Kicking his feet and splashing with his hands, he ducked his head underwater to rinse his hair. Something brushed against his leg, a cold ripple like a slick stem of waterweed, but he paid it no attention.

Refreshed, Gilgamesh swam to the side of the pond, wading out. The rustling through the roots of the reeds drew his glance, the wet black wriggle of a snake slithering toward the pool. Then he saw the flash of bright green, and the sweet scent struck his nostrils—the scent of the plant of renewal, which the snake bore in its mouth.

Crying out, Gilgamesh lunged for it, but his foot slipped in the mud, his fingers barely grazing the slick scales. The snake turned like a whip cracking, flicking away. Gilgamesh scrambled through the reeds after it, snatching out again and again, but it whispered away from his grasp like an eddy of wind. At last it turned, making for the pool. Gilgamesh dived after it, lunging full-length to grasp its tail.

Yet even though he could see that he held the snake tightly, its tail-tip flicking black from the end of his fist, it seemed to Gilgamesh that he could feel it wriggling from his grasp. Then he saw: the scales of its head had split as it stretched its jaws over the plant, the snake slipping from its skin as if from a worn-out garment and away. A shimmering rainbow played over its black scales in the second before it slithered into the pond; then it was gone, and with it, the plant of renewal.

Gilgamesh opened his hand, dropping the weightless burden of the cast-off skin. He looked into the waters of the pool, muddy from his bath, but saw nothing. The snake must lair somewhere within the pond, or the freshwater stream leading to it. And it was too late to snatch the plant from its jaws now.

He walked back to the campfire, sitting down on a rock beside it. For a little while he could not speak, his disappointment too deep to form into words.

*A snake*, Gilgamesh thought. A beast that could not see death before it, like the walls of a city rising at the end of a long road, that would never know, even as it came newborn from the tatters of its old skin, that it was reborn. So close to Erech, with the precious reward toiled for and won, how could it have been snatched from his hand like this? No decree of the gods, not even the act of a foe, but only blind chance: a monstrous randomness, stealing the hope of which he had already made sure, like a wild pig breaking through a fence to snout up a garden that had already sprouted and begun to burgeon with leaves. And here he was left coming back to Erech with nothing, all his wanderings gone to naught. *I should have stayed at home*, Gilgamesh thought, *to rule even as I mourned, had I known that there would be such an empty repayment for all my pain . . .*

The tears welled up in his eyes, running down along the sides of his nose and spilling freely over his face. Urnashabi, still chewing on a dried apple, looked curiously at him.

"Why do you weep?" the ferryman asked. "What more have you to trouble your thoughts?"

"For whom, Urnashabi, do my arms toil? For whom has the blood of my heart dried up?" Gilgamesh asked bitterly. "I have not won any good for myself, but done a good deed only for the snake, the lion of the ground—by now the flood tide has pushed it twenty leagues away. I learned my place when I entered the channel; what will serve as a sign-post for me now?"

Gilgamesh looked out over the Buranun. Though the land around it had darkened, the slowly curving length of the river still shone blue between its shadowy banks, reflecting the last brightness lingering in the sky. As though his eyes had cleared, the land no longer seemed strange to him: as Urnashabi had said, they were not far from Erech. He had ridden these roads before, many times. Soon they would reach the plain where Agga's troops had gathered, and then be within sight of the walls of Erech.

"Let us withdraw from the river," Gilgamesh said thoughtfully, "and leave the boat by the shore—we may as well go on to Erech by foot."

THE WALLS OF Erech rose high over the plain, the cedar gates gleaming above them. Even from afar, where the rich smooth patterns of their ruddy grain and the fine carvings along their height could not be seen, the gates were beautiful, a sign of welcome to travelers from afar. Gilgamesh could see the figures walking along the walls, glints of gold and bronze sparking from them in the morning sunlight. Despite the heaviness in his breast and the aching in his hand where the thorns of the lost plant of renewal had bitten deep, he felt his pace quickening, felt a sudden hunger to go along the streets of his city, to sit in the shade of the judgment hall, with Enatarzi bringing him beer in his own cup. "I am home," he said to himself. "Soon, in only a little while, I shall be within my walls."

Yet Urnashabi held back, grumbling into his beard, and shortly had fallen several paces behind Gilgamesh.

"I think I will go no farther," the old ferryman said when Gilgamesh stopped and turned to him. "I have not entered a city's walls in many generations, nor have I spoken with men in the marketplace. I shall leave you now, and go back to my boat and my accustomed work."

"No." Gilgamesh gestured at the city with a grand sweep of his arm—a gesture of pride, for he could not help feeling proud at the splendor he saw before him, the great walls and the matchless gates. "Rather, Urnashabi, you should go up onto the walls of Erech and walk about. Look at its foundation, inspect its brickwork. Is not the very core made of oven-fired brick, and did not the seven sages lay out its plans? In Erech, the house of Inanna, one part is city, one part orchards, and one part clay pits—those are the three parts that make up Erech."

Urnashabi grumbled a little more, but he did not stop walking beside Gilgamesh, nor turn back when they stepped onto the wagon-rutted road that led to the cedar gates. Now that they were closer, Gilgamesh could see that it was the New Year's procession that walked the walls. The folk of temple and town paraded in all their finery—the young pleasure-priests of Inanna draped in colored scarves, the maidens and priestesses lifting swords and double-edged axes, the young men carrying their wooden hoops and the colored cords for their dancing games and rope-competitions. The sounds of horn and drum floated out over the plain, together with snatches of song. *The people of Sumer parade before you, they play the sweet* ala-*drums before you . . . I say "Hail!" to Inanna, Great Lady of Heaven . . .*

As they came toward the city, the cedar gates swung open to the deep blowing of rams' horns, and two people walked out. The Shamhatu, her slender body draped and veiled in bridal finery, led a pair of tawny creatures: at first Gilgamesh thought they were dogs, but then, as they tugged at their leads and scampered forward beside her, he saw that they were great-pawed lion cubs. Beside her was Shusuen, dressed in a white robe like Gilgamesh's own, with his striped cat riding on his shoulder. He wore the high, many-horned cap of rulership on his thick dark hair, and carried a staff in his hand—Gilgamesh's staff, the great staff of the Ensi; and the En's great electrum medallion, clear stones glowing bright between the deep sheen of the black cabochons, shone upon the scribe's narrow chest.

A dreadful thought came over Gilgamesh as the two of them came closer. He had been gone for months, with no one knowing where he went or if he would ever return, and a city must have a ruler. Had Shusuen claimed the title of the En and been anointed and exalted as Ensi already? Was there any place left for him in Erech, Gilgamesh wondered, or would he have to wander yet farther—or set the city to battling in its own streets, if he wished to take its rule again? For Shusuen could have declared him an outcast already. Nothing would have been easier than for the scribe who had seen to and carried out all his decrees to make himself sole ruler and final authority: he even held the Ensi's cylinder-seal already.

Gilgamesh stood still, his hand dropping to the axe in his belt. It would be easy, out here with no guards, to cleave Shusuen's body from shoulder to hip. But his fingers could not close upon the weapon. He had wandered too far, he had seen too much—and looking upon the scribe's pale face, the familiar lines of delicately squared jaw and pointed chin, his blue eyes grave beneath flaring dark eyebrows, Gilgamesh knew that he would give up his throne rather than send his old friend down the long road to the halls of dust. If it were so set that Shusuen would go into Inanna's bridal shrine that night, leaving him to wander outside the walls of the Eanna as a simple man of Erech . . . then so it would be. He was done with fighting against fate.

Yet, for all his thoughts of resignation, Gilgamesh felt a great sigh of relief and joy flow from his lungs as he heard Shusuen's first words. "Hail and welcome, Gilgamesh, Ensi of Erech, exalted one of Inanna and Anu! The New Year's feast is upon us, and we are gladdened by your return."

Writhing around Shusuen's neck, his claws kneading into Shusuen's shoulders until the young man winced, the cat gave a chirruping cry of greeting. The Shamhatu's two lion-cubs struggled against their leashes, their pounces tugging her forward.

"Inanna bids you welcome, Gilgamesh . . . oh!" she cried as one of the cubs darted backward, the sudden jerk on the lead nearly pulling her from her feet. Shusuen reached to steady her with a quick hand on her elbow. Recovering, the Shamhatu straightened up, gathering the leads in closer to her body. One of the little lions sat down, bending to wash a hind leg; the other lay down with its chin upon its paws, tail twitching as it watched Gilgamesh and Urnashabi. "I, and the En of Erech," she went on with an air of unruffled dignity only spoiled slightly by her breathlessness, "welcome your return."

"The En of Erech?" Gilgamesh asked, looking at Shusuen. He nodded. "So the old man has given over his duties at last."

"He is dead," Shusuen answered. "He died less than a month after you left. The Shamhatu and I have been doing what we could in your absence, waiting to hear what had become of you."

Gilgamesh looked wonderingly on his scribe, overwhelmed at all Shusuen's words told him. Waiting with little hope, the rulership easily within his grasp—yet Gilgamesh remembered the long night in the mountains, the scribe following him even to Huwawa's gates. The shock of Shusuen's endless trustiness did not wring his heart now; instead he felt the hot blood of guilt scorching his cheeks, for having doubted, and for . . . *I did not earn this,* he thought. *Why is he so faithful to me?*

*Because he is as he is, and I am as I am,* Gilgamesh answered himself. Then, *What can I do to earn this trustworthiness? Only enter the walls of my city again, and rule as best as I can.*

"You have done very well—better than I deserved. I shall not go away again."

"Good."

Shusuen handed Gilgamesh the Ensi's staff, then took the tall horned cap from his head and the medallion from around his neck, holding them out as well. Gilgamesh shook his head.

"You are still the En," he said. "I shall not take that from you—have you not more than earned it?"

"The En is Inanna's husband," Shusuen replied. "My great-grandfather kept these in trust from Lugalbanda, that you should receive them and be anointed upon your ascension."

He seemed about to say more, but the lion-cub that had been lying down raised its haunches into a crouch, then suddenly sprang at Gilgamesh, dragging the Shamhatu forward. Its paws wrapped around his leg; if the claws had not been blunted, it would have taken his calf half off, but though it rubbed its whiskery face hard against him, it did not try to bite. Gilgamesh looked looked down and could not help laughing.

"Where did these come from?" he asked her.

The Shamhatu raised her eyes to Gilgamesh's, tugging the other cub forward as she came toward him. "Akalla came upon them in his hunting one day; near the walls of the city he saw a queen trying to protect her cubs from a strange male. And he recognized the markings upon their brows—look you there." She bent down, tracing the double-pointed arch that showed black on the cubs' foreheads—the same mark as on the head of Enkidu's lion. "He frightened off the invader, and brought the two surviving cubs to be raised in the shrine."

Gilgamesh crouched down, and the second cub scampered to him with a soft deep chirp of greeting, batting at his hand and tilting its head for him to scratch its ears. "Enkidu's children," he murmured. "And Inanna's lions, the lions of Erech's Ensi . . . my *pukku* and *mikku*."

The eyes of the lion-cubs, green as Enkidu's and shot through with the same crystal-slivers of gold, looked up at Gilgamesh. "Pukku and Mikku," he repeated thoughtfully, stroking each of their heads before he stood again, letting the Shamhatu hand him the leads. Then Gilgamesh reached out for the medallion the En held, dropping it around his neck, and the horned cap, which he set upon his head. Staff and lion-leads in one hand, he took the Shamhatu's hand in the other, drawing her close to him, then laid his palm upon her heart, feeling its fluttering thump beneath the warm curve of her breast, her nipple hardening beneath his fingers. For the time had come for his return to Erech, and Gilgamesh knew that this must be his wedding night.

"My sister," he said, the words of Dumuzi's song slipping easily into his mouth at last, like fresh offering-milk flowing over his tongue, "I would go with you to my garden, I would go with you to my orchard, I would go with you to my apple tree. There I would plant the sweet, honey-covered seed."

"Let the bed that rejoices the heart be prepared," the Shamhatu answered. "Let the bed that sweetens the lions be made ready. Let the bed of the Ensi be prepared, let the bed of queenship be made ready. Let the rulers' bed be prepared."

The Shamhatu's dark eyes glistened as they met his, and though she was smiling, Gilgamesh saw the faint quiver at the corner of her lips. The words of the rite no longer seemed enough to shape the feelings in his heart, nor to mark the end of the road to which he had come. Instead he bent to kiss her, holding her slender body to him as their lips met for the first time.

"The rulers' bed is made ready for you," said Shusuen, and it seemed to Gilgamesh that he heard a hint of laughter in the dry baritone voice as the new En spoke the ritual words. "Come into the sheepfold, and let Erech overflow with your blessing."

Gilgamesh, the Shamhatu, and Shusuen stepped through the great cedar gates, with Urnashabi trailing behind them and the lion-cubs pouncing beside. As they entered, the singing rose up around them, all the voices of Erech blending together into a single cry of resounding joy; and the three of them opened their mouths to join in.

"My lady looks in sweet wonder from heaven,
She looks in sweet wonder from all the lands,
And on the people of Erech, as numerous as sheep.
I sing your praises, holy Inanna,
Brightly in Erech shines the Queen of Heaven . . ."

# AFTERWORD

The epic of Gilgamesh is one of the oldest heroic epics known. The historical Gilgamesh was apparently a Sumerian king of the Early Dynastic period, ruling circa 2700 B.C.E. The text telling of his deeds was written in the first millennium B.C.E., and consists of twelve tablets, the last of which gives an alternate version of the death of Enkidu. It, in turn, was based on an earlier epic written in the Old Babylonian period (1800–1600 B.C.E.). In addition to the epic, there are several Sumerian poems about incidents in Gilgamesh's career, produced during the reign of Shulgi, around 2000 B.C.E.

In writing this book, we have largely followed the standard text, using the translations of Maureen Gallery Kovaks (*The Epic of Gilgamesh*, Palo Alto: Stanford University Press, 1989) and John Gardner and John Maier (*Gilgamesh*, New York: Vintage Books, 1985). Gilgamesh's war with Agga is not in the epic; it comes from the Sumerian poem "Gilgamesh and Agga," translated in Samuel Noah Kramer's *The Sumerians: Their History, Culture, and Character* (Chicago: University of Chicago Press, 1963).

Tablet XII of the standard text, which tells the story of Gilgamesh's loss of the *pukku* and *mikku* and Enkidu's subsequent descent to the Netherworld, presented a special problem, since it was obviously incompatible with the other tablets of the epic. In order to be faithful to the traditions while still telling a coherent story, we chose to exercise artistic license by incorporating it in the form of visions experienced by Gilgamesh during the events of Tablets IX to XI. The precise identity of the *pukku* and *mikku* is a matter of much scholarly debate: their use in the text suggests drum and drumstick, but others have thought that they may be the rod and the ring, symbols of rulership.

The hymns to Inanna are largely drawn from *Inanna, Queen of Heaven and Earth: Her Stories and Hymns from Sumer* (London: Rider, 1984) by Diane Wolkstein and Samuel Noah Kramer. We also used texts from *The Ancient Near East*, vols. I–II (Princeton: Princeton University Press, 1973–75), edited by James B. Pritchard.

The behavior of the various lions throughout the book is drawn from the observations in *The Serengeti Lion: A Study of Predator-Prey Relationships.* (Chicago: University of Chicago Press, 1972) by George B. Schaller and *The Tribe of Tiger: Cats and their Culture* (New York: Simon & Schuster, 1994) by Elizabeth Marshall Thomas. Cats were known to the Sumerians as controllers of pests, though they played no particular role in Sumerian religion and culture (the mutual influence between Sumeria and Egypt was surprisingly limited, although a certain amount of interaction and trade did take place). The Sumerian cat may well have been of the long-haired Eastern type, rather than the shorthaired Egyptian cat—the En's fictional cats are unique, and would probably have required a special temple dispensation as a gift to a respected foreign priest; one may, for instance, compare the history of the first Siamese cats to leave Siam. Interestingly, the lion was classed as a canine by the Sumerians—it is, as the En notes, observation rather than general knowledge which leads some of the characters in this book to compare it to the domestic cat.

In general, we have tried to present the epic in its Early Dynastic historical context. However, the time of its writing and the nature of the materials available have made it virtually certain that our *Gilgamesh* contains a number of conceptual and practical anachronisms: for instance, the Inanna of Gilgamesh's age was probably much less aggressive and martial than her late incarnation, the Akkadian Ishtar. Readers of direct translations of the epic will notice that the god-names here are different from those in the poem (Inanna for Ishtar, Utu for Shamash, Enki for Ea, and so forth). This is because we have tried, whenever possible, to use Sumerian name-forms, though in a few cases we have preferred the standard versions: obviously, for instance, we rejected the early Sumerian form "Bilgamesh" as more correct for the hero's name. We apologize to all specialists in Middle Eastern studies for any grating linguistic or historical mistakes we may have made.

Mesopotamian religion, on the whole, is a subject of extreme complexity. It certainly underwent some changes between the Early Dynastic period and the time-period in which the epic of Gilgamesh was written down. Some deities increased in significance, while others decreased; cultic practices and iconography also undoubtedly shifted a great deal. Our knowledge of Sumerian religious beliefs comes from a combination of recorded myths, hymns and votive inscriptions, and artworks. Although there is a great deal of surviving material, much of it is incomplete, sometimes contradictory, and open to a great deal of interpretative scope. A number of cultic titles and terms are known, some of which are easily identified (and cover a range of functions from diviners, purification-priests, and practitioners of ritual sexuality to temple cooks and brewers), others of which remain mysterious.

Overall, a large part of the Sumerian view of deities and their relationship with humans is similar to the beliefs appearing in the Old Testament. Perhaps the best-known point of overlap is that of Utnapishti's Flood, which, of course, shows up as the biblical myth of Noah. The Sumerian corpus also includes a Joblike dialogue (predating the biblical Job by roughly a thousand years) entitled "A Man and His God," wherein a virtuous man bemoans his woe. His answer includes, among other things, the statement, "Never has a sinless child been born to its mother . . . a sinless youth has not existed of old." The distinction between gods and humankind, particularly the power of the former and the powerlessness of the latter, is made very clear. In addition to the great gods, however, the Sumerians also practiced a certain degree of ancestor-worship, characterized particularly by offerings to the dead and the expectation of their help, in this world or the next. Every person was likewise thought to have a "personal god," the equivalent of a "guardian angel" (perhaps the helpful spirit of a deceased ancestor, as suggested by the identification of Lugalbanda as Gilgamesh's personal god), who interceded for them with the great gods.

The Sumerian gods were usually identified with the particular city-states in which their cults were dominant: Inanna in Erech, Enlil in Nippur, Enki in Eridu, and so forth. The temple controlled quite a lot of the economic and social life of the city, but did not by any means have a monopoly upon it. The three chief titles of rulership, En, Ensi, and Lugal, offer a fascinating view of the ways in which the Sumerian city-state could be ordered. The En was the high priest or priestess who acted as the spouse of the city's deity; the Ensi seems to have been a general leader; and the Lugal was specifically a war-leader. One person could hold any of the roles, separately or together, as appropriate under the particular circumstances. Although Gilgamesh is often described in modern translations as a "king," we have avoided using the word altogether, since it does not correspond accurately to any of the Sumerian titles, and would only confuse the reader about Gilgamesh's situation.

From the point of view of historical legend, we were particularly fascinated by the way in which the biblical story of Lot and Abraham fit into the Sumerian context. It was quite a normal arrangement for one male relative to set up in a Sumerian city, while the other continued the Semitic herding-lifestyle outside the city walls. Having observed this, it was irresistible to include Lot's letter . . .

For those interested in finding out more about Sumerian culture, we strongly recommend Kramer's *The Sumerians* (cited above) and George Rouex's *Ancient Iraq* (Harmondsworth: Penguin, 1980). On the subject of religion in particular, Thorkild Jacobsen's *The Treasures of Darkness: A History of Mesopotamian Religion* (New Haven: Yale University Press, 1976) is a good introduction, while Jeremy Black and Anthony Green's *Gods, Demons, and Symbols of Ancient Mesopotamia: An Illustrated Dictionary* offers an extremely useful general reference.

Much of the later portion of this book was written under the light of the Hale-Bopp comet, which last passed through our skies long after the death of Gilgamesh, but at a time when his tale was still very much current and growing, circa 2000 B.C.E. It pleases us to think that an Akkadian scribe might have looked up at the great tailed star just as we did, retelling the story of the ancient hero-king and his struggle against death. It should be noted that while Babylonian astronomy was a very highly developed art, so that the eclipse would have come as no surprise in the later period, it is unlikely that the astronomers of the Early Dynastic period would have reached the point of being able to predict eclipses, so that the one in the book is unexpected and startling. For those who might think that a lunar eclipse and a comet together is stretching literary coincidence a little too much: a partial lunar eclipse occurred under one of the brightest nights of Hale-Bopp, and a full one in 1996, beneath the previous comet.

Gilgamesh's son Ur-Lugal is mentioned in the early king-lists, and is recorded as having conquered Kish, extending Erech's sovereignty over Sumer for a time. As for Gilgamesh himself: a Sumerian poem entitled "The Death of Gilgamesh" tells how, in due course, he made his offerings to the gods of the underworld and the important dead. A later poem, describing the death of the important Sumerian king Ur-Nammu, mentions the deceased Ur-Nammu making offerings to the "seven gods" of the underworld, including both Gilgamesh and Dumuzi, and tells of how Gilgamesh welcomed him into the Netherworld and explained its ways to him. Although he failed in his quest for eternal life, Gilgamesh—perhaps as a result of his quest to learn the secrets of life and death—seems to have become a being of great influence in the Netherworld. Thus, in respect for the dead and our Sumerian cultural forerunners, if you, reader, have enjoyed this story, we invite you to pour out a beer on the earth for Gilgamesh and his beloved Enkidu.

—Stephan and Melodi Lammond Grundy
April 15, 1997 C.E.

# GLOSSARY

*abzug*—the freshwater sea believed to be beneath the earth, the dwelling of Enki.

**An (Anu)**—god of the sky, a rather remote figure, seldom personified or active in human affairs.

**Aruru**—a mother goddess.

**Basthotep (Egyptian)**—"Altar of Bast," an unattested name formed for a rather special cat.

**Buranun**—the Euphrates.

**Dumuzi (Tammuz)**—an early ruler of Erech, who becomes a dying and returning god. His worship proved enduringly popular: in the sixth century B.C.E., Ezekiel chided the women of Israel for mourning him, and Kramer observes that "one of the months of the Jewish calendar bears his name to this day, and the fasting and lamentation which mark its seventeenth day no doubt hark back to the Sumerian days of the distant past." (*The Sumerians*, p. 45) One of the king-lists has him as the son of Lugalbanda and the father of Gilgamesh, but the literary traditions tend to prefer Lugalbanda as Gilgamesh's father.

**Eanna**—the temple precincts in Erech. The name means "house of heaven" or possibly "house of An."

**En**—the priestly spouse of a city's patron deity (see discussion above).

**Enki (Ea)**—god of words, trickery, and freshwater.

**Enlil**—one of the chief gods of Mesopotamia and often presented as preeminent among them, frequently associated with the wind.

**Ensi**—the ruler of a city (see above).

**Erishkegal**—goddess of the Netherworld.

*gala*-**priest**—a priest specializing in ritual singing.

*galla*—a spirit of the underworld.

*gidim*—a restless ghost.

*gipar*—the residence of a city's En and the administrative center of the temple.

**Gula**—a goddess of healing.

**Idiglat**—the Tigris.

**Inanna (Ishtar)**—patroness of Erech, her chief attributes seem to have been love and war. The most important of her rituals was the Sacred Marriage, reenacted at the New Year's celebrations which took place in early spring.

*ishib*-**priest**—purification/sacrificial priest.

*kur*—"mountain" or "underworld."

*lilitu*—a female demon thought to prey particularly on pregnant women and infants, perhaps related to the Lilith of Jewish tradition. A male form, *lilu*, is also known.

**Lugal**—war-leader.

*me*—a plural noun, referring to all the special gifts of knowledge, craftsmanship, and power that Inanna tricked Enki into giving her while he was drunk, and brought back for human beings.

**Nanna**—god of the moon.

**Nergal**—husband of Erishkegal.

**Ninurta**—god of war, also a god of farming.

**onager**—the horse had not been introduced into Mesopotamia in this period. The "onagers" referred to are actually onager-donkey hybrids, since the wild onager cannot be tamed. The donkey itself was viewed in a much more exalted light by the Sumerians than it is today: in "The King of the Road," a hymn of self-praise composed by the king Shulgi to boast about his prowess as a runner (among other things), Shulgi calls himself "a princely donkey all set for the road . . . a noble donkey of Sumugan, eager for the course."

**Shakkan**—god of wild animals and hunting, also sometimes associated with the underworld, perhaps due to the close connection in the Mesopotamian mind between the underworld and wild places.

**Shamhatu**—the woman who seduces Enkidu into humanity has been variously interpreted as everything from a professional tavern wench to a high priestess whose duties include ritual sexual relations. We have obviously taken the latter reading, and regarded the description as a title.

**Utu (Shamash)**—god of the sun, Inanna's brother. His importance to the story varies in different versions of the Gilgamesh cycle, being particularly prominent in the Old Babylonian, but overall he seems to be one of the most active and well-disposed of the gods.